May
2015

Excellent!

COLD SASSY TREE

———

LEAVING COLD SASSY

BOOKS BY OLIVE ANN BURNS

Cold Sassy Tree
Leaving Cold Sassy

Cold Sassy Tree

Leaving Cold Sassy

OLIVE ANN BURNS

Houghton Mifflin Harcourt

BOSTON · NEW YORK

2011

For information about permission to reproduce selections from this book, write to Permissions, Houghton Mifflin Harcourt Publishing Company, 215 Park Avenue South, New York, New York 10003.

www.hmhbooks.com

Library of Congress Cataloging-in-Publication Data
Burns, Olive Ann.
Cold Sassy tree - Leaving Cold Sassy / Olive Ann Burns.
p. cm.
ISBN 978-0-547-57755-5
1. Families — Georgia — Fiction. 2. Country life — Georgia — Fiction.
1. Burns, Olive Ann. Leaving Cold Sassy 11. Title.
PS3552.U73248C64 2011
813'.54 — dc23
2011029337

Book design by Melissa Lotfy

Printed in the United States of America

DOC 10 9 8 7 6 5 4 3 2 1

Cold Sassy Tree

To Andy
My Beloved

To Becky and John
Our grown children

And to my father
Who was fourteen in 1906

Acknowledgments

Cold Sassy is a lot like Commerce, Georgia, at the turn of the century. I couldn't have understood small-town life in that era without the oft-told tales of my late father, William Arnold Burns. He grew up in Commerce, was fourteen in 1906, and, like Will Tweedy, could always make a good story better in the telling. Another rich source of information was the delightful *History of Harmony Grove–Commerce, Jackson County, Georgia, 1810–1949*, by Thomas Colquitt Hardman. I am indebted to the Atlanta Historical Society for access to old Atlanta newspapers, and to C. Vann Woodward's *Tom Watson: Agrarian Rebel* (The Macmillan Company, New York, 1938) for filling the gaps in my knowledge of conditions in Georgia at the time of this book.

I have many reasons to thank my husband, Andrew Sparks; also the children's book author Wylly Folk St. John, who for years urged me to try a novel; Norma Duncan, my neighbor, who saw what was right and wrong with the early manuscript; Eleanor Torrey West at Ossabaw Island, Mary Nikas at the Hambidge Center and Dr. and Mrs. T. E. Reeve, who provided places where occasionally I could get away from home to write; Menakhem Perry, literary critic and University of Tel Aviv professor, who read the first four hundred pages and helped me believe it was good; Anne Edwards, author of *Road to Tara*, who recommended it to her publisher, Ticknor & Fields; Chester Kerr, former president of Ticknor & Fields, and his wife, Joan, without whose encouragement I would still be finishing the manuscript; Katrina Kenison, my editor at Ticknor & Fields, and Frances Apt, manuscript editor, both of whom helped make *Cold Sassy Tree* what it is today.

I

THREE weeks after Granny Blakeslee died, Grandpa came to our house for his early morning snort of whiskey, as usual, and said to me, "Will Tweedy? Go find yore mama, then run up to yore Aunt Loma's and tell her I said git on down here. I got something to say. And I ain't a-go'n say it but once't."

"Yessir."

"Make haste, son. I got to git on to the store."

Mama made me wait till she pinned the black mourning band for Granny on my shirt sleeve. Then I was off. Any time Grandpa had something to say, it was something you couldn't wait to hear.

That was eight years ago on a Thursday morning, when Grandpa Blakeslee was fifty-nine and I was fourteen. The date was July 5, 1906. I know because Grandpa put it down in the family Bible, and also Toddy Hughes wrote up for the Atlanta paper what happened to me on the train trestle that day and I still have the clipping. Besides that, I remember it was right after our July the Fourth celebration—the first one held in Cold Sassy, Georgia, since the War Between the States.

July 5, 1906, was three months after the big earthquake in

San Francisco and about two months after a stranger drove through Cold Sassy in a Pope-Waverley electric automobile that got stalled trying to cross the railroad tracks. I pushed it up the incline and the man let me ride as far as the Athens highway.

July 5, 1906, was a year after my great-grandmother on the Tweedy side died for the second and last time out in Banks County. It was six months after my best friend, Bluford Jackson, got firecrackers for Christmas and burned his hand on one and died of lockjaw ten days later. And like I said, it was only three weeks after Granny Blakeslee went to the grave.

During those three weeks, Grandpa Blakeslee had sort of drawn back inside his own skin. Acted like I didn't mean any more to him than a stick of stovewood. On the morning of July 5th, he stalked through the house and into our company room without even speaking to me.

Granny never would let him keep his corn whiskey at home. He kept it in the company room at our house, which was between the depot and downtown, and came by for a snort every morning on his way to work. I and my little redheaded sister, Mary Toy, always followed him down the hall, and he usually gave us each a stick of penny candy before shutting the company room door in our faces. While our spit swam over hoarhound or peppermint, we'd hear the floorboards creak in the closet, then a silence, then a big "H-rumph!" and a big satisfied "Ah-h-h-h!" He would come out smiling, ready for the day, and pat Mary Toy's head as he went past her.

But this particular morning was different. For one thing, Mary Toy had gone home with Cudn Temp the day before. And Grandpa, instead of coming out feeling good, looked like somebody itching for a fight. That's when he said, "Will Tweedy?" (He always called me both names except when he called me son.) Said, "Will Tweedy? Go find yore mama, then run up to yore Aunt Loma's and tell her I said git on down here."

Lots of people in Cold Sassy had a telephone, including us. Grandpa didn't. He had one at the store so he could phone orders to the wholesale house in Athens, but he was too stingy to pay for one at home. Aunt Loma didn't have a phone, either. She and Uncle Camp were too poor. That's why I had to go tell her.

I ran all the way, my brown and white bird dog, T.R., bounding ahead. As usual when we got to Aunt Loma's, the dog plopped down on the dirt sidewalk in front of her house to wait. He couldn't go up in the dern yard because of the dern cats, of which there were eighteen or twenty at least. They would scratch his eyes out if he went any closer.

I found Aunt Loma sitting at the kitchen table, her long curly red hair still loose and tousled, the dirty breakfast dishes pushed back to clear a space. With one cat in her lap and another licking an oatmeal bowl on the table, she sat drinking coffee and reading a book of theater plays.

Mama never knew how often Aunt Loma put pleasure before duty like that. Mama liked to stay in front of her work. But then Loma was young—just twenty—and sloven.

When I told her what Grandpa said, she slammed her book down so hard, the cat leaped off the table. "Why don't you just tell him I'm busy." But even as she spoke she stood up, gulped some coffee, set down the cup still half full, and rushed upstairs to change into a black dress on account of her mother having just died and all. When she came down, carrying fat, sleepy Campbell Junior, her mass of red hair was combed, pinned up, and draped with what she called "my genteel black veil."

Campbell Junior pulled at the veil all the way to our house, and Aunt Loma fussed all the way. When we got there, she handed the baby over to our cook, Queenie, and hurried in where Grandpa was pacing the front hall, his high-top black shoes squeaking as he walked.

I couldn't help noticing how in only three weeks as a widower he already looked like one. His dark bushy hair and long

gray beard were tangled. The heavy, droopy mustache had
some dried food stuck on it. His black hat, pants, and vest were
dusty and the homemade white shirt rusty with tobacco juice.
Granny always prided herself on keeping his wild hair and
beard trimmed, his shirts clean, his pants brushed and "nice."
Now that she was gone, he couldn't do for himself very well,
having only the one hand, but he wouldn't let Mama or Aunt
Loma do for him.

"Mornin', Pa," Aunt Loma grumped.

"Is that y'all, Will?" Mama called from the dining room,
where she was closing windows and pulling down shades to
keep out the morning sun. We waited in the front hall till she
hurried in, her hair still in a thick plait down one side of her
neck. I always thought she looked pretty with it like that—almost like a young girl. Mama was a plain person, like Granny,
and didn't dress fancy the way Aunt Loma did every time she
stuck her nose out of the house. Even at home Aunt Loma
was fancy. She wouldn't of been caught dead in an apron made
out of a flour sack, whereas Mama had on one that still read
Try Skylark Self-Rising Flour right across the chest. The words
hadn't washed out yet, which I was sure Aunt Loma noticed as
she said crossly, "Mornin', Sister."

Taking off the apron as if we had real company, Mama said
to me, "Son, you go gather the eggs, hear? With Mary Toy
gone, you got to gather the eggs."

"Yes'm." My feet dragged me toward the back hall.

"Let them aiggs wait, Mary Willis," Grandpa ordered. "I
want Will Tweedy to hear what I come to say. He'll know soon
enough anyways." Then he stomped toward the open front
door and put his hand on the knob as if all he planned to say
was good-bye—or maybe more like he was fixing to put a
match to a string of firecrackers and then run before they went
off.

My mother asked, nervous-like, "You want us to all go sit in
the parlor, sir?"

He shook his head. "Naw, Mary Willis, it won't take long enough to set down for." He took off his black hat and laid it on the table, pulled at his mustache, scratched through the white streak in his beard, and turned those deep blue eyes on Mama and Aunt Loma, his grown children, standing together puzzled and uneasy. When he began his announcement, you could tell he had practiced it. "Now, daughters, you know I was true to yore mother. Miss Mattie Lou was a fine wife. A good cook. A real good woman. Beloved by all in this here town, and by me, as y'all know."

Hearing Grandpa go on about Granny made my throat ache. Mama and Aunt Loma went to sobbing out loud, their arms around each other.

"Now quit yore blubberin', Mary Willis. Hesh up, Loma. I ain't finished." Then his voice softened. "Since yore ma's passin' I been a-studyin' on our life together. Thirty-six year we had, and they was good years. I want y'all to know I ain't never go'n forget her."

"Course you w-won't, Pa," said my mother, sobbing.

"But she's gone, just like this here hand a-mine." He held up his left arm, the shirt sleeve knotted as usual just below the elbow. Grandpa's blue eyes were suddenly glassy with unspilled tears. He struggled to get aholt of himself, then went on. "Like I said, she's gone now. So I been studyin' on what to do. How to make out. Well, I done decided, and when I say what I come to say I want y'all to know they ain't no disrespect to her intended." Grandpa opened the door wider. He was about to light his firecrackers.

"Now what I come to say," he blurted out, "is I'm aimin' to marry Miss Love Simpson."

Mama's and Aunt Loma's mouths dropped open and their faces went white. They both cried out, "Pa, you cain't!"

"I done ast her and she's done said yes. And Loma, they ain't a bloomin' thang you can do bout it."

Aunt Loma's face got as red as if she'd been on the river all day, but it was Mama who finally spoke. In a timid voice she said, "Sir, Love Simpson's young enough to be your daughter! She's not more'n thirty-three or -four years old!"

"Thet ain't got a thang to do with it."

Mama put both hands up to her mouth. With a sort of whimper, she said, "Pa, don't you care what folks are go'n say?"

"I care bout you carin' what they'll say, Mary Willis. But I care a heap more bout not bein' no burden on y'all. So hesh up."

Aunt Loma was bout to burst. "Think, Pa!" she ordered, tears streaming down her face. "Just think. Ma hasn't been d-dead but three w-w-weeks!"

"Well, good gosh a'mighty!" he thundered. "She's dead as she'll ever be, ain't she? Well, ain't she?"

2

I THOUGHT Mama was going to faint. She stumbled toward her daddy, arms outstretched, but Grandpa glared at her and she stepped back.

"I'm lonesome." He said it kind of quiet. Then he hugged each weeping daughter and walked out the door, hitching up his trousers with the stub of his left arm.

On the veranda, Grandpa turned back and spoke his defense. "I ain't go'n be no burden on y'all. Not ever. Which means I got to hire me a colored woman or git married, one, and tell you the truth, hit's jest cheaper to have a wife. So I'm a-go'n marry Miss Love. And I ain't got but one more thang to say. All y'all be nice to her. You hear?" He said *all y'all*, but it was Aunt Loma he glared at when he said it.

With that, my grandfather stalked tall down the steps. We watched as he strode past Mama's pots of pink begonias and Papa's life-size iron stag and walked through the iron gate. Banging it shut, he passed the tall pink crepe myrtles that lined the dirt sidewalk in front of our house, crossed the dirt street called South Main, went over the railroad tracks onto North Main, and headed for the store.

Soon as Grandpa got out of sight it was as if somebody had wound Mama and Aunt Loma up and let go the spring. Mama wailed that she could never show her face in Cold Sassy again, she was so embarrassed. Aunt Loma was just plain mad. "Remember Ma's funeral headline, Sister?" She spat out the words.

Mama nodded into her handkerchief. "Y-yes, of course I do. It said, 'Grieving Husband Left to Walk Through Life Alone.'"

"I can just see the engagement notice: 'Grieving Widower Finds Woman to Walk With.'"

"You know Bubba wouldn't do that!" Mama cried. Bubba Reynolds was editor of the *Cold Sassy Weekly*.

"He will if he thinks of it," said Loma. "Sister, that woman ought to be ashamed. And I'm go'n go tell her so."

Mama was alarmed. "Now, Loma, once you get started, you don't know when to hush." Then she added, "But it might do some good to tell her how stingy Pa is, and how hard he is to cook for. That might make her think twice."

There was a silence, except for Aunt Loma pounding her right fist into her left hand, bam, bam, bam, glaring at me as she did it. Finally she said my daddy might could talk Grandpa out of it.

Mama didn't think so. "Hoyt don't even dare ast Pa to raise his pay. Get your Camp onto him." She was being sarcastic. I'd heard her say that Grandpa thought Uncle Camp was still in knee britches. Aunt Loma didn't answer. She knew — they both knew — that nobody could stand up to their daddy.

Then Loma shook both fists in the direction of the store. "Dog bite your hide, Love Simpson!" she screamed. "And dog bite yours, Pa!"

"Loma, hush. The neighbors will — "

"How could he do it, and her a Yankee!"

Mama was always fair, even when flustrated to distraction. "Now, Loma, everybody calls Miss Love a Yankee and she does kind of talk like one. But Maryland is not a Northern state." Then, as another thought struck her, Mama collapsed onto the leather davenport there in the front hall. "Loma," she wailed, "Pa didn't have on his black armband!"

"Well, should he, Sister? When he's engaged?" Aunt Loma like to choked on the word *engaged*.

"But they cain't marry for a year or more. I don't see why Pa couldn't wear an armband for Ma."

"While Love Simpson wears an engagement ring for Pa?"

"Surely he won't give her a ring! He just said he wanted us to know, not the whole world!" Mama jumped up and stuck her nose right in her young sister's face. "Now you listen to me." Loma backed off a little. "I want you to keep your mouth shut. It may all blow over, and nobody'll ever know. Maybe—maybe Pa just thought she said yes."

"Grandpa ain't hard of hearin'," said I, but they didn't seem to notice.

I was amazed at Mama. She was usually just the mildest sort of person. Ordinarily if anybody was saying hush up around here, it was Aunt Loma, despite she was fourteen years younger than my mother. No doubt Aunt Loma marveled, too, because she didn't say anything sassy back. Just jerked off her genteel black veil and threw it hard as she could towards the front door.

"Sister, I was fixin' to ast Pa for Ma's piano," she burst out. Tears of flustration wet her red face. "And I want the mirror that Cudn Pearl painted Saint Cecilia on. Just think, while I was waitin' a decent time to ast for a piano and a mirror, come to find out he was astin' for a wife!" Screaming the words out, she stomped her foot.

I knew Mama wanted the piano so Mary Toy could take music lessons. Mama always liked the Saint Cecilia mirror, too. Everybody in Cold Sassy except us had Saint Cecilia painted on something. And though Mama wasn't the kind to ask for things, I'd heard her tell Queenie she was go'n see if her Pa would let her swap our mismatched parlor furniture for Granny's nice parlor suit. She knew he wouldn't care one way or the other.

"I just cain't understand it," Mama fumed, getting up to pace the hall just the way Grandpa had. "I thought Love Simpson would marry Son Black. I know his mother don't approve, but he's not gettin' any younger, and they been courtin' a year or more."

"And Love deserves him," said Aunt Loma. She used to be sweet on Son Black herself, so I reckon she knew what she was talking about when she added, "Son's right nice-lookin' and smart, but his mouth sure isn't any prayer book. And he's meaner'n a snake."

"Yeah," I chimed in. "I heard he had him a pet snake one time that bit him and the next day the snake died."

They ignored that. Mama said, "Love is too used to town life and dressin' fashionable. Maybe she don't care to stay out there on the farm with Son's mama and raise chi'ren. Maybe she thinks she's too good to marry a farmer."

"Shoot," retorted Aunt Loma, "what about that rancher out in Texas she was engaged to before she came here? A rancher has lots of land and money but he's a farmer just the same. Lord, I wish to heaven she'd married him. If only he hadn'—"

"Sh-h!" Mama nodded toward me.

I knew Loma was fixing to say "If only he hadn't got Miss Love's best friend in trouble and had to marry her." Everybody in town knew that story. I don't know why Mama thought I didn't.

Nobody asked my opinion, but I had always admired Miss Love, with all that wavy brown hair piled atop her head, and that smiley, freckledy face and those friendly gray-blue eyes. She was a merry person, like Grandpa. Always wore big flowered hats and bright-colored dresses, never "quiet" clothes like nice ladies were supposed to wear on the street. I could see how Miss Love could cheer up a man whose wife was short of breath for four years, dying for ten days, and dead for three weeks.

Aunt Loma's face suddenly went redder than ever. Clearly she'd had a new thought. "Sister, with Love bein' Pa's milliner, and them seein' each other down at the store every day, people are go'n say—"

"Will, I thought I told you to go get the eggs," Mama interrupted with a mad sound in her voice. "Now go on, right now. Mind me."

I minded her. But she needn't think I didn't know what Aunt Loma was driving at. Well, there couldn't have been any carrying-on down at the store or we'd have heard about it long time ago. Anyhow, Miss Love wasn't that kind and neither was my grandfather. And heck, he loved Granny. Even now I couldn't hardly imagine him kissing another lady, or slapping her playful on the backside like he used to do Granny when he was in a teasing mood. I guess what I really couldn't imagine was Miss Love kissing him, much less marrying him. It was easy to see he needed looking after, but what did she need that an old man could give when she already had a beau her own age who was anxious to marry her?

3

I SAT down on the back steps to think. I didn't see why Mama and Aunt Loma weren't glad Grandpa Blakeslee had found him a lady to marry. The sooner the better, if you asked me. The wedding couldn't be for a year or more, of course, but after that he wouldn't have to keep coming to our house for dinner or to Aunt Loma's every night for supper, which he'd been doing ever since Granny passed away. And Miss Love wouldn't have to bring a quart Mason jar full of hot coffee down to the store for him every morning like she'd been doing.

Papa kept trying to get Grandpa to eat breakfast with us, being as he came by home anyhow for his snort. It wouldn't of been much trouble for Mama; all Grandpa ever wanted in the morning was four cups of coffee and some yeast bread, toasted hard and dipped in boiling water and then buttered. But when Papa said, "Sit down and have a bite with us, Mr. Blakeslee," Grandpa would say he just et. I reckon he thought if he took dinner and breakfast both at our house, it wouldn't be any time before Papa would be after him to move in with us.

Well, this time next year Grandpa would be married, and if he didn't like what was put before him it would be Miss Love's little red wagon, not Mama's or Aunt Loma's. Also, they wouldn't have to see after him if he got sick. He was hard to take care of when he was ailing. Liked to groan and carry on. He'd lie down before supper on the daybed, moaning, "Oh, me, me. . . . Oh, me, me," and Granny just about went crazy listening to it, knowing that next morning he'd go on to the store anyway. The last year or two, no matter how bad he felt you couldn't make him stay home. He could have a cold so bad it sounded like pneumonia rattling around in there but he wouldn't stay home.

That really used to worry my grandmother. She'd beg him not to go to work. "Mr. Blakeslee, I nurse everybody in town but my own husband. Please stay in bed t'morrer. Hear?"

But he'd say, "I ain't thet big of a fool, Miss Mattie Lou. Ain't you ever noticed? Folks die in bed."

Anyhow, now there wouldn't be any more worrying about Grandpa living by himself.

Aunt Loma had already declared he couldn't live with her. Said she didn't have room. I don't know how she could say such as that when her daddy had given her husband a job and provided them a house to live in. Mama couldn't have said it — even if he didn't own our house, too, and even if Papa didn't work for him. Papa had been keeping the store ledgers since he was sixteen.

Grandpa wouldn't of lived with Aunt Loma, of course, on account of her cats. The first time he went there for supper after Granny was buried, the next morning he started fussing about her cats the minute he got to our house for his snort. "I swanny to God, I seen one a-them cats jump up on Loma's kitchen stove last night! Tiptoed across thet red-hot stove on his dang claws and et right out of the pot!"

I had been hoping Grandpa would come live with us. But even though she never said so, I knew Mama dreaded that possibility. Tell the truth, she was scared of her daddy, as if she wasn't sure he'd got over her not being a boy and her marrying a Presbyterian—though the way I heard it from Cudn Temp, Grandpa was all for her marrying my daddy, and had a fit when the Baptist deacons tried her for heresy.

Heresy was his word for their word for her marrying a Presbyterian.

According to Temp, the deacons voted to put it in the church records that "Mary Willis Blakeslee has swapped her religious birthright for a mess of matrimonial pottage." It made Grandpa mad as holy heck. "Anybody calls Hoyt Tweedy a mess of matrimonial pottage," he roared, "thet man is a-go'n answer to me." The deacons struck the pottage part from the record. But they turned Mama out of the Baptist communion just the same, and her only seventeen.

That was one reason I didn't like the way Mama was carrying on so about Grandpa getting engaged. He had stuck up for her when she wanted to marry Papa. Why wouldn't she stick up for him now?

I wasn't surprised at Aunt Loma, of course. She was the only child of Granny and Grandpa's to live more than a few years, besides my mother, and she'd been spoiled all her life. I reckon they thought they had to keep rewarding her for not dying. Anyhow, Loma never could think about much else for thinking about how to get her own way. Despite she was married now, and a mother, she hadn't grown up any that I could see. If it didn't suit her for her daddy to marry again, why, he just wasn't going to.

Miss Love having worked for Grandpa at his store for two years or more, she must already know he was stingy and set in his ways. She also knew that, because of his having just the one hand, he needed special looking after. He bit off his fingernails, so keeping them short was no problem. But tough meat had to be cut up for him, and he needed help with his high-top shoes. Timmy Hopkins had been coming by to tie Grandpa's shoelaces ever since Granny took sick.

But though Miss Love might not be a good cook after

boarding so long, and probably couldn't of outworked Granny in a vegetable garden or rose garden or sickroom, most anybody could outdo Granny with a broom and a feather duster. She used to say "A house will keep, whether you weed it or not, but that-air yard will git away from you in the bat of a eye." The only thing she liked to do indoors was cook and tend the sick. I remember one time she pulled off her apron after two days and nights nursing a neighbor lady and said, "They ain't no feelin' in the world like takin' on somebody wilted and near bout gone, and you do what you can, and then all a-sudden the pore thang starts to put out new growth and git well."

I hadn't ever heard of Miss Love nursing the sick. But that wasn't any reason for Grandpa not to marry her. I just couldn't see why Mama and Aunt Loma were having a fit about it. The fact that I liked Miss Love didn't mean I hadn't loved Granny, and I figured it was the same with him.

I was just fixing to get up off the back steps and go gather the eggs when Campbell Junior started squalling in the kitchen. I heard Aunt Loma go in there. "I got to get on home," she told our cook.

"Yas'm," said Queenie. "B'ess his li'l heart, he be's hongry."

"And I be's full as a Jersey cow," said Aunt Loma, mocking her. "Seems like all I do is nurse this bloomin' baby."

"Shame on you, Miss Loma, talkin' lak dat. Some peoples cain' nuss dey baby, and some ain' got nary baby to nuss. You be's lucky."

"Humph," said Loma, and left.

Before I had a chance to move, Mama came out and lit into me for sitting there doing nothing. Said I was no-count and shiftless and why hadn't I gathered the eggs and I was supposed to have weeded the lower garden two days ago and to go do that "but first you gather the eggs like you been told to. You go'n let the rats get'm. Or that no-count egg-sucker dog of yours."

I resented that. T.R. didn't suck eggs. But I said yes'm.

Mama went inside, and I was hardly down the three back steps before she stuck her head out of her bedroom window upstairs and hollered to me to watch for Papa and my grandpa when it was time for them to come to dinner.

"Yes'm."

"I got a sick headache," she said, like it was my fault, and put her hand up to her forehead as she faded back into the room. The window slammed shut and the shade came down to keep it cool in there.

In a kind of furious daze, forgetting the eggs, I got a big old gray peach basket off the porch and dragged it down the path. The garden was to the left of the barn and the pasture, hidden from the house by the smokehouse and a pecan grove and a row of little peach trees that because of the drought had dropped hard knotty fruit not even fit to make spiced pickle with.

Gourd leaves that yesterday drooped down like a hundred little half-closed umbrellas were now freshened with dew. But it was already hot, great goodness, and the dirt was powder-dry. I hadn't weeded since the last rain. I started pulling up the grass and weeds as if they were Miss Love Simpson—like I thought getting rid of them would get rid of her and bring Granny Blakeslee back from the grave and let us be a normal family again.

Nothing had been normal since Granny died. Mama was grieving herself to death, Papa was sterner than ever, Aunt Loma was meaner, the laughter had gone out of Grandpa, and if he was about to sell the store, it wouldn't of upset everybody any more than him aiming to marry his milliner.

Worst of all, for me, was being in mourning.

I just didn't think I could stand any more mourning. For three whole weeks of summer vacation they hadn't let me play baseball or go fishing or anything. I couldn't mention the camping trip I'd been planning all spring with Pink Predmore and Lee

Roy Sleep and Smiley Snodgrass, and I had missed a chance to ride in a Buick automobile all the way to Atlanta. Pink's uncle over in Athens invited him and me to go so we could fix his flat tires and push the car up hills—and out of ditches if it rained and the roads got slick. Pink went, but Mama wouldn't let me go. Also, I didn't get to go downtown for the Fourth of July parade, and they hadn't let me read the funny paper since the day Granny passed on.

Papa never had let us read the funny paper on Sunday. That was a sin. We had to save it till Monday. But now we were having to save the funnies indefinitely, and sometimes the newspaper got taken to start a fire with before I could tear out the page. The Katzenjammer Kids had dropped clean out of my life. Seems like I missed them about as much as I missed Granny. Maybe more. They were up there on the shelf in Mama's chifforobe with things happening to them, whereas Granny wasn't anywhere.

I wished she could come back for just a minute. I'd ask her wouldn't she hate my giving up the funnies and the automobile trip when there wasn't a thing I could do for her anymore. Despite she had wanted a nice funeral, I knew she wouldn't expect a boy to walk around with a long face the rest of his life.

I was just fixing to quit weeding and rest a spell under the big hickernut tree when I noticed my shadow was underfoot, nearly straight down. It must be right at dinner time. Gosh, Mama had told me to watch out for Papa and Grandpa. Dashing past the barn, the smokehouse, and Mama's flower pit, I ran through the house and got to the front door just as Papa hurried up the walk. He was by himself.

"Where's Grandpa at?" I asked.

"Where's Mama at?" he asked. He was sweaty and red-faced from rushing home and he looked upset.

"She's gone to bed, sir. I think she's sick."

Even now, eight years later, I remember how my papa looked

that day—like a thundercloud, but also like a pitiful, lightning-struck tree. Taking the stairs two at a time, he didn't even no-tice me following behind.

As he burst into the darkened second-floor bedroom, he said, "Mary Willis, guess what! Your daddy just left in his buggy with Miss Love Simpson! Said they were off to Jefferson to get married!"

Mama bolted up. "You mean already?" she screeched. "To-day?"

"You knew it?" roared Papa. "Why didn't you tell me?"

"I didn't dream he meant today!" Then she blurted out what all Grandpa had said that morning. "Hoyt, he said it didn't matter, said Ma havin' just passed away didn't matter! He said . . . he said Ma was d-dead as she—" she started crying. "Dead as—oh, Hoyt, I c-cain't bear to repeat his w-words! He said . . . Ma was dead as she'd ever b-be!"

Peeping in the doorway, I saw my mother was laying across the bed, on her side, pressing a handkerchief to her mouth. Papa had sat down by her and was patting her shoulder. He kissed her forehead. "There, there, Mary Willis hon. Don't carry on so. I admit it, I was surprised myself. But Lord knows, Mr. Blakeslee needs somebody to see after him. Hon, I'm sure Miss Love will be good to him. She'll—"

"She'll get the store, that's what she'll do!" cried Mama. "And this house! Maybe everything he owns! What if she has a baby, Hoyt? Did you think about that? And what if she marries again after Pa dies? Oh, Hoyt. . . ."

I knew my mother thought the marriage was a scandal, but this was the first I guessed that she saw Miss Love as a scoun-drel, a villain, out to steal hers and Aunt Loma's inheritance.

Slowly it dawned on me that if Grandpa Blakeslee died and left Miss Love the store, she really could marry again and let her new husband run it. And if he was somebody like Son Black, he might just push my daddy and Uncle Camp clean out. The threat was sobering even to me.

But somehow the picture didn't fit. Maybe Grandpa didn't care what folks said or thought about him, but he cared a lot about Mama and Papa and Aunt Loma. I mean, he didn't *like* Aunt Loma a lot, but he loved her. Also, he set great store on a man doing right by his family.

Peeping in again, I saw Papa had his arm around Mama. She was crying. "When a woman m-marries a man old enough to be her f-father," she said, "you can b-b-bet your . . . bottom dollar it's for . . . w-what she can g-g-get out of him. . . . Pa's a fool, Hoyt! And I just don't see h-how we can start all over when he d-dies. Oh, Hoyt. . . !"

She kept wailing and Papa kept patting her. I didn't know what to think about all that, but I knew I didn't want them to catch me out there listening. Tiptoeing around to the other side of a golden oak bureau that was in the hall near their bedroom door, I squatted down.

"I'm sick over the whole thing," Mama muttered. "Just sick! No tellin' what kind of fam'ly she comes from. There's a milliner in Athens who trained with Love in Baltimore and she says Love's daddy fought on the Union side in the War. That by itself should of made Pa think twice, feelin' like he does about Yankees. Hoyt, we don't even know what her father does, for heaven's sake, or whether the fam'ly has any education or background, or any standin' at all in their community." Mama was a great one for not marrying beneath yourself.

Papa argued that the family surely must be educated, judging by the way Miss Love talked so proper. "She seems like somebody with background."

"Well, one thing I know, Miz Predmore says the only letters Love Simpson gets from Baltimore are from the millinery company that trained her. The postmaster told her. We figure she must be ashamed of her folks. If she don't write them and don't hear from them and don't ever say pea-turkey about them to anybody, something's wrong."

"Please, hon, don't let yourself get all wrought up."

"Her fam'ly could be common as Camp's folks, for all we know. Ignorant. No-count. Even low-down. I still don't see how Loma could of married into that sharecropper white trash. With all her education and advantages, she's got a daddy-in-law who cain't read or write and a mother-in-law who dips snuff. And Camp's sisters work in the fields just like colored girls. Thank the Lord they didn't come to the weddin'."

Papa couldn't stand it when Mama got to low-rating Uncle Camp's people. "Now, hon, that don't have anything to do with your pa."

"It does, too. Even if Love's folks ain't ignorant, they could be dead-beats. Jesus said take up your cross and follow Me, but He didn't ast us to go out and nail ourselves to a board. Some fine day, mark my words, Love's fam'ly will get off the train from Baltimore to come live off of Pa. Just like Camp's folks are go'n be livin' off of he and Loma before it's over. Or maybe livin' with them. Only reason Loma married Camp, she was mad cause Pa wouldn't let her go off with those actors. That's just exactly why. She was bound and determined to get her way about something—just to spite Pa."

It was true. A touring Shakespeare company had let Loma try out after their performance in Cold Sassy's brush arbor and then asked her to join the troupe. Everybody in town said Lord help Loma if she ends up an actress. Even if she got rich and famous and did command performances for Edward VII, like she said she would, she couldn't ever live down the taint.

But Grandpa said, "Loma, I ain't a-go'n let you do it. Ain't no tellin' what kind of a life you'd live with them kind a-folks."

She stomped and cried and carried on something awful. "I wish I was a boy so I could go off on my own!"

"I wish you was a boy, too, but you ain't," Grandpa retorted, "and you ain't go'n be no actress, neither. So hesh up." Loma went to her room and threw things, but Grandpa didn't hear it. He had gone on back to the store.

I myself used to wonder why Loma didn't find some more

actors to run off with—a thing she wanted to do—instead of marrying Campbell Williams just to spite her daddy. Well, and now her daddy had married Miss Love—maybe partly to spite Cold Sassy.

"Loma and Pa, they're just alike." Mama was fuming. "They don't ever consider anybody else. Neither one of them. When I think of the nice widders Pa's age who'd be happy to marry him, I don't see why he had to pick an old maid from Up North who's had to work for a livin'."

In Cold Sassy, ladies who work for pay are looked down on—except schoolteachers or widder women with no close kinfolks to turn to. Milliners are considered in a class with store clerks and telephone hello-girls.

"Why wouldn't Pa let me look after him?" Mama went on. "We could of moved up to his house."

"And go back to usin' lamps and privies?" asked Papa irritably. "And give up Queenie?" Grandpa didn't have electricity or running water and didn't believe in hiring colored help.

That silenced my mother, but only for a minute. In a new burst of tears, she said, "Hoyt, Pa has disgraced the whole f-f-fam'ly. The whole t-town!"

Most likely Papa was patting her shoulder again. "It's go'n turn out all right, hon. Just don't forget I work for him, and Camp works for him. Y'all have got to be nice to Miss Love. Now, hon, I need to get back to the store. Please, let's go eat."

"You and Will eat." Mama's muffled voice came out of her pillow. "I'm not hungry. The nerve, that woman thinkin' she can take Ma's place! And everybody's go'n say—you mark my words—they go'n say Pa must have been sweet on her from the day he laid eyes on her. It's like he just couldn't hardly wait for Ma to p-p-pass!"

I guess my mother didn't notice that Papa had left the room. I waited till he got downstairs before I crept down myself. I couldn't stand hearing her keep on talking against Grandpa.

4

I USED to try to undress Grandpa Blakeslee's face in my mind and think how he'd look clean-shaved. I never could picture him like that, but I liked looking at him the way he was—his eyes merry, his upper lip hidden under the droopy mustache, his bushy gray beard usually stained here and there with tobacco juice.

Most people thought I was his spittin' image. Granny used to say I walked like Grandpa, twitched my shoulders like him—"cain't neither one a-y'all set still"—and looked like him "cept for yore eyes bein' brown and his'n so blue, and the fact yore nose ain't humped." Grandpa's nose had got broke three times, and it showed. First time, he was trying to fly: "I was maybe twelve year old. Jumped out'n a hayloft holdin' a dang umbrella and it turned inside out." The other two times, his nose got busted in fistfights.

At fifty-nine, Grandpa still had all his teeth, which should be a comfort to Miss Love. He only wore glasses to read. He was lean, strong, straight, and taller than most men—the way I was taller than most fourteen-year-old boys. My grandmother was small. She could stand under his arm if he stuck it straight out, and never could keep up with him when they walked together. His long legs swung in giant strides; she trotted at his heels like a good little dog.

Grandpa was a buster all right.

He was a Democrat, a Baptist, and a devout Confederate veteran. The words *Abraham Lincoln* couldn't be spoke in his presence. His only hand was soft and smooth, not like the rough, red, calloused hands of farmers. In a fight he used the elbow of his left arm as a deflector and his "fightin' right" to punch with.

The fights were embarrassing to the family but real entertaining to the Baptists, for he would stand up at the next Wednesday night prayer meeting, in the testimonial and confessing part, and tell the Lord all about it. One Wednesday night he ended a long prayer with "Lord, forgive me for fittin' thet man yesterd'y—though Thou knowest if I had it to do over agin I'd hit him harder."

Grandpa was a good shot with a pistol. He never went hunting, but he could prop a Winchester rifle on a fence and shoot into the mouth of a Coca-Cola bottle fifty feet away and not even chip the glass, except for the hole at the bottom where the bullet came out.

I never could figure why Papa and Mama let him keep his quart jars of moonshine in the closet in our company room. At the time, Papa made and drank locust beer, and Mama made scuppernong and blackberry wines for church communion. After the Georgia legislature declared a prohibition against alcoholic beverages in 1907, Papa quit making or drinking beer—he believed in being law-abiding—and the churches started using fruit nectars instead of wine. But even before Prohibition, neither Papa nor Mama could stand whiskey-drinking.

Yet there stood those jars of corn whiskey on our closet shelf.

Why couldn't my daddy ask him to keep them down at the store? Or after Granny died and wasn't there anymore to disallow it, why didn't he take the stuff to his own house?

My parents never once spoke of his drinking in front of me or Mary Toy. Acted like he just went in the company room to hitch up his suspenders or something. But I doubt they could of said anything even if he hadn't been Mama's papa and Papa's employer. Grandpa had the manner of a king or duke: when he said do or don't do something, you said yessir before you thought. And if he said he meant to do something—like keep his corn whiskey in your closet or marry Miss Love Simpson—if you couldn't say yessir, you sure-dog didn't say no sir. Not out loud.

What I admired most was his flair for practical jokes. That was a way of life you could learn early, as I discovered when I was little bitty and Cudn Doodle told me to lick a frozen wagon wheel and my tongue stuck to the ice. Playing jokes didn't have to stop because you got grown. Grandpa must of been twenty-five at least when he turned over the privy at the depot with a Yankee railroad bigwig in it.

I didn't want to be like my grandfather in all ways. I thought I wanted to be like Papa, at least sometime in the distant future. But right now Grandpa was more fun than Papa and didn't worry near as much, if at all, about sin. And he was real proud of me. I was the son he never had.

While I was still in dresses he put me to sorting nails at the store and getting out rotten apples and potatoes. By time I was seven, he let me make deliveries for him in my goat cart. It was his notion that when I got grown, he would give me an interest in the store and take me into partnership.

It was my notion to be a farmer. Papa wanted to buy the old home place out in Banks County from his daddy and let me run it. But at the time Grandpa Blakeslee married Miss Love, I still hadn't got up the nerve to tell him my plans.

Most folks thought, as Miss Effie Belle Tate put it, that Grandpa was "both rich and well-to-do." For sure he was one of Cold Sassy's leading merchants. Had him a big brick store

with mahogany counters, beveled glass mirrors, and big colored signs for Coca-Cola, Mother's Friend *(Take to Make Childbirth Easier)*, Fletcher's Castoria, Old Dutch Cleanser, McKes-
son and Robbins liniment, and all like that.

I liked to look at the advertisements in the mail-order catalogues he kept by the cash register. *Manhood Restored* was my
favorite:

> Nerve Seeds guaranteed to cure all nervous diseases
> such as Weak Memory, Loss of Brain Power, Headaches,
> Wakefulness, Lost Manhood, Nightly Emissions, ner-
> vousness, all drain and loss of power in generative organs
> of either sex caused by over-exertion, youthful errors, ex-
> cessive use of tobacco, opium or stimulants which lead
> to infirmity, consumption or Insanity. Can be carried in
> vest pocket. $1 per box address Nerve Seed Co., Masonic
> Temple, Chicago, Ill.

Grandpa had him a big sign out front over the entrance to
the store. In fancy red letters outlined in gold it said:

GENERAL MERCHANDISE
Mr. E. Rucker Blakeslee, Proprietor

Besides keeping the store's ledgers, my daddy took a lot of
the buying trips to Atlanta and Baltimore and New York City. I
went to New York with him one time when I was little bitty. I'd
heard about damnyankees all my life and there I was in a city
just full of them. It scared me to death.

Granny's Uncle Lige Toy, who used to have a restaurant
business feeding county prisoners, was in charge of Grandpa's
cotton warehouse, one of the biggest in north Georgia, and
also the store's cotton seed business. Uncle Lige was the one to
talk to if you wanted to put your bales in storage till you could
get a better price.

A third cousin of Papa's, Hopewell Stump, from out in
Banks County, clerked and took care of the chickens that folks

brought to trade out for nails, flour, sugar, coal oil, coffee, and chewing tobacco. There used to be smelly chicken coops out on the board sidewalk in front of every store in town, but after Cold Sassy was incorporated in 1887, the Baptist missionary society ladies petitioned the town council to get rid of them. So when Grandpa built his brick store in 1892 he put a great big chickenhouse in back, and every Friday Cudn Hope shipped hens, roosters, and frying-size pullets to Athens or Atlanta on the train.

Uncle Camp mostly swept the floor and put out stock, and in the wintertime broke up wooden shipping crates to burn in the stove. Grandpa called him "born tired and raised lazy." Said getting him to finish something was like pushing mud. "Money don't jump out at you, boy," he'd say. "You got to work for it."

Campbell Williams was Uncle Camp's whole name. He was a pale thin fellow with pale thin yellow hair and a pale thin personality. He was always checking the time so he could show off his gold pocket watch.

He wasn't but nineteen when he came to Cold Sassy from over near Maysville, Georgia. The day Camp walked into the store and asked for a job, Grandpa took one look and said he didn't need no hep right now. Camp got him a job at the tannery, working for Wildcat Lindsey, but soon lost it, and then worked a while at the gin. Grandpa didn't bring him into the store till after he married Aunt Loma, and never did have any respect for him.

Love Simpson was the first woman Grandpa ever hired. She grew up in Baltimore and had never married but didn't look or act like any other old maid in town. She was tall, plump, and big-bosomed, stood very straight, moved lively, and wore flouncy, fashionable clothes. Miss Love had a sparkly way of talking and she laughed a lot.

I remember the first time I saw her. I had been standing in front of the store watching a flock of turkeys trot through town. If a turkey strayed, a man would snap a long whip around its neck and pull it back in line.

When I went inside, there was the new milliner, seated at a table littered with feathers, bird wings, satin bows, stiff tape, bolts of velvet, linen, silk, and so on, and several life-size dummy heads. She had one of the heads in her lap, wrapping folds of pink velour around it and sticking pins here and there to hold the cloth in place. Looking up, she saw me, smiled and said, "What's all the commotion outside, honey?" She had two pins in the corner of her mouth and had to speak around them.

"A turkey drive, ma'am. The men are rushin' to get'm through town before first dark, cause when it's time to roost, they go'n fly to the nearest tree and they ain't go'n budge till daybreak."

I was only twelve then. It was before I got long-legged, so with her sitting down and me standing, my head was just about level with hers. I forgot all about the turkeys, I was so busy smelling her perfume and looking at her freckles. They were like brown pepper. She had gray-blue eyes, long black lashes, a tilted-up nose, a big smiley mouth, and thick wavy brown hair piled high and perky on her head.

Miss Love took the pins out of her mouth. "I guess you live here in Cold Sassy," she said, smiling extra friendly.

"Yes'm. I'm Will Tweedy, ma'am. You must be the new milliner."

"And you must be Mr. Hoyt's boy." She nodded in the direction of Papa, who was over by the cash register.

"Yes'm."

"He is a very nice man, and good-looking, too." That pleased me. Papa was stocky, not tall, but he was neat about his clothes, had a handsome face, and shaved every morning. Most men in Cold Sassy had a beard or just shaved on Saturday night to get ready for Sunday.

Miss Love held up the dummy head with the pink velour

wrapping, turning it this way and that to get the effect. "You like this hat, Will Tweedy?"

I didn't have much opinion about hats, or much interest either. "Well'm," I mumbled, "I cain't hardly tell what it's go'n look like yet."

Miss Love laughed. A hearty laugh. Her lips were so red they looked painted almost. "You're a good diplomat, Will Tweedy."

One thing I noticed that day was how proper Miss Love spoke. Till then, I never met anybody who could talk as proper as Aunt Carrie. Aunt Carrie was taught to speak cultured at a private school in Athens run by a French woman, Madame Joubert.

I found out later that Miss Love learned to talk right from a rich educated lady in Philadelphia that she used to go stay with every spring and fall, making hats for her and her daughters.

"Mrs. Hanover was always correcting my grammar and pronunciation," Miss Love told me. "If I mumbled or made the least little mistake, I had to say it over and over till I got it right. I guess Mrs. Hanover liked me. She said that with my flair for fashion, her friends couldn't tell me from one of them till I opened my mouth. 'Cultivate good speech, Miss Simpson,' she'd say, 'and you can marry above yourself.' She gave me her finishing school grammar book. I still have it. I felt certain if I memorized that book I could marry the Prince of Wales—or at least a railroad president."

Grandpa was real proud of the store having a milliner trained at the Armstrong and Cater Company in Baltimore. In 1901, the company had sent Miss Love and her best friend out to a big store in Texas. When she wanted to leave Texas, Armstrong and Cater sent her, sight unseen, to Grandpa. He had written asking for a milliner and Miss Love was available, so that's all there was to it. But for weeks after she came to town, men would poke Grandpa in the ribs, nod toward the milliner's table, and say, "You shore know how to pick'm, Mr. Blakeslee," or, "You got you a real looker, ain't you?" Grandpa would grin and say you dang right.

At first Miss Love stayed at Granny and Grandpa's house, in their company room. Later she boarded with Mr. and Mrs. Eli P. Crabtree, whose son Arthur was bad to drink and took an overdose of laudanum in the cemetery one cold night. They found him dead the next morning, huddled up against his sweetheart's tombstone, and now Miss Love was renting Arthur's old room. The Crabtrees thought she was real nice, but she didn't tell her business to them or anybody, and didn't have close friends. The only thing Cold Sassy knew about her was what that milliner in Athens told Aunt Loma.

Besides about her daddy being in the Union Army, the woman told it as gospel that after Miss Love got engaged to a rich Texas rancher and went home to Maryland to make her trousseau clothes, her best friend got you-know-what by her fee-ance, and they eloped. Aunt Loma said if her fee-ance and her best friend were that kind of trash, "it don't speak so well for Love Simpson."

You have to take into account that Aunt Loma was just eighteen when Miss Love hit town, and the jealous type. Aunt Loma was blue-eyed and had the thickest long curly red hair you ever saw, with little tendrils around her face that made her look sweet and innocent. Till Miss Love came, she was considered just the prettiest thing in Cold Sassy, and also the most fashionable. While visiting one time in Atlanta, Loma went to M. Rich & Bros. and bought herself some handmade French drawers with lace-edged ruffles, and also what she called "a blue poky-dot foulard dress with an overskirt of Georgette crepe." Grandpa like to had a fit about her spending the money, but after she cried, he let her alone about it. The only thing not fashionable about Aunt Loma was her bosom.

She was so flat you didn't have to be big to be bigger, and Miss Love Simpson was definitely bigger. At some point Miss Love made the mistake of remarking that Loma had just the

perfect figure for the stylish new shirtwaists with lots of tucks
and ruffles in front. That was because of Loma's flat busts, so
though it was meant as a compliment, she was insulted. She
hadn't had much to do with Miss Love since, especially not after one Saturday when she wanted to buy a little blue hat with
white bird wings on it that Miss Love was wearing and didn't
want to sell. I heard what was said because I was down at the
store washing fly spots off the show window.

"You've sold hats off your head before," Aunt Loma argued,
pushing out her bottom lip.

"I know," Miss Love answered sweetly. "But I made this hat
special to go with this dress. Let me fix up something else for
you."

Aunt Loma's face flushed red as her hair, she was so mad,
and she flounced off acting like a store-owner's daughter to a
hired hand. "I must say, Love Simpson," she hissed, "you'd do
well to quit thinking you're good as your betters!"

As they say in Cold Sassy, Aunt Loma was behind the door
when they passed out the tact. And her temper was such that if
King Edward VII or the Lord God Almighty Himself had been
around when she got mad, she wouldn't of talked any less awful. In fact, she'd of been glad of the extra audience.

I just couldn't stand Aunt Loma. As long as I could remember, she'd bossed me like I was her slave. She was only six years
older than me, for gosh sake, which to my mind didn't give
her any right to lord it over me like she was a hundred. God
help Miss Love Simpson if she really had gone off and married
Grandpa against her will—against Aunt Loma's will, I mean. I
hoped Miss Love understood what she was up against. I could
of told her, because I had been up against Aunt Loma all my
life.

There were some people in Cold Sassy who called Miss Love
"that Yankee woman" or made fun of her for being a suffrag-
ette. Not a man in town thought it mattered a hoot about

women voting, and only two ladies went to the first women's suffrage meeting Miss Love set up. Either nobody else was interested or their husbands wouldn't let them come, one. After that meeting, most folks felt a little uneasy about Miss Love. Still and all, just about everybody liked her.

The men liked her because she was pretty and friendly and, as Mr. Cratic Flournoy put it, full of ginger and pepper.

The ladies liked her because she made hats that could of come straight out of New York City. Also, she had a pattern book of the newest styles and would order patterns for anybody who wanted her to, and she showed the ladies how to fix their hair fashionable.

The congregation at the Methodist Episcopal Church, South, liked her because her piano-playing was loud and lively. Ever since Miss Love started playing for preachin', folks had sung out good, patting their feet and generally getting in shape to shout and amen during the sermon.

Just the same, Cold Sassy thought it was one thing to like Miss Love and another thing entirely to marry her. Especially if your wife died just three weeks ago.

5

AS MAMA expected, there wasn't anybody in Cold Sassy who didn't wonder if Grandpa hadn't been sweet on the milliner a long time, and maybe was relieved to get shet of Miss Mattie Lou so he could marry Miss Love.

For sure Miss Love wasn't a bit like Granny, except they were both feisty. Granny always wore her skimpy gray hair pulled straight back behind her ears and fastened in a ball. I never saw a frill or ribbon on her and I figured she had never been pretty. She told me that when she and her cousin were young, they walked by the harness shop one day and chanced to hear an old man say what nice girls they were. Another man said, "Yeah, but one of 'm shore is strange around the eyes."

"We never knowed which'n he meant," Granny said, laughing.

I knew which'n. It was Granny. Her eyes were the farthest apart I ever saw. She had big ears, too, and the last few months a peculiar knot came on one side of her throat. It wasn't a goiter. Doc Slaughter said blamed if he knew what it was. Grandpa teased her about it. "You look like you done swallered a goose aigg, Miss Mattie Lou, and it got stuck in yore goozle."

She just laughed. She was kind of worried about the knot, but really didn't care how it looked, and Grandpa didn't either.

Her not having a boy baby was the only thing Grandpa ever threw up to her. Once I saw tears come in her eyes when he mentioned it.

Granny used to say she never did see why Mr. Blakeslee married her. "When he come back to Cold Sassy after the War, he was the handsomest man you ever seen and I was a old maid. Twenty-one year old and never had a beau in my life. I was fixin' to go in to church one Sunday mornin' when this good-lookin' feller, he tapped me on the shoulder and said, 'Ain't you Miss Mattie Lou Toy? You don't need no sermon today. Stay out here and le's talk.' I ain't seen him since the fourth grade but I knowed it was Rucker Blakeslee. So we stayed in the churchyard, like a reg'lar courtin' couple, and talked one another's ears off. Afterwards it was dinner on the grounds, and we talked some more. Fore that day was over Mr. Blakeslee said he was a-go'n marry me, soon as he come back from peddlin' in the mountains." I remember she laughed about how quick Grandpa could make up his mind. "Maybe he thought I was rich," she added, laughing again.

There were those in Cold Sassy who had the same idea. They said the land Mattie Lou's daddy owned was why Ruck Blakeslee was so taken with her. She knew they said that, but it never worried her.

She always called him Mr. Blakeslee, and I never heard him call her anything but Miss Mattie Lou. Once when I was little bitty and Papa and Mama went to Atlanta on the train to buy for the store, I stayed at Grandpa's house and slept on the day-bed in the back hall. About daybreak I heard him stand up to use the pot. The bed creaked as he flopped back down, and I heard him say, "Turn over, Miss Mattie Lou, so I can put my feet up to yore stomach. They's cold."

At the time, I wondered how Grandpa could get his feet up that high, tall as he was and short as she was. Only when I was older did I think how funny for a man to call his wife Miss Mattie Lou when it was just the two of them in bed. Papa called my mother Miz Tweedy in front of Queenie or neighbors, and Mama in front of me and Mary Toy, but I knew she was "hon" or Mary Willis when they were by themselves.

Everybody in Cold Sassy admired my grandmother. At her funeral, I heard somebody say, "Miss Mattie Lou just reeked of re-fine-ment, didn't she?" and I knew what was meant.

Her refinement wasn't like Aunt Carrie's. Granny didn't sit on the porch reading Greek and Latin and Shakespeare, or get up lectures for children, or recite poetry. She didn't think she always knew best, the way Aunt Carrie did, and didn't throw off on people who said "I seen" or "I taken," like Aunt Loma, and didn't make children practice manners, like Mama. But Granny was a fine lady anyway, never mind her grammar or her country ways and never mind how plain she was.

To my thinking, it was refined that she didn't fuss at Grandpa about not having the house wired for electricity. When Mr. Sheffield, the mill-owner, bought a Delco generator for the mill and contracted with the town to install twenty street lights and run wires to all the houses and stores on both sides of the railroad tracks, practically everybody got electricity except Grandpa and the mill workers and the colored folks in Pigfoot Bottoms. But you didn't hear Granny complain about having to trim wicks, clean smoked-up lamp chimneys, and fool with kerosene when other ladies could just pull a ceiling cord to get light.

Grandpa wouldn't pay to hook into the new water main and sewer system, either. Said he didn't mind going to Egypt, which was what everybody in town called privies. He never seemed to notice that Granny was still drawing well water and emptying slop jars after other women were turning faucets and pulling tank chains.

Still and all, Grandpa loved Granny. Nobody would doubt it if they'd been down there with him and her like I was after she had her stroke.

She got took one night early in June. I remember I was at a magic show in the brush arbor and they called me out.

The family sat around Granny's bed till nearly daybreak. She moaned a lot and hiccupped, but never spoke a word. Not even to Grandpa. We went home for breakfast, and I remember how Papa kept patting Mama's hand. "Please, God, don't take her," she prayed between bites.

We could hear Queenie moaning in the kitchen as she fried salt mackerel, her tears splattering in the hot grease. Then she went to singing a Nigerian grief song learned from her daddy, who was lured onto an illegal slave ship in 1848, when he was only twelve. The slavers brought him to an island off the Georgia coast and hid him there till he got bought for Mr. Bubba Tate; that's how he ended up in Cold Sassy. Queenie always sang her daddy's African words, but you knew by the wailing and moaning that they meant death.

"Don't you dare sing that!" Mama yelled from the breakfast room.

Soon as we could, Papa and I hurried to the store. We knew Grandpa wouldn't get down there that day.

We were so busy we none of us went home to dinner, not even Miss Love, who put aside her hats to help wait on customers. All we had was crackers out of the barrel and rat cheese off the wheel. Dr. Slaughter came by the store from the sickbed about one o'clock. He told me Granny was "tol'able." But when he went over to the cash register where Papa was, he said, "Hoyt, she's dyin'. And she cain't stop hiccuppin'. Hit's wearin' her out."

You have to understand that Dr. Slaughter was a fine physician. He had not only read medicine for six months under a doctor over in Athens, he'd gone two whole years to medical school up North. So if he thought Granny was dying, I never doubted it was going to happen. "God's mercy is our only hope," he said as he went out.

I went back to the storeroom and knelt down on a sack of cow-feed and prayed harder than I ever had before in my life. "Oh, Lord Jesus Christ, have mercy on Granny Blakeslee," I begged. "Please, God, spare her. If Thou wilt just let her live, I promise I'll be a better boy. Please, God. Please. . . ."

6

IT WAS all over town about Granny's stroke. Several ladies who went down to the house came by the store later and told us how she was, but at three o'clock we still hadn't had any direct word from Grandpa or Mama or Aunt Loma. Papa said he sure did wish Mr. Blakeslee had a telephone at home. Finally Miss Love said, "Mr. Hoyt, why don't you send Will up there?"

So Papa said, "Will, run and see how your granny is and how Mama's holding up. And ask Mr. Blakeslee if that case of Castoria ever came in from Athens. Chap Cheney's wife needs some for the baby."

Aunt Loma was at the door to greet people. When she saw it was only me, she turned away without speaking. Her eyes were swollen and she held a handkerchief to her mouth. As I went in, Mrs. Means came out with her baby, who had not only spit up but had soiled his diaper, I could tell. The front hall and parlor were full of neighbor ladies, but instead of it being a gaggle of sound like at church meetings, the talk was all whispered. My mother hurried toward me. I was fixing to ask her about Granny, but her face told me.

"Pa won't let anybody in the sickroom," she whispered. "Not even me and Loma." Tears welled up in her eyes. "But he'll want to see you, Will."

"Is she still hiccuppin'?" I whispered back.

"No, it fine'ly stopped, thank the Lord."

Granny was propped up on pillows in the big high-back walnut bed. Her eyes were closed. Her face looked gray. I thought she was dead, but when I stared hard at her chest, I saw a faint rise and fall. Not knowing what to say or do, I tiptoed in and just stood at the foot of the bed, one bare foot on top of the other, and looked at her and Grandpa.

He hadn't seen me come in. Sitting in a cane-back rocker pulled up by the bed, he was resting his left elbow near Granny's head. The empty knotted sleeve lay crumpled against her gray hair, and he held her small right hand in his big bony one. He was staring at Granny like she could hold on to life if only he didn't blink. But all of a sudden Grandpa's chest started jerking in the strangest way, and his eyes squeezed shut. Between the heavy mustache and the bushy, white-streaked beard, his mouth stretched across his teeth in a fierce smile. Then his lips squeezed shut. Though he made no sound, his chest kept jerking. I didn't know what to think. It scared me.

But then he gasped, and tears ran down his cheeks as he buried his face in his hand.

I had never in my life seen a grown man cry that way. Preachers and sinners cried at revivals, and old Chickenfoot Creesie, a colored man, would cry when he came to our back door begging vittles for his children on a cold winter day. But not silent like this.

Grandpa would of hated being seen. I sneaked out of the room, went out on the back porch, and stood watching Granny's White Leghorn rooster chase the dominecker hens and the Rhode Island Reds. Then I went in the kitchen, where several ladies were talking. The table was just full of good things folks had brought in, and I ate some fried chicken and a piece of lemon meringue pie.

When I peeped into the sickroom again, Grandpa was bent forward in the rocker, his arms and head resting on the bed by

Granny's side. Her eyes were still closed, but her right hand brushed across his mane of dark hair.

"You need . . . y' hair . . . cut . . . Mr. Bla'slee. . . ." Her words came weak and slurred. The left side of her mouth drooped like a rosebud gone too long without water. "Soon's I git . . . better . . . I'm go'n . . . cut it . . . trim y' beard."

At which Grandpa got up quickly and stood a spell before the window, getting aholt of himself. After he sat back down in the rocker, he gently pushed the hair off Granny's damp forehead, then blew his nose loudly—like a foghorn, tell the truth—and said, "I seem to of caught a li'l cold, Miss Mattie Lou."

That's when he saw me standing in the doorway.

"Grandpa," I said, "why don't you go get you some lemon meringue pie? I'll sit with Granny."

He started to argue, but Granny smiled a tiny one-sided smile and said, "Let Willy . . . I ain't hardly . . . seen . . . m' Willy. . . ."

Soon as he tiptoed out, she closed her eyes. I think she slept. In a few minutes Grandpa was back with a dark red rose in his hand, biting off the thorns and spitting them out as he walked toward the bed. When Granny roused a little he held the rose close to her face. His hand was trembling. He said gruffly, "Here."

She tried to take the blossom but it fell to the sheet. Picking it up, he sat staring at it, then spoke real low to her. "I remember you had a red rose like this'n in yore hair the day I decided to marry you. Recollect thet Sunday, Miss Mattie Lou?"

She kind of nodded and just barely smiled, her mouth listing to the left.

"I hadn't laid eyes on you since you was a li'l girl, till thet day. You was sech a sweet thang," he said softly, his face close to hers, his hand caressing her cheek. "Yore eyes was all feisty and yore feet patted out the organ music whilst we talked. Was thet really the first time you ever set outside with the young folks, Miss Mattie Lou?" There was a twinkle in his eyes, a slight teasing in his voice, almost like he'd forgot how sick she was. "Gosh a'mighty, girl, thet rafter-rattlin' preacher give us plenty time to git acquainted thet day, didn't he? And I was after you like a charged-up bull. You recollect thet day, Miss Mattie Lou?"

She struggled to speak, her voice a whisper. "'Member . . . the brush arbor . . . Mr. Bla'slee?"

As Grandpa held her hand tight and tears rolled down his cheeks, I thought how Granny used to tell me about them camping out under a thick brush arbor their whole first married summer while Grandpa and Uncle Ephraim Toy built her a two-room house out of poplar logs so big it took just five to make a wall.

I had figured out long time ago that my mother must have been conceived under the brush arbor—and I blushed to think about that now. Whether such memories were stirring in Grandpa, who can know. What he said next was "Miss Mattie Lou, try real hard and git well. You hear? Please git well. I don't want to live 'thout you."

But Granny was asleep again, and soon was breathing so loud and deep it was like—I don't know what it was like. I'd never heard anybody breathe that way.

He looked over at me. "Will Tweedy, git on yore knees, son. Hit's time to pray."

I knelt down on one side of the bed and Grandpa on the other. Holding Granny's right hand, he rested his bowed head wearily against the edge of the feather mattress. Then for all the world like we were at testimonial time at the Baptist church with forty-five people listening besides God, he commenced to pray.

The way Grandpa prayed wasn't like other people prayed. You'd of thought God was an old crony of his instead of somebody who could strike you down dead if He had a mind to. "Lord?" he began, then stopped to honk his nose into a handkerchief. "Lord, I'm tempted to ast You to make Miss Mattie Lou well, like You was one a-them Atlanta doctors, or maybe Santy Claus and her a Christmas present You could give me if'n You jest would. I know Thou don't mind me hopin' she'll git well, Lord, or wishin', but hep me not to beg You to spare her. . . . Oh God, You know my sin!" he cried suddenly. His voice had an awful sound, like he was about to break half in two.

What could be his sin?

Granny's harsh breathing and the hushed voices in the parlor filled the silence. Finally he went on. "If'n she lives, Lord, I'll be thet thankful. If'n she don't pull th'ew, I ain't go'n say it was Thy will. You wouldn't kill her, Lord, to punish me. . . . Hep me remember my faith that Yore arrange-ment for livin' and dyin' is good. Hit ain't fair or equal, Lord, but it keeps thangs movin' on. Hep me not forgit my faith thet whatever happens, it's all right. . . . Hep Will Tweedy here see thet we got to accept dyin' in exchange for livin' and workin', and havin' folks like Miss Mattie Lou to love. And be loved by."

My grandfather's voice was stronger and calmer now. "Lord," he added, like it was a postscript on a letter, "please forgive the ways I ain't done right by Miss Mattie Lou. Please, forgive me. She don't know, and ain't nobody else knows, but I know and You know, Lord, what I'm a-talkin' bout. And please hep her stand the sufferin'. Hep her not be skeered. And wilt thou please comfort them grievin' daughters in the parlor, Lord, and Will Tweedy here, and li'l Mary Toy. Give them heart's ease. And me, too, Lord. A-men."

Granny didn't die that day. Next morning she was better. She could talk clearer and she took some chicken broth and sassa-fras tea when Mama brought it in to her.

Everybody except Grandpa said it was God's will. Some said He spared Miss Mattie Lou because so many folks were pray-ing for her. The Presbyterians said her getting well was preordained. Brother Belie Jones, the Baptist preacher, said God just wasn't ready to take her Home, praise Jesus, or else He had something more for her to do here before she passed into the Great Beyond.

Grandpa didn't say anything at all. But there wouldn't of been more joy on his face if he'd just won a fist fight or made a hundred dollars on a land deal. If Cold Sassy folks would bother to remember that day and how happy he looked, they'd know Miss Love was nothing more to him at the time than a way to make a profit on ladies' hats.

7

MRS. Avery down the street kept saying, "Now don't y'all git your hopes up too much. I seen it many a time—a sick person gits better just fore they go'n die."

We didn't pay her any attention. Granny really was better, no doubt about it. In the days that followed she slept a lot, but not with that awful unnatural deep breathing, and she could talk plainer and move her left hand, and the left side of her face wasn't dead-looking.

The first sign that Mrs. Avery might be right, or at least that there was a change, started one evening about a week later. It was about five o'clock. I was the one sitting by the sickbed. Granny had been dozing when all of a sudden she roused up and grabbed my arm. "Willy, look-a-there at them two coats fightin' in the corner! That littlest coat don't have a gnat's chance!"

Before I could answer, she whispered, "They's a old woman in Mr. Blakeslee's cheer. Go away, woman! She's hid-jus, Willy—face all puckered like them doll heads made out'n dried apples. Go on, git!"

"Ain't nobody in the chair, Granny."

"Ain't now. I got rid of the old booger." She sounded proud

of herself. Then in a panic she whispered, "Willy, she didn't leave! She's up on the wall!"

I was scared. I didn't know what to do. Mama had gone down to our house to change clothes. Grandpa, wore out, was sound asleep on the narrow daybed in the back hall. I was just fixing to call him when Granny smiled and said, "Old booger's gone, thank the good Lord!" Then she drifted off into a per-spiry sleep.

Trying to cool her off some, I picked up the cardboard fan that said BIRDSONG'S FUNERAL PARLOR in big letters and under it *Rest in the Lord.* The fan seemed like an omen. A chill goose-bumped my arms. I fanned fast so as not to read the words, but they had already brought to mind Great-Granmaw Tweedy, how at her first funeral she sat up in her coffin at the graveyard and screamed. They were fixing to close the lid on her and nail it down, and she wasn't dead.

I shuddered, and just then Granny Blakeslee's eyes opened wide in a horror of her own.

"Willy?" she whispered. "What's them two men doin' over yonder? See? Look on the far side a-the cemetery." She pointed. "They got shovels. They comin' over here! They go'n steal me!" Grabbing my arm, she pulled me down on the bed—pulled so strong that if she'd really been pulling me into her grave, I wouldn't of been scareder.

"Grandpa!" I yelled. But then she loosened her hold and looked up past me, as if seeing a wonderment. "Y'all come for me?" she called out, real friendly.

Granny listened, like to somebody talking . . . looked dis-appointed . . . then smiled politely and said, "Well, when y'all ready for me, just holler." Then in a strong, trembling voice she said, "Ain't they a sight, Willy!"

"Ma'am, I don't see nothin'."

Granny kept nodding and smiling, like greeting folks at church, and reached up like to touch somebody.

"What you see?" I asked eagerly.

"Angels! Son, this here room's just full a-angels!" Her voice sent another thrill up my spine. "They got lacy wings, and they's all dressed up in quilted robes. . . . The softest, prettiest colors, Will! Lordy, they keep a-comin'. They's flyin' out'n the quilt chest! You cain't see'm? They come out, and then they float up and on off—clear th'ew the ceilin'! They's just beautiful, son! Bye-bye now," she called. She kept looking this way and that, smiling and waving. "Y'all come see me agin, hear." Every time one batch of angels left, another batch came out of the chest.

"Go git your grandpa," Granny ordered. "I bet he can see'm. They's just everwhere. . . ."

When Grandpa stumbled in, rubbing his eyes, she said to him, "Lookit the quilted angels, Mr. Blakeslee! . . . Aw, shoot, they done gone." Granny sagged down weak against the pillows, exhausted, her fingers plucking the sheet.

Mrs. Avery always said you know death's on the way when a sick person goes to picking at the covers.

"Mr. Blakeslee, I seen the most beautiful bein's. . . ." As Grandpa plopped down in the rocker, she went to telling him about it and got all excited again. "I wouldn't take a pretty for them angels!" She said it over and over. "I just wish you—"

"Forgit all thet, Miss Mattie Lou." Grandpa said finally. He spoke soft to her, like you would to a child. "Hit were jest a dream. You all tangled up in yore mind. Go to sleep now." He slid his left elbow under her neck, circling his other arm around her, and pulled her close to him, rocked her against him.

"Mr. Bla'slee," she mumbled, "if you'd a-come . . . a mite sooner . . . you'd a-seen'm. . . . I seen a. . . ."

"Sh-h-h. Go to sleep now, Miss Mattie Lou," he whispered, his strong arms holding her, gently rocking, slow and gently rocking. "You all tuckered out. Sleep now. Go to sleep."

She drifted quickly into a deep snoring stupor. By next day you could hardly wake her—and if you did, a minute later she'd go right back into that loud, awful breathing. The last time Grandpa got her roused up, she looked scared and said, "Sump'm terrible. . . . Sump'm awful's a-matter . . . w' me. . . ."

Grandpa smoothed the damp hair from her forehead, spoke soft. "Tell you the truth, you been pretty sick, Miss Mattie Lou. But you gittin' better now. You jest real tired and need to rest. So go on back to sleep, hear. I'll set right here by you. I ain't go'n go leave you, Miss Mattie Lou." He choked up. "I ain't ever go'n leave you. . . ."

But she left him. That night the angels came back for her, like she'd asked them to.

And nobody who saw the heartbreak on Grandpa's face when Granny breathed her last would have thought for one minute that he was glad to get shet of her so he could marry Love Simpson.

8

AFTER Grandpa and Miss Love eloped, a lot of people felt sure he had never so much as looked at the milliner till after Granny died and he needed a housekeeper.

But those same folks were sure as certain that Miss Love had had designs on him ever since Miss Mattie Lou took sick, and was after him from the minute he became a widower.

"I was onto Love Simpson from the beginnin'," skinny old Miss Effie Belle Tate told Mama after the elopement. "Nobody else suspicioned what was goin' on, but I did." Because of living next door to Grandpa, Miss Effie Belle acted like God had sent her a special delivery letter explaining all the goings-on. "Miss Mattie Lou's body wasn't hardly gone to the funeral parlor before that woman was down to your pa's house, washin' and moppin' and dustin' and sweepin'." The pink wart quivered on her thin upper lip. "I knew the minute Miss Love got out a broom that she was after the nearest of kin. Why else would a white woman go over to your daddy's house to get it cleaned up for the funeral?" she asked Mama. "Hit wasn't like he didn't have you and Loma to do for him."

But at the time of Granny's funeral, Miss Effie Belle had sung a different tune entirely. I remember how she talked across the coffin to Mama. "Ain't Love Simpson sweet to pitch in like this? After workin' for your pa two years, I reckon she knows how economical he is. He ain't go'n hire nobody to hep, and Lord knows, you and little Loma got your hands full. Not to mention your hearts bein' full to overflowin' with grief."

All Miss Effie Belle did for Grandpa that day was bring over a chocolate cake and a caramel cake. Being eighty-nine years old, she'd had plenty of practice and was by far the cake champion of Cold Sassy. Still and all, two cakes weren't anything like equal to the trouble Miss Love went to on the day before the funeral. Besides all the cleaning, she had washed and dried dishes for hours in Granny's hot kitchen. The house was full of sad people, come to cry and eat and drink tea, and Granny didn't have enough dishes without somebody being in the kitchen to wash each plate and glass as soon as it got set down.

If Miss Love had notions about Grandpa that day—the way Miss Effie Belle claimed later—having to use a privy and draw well water and go to the back porch to throw out the dirty dishwater would have been enough to make her think twice.

That night after supper, Aunt Loma, Uncle Camp, us Tweedys, and Grandpa sat in the parlor with the remains and the visitors. But Miss Love was still working in the kitchen—by lamplight, I might add. I remember Grandpa went back there two or three times to tell her to quit. She said she wasn't tired a bit, but she must of been about to break half in two.

Mama and them had expected we would all sit up with Granny that night. But at ten o'clock, when Miss Love finally got through and came in the parlor and asked if there was anything else she could do, Grandpa not only told her to go on home, he told all of us to. "Ain't nobody go'n set up with Miss Mattie Lou but me."

"Pa, we don't mind a bit," my mother said. "We want to. You need us."

"I don't need nobody but yore ma."

While we were saying good night, I saw Miss Love put her hand on Grandpa's arm.

"You done too much," he told her gruffly.

"Not at all," she said. "Sir, the first winter I was here, when I had the flu, Miss Mattie Lou came and bathed me every morning —like she was my own mother. I won't ever forget that. I want to do anything I can to help you now." She said it so sweet, with tears in her eyes.

Grandpa blew his nose loud. "Uh, well, good night, Miss Love. I'm much obliged."

When I was halfway down the front steps, he called me. "Will Tweedy? Git up here fore sunup, boy. I want you to hep me."

Anybody who had been with us next morning wouldn't ever wonder how Grandpa had felt about Granny—before she died or after.

I got there at daybreak. The parlor door was shut where Granny was, and I could see the flickering glow of lamplight under the door as I walked down the cool dark hall. I wanted to go look at her, but I was scared to, by myself. I hurried to the back porch.

In the half-light I could see Grandpa out in Granny's rose garden. He was cutting rosebuds, which for him wasn't easy with just the one hand, and dropping each one into a big zinc tub. Without even a howdy or good morning as I walked toward him, he called, "Git out yore pocketknife, Will Tweedy."

"What you want me to do, sir?"

"Hep cut them roses."

When it came to feeling close to Granny, being in the garden was a sight better than sitting by her coffin. Out there amidst all the growing things, it seemed like maybe she'd just gone to the shed room to get a hoe instead being off in Heaven.

I stood and looked for a long time. Over yonder were what she called her "word plants"—the wild flowers she planted because they had names she liked. Creepin' Charlie, Lizzie run by the fence, love's a-bustin', fetch me some ivy cause Baby's got the croup. . . . In the next bed were medicinal herbs she used in potions for sick folks: squaw weed, hepatica, goldenseal, ginseng for the brain, jewelweed for poison ivy rash, wolf milk for warts, and fleabane and pale bergamot, which Granny would rub on her face and arms to keep off mosquitoes and gnats.

But on that early June morning, the heavy scent of roses was what made my heart ache. It was hard to believe the roses could be so alive and her so dead.

"Make haste, son. Come hep me." Grandpa was impatient.

"How many we go'n pick?" I asked, coming up where he was.

"All of'm," he said, waving his arm stub over the big garden. It had been a late spring and there were still masses of roses. Red, white, light pink, dusky pink, yellow. All colors, all kinds. The garden had a border of climbing Seven Sisters on the west side, a hedge of red roses on the side next to Miss Effie Belle's house, white roses against the henhouse, and yellow tree roses at the far end. "Just git the buds," ordered Grandpa. "The wide-open ones won't last out the funeral."

Grandpa had him an idea.

I toted tubs full of roses to the back porch. Drew buckets and buckets of well water to pour over them. And about time the first rays of sunlight hit the back steps, I sat down out there with my grandfather.

First he took a square of Brown Mule out of his pocket, bit off a plug, and settled it in his left cheek. Then he leaned his chair back against the porch wall and got to work. While I trimmed off the lower leaves and thorns, Grandpa took a big split-open croker sack and poked each rose stem into the loose burlap, weaving it in and out, then in again, like a pin being stuck into cloth. In no time at all he had him a solid blanket of roses. It was beautiful.

I noticed for the first time the pile of big croker sacks by his chair.

He spat tobacco juice in an arc that just missed a Rhode Island Red pecking dirt in the swept yard. The hen shrieked, flapped her wings, and ran off. Handing me what he had done, Grandpa said, "Now, son, git this here thang down under some water. Yore granny always soaks roses under water fore she puts'm in a pitcher." He didn't notice he was talking as if Granny was in her kitchen, fixing to cook us some grits, instead of laid out in a coffin in the parlor.

It will help to show what Granny meant to Grandpa if I point out that it wasn't a cheap homemade coffin she was in. It was a fine readymade one he'd ordered years ago when rich Mr. Sheffield was thought to be dying and didn't. It had been upstairs at the store ever since, alongside the stock of corn planters, fertilizer spreaders, mule collars, iron washpots, hat trees, and extra brass racks for readymade dresses. When I was little bitty, I used to close my eyes whenever I had to walk by that coffin.

There were some who said later that Grandpa, stingy as he was, wouldn't have used that expensive coffin for Miss Mattie Lou if he wasn't trying to make it up to her for something he'd done wrong—such as lusting in his heart after Miss Love or being too stingy to give Granny electricity and a bathroom.

If he wasn't ashamed about the lights and plumbing, maybe he should of been. But personally I didn't think guilt had anything to do with the nice coffin. I thought he used it because he loved her. Despite all I found out later, I still think so.

Grandpa told Granny one time that dead folks ought to be put right in the ground as the Lord intended. I was there and heard it. "And I want me a party when I die, not a funeral. Remember thet."

She didn't act shocked like Mama would of. As a matter of fact, she laughed. "Don't go talkin' bout dyin', Mr. Blakeslee. I druther live in the past than dwell on that part of the future. Still, since you brung it up, I'll say this: my feeling bout buryin' ain't the same as your'n. You remember that." She said the dead body was sacred, it having been a house for the mind and soul, and as such it deserved proper respect. "A nice funeral is a sort of thank-you," she added. "A person's body oughtn't to be treated like no old dead dog."

What she said didn't change Grandpa's thinking about buryings in general, but that being the way she felt, then he was going to see to it she got her thank-you. For Grandpa, that was a sign of love, because usually he did what he wanted to and never noticed that Granny might welcome a little consideration.

By the time he finished covering another sack with roses, he was as excited as a little boy digging worms to go fishing.

They were really something, those rose blankets. It seemed a shame to plan on covering up a fine coffin with them, but they were sure pretty.

I stood up to stretch and scratch. I was hungry. After milking that morning, I had poured me a big glass of sweetmilk, warm right out of the cow, but that wasn't enough to call breakfast. I slumped down in a chair, tilting it against the side of the porch. "We picked way too many roses," I said, yawning.

"No, we ain't. Now make haste, son. I don't want no kinfolks or neighbor ladies seein' what we done and buttin' in with suggestions. Fore you know it, half a-Cold Sassy'll be down here a-cryin' and carryin' on, tryin' to see how I and yore ma and Loma is a-takin' it. I cain't stand thet. So we got to git th'ew."

I figured the real reason he didn't want anybody to see the rose blankets, it would spoil his surprise for the funeral. But of course he couldn't admit that.

Before long we heard somebody at the front of the house. Probably Mama, but I knew he was scared it was Aunt Loma. He made me drag the zinc tubs full of watered-down rose blankets into the shed room by the back porch. Then, with me on one side of the tub and him on the other, we toted the rest of the roses to the barn and finished out there.

When he thought we had enough, he told me to cut a sack half in two for him. Leaving an oval space the shape of a head on a pillow, he put the last rosebuds around the oval. I guessed what he aimed to do with it.

First I had to go ask Mama to clear folks out of the parlor where Granny was. Then me and Grandpa went in there from the dining room. I couldn't believe how many big vases and baskets of yard flowers had been brought in and set on tables and on the floor around the coffin.

It gave me the creeps, helping Grandpa slip his pillow sham of roses under Granny's head. But touching her didn't seem to bother him. He patted her face and smoothed her hair, and even pried up her stiff hands and moved them a little. Then all of a sudden his face scrooched up, and in a choky voice he ordered me to leave and tell Mama not to let nobody come in on him.

It was ten o'clock, and like I say, I was hungry. Folks had already brought over more cakes and pies, and platters of fried chicken and ham, and their good china bowls full of string beans, butterbeans, okra, and tomatoes. Enough to feed a ox, really. So I ate. I was in the kitchen finishing a piece of Miss Effie Belle's caramel cake when Grandpa found me again.

My mother stuck a glass of buttermilk in his hand and he drank it, but I'm not sure he even noticed. He was all business. "Will Tweedy?"

"Sir?"

"Go hitch up Big Jack."

"Yessir."

He walked with me to the back porch. As soon as we were out of earshot of the others he said, "When you git Jack hitched, lay them rose thangs in the buggy and bring it on up here."

"Yessir."

When I got back with the buggy, Grandpa was out on the porch picking long nails from a dusty glass jar on the long-legged, blue-painted old slab table. A hammer handle stuck out of his pants pocket. "Load up, son."

"Yessir."

The mourners were all up front with the corpse—admiring the roses that framed her head, I expect. So not a soul except Mama saw me bring the zinc tubs out of the shed room. She marveled, I could tell, but said nothing as I dragged each one to the edge of the porch, tilted it to drain the water out, then loaded "them rose thangs" on the back of the buggy. I didn't know how many blankets we had, but I was sure it was too many.

Grandpa said, "Naw, son, it's jest enough."

Enough for what? He didn't say, I didn't ask, and neither did Mama, who watched as we drove off.

He let me keep the reins. Said we were bound for the cemetery—"but first, son, we'll go by yore house." I didn't have to wait till the whiskey was on his breath to guess why.

The grave was already dug, of course, close behind all his and Granny's children that hadn't lived to grow up, and just a little ways from the Toy plot, where Granny's daddy was buried between her mama and his second wife. He had a granite tombstone. His wives had slabs of brown marble off of washstands.

I always thought a single marker joining the graves of a man and wife looked like the head of a double bed. In the moldy old Crane plot was a wide granite headstone that joined three graves—like a triple bed, you might say. This is what it said:

Here Lies Luzon Theophilus Crane
A Good Man

| *Eugenia Lamson Crane* | *And Lucy Wylie Who* |
| *His Wife* | *Should Have Been His Wife* |

"Did the Wylies put that up, Mama?" I asked her one day. "I know it wasn't the Cranes did it."

"Aw, shah!" she snapped, jabbing a cone-shaped tin cemetery urn into the ground for the jonquils we brought. "Quit readin' that trash and bring me that quart jar of water for the urn."

Not far from Mr. and Mrs. Crane and Miss Wylie was a little

bitty headstone that said *"In Memory of Tweety, Jan. 4, 1894."* I
used to think that was a baby cousin of mine with the Tweedy
name spelled wrong, but Mama said it was somebody's pet
canary. "The Tweedys are always buried at Hebron," she reminded me. "I mean the older generations. This family"—she
solemnly indicated the grave of my baby brother—"has started
bein' buried here."

Always before, the graveyard had seemed real interesting and
peaceful. Just a quiet and reverent place. But in mid-June, 1906,
the deep yawning hole that would swallow up Granny looked
horrible, like it could suck me down.

"What we go'n do, Will Tweedy, we go'n line yore grandma's grave with these here roses."

It took two of the blankets to cover the floor of the pit. The
others he nailed into the grave's damp red-clay walls while
both of us lay on the grass, me holding a croker sack blanket
and a long nail, him propped on his left elbow, hammering. It
was only as the last nail went in that Grandpa sagged. As if he
was too tired to get up, he lay there looking down, and so did
I. It wasn't awful anymore. The heavy smell of roses drifted up,
and I thought I'd never seen anything as beautiful.

A tear dropped off Grandpa's nose and watered a red rose.
Seeing that, I choked up. I ached for Grandpa, grieving. And
for Granny. I knew she wouldn't want to be dead. And then
I thought about my friend Bluford Jackson, the one who got
lockjaw after firecrackers burned his hand last Christmas. He
had died soon after New Year's Day and now nearly six months
later I was just finally seeing that Blu was gone for good.

"Why'd Blu Jackson have to go and die, Grandpa?" I hit my
fist on the grass. "Why'd God take him like that? He hadn't
lived yet. He wasn't old like Granny. He had so many things to
do. . . . He was scared of dyin'. . . . I bet Granny was scared of
dyin', too."

Grandpa put his arm stub around me, and we lay there, staring down into the grave. "Like they say, the old must die and the young may die," he muttered softly. "Hit's what you git for livin'. But thet don't seem so awful as you grow older, son. You'll see." He gave a deep sigh.

"How you go'n stand it, Grandpa? I mean goin' home every night and she ain't there."

"Thet's what I don't know, son. Thet's what I don't know. Yore granny was—" He choked up again. When he could go on, he stretched both arms down into the grave, dropped them, helpless-like, and said, "But do I got a choice, Will Tweedy? I got to stand it, ain't I? Livin' is like pourin' water out of a tumbler into a dang Coca-Cola bottle. If'n you skeered you cain't do it, you cain't. If'n you say to yoreself, 'By dang, I can do it!' then, by dang, you won't slosh a drop."

We lay there a while longer. Finally Grandpa sighed again and said, "I wouldn't ast the Lord to steady my hand for a thang like pourin' water into a Coca-Cola bottle. But I'll be astin' Him for hep on this." He indicated the grave. After a moment he said, "Miss Mattie Lou shore was a fool about roses." Silence again. "Two or more year ago she was out workin' in her rose garden one mornin'—did you know, boy, she's got over sixty different kinds out there?—and she said to me, said, 'Mr. Blakeslee, I wouldn't even mind dyin' if'n I could be buried in a bed of roses.' Thet's jest the way she put it. I laughed and said it would be her luck to die in the dead of winter. . . . Well, son, we better go git cleaned up for the funeral. Wisht it was over with. I'm plumb wore out." We both got up. "If'n I had my way, wouldn't be no sech a thang as funerals. They's jest a long hot time full a-hypocrites and kin-folks—grievin' some maybe, but mostly bein' glad to be alive theirselves and tryin' to pretend they ain't havin' a good time seein' one another."

"It wasn't like that at Blu's funeral."

"No, course not. They ain't no hypocrites at a youngun's funeral."

When I brought up the buggy, Grandpa stood by old Jack,

absently stroking the huge gray forehead, and looked back at the grave site. Then he spat a wonderful stream of tobacco juice and climbed in beside me. "She was a plumb fool bout roses," he said softly.

Later, remembering that morning, I had no question in my mind: Grandpa's eloping wasn't a matter of him not loving Granny or not respecting the dead. He just needed a cheap cook.

9

T O ME, all that went on during Granny's sickness and dying and getting buried was more like a dream than real, till we got back from the cemetery and I watched Grandpa stop at the little pine desk in the front hall and write down her end in the Toy family Bible.

Miss Love Simpson was standing nearby, come to think of it, as Grandpa put on his glasses and opened the Bible to the page where his and Granny's life together was written down in different handwritings and different shades of faded ink. Miss Love and I watched as he read it, muttering out loud to himself.

> "*Matilda Louise Toy, born April 10, 1850, in Cold*
> *Sassy Community, Jackson County, Georgia*
> *Married Enoch Rucker Blakeslee May 27, 1871.*
> *Children:*
> *—Mary Willis, born March 5, 1872.*
> *—Trix Esperance, born Jan 19, 1873.*
> *Kicked by a mule and died July 1, 1880.*
> *—Rachel Aleez, born Nov. 25, 1875. Died April 5, 1877, of*
> *the smallpox.*
> *—Emma Frances was born Dec. 29, 1876. Died April 30,*
> *1877. Pneumonia.*

—*Missouri Mathis, born Wednesday Spt. 2, 1878. Died
Spt. 5, 1878, of water on the brain.*
—*Loma Louise was born Dec. 6, 1886.*
—*Fannie Marie was born January 28, 1888, died a little
Lamb of God the same day."*

Then Grandpa wrote in fresh, black, final-looking ink beside Granny's name: *Died June 14, 1906.*

The *Cold Sassy Weekly* said it was "one of the saddest deaths that
has ever grieved the people of Jackson County, because Mrs.
Blakeslee was so beloved by so many."

I saved the write-up. It had a black border and was long and
fancy, beginning,

> *Asleep in Jesus, blessed sleep From which none ever wake to
> weep.* . . . Mrs. Mattie Lou Blakeslee, a sacred mother of
> Israel, has gone to receive the crown of righteousness
> which God has promised to all those who love His ap-
> pearing. Born Matilda Louise Toy, great-granddaughter
> of Capt. Josiah Toy who pioneered the settlement of Cold
> Sassy in 1804, she embraced the religion of our Blessed
> Master when young. Since that time her life and charac-
> ter has been that of a pure Christian ministering to the
> comfort of all, especially her beloved husband and con-
> sort, E. Rucker Blakeslee of this city, who now must walk
> alone. She gave up this life *"As one who wraps the draper-
> ies of his couch about him and lies down to pleasant dreams."*
> We must believe that the gates of Heaven were thrown
> open to receive her ransomed spirit, and that a crown re-
> splendent with glory was placed upon her peaceful brow
> whilst the plaudit *"Well done, thou good and faithful servant"*
> echoed and re-echoed through the mansions of bliss.

There was a lot more. Grandpa read it all, but instead of
tearing it out to put in the Bible, he just dropped the newspaper

on the floor, the way he always did when he was through with it, put his glasses in his pocket, and got up to go feed his mule.

He went back to work the day after the funeral, which most folks thought not fitting. But as I said before, he wasn't the same. No laughter in him. No jokes or funning. No neighborly talk, and wouldn't talk about Granny, either. If a customer started saying her condolences, Grandpa would nod and cut her off with "You be needin' anythang else, ma'am?"

He treated Uncle Camp awful during that time. One morning Grandpa pointed to a keg of nails and said, hateful, "Camp, see thet keg? I want you to roll it from one end of the store to the other till I say stop." He made Uncle Camp roll the keg all day long. When Papa asked what it was all about, Grandpa said, "I'm jest sick a-watchin' thet boy do nothin'."

I didn't like my grandfather much that day. But I didn't like Uncle Camp, either. If he'd been a real man, he would of refused, and then either walked out or set to work like his job depended on it.

We soon found out that Grandpa didn't go home at night when he left Aunt Loma's after supper. He went to the cemetery.

"Yore pa walks by here and we're settin' on the veranda but he don't speak or so much as nod in our direction," Miss Alice Ann Boozer told Mama. "He don't even see us. Just turns at them iron gates and disappears like a ghost. We always stay out there till the night air cools off, you know, and many a night he still ain't come back by time we go to bed. It ain't good for Mr. Blakeslee to be by hisself at the cemetery in the pitch-black dark—or in a full moon, either, for that matter."

I've mentioned Miss Effie Belle Tate, who lived next door to Grandpa. She told Mama that sometimes Grandpa's lamp was still on in his bedroom at two and three in the morning. "And lots a-times he goes out there to Miss Mattie Lou's rose garden in the middle of the night to pace them paths. If it's a moon I can see him just a-walkin'. Up and down, down and up. Pore man, he's a-grievin' hisself to death. One night I come close to takin' some sweetmilk and cookies out there to him, but I didn't know what to say. He's shut us all out. I keep out'n his way."

Miss Effie Belle wasn't the only one who didn't know how to take Grandpa.

Folks felt a lot more easy with Mama and Aunt Loma, who would sit and cry with them and carry on about God's will and how He surely had a purpose in letting their ma die or else needed her in Heaven, one. They'd talk on and on about the final illness, the dying, the funeral, and especially about the grave being lined with roses. "Such a sweet thing," folks would say. "Such a sweet thing Mr. Blakeslee done."

Nobody seemed to of been told that I helped.

Then somebody would bring up about Granny's ancestors leading a wagon train from North Carolina, how they camped here on the ridge under some big sassafras trees while they were building their houses. If somebody didn't know how come the settlement was named Cold Sassy, it would be explained that mountain wagoners on the way to market used to call the place "thet cold sassyfras grove" or "them cold sassy trees."

As often as not, before the conversation got back to Granny, somebody would say, "I think we done outgrowed the name Cold Sassy. Hit's old-fashion and tacky. We ought to do like Harmony Grove and git us a name like Commerce."

Then they'd talk a while about how hard Miss Mattie Lou worked all her life, hinting but not exactly saying out loud that she had worked herself into an early grave—which was the same as saying Grandpa could and should of hired her a cook and a colored boy to work her garden.

Nobody mentioned that all my life I had been her colored boy. Knowing Grandpa wouldn't hire anybody, Papa had expected me to put in a piece of every day down there. And I didn't mind. What I did mind, now that she was dead, was being in mourning.

Because of her hair, my sister didn't feel like I did. She was glad to hide at home. What happened, while Granny was on her deathbed, Mama got up a black outfit for Mary Toy to wear to the funeral—black taffeta dress, black stockings, black slippers, and a little black bonnet. "It'll give her something to wear on trips later," said Mama. "If everything is black already, the train sut won't show."

Unfortunately, Aunt Carrie decided early the morning of the funeral that Mary Toy's fiery red hair looked "inappropriate" for such a sad occasion. Her solution was to dye it black. "Just for today, sugarfoot," she said when my sister had a conniption fit. "We'll rinse it out tomorrow." By time Mama heard about it, it was too late to argue. And anyhow, who could argue with Aunt Carrie?

She wasn't really kin to us. She had latched on to Granny's mother long time ago. Granny inherited her, and now she was ours—for Christmas and Thanksgiving and all the Sundays between. She used to be rich, but wasn't anymore, having lost everything during the War, including her husband. But she still acted rich and, like Grandpa, had the manner of one who expects to be obeyed. She lived in an old three-story, rundown plantation house with morning rooms and sun rooms, and porches wrapped around every floor. Aunt Carrie looked rundown herself, in her frayed sweaters and canvas and rubber Keds shoes. She wore her thin hair in a knot, and except in winter always had a flower stuck behind each ear.

One summer she held weekly "cultural gatherings" for children. You had to recite a poem to get in. She gave us lectures on women's suffrage, Shakespeare, Beethoven, English history, and horticulture, and always had two freezers of homemade ice cream, which was why we all went. Her last lecture was on what she called "human excrement." Taking a rose out of her hair, she said it wouldn't be nearly so lovely if it weren't for human excrement, and told us children to go home and get our folks to empty our slop jars into our manure piles. Nobody let their children go to Aunt Carrie's gatherings after that, but she kept letting everybody know what happened to the excrement at her house. Aunt Carrie was stubborn.

Which is why nobody thought to argue with her when she decided to dye Mary Toy's hair black for Granny's funeral.

Halfway through the service Mary Toy got to sweating. Trickles of black liquid started running down her face. Seeing it, the preacher could hardly keep his mind on how good Granny had been or how it was God's will and all. Mama kept glancing at Mary Toy and finally dabbed at her face with a lace handkerchief.

About then, Mary Toy noticed the black that was smearing off her hair onto her sweaty arms. Thinking it was black blood, she went to wailing. People in the pew behind the family said later they thought she was just missing her granny, pore child.

Soon as we got to Grandpa's from the cemetery, Mama took Mary Toy's taffeta dress off and stuck her head in the wash basin on the back porch. The black leached right out, just like Aunt Carrie said it would. Only thing, her hair wasn't red anymore. It was purple. Soon as she looked in the mirror, Mary Toy went into mourning for her hair. She cried for hours and then days. It was a relief to everybody when, after our Glorious Fourth celebration, Cudn Temp said to her, "Sugarfoot, come on home with me and stay till the color grows out." Cudn Temp lived out on a farm in Banks County.

Like Mary Toy, my mother was partly in mourning for herself. Because of Granny's dying, she couldn't go to New York City with Papa on the buying trip they'd been planning ever since February, when a wholesale house in New York offered the store two free tickets on the boat from Savannah and Grandpa said for Mama to go. The morning after the funeral, she insisted she wouldn't even want to go now. But tears were brimming in her eyes and all of a sudden she left the room and ran upstairs, I guess to cry. I felt sorry for her, and I knew she couldn't help feeling sorry for herself. Mama had never been anywhere much except to Atlanta, once to Raleigh, and once to Social Circle, Georgia, for a two-week visit the summer before she married.

At first I didn't mind being in mourning. I didn't want to do anything anyhow but think about Granny. It was like I was trying to memorize her.

One thing I already missed was pork. Granny had been providing me with ham and sausage ever since Papa decided if the Lord thought hog meat was bad for the Jews, then we weren't going to eat it, either. "Southern Presbyterians are as much God's Chosen People as Jews are," he said.

Grandpa had laughed about that. Said he heard Presbyterians were God's Frozen People, haw. He and I thought that was funny, but Papa didn't. Anyhow, we gave up pork and got sanctified. I reckon us and Mr. Izzie, Cold Sassy's only Jew, were the only folks in town who never ate a piece of fried ham for breakfast. Well, and my friend Pink Predmore's mother. Pork gave her the trots. Mrs. Predmore was the last of seventeen children and always said the family gave out of strong stomachs before it got to her.

Well, Granny saw to it that Mary Toy and I had our share of hog meat. After Papa's big decision, she kept leftover sausage or ham or fried steak-a-lean in her warming oven in case we came by after school. Pork didn't matter all that much to me, but the fact Granny saved me some mattered a lot. It was like getting hugged, or knowing that at the Friday speakings she would be out there in the schoolyard with Mama, sitting on a sawmill puncheon and perking up when it was Mary Toy's turn to quote from "Lord Ullin's Daughter" or my turn to give an oration from Demosthenes. No matter how bad we recited, Granny always clapped loud.

I went up to her house about a week after her passing. I guess I hoped she would seem less dead there.

Everything was a mess. Grandpa's bed looked like he got caught in the cover when he flopped out that morning. The top sheet trailed onto the floor. His bureau drawers were all open, and the clothes jumbled. His spit cup on the night stand was full of stale tobacco juice and smelled awful. A pile of *Atlanta Constitution Tri-Weeklys* littered the floor by the cane-back rocker.

In the kitchen I found coffee grounds spilled all over the table and burned toast in a pan on the cold stove.

Like I said, it had never been a spic-and-span house. Granny wasn't much for cleaning up. But though her windows didn't shine and her curtains drooped with dust and nobody could of eaten off her floors, she kept the bed made, the dishes washed, and things in place. She always said if a house looked neat, folks didn't notice cobwebs in the corners or dust on the mantel-piece.

Well, it was a sight now. I guess Grandpa had been looked after for so long, he didn't know how to do for himself. Mama had tried to help him. A week after the funeral she went up there and cleaned, but next morning when Grandpa came by for his snort, he told her she had her own place to see after "and anyways, I ain't a-go'n let you work like a colored woman at my house. Hit was yore ma's duty. Hit ain't yore'n." The place looked so lonesome without Granny that I couldn't stand it. My feeling was that if I called out, she would answer from the next room. But my knowledge was that I could go from room to room all day long and never catch up with her.

Despite I used to scour the porch for Granny and row her garden and all, I'd never done woman's work there or anywhere. But I did it that day. I wiped the kitchen table, rinsed out the spit cup, put clean sheets on Grandpa's bed, picked up clothes and newspapers. After which I just had to get out.

In the backyard, the hens clucked and murmured as they scratched for bugs or pecked at the last dirty crumbs of wet cornmeal that Grandpa had put out for them. The chickens didn't seem to miss Granny. The garden and the flower beds did. It being June, nothing looked tired of growing yet, but it all looked neglected.

I should of gone to weeding. Instead, I got Granny's gall-berry brush-broom off the back porch and swept the dirt clean around the steps. Then I sat down on the bottom step, put my face in my hands, and commenced to mourn.

To mourn is not the same as *to be in mourning*, which means wearing a black armband and sitting in the parlor, talking to people who call on the bereaved. At first you feel important. The armband makes you special, like having on a badge. But after a day or two it stops meaning anything.

But *to* mourn, that's different. *To* mourn is to be eaten alive with homesickness for the person. That day, I mourned mostly for Granny, who had lost more than any of us, but also for Grandpa, for Mama, and for myself. I didn't want to visit Granny at the cemetery like Grandpa was doing. That was just her empty shell over there, whereas here I could touch things she had touched, look out on the flowering plants she had looked at, and walk through her house. Of course, it never dawned on me then that another woman was about to come in and take over.

This had been the Toy home place ever since it was built in 1837. Granny lived here till she got married. It was still a farmhouse in 1890, when her daddy died and her stepmother went to live with a grown son, Mr. French Gordy. Granny moved back there with Grandpa and Loma, who was four years old at the time. Mama had already married, so she never lived in this house.

A long time later, when I was telling Miss Love about the home place, she asked me what happened to all the Toy farmland.

"Grandpa chopped it to pieces," I said. "He'd always made his living selling things, so when all that land was left on his hands, why, the only thing he knew to do with it was sell it." The railroad was finished in 1877 or around then, I explained, and with new businesses starting and folks wanting house lots close to town, the Toy farm that used to yield cotton was soon sprouting homes, outhouses, gardens, stables, and small pastures.

Granny never questioned Grandpa's selling her land or using the money to build the brick store. But as she once admitted to me, "I looked at him kinda hard one day and said, 'Cain't we use part a-that money to make the house modrun?'" She had been cooking in the dining room fireplace—that was easier than going outdoors to the old kitchen—and she wanted to join the old kitchen to the house. So it was placed on logs and rolled close to the dining room, and what they called a "butler's pantry" was built between. While he was at it, Grandpa also bought her a new walnut bedroom suit and a big iron coal-burning stove. He put in a nice new privy, and had a new well dug right by the back porch so you didn't have to go in the yard to draw water.

But that was the last time he ever put a dime into improvements.

Now that Granny was dead, you'd think he'd ask the Lord to forgive him for not letting her have plumbing, electricity, and a telephone. But I doubted he could repent of that. He had skimped so long to get ahead, he didn't even notice how stingy he was—something like the way my daddy had gotten everything wholesale through the store for so long that he didn't notice how much he spent anymore; just noticed how much he saved over retail. When Grandpa wouldn't even put in one bathroom, my daddy had put in two—one on the porch upstairs and another on the porch near the kitchen. The same year, Papa replaced our old-fashioned white picket fence with a fancy iron one and set up the iron stag between the pittosporum bush and the elaeagnus.

Well, so Granny had died without ever getting much she wanted. But she had sixty varieties of roses, and most everybody in Cold Sassy was beholden to her for nursing a relative back to health or laying out the body for burial.

If she'd been a man, Granny Blakeslee would of made a dandy doctor or undertaker, either one.

One thing I got onto that morning, with the house full of Granny and empty of her at the same time, was the notion that she'd of hated dying so plain.

Like doctors and undertakers, she really told good dying stories. There wasn't a grown person in Cold Sassy who couldn't pass away the time after Sunday dinner by recollecting who'd died of what when, but Granny was the only one I ever heard be interesting about it.

Just for instance, her aunt Beppy—the one they say had the power of levitation—died with typhoid fever. That by itself wasn't enough to mention. Lots of folks died of the typhoid. But Beppy died at seventeen, on her wedding day. "They give her Bible to Mr. Billy," Granny would say.

She used to tell about a Confederate soldier from Cold Sassy who got sent to Andersonville to guard Yankee prisoners and passed away in the smallpox epidemic there. He was buried at Andersonville. His family never forgave the Confederacy for not marking his grave. "In that cemetery," said Granny, "you couldn't tell Abner from a dead Yankee."

If Aunt Carrie wasn't there, Granny would tell how Carrie's husband, Mr. Horace, went to the War right after they married and never was heard from again. "Everybody figgered he died on some Yankee battlefield, but you cain't be sure for certain," said Granny. She never liked Mr. Horace.

Granny's cousin Selah Toy had been a boatman on the Savannah River and named his daughter Vanna, after the river. Not long after he got the top of his head shot off in the Battle of Chickamauga, Cudn Vanna married an Englishman, a blockade-runner for the Confederates. When the Yankees caught him, they stood him up on a barrelhead and, without a trial or anything, shot him. After the War, Cudn Vanna married three more husbands and lived to bury them all, even the one that was forty years younger than she was.

Uncle Buson was the one I liked to speculate on. He didn't die. He just disappeared.

"We never knowed what happened to him," Granny would say cheerfully, "but he was dead to the fam'ly from the day they read Grandfather's will. Hit said, 'My son Buson has not acted in a becoming manner so I leave him nothing.' That night, Uncle Buson he took off on my granddaddy's best horse and ain't nobody in Cold Sassy ever heard pea-turkey from him since. Somebody said he went out West and married one a-them Mexican women, but we never knowed if it was so or not." Once I asked Granny what Uncle Buson did that was so bad, but she wouldn't tell me. Said I was too young to hear such. It must of really been worth hearing about if it was too awful to mention.

Granny's favorite was the Stokeses. "They was mighty wrought up about the South losin' the War," she would begin. "When the carpetbaggers commenced takin' over, them Stokeses built a rock wall around the fam'ly graveyard and took off for Brazil, lock, stock, and barrel. The whole lot of'm went, and never wrote one word back to Cold Sassy. Hit was like ever last one had passed away."

When Granny passed away herself, I thought how dying was a lot like what happened when the Stokeses went to Brazil or when Uncle Buson rode off into the night. Whether you were up meeting God, down in Brazil hating Yankees, or out West somewhere loving a Mexican woman, to those left behind, you had just plain disappeared.

The morning I was mourning up at Granny's house, I thought how disappointed she would be to of died so ordinary. She wouldn't call heart trouble, a stroke, kidney failure, and malignant spring fever worth mentioning alongside having two funerals, like my great-grandmother Arminda Tweedy, or being buried alongside Yankees at Andersonville, or dying on your wedding day.

But after Grandpa went off to Jefferson in the buggy with Miss Love, it dawned on me that now Granny's passing wasn't so plain after all. Like everybody else in Cold Sassy, she would call it worth mentioning that her husband got married just three weeks after she went to her grave.

10

PURELY on account of being in mourning, my family missed most of the July the Fourth parade.

Grandpa had thought up Southern Independence Day way back in February as a practical joke on the United States of America. Like everybody else in Cold Sassy, he still carried a grudge against the Union, and I reckon he had a right to. Grandpa was just fourteen when he joined the Army of the South with his daddy. They served all through the War in the same outfit: Echols Battery of Georgia Light Artillery, Company K, 6th Georgia Regiment.

Grandpa went in as a drummer boy, but one morning when the 6th Georgia was in retreat, he put his drum in a supply wagon and took up a gun, and that was the last he saw of the drum.

His lieutenant told them one time not to get captured. Said the Yankees would hang you by your heels and split you down the middle like a dang pig. Grandpa claimed he never believed that. But he believed starving. They got so hungry, one night his daddy roasted a rat and parched some acorns, "and we was glad to git it. But right then I made up my mind, if'n I got home alive, I never was go'n eat nothin' I didn't like agin. And I ain't."

One time when my mother complained about him being so hard to please about food, Papa said, "Hon, what if you'd had to eat a rat?"

Besides losing his appetite and his drum, Grandpa always said the War cost him half his left arm. He claimed a damn yankee shot it off. Granny told me it happened in a sawmill accident after the War. "But they ain't a bit of use mentionin' that in front of your granddaddy," she said. "For one thang, it don't matter. For another, you know how he is. He tells a thang a few times, he believes it hisself. For another, when that-air arm goes to hurtin' on a cold winter night, it's a comfort to him to cuss the Yankees. A man cain't hardly cuss no sawmill."

Be that as it may, 1906 was the first and only year we've ever celebrated the Glorious Fourth. Usually nobody even mentions it.

Cold Sassy is the kind of town where school teachers spend two months every fall drilling on Greek and Roman gods, the kings and queens of England, the Crusades, the Spanish Inquisition, Marco Polo, Magellan, Columbus, the first Thanksgiving, Oglethorpe settling Georgia, and how happy the slaves were before the War. A good teacher could cover the history of the whole world in two months and spend the rest of the school year on the War of the Sixties and how the Union ground its heel in our faces after it knocked us down. Seems like we never got much past the invasion of Yankee carpetbaggers before school let out for the summer.

The Declaration of Independence and the Revolution were mentioned at school, of course, but just barely. In Cold Sassy, nobody under forty had ever made or waved an American Flag. Even today, in 1914, there's not but one United States flag in the whole town. The post office being in one corner of the drug store, Dr. Clark is required to fly a U.S. flag. On July 4, 1906, he put it down to half-mast.

Just the way Grandpa planned it, all the stores closed that day, and folks white and colored lined North Main and South

Main, waving their Confederate flags. The parade was led by the town band and the Negro band, which rode in a mule-drawn wagon. Both bands were playing "Dixie," but not in the same style.

Our cook's husband, a giant, tar-black Negro named Loomis Toy, blew the alto horn in the Negro band. His trick was to sit with the horn in his lap for the first half of a piece, then start at the beginning and, tooting double time, hit the last note right with the others.

Behind the bands came a big cotton wagon draped with Confederate bunting and pulled by a double team of mules. It carried Cold Sassy's disabled veterans and the moldy old ones. Most were in uniform, sitting up there stiff and proud in rows of chairs. As the wagon rolled slowly along, grown men and women watched silent, with tears in their eyes.

Next came old Ab Pulliam in his goat cart, the pants of his gray uniform folded under his thigh stubs. He had a double sign hung across the goat's back that said, WE LOST THE WAR BUT WE AINT ON OUR LAST LEGS!

Behind him walked Miss Love Simpson and Aunt Carrie, Cold Sassy's only suffragettes. The banner stretched between them read, "Ladies, How Long Must We Wait for Liberty? Demand the Right to Vote!"

Grandpa Blakeslee was supposed to be next, leading the column of younger, gun-toting veterans who were to charge up North Main Street, playing like this was the Battle of Gettysburg. He had planned on riding a bicycle, just to be funny, and even went so far as to order one from Sears, Roebuck and Co. But him never having ridden anything smaller than a horse, buggy, or train, the bicycle scared him to death. After one try, he fell off and wouldn't get back on. Said he would lead the charge bareback on old Jack, his mouse-colored horse-mule.

In the planning stage, Grandpa said I could be the drummer boy and march right behind him. As it was, because of our being in mourning for Granny, Mama wouldn't let me so much as follow the army downtown, much less beat the drum. I just watched what I could from our front veranda.

Grandpa wasn't in the parade, either. When Granny took sick, he said he didn't have any heart for the battle and wouldn't be in it. Mr. Toot Withers took his place, riding a high-stepping white stallion, and waving a sword in one hand and a big Confederate flag in the other. Mr. Toot being drunk, as usual, nobody knew how he stayed on a horse that didn't like rebel yells, drumbeats, rifle fire, or firecrackers, all of which erupted when he shouted "Charge!" and the marching soldiers went into action—dashing, tottering, or limping back and forth across the railroad tracks, firing their guns toward the sky and poking bayonets at imaginary damnyankees.

It was a grand sight!

At that point I do believe Grandpa would have left our porch swing and joined in if he could of found his uniform right quick. But only Granny knew where she had packed it away, and Granny was dead.

The very next day, Grandpa got married.

11

MAMA didn't come down to dinner at all after Papa told her Grandpa and Miss Love had run off to Jefferson together.

I wasn't hungry, and Papa's appetite was down, too, judging by the way he picked at his food and picked at making conversation.

He had a habit at meals of telling things he'd heard at the store or read in the paper. But whereas I thought the big news today was Grandpa's eloping, the first thing Papa said was something about the average life span in America being forty-seven years.

Thinking any minute he would tell me what was really on his mind, I just said, "I declare." But what little he talked, it was about other things. Like for instance Papa said old man Plunket told him the train hit a mule and a cow at the same time yesterday just outside of Cold Sassy. "Killed'm both," Papa said, and reached for the pully-bone, my favorite piece of fried chicken except for the head. "And might-near wrecked the train."

By then I was just barely listening, because it had dawned on me that our time of mourning must be about over. If Grandpa could go get married, maybe I could go fishing.

Well, I'd just go. Today. I'd go to Cussin' Creek. Leave just soon as Papa went back to the store.

I never did like to fish by myself. So after whistling my dog out of the garden, where he was digging a hole to lay in and get cool, I went by the Predmore house to find Pink.

"He ain't to home," his little brother Harkness told me. "Him and Daddy rode the train down to Athens this mornin'."

Pink's mother was in the yard, hanging out clothes. "I was hopin' Pink could go fishin' with me," I told her.

"Well, he's gone to Athens."

"That's what Harkness said."

Mrs. Predmore didn't even mention Grandpa and Miss Love, so likely Mama was all wrong about folks being scandalized.

But when I got to Smiley Snodgrass's house I found out Mama was likely right. "What's this I heerd 'bout yore granddaddy, Will?" asked Mrs. Snodgrass, wiping her hands on her long white apron as she came to the door.

I couldn't tell how much she knew, so I just said, "I don't know'm."

"When they gittin' hitched? Not any time soon, I reckon."

"I don't know'm." They were already hitched, more than likely.

"I hear tell Loma's bad-mouthin' thet Simpson woman all over town. You cain't blame her." She waited for me to say something. When I didn't, she said, "Pore Loma. Pore Mary Willis. What a cross to bear, and Miss Mattie Lou not hardly cold in the grave. How's yore ma a-takin' it, Will?"

I couldn't make out whether Mrs. Snodgrass was embarrassed for pore Loma and pore Mary Willis or if she was thinking Mama and Aunt Loma would be pore in the future if Miss Love got aholt of their inheritance. One thing I did know, my mother sure would be upset when she found out Aunt Loma was talking outside the family—especially now that there wasn't any chance of changing Grandpa's mind. Mama thought private family matters ought to be just that. Private.

"Mama's takin' it all right, I s'pose," I said, as if widowers getting hitched right after the funeral was an everyday thing.

"I betcher Son Black's madder'n a wet hen, losin' Miss Love to a old man."

"I don't know'm. . . . Miz Snodgrass, where's Smiley at?"

"Down to the barn, cleanin' out the stalls. Bein' punished for back talk, so don't you go git him to slip off. You hear?"

"Oh, no, ma'am." I backed off the porch. Knowing that Mrs. Snodgrass would likely watch to make sure I left, I struck off down the street, pitching sticks for T.R. to go fetch. But after passing by the French Gordy house next door, I ducked around back to the Gordy stable and went through it to the pasture.

Mr. French had three cows. One of them, a tan Jersey named Blind Tillie, was Cold Sassy's champion milk producer. Born with milk-glass eyes, she was named for Blind Tillie Creek, where I sometimes fished. She always walked with her chin resting on the rump of another cow. That day, Tillie and the other two cows and I were all headed for a big oak tree near the barb wire fence, on the other side of which the Snodgrass's mule-headed Jersey cow had already laid down to chew her cud in the shade.

I crawled under the barb wire, stepped around a wet cow splat, and headed for the Snodgrass barn. There was old Smiley, leaning against a fence beside a big pile of manure, staring at the sky with his mouth open and his hands resting on the pitchfork handle—dreaming about girls, most likely. Seeing a pile of dried horse biscuits, I got me one and threw it just as Smiley's mouth stretched in a wide yawn. It went in nice and neat, like a baseball into a glove.

Boy, was he mad. He and I had us a great manure war then, throwing dried cow cushions and sheep pills and horse biscuits at each other and dying laughing. Just as I was fixing to talk about fishing, Mrs. Snodgrass yelled from over near the smokehouse for Smiley to come catch her a chicken. So that was the end of that.

Lee Roy Sleep was still out of town. He and his folks were up in the mountains at Tallulah Falls, visiting his grandmother. I thought about Dunson McCall, but remembered Dunse was picking peaches for Mr. Angus Tuttle, the depot man, who had an orchard out on the edge of town.

Mr. Tuttle hadn't offered me a picking job since that time us boys pulled up an acre of his onion crop to dam the stream between his pasture and ours. We were making a swimming hole. Our daddies paid for the onions and we all worked out the money, but Mr. Tuttle never forgave us.

Well, so I didn't have a soul to go fishing with but T.R.

T.R.'s real name was Theodore Roosevelt. He was just a puppy when Papa took me to Atlanta to hear the president speak; I named him Theodore Roosevelt when I got home that day—then shortened it to T.R. so folks wouldn't think my dog was a Republican.

Naturally I didn't carry a fishing pole. No use looking disrespectful of the dead. In one pocket of my overalls I had me a line, and my sinkers and my hooks stuck in a cork. Stuffed in another pocket were some biscuits, to wad up into dough balls to bait the hooks with, and five pieces of Queenie's fried chicken in case I got hungry. I would cut a pole at the creek.

Cussin' Creek was where us boys usually fished when an hour or two was all we had between chores. It wasn't far. Just a piece down the railroad tracks near Mr. Son Black's farm. Our train was a branch line of the Southern Railroad, which ran north from Athens through Cold Sassy, Commerce, and Maysville, connecting at Lula Junction with the Airline Railroad, which went on to Atlanta and Charlotte. I would get on the tracks at the depot just past the Cold Sassy tree.

That tree was close to a hundred feet tall and the only sassafras still left of the big grove our town was named for. On a bright fall day when the sun lit up its scarlet leaves, you never

saw anything to equal it. People would ride the train to Cold
Sassy just to look. Usually they'd read the plaque that was
nailed to its trunk: "Sassafras: family *Lauraceae*, genus *Sassafras*, species *S. albidum*. Note how the leaves vary in shape on
the same twig, some having no lobes, some two or three." Considering the number of train travelers we had, I thought the
plaque ought to tell how unusual tall the tree was and something about how Cold Sassy got its name.

We used to have another big sassafras tree, which stood next
to this one and had a knothole where bluebirds nested. Us boys
used to rob the nest of its bluish-white eggs and blow out the
insides. The railroad had taken that sassafras down some years
earlier to make room for a bigger depot platform.

I saw Mr. Angus Tuttle out there on the platform now, but
he didn't see me. He was too busy arguing with a fat old farmer
in overalls. Like all depot agents, Mr. Tuttle was cow coroner
for the railroad, so I guessed right off that this was the farmer
whose cow and mule got killed yesterday. Death by train isn't
unusual out in the country. Farmers don't keep their livestock
tied or pastured up like we do in town. I gathered from the argument, which was getting pretty loud, that the farmer was
mad about the amount Mr. Tuttle had offered to settle the
claim against the railroad. I could still hear those two fussing
after I passed the foundry, but then everything got drowned
out as the 1:10 from Athens approached.

Stepping off the tracks to let it pass, I watched as the engine
screeched and ground to a halt at the depot, belching smoke
and steam. Back on the tracks and heading toward open country, I had a thought. "T.R., hot day like this, ain't no fish go'n
bite at Cussin' Creek." I remembered then that Queenie's husband, big Loomis, said they were biting real good now under
the trestle at Blind Tillie Creek.

There were hazards. The shortest way to get there was to
follow the tracks in the opposite direction, which would not
only take me back past the depot but also past our house and

Grandpa's store, where I might be seen. Also, I'd have to go through Mill Town.

I had walked through Mill Town plenty of times, but never by myself.

I was about to call it a dern fool idea when it came to mind I might see Lightfoot McLendon. I hadn't laid eyes on her since school let out for the summer. Whistling to T.R., I turned and headed back—past the foundry, past Grandpa's house, past the Cold Sassy tree and the depot, past our house, which I detoured around, and on toward the hotel and the block of stores.

Walking along, I wondered about Grandpa and Miss Love. When would they get back? Would she come in and work on her hats, or would Grandpa drop her off at his house so she could sweep up some and cook his supper? Or since he was used to eating supper at Aunt Loma's, would they both go over there tonight?

I wondered if an old man who just buried his wife would take his bride on a wedding trip. I decided he wouldn't. Not just because of being stingy but also because, at fifty-nine, Grandpa had his mind on the store and not on what Queenie called "de sweet'nin' on de gingercake."

Well, right now my problem was not Grandpa and Miss Love but how I would get past the batch of stores without Papa and them seeing me, or old Crazy Tatum, who always sat in a rocking chair by the door to keep people out of his store. He put the chair just inside if it was cold, and out on the sidewalk if it was summer. If it looked like you might try to come in, he'd flap his arms like a bird and leap around, hollering and whooping. I knew if he went to whooping at me, Papa might chance to look out the store window and wonder why I wasn't weeding the garden like he said to.

I had figured on going behind the brick stores till I was clear of them, but when I saw the 1:10 leave the depot, headed towards us on its way to Lula, I whistled to T.R. and got off the tracks on the South Main side. Seeing me, the engineer put an arm big as a leg of mutton out the window and waved.

Since the store was across the tracks on North Main, we were hidden behind the moving boxcars, and I decided to keep on walking. The train was so long that before all of it passed us we were beyond the stores, the Confederate monument, the livery stable, the tanyard, the cotton gin, and Sleep's Ice and Coal, and nearly to Mill Town.

The factory soon came in view and, just beyond it, the river that powered the machines. On a railroad siding off the main tracks, men in linty overalls were loading big pasteboard boxes full of cotton thread onto a freight car. At a huge square opening in the factory wall, other men were taking bales of cotton off of a wagon. I recognized old Charlie Rowley up there on the driver's bench of the wagon. Old Charlie and his mule were both string-halted, each having a tight ligament in the leg that made him limp. But that didn't keep them from hauling for Grandpa's big warehouse—delivering to the mill or depot when farmers who stored their cotton with us finally sold it.

Charlie saw me and waved, and I waved back. Too late, I realized if he saw Papa later he might chance to mention seeing me on the train tracks going through Mill Town.

Hurrying by the factory, I came to where the mill hands lived in close-together little shotgun houses—three rooms in a row, like long boxes, with public wells and privies that served two or three houses each.

Cold Sassy was proud of its cotton mill, just as it was proud of the trains coming through. "Get you a railroad" and "Get you a cotton mill" was what big businessmen in Atlanta advised any town that wanted to grow. Having both, we were bound to grow, but Grandpa said he didn't see how the population could change any. "Ever time a baby's born, some boy joins the Navy." Still, Cold Sassy was considered up-and-coming. And like I said, already folks were talking about changing its name to something less countrified, the way Jugtown had been re-named Winder, and Garden Valley was now Pendergrass, and just four years ago Harmony Grove became Commerce—all of which, to my mind and Grandpa's, were awful improvements.

Our mill houses were a long sight better than in lots of places, but they looked more like repeating blobs of white than homes. There weren't any trees. No shrubbery. Families sat crowded on the hot little porches, cotton lint from twelve hours in the mill still clinging to their hair and overalls and dresses. I guessed they were night workers who hadn't gone to bed yet. Who could go to bed in those little houses on a hot day in July?

I kept glancing at the blank, stony, pinched faces of the men and women staring at me from steps and doorways, and at the children, all white-headed just like you see them in the Appalachians. They stared at me with sullen, mean eyes, like I was a strange animal. But whenever I looked right at them, their gaze dropped to the ground.

Mill Town was watching the Town Boy pass.

Nervous, I hurried my steps on the crossties. And T.R., who'd been running ahead like a brown and white flash, now walked stiff-legged close beside me, growling at any bony mangy dog that slunk too near. I went from hoping I'd see Lightfoot to hoping I wouldn't. It was one thing to like her at school and nobody know it. Here in Mill Town on my crosstie stage, folks would suspicion her if they saw me acting friendly. Also, I knew I'd be embarrassed if she was sweaty and lint-headed from the factory or if, Lord forbid, I saw her coming out of a privy.

I decided it was a lot harder to walk through Mill Town than to have our school cluttered up with snot-nosed children who had cooties and the itch, and who at dinnertime stayed at school to eat biscuits and syrup, making us town children feel guilty for going home to a big hot dinner. The mill boys were always picking fights with town boys—tripping us up or calling us names. Of course we did our share of tripping and worse. But it was our dern school, for gosh sake.

Before Lightfoot, I had a healthy disrespect for all mill children. Since Lightfoot, just being around them was like getting fussed at for wearing shoes in winter and having a cow and a family cook.

Lightfoot wasn't like the other mill children. Wasn't like any girl I ever knew, for that matter. Wasn't silly, wasn't always twiddling her plaits, didn't tattle or gossip, didn't hit boys over the head with books or scrape the back of your neck with a sweetgum burr when you weren't looking. She was quiet and sweet and smart. Ragged, of course, but real clean, and thin without having the bony-faced, sunk-eyed look of mill children who've been hungry all their lives. Lightfoot had what I thought of as the fresh free look of the hills on her.

The way I got to really know her, I had to stay after school one day for flipping spitballs, and she was staying late so Miss Neppie could help her catch up. This was back in January, soon after she came to Cold Sassy from the foothills of the Blue Ridge. At some point, when Miss Neppie went to Mr. McCall's office, I asked Lightfoot how come she left the mountains. "My mama always wanted us to move to Cold Sassy," she said. "My mama she had the TB, you know. Last summer, jest fore she passed, she wrote her brother in Mill Town and he said we was more'n welcome to stay with them. Mama kept sayin' Pa would have steady work in the mill and I could git me a good education and amount to something."

The girl didn't seem to have heard yet that nobody in Mill Town ever amounted to anything.

"So after the fall crop come in, my daddy he sold his plowin' steer and his piece a-land, and we caught the train to Cold Sassy."

"You got any brothers and sisters in the mountains?" I asked.
"Yeah, lots of'm. But they all married or dead, one."

As T.R. and I walked the railroad tracks past the sweaty, dirty, hostile faces of Mill Town, I couldn't help wondering if a summer of slaving at the spindles would take away Lightfoot's hopes—and my notion that she walked in a cloud of fresh mountain air. Fixing my eyes on the repeating crossties, I walked fast. And even faster as it dawned on me just how much I didn't want to see Lightfoot McLendon with lint in her hair.

I also didn't want to see Hosie Roach, a snot-nosed twenty-one-year-old mill boy in my class who stunk like a polecat and had tow-colored hair so thick and tangled it looked like a cootie stable. Hosie wasn't big as me, but whenever we had a fight—about once a week—he usually won. Gosh, what if he and a bunch of other mill boys ganged up on me.

Getting beat to a pulp might have been better than what happened later at the trestle. But of course I didn't know it at the time, so it was a grand relief when my dog and I got past all chance of seeing Hosie or Lightfoot, either one.

Once we were out in the country, we had a high old time. The dog romped through the daisies and weeds and tall grasses growing along the tracks. He scared up rabbits, barked at terrapins, caught gnats and flies in his mouth, and every few minutes looked back to be sure I was still coming along behind. Two bobwhites scooted across the tracks right in front of us, heads up and backs straight as tin soldiers', but they flushed before T.R. could point.

That dog must of wet every black-eyed Susan and every head of white Queen Anne's lace we passed. I never saw such a dog for doing Number One. Grandpa called it the sweet-pee trick. I know that's how dogs stake out territory and also how they find their way home, but looks like T.R. would know by now that all we had to do to go home was turn around and follow the train tracks.

Two or three times he stopped and stared back like he thought somebody was coming behind us. But then he would lower his head for a new scent and run ahead.

We saw a few mill people near the tracks, picking blackberries into lard buckets, and a whole family of colored people. The Negroes smiled and waved and held up their buckets for me to see. The mill people didn't.

It was hot, good gosh. My straw hat shaded my eyes, but that was all in the world good it did. "I guess I got about two hours," I muttered out loud. I knew the southbound train would cross the trestle over Blind Tillie Creek about when I ought to head home to milk.

You couldn't exactly tell time by that train, but it would be close enough. It always came back through Cold Sassy with a load of lumber from the sawmill at Lula, bound for the lumberyard in Athens, and usually there were some passenger cars carrying folks who'd been to Atlanta. In the fall there were always cotton buyers, and usually four or five drummers who would set up their merchandise in a hotel room, stay a few days, then move on to another little town. Grandpa called them "Knights of the Grip." When Mama and Aunt Loma were young, he never let them hang around the depot. Drummers liked to flirt, were fresh-shaved, and wore suits, patent leather shoes, and big smiles. Girls always liked them.

Less than a mile past Mill Town, I rounded a bend and saw the train trestle up ahead, marching through the air high above the wooded gorge where Blind Tillie Creek ran. Just before we got to the trestle I whistled for my dog and went slipping and sliding down a red-dirt path, past dusty briar bushes that reached out to scratch me as I ate my fill of blackberries.

It was a sight cooler by the creek than up there on the tracks. I cut me a pole and was soon perched on a stump, fishing and eating fried chicken. Later I cut a blackgum twig to chew on and settled myself comfortable on the ground with the stump for a back rest.

It was nice and peaceful there. Watching the shallow water splash and churn over rocks, I almost forgot how mad I was at Mama for making me stay in mourning, how mad I was at her and Aunt Loma for fussing about Grandpa marrying when he clearly needed a housekeeper, and how mad I was at him and Miss Love for not caring how the family felt. But then I got mad at Papa. Here I was at last—fishing—and I couldn't enjoy it for feeling guilty.

I had sense enough to know my daddy really needed me to be home working the garden. But I wished he knew what it felt like to have fun. All Papa had ever done was work. Before he was knee-high to a gnat, his own daddy had him picking bugs off of cotton plants, and he was hoeing as soon as he knew the difference between a weed and a cotton stalk, and milking soon as his hands were big enough to squeeze a cow's tit. I bet he never in his life had sat in the shade of a train trestle holding a fishing pole and watching dragonflies walk on water.

Grandpa Blakeslee bragged a lot about my daddy being such a dandy worker. I was proud he wasn't lazy like his own daddy, who spent the summer days on his porch swatting flies and even had him a pet hen to peck up the dead ones. Grandpa Tweedy always claimed he couldn't work. "My veins is too small," he'd say. "My blood jest cain't git th'ew fast enough to let me do much." Naturally he had a beard. He was too lazy to shave. He was even too lazy and self-satisfied to go anywhere, except to preaching over at Hebron or to Cold Sassy to sell his cotton. Wasn't ever on a train but once, when he went to Dr. Mozely's funeral in Athens. All of us went, but first Grandpa Tweedy and my daddy had to decide if it was all right to ride that train. Being Sunday, it might be a sin.

Like Grandpa Tweedy, Papa worried all the time about sin on Sunday. He never let us read anything but the Bible and the *Christian Observer* on the Sabbath, and once talked Mr. Tuttle into locking up everybody's Sunday Atlanta papers at the depot till Monday morning. The fact that Cold Sassy put up with that for a month or more shows how much they respected my father. I respected him, too, as I said before. But I wished he knew what it felt like to need to go fishing.

My bait was gone again. I wasn't going to catch anything here. It was too hot and the creek too low. Might as well go home and get to work. But glancing around, I saw a mess of logs and brush on the other side and remembered the deep hole there. If any fish were in Blind Tillie Creek, that's where I'd catch them. I was just fixing to get up and wade across when I chanced to look up at the train trestle.

I had walked trestles plenty of times. I used to play on one out in Banks County with Cudn Doodle and them. But I'd never been on Blind Tillie Trestle. From where I sat, leaning against my tree stump and looking up, it seemed higher than a Ferris wheel. Higher even than the new Century Building in Atlanta, and it spanned a wide, deep gorge.

Miss Bertha at school had told us about the si-renes—the mermaids who used to sing to Greek sailors and they'd go off course to follow. Looking at that trestle, I felt like I was being sung to. Or maybe it was more like when the fire bells clang on Cold Sassy's horse-drawn fire engine and you just got to go chasing after it to where the smoke is billowing up.

That's how Blind Tillie Trestle called to me that day.

The longer I stared up at it and the blue sky and fleecy clouds beyond, the more it seemed like a bridge across the world. I wanted to see how things looked from up there. I don't even remember winding the fishing line around my pole, but all of a sudden I was clambering up the bank. Old T.R. raced me to the top and then barked at me till I got up there.

At the edge of the trestle, a brisk breeze had whipped up, and the tracks seemed to soar across the sky.

It never once occurred to me to be scared. But it occurred to the dog.

12

FOLLOWING behind me, T.R. crouched low and took a few careful steps onto the trestle. Then, whining, he turned and crawled back to solid ground, tail between his legs, and commenced begging me to come back, too.

When the dog saw I was laughing at him, he wet on the rail, scratched with his back paws in the dirt, and dashed off, trying to get me to play chase. After that didn't work, he bounded down the brambly path to the creek below, where we had just come from, and splashed over to the other side, trying to show me a better way to get there. Standing in the shallow water, T.R. barked and bragged his white-tipped tail like he'd done something to get praised for.

"Old yeller belly!" I called down to him, laughing. My voice echoed spooky between trestle and water and gorge. I sure wished Pink Predmore and them were up here with me.

I put one bare foot on the rail. It was hot but not enough to burn, so I walked on it a piece, arms spread-eagle, balancing with my fishing pole like a tightrope-walker at the circus. I remember wondering if any birds ever walked through the sky up there instead of flying over the gorge. I soon passed the sand barrel that was bolted onto the trestle beside the tracks. People have been known to jump into a trestle barrel if a train comes at the wrong time and they get trapped.

Two thirds of the way across, I stepped off the rail onto a crosstie and sat down, elbows on knees, to look around. I thought about putting a penny on the tracks for the train to flatten, then decided not to. The penny would fall in the creek. So I just sat there, looking way off, and tried to think who lived in that little white farmhouse with green shutters down in the valley. From up here the house looked like a fresh-painted toy. I wondered why nobody ever painted their houses out in Banks County, where Grandpa Tweedy lived. He didn't know what a can of paint looked like.

Enjoying the breeze, I stretched out, face down, to look through the crossties at the water below. Leaves floated on the creek like tiny boats. And here came a long stick, a wake trailing behind it. When the stick turned against the current to swim toward the bank, I saw it was a water moccasin and threw a cinder at it. I missed the snake, but my next cinder hit the white spot on old T.R.'s rump. He barked at me till he got distracted by a big terrapin crawling on the creek bank.

It sure beat being in mourning.

All of a sudden I saw T.R. raise his head to listen. Then he dashed up the path on the far side of the creek, barking all the way, and went to jumping around at the edge of the trestle. He like to had a fit for me to come on. Shoot, you'd think he heard the train or something. Wasn't near time for the train. I didn't hear anything myself except that dern dog barking.

But just to make sure, I moved my head over to the rail and put an ear against it, lazy-like, and—I could hear the clickety-clack! The train was coming! Well, I could make it easy. But as I scrambled to my feet, the fishing pole got wedged somehow between the rail and crosstie. Couldn't leave it that way. Might derail the train. By the time I got it loose, the clickety-clacks were plain as day and getting louder, *louder*, LOUDER!

I stumbled and fell. Jerking myself up, I saw I couldn't possibly get off the trestle before the train moved onto it. Like a fox who runs into a hound, I turned and sprinted the other way. From somewhere, as in a dream, I heard a scream and looked back just as the big smoking engine roared around a bend.

I knew the engineer saw me. His whistle was going *whoo-whoo-whoo* in quick fast blasts. The trestle shook like a leaf as the train hit it.

I thought to aim for the sand barrel.

God A'mighty help me, I wasn't go'n make it! *Jump!* No, too far, creek too low. . . . Whistle screeching in my ears. . . . Train heat almost at my heels. . . . *Whoo-whoo-whoo!*

At that moment I thought FALL!

Like a doll pushed from behind, I fell face down between the rails and lay flat and thin as I could, head low between crossties, arms stretched overhead. As I was swallowed up in fire and thunder, I hugged my arms tight against my ears.

The engine's roar pierced my eardrums anyway, making awful pain. I was so scared I could hardly breathe, and there was a strong smell of heated creosote. Hot cinders spit on me from the firebox. Yet even as the boxcars clacked, knocked, strained, ground, and groaned overhead, it came to me that I wasn't dead. If there wasn't a dragging brake beam to rip me down the back, I was go'n make it!

Boy howdy, I did some fancy praying. All it amounted to was "God save me! Please God save me!" And then it was "Thank you, Lord, thank you, God, thank you, sir. . . ." I guess what made it seem fancy was the strange peaceful feeling I got, as if the Lord had said, "Well done, thou good and faithful servant," or something like that. I wasn't dead! Boy howdy, boy howdy, boy howdy! I was buried alive in noise, and the heat and cinders stung my neck and legs and the bottoms of my feet. Still and all, that was what kept reminding me I wasn't dead.

I found myself counting boxcars, by the sound of them, which was a long sight different in this position, with my eyes shut tight against the dust and cinders, from being in Cold Sassy waiting for the train to get by so I could cross from South Main to North Main. The train had to end. Trains always do. It seemed like this one never would, but brakes were screeching and the clickety-clacks on the rails were slowing, so I knew the engineer was trying to stop.

I felt blistered from the heat. My straw hat was gone. My arms were so tight against my head that my ears felt numb, yet it wouldn't have hurt more if knives were being jabbed into my eardrums.

But boy howdy, I was alive! Thank you, Jesus.

All of a sudden I felt sunshine overhead. Opening my eyes and raising my head, I saw the red caboose getting smaller and smaller as it neared the end of the trestle. The shaking of the trestle stopped. All sounds were muted, as if I had a wad of thick cotton in both ears or was shut up in a padded closet. I felt limp and dizzy. And as knowledge of what could of happened hit me, I started shaking and crying.

I heard T.R. barking from what seemed like far off, but all of a sudden his tongue was on my face! By gosh, he had run out over that trestle he was so scared of! I grabbed and hugged him, crying, "Good ole dog, good ole T.R.!"

When the train finally stopped, its caboose was maybe a hundred feet beyond the trestle. Just then, despite being deafened, I heard a girl's voice scream out, "Will! Will Tweedy! You awright, Will?"

And then she was on the trestle running toward me, her arms outstretched. "I'm a-comin', Will!" she called. "I'm go'n holp you!"

13

THE girl running toward me was Lightfoot McLendon, which didn't surprise me at all. If you've been run over by a train and you're alive to know it, what can surprise you after that?

She ran over the crossties barefooted, surefooted, light-footed like her name. I wanted to quit crying and shivering, but what did it matter, anyhow? I was alive!

I no longer felt so boy-howdy about it, though. I was numb, I was half-deaf, I was sick, shaking, stinging, and smudged with dirt and oil. I fixed my eyes on Lightfoot as if she was one of Granny's angels come to fetch me, and put my arms tight around T.R. He crowded me—licking, wagging, whimpering. When Lightfoot reached us, I grabbed her, too, and the dog licked both faces. Hers and mine, hers, mine, hers, mine. She was crying, too.

She said something that must of been "Lemme help you up, Will," and tried to pull me to my feet. WHOOP! Both of us nearly toppled off into the creek below. I tried not to look down.

"I don't . . . I cain't . . . I don't know if I can stand up," I mumbled. My voice came out of a well inside my head. She said something I couldn't understand.

Lightfoot bent so close that her long flaxen hair brushed against my face. It was tied with a string instead of plaited and I can still remember how sparkly white it looked in the sun. She yelled into my ear, "Kin you crawl, Will? If you cain't, them men comin' out'n the train can holp you."

I looked up to see men, women, and children rushing towards the trestle, and others swinging themselves out of passenger cars. Reminded me of bugs pouring out of a rotted cantaloupe if you kick it on the ground. The sight was enough to get me moving. Nobody was go'n tote me off that trestle.

"You go on first, Lightfoot!" I yelled. I reckon I was thinking if I couldn't hear her very good, she couldn't hear me, either. "I'll come behind you!" Grabbing a rail, I pulled myself up to a squat—but didn't have the nerve to turn loose and stand up. I was still shaky. The girl stood up, but swayed and then dropped down to her hands and feet, like me, and we moved on all fours, holding to crossties. Later somebody said we looked like spiders coming off that trestle.

As we neared the end of it, there were shouts and whistles and cheers from the folks crowded there, and finally a burst of clapping. The last few steps of the way, hands reached out to pull us to our feet. Then I was caught up in the arms of a huge man wearing overalls and a train cap—the engineer who'd waved at me in Cold Sassy. Giving me a bear hug, he shouted, "God a'mighty, boy! God a'mighty!" It was like I was his own son. He'd never even seen me before that day, I don't think, but it was like I was his own son.

In bed that night, going over and over what all happened, it dawned on me that by saving myself, I had saved the train engineer from running down a life, never mind it wouldn't of been his fault. That's why he was so glad to see me.

He was still holding me tight when I looked back and saw that T.R. was right out there where we'd left him on the trestle. Yelping and whining, he crouched forlorn between the rails, yearning towards us but not moving.

"T.R.!" I yelled, pointing at him, and the crowd took it up.

"Come 'ere, boy!" a man called, giving a loud piercing whistle.

"Here, boy! Here, boy!" from someone else.

"Come en, pup, you kin make it!"

More whistles. Arms outstretched toward him. And me shaking worse than ever, too weak to yell again. The dog wouldn't budge. Howling, barking, whimpering, he finally tried to crawl, but quit when one hind leg slipped through the crossties. He just let it hang there. He was frozen.

"Won't somebody g-go get him?" I was weeping now. "That's my dog!"

But the engineer, one bulging arm still around my shoulders, suddenly yanked me towards the train. "We gotta git outer here, boy! Come on, folks, git back on the train!" he hollered. "They's another'n comin'!" Then, handing me over to the conductor, he and the fireman sprinted toward the engine, way up the tracks.

The conductor, a tiny man in a beaver hat and Prince Albert coat, was jumping up and down like a tin clown. "Make haste, folks!" he yelled, waving his hat and pushing me toward the caboose. "We had to put on two trains! Other'n will be along any minute! Got to clear the tracks!"

"I ain't go'n leave my dog!" I said, turning back.

Lightfoot sprang forward. "I'll go git him, Will!"

The conductor grabbed her. "We ain't got time! I ain't go'n let you be on that-air trestle for the next train to hit. Besides, you cain't tote that big dog, honey. You too little bitty."

A new voice swept by like a wind, deep and booming. "I's gwine git him, Mr. Will!" It was big black Loomis, Queenie's husband, six feet six and three hundred pounds, hat on and coattails flapping. Racing by me, without even slowing down he hit the trestle like it was no different from the tracks in Cold Sassy. T.R. recognized Loomis right off and started crawling in, belly scraping the crossties.

Some of the passengers rushing to get back on the train stopped to watch as Loomis loped over the trestle. It was like they were hypnotized. But the conductor and the regular train travelers sure weren't hypnotized. They kept yelling for us to come on.

As the crowd pulled and pushed me toward the cars, my head corkscrewed back just in time to see the black man swing T.R. up and drape him around his neck, like in the Bible picture of the lost lamb and the shepherd. Then I got handed up to the conductor, who stood on the steps of the caboose—Lightfoot right behind me. The conductor was screaming for folks to run on up to the other passenger cars. "Ain't room for nobody else on this here caboose!"

But they let big Loomis on. He handed up the dog. Then, ducking, he swung himself through the door just as the train lurched forward. T.R. licked my face, wagging his tail into a blur, while I and the others cheered the black giant.

Some of the passengers didn't make it back onto the train. We saw men, and women, and children pull back into the bushes and brambles as the train got rolling. They looked anxious but most smiled and waved. Those of us who were by a window waved back.

Big Loomis had moved onto the little platform at the back. I figured he didn't feel right, being in the same car with white folks, though Lord knows nobody cared right then. All of a sudden Loomis yelled, "Jesus save us, dare's dat dar udder train! He ne'ly at de trestle!"

Fear spread over faces. A lady screamed. I felt like screaming. Clapped a hand over my mouth so I couldn't. Lightfoot caught my other hand and held it tight, her eyes wide, her face gone white. Somebody yelled, "Conductor, cain't you run faster?"

The oncoming engine hit the trestle, whistle screaming WHOO-WHOO-WHOO. The question was could it be braked fast enough and could we speed up fast enough. . . . The chasing engine got bigger and bigger as the gap between us closed,

then shrunk as our engineer picked up speed. The last I saw before we rounded a bend, the other train had stopped and was
picking up everybody we'd left beside the tracks.

Lightfoot sat by me on the short run to Cold Sassy. T.R. lay
across my feet. Loomis had come back in, and he stood with
one hand on my shoulder, his black face shining with pride
and sweat. Hot as he was from running, he kept on the long
black jim-swing coat till he saw me shivering, and then he put
it around me. Queenie had sewed that coat. Weren't any white
men in town big enough to where Loomis could wear their old
clothes, so she had to make nearly everything he had. The cloth
smelled sweaty, but I didn't care. I didn't know there was lubri-
cating oil on my overalls and in my hair, where it had dropped
off the engine parts, and I'm afraid it got on the coat that Loomis
was so proud of. Shouting above the train noise, I told him
much obliged for saving T.R.

"You be's welcome, Mr. Will. You know dat."

I loved Loomis. His whole name was Annie Mae Hubert
Knockabout Loomis Toy. After his mama had ten boys, she said
the nex' baby gwine be name Annie Mae no matter whut. She
always called him Annie Mae, but nobody else did. His daddy
was owned by the Toys is how he got his last name. Loomis
worked for us off and on all my life—milking till I got big
enough, plowing the garden till I got big enough, fixing fences
and chopping wood till I got big enough. He beamed down at
me now, showing his two gold front teeth, and rolled his eyes
toward Heaven. "You sho got you a frien' Up Yonder, Mr. Will.
Sho nuff! I speck it cause yo daddy and mama be sech good
peoples. Lawdy, Lawdy, it gwine be a happy time at yo house
t'night!"

I hadn't thought that far. Good gosh, Papa would be mad as
heck about my sneaking off!

The train rocked on toward Papa.

Lightfoot was scrooched up in the corner of the bench, swaying with the motion of the train. I looked over at her, red-faced

from the heat and sweaty and dirty as me. Her long whitey hair hung in damp strands and there were briar scratches on her hands. Tears brimming in her blue eyes suddenly spilled over. I figured she was picturing me flattened like a penny on the trestle rails. But what she said, in a wail hard to understand over the train racket and me still part deaf, was "I left my bucket in the blackberry bushes, Will! Hit were might near full!"

I couldn't think what to say. If she hadn't rushed to help me, she wouldn't of lost the bucket, and I knew those blackberries weren't picked to make a pie with or to put up as jam or jelly or wine. They were for supper. Like as not, all else her folks would have was fried fatback, cream gravy, and corn pone.

The girl blushed, like it just dawned on her that she had let out how poor and hungry she was, and turned her face away from me.

Trying to sound like I thought berry-picking was just something she did for fun, I said, "Why'n't we go pick some more early in the mornin? Mama's been astin' me every day when am I go'n get her some blackberries."

As a matter of fact, Mama never asked me to pick anything anymore, except in our garden. Between her and Papa and Grandpa I was too busy with home chores and store work to go hunting wild fruit. Mama bought our blackberries and yellow plums and muscadines from little colored boys who came by, or from doddery old colored men, or from fat black women with shy stair-step children, each toting two lard buckets full.

"If we go back to Blind Tillie Trestle we can find your bucket," I said. "How bout tomorrow?"

Soon as that was out of my mouth I didn't know why I said it. For one thing, I didn't particularly want to walk through Mill Town again. For another, I felt sick. Sick at my stomach. For another, I'd never hear the last of it if Pink and them somehow found out a girl was waiting for me under Blind Tillie Trestle. Guffaw and haw!

And if Mama and them found out it was a mill girl, I'd be

hard put to explain it. No town boy or girl from a nice home would be caught dead with a linthead.

I was about to make up some excuse when I felt the clickety-clacks slow down and saw Cold Sassy going by the train windows. Remembering Papa, I forgot all about Lightfoot's blackberry bucket. Him laying on the strap wouldn't be the half of it. He'd keep me in the store, garden, and stable the rest of the summer.

Sick at heart, I knew I didn't even want to meet Lightfoot tomorrow.

I tried to think up some excuse, but no matter what I said, it was such in Cold Sassy that she would read *mill girl/town boy* written all over me and she'd hate me the rest of her life, despite she had helped me up from under the wheels of death, so to speak.

Passing the Cold Sassy tree, I felt a new wave of nausea. Amidst the jolts and grinds and the whoosh of steam as the engineer braked into the depot, big Loomis pulled me to my feet and said again, "Lawdy, Mr. Will, yo ma and pa dey gwine be sho nuff proud dis eeb'nin'."

I never found out why Mr. Tuttle was way back there at the caboose when the train pulled in. I just knew that when I looked out the window I found myself staring right into his hard little eyes.

Loomis half pushed, half carried me to the door. I was shaking like the palsy and scared to death I'd puke or start crying. If the earth had opened up and dropped me clear to China, that would have been just dandy with me.

14

WHEN I try to put together the rest of July 5, 1906, it seems hazy. And not just because eight years have gone by now. It was hazy at the time.

I remember worrying after I got to bed that night about not telling Lightfoot good-bye or thanking her. I guess she followed me and Loomis and the dog off the train, but I never saw her after I got surrounded by the other passengers. They were touching me, patting my arm, congratulating me. A tall old man with bulging eyes and a big goiter on his neck pressed a five-dollar gold piece in my hand and got back on the train without saying a word. One little boy begged for a piece of my shirt. I felt foolish, but I pulled off a loose button and gave it to him.

Loomis pushed me through the crowd, bowing and scraping to the white folks, but pushing all the same. "Pleas'sir, let dis here boy pass. . . . Please'm, we's gotta git dis here boy home."

There were Cold Sassy folks at the depot and of course they were puzzled why I was such a hero. I saw Shoeshine Peavy, a young colored boy. He was staring at me, and so was the dwarf, little old Thurman Osgood, who always watched the trains come in. Mr. Beach drove up in his buggy, bringing his wife and little girls to catch the train to Athens. They and others pressed around me, asking questions. "What happened, Will?" "You git hurt?" "Somebody tell us what happened!"

"Please, white folks, let dis boy pass. He don't feel lak talkin'. . . ."

Then the big engineer ran up. "Lookit this 'ere boy!" he shouted, like he was a barker at the county fair and me the prize pig. Waving in my direction, he boomed out his news: "This 'ere boy just now got run over by this 'ere train! Look at him good, folks! Ran over by a train on the trestle and livin' to tell it! Not a hair on his head hurt, folks, not one Goddamn hair, praise be the good Lord!"

Normally I didn't mind being on stage. But what with shaking and shivering and about to cry and vomit and all, I just wanted to get home. It was awful, everybody crowding around like I was a side show, asking how'd it happen and what was I doin' on the trestle anyhow, and what you mean, ran over?

"Mr. Will he ain't feelin' too good," Loomis kept insisting. "He need to git on home." He was still talking polite, but not smiling.

About then Mr. Tuttle got to me. "Engineer said you was on Blind Tillie Trestle. You know you shouldn' a-been up there, boy!"

I didn't answer. I figured Mr. Tuttle was picturing me cut to pieces and himself down at my house trying to settle, cheap, my folks' claim against the railroad. Gosh, would I be worth any more than a dead cow and mule? Or would Mr. Tuttle have sat in our parlor and argued about it.

When Mr. Beach offered to carry me home in his buggy, I said, "Thank you, sir, I'd sure be much obliged." We just live across the street and two houses down from the depot, but I wasn't certain I could walk it, and I sure as heck didn't want Loomis totin' me like a sick calf.

You can imagine how it was when we got to my house and Mr. Beach told Mama what happened. Trying not to cry, she

led me in and made me lay down on the black leather davenport in the front hall. I was shivering like a wet dog; she put a
heavy quilt over me. She was wiping the dirt and grime from
my face with a wet washrag when Papa tore through the front
door.

"Loomis said——" he began, then must have been too mad to
say any more, because he just stood over me. Fastening my eyes
on his knees, I saw they were shaking. I waited for him to take
off his belt. When he didn't, I got the nerve to look up at him.

Tears were streaming down Papa's cheeks. He had his straw
hat across his chest like folks do when a Confederate veteran's funeral procession passes on its way to the graveyard. I
stared up at him, tears wetting my own cheeks. Suddenly he
knelt down beside Mama, put his hat on the floor, grabbed my
right hand in both of his, and held on like he'd never let go. I
couldn't help it; I sat up and threw my arms around my daddy's
neck. He held me tight for a long time, till I quit shaking. He
didn't say a word.

Papa hadn't hugged me I don't reckon since the day I was
twelve years old.

Well, then he put his arms around Mama. "Oh, Hoyt," she
whispered. "The little grave we've got in the cemetery . . . I
don't think I could stand it if—oh, Hoyt, our boy is alive!"
Then she grabbed aholt of me and cried like I was dead.

At some point my daddy walked toward the back hall and
was gone a while. When he came back in he said, "You don't
have to worry about the milkin', son. I did it."

It's not to my credit that I had forgot all about the cow. Well,
I reckon he needed to go get aholt of himself.

I didn't want any supper, and they didn't, either. Mama just
brought some buttermilk and cold corn lightbread and they sat
there by me in the hall to eat it.

About first dark, Cold Sassy arrived.

Good ole Loomis, he must of galloped all over town telling about my escape on the train trestle, because everybody seemed to know all about it. Just the same, they kept asking questions that I didn't feel like answering.

Lots of ladies brought cake or pie—like if somebody had died.

I wanted to see Grandpa Blakeslee. I almost asked if him and Miss Love were back yet from getting married, but there wasn't any use giving Mama another headache.

I remember Aunt Loma and Uncle Camp coming in. The baby, fat and sweaty and dumb-looking, was fast asleep on her shoulder. I don't know if I mentioned it before, but Campbell Junior was the fattest baby ever seen in Cold Sassy. Aunt Loma looked furious. She didn't so much as ask how I was feeling. Why would my getting run over make her so mad? Maybe she was mad because I'd lived to tell it.

But for once it wasn't me she was mad at. "How could Pa have run off with That Woman!" she whispered to Mama.

"Hush, Loma," said Mama, placing her hand on my arm. "That's not important right now. Not compared to Will."

I felt like the Prodigal Son. When my mother headed for the dining room, her eyes shining with joy, I knew she was fixing to get out her gold and white china dessert plates.

Pink and Smiley and Dunse McCall came in, tiptoeing over to me like I was a haint or a corpse, or like they planned to yes-sir and no-sir me from now on. Finally Pink mumbled, "You didn't have to go do a fool thing like that, Will." He was proud of me and jealous both, I could tell.

"Aw, go get you a piece of pie," said I. Propped on my elbow, holding up my head with my hand, I grinned at the three of them. They grinned back, and Smiley kind of joshed my shoulder as they moved toward the dining room, where Aunt Carrie and Miss Sarah, French Gordy's wife, were slicing cakes and pies. I could hear the dessert plates rattling as Mama took them out of the china cabinet.

I could also hear several ladies talking low over near the front door. I knew by the crackledy voice that Miss Alice Ann Boozer was one of them. She said somebody seen Rucker Blakeslee and the Simpson woman havin' supper at the ho-tel. "A weddin' supper, I s'pose you'd call it. Rucker didn't never spend one dime takin' Mattie Lou to no ho-tel. Bet you she haints them two t'night."

"Well, I heard little Loma threw a pure fit down at the store today," said somebody else. "You want my opinion, Rucker's been hopin' to git shet a-Mattie Lou ever since he laid eyes on the milliner. But be ye not disencouraged. The Lord says vengeance is His'n."

Miss Sarah heard this last as she came through the hall with the big plate of sliced cake. Going over to the talking ladies, she whispered, "I saw her and Rucker right after they come in from Jefferson. He called me over to say they'd just got married. 'She wants a weddin' pitcher,' he said, and they went in Mr. Hale's photo shop. I couldn't believe the nerve."

"I heard Mr. Hale refused to take the pitcher," said Miss Alice Ann.

"Well, good for him," said somebody. "Imagine, a weddin' pitcher this soon after Mr. Hale took a funeral pitcher of Mattie Lou laid out in her coffin and all them baskets of flowers around her."

I knew Mr. French would be upset about the wedding. His mother having married Granny's daddy, they grew up together like brother and sister. The day Granny died, Mr. French said to Mama, "Mr. Blakeslee is a good decent man. But Mattie Lou done all the givin'."

The talkers moved on then, because a covey of Presbyterian ladies were coming in. I shut my eyes like sleeping as they marched over to stare at the corpse.

"Dear boy, hit just wadn' his time to die," Miss Looly said softly.

"S'pose it wadn' his time to die but it was that trestle's time to fall?" her sister breathed, touching my cheek. "Or what if it was that train engineer's time to die? What would of happened to Will?"

"Shet up, Cretia," whispered Miss Looly. "Hit ain't for us to ast sech questions. Hit were the Lord's will for the boy to live. All we got to do is be thankful."

For a moment I swelled with importance, getting talked about like that. Then for no good reason I saw myself as Raw Head and Bloody Bones, spinning into nothing under giant wheels and thunder. I felt sick again, and scared. I didn't want to be a nothing.

I wished Grandpa would come, but I knew he wouldn't. Not on his wedding night.

15

WHO came instead of Grandpa was the Methodist preacher. Standing over me, he said, "Son, John Wesley got saved from a fire as a boy and he started the Methodist church. Now you been spared, Will. Miraculously spared. Maybe the Lord's got special plans for you, too—like preachin' the gospel."

Miss Lizzie Mae Tuttle came in the door as he said that. She hooted. "God sure better get to work if He's got in mind to make a preacher out of Will Tweedy." Everybody laughed, including me. "Mr. Tuttle's go'n be on over terreckly," she added, like she thought I'd asked for him personal.

Cudn Hopewell Stump spoke up from the parlor. "God spared Li'l Beulah Samples in that cyclone back in 'eighty-four. Y'all recollect them Sampleses? Used to live over on the Athens road."

Raising my head, I saw Cudn Hope lean forward in his chair, taking aim at the brass spittoon on the hearth. But him being known as a poor shot with tobacco juice, I reckon Mama cringed, because he said, "Jest a minute, folks," and went outside to spit over the banisters.

When he got back, his wife, Cudn Agnes, had taken over the story, telling how Big Beulah sent Little Beulah over to take

Miss Winnie Blalock a basket of sweet potatoes. Miss Winnie lived in a sharecropper house on the Stedman farm. "Jest fore Li'l Beulah got thar, a storm come up and hailstones big as this commenced a-fallin'." She made a circle with her plump thumb and forefinger.

"Lord, some them hailstones was big as teacups and weighed a pound," Cudn Hope said, sitting down again. "I seen'm. If one had a-fell on Beulah's head, she'd a-been with Jesus 'thout ever knowin' what hit her."

"Pore thang had jest jumped under a bridge to git shelter from the hail," said Cudn Agnes, "when here come a great big ole dark funnel-shape cloud, full a-planks and trees and dust. Hit was a-roarin' like a freight train!"

Cudn Hope grabbed the story back. "First it sucked up the Stedman house, like 'tweren't no more'n a leaf, and—"

"And after that house went whirly off into the sky, dipped down agin and tuck Miss Winnie's house—and her in it!"

Cudn Hope said, "Li'l Beulah had to watch whilst Miss Winnie went flyin' off to Kingdom Come. Next thang she knew—"

"Next thang she knew, the cyclone was liftin' the bridge right up from over her, like it was a piece a-paper." Mama, who had come to sit by me on the davenport, put her hand on mine and kept it there while Cudn Agnes finished the story. "But nary a hair on that chile's head got tetched. The good Lord spared her. And when she was seventeen, God called her to China as a missionary. Pore thang got over thar and died of the smallpox two months later."

But Cudn Hope got in the last word. "Us that knowed her," he said, "never doubted she saved some Chinamen first."

"I swannee to God," somebody breathed, and the room was quiet for a moment.

"Is that cyclone why the woods around here are full of up-rooted pine stumps?" the Methodist preacher said finally.

Cudn Hope said naw, that happened around 1882. "We had a big wind and rainstorm one night and near all the pine trees blowed down. Peeler and Lovin Comp'ny put a sawmill in there and sawed'm up."

Papa told the preacher, "The stumps all point northeast to southwest. You can hunt coons in those woods at night and never need a compass."

It was after somebody brought in lemonade that they started on hit-by-the-train stories.

Mr. Gordy told how, back in aught-one or aught-two, Cold Sassy's first steam fire engine got hit crossing the tracks to the old Sanders Hotel fire. The engine was smashed and both horses killed, and a fire hook stabbed young Addis Morgan in the head and spilled his brains out.

"Next day they found one a-them horses' hoofs up past the depot," remembered old man Frazier. "It was already crawlin' with maggots."

"Oh, Lord, Will," whispered Mama, and got up and hurried toward the bathroom. Knowing Mama, I figured it was to vomit. In my mind I pictured that horse hoof. Then I pictured somebody finding my own foot at the water's edge on Blind Tillie Creek. About then Mr. Cratic Flournoy came out in the hall and noticed how pale I was, I reckon, and deliberately told one you could laugh at, about Mr. Farnam's brood sow getting picked up on the train's cowcatcher, and all it amounted to was the sow had a free ride to town. Wasn't hurt a bit. When somebody sent word to Mr. Farnam, why, he just walked into the depot and led her back home to her pigs.

Toddy Hughes lumbered in. Besides working at the foundry, he was a young stringer for the *Atlanta Constitution Tri-Weekly*. Said he wanted to write me up. Nobody in our family had ever been written up in the Atlanta papers. I was real excited, but Mama said he better wait till tomorrow. Oh, gosh, he might change his mind or forget about it. But he promised he'd be by right after breakfast.

And here came Mr. Tuttle, acting like he'd personally saved me and like maybe I was his favorite young friend. After he inquired how I was, somebody asked him about the cow and mule that was killed yesterday. Then he told about one time ten or fifteen years ago when the southbound train ran over a bull yearling on a curve. "Two or three boxcars turned over and rolled down into the ravine. Spilled a mess of flour and sugar and I don't know what-all."

My daddy remembered riding his horse out there to see the wreck. "It looked like snow had fell down that embankment."

"When I ast the farmer how much he wanted for his dead yearlin'," said Mr. Tuttle, laughing, "he stood lookin' out at all that flour and stuff spilled broadcast down the bank and said, 'Tuttle?' he said, 'Tuttle, I'm willin' to strike off even, if you are. I think my bull got the best of it.'"

In the midst of the ladies' shrieky laughter and the men's guffaws and haws, Dr. Slaughter hurried in. "How you feelin', son?" he asked. "I just heard, Mary Willis. I been out in the country all day. I want to be sure Will's all right."

While he poked around on my stomach, felt my bones, and told Mama not to give me anything but liquids tonight, we heard a commotion at the door and Grandpa's voice boomed out from the veranda: "Gosh a'mighty! If'n I'd a-knowed y'all had made up a party for us, we'd a-got here sooner!"

16

I FOUND out later that Grandpa and Miss Love knew about the train running over me. After Loomis spread the word all over town, Mr. Jimmy Dan Allsup had rushed into the hotel dining room to tell Grandpa, who was sitting at the little round table with Miss Love, eating a wedding supper of fried catfish and banana fritters.

Next day Mr. Allsup told French Gordy that Grandpa turned white as a sheet. Soon as he found out I was all right, though, he said they might as well finish supper. He'd have to pay for it anyway, and besides there wasn't anything at his house for Miss Love to cook. But Grandpa didn't let on to the crowd gathered at our house but what he thought they were all there to celebrate the wedding.

It's hard to believe how he carried that off.

It was like he didn't hear the silence that greeted them and didn't see Mama go pale or Aunt Loma flounce out of the parlor and down the hall, handling the baby so rough he woke up squalling. Grandpa walked in like it was the usual thing to go off and get a new young wife before your old wife is cold in the grave. Like it never dawned on him anybody would mind.

It's not easy for a pretty lady with her chin in the air to look flustered, but Miss Love did.

She was wearing a hand-embroidered blue dress, her brown hair in a big pompadour, and had on a little blue hat with white bird wings—the same hat Aunt Loma tried to buy that time. And as Grandpa pushed her forward, it was on her that all the eyes fastened. One by one the men stood up, the way you're supposed to when a lady comes in, but they looked uncertain what to say.

There was no uncertainty about Grandpa. "By golly, I'm shore glad to see you folks!" he said, ushering Miss Love toward the parlor door and ignoring me on the davenport in the hall. His blue eyes twinkled with excitement. First time I'd seen any life in him since Granny took sick.

Like there was no way in creation that anybody could know what he and Miss Love had been up to, Grandpa said, "We got a surprise for all y'all." Standing in the double doorway to the parlor, his back to me, he put his right arm around Miss Love's shoulders and said, "We'd like to announce we done got married this evenin', over at Jefferson. Folks, meet the new Miz Enoch Rucker Blakeslee! Mary Willis? Where's Mary Willis?" Mama was right there, but he hollered like she was way at the back of the house. "Mary Willis, come kiss the bride. Loma?"

What else could a daughter do? Mama walked over and pecked Miss Love on the cheek. Loma stalked into the room, her face beet-red, and did the same. But they nor the bride said a word. Everybody else was quiet, too. Watching. All you could hear was the clock ticking and Mr. French's fork tapping his dessert plate. He and the other men were still standing, waiting for Miss Love to sit down.

"Where's the chi'ren?" Grandpa boomed out. "Y'all come kiss yore new granny." He turned to Miss Love and laughed. "Haw, I didn't think till now, but I done made you a granmaw!" To the company he said, "I reckon she's jest about the prettiest dang granmaw in Jackson County, ain't she, folks?" He looked around the room then. "Mary Toy, where you at, girl? Will Tweedy?"

"Cudn Temp took Mary Toy out to the country after the parade yesterday, Pa. And Will, h-he . . ." Mama started crying. With his arm around her, my daddy told Grandpa what happened on the train trestle.

"Good gosh a'mighty!" Grandpa turned toward me, his face beaming. "Now ain't thet jest like you, Will Tweedy! Always a-doin' something different. Well, son, I reckon if'n you jest got to git ran over by a train, how you done it was the best way." Ambling out of the parlor, he came over to me, grinning, and touched my shoulder.

I was starving all of a sudden. I sat up and said I was ready for a piece of pie.

"Dr. Slaughter wants you just to have liquids, Will," Mama said anxiously. "He said not give you any solid food tonight."

"Doggit, let'm have his pie," ordered Grandpa, slapping me on the back. "If'n a boy wants a piece a-pie, he cain't be all thet bad off. Come on, Will Tweedy, let's go git us some."

I do believe he forgot all about Miss Love. As we went toward the kitchen, I looked back and saw that Cudn Hope had offered her the green velvet rocker and everybody was sitting down again.

Grandpa, laughing as if the triumph over the train had been as much his as mine, grabbed what was left of a chocolate pie from the dining room table and pushed me through the door into the kitchen. When the door swung to, it shut out everybody in the house but us.

I could hear voices in the parlor, but not what they said, and I could tell that nobody was saying a whole lot. Miss Love must have felt like a cat cornered by a pack of dogs. At the time nobody knew what a cat she could be when cornered. From what I heard tell later, though, she tried to be real nice that night.

While I served out the pie and poured me some sweetmilk from the pitcher on the table, Grandpa slipped into our company room closet for you-know-what. Then, seated across from me at the kitchen table, his face flushed with whiskey and pride, he said, "Tell me about it, son."

And I did. On the davenport in yonder I hadn't even wanted to think about what happened on the trestle, but with Grandpa I didn't feel like that. I told him how I was tired of being in mourning and got mad at Papa and slipped off, how grand it felt up there on the trestle, how awful it was when the engine commenced chasing me. I told him about the cinders hitting my back, the smell of hot creosote, and the huge roar as the train straddled the rails above me. "I felt like somebody was stabbing my eardrums. It was like I'd gone crazy, Grandpa. Like I was drownin' in sound."

Grandpa heard me out, his blue eyes intent. I even told him about "this mill girl I know at school" who was picking black-berries near the trestle and helped me off the tracks. "And you should of seen ole Loomis, Grandpa, sprintin' onto the trestle to get the dog. Loomis knew another train was comin', and went and got him anyhow! . . . Grandpa, uh, I cain't eat my pie." Couldn't even stand to look at it. Pushed it away, and the milk, too. But Grandpa didn't notice.

I knew he was real excited, because he kept scratching his head fast. But he didn't act like I'd been snatched from hell or go on about a maggotty horse hoof on the railroad tracks or how I had to pray God to use the life He had so mercifully spared. Grandpa reached across the table and put his hand on my arm, just for a second, then poked me in the ribs and said, "By George, gittin' ran over by a train must a-been some experience!" He acted like it was something to remember instead of something to forget.

With the way he took it so casual, and the relief of getting it told, I felt like I'd been stuck back together. But one thing worried me. "Grandpa, you think I'm alive tonight cause it was God's will?"

"Naw, you livin' cause you had the good sense to fall down 'twixt them tracks."

"Maybe God gave me the idea."

"You can believe thet, son, if'n you think it was God's idea for you to be up on thet there trestle in the first place. What God give you was a brain. Hit's His will for you to use it—p'tickler when a train's comin'."

Resting my chin in my hand, I thought about that while Grandpa finished up his pie. I felt awful tired. "Sir, do you think it was God's will for Bluford Jackson to get lockjaw and die?"

Grandpa spoke kindly. "The Lord don't make firecrackers, son. Hit's jest too bad pore Blu didn't be more careful when he was shootin'm off."

"You don't think God wills any of the things that happen to us?"

"Maybe. Maybe not. Who knows?"

"Mama and Papa think He does."

Grandpa licked some meringue off his fork while he pondered. Finally he said, "Life bullies us, son, but God don't. He had good reasons for fixin' it where if'n you git too sick or too hurt to live, why, you can die, same as a sick chicken. I've knowed a few really sick chickens to git well, and lots a-folks git well thet nobody ever thought to see out a-bed agin cept in a coffin. Still and all, common sense tells you this much: everwhat makes a wheel run over a track will make it run over a boy if'n he's in the way. If'n you'd a-got kilt, it'd mean you jest didn't move fast enough, like a rabbit that gits caught by a hound dog. You think God favors the dog over the rabbit, son?"

I shook my head.

"I don't neither. When it comes to prayin', we got it all over the other animals, but we ain't no different when it comes to livin' and dyin'. If'n you give God the credit when somebody don't die, you go'n blame Him when they do die? Call it His will? Ever noticed we git well all the time and don't die but once't? Thet has to mean God always wants us to live if'n we can. Hit ain't never His *will* for us to die—cept in the big sense. In the sense He was smart enough not to make life eternal on this here earth, with people and bees and elephants and dogs piled up in squirmin' mounds like Lorna's dang cats tryin' to keep warm in the wintertime. Does all this make any sense, Will Tweedy?"

"Yessir, Grandpa." I wanted to go lay down. But I also wanted some more answers. "Grandpa, uh, why you think Jesus said ast the Lord for anything you want and you'll get it? 'Ast and it shall be given,' the Bible says. But it ain't so." I felt blasphemous even to think it, much less say it out loud.

Grandpa was silent a long time. "Maybe Jesus was talkin' in His sleep, son, or folks heard Him wrong. Or maybe them disciples tryin' to start a church thought everbody would join up if'n they said Jesus Christ would give the Garden a-Eden to anybody believed He was the son a-God and like thet." Grandpa laughed. Gosh, I'd get a whipping if Papa knew what was going on with the Word in his kitchen. "All I know," he added, "is thet folks pray for food and still go hungry, and Adam and Eve ain't in thet garden a-theirs no more, and yore granny ain't in hers, and I ain't got no son a-my own to carry on the name and hep me run the store when I'm old. Like you say, you don't git thangs jest by astin'. Well, I'm a-go'n study on this some more. Jesus must a-meant something else, not what it sounds like."

"Grandpa, I think maybe I better go back in yonder and lay down."

"Yeah, you better. But I got one more thang to say. They's a heap more to God's will than death, disappoint-ment, and like thet. Hit's God's will for us to be good and do good, love one another, be forgivin'. . . ." He laughed. "I reckon I ain't very forgivin', son. I can forgive a fool, but I ain't inner-rested in coddlin' hypocrites. Well anyhow, folks who think God's will jest has to do with sufferin' and dyin', they done missed the whole point."

I stood up, weaving a little. That brought Grandpa out of his sermon. "Gosh a'mighty, pore Miss Love! You reckon they've et her up alive in there?" He leaped to his feet and burst through the swinging door to the dining room.

We got back to the parlor just in time to hear my daddy, in a strained and formal voice, making polite conversation by telling Mrs. Love Simpson Blakeslee what was coming along in our garden in the way of vegetables.

You could tell that Miss Love and Papa both were mighty glad to see Grandpa. Everybody else was, too. It's not easy to keep up a conversation with somebody you'd rather not even be speaking to.

Miss Love stood up and moved toward us, and all the men rose, polite but stiff.

"Well, folks," said Grandpa, taking aholt of her elbow, "I reckon we best mosey on home now. Hit's been a long fancy day."

Miss Love looked at me. "How are you feeling now, Will?"

"Pretty good, ma'am."

"Fore we go," said Grandpa, "I'd like all y'all to join me and my wife in a word a-prayer."

You can't hardly refuse a man that.

In stony silence they all bowed their heads, where they stood or sat. With his right arm around Miss Love and his left arm stub laid across my shoulder and me facing the two of them, Grandpa prayed.

I didn't close my eyes. I was too busy watching faces—Mama's and Papa's and Aunt Loma's and, of course, Miss Love's. Clasping her hands together, she closed those gray-blue eyes and ducked her head down and all I could see then was the big mass of wavy brown hair and the little blue hat. I noticed for the first time that her hair had a lot of gray sprinkled through it.

After what Grandpa had been saying to me in the kitchen, I

should of been prepared for what he said to God in the parlor: "Lord above, afore this gatherin' assembled, I ast You to bless the memory of Miss Mattie Lou."

Everybody gasped. Nobody expected him to bring *her* up.

Grandpa didn't seem to hear the gasps. "Please God, forgive me all the ways I ain't done right by her. Thou knowest what she meant to me and our chi'ren, Mary Willis and Loma," he continued, "and to Will Tweedy and li'l Mary Toy." There was a pause, his face working like he might not could go on, but he did. "And now I ast yore blessin' on this here girl I married today." Miss Love raised her head and stared up at Grandpa, mouth agape. I do think his were the only eyes in the room still shut. "Lord, hep me be good to her. You know I need Miss Love. Hep her to need me likewise. And give her the grace to unner-stand thet if'n they's aught to respect in me, it's because a-thet one in the grave out yonder, what all she learnt me."

Tears were flowing down Miss Love's cheeks. I never before saw anything so beautiful as the way she reached up and put her left hand over the big bony hand that clasped her right shoulder. Grandpa opened his eyes then and looked a long time into hers—till finally, like he'd just remembered God and the other people in the room, he bowed his head again. "And last, bless my daughters and their fam'lies. Specially Will Tweedy, who as You know didn't git kilt today. We're mighty proud to still have him." His voice broke. My own throat swelled and ached. Even with all Grandpa had said in the kitchen, I half expected him to thank God for sparing me, but he didn't. Somebody in the room started sniffling. I couldn't tell who, but I knew it wasn't Aunt Loma.

Grandpa had made the Lord seem so real, I wouldn't of been surprised if he'd said good night to Him. But after a long pause he just said a-men.

It was a strange thing happened then. My mama went up to her pa and kissed him and, crying, hugged Miss Love, who, crying, hugged her back. My daddy kissed Miss Love on the cheek and then shook hands with Grandpa. Uncle Camp naturally did the same thing. So did Mr. French Gordy, Granny's stepbrother. After that all the friends and neighbors filed by—it was still more like a funeral than a wedding party—and shook hands with Grandpa, and either hugged Miss Love or clasped her hand.

I saw Mama whispering to Aunt Loma. Mama believed you had to be nice even to a rat if it was a guest in your home. But Loma shook her off and stalked past Miss Love and Grandpa to join Uncle Camp, who had taken Campbell Junior out on the porch. She didn't even make a polite show of wishing them well. Didn't say good night, even. But I couldn't tell that Grandpa noticed or cared.

In the back of my mind I'd been thinking I had saved him and Miss Love from the gossipers. I mean I figured everybody would be talking about me getting run over by the train instead of about them eloping. That just shows how swell-headed I was, and how I underestimated Grandpa. If I had deliberately planned on nearly getting myself killed just to help him out, it would of been a waste of time.

Grandpa was equal to anything.

17

THAT night in a dream I stood on the tracks at the edge of Blind Tillie Trestle. Lightfoot McLendon was way out at the middle, over the deepest part of the gorge. Her hair, white-gold in the sunlight, hung loose down to her hips. She looked like a doll out there, and her voice echoed as she kept calling my name. "Come on, Will! It's so pretty up here? . . . Don't be skeerdy!" I put one foot on the trestle, then pulled back. "Will?" she called. "Will?" Then, oh gosh, she unbuttoned her shirtwaist, let it drop to the rail, and stretched her arms toward the sky. "Come on, Will," she teased, and went to swaying.

Later, remembering the dream, I thought about a porcelain lady with no head or arms that I saw one time in a shop in Atlanta. All she had on was a cloth, draped around her hips, and I could hardly take my eyes off of her. In the dream I could hardly take my eyes off of Lightfoot, swaying out there on the trestle. Then I saw the train loom up behind her. It made no sound, and Lightfoot didn't see it coming. I tried to yell, but like the train I had no voice. I wanted to save her, but my legs wouldn't move.

Swaying her hips, she all of a sudden dropped her skirt and

was stepping out of it when the engine hit and exploded her into a thousand pieces. They fell in a slow shower to the creek below.

She shattered without any blood, as if she'd died without ever living.

I screamed. . . .

"Will! What's the matter, sugar?" Mama was shaking me awake.

I told her I dreamed the train hit somebody. I didn't say it was a naked mill girl.

I had another nightmare that night. I was running for my life, the train nipping at my heels, but I was winning the race! The end of the trestle was only a few feet away, and I was like a wind-up tin man with four legs spinning. This time, boy howdy, I was go'n make it! Then Loma appeared on the trestle, barring my way, flapping her arms at me like a farm wife trying to keep a goat out of the garden. "Move!" I shouted. "Get out a-my way!"

"Call me Aint Loma and I'll let you by!" she yelled in a high, child voice.

"I won't! Move!"

"Say Aint Loma!" With every flap of her arms, her body swelled, till she and the train were the same size, and me caught between.

"You ain't my aunt! MOVE!"

Struggling out of the dream, I heard myself babbling sounds that made no sense. Gosh a'mighty, if only I'd had time to grab Loma and push her off into the gorge or under the train wheels! I was so mad it took me a minute to see that I was safe and alone in my room at home. In the next instant, a time out of my childhood flashed before me: the day Loma turned twelve. It put light on what had long been a dark puzzlement.

Up till that birthday we were like a sister and a little brother. She'd get mad and hit me if I crossed her or sassed her, and I'd do meany things to her, like tripping her up or putting sugar in her salt cellar. Still and all, we got along about like you'd expect till, on the day she was twelve (I was just six), she ordered me in a growny tone to start calling her Aint Loma. "Say it. Call me Aint Loma." She raised her fist over my head.

"Silly, you ain't my aunt."

"I am so, too. Ast Sister." Sitting smug in the porch swing, she cut herself another piece of chocolate birthday cake.

"I want some, Loma." I held out my hands.

"If you say Aint Loma and ast me nice."

Jerking her braids, I ran upstairs to my room and slammed the door. Later, coming out, I nearly stepped on my lead soldiers, which Grandpa had ordered for me from London, England. They were in a pile by the door. All broken.

I never forgot the pitiful sight of those dead soldiers, some without heads or arms, some with legs missing, and rifles bent or snapped in two. But I had forgotten why Aunt Loma did it.

After the dream I remembered everything: how I cried till suppertime about the soldiers but still wouldn't say Aint Loma. How she taunted me, singsonging, "Crybaby, come let your Aint Loma hold you."

"I'm go'n tell Mama on you!" I yelled.

"You do and I'll say you done it. And who you think she'll believe, smarty crybaby? She's seen you get mad and tear up things before."

I spat in Loma's face.

She told Mama on me for spitting at her. I said she broke my lead soldiers. She said I did it. Mama believed her instead of me, and Papa whipped me good. That night when she tucked me in, Mama said, "Will, sugar, try to be a better boy tomorrow. Hear?"

"Yes'm. But tell Loma to quit sayin' she's my aunt. She says I got to call her Aint Loma."

"We'll talk about it tomorrow, son. Go to sleep now."

You need to understand that in Cold Sassy when the word "aunt" is followed by a name, it's pronounced *aint*, as in Aint Loma or Aint Carrie. We also say *dubya* for the letter "w", *sump'm* for something, *idn'* for isn't, *dudn'* for doesn't, *raig'n* for reckon, *chim'ly* for chimney, *wrench* for rinse, *sut* for soot, as in train or chim'ly sut, and *like* for lack, as in "Do you like much of bein' th'ew?" Well, I know that how we speak is part of what we are. I sure don't want Cold Sassy folks to sound like a bunch of Yankees. But I don't want us to sound ignorant, either, and pronunciations like *sump'n* and *id'n* sound ignorant. So I'm trying to remember not to use such—except right now to tell how Loma became Aint Loma.

The morning after our fuss about it, Mama sat me down for a talking-to. "Now, sugarfoot, you got to get something straight," she began. "Loma is my sister, which makes her your aunt. And it's high time you started callin' her that. She's twelve now, a young lady."

"Then how come she's still goin' barefooted?"

"Well, she cain't go barefooted anymore. And you got to start showin' her proper respect. You hear? Take in that lip and answer me."

"Yes'm."

"Look at me when you answer me."

"Yes'm."

"Now if I hear of you and your Aint Loma fussin' about this again, you go'n get another whippin'. You understand?"

"Yes'm."

Loma was at our house as much as at her own, I reckon, and for a long time after Mama laid down the law I didn't call her anything. But because Mama and Papa and Grandpa and Granny started speaking of her to me as "your Aint Loma," I gradually thought of that as her name, and after the awful first time, saying it wasn't much harder than saying doodly-squat or Peter Rabbit. By time Mary Toy was old enough to talk, Loma was Aint Loma to both of us. And though I finally forgot *why* she broke my soldiers—until the nightmare—I never forgot or forgave her for doing it.

When Miss Love came into my life, Aunt Loma was still my prime hate, and getting even with her was still my prime goal.

Mama thought hating folks was sinful. She could make allowances for anybody. When I'd get to fussing about Aunt Loma, she'd say, "Your Aunt Loma means well, son. I know she's hateful sometimes, but she's got a good heart."

Good heart, my foot. Aunt Loma's heart was down on a level with Mr. Angus Tuttle's, and he had caused me more whippings than I could count. Us boys were always trying to get back at him. Just for instance, one day we sneaked into his barn, just fooling around, and chanced to see a gallon of the yellow paint that he put on the handles of all his farm tools so if somebody showed up with a yellow-handled hoe, everybody would know it was stolen from Mr. Tuttle.

Well, it was real cold the day we went in there, and his barn was full of mules, horses, and cows brought in from his farm; sharecropper tenants being bad to steal, if you live in town, it's the custom to bring in all your animals, wagons, and farm tools for the winter. What we did, and it was my idea, we dipped every horse, mule, and cow tail in that yellow paint. When one flipped, good gosh it sent a spray of yellow all over the dern animal, the stalls, the hayracks, everything. Then we got the idea to paint all the hoofs yellow, too, and the cows' horns, and we caught a rooster that was up on the rafters and painted his beak and toenails.

You never saw anybody mad as Mr. Tuttle when he got home, and he never doubted who'd done it. That night Mama didn't just ask me to be a better boy; she insisted on it.

If I had told her just how much I hated Mr. Tuttle, she wouldn't of believed it. But compared to the way I felt about Aunt Loma, he was like a favorite uncle.

There were a few other people I couldn't stand, like Hosie

Roach, the mill boy in my class at school. Most mill children went to school just two or three years, then dropped out to work at the spindles. If they were too little to reach the spindles, they stood on boxes. Children caught playing on the job got a whipping from the supervisor. I didn't like to think about that. I didn't like to think about mill children at all, and never had to as long as the mill ran its own school. Then a few years back, though the *Cold Sassy Weekly* ran editorials against "allowing cotton mill folks to mix and mingle with the children of our fair city," the school board voted to close the mill school and let the lintheads come to ours. Papa was one of the board members in favor. If he'd had to sit next to Hosie, I bet you he'd of thought twice.

Hosie was still not through high school, even though he was twenty-one. He'd work a few months in the mill, then come to classes a few months. Sometimes he worked at night after being at school in the day. So he hadn't been promoted regular, despite he was right smart for a mill boy. Our superintendent kept trying to get him to quit school, but Hosie vowed he was go'n graduate if it took him till he was thirty years old.

We were always fighting at recess. I really hated him, and the feeling was mutual. But compared to Aunt Loma, Hosie Roach seemed like a best friend.

Then there was Grandpa Tweedy, my daddy's daddy out in Banks County. He talked hard times morning, noon, and night. Called himself a farmer, but you never saw him behind a plow or driving a team. Lazy, great goodness. Like the lilies of the field in the Bible, he toiled not, neither did he spend his own money. He was always asking Papa to help him out. All he ever did was sit on the porch and swat flies, and like I said, even had him a pet hen to peck them up.

When Papa left the farm at sixteen to go work for Grandpa Blakeslee, he made twenty dollars a month and had to send half of it home to pay the field hand who took his place. That was the custom. But even after Papa married at nineteen, making forty dollars a month, he still had to send Grandpa Tweedy ten of it till the day he was twenty-one. My mother never said she didn't like her father-in-law, but I could tell she didn't, and that may of been why.

What started me hating him, he wouldn't let me fish on Sunday. Said it was a sin. I remember I put out some set hooks late one Saturday, thinking if I caught a fish, it wouldn't be a sin to take him off the hook next morning. End his suffering, you know. Early Sunday I ran down to the river and one of the lines was just a-jiggling! But when I ran up the hill and asked Grandpa's permission to get my fish off the hook, he said, "Hit'll still be thar t'morrer, Lord willin'. The Lord ain't willin', it'll be gone. Now git in the house and study yore catechism till time to leave for preachin'."

Of course the fish was gone Monday morning. But I got back at Grandpa Tweedy. I'd noticed a big hornet's nest in the privy, just under the tin roof, so I bided my time behind a tree till I saw him go in there. Giving him just long enough to get settled good, I let fly a rock and it hit that tin roof like a gunshot. Grandpa burst out of there in a cloud of hornets, trying to swat and hold his pants up at the same time. He knew I'd done it. "Will Tweedy, I'll git you, boy!" he yelled. "I'll git you!"

I just couldn't hardly stand him. One time when he was fussing about tenants stealing out of his woodpile, I watched while he drilled holes in several sticks of stovewood, filled the holes with gunpowder, sealed them over with candlewax, and put them on top of the woodpile. "What if somebody gets kilt?" I asked him.

I was just a little bitty boy, so I believed him when he said, "Ain't go'n hurt nobody. Hit'll jest scare the livin' daylights out of 'm."

Next morning at breakfast we heard a big WHOMP, BOOM from the tenant shack. A few minutes later, the cook rushed in and said, "Mist' Tweedy, one them white-trash chillun's hand done got tore up, po li'l lamb, an' dey stove's ruint."

Grandpa saucered his coffee and took a big slurp before he spoke. His voice was hard. "Well, then I reckon they won't steal no more a-my f'ar wood."

You can see why I despised Grandpa Tweedy and didn't have a dab of respect for him. But compared to Aunt Loma, he was King Arthur and I was a Knight of the Round Table.

Lying there in the dark, thinking about Aunt Loma, I got really mad. She could of at least pretended to be glad I'd escaped from the jaws of death on that trestle. It wouldn't of hurt her. But she hadn't said one word, and then flounced off without so much as a good night to Grandpa and Miss Love.

I wondered would she meet her match in Miss Love. Or would Miss Love do like Mama and kowtow to Loma for the sake of peace in the family?

18

I T'S not to my credit that the next morning I forgot all about telling Lightfoot we'd pick blackberries.

I couldn't of gone. I had to wait for Toddy Hughes to come by and interview me for the Atlanta newspaper. Also, I felt awful tired, and Dr. Slaughter had said I better stay quiet and not get hot. Mama would have a fit if I tried to go off somewhere. She wouldn't even let me milk that day. Got Loomis to do it.

There wasn't any way to let Lightfoot know, but I should of at least remembered.

I guess what messed me up was so many folks coming to call, from right after breakfast on. If they weren't asking me about getting run over by the train, they were asking Mama about Grandpa and Miss Love.

I was on the front veranda with young Toddy Hughes about ten o'clock when Mr. Son Black rode up bareback on his red mare mule. He had unhitched her from the plow and she still had on her collar, the traces draped over her neck. Wearing an old felt hat and dirty overalls, Son sat sideways, slumped, with one leg crossed over the mule's shoulder and the other hanging loose. He looked so seedy I wondered what Miss Love, or even Aunt Loma, had ever seen in him.

"Whoa, Lucy," he said to the mule, then kicked her halfway up our walk and asked where my granddaddy was. He sounded mad. "I want to see him. He ain't come in yet at the store."

"That ain't surprisin', Son," Toddy Hughes said with a leery grin, "bein' as yesterd'y was Mr. Blakeslee's weddin' day. Or ain't you heard?"

Son spat. "I heard."

"Well, and I just guess they slept late," Toddy called as the mule turned away and trotted down the walk.

"Mr. Hughes!" snapped Mama, who came out on the porch in time to hear that.

Toddy stood up quick, blushing, and said, "Sorry, ma'am. Sorry. Well, I'll mosey along. Got to go write this up and put it on the telegraph to Atlanta. I, uh, reckon they'll use it right away, Will. The paper ain't likely to of had anything like bein' run over by a train and lived to tell it before. Uh, be seein' you, ma'am." He tipped his straw hat to Mama. Looked like he couldn't get away fast enough.

He was gone before I remembered I was going to tell him about Lightfoot McLendon running out on the trestle to help me off and about Loomis saving my dog. Likely they wouldn't of put Loomis in the paper, him being colored, but I meant to ask Toddy to try.

It's no credit to me that I was sort of glad he rushed off before I could tell him about Lightfoot. I didn't want to hear what Pink and Lee Roy and them would say about me and her if they saw her name in the paper. Also, it would take Mama and Papa a month to convince folks that, no, I wasn't at the trestle with a mill girl. She just happened to be picking berries nearby.

Aunt Loma spent most of that morning at our house, fussing about Miss Love and jerking the baby around like it was all his fault that his grandpa had disgraced the family. She kept saying, "I'm go'n get even with Love Simpson if it's the last thing I ever do."

· · ·

Despite everybody acting so nice the night before, nobody went to call on Grandpa and Miss Love—at least nobody that I heard of. Even the few who weren't mad for Granny's sake likely didn't know what to say, under the circumstances, and nobody was going to risk criticism by paying a formal call or taking a wedding present. Not even those who had hugged her the night before would do that.

I wondered if the newlyweds had anything to eat. I knew Miss Love could make coffee, but after boarding so many years, she might not know how to cook anything else. "You go'n send them some dinner?" I asked Mama. "I could carry it up there."

She said, "You got to rest, like Dr. Slaughter told you. And I'll say it right now, Will: you are not to go runnin' up there all the time like you used to. We don't owe Love Simpson any favors. And you can see your granddaddy at the store. You understand?"

I understood, all right.

But Grandpa didn't.

He never appeared at the store at all that day, or at our house, either. When he didn't even come by for his whiskey, I and Papa and Mama must of each thought Miss Love didn't object to a man's having a little toddy at home. But then real early Saturday morning he stopped in as usual before work, like he still didn't have a closet of his own, and came out of the company room scratching his head and hitching up his trousers with his arm stub, the way he always did when he was excited or upset. Right in front of Mama, he said, "Will Tweedy, git on up home, son, and see can you hep Miss Love any. She's a-tearin' the place apart! Scourin' floors, washin' winders and curtains, and scrubbin' furniture like they's cooties or bedbugs in ever piece. She had me workin' all day yesterd'y."

"You, Pa? Housework? Shah!" Mama didn't believe it.

"Yes'm. Sunup to bedtime." A sheepish look came on his face. Pulling at his bushy beard, he announced, "Mary Willis, you and Loma got to come go th'ew yore ma's thangs."

Mama didn't answer.

"I ain't never see sech a one for cleanin' house as Miss Love." He spoke with a pride that he tried to hide. "You got time to hep her any, Mary Willis?"

"No, Pa, I haven't," she said. "Queenie and I are cannin' soup vegetables today. We got to, or lose everything, one." I was surprised she spoke up to him. She never had before. "And," she added firmly, "I'm countin' on Will to pick the vegetables."

Grandpa was a little taken back. "Well," he said. "All right. But send him on up soon as he gits th'ew."

My mama was really something when she got mad. Blue eyes blazing, hands on hips, she watched her daddy go down the walk and cross the railroad tracks. "Tearin' into that house like it was hers!" she muttered.

I thought Grandpa had prayed away all the town's hard feelings, and maybe he really had. But that was Thursday night and this was early Saturday morning, and he'd just showed he didn't know pea-turkey about how grown daughters feel when a young stepmother is brought into the family, or how they feel about being told to clear out their mama's personal belongings to make room for the new wife's things.

I saw what was going through Mama's mind like she was in the funny paper with a balloon coming out of her head:

It's enough he up and married like he did, said the balloon. *It's enough they neither one, Pa nor Love, went anywhere the day after the weddin' and now everybody's sniggerin' about it. But to find out Miss Love cain't wait a minute to take over Ma's house is too much and then some.*

Even I could see that for the bride to start fall cleaning the day after the wedding, in the middle of the hottest summer on record, was the same as announcing to the world that the first Mrs. Blakeslee was sloven and her house too dirty to live in — and that the Blakeslee daughters hadn't cared enough for their poor bereaved papa to keep it clean for him.

Mama and Aunt Loma always did think Grandpa should of

hired a cook for Granny. Aunt Loma said as much to her daddy one time, but he just laughed. "Last buyin' trip I took," he said, "a New York feller got to talkin' 'bout Southern ladies rockin' on the porch at five o'clock ever evenin'. He called it a waste of woman power. Thet's the only time I ever seen eye to eye with a Yankee. Anyhow, Loma, yore ma had a long sight rather be a-workin' than a-settin'."

I was fixing to ask Mama what I was to do—I mean, was I to mind Grandpa or her—when she said in a spitting voice, "Will, pick everything that's ready and then make haste on up to your grandpa's."

She was scared she had gone too far in crossing him. And she was mad at herself for giving in.

I never in my life stripped a garden so fast, and my feet raced each other past the depot and the Cold Sassy tree and the nine houses between Grandpa's house and ours. I was about even with the Tate house when I caught the first muffled sounds of "Ta-Ra-Ra-Boom-de-Ay" on Granny's piano.

Miss Effie Belle's 102-year-old brother was sitting on their front porch, his square, moldy, splotched face unsmiling and vacant. I knew he couldn't hear Miss Love's music, not without his ear trumpet. But Miss Effie Belle could. Eighty-nine, and skin and bones like a mummy, she stood listening at her open front door, hands on hips and very grim of face.

Miss Effie Belle had a grim face any time, punctuated by a big pink wart that stuck out from the side of her upper lip like the feeler of a bee. She being the kind that put down newspapers so old Mr. Tate wouldn't track in dirt on her floors, you can imagine that she wasn't taking kindly to Miss Love's music. She would be thinking that when you've married somebody else's husband, if you play on her pi-ana it ought to be a contrite hymn that starts, "Lord, my sins be as scarlet" or "Too shamed to lift my head, Lord, too stained to hope for Heaven." Miss Effie Belle would call Miss Love awful to be playing dance-hall music.

I reckon the bride thought that with the parlor windows shut, nobody could hear it. That did dull the loudness, but not the joy and bam with which she played. The music really wasn't fittin', under the circumstances of Granny being dead and all, but it sounded mighty fine.

I didn't know whether to knock or just go on in, like I used to when Granny was alive. I knocked. But of course Miss Love couldn't hear me over the racket, so I tiptoed into the hall. Just then she went to singing, for gosh sake. "Ta-ra-ra-BOOM-de-ay! Ta-ra-ra-BOOM-de-ay!" I stood listening to the deep, rich good-times voice. Without a pause after the last "BOOM-de-ay," she burst into a chorus of "I'm Only a Bird in a Gilded Cage" and then sang "It'll be a HOT time, in the OLD town, to-ni-ight!"

I sure would of missed something if that train had of killed me!

I stepped over the parlor rug, which was in the hall, rolled up like a long log. Nearby was a pile of dusty ragged sheets that Granny had kept draped over the upholstered parlor furniture. Following the song to the parlor, as if Miss Love was a Pied Piper, I stopped at the door in pure amazement.

The room, pounding with music, was so bright with sunlight it might near put my eyes out. It had always been dark and cool in there. I'd never seen the rich red velour on the love-seat and side-chairs or on what Granny called "my gentleman's and lady's chairs." Of course the sheets weren't on the furniture when Granny had lain in state in there, but even then, because of her being dead and all, the blinds were closed and the draperies drawn.

Today, despite the windows were closed, Miss Love had opened the shutters wide. And the dark heavy draperies weren't just pushed apart; they were down and laid across a chair, like a sweaty dress after Sunday morning preachin'.

The good smell of wet wood rose from the floor, still damp after being scrubbed. Granny's big upright grand piano had been pulled way out, at an angle to the wall, and I saw Miss Love's new gold wedding band on the piano top beside a rag and a square of beeswax in a saucer. I guess she had been about to polish the rosewood but sat down to play instead. The rug being out and the draperies down, the piano sounded tinny and alive.

Miss Love had started playing "All Hail the Power of Jesus' Name" with a strong marching beat and lots of walking bass. She still hadn't seen me, though I had a good side view of her. I stood by the door while she finished the hymn and ran through choruses of "Maple Leaf Rag," "Georgia Blues," and "Good Ole Summertime," which she hummed, then played again, singing the words. After that she bammed out "Meet Me in St. Louis, Louis," as if her purpose in life was to play loud enough for old man Tate to hear through the shut windows.

I don't know what I was most flabbergasted at, the bright sun in the parlor (already fading the furniture, I was sure) or the bing-bang music (which I knew she would quit playing as soon as she saw me) or Miss Love herself, seated on the round stool, legs apart, long skirt hiked up above her knees (to be cooler, I reckon), and her heels and toes rocking the way I imagined a piano player's would in a cabaret.

Maybe it was her clothes. I had never seen Miss Love when she wasn't dolled up like one of those M. Rich & Bros. fashion advertisements in the Atlanta newspapers. Working at the store or playing for preachin' on Sunday at the Methodist Episcopal Church, South, she wore perfume and a hat, and her hair fixed fancy, and was always corseted and gusseted or whatever it was ladies did to shape their hips and bosoms.

But today she looked like a girl instead of a lady.

Her heavy brown hair was bound up and covered with a kerchief made out of a rag—actually a piece of Granny's old white outing nightgown. Mama always wore loose housework dresses at home, but Miss Love had on an old pink afternoon dress with white eyelet embroidery and a low-cut neckline. If she'd of bent down in that dress, her bosoms would of looked like two puppies trying to climb over a fence. Whenever her hands hit bass and treble chords at the same time, the bodice stretched tight across her bust, and on fast pieces, the jiggle was something to see! I tried not to stare, but I couldn't exactly help it.

With all that and her rollicking songs, I was on fire. My bare left foot patted to beat the band while she was singing "Yes, Sir, That's My Baby." Then she repeated the last line real slow and soft, except this time she sang, "Yes, sir, it's my baby . . . yes, sir, this house is . . . my baby . . . now-ow . . ." She ended with a slow, subdued flourish of treble chords and finally one soft single bass note, like a Graphophone winding down.

"Boy howdy, Miss Love!" I exclaimed.

Surprised, she swung toward me on the piano stool, clutching her low dress front with one hand and flipping down the long pink skirt with the other.

"Will Tweedy!" she exclaimed, the way a child caught with his hand in the cookie jar might say "Mama!"

"I, uh, knocked, but you didn't hear me," I said. She blushed. I reckon she was embarrassed at being caught with her knees showing, or being caught so happy when her husband's real wife wasn't yet cold in the grave.

"What can I do for you?" she asked, as if this was the store and I was a lady come in to order an Easter hat.

"Uh, Grandpa said you could use some hep," I offered, hitching my overalls and scratching my left heel with my right big toe.

"I hadn't expected your mama could spare you."

"Grandpa told her to send me up here."

"That man! I never saw anybody get away like he did this morning." She laughed gaily, her hand still clutching the low dress front.

"I reckon he was scairt somebody would see him doin' housework," said I, grinning. "He don't know doodly-squat about cleanin', you know. The one that always hepped Granny was me. Uh, excuse me, ma'am," I said lamely. "I shouldn't of mentioned my grandmother."

Waving a hand in protest, Miss Love got up from the piano stool. She looked a little flustered, as if trying to decide what to say and how to say it. "Look here, Will. Miss Mattie Lou was nicer to me than anybody else in Cold Sassy. Even if she weren't all around me in this house, I'd never forget her. So please don't think I expect to take her place. I'm—well, I'm just going to try to look after your grandfather."

"Yes'm."

We talked a little about me on the train trestle. She asked if I felt all right and I said yes'm. Then she went to get a gold bar pin for her dress front, to make the neck higher, and I went out to the porch for a drink of well water. On the way back up the hall, I chanced to look in Grandpa's room and saw that the bed in there wasn't made up.

Mama wouldn't ever start anything else without she made up the beds first.

Miss Love had raised the parlor windows by time I got back. "First," she said cheerfully, "I'd like you to shake these dusty draperies outside. I want to make new ones, soon as I can get around to it; the room needs brightening. But these will do for now."

How was Granny going to stay all around Miss Love if she got new parlor draperies?

Next I hefted the rolled-up parlor rug over my right shoulder and started out to hang it on the line. "When you get through beating it, leave it out in the sun a while," she said.

"Uh, won't it fade in the sun? Mama always says sun will fade a rug." It didn't matter to me personally, but I knew what Mama and Cold Sassy would say if Miss Love ruined Granny's things.

It got her dander up, my saying that. "The rug is moldy, mildewed, and full of moths, Will," she snapped. "That's what happens when a room stays shut up. The sun may fade it a little, but at least it won't smell musty."

To my mind she was same as saying that Granny was a dirty housekeeper. I lacked the nerve to explain about Grandpa not hiring help. As if reading my mind, Miss Love came over and patted my arm. "I didn't mean to be passing judgment, Will. When a woman gets sick, the house gets sick, too."

She was in the dining room when I came in from beating the rug. "I'd like you to take down the curtains in here," she said, "and put them out to burn. They're rotten. Then please sweep the walls and the ceiling in here, and when the dust settles, we'll wash the windows and the floor. But first, Will, take the coat rack and the little pine desk out of the hall into the parlor. I've already washed and waxed them."

Toting the desk into the parlor, I saw that Miss Love had laid the big Toy family Bible on Granny's loveseat. Seeing it, I longed for Granny. It sounds crazy, but I still found it hard to believe she was gone, and half expected that her death wasn't really written down in the Bible.

It was there, all right, in Grandpa's bold handwriting: *Died June 14, 1906.*

And below it, there was a new line. In a fine ladylike hand it said, *Enoch Rucker Blakeslee married Love Honour Simpson in Jefferson, Georgia, July 5, 1906.*

Gosh, Mama would sure be mad! This was the Toy Bible, not the Blakeslee Bible. To my knowing there wasn't any Blakeslee Bible. And I had heard Mama tell Aunt Loma right after the funeral, "I'm go'n bring Ma's Bible over here, if Pa don't mind."

I wondered if Grandpa knew Miss Love had put her name in it.

All the walls in Granny's house were horizontal pine boards, painted to look like plaster. I swept those in the dining room, like I was told to. When I came out, Miss Love was down on her hands and knees, scrubbing the hall floor, and humming like it was the most fun she'd ever had in her whole life.

She had just fired up the stove and put the kettle on when Grandpa walked in to eat dinner. Not a blessed thing fixed! He always was one to want a big meal in the middle of the day, and he told Miss Love so.

You never saw the like of how she took it. Instead of getting her dander up like Loma would, or being upset and apologizing the way Mama would, Miss Love, just calm and cool as you please and with a happy smile on her face, said, "Goodness, Mr. Blakeslee, cleaning this wonderful house made me forget all about time!" Her eyes were glowing. "Look, I'll cook you a real good supper. But for now, we can have the apple pie left from yesterday, sir, with a big hunk of that rat cheese from the store on it, and some cool milk. Is that all right?"

I expected him to explode. Instead he just went out on the back porch, poured some water from the bucket into the gray enamel basin on the shelf, washed up, came on in, sat down at the table, and said the blessing over the pie and milk. He didn't fuss at all, and didn't seem to notice she wasn't wearing the gold wedding band, which was still on the piano. She'd told me the ring was a little big and kept slipping off when her hands were in the soapy wash water.

While I bolted down my pie, Grandpa blurted out that Son Black had come in the store that morning. "He says you and him had a unner-standin'. He's talkin' bout breach a-promise. He got any call to think you was go'n marry him?"

Miss Love looked startled. "If he did, it was all in his own head. He talked about us getting married, but I always just passed it off as a joke."

"Thet's all I need to know," said Grandpa, finishing up his pie. "Miss Love, you think you could trim my hair some?" He tried to smooth it down with his hand, but it was too thick and bushy to mind anything but scissors.

"I'd love to trim your hair, Mr. B." There in the kitchen she danced around, studying his face this way and that, and finally burst out, "Mr. Blakeslee, you don't know how long I've wanted to see what's under that shelf of a mustache and that old gray beard!"

He jerked his arm across his face. "I didn't say cut my beard off, woman. I said cut my hair. I reckon the beard could use a li'l trimmin', but thet's all, hear. I ain't fond a-shavin'."

She didn't give up. "With a close haircut and a thin mustache and no beard, sir, you'd look—distinguished! Can I? Oh, please, Mr. Blakeslee?"

"I don't think so. I ain't seen my face in so long I mightn't know me."

"Wouldn't nobody know you, Grandpa," said I, pitching a hunk of cheese in the air so it dropped into my mouth. "Cain't you just see my daddy and Uncle Camp and Cudn Hope if you walked in the store shaved? They'd take you for a stranger and sell you a mule collar or something."

The idea really appealed to him. "By dang, Will Tweedy, you right. They wouldn't know me from Adam!"

"But you won't look like somebody who needs a mule collar," Miss Love protested. "You'll look like a judge who's come in for fine tobacco. All right, Mr. B.?" She was real excited. "Can I? Please?"

"By George, yes!" he said, slapping his knee. "If'n you can fix a lady's hair to go with them fancy hats, Miss Love, I reckon you ain't go'n make me look no worse'n I already do. Will Tweedy, go git the strop and my Wade and Butcher razor. Hit used to be my daddy's," he told her. "And, son, find them haircuttin' scissors yore granny always used. They's somewhere on my bureau."

Miss Love cut off most of the thick gray beard with the scissors, after which Grandpa wrapped a steaming towel around his face to soften the stubble. He shaved kind of awkward, nicking his face in several places. Then Miss Love trimmed the mustache into a pencil-thin line and cropped his hair down from a mane to short as mine.

Boy howdy, I couldn't believe what a difference! His hair and mustache being dark, he looked years younger without the gray beard. His face was lean and handsome. He looked like a fine gentleman.

Later, considering who arrived on the train that same evening, I couldn't help thinking how glad I was that Miss Love got Grandpa changed from a bushy-headed, bushy-faced old country man to somebody she could be proud to stand beside and introduce as her husband.

19

G RANDPA couldn't stop looking at himself in the mirror. Preening like a rooster, he kept saying things like "I do recollect seein' thet feller somewheres before. Ain't he a buster though!"

Miss Love was so excited she hugged him.

I could tell the hug surprised her as much as it did Grandpa, who looked like he didn't know whether to hug her back or not, which he didn't. But he seemed mighty pleased, and didn't object when she said, "Mr. B., don't go back to the store wearing that same tobacco-stained shirt, or you won't fool a soul."

Grandpa generally wore just two shirts a week, and Saturday wasn't his day to change. But he went to his room and came out buttoning a clean one. Then as he pulled up his suspenders, he said, real formal, "I'm much obliged to you, Miz Rucker Blakeslee."

He hardly ever thanked anybody for anything. Gratitude embarrassed him. I guess the words popped out because he was so pleased to see how good he looked after all these years.

While he dusted off his hat, Miss Love said, "You'd really look spiffy in a new cut of suit, Mr. Blakeslee."

"Cain't afford no new suit," he said gruffly.

"I'll make you one."

"Thet'd be a dang waste a-time. I wouldn't live to wear it out. Will Tweedy, you think they'll know me at the store?"

"No, sir! Specially if you walk in kind of sideways, so they won't see your arm off."

He looked at the clock on the mantelpiece. "I better git on back. Camp'll go to sleep if'n I ain't there." He set his hat at a jaunty angle and raised his hand good-bye. Reminded me of a little boy going off by himself for the first time.

We stood watching as he walked across the tracks, a new sort of strut in his long stride. "Boy howdy, Miss Love," said I, still amazed at the change. "If I was at the store and Grandpa walked in, I wouldn't know him. I might think I'd seen him somewhere, but I wouldn't know him."

She turned towards me, beaming. "He likes it, Will Tweedy! And isn't your grandfather a handsome man! You and him—I mean you and he—you look a lot alike, Will. I never realized it before."

"Granny always said so."

"It's the mouth and the shape of the jaw, and—" She put her hand on my shoulder, turned me toward her, and studied my face. Blushing, I bent my head. "No, look at me, Will. It's also your eyes, big like his. And your brows are arched like his."

Soon as Miss Love went to the kitchen, I went hunting for the painted mirror that usually hung over the marble-top table in the front hall—the mirror Aunt Loma and Mama both wanted. I found it laid across a table in the parlor. Bending over the glass, I stared around Saint Cecilia at the organ and all the painted angels and flower garlands to see if something of Grandpa would stare back at me.

Well, gosh, yes. Now that I had finally seen his face, I could say I did look like him. A lot like him. When I grinned at myself, the lower lip turned up at the corners, just like Grandpa's. His mouth was like a boy's anyhow, except looser. I preened a while, this way and that. If I looked like Grandpa, and Miss

Love thought he was handsome, then that meant I was handsome, too.

Lee Roy and them might not think so, but Miss Love did.

I combed my hair down with my fingers, squeezed a red sore place on my chin, and examined my upper lip to see if my mustache was any more ready to be shaved than yesterday. Hearing Miss Love coming, I sort of waved good-bye to myself and straightened up. She said, "Will, bring those pasteboard boxes in off the back porch to the company room, and I'll tell you what to do next."

When I came in with the boxes, I asked, "Ma'am, what you want me to do with'm?" I couldn't see her over the high stack I carried, but I knew she was in there. I could hear her opening drawers.

"I want you to pack up everything in this bureau," she said evenly. "And the things in the wardrobe, too."

"Everything?" I dropped the boxes. They fell with a thick dull clatter. I couldn't believe it. Without so much as a by-your-leave from Mama or Aunt Loma, Miss Love was planning on getting rid of Granny's belongings!

"Yes, everything. Mostly it's stuff that was packed away—old quilts and things your grandmother obviously wasn't using but I suppose hated to get rid of. The clothes she was wearing are all in Mr. Blakeslee's room. He wants everything in there to stay the way she had it."

I couldn't think what to say to that. So I asked, "Where we go'n put what's in here, Miss Love?"

"I want you to take it home. Your mother and Loma can go through it and throw stuff out or give it away. I need the space for my things, you see. It's—uh, this will be my room." She blushed.

It slowly dawned on me that it already was her room. Several of her dresses hung on wall nails, and also her nightgown, and she had pushed back a blue thousand-eye tray on the princess dresser to make room for a shoebox full of her combs and ribbons and doodads. Why, she had already brought over her things from the Crabtrees'! Two big trunks sat in front of the fireplace.

Looking around, I noticed a small poster tacked on the wall, advertising a women's suffrage speech in Baltimore in 1888. It said:

> *The Subject: Throw Off the Yoke of Oppressor Man!*
> *Miss Hannah Lee, The Long-Tongued Orator*
> *Will Emit Impassioned Yawps at Borough Hall*
> *7 O'Clock Monday Night!*
> *The Belva E. Lockwood Quartette*
> *Will Furnish Discord!*
> *Come One, Come All*
> *And Bring Your Chewing Gum!*

I didn't want to offend Miss Love, but I thought that was the silliest thing I ever read. Seeing I was trying to keep a straight face, she giggled. "Go on. Laugh. Your grandpa did. I laugh myself, every time I look at it. That's why I put it up."

"I thought you wanted women to get the vote, Miss Love."

"I do. Oh, I do. But that doesn't mean I can't laugh."

"'The long-tongued orator will emit impassioned yawps,'" I read. "Haw, I sure would of liked to hear that! Was she chewin' chewin' gum while she talked?"

Miss Love laughed. "I doubt it, Will, but I wasn't there. I found that poster on the sidewalk later. For a long time I tried to figure it out. I didn't know whether Miss Hannah Lee thought the suffrage movement was getting too grim and made this up to poke fun at herself and the rest of us, or whether some printer did it as an insult. I just know that every time I start taking life too seriously, I can look at that silly poster and get my sense of humor back."

Laughing merrily, she started out the door, then turned and asked, "Did you ever hear of Belva E. Lockwood, Will?"

"No'm. Was she that lady scientist over in France? Well, no, I see she was a singer." I nodded toward the poster.

"More than a singer. She ran for president that year."

"Of what?"

"The United States. I campaigned for her. She was a lawyer in Washington, and I thought she had a lot of sense."

Miss Love left the room. I read the poster again, then looked around at her clothes and at the bed. Maybe Miss Love and Grandpa were sleeping in here out of respect for the dead. I mean, maybe they were trying to show respect by not using the bed where the dead had died. But then I remembered that the big bed Granny and Grandpa shared wasn't made up. That must mean Grandpa slept in there last night. Maybe on his wedding night, too.

Who ever heard of a married lady wanting to pretend she was still an old maid — even to having a room to herself? Was this her idea of "throwing off the yoke of oppressor man?"

Well, her sleeping like an old maid did prove one thing: she and Grandpa hadn't been sweet on each other before Granny died. I couldn't wait to go home and tell Mama.

"See?" I'd say. "They weren't courtin' on the sly or anything like that. The fact Miss Love is usin' the comp'ny room proves it. They just got married so she could stay there and keep house."

Aw, I couldn't say that to Mama.

For one thing, it wouldn't help. She'd get another headache trying to decide all over again what Miss Love wanted out of her daddy. If she didn't intend to have babies, what had made her willing to marry an old man? She wouldn't do it just to keep house for him.

Also, Mama would worry that somebody else might find out about the sleeping arrangement and start sniggering the way they did about Mr. and Mrs. Abernathy, who hadn't slept in the same room for thirty years. The Abernathys each claimed the other one snored, but nobody believed that was the real reason.

As I wiped the sweat off my face and picked up a pasteboard box, I knew I couldn't mention such to Mama anyway—about the beds, I mean. In her mind, I didn't know what went on in bedrooms.

Which I didn't. Not exactly. When I was little I asked Papa one day where babies came from and he said ask him again when I was ten and he'd tell me. As soon as we sat down to breakfast on my tenth birthday, I said, "Well, Papa, I'm ten!"

He said, "Yes, I know, son. Happy birthday!"

I waited for him to explain about babies, but he just kept eating. On his second cup of coffee I said, "Papa, you said when I got ten, you'd tell me where babies come from. Remember? You said—"

Mama blushed and picked up little Mary Toy, who was four, and took her out. Papa blushed and said, "Well, uh, let's see, son. It's kind of like the way hens lay eggs and then biddies hatch out of the eggs." He stood up and wiped his mouth on his napkin.

"But what about the rooster? Don't he have something to do with it? Bluford says the rooster does something when he lights on a hen. What—"

"I got to get down to the store, Will." It didn't dawn on me till after he left that I still didn't know any more about ladies having babies than I did yesterday when I was just nine.

Filling one of Miss Love's boxes, I remembered one time Smiley said his folks were gone off and he'd get his little sister to go down to the barn with us. He wanted to show me what "it" was like. I was twelve. His sister was only five and wouldn't know what it was all about, he said. But just the idea scared me so bad I made up that Papa had told me to build a shelf on the back porch for Mama's flower-potting stuff.

By then I understood how it was with roosters and hens, of course, and cows and dogs and cats. And because of all the smutty stories I'd heard, I had a pretty good guess about people. I certainly knew that getting married meant you were supposed to sleep in the same bed, and that the bed had a lot to do with having babies. When Aunt Loma got married, she and Camp didn't have but one bed. Still and all, I used to look at her and wonder if they had done "it." The day I found out she was in the family way, I finally knew for sure they had.

Well, it looked like Miss Love and Grandpa weren't aiming to do it or anything else—have a baby or sleep in the same bed, either one.

I could hear Miss Love in the kitchen, getting Grandpa's good supper started. I emptied a bureau drawer full of ragged, baby-stained old quilts into a big box. In the next drawer was a stack of baby clothes, ironed and done up nice, like for the next birthing. Why come Granny hadn't given all that to Mama when I was born—or when Mama was expecting the baby that died or when Mary Toy came? Or at least why didn't she give the clothes to Aunt Loma? By time Campbell Junior came along, Granny surely wasn't still hoping to have another baby herself.

I kind of wished the little gowns and lacy caps could stay here in the bureau. With a new young wife, Grandpa might still get him a boy. But this was Miss Love's bed in here, and his bed was in yonder, so I knew it wasn't ever going to happen. Anyway I, Will Tweedy, was his boy. And I was certain that's the way Mama and them wanted it to stay.

I reckon I did, too, I'm ashamed to say.

Miss Love brought me some sweetmilk just as I emptied one of the small top drawers into a box. It was full of old brass keys, old receipts, yellowed letters tied in bundles, hairpins, tintypes, and at least a dozen pairs of gold-rimmed spectacles with bent or missing rims, and some with the glass missing. I pointed out Grandpa's medal from the Confederate Veterans' Reunion in 1875. Miss Love picked it out of the pile. "I suppose we should put this in a drawer in his room. But take the rest of it home, Will."

Her face was flushed with heat, and the pink dress was so

soaked that it stuck to her skin in the back. She had the same cardboard fan in her hand that I'd fanned Granny with when she lay dying. Miss Love fanned hard, and BIRDSONG'S FUNERAL PARLOR became a blur. "I'm so hot, Will. And I'm tired. I think I'll go lie down a while."

"Yes'm, you look like you could use a rest." I gulped down the sweetmilk. "Most ladies take a nap after dinner."

"Take what?" Miss Love hadn't heard a word I said.

"A nap, ma'am."

"I have never napped in my life."

"Mama says a nap makes her feel better."

"How could I feel any better?" she asked, laughing. "Anyway, I'm not planning to sleep. I'm just going to lie down a minute."

"Yes'm." I drained the glass. My thumb accidentally touched her forefinger as I handed it back. "Thank you, ma'am."

Miss Love had hardly sat down on the daybed in the hall before she hopped up and said maybe we ought to bring the parlor rug in out of the sun. We did, and then she decided we should place the parlor furniture. I saw right off that she didn't plan on putting anything back just like Granny had it.

"I want this over here, this over there," said Miss Love, pointing first to the loveseat, then the marble-top table. After I moved them, she got at one end of the piano to help shove. When the furniture was all changed around, she asked, smiling and fanning, if I thought my mother and Loma would like it.

"You think Grandpa will?" It was just as well not to say about Mama and Aunt Loma.

"Men think they don't like changes, but they can get used to anything. Besides, I think furniture likes to be moved. Wouldn't you say so?" I thought that sounded foolish, till I saw she was just teasing.

"I reckon." Grinning, I glanced around the room. It did look nice. "Want me to hang the pictures back up, Miss Love?"

"Well, uh, I'm going to let you take those to your mother and Loma. All except the round print of the three horses' heads over there. I want it. Did you know it's part of a big battle scene? I saw the whole picture once, in a book. Look at those flaring nostrils and wild eyes, Will!" She held the picture up to show me, as if I hadn't been seeing it all my life, then traced her finger over the profile of the biggest horse. "I rode a lot when I was out in Texas. I haven't seen any ladies riding in Cold Sassy except Mrs. Sheffield."

"That's because she's the only one that does."

Miss Love fanned some more. "Golly Pete, Will, it's so hot!"

Later I couldn't of told you to save my neck why I asked her what I did then. I was thinking with my mouth, not my brain. But after she took off the dusty head rag, her brown hair came tumbling down around her flushed face, and she was so pretty that I couldn't for the life of me figure out why in the heck she would marry an old man.

Anyhow, I said it: "How come you married my grandpa?"

The question blurted out like a pitcher's fast ball, and I knew right off that I had overstepped.

20

BLUSHING, I stammered out that it was none of my business and please forget I asked.

Miss Love blushed, too. Didn't say a word. She fanned fast for a minute, then sank down in Granny's big rocker, the high-back one with apples and pears carved on it. I knew she must be furious.

But as it turned out, she was busting to talk. I think if I was a frog she'd of talked to me just the same, once I got her started with that smart-aleck question. Twisting her hair into a topknot and fastening it with three big tortoise-shell pins, she said, "Sit down, Will." I sat. "Partly I married your grandfather to have a family." Oh, Lord, that's what Mama was scared of. But Miss Love didn't mean babies. "I don't think of myself as a step-mother to Mary Willis and Loma, of course. But I hope they'll come to regard me as—well, like a sister. I want so much to be-long in this family. I want kinfolks."

"You ain't got any?"

"My mother died when I was twelve. Cousin Lottie raised me, and she died last year. She was eighty-five. I'm my own last living relative, so to speak."

Gosh. It would be awful not to have folks. "Your daddy, what about him?"

A hard look came on her face. "I have no living relative." Then, taking a deep breath, she said, "My father was a drunkard. I decided a long time ago to pretend he never existed. But enough about my people. Will, I'm aware that I've given Cold Sassy plenty to gossip about this week, and I know your mother and Loma are upset. I wish I could apologize but . . . I don't know how to approach them."

I didn't know either, so I didn't answer.

"I hate being talked about. I hate feeling disliked. I hate it that your folks are embarrassed." I wondered if she knew *scandalized* was more the word for it. "But Mr. Blakeslee thinks the talk will die down if I don't feed it. He says just keep my mouth shut."

And get Aunt Loma to shut hers, I thought. "Yes'm, he's right. He gets away with a lot that way. And if he don't want to hear about something, he just changes the subject or makes a joke."

She smiled. "Yes, I've seen that happen at the store. People will be arguing politics or complaining about the weather and he'll say, 'What time will the sun set this evenin'?' or, 'I been tryin' to remember when was the Battle of Chickamauga.' But I'm not answering your question, Will. I married him because — "

"You ain't got to answer, Miss Love." I fumbled with the rusty wire on the back of the horse picture, twisting it back in place. "I shouldn't of ast that."

"But I want to tell you. Usually people who don't approve of what you do never wonder or care why you did it. I appreciate your wanting to know."

"Ma'am, I didn't say I disapprove. It ain't my place to say."

"But of course you disapprove." She was rubbing sweat off her face and neck with the dusty head rag. It left a grimy smear down one cheek. She took a long breath, like before diving into a swimming hole. "So I am going to tell you how it happened. I went back to the store last Wednesday after the parade. Nobody else was there. The store was closed, of course, but Miss Pauline was anxious to get her hat, so I was going to finish it. Then your grandfather walked in. He came right over to the millinery table and asked if I would marry him." She blushed. "Said it would be a marriage in name only. I'd just be his house-keeper. He made it clear he didn't love me or anything, and said of course I didn't love him. 'But I always liked havin' you around the store,' he said, 'and I figger you like me all right, bein' as you ain't quit or nothin'.' You know how he talks."

"Yes'm."

"And he said he liked my coffee. I reminded him it was Mrs. Crabtree's coffee. Mr. Blakeslee was coming to work every morning without breakfast, Will, and I got worried about him and asked Mrs. Crabtree if I could take him some coffee. I got him to eat store cheese and crackers with it."

"Yes'm. I heard."

"You did? How?"

"Well'm, Papa told us. He knew Mama was worryin' about Grandpa not eatin' breakfast. He was glad you'd thunk it up."

It didn't seem polite to tell her what Miss Effie Belle Tate said, namely, that every old maid and widow woman in town had been bidin' her time, tryin' to wait a decent period after the funeral before invitin' Rucker to Sunday dinner. "But wouldn't you know Love Simpson got to him first with a quart jar a-cof-fee!"

Miss Love was talking on. ". . . so it would just be a business arrangement. I was to cook and clean up and wash. In exchange he would deed the house over to me. He said that seemed fair enough. Will, I decided he had to be joking, so I joked back. I said, 'Now, Mr. Blakeslee, that sounds fine, but you'd have to deed over the furniture, too. After you pass on, what good would the house do me without a bed to sleep in?' He said, 'Gosh a'mighty, woman, you're astin' too much.' I laughed and said, 'Take it or leave it, Mr. Blakeslee.'"

Miss Love said she was still just carrying on. "It didn't seem appropriate to be joking like that, Will, Miss Mattie Lou being so recently dead. But I didn't know how else to handle it."

After pondering a minute, Grandpa had agreed to give her the furniture with the house. "Thet way, when I die they won't be no big fuss bout who's to have what."

"Will, that's when I realized he really meant to marry me," said Miss Love. "I was flabbergasted. I told him, 'I'll have to pray about it, Mr. Blakeslee. I've never made an important decision in my life without praying about it.' 'Well, kneel down,' he said. 'Let's go to prayin'.' He had one knee bent toward the floor when I said, 'Don't rush me, Mr. Blakeslee—me or God, either.'"

Miss Love put her hands up to her cheeks and closed her eyes for a minute, then talked on. "I couldn't believe this. Two years ago I—I almost married somebody, Will. When things didn't work out, I felt that God was trying to tell me I shouldn't ever marry. But—well, if I was just to be a housekeeper, that would be the same as not marrying, except I would have a home. On the other hand, it was a proposal that blasphemed holy matrimony. I sat there not saying a word, my mind a jumble. I guess Mr. Blakeslee thought I wasn't sold on the idea, because he put some more icing on the cake. Said, 'Well, and I'll set aside a little cash money for you in my will, Miss Love. Say two hundred dollars.'"

"Grandpa must of been mighty lonesome, or else mighty anxious to get the house cleaned up," said I. "It ain't like him to pay that much for anything."

"Well, he made it plain he had offered as much as he was going to. He also made it plain that the store and all his other property would go to your mother and Loma."

Oh, boy, I couldn't wait to tell Mama. I grinned. "Well, it ain't hard to figure out you said yes."

"I told him I couldn't possibly give him an answer, just like that. He said if I needed a while to think it over, I could let him know next day."

All of a sudden Miss Love hopped up like she'd sat on a pin, plopped herself down on the piano stool, and went to playing chords. I thought she'd gone loose in the head. But I soon saw she was playing music to go along with what she was saying, like at a picture show. Glancing over her shoulder at me, she slowly walked two fingers of her right hand up and down the keyboard. "This is me thinking," she said, nodding toward the two fingers. "Trying to sort out all Mr. Blakeslee said. . . . Now this is me talking." Accompanied by a *plink-a-plink* up above middle C, she quoted her answer: "'What's the rush, Mr. Blakeslee? We'd have to wait a year anyway.'"

With bass notes and a deep voice, Miss Love became Grandpa: "'I ain't talkin' bout no year. I'm talkin' bout t'morrer, Miss Love. Marryin' t'morrer. I got to go on and git married or hire me a housekeeper, one.'" Gosh, she sounded just like him. Even looked like him, using her tongue like a wad of tobacco being switched from one cheek to the other.

"I said,"—*three stiff, prissy notes*—"'It's not proper, Mr. Blakeslee. It's not even right.'" *A pause, then sad chords.* "'Sir, Miss Mattie Lou has been dead only three weeks.' What he said then sent chills down my spine, Will." *Heavy bass notes followed by harsh discords.* "He said—"

"She's dead as she'll ever be?"

Bam! "That's it exactly. How did you know?"

"That's what he said to Mama and Aunt Loma and me."

Miss Love had been as stunned as we were. "I told him he hadn't had time for her to die in his heart or his mind and I was afraid he'd regret rushing into something like this. 'Well,' he said"—*discords in the bass*—"'I ain't go'n spend the rest a-my life sweepin' and arnin' shirts. And I ain't go'n move in on Mary Willis and them—or Loma, either. Loma's got too many cats and talks ugly, and Mary Willis would worry me to death. She fusses over me like a old hen. Besides, I don't want to be no burden on'm.' He said marrying was the only solution he'd been able to come up with, and I and one other woman in town were the only ones he thought he could stand to have around the house."

I wondered who the other lady was.

Miss Love wiped her sweaty hands on her dress, closed her eyes, clasped her fingers tight around her knees, and stopped talking, like she'd forgot I was there. But then her long black lashes fluttered open, and in a soft, sad voice she continued, "I was so shocked, I could hardly take in anything he said."

Her hands went straying around the keyboard, found "Abide With Me," and played a few lines, real quiet. "I remember Mr. Blakeslee said I could keep being a Methodist. 'Go ever Sunday,' he said, 'but don't ast me to go, not to the Methodist or Baptist or any of'm. I'm done with it. I went to preachin' with Miss Mattie Lou for jest one reason. Hit made her happy. But thet don't matter now, and I'm tired a-preachers. They talk tithin' all the time'"—*sharp, stingy single notes*—"'and say thangs like if a man sins, God's go'n punish him by takin' his wife or his son or his biz-ness.'" *Discords in the bass, and fire in Miss Love's eyes, just like Grandpa's.* "'I'm tired of'm tryin' to scare folks to Heaven with all thet hellfire and damnation. I want to hear bout the lovin', forgivin' God thet Jesus preached. But all you git at Christian churches is Old Testament vengeance: watch out and be good or the Lord will smite you down.'"

Lost in thought, Miss Love played a chorus of "Faith of Our Fathers, Living Still." Then she said, "I told your grandfather that the church was very important to me. He said, 'Well, you go on by yoreself, jest like you been a-doin'.'" Thinking how pretty her hands were, despite they were red from scrubbing floors, I watched her fingers move dreamy up and down the keyboard. "Mr. Blakeslee said he never told your grandmother how he felt about the church. 'Hit would a-hurt her feelin's, same as sayin' I didn't like her daddy or her roses.'"

She twirled around on the piano stool, facing me, and I saw

her eyes were glistening with tears. Wiping them in a quick motion with the back of her hand, she smiled. "He must have loved your grandmother very much."

"Yes'm, he did."

"Well, he went on to say he'd lived fifty-nine years by other people's rules—'but from now on, I'm a-go'n do what I dang want to. Startin' with marryin' you, Miss Love, if'n you'll have me. I'll deed over the house and furniture when we go to the courthouse to git married, and I'll write a new will. But when I'm th'ew with thet, don't try to tell me what to do or make me over. If'n the way I want to live don't suit you, then don't marry me.'

"I said, 'Well, I don't suppose what you do or don't do would affect me the way it might a real wife.'

"'Thet's the way I look on it,' he said."

For several minutes I didn't say anything, and Miss Love didn't, either. Finally she spoke. "I'd quit praying for a husband two years ago, Will. But I've prayed all my life for a home of my own—and for this." She patted the sounding board of the piano. Defensive, she added, "It was going to be me or some-body else. He said so. Folks will talk, I know, but. . . . You ask why did I marry him? Yes, for a house! Can you imagine what this means to me, Will Tweedy? All my life I've lived in rented upstairs rooms with ugly rented furniture. Cousin Lottie used to say we were so poor that we didn't have a pot to throw out the window, and we didn't. We had to move every time the rent was overdue."

"But when you went to work—"

"Milliners make room money, Will. Not house money."

"Yes'm, I s'pose so."

"But after it seemed to be God's will that I never marry, I gave up hope of ever having a home. . . . Does it sound so aw-ful, Will, to marry for worldy goods?"

"No'm. It don't to me. Maybe to some folks."

"The Lord answers prayers in strange ways."

I nodded to show I understood. Then, stretching, I tried to figure some way to lighten up the conversation. "Too bad you didn't hold out a little longer. Grandpa and God might of give you a ridin' horse, too."

She laughed. "If I'd tried to get everything I ever wanted, Will, I'd have asked for a diamond necklace and a motorcar and—"

"Yes'm but he might of married that other lady."

Miss Love smiled, but it was a weak smile. The steam had gone clean out of her. "Will, do you think they'll let me in? Your family?"

I didn't know how to say what she wouldn't want to hear. So I said, "There's just one thing I cain't figure, ma'am. Why didn't you get married long time ago? A lady pretty as you, I bet the Lord didn't have no trouble givin' you chances. For instance, why didn't you marry Mr. Son Black? He's got a nice house."

Miss Love stood up, so I did, too. She said, "I knew God didn't want me to marry a man like him. He talks tough but inside he's just a little bitty boy, scared of his mama. And anyhow, it's her house." She was silent a minute, then laughed and made a joke. "Reading King Arthur is what made me an old maid, Will. I kept holding out for a hero, a knight in shining armor. I really thought some rich, exciting man would come riding up on a white horse and rescue me from being poor and unhappy. After I fell in love with the man in Texas. . . . Well, he was rich and had a white horse, but he was no knight. And neither is Son Black. He couldn't qualify as the hero in a cheap novel."

Glad to be on a new subject, I said, "I been readin' a novel, Miss Love, one called *Damaged Goods*. I got it hid in the barn. Papa would have a fit, but it's got a good moral lesson. I think books like that are good for a boy if he has the right mind. You want to borrow it when I get through?"

She didn't laugh at me. "Well, uh, maybe." She sighed. "Do you know what I'm talking about, Will?"

"Yes'm. Maybe."

"I'm saying that after I missed the love boat, I wasn't going to settle for a raft—meaning somebody like Son Black. But I'm glad to settle for a man I can respect, and a family I'm proud to be part of. I think Mr. Blakeslee is probably the only completely honest man I've ever known. He drinks a little, but"—she hesitated—"not like my father. Whiskey isn't important to Mr. Blakeslee."

"No'm. I think Grandpa mostly takes that one drink to prove he's got a right to." And maybe, I thought, he married you to prove the same thing.

Miss Love looked at her hands. "My nails are a sight from all that scouring," she said, taking a long file off the mantelpiece and smoothing a frayed thumbnail. Then, meeting my eyes, she sighed and said, "Now, Will, have I answered your question?"

"Yes'm, thank you, ma'am. I understand." I was so flattered, the way she'd poured out her heart. "Miss Love, why don't you go lay down now? You look wore out."

"Never say *lay*, Will." She was teasing. "I will not lay. But I think I may *lie* for a while. I really am tired." Walking slowly to the hall, where there was a little breeze, she stretched out on the daybed and went to filing her nails.

I went to her bedroom and started filling up the boxes. I was pulling moldy old-timey dresses and frayed coats and hats of Granny's out of the wardrobe when I chanced to look out the front window and saw a well-dressed stranger pass by on the dirt sidewalk.

Hung over his right arm was a fancy saddle with silver trim that gleamed so bright in the sun, it just about put my eyes out. That saddle wasn't like anything you'd ever think to see in Cold Sassy, then or now. Neither was the man.

And suddenly he paused and looked towards Grandpa's house.

21

I HAD seen pictures of cowboys in books and magazines, and this fellow didn't exactly look like a cowboy. I mean, he wasn't dirty, didn't have on spurs or cowhide chaps or a red bandanna around his neck, and didn't carry a lasso. He looked like he'd just had a bath and a shave, and he was wearing an expensive black suit. But he was a cowboy, all right. I knew by the high-heeled, tooled-leather boots, the big white felt hat, and the pistol in a holster on his hip. When a Cold Sassy man carries a pistol, he straps it across his chest under his shirt and you don't see it.

The main thing, though, was that tooled-leather Western saddle he toted, which like I said was ornamented with silver. The stranger held it careless, as if it weighed no more than a rooster, though even to a horse it would of been heavy as lead.

What I could hardly believe was the man himself. His legs were so long it seemed like they swung from his waist. His body was long, too, and his arms and hands, and even his craggy, sun-browned face. He must of been six feet three at least and walked with a different gait altogether from the men in Cold Sassy.

After pausing and squinting hard in my direction, the stranger walked on. I rushed to the front door to get a better look. I watched as he stopped little Timmy Hopkins, who was rolling a hoop in the street. They talked a minute, Timmy pointed toward Grandpa's house, and the stranger, shifting the saddle to his other arm, came back.

"Miss Love!" I called softly. "Come 'ere, quick!"

I pointed down the street as she came up beside me. "Lord, it's hot," she mumbled sleepily, rubbing the small of her back. "Will, what are you staring at?"

"Look at that feller."

Her gaze focused where my finger was pointing. "Oh, my God in Heaven!" she gasped. Both hands flew to her mouth. "Oh, Lord, what can I do?" She ran back a few steps into the hall, whirled around. Her face had gone so white, the freckles stood out like tiny brown poky dots. "Don't let him in, Will!"

But even as she said it, she bent down to wipe the sweat off her face with her skirt, then tried to smooth her hair. "Oh, Lord, he mustn't see me like this! Will, say I'm not home."

But the man was already up the steps and, before she could escape, had either heard or seen her. Without so much as a knock or a by-your-leave, he stalked through the door, brushing past me, eased the saddle to the floor, and, seeing nothing but her, moved down the hall toward Miss Love.

She stood there like she'd gone numb, her hands on her mouth. When he got to her, they just stood staring at one another. He took off the big hat, real slow, his eyes never leaving hers, dropped it on the daybed, and took her hands and kissed them. Then he put his arms around her and kissed her, right on the mouth! Kissed her like he was starved and she was something to eat.

I never in my life dreamed of a kiss being like that. It sure wasn't that time I kissed Mary Riley St. John behind the door at Oralee McGibboney's party, and it sure wasn't like that when Papa kissed Mama good-bye after breakfast. Mama was usually still eating, so he'd bend down and wait while she wiped her mouth, then smack her one, and that's all there was to it.

Well, this man kissing Miss Love, he didn't just kiss her. He kept on kissing her. A string of kisses a mile long melted together as his lips brushed her ears, her neck, her arms, her hair, and then got back to her mouth again. And Miss Love was kissing him back, no doubt about it. I didn't know what to do. I stood on one foot, then the other, and if I'd had a third foot, I'd of shifted to it. For sure I was in the way and I ought to slip on out. But I was pinned to the sight.

Oh, gosh, what if Grandpa walked in! Like it was me that was guilty, I glanced through the open door, half-expecting to see him. Who I saw instead was Miss Effie Belle Tate from next door, hurrying up the walk with a frosted coconut cake!

I first thought she was bringing it to Miss Love as a welcome-to-the-bride present. But in her hurry to get over there, Miss Effie Belle had forgot to change out of her bedroom shoes, so I knew right off she hadn't planned a social call. What happened, I guessed, was that Miss Effie Belle saw the tall stranger walk into Grandpa's house with the saddle and, as an excuse to get a good look at him, had grabbed up the cake she just frosted.

Bursting out onto the veranda, I met her at the top step. "Sure is a hot day, ain't it, Miss Effie Belle?" I talked loud as I could. She wasn't deaf or anything, like her brother, but I was hoping if Miss Love had any ears left, she would hear me and run sit down prim and proper in the parlor. If the stranger sat clear over on the other side of the room, they could make like they'd just been talking.

As Miss Effie Belle marched toward the doorway, I kind of stepped in front of her and yelled, "Did you see that tall feller that's come callin', Miss Effie Belle? Ain't he a buster! Uh, I think he's her lawyer or somebody." I had my voice aimed halfway at the coconut cake and halfway into the hall. "Miss Love would have more time to set a spell if you'd come back later, Miss Effie Belle."

"Oh, shut up, Will," she said. But she stopped at the door,

chewed on her bottom lip like she was thinking, and then seemed to change her mind about barging in. The way the big pink wart on her upper lip quivered, I couldn't tell if she had seen them kissing or just lost her nerve. At any rate, she turned on her heel, nearly losing a bedroom slipper, and without a word and without so much as handing me the coconut cake—though I reached for it—she marched down the steps and took her cake back home.

I sure hated that. And her forgetting to give it to me made me think for sure she'd seen the kissing.

About time I got back in the house, Miss Love came to herself and opened her eyes, and the fireworks started!

The stranger just laughed when she tried to push him away. Didn't back off till she scratched his neck with claw fingers. "You ain't changed a bit, Love." He rubbed his neck, but he was still laughing.

"You ain't either, you devil!" she screamed, bursting into tears. That was the first time I ever heard her say *ain't*. "Why did you c-come here? Get out of m-m-my house!"

"Your house?" He looked around the front hall, took in all the signs of cleaning, ambled over and peered into the parlor, and put on an exaggerated mock expression of being impressed. "Millinery sure must pay good in Georgia." He strolled towards her.

She backed back. "You put your hands on me again, Clayton McAllister, I'll gouge your eyes out! I'll kill you!" She grabbed the long nail file off the daybed.

He laughed again, but not with his whole face, I noticed. "That's what I like about you, tiger," he drawled. "You got spirit. But if you kill me, honey, you'll be killin' the man that's gonna take you out of this hick town. Love, I come to get you!"

She stared at him, dumfounded. "Get me? What're you talking about?"

"If you'd opened my letters stead of sendin'm back, you wouldn't be so surprised. Lord knows I've written you enough."

Whatever Miss Love felt when he was kissing her sure had evaporated. The gold pin was undone and she hadn't even noticed—though I expect he had, standing where he could look right down that low-cut pink dress.

I knew I ought to leave. "Miss Love," I said, "I got to get on home and milk the cow."

She exploded like a fireworks rocket. "Don't you dare, Will Tweedy! You leave me alone here with him and nobody in this town will ever speak to me again!"

"Go 'long home, boy," said Clayton McAllister, as if he'd known I was there all the time. "It won't matter if nobody here speaks to her again, cause she won't be livin' here no more."

Miss Love swung around, her hands clenched, face red, those gray-blue eyes hard as steel, and the fanciest gosh dern words coming out of that big mouth you ever heard. She didn't yell. She spat words. I can't remember all she said, but Mr. McAllister got the message that she had made the mistake of loving him once and she sure wouldn't ever make that mistake again, and why did he think she would run off to Texas with him, for heaven's sake.

He wasn't laughing now. "You don't know what you talkin' bout." He was mad. "I'm astin' you to marry me, not run off with me."

"You asked me once before, if I remember correctly." She blazed away like a six-shooter, hitting him with words. "And off I went to Baltimore, all dreamy-eyed, to sew my trousseau. Cousin Lottie and I were finishing up the wedding dress when your letter came. It just about killed me, Clayton McAllister." (Gosh, that must of been how she found out he'd eloped with her best friend!) Miss Love sat down on the daybed. "Oh, how I've hated you!"

"I deserve it, Love." He looked miserable. "But I've come to tell you, I'll make it up to you if you'll let me."

She stood up and said, "Well, that's settled. So good-bye."

He took a long breath and pointed at the saddle. "I had that made for you, remember? It's been in the tack room all this time. Nobody's used it. I want you to have it."

"I don't want it. I don't want anything of yours—especially not a saddle that was an engagement present, for heaven's sake! Take it back to Texas."

"Love, I've brung it back to be your engagement present agin. Cain't you understand?" (Gosh, that must mean Miss Love's best friend had died.)

Her lips were trembling like she might cry. She sank down on the daybed again. "Lord, Clayt, you don't have a grain of sense. You write me I'm not good enough for you, and now two years later you—"

"I didn't say that, damnit!"

"Don't you curse at me. Whatever it was you said, that's what you meant." She didn't look about to cry now. She looked mad. "How a philanderer like you could sit in judgment on me, I'll never understand!"

"I felt like you were—like you'd been pretending to be something you weren't. That's why I got so mad at you. How pride could of made me hurt an angel like you—" He moved towards her. There was the same look on his face as on Grandpa's when Granny's hand went limp in his. But there was hope, too. "Love," he whispered, "you're the only woman I could ever marry. You know that." (Gosh, then he'd never eloped with Miss Love's best friend! Loma must of made that up.) "There's been other women in my life," he admitted, "but nobody I wanted to marry but you."

"Ha. What you mean is that the pickings are slim in Texas. You've given up on finding somebody decent out there. Well, if the only white women you know are married ladies or white trash, or both, that's your worry, not mine. Get you a Mexican wife. Get you a squaw. Or spend the winter in town again. Remember my friend Edna Mae? She wrote me they've sent in another milliner from Baltimore."

"But I want you, Love. Only you. And you still care for me. I can tell. Please, Love, forgive me."

I do think that for a moment Miss Love yearned towards him. Then all of a sudden she laughed out loud. "Clayton McAllister, what's there to forgive? Will, you've heard all this. Do you see anything to forgive?"

All this time I was standing in the darkest, out-of-the-way corner I could find. I thought they'd both forgot I was there. "I don't know'm," I mumbled.

"Well, there's not. You did me a favor, Clayt. If you had even pretended to be a forgiving Christian gentleman, I'd now be the lonely wife of a rich, stuck-up philanderer. Meaning you, God help me. Because that's all you were when we met and that's all you were when you asked for the ring back, and that's all you are now. Edna Mae wrote me all about you and that married woman you've been—"

He was real mad. "Whatever Edna Mae said, it ain't true."

"But I believe her. You wanted to marry me in the first place, Clayt, because I wouldn't . . . I was just a challenge. You always did want anything you couldn't get. Then when I told you what you didn't want to hear, you—" She stopped, biting her lip. "Well, so here you are again, all the way from Texas. I guess your pride's hurt because I wouldn't read your letters, much less answer them. It's a helpless feeling to get letters back un-opened, isn't it, Clayton? I know. In case you don't remember, I wrote you after you asked me to send back the ring. I poured out my heart in that letter. When it came back in the mail, I opened it and read it. Lord, I was glad you never knew how I had groveled at your feet!"

"Love, I'm grovelin' at yours now. Please, listen to me."

Ignoring him, she said brightly, "I just had another thought. Maybe that married lady friend is what has brought you back to me. Is she after your money, Clayt? Is she talking about di-vorcing her husband? She's got you scared, hasn't she? You'd rather marry somebody like me than a divorced person, and if you can take me to Texas, she'll be off your back. Is that it?"

Mr. McAllister was furious. "Love, will you shut up? I've come back for just one reason. *I love you.*" He reached to touch her arm. She jerked away. Her hands were shaking. She hid them in her skirt.

"I've changed, Love. God knows it."

"Well, I don't. So you just pick up that saddle and ride it out of here. I don't want it. It's tainted."

"You're comin' with me, Love Simpson. You still love me and you know it." It looked like he was fixing to grab her for another ten-minute kiss. Gosh, I didn't think I could watch that again. And had she forgot all about Grandpa? Why didn't she just tell Mr. Cowboy she was already married?

Right then she came out with it. Almost laughing as she looked up at him, she said sweet and easy, "If you were the last man on earth, Mr. Clayton McAllister, I wouldn't go a mile with you. Even if I was free to."

"What do you mean?"

She held the back of her left hand up to his face and wiggled the fourth finger. Then I guess she remembered her wedding band was still on top of the piano. She tapped the finger. "I've got a wedding ring goes on this." A sound on the porch made her look toward the front door. "And I do believe," she said, cool and calm as you please, though I bet her knees were shaking, "I do believe here comes my husband now!"

Of course somebody must of gone to the store and told Grandpa there was a tall stranger with a silver-trimmed saddle up at his house. And something about the way it was said had made him hot-foot it home, else why would he leave the store on a busy Saturday?

When I saw him walk in with that clean-shaved face, close-cut dark hair, and thin mustache, my first thought was to wonder if it was really Grandpa. My second thought was to be proud of him, especially for Miss Love's sake. My third thought was that Miss Effie Belle—unless she took Grandpa for another stranger calling on Miss Love—must of run out and told him about the kissing.

Gosh, in that case he might bust Mr. McAllister's head wide open!

22

I DIDN'T know then whether Miss Effie Belle had got to Grandpa or not. But I found out later that white-haired old Mr. Boop had. Papa told us that night how Mr. Boop ran over from the hotel to say a feller wearin' a Stetson hat and cowboy boots had come in on the train from Lula.

"Where's Rucker at?" Mr. Boop asked, picking up a can of pipe tobacco and handing Grandpa the money.

"You talkin' to him, Amos." Grandpa grinned and ran his hand over his smooth-shaved face. Papa and them laughed out loud as Mr. Boop stared. "Hit's me all right, Amos. See?" Grandpa held up that left arm and dangled the knotted sleeve in his face.

"Well, I be-dog. Ain't you a sight! I was just a-wonderin' how Rucker could a-hired a new man and I ain't heard bout it. Well, I want to tell you bout this here stranger, Rucker. He come in the ho-tel totin' a fine brown and white cowhide grip and the fanciest dang saddle you ever seen. Silver dohickies all over it. The feller said he needed to shave and git a bath but might not be stayin' for the night."

"What's his bizness here?" Grandpa asked, real interested.

"Didn't state his bizness. But pretty soon he come back to the ho-tel dest. He was cleaned up, slicked down, and wearin' a nice black suit—and still carryin' that dad-gum saddle. You know what he ast, Rucker? Ast where did Miss Love Simpson board at, or would she be at work." After letting that soak in on Grandpa, Mr. Boop said, "I pointed the way to yore house, Rucker, but I didn't bother tellin' him she'd got marrit. Didn't seem to me it was any of his bizness. But I thought you ought to know that a tooled-leather saddle orny-mented with Mexican silver is headin' up North Main towards yore house."

"Is thet so," said Grandpa. According to Papa, he didn't even look up.

"This man's so good-lookin', Rucker, I bet he has to use tar soap to keep the ladies from lassoin' him!"

"Is thet so," said Grandpa.

"You goin' down there, Rucker?"

"I ain't got time right now. I reckon Miss Love knows how to make a stranger welcome."

Mr. Boop having felt Grandpa's right fist on his jaw one time, he was probably hoping a good fight would come out of the situation.

But I wasn't hoping it when Grandpa sauntered through the front door of his house. I couldn't think of anything worse for an old man than getting beat up by his wife's former fee-ance. Maybe Grandpa wasn't in a fighting mood that day, or maybe he took one look at Mr. McAllister and figured discretion was the better part of valor, as the saying goes. He not only didn't pitch Mr. McAllister out, he shook hands nice as you please, saying where you from and why don't we go set down in the parlor.

"Miss Love, see if'n they's some a-Miss Mattie Lou's scup'non nectar in the pantry, hear," said Grandpa, taking the rocking chair and motioning Mr. McAllister to Granny's gentleman's chair. "Fix us a drink with thet, Miss Love."

After she went to the kitchen, Grandpa winked at Mr. McAllister and said, "Sorry I ain't got no locust beer to offer you. My son-in-law, he makes it by the barrelful. Ever had locust beer?"

"Never cared for it much," said Mr. McAllister. "The other'll be fine, Mr.—uh, what's your name, sir?"

"Blakeslee. E. R. Blakeslee."

"Clayton McAllister, sir."

They stood up and shook hands again, like they'd just met, and went on talking.

Miss Love was gone a good while. When she finally brought in a tray with the pale gold drinks, she had on lots of perfume and a clean yellow dress with a high neck, and her hair was fixed nice. She looked real fresh and pretty.

Grandpa was just the friendliest host you ever saw. He asked how long was the train trip from Texas, spoke of the drought, and discussed the difference between Texas barbecue and the Georgia kind. Then they got to talking hard times, but I couldn't listen for wondering if Miss Love was thinking about Mr. McAllister kissing her. If she was, she didn't let on. But that's what I was thinking about. If God had sent this man all the way from Texas to barge in and tempt her, she sure had been found wanting.

From there I got to thinking about predestination. The Southern Presbyterians believe that what is to be is to be and you can't do a thing about it. I mean, they think that from the day you're born, God knows everything that's going to happen to you. Preordains it, the preacher keeps saying. It hasn't ever made any sense to me to try so hard, or even to pray for something, if God is either going to make it happen despite all your prayers and all you do or don't do, or else make it not happen despite everything. For instance, suppose Mr. McAllister hadn't got mad and called off the wedding, and Miss Love had married him despite his reputation for philandering. Would that mean God preordained them to marry no matter what? Or would it just mean Miss Love wanted to marry him no matter what? I sure wished I could ask Papa how to fit predestination into this puzzle.

Well, suppose the Lord wanted Miss Love to marry Mr. McAllister, hoping she could save him from his sinning ways, and suppose she *had* married him, but then he just kept right on chasing women? Could she ever again have counted on God to steer her right?

It's a pity God ever let Miss Love out of Baltimore. If she'd never met up with Mr. McAllister, she wouldn't of had to get that nasty letter from him so God could show her He didn't approve of the match, and Granny wouldn't of had to die so God would find Miss Love a house. When I tried to make sense out of all that, it seemed like the Bible was right. The Lord does work in mysterious ways His wonders to perform.

Grandpa had gone to talking politics. He was telling Mr. McAllister about the winter morning when Brother Belie Jones's wife fired up her stove and shut the oven door, not knowing her cat was asleep in there. "By the time Miz Jones opened the oven and found Essie, the dang cat was cooked. Later Miz Jones come down to the store jest a-cryin'. Said, Pore Essie. She must a-slept right th'ew. Else why wouldn't I of heard her holler?' Sometimes I think us folks in the South are jest like pore Essie. We sleepin' right th'ew them unfair freight rates, for instance, when we ought to be hollerin' all the way to Washington."

Mr. McAllister laughed. Miss Love laughed, too, but uneasy — like at the circus when the man puts his head in the tiger's mouth and you giggle when what you want to do is cover your eyes.

The husband and the fee-ance really liked each other, I could tell. Grandpa even asked Mr. McAllister to take pot luck and stay to supper. Practically insisted. "We don't git folks from Texas here ever day," he said in his best hospitality voice.

Knowing what I knew and not knowing what if anything Grandpa knew, all this funning and politeness gave me the creeps. Lord knows what it was doing to Miss Love, who had hardly said a word since Grandpa walked in. But the invitation brought the Texan back to the situation at hand. "Thank you, sir, but I got to catch the train to Atlanta. I better get on back to the ho-tel and pick up my grip."

He stood up, and Grandpa and Miss Love stood up, and I did, and there was an awkward minute till Grandpa said, "Well, I wisht you'd stay on, sir. We could put you up for the night."

That must of give Miss Love a start. Picking up the big white hat off the daybed, she handed it to Mr. McAllister and said, nervous as a witch, "He was just leaving when you came, Mr. Blakeslee. He's got business in Atlanta."

The long tall man flipped his hand in the general direction of the saddle laying on the floor. He said, kind of casual, "This here belongs to your wife, Mr. Blakeslee. I come by to bring it to her—bein' as I was in the vicinity, so to speak."

"You shouldn't have gone to all that trouble, Mr. McAllister," said Miss Love, real formal. "I don't have a horse. You take it on back to Texas."

"Naw," he said. "If you don't want it, Miss Love—I mean Miz Blakeslee—why, sell it. And it wasn't no trouble, you bein' such a friend of the fam'ly while you were out in Texas. The saddle was a good excuse to drop by. And, uh"—he actually winked at her—"if you and Mr. Blakeslee ever get out my way, y'all be sure and look me up. I'd like to feed Mr. Blakeslee some Texas barbecue."

Ignoring the invite, Miss Love said, "It's been nice to see you again, Mr. McAllister." She looked up at him like he was no more to her now than some ten-year-old boy come in for penny candy at the store. Then she placed her trembling hand on Grandpa's good arm, smiling up at him like he was made out of money and honey both. Boy howdy, you wouldn't guess that fifty minutes ago she had been kissing this other man!

Grandpa walked the Texan out to the street, clapped him on the shoulder, good-natured like, and pointed directions to town.

It wasn't till my grandfather came back in the house that he really looked at the saddle. Going over where it lay on the floor, he hooked it up with the toe of one high-top shoe to see it better. "Miss Love, I think—"

"Mr. Blakeslee, I was once engaged to marry Mr. McAllister. He had that saddle made for me. It was his engagement present." She was talking fast, like if she slowed down she might lose her nerve. She told Grandpa in a small pinched voice that what Mr. McAllister really came for was to get her to marry him.

Then Miss Love flung herself face down on the daybed and went to crying. "I-hate-him-I-hate-him-I-hate-him!" She beat her fist on the thin mattress in time to the I-hate-hims.

"She sure told him off, Grandpa," said I, trying to be helpful. "You should of heard her."

Grandpa didn't answer. Just stood there, looking down at the fancy saddle.

"I was a f-fool, Mr. Blakeslee." Her words were muffled sobs. Now it's coming, I thought. She's going to tell Grandpa about the kissing. Instead, she said, "How I ever th-thought I wanted to m-m-marry him, I don't know. I was such a fool. And old enough to know b-better. . . ."

Grandpa sighed and sat down by her on the daybed. "Best fool knows he's a fool, Miss Love. I don't know a soul who couldn't see a fool jest by lookin' in the glass. I been one myself, once't or twice't. So hesh up now. Cryin' ain't go'n do no good." Grandpa just couldn't hardly stand to watch a woman cry.

Well, plainly Miss Love wasn't a big enough fool to mention getting kissed. But thinking to kind of warn her, in case she didn't know that somebody besides me may have seen the peep show, I butted into the silence.

"I thought y'all were go'n have a coconut cake for supper, Grandpa. Miss Effie Belle came over with one just now."

Miss Love shot to a sitting position, her hands covering her mouth and the whites of her eyes showing. "Miss Effie Belle? She came over here?"

"Yes'm. I reckon she wanted to get a good look at Mr. McAllister. But I went out on the porch and told her y'all were talkin' bizness and maybe it'd be best if she came callin' tomorrow."

"Oh, Lord." Miss Love moaned.

"She forgot to hand me the cake."

Miss Love wasn't interested in the cake. "Did she . . . uh, did she see Mr. McAllister?" I could tell she was really worried and dying to find out what else I knew. Importance swelled me up inside.

At that point Grandpa held up his right hand like a policeman. "Y'all shet up. Lemme think a minute. Hear?"

Well, Miss Love and I shut up, and Grandpa commenced pacing the floor. I couldn't take my eyes off of him. From the neck down he was the same old Grandpa Blakeslee; from the neck up he was a distinguished, smooth-faced stranger who looked kind of familiar. After while he slowed down to bite off a plug of tobacco and move it into his cheek. Then he paced some more. Finally he stopped in front of the saddle, shoving it with his foot.

Just to look at Grandpa, most people wouldn't know he was upset. But I could tell. All the time he was pacing, his shoulders kept twitching forward, one or the other or both—a sure sign—and every minute or two he stopped to scratch his head hard and fast.

When he finally spoke, what he said was "Miss Love, you want to marry Mr. McAllister?"

Why would he ask a thing like that when she was already married and also had just finished saying how much she hated the man?

She was as surprised as I was. Too surprised even to answer. Just sat on the daybed staring at Grandpa with wide-open eyes and a wide-open mouth.

"Cause if'n you do, or if'n you have a mind to after you git over bein' so mad at him, why, we could git this'n annulled. Folks in Cold Sassy will have a good time talkin', but if you go on off to Texas, why, you won't have to put up with nothin' on account of it. So you want to marry him or don't you?"

23

MISS Love rose to her feet, looking just about as stunned as old Cholly Smith did after he sold the family home place and heard the new owner had found a bag of gold coins behind a square of crumbling plaster in the dining room.

Walking slowly toward the back door, she stood looking out for a long time, twisting her hands and saying nothing. Finally she turned and spoke, sounding like a wrung-out dishrag. "Mr. Blakeslee," she said, her eyes cast down, "I don't want an annulment. If I weren't married to you, I still wouldn't marry him."

He went over close and she looked him square in the face. "I reckon you done answered my question," he said.

But then Miss Love's hands were on her mouth again. "Oh, Lord! Maybe you were trying to say—maybe what you mean is that you, sir, want an annulment. I don't blame you. I've embarrassed you before the wh-whole t-town." Big new tears streaked down her cheeks. "You want me to l-leave, don't you, Mr. Blakeslee?"

"God A'mighty, why would I want thet?" I could see him thinking he would have to hire him a housekeeper if she left. "If'n it was in my mind to ast you to leave, thet's what I would a-said, Miss Love. So in which case the subject is closed. Now what bout thet there saddle?"

"I don't w-want it." Trying to stop crying, she snuffled and blew her nose.

"Well, now," said Grandpa. Sitting down, he lifted the saddle onto his knee and looked close at the silver and the tooling. "Hit shore is a handsome thang."

"I don't care." She glanced at Granny's clock on the mantelpiece. "Will, I want you to run up to the hotel with it. If he's not there, take it to the depot."

"Now let's think about this a minute, Miss Love," said Grandpa, motioning me to wait.

"I don't want it."

"Thet ain't the point. A man with a bad conscience, and stubborn enough to lug something this heavy all the way from Texas, he ain't a-go'n lug it back home. You send it up to the ho-tel, why, he'll have to bring it back down here. Miss Effie Belle's neck will break off, tryin' to keep up with all the back and forths. Besides, Mr. McAllister might miss his train." He grinned. "You keep it. Then thet will be the end a-thet and you won't need no more truck with him."

Miss Love was speechless.

Thinking to get in a lick for her, I said, "Gosh, Grandpa, what good is a saddle without a horse? Haw, I can just see Miss Love sittin' up on that fancy gee-gaw on your old mule."

"Haw, yeah, old Jack'd pure die from embarrass-ment," said Grandpa, laughing for the first time since Mr. McAllister left. "But I cain't afford no hoss. Miss Love, I reckon you'll jest have to hang up thet saddle for a orna-ment."

She didn't answer. Just kept snuffling.

Grandpa was pacing around nervous, scratching his head hard and fast again. "Shet up, hear?" he finally said to Miss Love. "One thang I cain't stand is a cryin' woman."

That made her cry worse.

All of a sudden Grandpa slapped his leg, excited. "Y'all, I jest recollected a letter I got from Cudn Jake, not long fore Miss Mattie Lou died. You know Cudn Jake, son."

"I ain't sure, Grandpa."

"Well, maybe you too young to remember the last time he come to Cold Sassy." He turned to Miss Love. "Jake lives jest this side a-Cornelia. Raises Thoroughbred racehosses." She looked up from her crying, curious to know what Grandpa was driving at. "Jake's near bout gone broke on them racehosses. Not from bettin'. He's got too much sense to bet. He jest cain't find much of a market for'm right now. Anyhow, he offered to give me a three-year-old if'n I'd come git him. Said the hoss had been broke to a halter and thet's all, but if I had a mind to fool with it I could have her for nothin'. Said it would save him feedin' thet big mouth another winter. At the time, the last thang I wanted was a dang racehoss. But . . . Miss Love, you want her?"

"I, uh, I never thought to want a racehorse, Mr. Blakeslee, but—"

"Think you could train him?"

"Didn't you say it was a her?"

"I don't recollect. Same difference. A gelding, maybe. Point is, could you train it to thet there saddle? I cain't pay nobody to train it, but Will Tweedy here could hep you. So you want a free hoss or don't you? If'n ole Jake ain't got shet of it already."

"Yes. Yes, I do want it! Oh, I do!" Miss Love was up and practically hopping, she was so excited.

"Then what say we let Will Tweedy go git him?" Grandpa looked at me and winked. "Son, what's today? Sarady?"

"Yessir."

"Well, early Monday mornin' I want you to hitch old Jack to my buggy and go git thet hoss. Maybe you could carry the Predmore boy along for comp'ny."

It was my turn to be hopping now. You'd of thought I'd been in jail for three weeks instead of in mourning. Boy howdy! Then I had another idea, which I didn't waste time presenting. "How about if I borrow Grandpa Tweedy's covered wagon, sir, and us boys go campin' in the mountains. We could go by Cudn Jake's on the way home. Can I? Please, sir?"

"Shore, if'n Mr. Tweedy can spare the mule team and yore folks say so. But it cain't be no long campin' trip."

"Sir?"

"Yore daddy's go'n be leavin' for New York City in two or three weeks. I don't recollect the exact date, but I don't want yore mama stayin' by herself whilst he's gone. I shore wish she'd change her mind and go on with him. Miss Mattie Lou would want her to. Hit'd do her good, and hit's jest a dang shame to waste a free boat ticket."

I was so excited I hardly noticed when Miss Love left the room. "We'll just camp a few days," I told Grandpa.

"Them mountains is the best place in the world to be in the hot summertime," he said. "I jest hope yore mother and them see fit to let you go."

"Yessir, I do, too." But I wasn't worried. With Grandpa practically ordering me to go, there wasn't any real question about it.

"Miss Love?" he called. "I'm a-goin' on back to the store now. Will Tweedy, you come on with me. I got a sack a-groceries I need delivered."

I'd of liked to stay and talk with Miss Love. I wanted her to know I wouldn't tell on her. Miss Effie Belle would, of course. But I wouldn't.

We were halfway to town when Grandpa said sternly, as if I was leaving for Cornelia in a few minutes, "Now you be careful with thet hoss, Will Tweedy."

"I will, sir."

"Tie him up good to the back of the wagon and don't let them fool boys try to ride it or git to cuttin' up with him or anythang. Or you, either."

"Oh, no, sir."

"Likely he's skittish and high-strung. Most racehosses are. If

I know Cudn Jake, thet free hoss may have more wrong with it than havin' to eat. How-some-ever, Miss Love needs something to take her mind off of Mr. Texas. Hope she can ride good as she says she can."

"I think Miss Love can do just about anything, Grandpa." I was thinking if she can marry you like she did, and turn you into a judge with just a shave and a haircut, and tell off a man like Mr. McAllister, then I reckon she can train a horse.

Grandpa didn't mention the Texan again that day. In his mind, Mr. McAllister was dead as he'd ever be.

Well, he wasn't dead to me. Even walking along beside Grandpa, I kept remembering the kissing. I figured Miss Effie Belle couldn't have helped seeing—but hey, with her coming out of the bright sunshine, maybe she couldn't see down the hall! I'd like to of comforted Miss Love with that possibility. It wasn't going to be easy for her to cook a nice supper for Grandpa when her reputation depended on the eyesight of a mean old lady with a lip wart and the loyalty of a fourteen-year-old boy who had never been known to keep his mouth shut.

Also, she must still be either hating Mr. McAllister like poison or else loving his eyes out and having second thoughts about not getting annulled. I wanted to tell her that I for one hoped she'd stay in the family.

24

I REALLY juned around when I got home that evening. I needed to lay in a store of good feelings as well as stovewood before asking permission to go camping.

At supper I was trying to think how to bring up the subject, when Papa did it for me. "Mary Willis, your daddy wants Will to go to Cornelia next week," he began. "Cudn Jake has offered him a horse if he'll send for it. And Mr. Blakeslee said maybe Will and the boys should go campin' for a few days first." Mama looked dumfounded. "I know it's mighty soon after your ma's passin', hon, but I think myself the trip would do the boy good. Get his mind off of that train trestle."

Looking tired and kind of forlorn, she said, "Well, if you think folks will understand. . . ."

Boy howdy! "Mama," I said, "a trip would do you good, too. Why don't you go on to New York with Papa?"

She ignored me. "Hoyt, why does Pa want a horse? He's got Big Jack. What does he need a horse for?" Then, sarcastic, "I guess it's Love that wants the horse. Ridin' in a buggy behind a mule ain't good enough for her. Will, were you down there today when that man from Texas brought her a silver saddle?"

"Yes'm." I reached for a biscuit. "But it ain't exactly a silver saddle, Mama."

"I heard it was a silver saddle. It's all over town about that saddle."

"Yes'm, but it's only trimmed with silver."

Her blue eyes flashing, Mama plonked down her fork and looked across the table at Papa. "Don't she care at all if folks talk? Hadn't she done enough already, without acceptin' an expensive gift like that from a man with a reputation so bad it rides ahead of him?"

"Mr. McAllister didn't give her the saddle, Mama," I said airily. "It was already hers. He just brung it to her. She didn't even want it, and told him so."

"I wish you'd quit takin' up for that woman," said Mama.

"Now, hon, Will's not—"

"It was Grandpa thought she ought to keep the saddle," said I. "Grandpa liked Mr. McAllister, Mama. Even ast him to stay to supper, and spend the night, too."

"Aw, shah!"

Not knowing what if anything Grandpa had told when he got back to the store, I was getting uneasy about shading the situation. It occurred to me to change the subject. "Papa, I bet y'all didn't reck-anize Grandpa when he came in without his beard and all."

Papa grinned and took another helping of potato salad. "Mary Willis, you ain't seen him yet, have you, hon?"

"No. But I heard." She spoke bitter.

"I took him for a stranger. Camp did, too. Camp just kept sittin' there on the counter swingin' his legs, and Mr. Blakeslee fine'ly yelled, 'Git down from there, boy, and find something to do!' I knew then it was him, but I couldn't hardly believe it! Mary Willis, you got you a young daddy. Miss Love shaved ten years off of him, gettin' rid of that long whitey beard and that mane of bushy hair."

"Is that so?" My mother didn't smile. "Well, Pa looked just fine to me the way he was. Seems like if Love Simpson cain't get him talked about one way, she does it another. Everybody will say she didn't want people thinkin' he's old enough to be her daddy. But he is."

We ate a while in silence. Then my mother said, real sarcastic, "Hoyt, y'all might as well put up a sign down at the store. Announce the widower is givin' his new bride a racehorse for a weddin' present."

"Now, hon, you know it's not like that." Papa reached over and patted her hand, but she didn't notice.

"Oh, Hoyt, however will it all end?" She pressed her napkin to her quivering mouth. "Ma would spin in her grave. . . ."

I had never in my life heard my mother speak out so bitter about anything or anybody. She was the one always took up for the preacher when folks complained about a dull sermon, and she always talked kind about old Mr. Tate if somebody laughed about him liking sugar in his buttermilk. Remembering how Mama had laid on her bed crying just two days ago, so scared Miss Love would get willed the store, I wondered if she could stand it when she found out Pa's house was already deeded over. Or if, Lord help us, she heard about Miss Love kissing Mr. McAllister.

I wanted to tell her the store was to be hers and Loma's. Instead, I found myself saying, in a small voice, "If it'll make you feel better, Mama, I'll give up the campin' trip."

"No, go on," she said. "Go on. Get it over with. You've been whinin' around about it ever since Ma passed." She started crying. "But, son, t-try not to have too good a time."

"I'll wear my black armband all the way, Mama," I said, eager to comfort her, but she left the table and ran upstairs. "Papa?" I asked. "What's the matter with Mama? It ain't like her to be so hard on folks."

"I think she's mad at your granny, son," he said, folding his napkin. He looked like he had a stomachache.

"Mad at Granny?"

"For dyin', Will. Mama never made a decision in her life without thinkin' would her mother approve of it or not. Ever since she passed, it's been like Mama's lost holt of the reins. Like she's bein' pulled along by a team she cain't control. And she don't see any sense a-tall in your granddaddy marryin' like he did. She don't know Miss Love, Will. Not like I do—from working with her. She's a nice lady and Mr. Blakeslee needs lookin' after. But Mama cain't see that yet."

I was so excited about the camping trip that I didn't worry as much about Miss Love as she deserved. But I did run up there for a few minutes that night, after I was sure it was too late for Miss Effie Belle to come tell on her. Miss Effie Belle didn't have a telephone, so she couldn't call, and she hadn't left home by herself after dark since she was eighty-five and stumbled on a tree root coming in from Wednesday night prayer meeting. So her not appearing at our house didn't mean yes or no about what she had seen. Just in case, I wanted to make sure Miss Love knew she could count on me. I'd cross my heart and hope to die before I'd tell on her to anybody.

I found her in the kitchen, washing up the supper dishes. Her eyes were still red from crying, she looked awful tired, and I didn't quite know how to get out what she needed to hear. "Where's Grandpa at?" I asked.

"Out at the barn, feeding the mule. He got in late, so I managed to get up a pretty good supper for him," she said. "Salmon croquettes, and slaw, and, uh. . . ." Forgetting what she was talking about, she just stood there with her hands in the dishwater. "I—I don't know how I let it happen," she said all of a sudden.

"You were just so surprised," said I, being helpful.

"Surprised? I guess I was. Will Tweedy, I swear I hardly knew what was happening. It was like being in a dream where you can't move."

"Miss Love, you can, uh, count on me." My words stumbled around. "Uh, I mean, uh, I know you couldn't hep what happened. He just overpowered you." She stared at me, saying nothing. "And, uh, I mean I ain't go'n tell Grandpa or Papa or anybody how Mr. McAllister and you—well, uh, you know."

I felt like a plumb fool, but Miss Love guessed what I was driving at. Blushing, she patted my arm and thanked me for being her friend. I felt so noble and generous.

"Don't you worry, now. If Miss Effie Belle says anything around town, I'll tell everybody it wasn't like that at all. I'll say it was just a brotherly kiss. And besides, I'll say, you really told Mr. McAllister off afterwards."

That got Miss Love nervous. "Don't, Will. Don't say anything at all. This is for grown folks. Anything you say might just make it worse."

I felt like a fool. Where Miss Love had been talking to me like I was a man, now she had cut me back down to size. "You go'n tell Grandpa?" I asked in a small voice.

"I don't know. I don't think I can face him if he f-finds out." And she burst into tears. She soon got aholt of herself, though, and went back to washing dishes. Holding a plate in midair, she looked at me kindly, smiling that big wide smile as if this was no bigger problem than getting the stove hot enough to fry the croquettes. "Don't worry about me, Will. I've been taking care of myself a long time. I just don't want to embarrass your grandfather, or the family any more than they're already embarrassed." She flushed. "I mean they're embarrassed enough over us marrying so quickly, without. . . . Well, we'll all survive." She straightened up.

"Yes'm. I reckon."

She saw that I didn't know what to say next. "Thank you, Will, for not wanting to be the one who spreads gossip. It shows you've got real character. I do hate gossipers." And with that, she kissed me on the cheek.

I practically danced home, thinking about her having confidence in me and about that little peck. By time I got to bed that night I was making like it was a kiss full on the mouth. From there I got to imagining what it would be like to kiss her the way Mr. McAllister did it, with kisses that ran together like a string of pearls.

That sure beat thinking about getting run over by a train, but I went too far with it. In the dark, alone in my bed, I tried sucking a knuckle of my finger and pretending it was her mouth. When I got so hot and squirmy I couldn't stand it, I tiptoed downstairs to pour me some sweetmilk.

With the glass still half full in my hand, I set my mind on Lightfoot McLendon, wondering if she would let me kiss her like that—the way Mr. Texas did it. But in no time at all I had my arms around Miss Love again.

It seemed so evil, I felt sick.

If it's true what the Bible says—that lusting in your heart after another man's wife is the same as if you actually did what you're thinking about—then I was guiltier than Mr. McAllister. When he was kissing Miss Love, he didn't know she was married. But I for sure knew, and it was my own grandfather's wife I was hankering after, which seemed like an awful sin. I was soon trembling with remorse as well as lust.

I purely made myself get out paper and a pencil and put my mind on the camping trip. Well, we'd take our shotguns, of course, to shoot game with. And fishing tackle. And a wood ax. Baseball and bat and gloves. Matches . . . flour, of course. Sugar and salt. A big iron skillet, some lard. . . .

There isn't anything like planning a camping trip to get your mind off of what it shouldn't be on.

Miss Effie Belle appeared next morning, just as we were fixing to walk out the door to go to Sunday school. "I would of come last night, but Bubba was feelin' po'ly," she began, all excited. "Well, I hate to be the bearer of evil, but I know y'all had a heap rather hear it from me than somebody else." And then with her pink lip wart quivering and her skin-and-bones face lit up like a Christmas tree, she proceeded to tell what the tall stranger had done besides bring Miss Love a saddle. "And her just two days past vowin' to cleave only unto Rucker! I swanny to God, these modrun women are something else." Her voice was shaking so bad that she had to stop a minute to breathe. Then she said, "Well, Mary Willis, I reckon now your daddy will ship her back to Baltimore. Pore man, look what bein' lonesome got him into."

After Miss Effie Belle hurried off to Sunday school, Mama and Papa lit into me. Did I see the kissing? Well, why hadn't I come straight home and told them? Did Grandpa know? Did Miss Love know Miss Effie Belle saw it? Sounding just like Aunt Loma, Mama said, "Her conduct proves it, Hoyt. That Woman ain't fit to be a servant in Pa's house, much less married to him."

Naturally Mama stayed home. Said she had a headache. Probably she did. But mostly she was too mortified to face the congregation. Papa would of stayed with her, except he had to take up collection.

It was just an awful day.

Miss Effie Belle's words flew from mouth to mouth in every churchyard in Cold Sassy. Then after folks talked about Miss Love cleavin' to somebody besides Grandpa, they had to speculate about her church affiliation. Her having married a Baptist, Cold Sassy naturally expected her to show up there that morning. The Baptists considered themselves above the rest of us. Most of them, including Aunt Loma, thought Miss Love would join their congregation with Grandpa "for the same reason she married him—to come up in the world." It must of been a relief to the Baptists when she didn't appear, because nobody knew whether to treat her like a grave robber or just a repentant sinner.

Since the Presbyterians weren't involved, there was no suspense at our preachin' service. Just pity for the shamed family.

The ones in a pickle were the Methodists. Most had thought Miss Love would go over to the Baptists right away or else hide at home, one. Well, she not only appeared at the Methodist Episcopal Church, South, but she wore a black dress, like she was in mourning for the one whose death had been her good fortune—and, as usual, sat down at the piano soon as she came in.

Miss Effie Belle stopped by after preachin' to tell us about it. "That Woman ain't got no respect for nobody. Wearin' mournin', for heaven's sake, and—"

Just the thought of it made Mama mad, but she tried to be fair. "It'd look a heap worse if she'd worn red," she said.

"Humph. Anyhow, we fixed her. Nobody sang. Well, Cratic and Agnes did. You know how they are. Them two were singin' by theirselves, though, I can tell you. Like we'd agreed to it ahead of time, the rest of us kept our mouths shut."

Aunt Loma came up our walk with Uncle Camp and the baby in time to hear that. "Did Love get the message?" she asked, hateful.

"By the second verse her face was red as the songbook," Miss Effie Belle said proudly. "Still, the nerve of That Woman ain't got no limits. She played all eight verses, right down to the a-men. But the preacher made certain sure she didn't get to do it agin."

"He ast her to leave?" asked Loma.

"No. He just didn't announce no more songs. Miss Love was still sittin' at the pi-ana waitin' for the next page number when he started his sermon. It fine'ly dawned on her he wasn't go'n let her play agin, and she jumped up and flounced out. Well, I better git on home and see about Bubba." Like an afterthought, she added, "Rucker didn't come to church with her, you know. I reckon he was shamed to. When I left this mornin', I seen him settin' on that big rock in Miss Mattie Lou's rose garden. Repentin' of his hasty puddin', I don't doubt."

25

I MET Pink early Monday morning in front of Clark's Drug Store to wait for Mr. Lias Foster, the rural mailman, who would be coming from Commerce in his buggy. "He's a talker," I warned. "If he cain't think of anything else, he'll say, 'Git yore foot away from thet aigg basket fore you bust them aiggs.'" We both laughed.

"What's he takin' eggs to country people for?"

"He ain't. They give him eggs for stamps. He puts stamps on their letters and then trades out the eggs at Grandpa's store or at Williford, Burns, and Rice in Commerce."

Mr. Lias made three buggy trips a week, delivering letters, newspapers, and Sears, Roebuck packages in Banks County. Out one day and back the next. The rural post offices were mostly in farmhouses, my Grandpa Tweedy's place being one of them.

We waited for Mr. Lias at the drug store because Cold Sassy's post office was in there, a big pigeonhole desk over where the telephone central switchboard used to be. They had moved the switchboard to Miss Lucille's house so that she could operate it nights as well as days. When Mr. Lias arrived, we followed him inside. Five or six old men were already sitting around in there, talking crops and fussing about the gov'ment in Washington while they cut one another's hair. A colored man named Henry had started a white barbershop in Cold Sassy a few years back, but these old fellers liked the drug store better. Folks coming in for their mail would stop and talk a while.

"Hey, Will, where y'all goin?" Mr. Tom Rainwater asked me.

"Out to Banks County, Mr. Tom. My Grandpa Tweedy's got a big blue North Ca'lina wagon, and we go'n borrow it and go campin'."

The ride started off as a high ole time, us laughing loud and cutting up behind Mr. Lias as the buggy racked out of Cold Sassy. Old T.R. trotted ahead or dropped behind or went dashing off across worn-out fields grown up in broom sedge. Pink and I talked about camping plans till the clip-clopping of the horses made him sleepy. Mr. Lias, contrary to his usual nature, said next to nothing. So I was left to myself.

I sat staring at his lean old hulk in the front seat and at the hind ends of the dappled-gray horses. I hardly noticed when one of the horses raised his tail and plopped in rhythm with the clip-clop. I didn't see the red dust that coated sassafras bushes and wild flowers by the roadside. I hardly noticed the blackberries that glistened among the brambles. All I saw was Bluford Jackson in his grave.

The camping trip had been Blu's idea. We were talking about it that morning we climbed up the water tower to throw down lighted firecrackers and scare people—the day Blu got the firecracker burn that gave him lockjaw.

Though I liked Pink just fine, I couldn't help thinking that if Blu hadn't of died, it would be him going out to Banks County with me this hot July morning. I wondered had he rotted down to bones yet. How long did it take? And what about Granny? Despite the fine hardwood casket, might she have worms in her already?

Lord help me.

I tried to think about Lightfoot McLendon's hair shining white in the sun, but that just set me to worrying about

whether she went to Blind Tillie Trestle on Saturday, expecting me to be there like I said I would. Dern, why hadn't I tried
some way to get word to her?

Right about then, Mr. Lias looked over his shoulder at me
and asked how did my folks take it when they found out Mr.
Blakeslee done got marrit.

"They took it all right." I knew whatever I said would be
written down in his mind to deliver with the mail.

"The milliner is a handsome lady, you can say thet for her."

"Yessir. How's Miss Ora, Mr. Lias?"

"Tol'able. Jest tol'able. She ain't never really got over her
pleurisy." He flopped the reins. "I been thinkin' lately on Sal,
my first wife. How she ruint my life."

"Ruint your life, sir?" I grabbed his words like they were a
rope to hang on to.

Mr. Lias clucked his cheek sideways and flipped the reins
till the horses picked up their trot. Then he waved at two old
country ladies sitting on their front steps picking through a little girl's hair for cooties. They waved back and stared after us.
I thought Mr. Lias would go on telling about his wife then, but
his tongue had already burned out. He just sat there, flopping
the reins every now and again or slapping at a fly or fanning his
leathery face with his straw hat. We passed a chain gang of Negro convicts grading the road. They had to step into the ditch
to let us pass. Then he spoke.

"I knowed hit were a mis-take, soon as me and Sal got marrit.
She warn't like any woman I ever seen before. A purty thang,
but when it come to washin' or cookin', if she'd a-moved any
slower she'd a-been goin' backwards. Everthang happened to
her was con-trary to nature. If she'd a-drownded, I'd a-gone
upstream to look for her. And she said sech dang-fool thangs.
When she was in the fam'ly way, her ma got worrit bout Sal
was losin' weight. You know what Sal said? She said, 'Ma, I
cain't see I've lost any. But course I ain't looked under my feet
yet, haw.' She thought thet was cute talk. I told her she sounded

like a idjit. 'For God's dang sake, Sal, shet up fore some jedge commits you to Milledgeville.'"

Another silence. Clip-clop, clip-clop, slap, flop, fan. Reins jiggling, horses snorting and pooling, buggy rocking and creaking, steel wheel rims hitting rocks, a caw-caw from a crow somewhere, T.R. way off in the woods, barking at something.

Another mile and Mr. Lias's gravelly old voice said, "I was pitchin' hay one mornin', Sal up thar on the wagon seat a-holdin' the reins, when here come Mr. James Henry's bull. A mean'un. Charged me, and got me down right by the wagon. My wife, she had two good wood axes up thar beside her, but she didn't do one dang thang to hep me."

He spat. After we passed the Antioch Baptist Church, I couldn't stand watching him think any longer. I poked him on the shoulder. "How'd you get away from the bull, Mr. Lias?"

"Huh? Why, I gouged his eyes out," he said, matter of fact. "Reached up and grabbed a horn with one hand and gouged with the other'n. Then I quick rolled under the wagon out'n his way. I would a-kilt thet bull if I could of. Dang thang run off a-bellerin' and a-bleedin' and a-bumpin' into haystacks and fences. Thet very next week, I found out my wife been runnin' round on me for five year with a sorry low-down good-fer-nothin' cropper on Mr. James Henry's place. I don't doubt a minute but he let thet bull out and sicked him on me."

Silence. The horses picked their way around a hole in the road. Mr. Lias spat again. "One night I got my gun and follered Sal straight to his house. Busted the door down and caught'm together, and had the dang hammer pulled back to shoot'm both when it dawned on me they warn't worth killin', neither one of'm. Eased the hammer back and lowered my gun and plain walked off. I went to live in Cold Sassy with my brother's fam'ly and got the mail route."

"What about Miss Sal?"

"Died. Got bit by a cottonmouth at a church picnic. Vengeance is mine, saith the Lord. Good riddance, saith I, and the next year I marrit a spinster lady over in Commerce with a nice house. Miss Ora. She's three inches taller'n me and six year older, but she tells me a dozen times a day how much she loves me."

By then I was barely listening. From the minute Mr. Lias mentioned Miss Sal carrying on with another man, I went to thinking about Miss Love carrying on with Mr. McAllister.

If Grandpa hadn't heard about the kissing yet, he was the only one in Cold Sassy still left to tell.

Gosh, what if he found out before we left for the mountains? If he decided to send Miss Love back to Baltimore, he sure as heck wouldn't want me to go on to Cornelia for any racehorse.

The buggy rolled between gullied slopes of red clay. Then we passed the gristmill built by my great-grandfather Tweedy around 1850 on the Hudson River, and rattled through the cool of the covered bridge he built across the river to join his land together. I wondered how a man smart enough to do all that could of had a son lazy as my Grandpa Tweedy, who couldn't even get around to treating his cows for hollow horn or when they got maggots under the skin.

One time I asked Papa didn't he think his daddy was lazy, leaving all the work to field hands or sorry no-count tenants and croppers. Papa said, "Your granddaddy's just fresh out of hope, son, like most farmers in Georgia these days."

I wished I could of known Grandpa Tweedy's daddy, but he died of the typhoid in 1867. He was too old to go fight in the War of the Sixties, but they made him a general in the local militia. General Tweedy, he was called. By time I came along, most everybody in Banks County thought General Tweedy had been a high monkity-monk in the Army of the Confederacy instead of just in the home guard. And I never heard any Tweedy, not even my own daddy, try to correct the impression.

Mr. Lias turned his team off the highway into the rutty lane that led up to the old home place. It, too, was built by General

Tweedy, out of hand-hewed logs and hand-sawed and hand-planed boards, and had portholes in the upper story for shooting Indians.

I poked Pink awake. "Someday I'm go'n farm this land," I bragged, gesturing in every direction. "Papa's go'n buy it and let me farm it."

Mr. Lias spoke up. "Everbody always figgered you'd go in the store with Mr. Blakeslee, Will."

"Well, I ain't. I like farmin'. All there is to store work is watchin' out for rice weevils and rotten potatoes, and keepin' the rats out of the seed corn." I was feeling real smart-aleck. "But on a farm it's always something to worry about or be excited about. Foot-and-mouth disease, weevils, too much rain, too little rain, hired hands goin' off in the night with half your tools. . . . I'm a gambler, I reckon, because the way I see it, farmin' is one big dice game."

"You talkin' like a dang fool, Will," said Mr. Lias. "Ain't nothin' excitin' bout a dang weevil, or plantin' fer seventeen-cent cotton and then cotton goes down to twelve cent cause everbody overplanted. I'm glad to be out of it. Ever now and agin you make enough to cover the mortgage and taxes and pay off the store thet give you credit. But even when it's a good fall, you might's well count on it, Will: fore the year's out yore mule's go'n die or yore barn burn down."

I wasn't discouraged. "I've heard farmers talk like that all my life, Mr. Lias. But, see, I aim to study agriculture over at the University and learn better ways. For instance, I ain't go'n buy corn from a store to feed my livestock. I'm go'n grow my own corn. And cotton ain't go'n be my only cash crop."

"Well, if it ain't, boy, you cain't git no lien from the store. And if'n you don't git no lien, you cain't buy no seed and guano. Well, *you* could, I reckon. Bein' who you are. Yore granddaddy'll give you good terms, and he ain't go'n charge you double when you send a nigger to town to git sugar and coffee on credit."

I didn't like him suggesting Grandpa overcharged, but I let that go by. Naturally Grandpa would give me favorable terms. But it was better farming methods I counted on to turn a profit. "I'll learn how to plan ahead," I said.

"See can you learn how to plan ahead for rain or drought, son. Do thet and they'll give you a prize over at thet Ag College." Mr. Lias clucked his team up to a trot. "Hope you don't never have to find out what it's like, bein' pore. But ain't no farmer in Georgie seen thet prosperity Mr. Henry W. New-South Grady used to write about in them Atlanta newspapers. When I was farmin', I'd go in town and them bankers and store men treated me like white trash. Since I got this here job carryin' the mail, I git some respect."

As we rode past the old barn, weathered gray and leaning into a clump of hollyhocks and daisies, I pointed toward the shed. "Our wagon's in there, Pink. It's got a cover that flares up four or five feet, front and back. My great-grandfather brought his whole family down to Georgia in it, even his old daddy. His daddy was a blacksmith with four forges, till he crippled his arm, and a missionary to the Indians besides."

"Gosh," said Pink, impressed.

"I knowed yore great-grandpa when I was a boy," said Mr. Lias. "General Tweedy was his name. He shore was a fine old man."

When we turned into the swept yard, I noticed for the first time how rundown the place looked. Almost like white trash lived there. Grandpa Tweedy wasn't white trash. He owned his land. But, like all farmers, he had to contend with high taxes, high freight rates, and land so worn out that he might spend more for guano than he could get for his cotton crop. Still and all, he got better terms at the store than most, on account of my daddy, and Papa helped out some with cash money. Times weren't as hard for him as they could be.

Grandpa Tweedy was sitting on the porch swatting flies. His

pet hen, a White Leghorn, clucked with excitement every time the swatter came down. I guess I saw him through Pink's eyes that morning, because I was embarrassed all of a sudden, how seedy Grandpa Tweedy looked in ragged overalls, his beard so long and scraggly.

While Mr. Lias walked to the back of the buggy to get out the mail, Pink and I went up on the porch. Before we could even say howdy, Grandpa Tweedy hollered to Miz Jones to put on two extry plates for dinner.

"Besides for Mr. Lias?" she called from inside the house.

"Yes'm," he yelled back. "Will's here, and another boy." Then he thundered his gravelly voice at me. "Will, answer me. 'What is God?'"

Without batting an eye I quoted from the Shorter Catechism in my best Sunday school voice: "'God is a Spirit, Infinite, Eternal and Unchangeable.'"

Grandpa Tweedy had been drilling me on the catechism all my life. "Now, tell me. 'What is a lie?'" He picked up his swatter off the floor, killed a fly on his arm as he said the word *lie*, and flipped the fly off for the chicken.

"'A lie is an abomination in the sight of God and . . .' uh, 'and a . . .'"

"And a what, boy?"

I knew the answer. I was just debating whether to give it or act smart and show off before Pink. I decided to act smart. "'A lie is an abomination in the sight of God,'" I repeated, "'and a very present help in time of trouble!' Ain't that right, Pink?"

Before Grandpa could bless me out for being sacrilegious, I told him about getting run over by the train. He said, "Thar you go, son, temptin' the Almighty Hisself."

Then I stated my business, namely, that Papa wanted him to let me use Big Red and Satan and the covered wagon. "Some of us boys are go'n go campin'."

Grandpa banged on the arm of his rocking chair. "What you arter be doin' instead, you arter be studyin' the catechism and the Bible. Ain't thet right, Lias? You ever see sech a smart-aleck boy?"

Coming up the porch steps, Mr. Lias grinned and said I was smart-aleck, all right. "But he ain't a bad boy, Mr. Tweedy."

"Then he must a-changed here lately."

Real respectful, I asked, "Is it all right for us to take the team and the wagon, sir? Papa said you might could spare'm."

"I need them mules." It was like he'd forgot Papa was the one that bought Big Red and Satan in the first place. "I need them and the wagon, both. You know good'n' well we use thet wagon ever fourth Sunday to go to Hebron for preachin'."

"We'll be back long fore time for Hebron, Grandpa."

"Well, anyhow, hit ain't all right with me. What y'all go'n go campin' for? Why cain't you jest lay out in some a-them woods around Cold Sassy a few days, or come out here?"

"Time for dinner, y'all," Mrs. Jones called from the door. "How you do, Will? Who's your young friend?"

She was a huge fat woman, Grandpa Tweedy's third wife, and I liked her. The reason she was still Mrs. Jones, Grandpa had called her that all the time they were courting—her being a widow woman—and after they got married he was too lazy to bother changing her name. Granny Blakeslee used to laugh about that, and she thought it worth mentioning that Mrs. Jones had kicked Mr. Jones after he was dead. Of course, Mrs. Jones hadn't known he was dead. She just thought he was snoring again. Doc said the snore was the breath going out for the last time.

As we started in to dinner, Grandpa Tweedy walked over to the edge of the porch and picked up a conch shell off the banister rail. "I ordered this'n from Savannah," he told Pink, and blew a loud blast. "Thet's to call the hands to dinner," he explained.

We had just sat down to the table when a rumble of colored men's voices suddenly drifted in from the kitchen. It was the field hands, coming in to eat. "Miz Jones, reach back of you

and shet the kitchen door," said Grandpa Tweedy. "Now, Willy.
Hit jest makes me nervous, the idee a-you takin' off in thet big
wagon. And shore as sin, if it ain't here we'll need it."

I knew he meant somebody might die. The covered wagon
was the hearse for anybody who needed one in that part of
Banks County. General Tweedy had taken his last ride in it
nearly forty years before, to the Hebron graveyard. His widow,
Arminda, my great-grandmother, had gone in it to the same
place just a year ago, and also when she died the first time.

Before Grandpa Tweedy could say any more about the
wagon, Mr. Lias said, "Y'all heard bout Will's other granddaddy gittin' marrit last week?"

"Is thet a fact," said Grandpa, helping his plate. "Seems like
it wadn't more'n a week or two ago, Lias, you come in with a
message from Hoyt sayin' Miss Mattie Lou had died. Rucker
shore acks fast."

Mrs. Jones wanted to know who was the bride, who married them, and all about it. Then she asked, "Will, is they any
more room in Mr. Blakeslee's cemetery plot? Besides for him, I
mean? You reckon they's room for this Miss Love in there with
him and Miss Mattie Lou?"

"Yes'm," I said, embarrassed. "I think so."

Grandpa Tweedy grinned. "Miz Jones worries bout where
I'm go'n put her down when the time comes, son. Hit bein' the
custom, I got to be buried twixt yore daddy's mama, Will, and
Miss Flo. But Miz Jones don't want to be put at our feet, which
is the only other space left."

"That's all right, Mr. Tweedy, I fine'ly figgered out a plan,"
she said, laughing merrily. "Want to hear?"

He looked up, suspicious. "Say it."

"I've decided I want to be put down settin' up. Settin' in a
rockin' cheer with a whole choc'late cake in my lap and a silver
fork to eat it with. And naturally it's go'n take a heap a-room,
me bein' a fairly large woman."

"Ain't no way to bury somebody settin' up in no rockin' cheer."

"Lemme finish now. Since they ain't that much room in yore lot, I just think I'll set beside Mr. Jones through eternity. I'm go'n ast the fam'ly when we go to Hebron next fourth Sunday."

It really made Grandpa Tweedy mad. He didn't say another word the whole meal, not even when the cook and Mrs. Jones were clearing the table. But a gleam came in his eye while he was spooning a mound of whip cream on his blackberry cobbler, and he started telling about when he was a boy and went to the mountains with his daddy, General Tweedy. "We was ridin' horseback, buyin' up cattle. Camped up there in the Blue Ridge for a week or more, gittin' maybe two-three cows from one farmer and six or seven from another. We drove home thirty-five head, just me and him. Son, you ain't never seen anythang pretty as them big blue Georgie mountains!"

The upshot of this remembering was that my grandfather not only went with us to the pasture and watched us catch Big Red and Satan, but got two of his field hands to come help us load the wagon bed with corn, oats, and hay. And all he said as we hitched up was "Y'all be good now. And come Sunday, find you a Presbyterian church to go to. You hear me?" I turned the team into the road, T.R. riding high on the seat between me and Pink.

"Y'all take good care them mules, Will!" Grandpa Tweedy hollered after us. "They's a matched pair and I'll be in a fix if'n anythang happens to'm! Be careful, hear."

"Yessir," I called back as the team broke into a trot. "Don't worry, Grandpa, I know all about handlin' mules!"

26

E IGHT years after our camping trip, I still can't believe how good I told that tale about Aunt Loma nursing a pig, not to mention the one about sticking a pin in her rubber busts.

Five of us boys went to the mountains: Pink, Lee Roy, Smiley, myself, and—at the last minute—Dunson McCall. His daddy, the school superintendent, had a two-horse farm near town and bought a lot of seed and fertilizer at the store, so Papa thought it would be "a nice thing to do" to invite Dunson along.

Dunse kept his nose in a book all the time and couldn't hit a baseball if you hung it on a string in front of his bat. And as the saying goes, he was a lost ball in high weeds when it came to hunting and fishing. But he was all right. We didn't mind having him.

Grandpa Blakeslee's house was on our way out of Cold Sassy. As we rolled past it, Smiley snickered and said, "How you like your new two-timin' grandma, Will?"

I raised the whip and said shut up. "If you got to talk like that, you just get out and go on back home. You and anybody else that thinks she's any of their business." I glared at the whole bunch of them.

By time we got out in the country, we were having a high old time, whooping, talking loud, and all like that. If we saw a creakity wagon up ahead full of country folks going to town, I'd cluck the mules to a smart trot and we'd all wave as we passed them. We knew the big blue-painted covered wagon was something to stare at, and five boys off for the mountains were something to envy.

I began to forget all about Miss Love and what Cold Sassy must be saying about her kissing another man two days after promising to cleave only unto Grandpa. I even forgot to hope she knew it was Miss Effie Belle that told on her and not me.

Our mothers had packed baskets of food to keep us going. Fried chicken and boiled ham, baked sweet potatoes, peach pickles, big buttermilk biscuits, cookies, cakes, apples, boiled eggs, I don't know what all. We traveled thirty miles that first day and never stopped eating. About two o'clock the second day, just past the little town of Clayton in the foothills of the Blue Ridge Mountains, we took an old logging road into the woods and picked out a site near a little branch. While I fed and watered the mules and staked them out under some trees, the other fellers made camp. We didn't know whose land it was, of course. Just so you didn't set the woods afire and weren't Gypsies, nobody minded. You didn't have to ask.

Though we counted on getting plenty of fish and wild game, we had a wooden grub box full of staples. Smoked ham, bacon, a bucket of salt mackerel, flour, cornmeal, grits, raw sweet potatoes, lard, coffee, a tin of butter, some store bread, and a can of beaten biscuits that Dunse's mama made.

That night we put the box out under a tree to make more room for us to sleep in the wagon. I'd barely closed my eyes good when T.R. went to growling and the mules commenced raring up and squealing. Boy howdy, we scrambled out quick to grab those mules. If they'd pulled up their stakes and run away, I'd never of heard the last of it from Grandpa Tweedy.

What happened, two great big black bears had busted into our grub box. We could see them in the moonlight, eating the ham and those raw sweet potatoes, breaking open cans, scattering coffee and meal—having just the best time you ever saw. Acted like we weren't even there.

Smiley got his gun and was fixing to take aim when I stopped him. "How you think we go'n hold the mules if you go to shootin'? These ain't huntin' mules." He raised the gun anyhow. "I'm tellin' you, Smiley! I rather be hungry than walk home!"

You talk about hungry, there's nothing like knowing your grub is off somewhere digesting in a bear to make you feel starved to death. At daybreak we scavenged in the wreckage of the box, but what hadn't been eaten was mashed into the wet pine needles. All we found was a little damp flour in the bottom of a busted can.

In the gloomy, misty, gray morning we grazed on blackberries. That was breakfast. We had blackberries again for dinner. Supper was a boiled goose that Smiley shot on a nearby pond after the sun came out. We had to skin him to get the feathers off, and he was tough, great goodness, despite we boiled him and boiled him and boiled him. But he made a meal, and we thought to skim the goose grease off the top of the water. Used it next morning to fry a few middling-size trout.

We ate blackberries off and on all that second morning, which was cold and damp and overcast. I managed to shoot a dove and a rabbit—not much for five boys—and at noon we roasted them on a spit over the fire. We'd just finished eating when the rain that had threatened all morning blew in over the mountains in heavy black thunderheads. We barely had time to string up some canvas over the mules before the storm hit.

Safe in the wagon, we had a fine time for a while, tussling in the hay and talking about girls and all. But as the day wore on with no let-up of rain, we started getting hungry and cold and miserable. We got even more miserable when Lee Roy noticed that Smiley had left our box of shotgun shells out under a tree. Wet shells meant the end of hunting anything except blackberries and dry wood, which we hadn't thought to collect any real supply of.

I was really mad at Smiley. Bluford Jackson wouldn't of been careless about the shotgun shells or the grub box, either. And he'd of thought to gather piles of wood when we first got there, instead of keeping just enough ahead for the next campfire. I groaned. My throat swelled and ached. Bluford Jackson was six feet under, and the camping trip he planned was deader than him.

Trying to put some life in the party, so to speak, I sat up and said, "Dunse, I don't think you've heard how my Uncle Johnny hung a cow by mistake."

"Aw, shut up, Will," said Lee Roy. "Dunse's heard it. We all done heard it. A million times." He found a blanket and started pulling hay over himself for warmth as the sky got darker. We sat some more, watching the rain drip off the back canvas. When it started down in sheets, I said, "Why don't I tell about Raw Head and Bloody Bones?"

"How about shut up, Will?" said Smiley. "We get tired of your damn stories."

"Don't you cuss me, dernit!"

"Well, shut up then."

There wasn't room in the wagon for a fight. "One time my daddy saw his ancestor who'd been dead a hundred years," I said, stubborn. There was a slight stir of interest.

Pink thought I meant Papa saw his ancestor's ghost.

"Naw, I mean he saw his actual great-great-dead-grand-daddy. He was in a brick crypt in a old church graveyard up in North Ca'lina. When Papa and a cousin of his went over to check on the crypt, so much ivy had grown in through the cracks, you couldn't tell if the vines were holding the bricks together or pushing them apart. So they went in, and there was their great-great grand-daddy. The coffin had rotted to pieces and his bones were just layin' there. Papa said the skull had a hatchet cut on the forehead."

"Goll-ee," Pink whispered.

"That ain't all. A little-girl skeleton was in the crypt, too, in a coffin with a glass top. Her bones were just so white and pretty—"

"How'd your daddy know it was a girl?" asked Smiley, suspicioning I had made up more of it than I really had.

"The bones had on a little white poky-dot dress that hadn't all rotted yet, that's how."

The drumming of rain on the canvas was easing up, which was a good thing; it had started to drip through on us. But I hardly noticed. Like an actor whose audience has stood up to clap, I didn't want to quit. And now I knew what bait to use.

I said, "I've told y'all bout Great-Granmaw Tweedy dyin' twice. The first time, you remember, she jumped out of the coffin just fore they were fixin' to nail the lid. The second time she stayed dead. But what I thought might inner-rest y'all right now, she rode to the Hebron cemetery both times in this very wagon." I knocked on the side of it. The hollow wooden sound like to busted Pink and Lee Roy clear out of the hay.

"Did you see her die, Will—either time?" Dunse asked in a hushed voice.

"Naw. But last summer they'd just pulled the sheet over her head when me and my fam'ly got out home. And I went in there where she was at."

Smiley gasped. "I wouldn't a-gone in there," he admitted.

"Me neither," said Dunse. "I never been that close to a dead person."

"A old colored woman was sittin' with the body. She said, 'Want to see yo granny, boy?' I shook my head, but she said, 'Miss Mindy ain' gwine hurt you,' and she pulled that sheet back. Granmaw was propped up on pillows. What little hair she had was damp and standin' out like a scairt cat's. Her mouth had dropped open and her eyes stared straight at me. I could a-kilt that nigger woman, showin' off like that, tryin' to scare me. I backed out of that room, I tell you.

"Miz Jones and Mama laid Granmaw out. Fixed her mouth shut with a handkerchief tied under her chin and over her head. Papa hepped my uncles finish makin' the coffin, and soon as the preacher came, we ate dinner quick and set out for Hebron, it bein' a hot day and her not embalmed or anything. And like I said, they carried her to the graveyard in this very wagon here. Used those same mules out yonder, Big Red and Satan. All the way to Hebron, Mary Toy complained about us havin' to miss the Ringling Brothers Circus over in Athens. Every time we had to walk up a hill to save the horses, she'd say why couldn't Granmaw have died last week."

It gave us the creeps, sitting there in that hearse. It was pitch-black dark before the rain finally drizzled away and the moon came out. Wispy clouds scurried across the sky like little ghosts.

I said maybe there was enough dry wood under the wagon to build a fire with.

The fire warmed us some, after we finally got it going, but it didn't cheer anybody up. "I wish we had some good old hot buttered arsh potatoes," said Lee Roy.

Every now and again somebody would say, "I ain't scared a-no old dead woman." Or, "Is all that so, Will?" Once Pink went shush and whispered, "Y'all hear that? . . . I thought I heard something. Over by the wagon. . . ."

"Just the wind," I said airily, holding a twig in the fire till it got red hot on the end, like a long cigar. I waved it in circles a while, thinking what I could tell next. Pink got up off his log and turned his back to the fire. As we sat listening to the katydids, singing loud as they came out into the wetness, the moon lit up a layer of fog below us.

Blu Jackson is dead, I thought bitterly. Granny Blakeslee is dead. And reckon what has happened by now with Grandpa and Miss Love? I wanted to go home.

Dunse was like-minded. "I'm sick of this dern campout." He groaned. "I'm hungry and I'm cold." Huddled in a blanket, he kicked at a log on the fire. It sent up sparks. The flaring of light made big shadows dance on the wet gray canvas of the hearse.

Suddenly it didn't make any sense at all to stay on here till next week, when all we had to do was leave. I said as much, and the faces lit by the campfire grinned with relief. So it was decided. We would set out for Cudn Jake's place early in the morning and get Miss Love's racehorse.

Not a one of the boys would sleep in or under the wagon that night, despite the ground was wet as heck. I had counted on that. I was going to have a bed of hay all to myself. But as I put one foot up on the axle to climb in, I decided I might as well stay out with the fellers instead.

That night Bluford Jackson came to me in a dream. He didn't look dead but said he was. Said he was damaged goods in the worst way. He wanted me to tell Emma Lee Crutchfield to let him sit by her at preachin' next Sunday and please to save a space for him in her family pew.

"How big a space do you take now, Blu? Same as before, or just a inch or two?"

He didn't answer that. Just said he'd need Sunday clothes, and would I find him some and leave them in the crotch of the maple tree in his backyard.

"What you need clothes for, Blu? If you went to church na-ked as a jaybird, nobody'd know it."

"Ain't that the least you can do for me, Will, considerin' it was your firecrackers?" That made me mad, but he kept talk-ing. "Will, I got lots of time now. If you want to be a doctor, when you get to medical school you can make room for me in your seat and I'll hep you with your lessons and all."

"I'm not go'n be a doctor. You the one was go'n be a doctor.

I'm go'n farm. I cain't live your life for you, Blu." Then I woke
up, frightened, and shivering from the cold.

I didn't tell my dream to the fellers, but weeks later I told it
to Grandpa Blakeslee. I said, "Grandpa, it was like Blu didn't
believe he was dead. Like he don't know what bein' dead means,
for gosh sake."

Grandpa studied on it a minute and said, "I think it's you
thet don't believe he's dead, son. I think it's you thet don't know
what bein' dead means. But who does? Only them as has passed
on."

Cudn Rachel was almost as big and fat as Mrs. Jones, and said
she could spot hungry boys a mile away. She and Cudn Jake
had already eaten, but her cook made us some big graham biscuits and fried half a ham, looked like, and a bunch of eggs, and
put a gallon of milk on the table. The cook, having heard about
our bears, said this blessing: "Lawd, hep us an' feed us, an' keep
our en'mies from us, cause some'll come upon us, an' take our
rations from us. A-men."

We ate it all.

Miss Love's horse turned out to be a tall, prancy black gelding with a star on his forehead. With him tied behind the wagon
on a lead rope, head held proud and high, we felt mighty fancy
on the down-go to Cold Sassy, and we made mighty good time.
The mules knew they were headed home.

We did lots of talking about whether or not Miss Love could
train him. And then for the first time since we left Cold Sassy,
the boys got to talking about her and Grandpa. Smiley started
it. He said his mother thought Miss Love must have money
and that's why Mr. Blakeslee married her. "My grandmother
always did think the reason Mr. Blakeslee married Miss Mattie
Lou was cause her daddy owned all that land."

That really made me mad. "Shut up!"

"Miss Mattie Lou was a old maid, wasn't she? Why would
anybody marry a old maid cept for land or money?"

"I said shut up!" I yelled

"Yeah, shut up, Smiley," said Dunse. "It ain't right to talk like that about the dead."

But they couldn't let go of the subject. And the more they got my goat, the worse things they said, especially about Miss Love. Things like "Hey, Will, how long you think they been sweet on one another?" and "You reckon Miss Love's too old to have babies?"

"They ain't plannin' to have babies," I burst out, furious. "Grandpa and Miss Love have a business arrange-ment."

"What you mean by that?" Lee Roy asked with a smirk.

"I mean Miss Love is sleepin' in the comp'ny room," I said. "She's just livin' down there to keep house."

"I don't believe it."

"Well, it's so."

"Says who?"

"Says her. She told me."

"Haw! Since when have ladies started sayin' such as that to a boy? Shoot-dog."

Then Smiley crowded close up behind the driver's seat to talk ugly about the rich-lookin' stranger from Texas. "I heard he tore her clothers half off fore he got done kissin' her."

"Well, he didn't!" I was really mad now. "And I ought to know. I was there."

The boys took to making up jokes then, saying things you wouldn't want said about your grandpa's wife even if you hated her. I decided to change the subject. I swear I didn't know when I opened my mouth that I would say what I said, but it changed the subject all right:

"Y'all want to hear about Aunt Loma nursin' a pig?"

"You mean Campbell Junior?" asked Pink Predmore.

"I ain't talkin' bout the baby." We had started down a steep hill. "Slow down, Big Red. Whoa, Satan! Lee Roy, push hard on the brake post! The wagon's go'n run over the team!" Careening downhill, bumping over rocks and dried mud holes, we like to shook apart before we got the dern wagon under control.

"Did you say Miss Loma nursed a pig?" Pink asked as soon as he was able.

"You mean she put a pig up to her tits and let it suck?" asked Smiley.

"If Miss Loma did that, she must be crazy," said Dunse. "Anyhow, Will, how would you know it?"

I didn't, of course. One time I overheard Mama and Aunt Loma talking about a distant cousin over in Athens that did it to keep her milk going while her baby was in the hospital, but I just made up that it was Aunt Loma.

"Well, you know Campbell Junior was born little," I began, thinking fast. "I mean he didn't weigh more'n a fryin'-size chicken. Born early."

"Funny, I don't recollect him ever bein' little bitty," said Lee Roy.

"Well, he was. To keep him warm they had to put him in a pasteboard box with hot water bottles wrapped in towels all around him." That part was true. You just couldn't get Aunt Loma's house warm in winter. The rest I made up as I went along. "He was too weak to suck good, so Mama showed Aunt Loma how to milk herself and they gave it to him with a eye-dropper. But seems like she never really had full bags. Not enough milk to feed a jaybird. And the baby bein' such a sorry sucker, they were scairt she'd go dry."

We were moving up a hill now, the mules straining forward. I flipped their rumps with the whip.

"Get to the pig," fat Lee Roy said impatiently. "Tell us bout the pig."

"Well, my daddy fine'ly got on the telephone and rung up a hospital doctor over in Athens and ast what to do. It was the doctor said get a pig."

"Naw!" The boys said naw like there was just one voice for the four of them.

"Yeah! The doc said a pig would really get her milk goin'.'"

"I don't believe any lady would nurse a pig," said Dunse. "Not even your Aunt Loma."

"You can believe it or not, it's so," said I, and at the moment I half-believed it myself. "They sent me out to Grandpa Tweedy's in the buggy to get one. His Poland China sow had just whelped a new litter. I got the runtiest and took it home in a box. Mama bathed it and wrapped it up in a blue blanket and took it in to Aunt Loma. Mama couldn't stand the sight, that little pig gruntin' and pushin', but I heard her tell Papa that Loma said it felt real good. You know how if a cow ain't stripped proper she gets a swollen bag and sore tits? Well, Aunt Loma had been hurtin' a lot, besides worryin' bout the baby starvin' to death. She nursed that pig a week or more, I don't remember how long."

"If the pig was nursin' her," asked Pink, doubting, "what was happenin' to Campbell Junior?"

I thought fast. "The way it worked," I said, "Aunt Loma would let the baby nurse her a few minutes. Then she'd milk herself into a bottle. Then while Mama went to work feedin' Campbell Junior with a eyedropper, Granny would wrap the pig up and take it in to Aunt Loma, to get her stripped good. After that, I or Mary Toy, one, had to take the pig and feed it some cow's milk with a baby bottle so it wouldn't starve to death. We had a three-ring circus goin' there for a while."

"What happened to the pig?" asked Lee Roy as we crested a hill.

"Granny cooked him."

"Taste all right?"

"Nobody could eat him," said I. "But from then on Campbell Junior got fatter and fatter, and it's all on account of Aunt Loma havin' so much milk from gettin' started good with that pig."

"How come nobody's heard all this till now?" Pink said after while. He had laid down back there in the hay. "I cain't figure

you knowin' something that good, Will, and keepin' it to yourself."

"Papa said I couldn't go fishin' for a year if I told it," I lied.
"Which reminds me, don't *y'all* tell it, or what I said about Miss
Love and Grandpa, either." All of a sudden I was real worried
about what Miss Love would think if she heard it, but they all
crossed their hearts and hoped to die.

It was really something to make up an outlandish story like
that. I thought up another one right off, but needing a little
time to work it out, all I said was, "Maybe I'll tell y'all about
Aunt Loma and the rubber busts."

"The rubber what?" asked Smiley.

"Aunt Loma's rubber bust set that she bought for her weddin'. But y'all got to promise not to repeat it."

They like to fell out of the wagon promising, but I said let's
wait till we stop to eat. Right off, Lee Roy commenced saying
how hungry he was, though it was only ten o'clock.

"Me, too," said Dunse. "I'm starved. Wonder what Miss Rachel put in the basket?"

We soon saw an old wagon road that led up to a lonesome
chimney and on to a shady creek. As we turned off the highway,
I said, "I'll tell y'all just one fact that's important to the story.
Until Campbell Junior was on the way, Aunt Loma was flat as a
battercake, so to speak. Before she got married, Grandpa used
to say he never could find a towel; Loma was always makin'
herself a bosom or a bustle, one."

First we had to tend to the mules and Miss Love's racehorse.
Then while Dunse pulled out Cudn Rachel's basket, I got shet
of my clothes and jumped in the creek. I was hot, for one thing,
and also I'd been remembering a floating trick Blu Jackson told
me about last fall. He said you won't sink if you stretch your
arms out on the water like Jesus Christ crucified, or like ten
minutes to two on a clock. Well, it worked, by gosh. I felt like
I was on a mattress. When I made my body straight and stiff,
even my toes rose out of the water.

"Bet cain't any of y'all float this good!" I yelled. They all took off their clothes, waded in, and laid down on the water, but their feet and legs sank straight down as usual.

It made Smiley mad. "You just layin' in shallows, Will. You ain't floatin'."

"I am, too. It's deep here. Come feel." And he did, whooshing his arm under my back to make sure. I rocked like a boat, my toes still sticking out of the water.

"You ain't never floated like that before," said Pink, still suspicious.

I tried making a pillow out of my hands, putting them under the back of my head, and that worked even better. Closing my eyes, I could of gone to sleep if the boys hadn't pounced on me and sent me under.

Without bothering to put on clothes, we opened up Cudn Rachel's picnic and ate, sitting on the mossy creek bank with our feet cooling in the water. When I finished, I lay back, feet still in the water, and said, "Now I'm go'n tell about Aunt Loma and the rubber busts!

"Well, when Aunt Loma was go'n get married," I began, "she ordered her this rubber bust set from Sears and Roebuck, but she couldn't get'm blowed up. It was nearly time for the weddin' and she couldn't get the bicycle pump to work, so she ast me to do it." I sat up, splashing my feet in the cool water. "Said she'd pay me a dollar. Also said she'd kill me if I told anybody."

"Specially us, haw!" said Pink, raising on one elbow to chuck a rock at a hickernut tree.

"Well, so I blowed'm up. But then I took a needle and stuck this little bitty hole in the left bust. It went *psssssssssssst* all through the weddin' and Aunt Loma had a flat by the last I-do! You never in your life saw a bride as mad as her, or one holdin' her bouquet as high up."

"She yell at you, Will?" Pink asked, grinning.

"She couldn't. The preacher was still marryin' them. But boy howdy, she shot me a look! She was so mad that when Uncle Camp had trouble pushin' the ring on her finger, she jerked her hand away and put it on herself. Uncle Camp is sort of a mouse, you know. When Aunt Loma fusses, he looks pitiful and says, 'I'm sorry, Loma Baby.' After they were man and wife, I heard him whisper, 'Loma Baby, what did I do?'"

We all guffawed and hawed.

"As you can imagine," I added, "I stayed out of the way till they got on the train to Tallulah Falls."

I didn't say so to the boys, but Aunt Loma thought Camp had made reservations at a nice honeymoon hotel, whereas he planned on staying with his aunt. He said they could go see the falls just as good from her house as from the hotel, and a whole lot cheaper. It turned out his aunt was a widow woman with ten children, living in a nasty, rundown old cabin on a turkey farm where you couldn't get to the privy without stepping in turkey mess. Aunt Loma stayed ten minutes and, holding her nose, said she was taking the next train home.

Before they left town, though, she dressed up in her first-day outfit and got a street photographer to snap a honeymoon picture of her and Camp smiling at each other in front of the biggest hotel in Tallulah Falls. But when the picture finally came in the mail, it wasn't her and Uncle Camp. It was another couple.

Getting mixed up by the photographer seemed to be the last straw. Aunt Loma was not only mad at Camp, she was furious at Granny and Grandpa for not forbidding the marriage. And now that she was stuck with it, she was mad at Mama for having married so much better than her. Despite Camp had grown up in a tenant shack, she thought he knew what was meant by coming up in the world. Now she knew he didn't.

27

W E ROLLED into Cold Sassy about five o'clock that
Saturday evening. As we neared my house, I said real
solemn, "Now if y'all tell about the pig or the bust set, I'll catch
heck." As if it was a casual afterthought, I added, "And don't
tell your folks about Miss Love stayin' in the comp'ny room at
Grandpa's house. Because if you do—" I glared at Pink on the
seat beside me, holding the brake post, and then at the others
lolling back there in the hay. "Because if you do," I repeated,
and they knew I meant it, "I'll make up something and tell it on
y'all, if you know what I mean." They hoped to die first.

With my threat hanging over their heads, I trusted them all
the time we unhitched and tended the mules, turning them out
into Papa's pasture for the night.

I trusted them while Queenie praised and patted the black
gelding, which Mama wouldn't even look at. Mama hovered
around, asking why did we come back so soon and how was
Cudn Rachel and them, did we have a good time and stay cool,
were we warm enough at night, and did we have enough to eat.
But she didn't ask one thing about the gelding.

I still trusted the boys when we all marched down to Grandpa's house, proudly leading the prancy horse to Miss Love, and
helped her put him in a stall. When we were leaving she took

my hand and said, "Will, he's just beautiful. Mr. Beautiful, that's what I'll name him. Thank you so much. Thank you."

All the time we were unloading the covered wagon, I believed the boys wouldn't tell on me. I still believed it while I took a bath. But about time I sat down to eat, it came to me with a sinking feeling that probably everything I'd said was being repeated right now all over town.

I wasn't too worried about Aunt Loma. Those were whacking good stories, if I do say so myself. And everybody would know they were made up. I'd made up things before. Anyhow, it would be worth a whipping to see Aunt Loma's face after she heard.

What made my stomach sink was knowing I had betrayed Miss Love. Folks would already be sniggering about those separate rooms. It was a strange thing to me that the same people who condemned her on her wedding day for taking advantage of an old man's loneliness would be condemning her now, just ten days later, for denying Grandpa his rights.

We were hardly through supper before here came Miss Sarah Gordy, saying I ought to be ashamed. Mr. French being Granny's stepbrother, his wife felt like they were kin and had a right to speak up in the family. After blessing me out, she took Mama in the house to tell her in private what all Mrs. Snodgrass said Smiley said I said. As they came out, Mama was nodding in agreement. "You're absolutely right, Miss Sarah. This time Will has gone too far."

After Mrs. Gordy left, Mama made me go to my room while she told Papa what Miss Sarah said Mrs. Snodgrass said Smiley said I said. Mama's furious voice drifted up from the porch, and pretty soon Papa came to the bottom of the stairs and hollered for me to get down there. He was already taking off his belt when I came out my door.

After the whipping, Papa said, "Son, we go'n go out to the barn, you and me. I think it's time I told you a few things."

Boy howdy, at last. But it was just another lecture about respecting ladies. "It's not fittin' to make jokes about a woman's—uh, womanhood," Papa began, looking stern. "If you got to show off before a bunch of boys by makin' up tales about a woman's—" He sputtered, unable to say the word. "Well, if you got to make up a story, Will, for heaven's sake don't pin it on anybody that anybody knows."

All in all, I came out about even on Aunt Loma that night. One beating and one lecture was about right for two good stories that would be told for a long time by old men playing checkers under the Cold Sassy tree at the depot. If Aunt Loma was mad, which she would be, that suited me just fine.

The next day at Sunday dinner, Papa had hardly finished serving the baked hen when my mother said, real pleasant, "I wonder who played the piano for the Methodists today."

"Miss Effie Belle," said Aunt Loma. Picking a curly red hair out of her sweet potato sooflay, she dropped it daintily to the floor. "They say there were lots of wrong notes and she played pretty slow, but they got by. Will, start the gravy. Don't just let it sit there."

Scared Aunt Loma might switch from Miss Effie Belle's piano playing to my camping trip, I asked, "Why didn't Miss Love play?"

"She wasn't there. That's one reason." Aunt Loma sounded like she'd just been weaned on a lemon.

Mama said maybe Love went to the Baptist church with Grandpa.

"If they came, I didn't see'm. Did you see'm, Camp?"

I said maybe Miss Love is sick.

"She's sick, all right," answered Aunt Loma, talking around a bite of chicken. "After two years of showin' off at the piano, your Miss Love has found out the Methodists can do without her. A committee of ladies went callin' on her last week, Will, to let our new Miz Blakeslee know that a married woman is expected to behave herself."

"It wasn't like that," protested Papa. "The ladies just—"

"—told her they didn't need her to play for preachin' any-more," Aunt Loma said, looking smug. "She tried to act like it didn't matter, but I bet after they left she threw things and cried her eyes out."

"Loma, you listen here—" Papa said sternly.

"Don't worry so, Brother Hoyt. What we're sayin' is in the bosom of the family." She looked straight at me then. "Unless Will here decides to tell it on his next campin' trip."

Just by the way Papa jabbed his spoon in the sugar dish, I knew something was coming. But he stirred his coffee good and put the spoon down before exploding. "I don't know why you're so happy about all that, Loma. Your pa sure ain't. Now I want you and Mary Willis both to hush up talkin' about her."

"You cain't make the whole town hush up, Brother Hoyt."

"Well, y'all don't have to join in. What's done is done, and we go'n live with it and be nice." I knew and they knew he was saying we got to remember which side our bread is buttered on down at the store, and who is buttering it.

"Brother Hoyt's right, Loma Baby," Uncle Camp said boldly. "We need to—"

"Oh, shut up, Camp, and pass my coffee cup to Sister. I just want a half a cup, Sister. Brother Hoyt, Love is the one you ought to say hush to. After her tirade down at the store last week, how can you think it's just me and Sister keepin' the town talkin'? It's mostly her."

"Your daddy don't see it that way," said Papa. "He says Miss Love's bein' tarred and feathered for what ain't nobody's business but his and hers." I was dying to ask what Miss Love said at the store, but I didn't dare.

Nobody spoke the rest of the meal except to say the gravy sure is good and please pass the muscadine jelly.

Mainly to get out of Aunt Loma's way before she could catch me alone and fuss about the rubber busts and all, I hurried to the pasture right after dinner. Papa wanted me to get the team and the wagon back to Banks County. Just as I was backing the mules into place on either side of the wagon tongue, here came trouble in the form of Grandpa Blakeslee.

Seeing him with short hair, and without that big droopy mustache and bushy gray beard, I was surprised all over again. I swear my granddaddy didn't look more'n eight or ten years older than my daddy.

It was the expression on his face that made me uneasy, and the sharp edge on his voice. "You fixin' to take thet rig back out to the country?" he asked.

"Yessir." I kept my eyes on the strap I was buckling. The leather was still damp from yesterday's mule sweat.

Grandpa didn't speak again for a minute. Then he said, "Yore daddy says you go'n stop by Temp's place on the way back and see Mary Toy."

"Yessir."

While I hooked the traces, Grandpa asked did my mother change her mind yet about going to New York.

"No, sir. Not as I know of. . . . Move over, Red!"

As I fastened the last strap, out there in the hot sun with the mules snorting and stomping and twitching off green flies, he finally said it. "Will Tweedy, I'm plumb shamed a-you."

I didn't have to ask why. I just stood there wondering who told him what I said about Miss Love taking over the company room. I even wondered how it was phrased to him. "Grandpa, I was just tryin' to—"

"I ain't inner-rested in what you was a-tryin' to do. What you done was bad enough. You done made a laughin' stock out a-Loma agin."

Loma?

Grandpa was mad about what I told on Aunt Loma?

"Now she does bring a lot on herself," he was saying. "Loma's so hateful sometimes I'm sorry to have to claim her. But you don't make her no nicer by outsmartin' her ever few days or makin' fun of her. Them stories you told ain't so, and ain't fittin' to be told on no lady. Loma may be hateful, but she lives

decent and you ain't a-go'n talk bout her like thet no more."
He spat his tobacco juice close to Big Red's front hoofs. "You
hear me?"

"Yessir." I felt about as low as O.K. Dunbar crawling home
drunk at midnight. I couldn't honestly say I was sorry, but I
hung my head.

I figured Grandpa would turn then and stalk off, but he
didn't. After ordering me in no uncertain terms to apologize to
Aunt Loma, he put his arm around my shoulders. "I sure want
to hear bout thet campin' trip," he said with a rough tenderness
in his voice. I felt like the sun had just come out.

"We had us a swell time, Grandpa!" There wasn't any use
saying otherwise. It's bad enough to be miserable on a camping trip without telling the world. Lighthearted now, I put one
foot on the wagon axle, whistled for T.R., and swung myself to
the driver's seat. The dog jumped up there beside me, landing
so hard—*zomp!*—he liked to knocked me over.

"Old T.R. knows you better be gittin' on if'n you go'n be
home fore dark," said Grandpa. Then, squinting up at me, he
went to talking like I had all day long. "We held church up at
the house this mornin'."

"Sir?"

"I was the preacher, Miss Love was the pi-ana player, and the
both of us made up the congregation. Hit was a real nice service." He enjoyed seeing I was confused. "Wish you'd a-been
there, son. We sang us some hymns, after which I talked to the
Lord a while, tellin' Him bout the week, and I then preached a
sermon. Tell you the truth, I think I upset Miss Love."

"Sir?"

"I didn't have no words thought out, you know, so I jest
commenced sayin' thangs I been a-thinkin' on lately—bout
the Virgin Birth and Resurrection and all like thet. I said don't
any a-them thangs matter. Well, Miss Love like to had a fit.
Said she warn't raised to think like thet. I said I warn't neither,
but thet didn't keep me from thinkin', and I ast her do Meth-

odists interrupt and argue with the preacher or do they sit and listen to what he's got to say."

"Gosh, Grandpa. You mean you don't think Jesus rose from the dead?"

"I'm a-sayin' thet did He or didn't He ain't important, son. What's important is thet when the spirit a-Jesus Christ come down on them disciples later, they quit settin' round a-moanin' and a-tremblin', and got to work. They warn't scairt no more, and the words they spoke had fire in'm. Compared to a miracle like thet, Jesus rollin' back a dang rock and flyin' off to Heaven ain't nothin'."

"What did Miss Love say to that, Grandpa?" I was real excited.

"Nothin'. I didn't let her interrupt me agin. I said thet same miracle is still a-happenin', right here in Cold Sassy, in July of nineteen aught-six. A crippled person or a invalid, or the meanest thief or the most despairin' misfit, why, if'n he can ketch aholt of the spirit of Jesus Christ, he can quit bein' scairt and be like risin' up from the dead. Once his soul gits cured, no matter what his body's like, why, he can start a new life. Well, next I preached bout the Virgin Birth. To my thinkin', the birth ain't the dang miracle. Hit's the fact thet a boy like Jesus was born to a mama who could leave Him be. Well, and then I talked to Miss Love bout Eternal Life. As you know, son, jest believin' we go'n live forever in the next world don't make it so—or not so."

I felt awful. "Grandpa, you don't think Granny's gone to Heaven? She ain't Up There waitin' on us to come?"

"I like to think so, son. If'n they is a Heaven, she's Up There, I know thet," he said softly. Then he laughed and slapped his hand on Satan's rump. "Ain't but one way to find out if she is or ain't, though. And I'm not thet curious." He sighed, spat, and said, "Havin' faith means it's all right either way, son. 'The Lord is my shepherd' means I trust Him. Whatever happens in this life or the next, and even if they ain't a life after this'n, God planned it. So why wouldn't it be all right?" He looked dead serious, then all of a sudden laughed again. "You know, if'n I was a real preacher, Will Tweedy, wouldn't nobody come to my church."

"I would, Grandpa."

"Well, I ain't shore bout Miss Love. She was expectin' the Lord to strike me down this mornin'. When I finished preachin', she brought in some lemonade and pound cake and I said it was the best Lord's Supper I ever et, and she didn't like my sayin' thet one bit. Said it was blasphemy. When I wanted to sing some barbershop harmony, she called it sacrilegious, bein' Sunday, but fine'ly I got her goin' on the pi-ana and we had us a real good time. Ever church ought to do thet—give God a good time stead of po-mouthin' and always be astin' Him to save us from temptation and sufferin' and death. If'n you live, Will Tweedy, you go'n be tempted, and you go'n suffer, and you go'n die. Ain't no way out of it. But with the Lord's hep, you can stand up to temptation, and live th'ew the bad times, and look Death in the eye. You remember what I say, son."

"Yessir. But I'd still like to hear you explain Jesus sayin' ast God for something and you'll get it. One time I prayed for a million dollars, to test Him, and didn't get one dime."

"Thet was jest wishin'. Hit warn't prayin'."

T.R. had long since jumped down to chase something, and the mules were restless, but I liked being with Grandpa like this, just him and me. I didn't want him to quit talking. "Did Miss Love think it up? I mean havin' preachin' at home?"

"Naw, son. I did. I—well, I expect you heard bout them Methodist ladies comin' to see her last week?"

"Yessir."

"Figgered you would." His tone was hard. "Miss Love was the maddest white woman you ever saw bout thet. She come down to the store a hour or so later and blessed out the whole dang town. Then yesterd'y she got a unsigned letter in the mail. Well, it warn't a letter, jest a old newspaper clippin' bout fallen women. Hit said thangs like 'A female by one transgression forfeits her place in society forever.' Miss Love cried all night last night."

Poor Miss Love.

"This mornin' she put on her Sunday clothes, but then she got to cryin' and carryin' on agin. I said to her, 'Miss Love, why'n't you stay home?' She said, 'I can't. They'll know I care.' So I put it to her plain. 'Miss Love, what *good's* it go'n do, mad as you are? If'n don't nobody speak to you or sit by you, you jest go'n be mad all over agin. We got a pi-ana. Let's have preachin' right here. Jest you and me.'

"Well, son, we had a heap better time than the dang Methodists, I gol-gar'ntee you. I unner-stand Miss Effie Belle played for them today. She's worse'n yore granny for losin' the place." Grinning, he smoothed his pencil mustache with one finger. "I made dang shore Miss Effie Belle got a earful when she got home. I said, 'The Lord loves a joyful noise, Miss Love, and here comes Miss Effie Belle up her walk. I want you to play "Ta-Ra-Ra-Boom-de-Ay" and rattle the rafters! Then she can tell it all over town how we desecrated the Sabbath.' And, son, Miss Love was mad enough to do it! The sound like to knocked Miss Effie Belle over. . . . Well, I reckon you really had best git started."

I bet Miss Love's bosom really bounced while she rattled the rafters. I wondered if Grandpa noticed. Naw, he wouldn't.

"Miss Love's already a plumb fool bout thet hoss, son," he said then. "Come up home t'morrer sometime, hear, and see can you hep her with him."

"Yessir," I said, but I wasn't happy about it. I didn't know if I could face her.

As the wagon rolled into the street, I thought how Granny would have enjoyed their preachin' service. If it could of been the three of them, I mean. Granny used to strike as many wrong keys on the piano as Miss Effie Belle. And she'd sing while she played, holding on to each note with her voice till she could find the next one with her fingers. As far as I know, she and Grandpa never sang together, just the two of them. But whenever Miss Love came for a family dinner, Grandpa would ask her to play hymns, and we'd all sing, and nobody enjoyed it more than Granny.

One thing I knew as the mules pulled out into South Main, I was not going to apologize to Aunt Loma. I'd just have to owe her one.

Turning onto the Banks County road, I was thinking what a difference a week can make. Before we went to the mountains, I felt sure Miss Love would tell me everything that happened while I was gone. I even planned to ask her did Grandpa find out about her kissing Mr. McAllister. But now I didn't think she'd ever tell me anything personal again. Even if she did, I wouldn't know what to say to her, or what not to say, or how not to say it, because now she wouldn't trust me.

"Giddy-up there!" I yelled, reaching for the whip. "I ain't got all day, dern you. Git up, Red! Git up, Satan!"

As we rattled toward the Banks County line, what really puzzled me was how come Grandpa blessed me out about Aunt Loma but didn't say pea-turkey about my discussing him and Miss Love with a bunch of snotty boys. Gosh, it must be he hadn't heard! Folks would snigger behind Grandpa's back but not many would dare repeat it to his face. They knew that hard fist.

I didn't find out till night that Miss Love sleeping in the company room just wasn't news anymore. While us boys were up in the mountains getting our food snatched by bears and cooking our goose and all, she had announced it herself!

28

I 'M BEGINNIN' to hate her with a passion," Mama said, and I hadn't a doubt who she was talking about.

Papa was still down at the church, making up his treasurer's report, so it was just Mama and me out there on the veranda in the dark, trying to get cool. I was bone tired. Not from walking the ten miles from Grandpa Tweedy's farm. That wasn't anything. It was from the camping trip. It had finally caught up with me. At the Sunday night preachin', my eyelids had been like heavy little windows flipping open and shut.

With me sitting in the swing and Mama in the tall porch rocker, she launched into a tirade about desecration of the Sabbath. "That Woman and your granddaddy were singin' dance songs at churchtime this mornin', Will. Miss Effie Belle heard them. Anybody who don't know or care if it's Sunday has to be common as pigs' tracks."

"Grandpa ain't common, Mama." I didn't dare say Miss Love wasn't common.

"It ain't him. It's her. He never did such a thing when Ma was alive, and you know it."

"Grandpa said they were havin' church," I told her. "Just him and her, Mama, in the parlor. He prayed and preached a sermon and they sang hymns and all."

"Aw, shah. You call 'Ta-Ra-Ra-Boom-de-Ay' a hymn?"

"That was after, Mama. They had church first."

Her chair stopped rocking. "How you know so much?"

"He told me all about it." I slapped at a mosquito, and the chains at the top of the swing jangled.

Mama rocked fast for a minute, then stopped dead. "Speakin' of common, did he tell you about Miss Love havin' a fuss with Miz Predmore down at the store last week?"

"Well'm, he mentioned it in passin'."

And so she told me. I knew she hoped it would make me quit taking up for Miss Love Simpson. "Miz Predmore was on the Methodist committee about the piano playin'," Mama began. "After they called on her, Miz Predmore stopped by Pa's store and was pickin' out some piece goods when here came Miss Love, hair done up fancy and dressed to the nines in a red dress and a straw hat with big red flowers on it." Mama's fan was just a-goin'. "Imagine, wearin' a red dress in public when the fam'ly's in mournin'."

Folks had criticized Miss Love the week before for wearing black as if she was grieving for Granny. Now she was awful to wear red.

As Mrs. Predmore told it to Mama and she told it to me that night on the veranda, Miss Love had flounced into the store like she owned it. She came in smiling big at two farmers who wanted Papa to extend credit for a new mule, and then greeted Mr. Cratic Flournoy, who was complaining of indigestion. Just as Camp walked in, carrying a glass of water clouded with baking soda for Mr. Flournoy, Miss Love spied Mrs. Predmore back near the millinery table, looking through bolts of cloth.

"Good morning, Mrs. Predmore!" she called, smiling her big wide-mouth smile as if Mrs. P. was her best friend and like she hadn't seen her in a week. Naturally Mrs. P. didn't speak or smile back. Fixing her mouth like saying prune, she just went on studying the piece goods.

But Mr. Flournoy, always the gentleman, lifted his glass

of soda water in greeting and, as Mrs. Predmore reported later, "spoke to that hussy like she was a queen or something. Hitched up his pants over that big belly and practically bowed to her. Said, 'Mornin', Miz Blakeslee. How's the bride?' "

"Fine, sir. But, uh, I have decided not to use Mr. Blakeslee's name, Mr. Flournoy," said the bride, speaking pleasant but formal, and loud enough to be heard in the piece-goods department. "Of course that is now my legal title, but for personal reasons I prefer to be addressed in the usual way." While Mr. Flournoy and everybody else, including Grandpa, stared at her, she flashed them all a great big nervous smile.

Grandpa was standing behind the counter, his one hand resting on the cast-iron string holder. Miss Love turned to him and said in a flirty voice, "Mr. Blakeslee, don't you agree it's not appropriate for me to be called Mrs. Blakeslee?"

A funny look came on Grandpa's face. Everybody could tell he was surprised. But he just shrugged his shoulders and laughed. "If you say so, Miss Love." Then he changed the subject. "I reckon you need some hep with yore millinery stuff. Camp, go git some a-them clean pasteboard boxes for our Miss Simpson here."

There wasn't much conversation in the store while Miss Love gathered up her hat-making gee-gaws. The way she threw things in the boxes, though, it began to dawn on everybody that, underneath the smile, Miss Love was boiling mad. Mrs. Predmore knew why, of course. The others could only guess.

When Miss Love and Uncle Camp went out to load boxes in the buggy, Mrs. P. put in her two cents' worth about a wife not using her husband's name. She thought Grandpa would welcome her opinion, but he just laughed. Acted like the whole thing was a big joke. "I look at it like this, Thelma," he was saying when Miss Love came back in. "Long as she cooks good and ain't aggravatin', I don't really care what she calls herself. Ain't thet how you see it, Hoyt?"

Papa was embarrassed and didn't know what to say. Miss Love didn't seem to notice. ("Too brazen to even blush," Mrs. Predmore told Mama.)

But a storm was brewing inside Miss Love. I figured later she was mad not only about the church piano stool being jerked out from under her, but about her whole life: having a drunkard for a daddy, getting jilted by Mr. McAllister, and being looked on in Cold Sassy as a Yankee outsider.

Still and all, she might not of gone as far as she went if Mrs. Predmore hadn't stalked over to Grandpa and let out exactly what she thought of him and her, both.

"Mr. Blakeslee, y'all ain't got no respect for the fam'ly or for this community, either one. It ain't decent, marryin' the way y'all done, with Miss Mattie Lou just barely dead."

It was like the smile on Grandpa's face dropped right off on the floor. "Don't you bring up Miss Mattie Lou, Thelma." He banged his fist on the counter. "And don't preach at me, or Miss Love, either."

Miss Love said, "For your information, Miss Thelma, we aren't indecently married. We aren't married at all." Giving her time to gasp, she added, "Except legally."

"Now ladies, now ladies. . . ." sputtered Mr. Flournoy.

Miss Love didn't even hear him. With her chin in the air, she said, "I keep house for Mr. Blakeslee, and that's all. In case you don't get my meaning, I'll say it plain: I'm sleeping in Mrs. Blakeslee's company room. It is not my plan to take her name or her place, except to cook and wash for Mr. Blakeslee and keep the—"

"Shet up, Miss Love!" ordered Grandpa.

She blazed out, "Don't you ever say shut up to me!"

"Hit ain't nobody else's bizness!" He was furious.

"I'll hush when everybody quits talking about me. And that won't happen till there's nothing else anybody can wonder about. Now, Miss Thelma?" She drew a deep breath and spoke like her words were sorghum syrup, "Be sure and repeat everything I've said. Tell it all over town. But do try to keep the facts straight."

During all this, the two farmers pretended to be looking at some hardware and Mr. Flournoy kept waving his hands and saying, "Now ladies . . . now ladies. . . ." And Mrs. P. kept dumping insults like she was emptying slop jars: "Love Simpson, you don't make no more sense than a chicken with its head cut off. If you're just comp'ny, like you say, and don't even want Mr. Blakeslee's name, how come you bothered to get married? I hear that up where you come from, lots of white servants stay with the fam'ly they work for."

Grandpa banged his fist again and yelled, "Thelma, you git outer my store!"

"I'm gettin'!" she shouted. "And I ain't comin' back, neither!"

Miss Love called, "Miss Thelma, let me say one thing more—"

"I ain't listenin'. It's trashy talk."

"Don't you want to know what I'll get out of this arrangement?" Her voice was impudent, but Papa told Mama she looked tired and her lips trembled. Papa said he felt sorry for her right then. As Mrs. P. paused near the door, Miss Love said, "Wait a minute and I'll tell you."

"Shet up, Miss Love!" Grandpa demanded again.

"I know what you gettin'," Mrs. Predmore retorted. "You savin' yourself from goin' single file all your life and havin' Miss on your tombstone. But bein' a wife in name only, and not even usin' the name. . . . Well, you really still just a old maid, ain't you?"

"He has deeded me the house," said Miss Love.

It took a few seconds for that to soak in. Mrs. Predmore put one foot out the door and said, "Well, call you Miz Greedy! First you grab Miss Mattie Lou's husband, then you grab property that should rightly be Loma's and Mary Willis's!"

Miss Love didn't answer as Mrs. P. marched out.

I need to say that for a long time Miss Love never answered those who called her Miz Blakeslee. Some folks who hadn't planned on speaking to her at all started saying, for meanness, "G'mornin', Miz Blakeslee!" But the only ones she spoke back to were the few who called her Miss Love or—for meanness—Miss Simpson.

Pink Predmore told me that what really burned his mother up was the way Mr. Blakeslee got to laughing. She heard him say, "Doggit, Miss Love, I'd shore hate for you to git mad at me. Wouldn't you, Hoyt?" Grandpa didn't give Papa time to answer before he added, "In case Thelma don't pass the word around, Miss Love, maybe you better git up at the next ladies' missionary society meetin' and say it agin. Or take out a personal advertisement in the *Cold Sassy Weekly*."

"The word will get around," Miss Love said, bitter.

After Pink's mother left the store, she went across the street to Clark's to get her mail, and was just coming out when Miss Love swept from the store with the last of her boxes and climbed into the buggy. As Mrs. Predmore put it, "She clucked at that silly mule like he was a horse, and drove off like that old buggy was a gold coach."

Miss Effie Belle was in her yard hanging out clothes when Miss Love got home. She told it around, with great satisfaction, that "That Woman was just a-cryin' all the time she unloaded the buggy. And late that night I seen Rucker pacin' the brick walk in Mattie Lou's rose garden. The lamp in Miss Love's room went off around midnight, but Rucker was still out there in that garden, walkin' back and forth, forth and back. I could see him by the moon. Pore Rucker, I reckon he was so upset after Mattie Lou died, he didn't hardly know what he was doin', marryin' That Woman. So I can forgive him. But not her. She could a-had the decency to refuse his proposition. Instead, she latched aholt. A grievin' man just ain't no match for a schemin' woman. Specially a pretty one."

29

I AGREED with Mama: there was just no excuse for the way Miss Love acted. No nice lady would pick a fuss in public like that, much less tell anybody and everybody her personal business. What on earth got into her?

Somehow it brought to mind the time I helped Smiley Snodgrass blow up a hen with a bicycle pump. We like to died laughing, watching that bloated chicken wobble around like a dern balloon. It's far-fetched to compare that to Miss Love blowing up Cold Sassy, but I'm saying it's one thing to embarrass a hen and another thing entirely to embarrass a family and a whole town.

Neither Mama nor I said much for a while. Just sat there on the porch in the dark, waiting for Papa. While the tree frogs croaked and the porch swing creaked, it came to me that there might not of been a fuss at the store if I'd told what Miss Love said the day I helped her clean up. Gosh, I'd felt so set-up and proud, her confiding in me like I could be counted on to keep my mouth shut, and all the time she must of been hoping I'd scatter her words broadcast like turnip seed.

Probably Miss Love thought Mama and them would take her right on into the family if they knew she wasn't a real wife and that all she'd ever get out of Grandpa was the house and furniture—not the store, not the farm lands or his other houses or the railroad stock and the cottonseed oil company stock.

Of course it could be she just needed to talk to somebody who was kind and understanding. If not me, who? Miss Love didn't have one close friend in Cold Sassy and no doubt was lonesome, being used to working around people at the store.

But tell the truth, she'd been lonesome ever since she hit town. Cold Sassy took pride in being hospitable to outsiders, so Miss Love had always got her share of invites. But she was still an outsider and acted like one. Despite being friendly and lively, like Grandpa she had always held a part of herself back. Close-mouthed, they called her.

So it just didn't make any sense at all for Miss Love to tell me about the arrangement unless she hoped I'd go home and set Mama and Aunt Loma straight—and through Aunt Loma, the whole town. If I was right about that, I'd sure let her down.

But now that Miss Love had declared war on Cold Sassy, where did that put me? Right smack in the middle that's where—between Grandpa on the one side and Mama and Cold Sassy on the other. I knew I still wanted to be her friend. Lord knows she needed one. And I couldn't help liking her. But I hated taking her part against Mama and them.

Papa was right. The family would just have to let bygones be bygones, and be nice no matter what.

That night Miss Love declared war on the family, too. She fired the opening shots at Aunt Loma.

Mama and I were still out there on the porch, waiting for Papa, when here came Loma and Camp—her carrying the baby, him carrying Granny's big mirror with Saint Cecilia painted on it. Boy, was Aunt Loma mad!

They had gone up to Grandpa's house straight from Sunday night preachin' at the Baptist church. "To pay a friendly Christian call, Sister. I was go'n try and show Pa that we weren't holdin' hard feelin's," said Loma. "Quit that, Campbell Junior." He was fretting and grabbing at her face.

"But Mr. Blakeslee warn't to home," Uncle Camp put in as Aunt Loma plunked herself down in a porch rocker, unbuttoned the shirtwaist of her mourning dress, and let the baby nurse.

"Love said Pa had gone to the store to make up his order," said Loma. "Workin' on Sunday, Sister! He never did that when Ma was alive."

"He sure didn't." Mama was disgusted.

"Well, after Love lit a lamp in the parlor, we all sat down. She took Campbell Junior and played with him a while, but then we just sat there. Sister, if Miss Love isn't a Yankee, she sure acts like one. You know the way they can sit for hours and nobody say a word? Drives you crazy. Finally I said isn't it a hot night and Camp said how much we could use some rain. Then I ast if she'd found out what was wrong with the horse Will brought her. I mean, you know, why would Cudn Jake give him away like that? Instead of answerin', she ast would we like some refreshments.

"With her gone to the kitchen, we could take a good look at the parlor. Sister, you wouldn't believe how she's changed things around. 'You sure have changed things around,' I said when she came in with lemonade and pound cake. But I spoke real nice, didn't I, Camp? I did tell her she better close the blinds every mornin' and keep the sheets on the loveseat and all. I reminded her about sun fadin' things."

"What'd she say?"

"She said she likes mornin' sun and doesn't intend to close the blinds at all. I ast her was that all right with Pa, her lettin' the sun fade Ma's things. She said she hadn't ast him."

Camp's voice spoke up in the darkness. "She shore does make a good pound cake, I'll say that for her. Loma Baby, I wish you'd make me some pound cake."

Loma Baby ignored him. "Then she offered to show us her room. She picked up the lamp and started across the hall, but I said, 'I'd like to see Ma's room, first.' 'All right,' Love said, 'but all I've done in there is sweep and dust. Your father wants it to stay just like Miss Mattie Lou had it.'"

"Maybe you hadn't ought to dust even," Camp told her. "Where somebody has died is a sacred place. Even the dust is sacred."

Miss Love had laughed at him! Said, "Camp, that's the silliest thing you ever said. Dust is dirt. There's no such thing as sacred dirt, for heaven's sake."

"The nerve," said Mama, "talkin' like that to Camp."

Shifting Campbell Junior to her other side, Loma said softly, "Well, we went in there, and Sister, it looked like Ma was still livin' in that room. Their weddin' picture on the wall over the bed, you know, and Ma's hair not even combed out of the brush, and her glasses still on her Bible on the night stand. . . . Love hasn't even thrown out that dried-up old rose in the bud vase. I hate dead flowers. I said, 'Love, you could at least throw out that old rose,' but she didn't answer me. Well, then I saw Ma's blue beads in the pin tray on the dresser."

"The weddin' beads that Pa gave her," Mama said, her voice choking a little. "We should of buried her in them. You know, Loma, I never saw Ma without them till the funeral. Did you? I'd sure like to have those beads."

"I already got'm, Sister," Aunt Loma said with an I-bid-first tone in her voice, and pulled them out of her pocket. "I told Love I wanted those beads and she said to ast Pa. Said she couldn't give permission. That really made me mad. 'I don't need your permission,' I told her, and I just prissed over and got them. 'Just tell Pa I have them.'"

"You tell him," Miss Love snapped, high and mighty, and hurried back up the hall to light the way to the company room.

"Sister, you ought to see what she's done to the comp'ny room." Aunt Loma was jealous, I could tell. Listening to her,

I felt jealous myself—for Granny's sake, I mean. Granny used to talk about fixing things nice but never had the time or the money, either one. Loma said the board walls in there were painted a bright yellow, and everything else was white: mantelpiece, door and window frames, iron bed, night stand, dresser, wardrobe, wicker chair—all white. There were ruffledy yellow and brown checked curtains at the windows and the same cloth was on the ceiling, glued up there like wallpaper.

Mama hooted. "Cloth on the ceiling? Who ever heard of paperin' with cloth!"

"I have to admit, it looks right nice," said Loma. "I ast her did Pa do all the paintin'. She said, 'Where would he find the time? I painted it myself.' Said she liked to paint. 'That's man's work,' I told her. I couldn't hep it; I said, 'Love Simpson, you remind me of a crowin' hen.' Well, anyhow, Sister, she's put Ma's tulip quilt on her bed. And she's got that little yellow, orange, and brown plaited rug beside the bed—the one Grandmother Toy made. And Ma's 'Yard of Yellow Roses' picture is hangin' over the mantelpiece. I told her, 'I want that picture. Miss Pearl Lozier copied it for Ma and I want it.'"

"What did she say?"

"She didn't answer, so I just let it go. I'll ast Pa for it later. I tried to remember that I was down there to be nice, pay a Christian call. So I inquired politely about the tintypes and photographs on the dresser. Who they were, I mean. One was her mother, and one was an old lady who raised her. A cousin, I think. At least she hadn't put out a picture of her Union Army daddy for Pa to have to look at. Well, Sister, then I spied a stirrup under the bed! I figured the silver saddle must be under there! But just as I bent down to look, Love said, 'Let's go back to the parlor where we can sit down.' Going across the hall with the lamp, she said, 'I have no family at all now. They're all dead.'"

Mama blew out a breath. "Well, that's a relief."

Back in the parlor with nobody talking, Loma had had time

to consider the situation. "The more I thought about it," she told us, "the madder I got. I mean the way she has just taken over. All of a sudden I said to her, 'Love Simpson, I cain't hep sayin' you sure got your nerve, movin' Ma's rooms around like this.' Camp said, 'Loma's right, Miss Love.' You know what Love said to him, Sister? She said, 'Campbell Williams, it's not your place to tell me anything.' I said he had more right to speak out in the fam'ly than she did. She said, 'Not in my house.' I said maybe it was her house, but it was still Pa's home. Boy, that shut her up."

Then Aunt Loma told Miss Love there were some things she wanted. "Things of Ma's. I don't mean old clothes and letters and ragged quilts like you sent over. I mean—" She almost lost her nerve, she told us, but had barged on. "I'm talkin' about things like the piano. I want the piano."

If she had said she wanted the whole house, I bet Miss Love wouldn't of been more shocked. "Why in the world would you want the piano, Loma? You don't play!"

"That don't keep me from wantin' it. Every house needs a piano."

"Well, you can't have it. I'm sorry."

"I'll ast Pa for it. He'll give it to me. He gives me anything I want."

"Go on, ask him! It won't do you any good." Miss Love was trembling, she was so mad. But she calmed down some and said, nice enough, "But maybe there's something else you want, Loma. Anything I can't use, you're welcome to it."

There was a silence till Uncle Camp spoke up. "She wants that mirror," he said timid, pointing behind the loveseat where "Saint Cecilia at the Organ" had been leaned against the wall.

"Shut up, Camp," Loma said. "I'm not go'n ast her for anything. I'll ast Pa."

"He'll just tell you to ask me," said Miss Love. It was too bad she hadn't made it clear that day at the store that Grandpa deeded her the furniture, too. She proceeded to make it clear to Aunt Loma now. "Maybe you don't know I own everything in this house."

Aunt Loma said she stood up so fast that the rocking chair nearly turned over backwards. Camp stood up, too, and so did Miss Love. "I ast her, 'Have you got that in writin', Love Simpson?'"

Miss Love said coldly, "Are you telling me your father would go back on his word?" Then she went over and pulled out the Saint Cecilia mirror. "Here, Camp, take this. I hate it. But, Loma, over my dead body you'll get the piano!"

And that's how the second Mrs. Blakeslee, alias Love Simpson, declared war on the family.

30

THE next morning I was sitting in Miss Love's kitchen, eating hot apple pie and cheese and hoping she wouldn't pick a fuss with me like she had with everybody else. If she did, or if she got to raving on about Cold Sassy treating her bad, I was go'n say, "Ma'am, I just remembered. Papa told me to paint the iron fence today. I better get on home." If she brought up that mess about keeping her maiden name, I'd say, "I reckon you got a right to, Miss Love. But it's foolish if you care a hoot about Cold Sassy acceptin' you as Grandpa's wife—or his housekeeper, either one."

I didn't get a chance to see if my nerve would hold up to my indignation, because she was just nice as you please. Besides that big piece of pie, she fixed me a glass of lemonade and some for herself, and sat down to talk. She asked right off how was the camping trip, which made me uneasy, I tell you.

"We had a swell time," I said. Taking a big slurp of lemonade, I changed the subject. "You sure make good lemonade, Miss Love."

"Well, I've got plenty. Help yourself."

"One time I ast Queenie why she drinks tea out of a quart Mason jar instead of a glass, and you know what she said? Said, 'Mr. Will, dat fust glassful always be's de bestis, so I makes it jes' big as I can.'" I laughed the way white folks always do when they tell something funny a colored person said.

Miss Love laughed, too. Then she said, "But of course you know the real truth about that, Will."

"What you mean?" My pie fork paused in midair on its way to my mouth.

"I mean colored cooks know white people don't want them using their dishes and things. That's why they all drink out of jars and eat out of old plates or pie pans."

"Ma'am?"

"Well, does Queenie use the same plates as the family?"

"Course not, Miss Love. It ain't the custom."

"And what's Queenie's joke about that?"

The color rose to my face. Clearly Miss Love didn't understand. Despite she wasn't exactly a Yankee, she was from way north of Cold Sassy. Before I could change the subject, she said, "Queenie uses an old knife and fork at your house, too, doesn't she, Will? And always washes them and her pan and her jar last—just before the dog and cat dishes? That's the custom, isn't it?"

"Queenie doesn't care what she eats out of, Miss Love. No more'n she cares if pot licker runs off of the turnip salad and soaks her biscuits, or if the cream gravy gets all over her mashed sweet potatoes. She likes usin' a pan. It holds more'n a plate." Being an outsider, Miss Love couldn't understand that Queenie really just didn't care. *Yankee*, I thought, burning. *Yankee, Yankee. . . .*

It was a hot day, but there came a chill in the air as I finished my pie. Miss Love chopped up two big carrots and put them in her apron pocket, along with some shriveled little yellow apples out of Granny's bowl on the work table. Then she reached into Granny's old brown crock for some sugar lumps.

She tossed me one.

I wasn't a child. She couldn't make up to me with a dern

sugar lump. "I'll save it for the horse," I mumbled, dropping it in a pocket of my overalls.

Miss Love took a green print sunbonnet of Granny's from a nail in the kitchen and we headed for the barn. Old T.R. sprang up from under Granny's boxwood, where he'd been cooling off, and ran ahead of us to chase Granny's dominecker hens out of the path. I didn't say a word all the way to the barn.

"Look, there he is!" Miss Love pointed to the gelding. He was cropping grass in the back pasture not far from Grandpa's mule. Mr. Beautiful raised his head and stared at us, and Miss Love squeezed my arm. "He's just so handsome, Will—that shiny black coat, and the white blaze on his forehead! And look how he holds his head!" I don't think she even noticed she had touched me, but the pit of my stomach might near flipped over.

Looking towards us, the horse sniffed the wind, started walking, then quickly picked up his gait to a fast trot. As he got near the barn, he shied at a rock in the grass, stumbled, rared up, and raced away, tail arched high. But he was soon back, nickering and snorting as he pranced sideways towards the pasture gate we were leaning on. Then he shot off again like an arrow.

Miss Love put her hands to her mouth, as if she couldn't believe him. She said softly, "That's got to be the fastest horse in Cold Sassy. Maybe the fastest in Georgia. . . ."

"Yes'm." Pride rose up in me for being the one that had brought him to her.

Every time the gelding came near, Miss Love held out a piece of carrot. Finally he stopped, walked slowly toward her, stopped again, came closer, and, glistening with sweat, stretched his neck to get the carrot. His breathing was hard. "Come here, Mr. Beautiful, I won't hurt you. Here, baby," she murmured, holding out an apple.

"Boy howdy, I cain't hardly wait to see that fancy Texas saddle on him!" I said. She blushed, as if she thought the saddle might remind me how she'd kissed Clayton McAllister. I blushed, too, because it did remind me of that. I said quickly, "Ma'am, I hope you ain't forgot. That horse ain't broke to anything but a halter. You won't try to ride him any time soon, will you?"

"I wish I dared. But no, I'm still just making friends. Here, boy," she called, walking along the fence.

"A big horse like him, he could kill you."

She met my eyes with her gray-blue ones and the long dark lashes didn't even flutter. She said, "Mr. McAllister taught me all about training horses, Will. It's done in definite stages. I helped him train the mare that was"—she hesitated—"the mare that was to be mine after we married. The one the saddle was made for."

Yeah, I thought, and I bet you kissed Mr. McAllister between every sugar lump and apple, and hugged him every time the mare did what you wanted her to. I hated Mr. McAllister.

I wished Miss Love would touch me again.

She didn't. It was the horse she kept touching. She rubbed his ears and his neck, talking soft and holding tight to the halter. Soon as she let him go, he was off again across the pasture.

We watched him a few minutes, then walked back towards the house. We were about even with Granny's flower pit when I stopped and asked the question that had been on my mind ever since I got there. "Does Grandpa know . . . I mean did anybody tell him about, uh, about the way Mr. McAllister, uh—"

There was an empty minute before she came right out with it. "Kissed me?" Her face was hidden under the bonnet, so I don't know if she blushed. But I did. "As a matter of fact, Will, somebody did tell Mr. Blakeslee."

"It wasn't me, Miss Love, I swear. Must of been Miss Effie Belle."

"Maybe she did. I don't know. But I told him first."

"You?" I couldn't believe any lady was that dumb. I said I bet he'd already heard.

She waved a honeybee away from her face. "No. This was

on Saturday night after Mr. McAllister was here. And if he had heard, he'd have said so as soon as he got home. Your grandfather is a very direct man, Will."

"Yes'm, he is."

"Still, I kept thinking what if he does know. I got nervous as a witch, wondering. But all he talked about at supper was the horse. Which stall it could have, which day you might get back with it, things like that. And he asked what did I know about breaking a horse. I could see he didn't know one thing about it himself."

"When did you tell him, Miss Love? About—you know."

"At one o'clock Sunday morning. We both went to bed early, but I just tossed and turned. I was so nervous I thought I'd scream. Finally I decided my only hope was to be honest and tell him myself, before you . . . I mean before Miss Effie Belle did, or somebody else."

"You called him out of bed? He don't like—"

"I just went to his door. It was open—for the breeze, you know. I stood there holding my lamp and called, 'Mr. Blakeslee?' He said, 'What you want? What's wrong?' So I told him how Mr. McAllister had barged in and was kissing me before I knew what was happening—and that Miss Effie Belle probably saw it. I said I'd pack up and leave as soon as it got light."

I kicked my bare foot at a bunch of tall grass. I had a glimmer of something I didn't like. Sounding bolder than I felt, I said, "Why'd you offer to leave, Miss Love? I thought you were hopin' if you were honest about it, he'd let you stay."

"Well, yes, Will." A wry little smile lit her face. "But I guess I thought I should at least offer to leave."

"Did you cry, ma'am?"

I think she sensed what I was driving at. Hesitating, she admitted she cried a little.

"What'd Grandpa say?"

"Nothing, for a minute. Then he told me to go to bed. 'Mr. McAllister's on the train to Texas, Miss Love, so that's the end of it. Effie Belle or no Effie Belle.' Then he raised up on his elbow and said, 'Now if'n you want to see me mad, Miss Love, jest let me git up for breakfast and you ain't made me no yeast bread like I ast you to.'"

We both laughed, ambling on towards the house. She said, "Tell the truth, I had forgotten all about making that bread. I was . . . well, it had been an awful day, as you know, Will, and I was worn out. But I went to the kitchen and got at it."

"In the middle of the night?"

"Yes. The oven was still warm from supper, so I mixed the dough and set it in there to rise. About three o'clock I got up to knead it, and at five I fired up the stove. I had the bread baked and toast ready when Mr. Blakeslee came in to breakfast."

I had to admire any lady that anxious to please.

Well, in all of that talking, Miss Love hadn't mentioned me gossiping about her on the camping trip, or her being taken off of the Methodist piano stool, or how she told off Pink Predmore's mama down at the store. She hadn't spoken Aunt Loma's name, much less Saint Cecilia's. But she'd told me the one thing I needed to hear if I was to keep coming up here: that Grandpa knew about her kissing Mr. McAllister. As long as I was wondering whether he knew or didn't, I'd of been worrying about what he might do to Miss Love when and if he found out, and how she would act toward me if she thought I was the one had told him.

On the back porch, she picked up the tin dipper that floated in the well bucket and started to drink.

"Here, I'll draw you some fresh, Miss Love," I said, emptying the bucket into the wash pan. With the well right up by the porch, I only had to lean over to let the bucket down. When I heard it splash, I turned the crank to draw it up and, feeling that I was being what Aunt Loma called gallant, offered Miss Love the first cool drink.

"Why, thank you, Will." She drank from the dipper, then

poured her leavings on a pot of begonias. "And thank you for being my friend."

Gosh, Miss Love sure knew how to make a boy feel like a man. Dipping up some water, I was careful to put my mouth where hers had been. I watched her over the rim of tin.

She hesitated as if trying to think of something to say, then asked, "Tell me, Will, uh, don't you think your mother will go on to New York City after all?"

"No'm. She ain't go'n go," I said as we left the porch and entered the cool hall. "She planned big on it all spring, you know. But not since Granny died."

"Are you very sure she won't change her mind? It would do her good to get away from here." Miss Love really cared about Mama, I could tell.

"Yes'm, I'm certain sure. Papa keeps tryin' to talk her into it, but she won't change her mind. She says it wouldn't be fittin'. Uh, I expect you been plenty times, ain't you, Miss Love? New York ain't all that far from Baltimore."

"I went just once. When I was a little girl." She smiled kind of wistful.

I reckon Miss Love was pure starved for company, because when we got to the front veranda, she sat down in the swing, patted the cushion beside her, and said come sit a while. "You went to New York with your daddy one time, didn't you, Will?"

"Yes'm, when I was seven, and I sure was glad to get back home. I'd heard about damnyankees all my life, and up there I was in a city just full of'm."

Miss Love really laughed.

"I been on lots of other trips with Papa," I bragged. "When I was ten, he took me to Atlanta just to ride a new street-car line to College Park and back. Another time we went to Atlanta to hear President Roosevelt. The speaking was in a place called Piedmont Park. Afterwards we took a street car to Davison-Paxon-Stokes Company, and then went to M. Rich and Brothers. You ever been in that store, Miss Love?"

"Oh, yes. They have very fashionable clothes."

"Yes'm. Well, while we stood outside lookin' at their show window, a man dressed up in a Sunday suit came out and greeted us. Then he opened the door wide, bowed to Papa with a big flourish, and said, 'Enter, sir! The store is yours!' It was Mr. Rich himself. Later I ast Papa why didn't he and Grandpa dress nice like that to go to work, and do like that. Bow, I mean, and open the door and say, 'Enter, sir, the store is yours.' Papa said, ''Cause if we did, Cold Sassy would think we were off in the head.'"

Miss Love was very entertained. "I guess you've been lots of places with your grandpa, too," she said, rubbing a chain link on the swing with her finger.

"No'm. He took me and Mary Toy to Maysville one time in the buggy to visit Aunt Fody, his youngest sister. The year he went to the Homer Celebration he took me, and since we were already halfway to Cornelia, we went on to see Aunt Clyde, his oldest sister. But Grandpa don't really like to go places. Last time he went to Atlanta was to General John B. Gordon's funeral, and that was two or three years ago. General Gordon was a Confederate general, you know."

"Well, your grandfather is so full of fun, I expect he has a grand time when he goes to New York for the store."

"I don't know'm. He ain't been since before you moved here. He feels about it like me; they got too many Yankees in New York. He said one time he'd just soon go to the bad place. That's why Papa's always the one goes on the buyin' trips."

I didn't find out till next morning that Miss Love wasn't just passing the time of day talking about New York City. She'd had an idea. An idea that just about tore our family to pieces.

31

WITH no inkling of what was to come, I left there on top of the world. I just had to do something, for gosh sake. So I decided to go apologize to Aunt Loma like Grandpa told me to. Not that I was regretting those titty stories. I was just in the mood to enjoy hearing Aunt Loma fuss and fume.

Every now and again she didn't react like I thought she would—for instance, that time she got Papa to make me paint her dining room. After I finished, I caught about ten of her cats, dipped their feet in the can of gold paint, and chased them around in the empty room. Boy howdy, the floor in there looked like a dern leopard skin! I expected Aunt Loma would be furious, but she said what a darlin' idea. Thought I'd done it to please her.

Well, she wouldn't be clapping her hands about the *pssssssssssst* and pig stories, which by now would be coming at her from every direction. She'd like folks saying what a bad boy I was, and how dirty-mouthed, but it would get her goat when they asked, "Loma, did you really nurse a pig?"

Her not fussing at me yesterday at Sunday dinner didn't mean she hadn't heard. She was just too busy low-rating Miss Love to fool with me. And last night she was too upset over not getting the piano.

And now as I came up on her back porch, Aunt Loma was the maddest white woman you ever saw. Her face was red. Her blue eyes spat fire. Her fists were clenched and her voice harsh. "I'm so mad I could die, Will!" That was her greeting. Boy howdy, I thought. But it wasn't me she was mad at. She said, "Come look what Camp's done now!"

Jerking up Campbell Junior from the kitchen floor, where he sat sucking a greasy chicken bone, Aunt Loma marched ahead of me to the parlor and pointed at the mantelpiece, gleaming with a new coat of hard shiny white enamel paint. "Just look!" she exploded.

"What's wrong, Aunt Loma? I think it's a big improvement."

"Go look. You'll see."

I looked and I saw. Without wiping off the mantelpiece at all, Uncle Camp had painted around a tin matchbox and right over a cockroach, a pencil stub, and a shirt button.

Trying not to laugh, I said, "Why didn't you make him get it up before the paint dried? Ain't nothin' harder than enamel paint."

"I only just noticed it, that's why."

"It's go'n be a job to scrape it off."

"I don't want it scraped off. I want Camp to be reminded how dumb he is every time he comes in this parlor. Will, I cain't bear to think I'm married to somebody that stupid."

"He ain't that stupid," I said, trying to make her feel better.

"Then he just don't care, and that's worse."

"Maybe he did it on purpose."

"You're crazy. He wouldn't have the nerve."

"Maybe he ain't got any nerve when you get to fussin' at him, Aunt Loma. But that don't mean he couldn't do this on purpose."

Her face flushed. She knew I was calling her bossy. "You know good'n'well if I didn't keep after him, he wouldn't ever do a blessed thing."

"Yeah, but that don't mean he likes bein' pushed around. And maybe for once he's showin' it. I feel right proud of him, Aunt Loma. Maybe you ought to be, too."

"Well, aren't you smart! I guess you got that notion from Miss Love Simpson Blakeslee. I'll thank her to keep her mouth shut, especially to you."

"Ain't nobody ever said nothin' out loud bout you hen-peckin' Uncle Camp, Aunt Loma. It don't take much brains to notice, though. If you treated a colored cook like you do him, she'd quit."

"Colored folks got more sense than Camp. Lord, Will, I had to show him the roach before he knew what I was mad about."

I would of laid a bet that when she got on him about it, Camp had looked down at the floor instead of at the mantel-piece. I bet he said, "I'm sorry, Loma Baby. I'm sorry."

I hated how he was and how she treated him.

"Grandpa said I had to apologize about those stories I told on you, Aunt Loma. So I'm apologizin'."

"Pa told you to?"

"Yeah, he did."

She looked real pleased. "Well, now! I never thought he'd take up for me against you, Will."

"He was mad as heck about it, tell you the truth. So I'm sorry. And soon as you finish bawlin' me out, I got to go."

She set the baby down on a plaited cotton rug by the fire-place and spoke sternly. "All right, I'll bawl you out: How dare you say I nursed a pig!" Then she giggled. "Will, you're awful. You ought to be ashamed. But my land, I haven't enjoyed any-thing this much since I left LaGrange College. It's almost like playin' the lead in a theatrical. Campbell Junior, come out of the fireplace! Get him, Will. He'll turn black before our eyes if he gets into that chimney sut."

I picked the fat baby up and swung him around. He squealed with pleasure. "You're your mama's little piggy, ain't you, Camp-

bell Junior?" I held him high above my head and he squealed
again. "So part of what I told wasn't no pig tale." Aunt Loma
laughed. It was like we were having a party. I put Campbell
Junior on my shoulder and rode him around, then tossed
him up.

"Will, I've decided. . . . Will, are you listenin'? Put the baby
down and listen to me."

"I'm listenin'." I tossed him one more time and put him back
on the floor.

"I've decided you ought to be a writer, Will. Those stories
you told on me, they're outlandish, but they'd be so easy to act
out. Those and all the other stories you tell. Will, I want you to
write plays." She said it as solemn as if she was a queen knight-
ing me with words.

I couldn't hide how pleased I was. I grinned from ear to ear.
Still and all, why couldn't Aunt Loma just be nice and compli-
ment me and let it go at that without saying what I had to be.
Long as I could remember, she'd been trying to direct me like
I was one of her dad-gum Christmas pageants.

It gave me some satisfaction to say "But I'm go'n be a farmer.
You know that, Aunt Loma, unless you ain't ever listened to
me talk. I'm go'n go to the Ag College over at the University.
Papa's aimin' to buy Grandpa Tweedy's farm, and I'm go'n
farm it."

"Anybody can be a farmer," she said, flipping away my
dream. "We cain't let a talent like yours go to waste, Will, and
I want you to start by putting down those stories you made
up about me. Do it right away, before you forget them." She
blushed a little. "I don't mean I think you could sell'm. They're
too—well, most editors would call them vulgar. But they'll do
fine for writing practice."

If I had pos-i-tive-ly decided to be a writer and at that moment had picked up a pencil to get started, I'd of put it down.
I just couldn't stand her telling me what to do. "I don't like to
write stories," I said stubbornly. "I just like tellin' stories. But

ain't nobody go'n make me do either one. Specially not you, Loma Blakeslee Williams."

Campbell Junior was crawling from her to me and back from me to her, but Aunt Loma didn't even notice him. All of a sudden she stood up and started singing, "Here comes the bride, dog bite her hide." We had sung it like that when we were children. Then she *dum-dummed* the rest of the wedding march. I didn't guess what she was doing till she made like she was adjusting a veil and mouthed I do and all, and then went *pssssssssssst*. Her eyes rolled with mock alarm and her hands quickly hid one side of her chest. Then she doubled up laughing. I was laughing, too. Campbell Junior must of thought we were a couple of hyenas.

"How in the . . . world . . . did you think up such a . . . thing as a . . . *rubber bust!*" She couldn't talk for ha-ha-ing and hee-hee-ing.

I was shocked that Aunt Loma had come right out and said *bust* in mixed company, but that just made it funnier. Between guffaws and gasps we moaned and clutched our stomachs. The poor baby sat staring at us, then dropped his chicken bone and commenced squalling. To her credit, Aunt Loma picked him up, sat down in the rocker, and unbuttoned her dress for him. I always watched close when she did that, hoping she'd be careless, but she never was. Like all the other nursing ladies in Cold Sassy, Aunt Loma would turn sideways to her audience or else cover herself with the baby, and also drape a clean diaper over herself.

I got up to go, but she told me to wait till she could put Campbell Junior down for his nap. She hummed the wedding march while she rocked him, only sometimes she had to press her lips together to keep from laughing out loud. "Is there any such a thing, Will?"

"As what?"

"As . . . well, you know. If there is, I sure wish I'd heard about it in time for my weddin'!" And we both died laughing again.

Except it was quiet laughing, so as not to distract the baby from nursing. In a few minutes she sat him up and he let out a loud belch.

"I really got to go, Aunt Loma."

"Oh, you can wait another minute. I got something for you." She laid Campbell Junior down on the rug by the fireplace, a clean diaper under his fat face, and he was asleep by time she came back downstairs, carrying a thick book.

"I made this before Campbell Junior was born." She flipped open the book, which had cloth-covered cardboard covers and blank pages inside. "I was go'n copy all my poems and plays in it. But as you know I never have a minute to call my own now." Her voice a little hard, she nodded towards the sleeping baby. "So I want you to have it, Will."

This was the nearest Aunt Loma had come to being nice since I was a little bitty boy, and I liked it, despite I also felt like she was trying to railroad me. When I hesitated, she held the book out to me. "You must write something in it every day." She nodded to cement her words. "Write down the stories you make up. Write poems and plays. Write down things that happen, and surprising things you see or hear about. Listen when people talk, and put their words down just like they speak. If you go'n be a writer, you got to practice, that's all there is to it. My professors preached that to me all the time at LaGrange College." Aunt Loma never missed a chance to mention La-Grange College, where she had studied elocution and expression.

"Well . . ." I took the book and flipped through the blank pages, then handed it back. "But I done told you, I ain't go'n be no writer. You be one."

"Fat chance," she said, bitter. "Camp won't ever be able to afford a cook. Not while he's workin' for Pa. And I cain't write without hep. I know that now. So you just do what I say, Will. Quit arguin'. Here, read this." Opening it to the first page, she forced the book into my hands again. "Look at this."

At the top of the page, in fancy printing, it said LOMA BLAKESLEE WILLIAMS, HER BOOK. Under that it said PRE-SENTED TO HOYT WILLIS TWEEDY, JULY 1906. "Do like I say, Will. And when you get famous, don't forget to mention it was your Aunt Loma that pushed you towards your destiny."

Bossy, same old bossy, I thought. But I was touched. And all of a sudden those empty pages were like the si-rene call I'd heard when I looked up at Blind Tillie Trestle and wanted to see how it was up there. I knew I wouldn't write any dang po-etry or plays. But right that minute I got the notion I'd like to keep a journal.

It's been eight years since Loma gave me that book, and not long ago I read through all I wrote down on its blank pages. That's why I can remember so much that happened to Miss Love and Grandpa, and what went on in the family and the town, and what people said and how they said it, and how I felt when it was happening. Reading my notes in the journal brings it all back.

I never knew before that Aunt Loma could be fun to be with—that, like Grandpa and me, she preferred three-legged chickens to the usual kind. What really surprised me was find-ing out I liked her. At least, that day I did. She was Grandpa all over again. She was hardheaded like him, wanted her own way like him, and had a sense of fun to match his. But of course she was mean and vindictive in a way Grandpa wasn't. At least that's what I thought right then.

Not till the next morning, when the matter of the trip to New York came to a head, did I suspect he had a mean streak that put Loma's in the shade.

32

I WAS still laughing in my mind at supper that night, like if Aunt Loma was there beside me going *pssssssssssst*.

Then Mama asked about the trip to New York City. "What day is it you are leaving, Hoyt?" In her black cotton dress she looked like warmed-over despair.

"Two weeks from today, hon." As Mama cut a bite of roast beef, looking pitiful, Papa reached across the table and put his hand on her hand that held the knife. "Mary Willis, hon, come with me. It'd be . . . well, like a second honeymoon."

She blushed, but looked him straight in the eye. "I wish I could, Hoyt. It sure hasn't been any honeymoon around here for a long time." She bit her lip, I guess to keep from saying anything against Grandpa or Miss Love that would upset my daddy. Then she kind of jerked, like people do at church trying to shake themselves awake. "You know I cain't go, Hoyt. It would scandalize the town."

Thinking with my mouth again, I said, "Mama, how could Cold Sassy be any more scandalized than it is already?"

Oh, for gosh sake, why did I have to say that?

But Papa took it up. "I say the same thing, Mary Willis. Please, hon, come with me, hear."

It seemed like Mama was weakening.

"Granny would want you to," I urged. "Not long before she took sick, she told me how happy she was about you gettin' this nice trip."

"Did she really say that, Will?" Quick tears came to Mama's eyes.

What Granny had also said, so wistful, was how she used to dream of going to New York with Grandpa, but he never saw why she wanted to. Granny said he always talked like it was just a long, tiring, boring time. Besides, he couldn't afford to pay her way and his, too.

"I couldn't get ready in two weeks," Mama was saying. "All those clothes I made back in the spring, they wouldn't do now. I'd need mournin' clothes. All I got for nice is two black dresses."

"That's all you need," said Papa, getting excited. "There's so many people up in New York, you could wear the same dress every day and nobody'd notice."

"Well, I'd notice and the hotel clerk."

"Listen, hon, I could buy you a readymade dress or two after we get up there. Get'm wholesale."

All of a sudden, Mama's face went from looking like nine miles of bad road to like somebody had left her a million dollars. "Oh, Hoyt, do you really think it would be all right?" she asked anxiously. "People wouldn't talk?"

"They might," he admitted, drinking the last of his buttermilk. "But Lord, Mary Willis, everybody knows what you been through lately. And it ain't like we'd be havin' a good time or anything. Still and all, there's enough to see and do up there to make goin' worthwhile. Ain't it, Will? You were so little when you and me went, though, maybe you don't remember much."

"I remember a lot, Papa."

"And Mary Toy's taken care of," he reminded Mama. "So all you got to do is get ready. Please say you'll come with me, hon."

Mama hesitated, then all of a sudden smiled and, clasping

her hands together, raised them and touched her thumbs to her forehead—a way she had of showing when she was happy. "I've decided! I'm go'n go, Hoyt! I'm go'n go!"

My daddy jumped up out of his chair, came around the table with his arms outstretched, grabbed Mama out of her chair, and kissed her hard. It wasn't like Mr. McAllister kissing Miss Love, but it wasn't the usual peck, either.

As we left the table, Mama asked him, "Hoyt, what do you think about—uh, do you reckon I could ast Miss Love to make me a new black hat? I don't want you to be shamed of me."

"Sure, ast her," said Papa. "Like I keep tellin' you and Loma, she's a nice lady. I know Miss Love, see. She'd be proud to hep you get off. And it might heal things over in the fam'ly."

I joined in. "Miss Love said just today how it would do you good to take the trip."

Mama looked surprised, but was too happy to say *aw shah*.

Next morning at breakfast she was downright ecstatic. "I didn't sleep a wink, Hoyt! Just laid there turnin' over and over in my mind what I'll pack and what all I got to do. My tail will be in the wind from now till we leave, I know that. First thing, I got to write Temp a postcard and be sure it's all right for Mary Toy to stay on till we get back."

"Maybe we could go see Mary Toy next Sunday," said Papa, sopping up sorghum syrup with his biscuit. "I miss my baby."

"I do, too, but I'm not sure we have time. Besides all the gettin' ready, I got to can some vegetables. If I don't, we'll lose too much. Goodness gracious, two weeks from now I may be too tired to go!" But despite Mama had a lot to worry about, there was a smile on her plain face and a light in her blue eyes that we hadn't seen in weeks.

Right after Papa left for the store, here came Grandpa Blakeslee.

As usual, he headed straight for the company room. His snort must of been pretty strong, judging by the redness of his face when he came out, calling, "Mary Willis? Mary Willis! Where you at? I got something to say."

Mama hurried down the stair steps, wearing a bright smile and carrying her nicest petticoats and nightgowns to hang out for airing. I knew she could hardly wait to tell Grandpa the good news. But before she got a word out, he said, "Mary Willis, since you cain't go to New York with Hoyt, I done decided to go myself. And I'm a-go'n take Miss Love. Ain't no use lettin' thet other free boat ticket go to waste."

Mama looked like a farmer seeing his barn burst into flames. While she stood there trying not to believe her ears, Grandpa said, "Miss Love thinks she can be a big hep in New York. She's go'n pick out the housewares and dress goods, and the ladies' ready-to-wear and all like thet."

"What, Pa?"

He raised his voice. "I said Miss Love thinks she can pick out what ladies want to buy better than a man can. Makes sense, her bein' fashionable and all. Anyhow, Mary Willis, I know Hoyt's go'n be glad not to go. He's been mighty worried bout leavin' you here by yoreself, grievin' for yore ma."

My mother didn't say a word. Just stood there staring at him, and then turned and took her petticoats back upstairs.

I followed Grandpa out the door. Before I could speak, though, he scratched his head hard and fast, like a dog scratching fleas, and said, "I ain't lookin' forward to New York, son, but Cold Sassy's been a-givin' Miss Love a hard time. I figger the trip'll take her mind off a-all thet mess."

"But Mama was—"

"I cain't live with thangs in sech a stew."

He was walking away when I said, "But Grandpa, Miss Love's got the horse. She's so excited about the horse. She don't even care what folks say anymore."

"Thet's what I thought, too, Will Tweedy." He stopped and looked at me. "But last night Miss Love was jest all to pieces.

She got to cryin' agin bout thet fuss she had with Miz Pred-more while you was gone, son, and said maybe she ought of went on to Texas so I could git some peace. And then it come to her all a-sudden thet her and me could go to New York on them boat passes. Git away for a spell. Now as you know, I ain't much on New York City. But I knowed yore ma warn't go'n change her mind and yore daddy had jest soon not go 'thout her. So when Miss Love kept a-beggin' me, I . . . well, I jest cain't stand to see no woman carry on like thet. I said we'd go if'n she could go cheap and not plan to stay at no fancy ho-tel."

Grandpa plopped his hat on and stalked off before I could tell him that Mama was the one crying now.

It was all my fault. Miss Love had questioned me, trying to make certain sure Mama wasn't going before she put on her act for Grandpa. Well, I'd go tell her how it was, that's what I'd do. She was so kind and understanding, I was sure she wouldn't stand in the way of Mama going.

I was right.

When I got there, Miss Love was in the kitchen at the wash table, scouring pans. Her face was more freckledy than usual, I reckon from being out with the horse, and she'd pulled her hair back in a tight knot. She didn't look pretty. I blurted it right out, how just last night Mama decided to go to New York with Papa after all, "only now Grandpa says you and him are go'n go."

She looked stunned. Her hands were sudsy from the dish-water but she didn't rinse or dry them before plonking herself down at the kitchen table. Her wet fists clenched and a hard look came on her face as the disappointment sunk in. Then she calmed down and said sweetly, "Will, I feel terrible about this. Your mother must go, by all means. She needs to get away. Anyhow, it's her trip."

"I was sure you'd say that, Miss Love, once you knew how it

was!" I could hardly wait to run home and tell Mama. When I was halfway out the door, Miss Love asked me what Grandpa said when he found out that Mama had decided to go.

"He don't know yet. Mama didn't tell him."

She seemed surprised. Giving a long sigh, she said, "Then I'll tell him at dinner. This was all his idea, you know. He said Mary Willis definitely wasn't going and it was a pity to waste a free boat ticket. You know how frugal he is. Well, he'll certainly want your mother to have the trip."

It struck me how different her explanation of how it came about was from what Grandpa said. I guess she was just too proud to admit to me how it had got to her, the way Cold Sassy was treating her. The important thing, Miss Love wanted to do right by Mama, just like I knew she would.

There's no way she could of guessed that Mama would say, "No, let Love go on to New York. Let her have a good time. It don't matter about me." Miss Love was just sorry as could be when neither Papa nor I nor Aunt Loma could talk Mama into going.

Aunt Loma was really furious about it. Soon as she heard —Camp told her when he came home to dinner that day— she rushed over home and ran upstairs, where Mama was crying in her room. Speaking so loud I could hear her from the downstairs hall, Loma said, "Sister, you cain't let Love Simpson go off like that with Pa! You know good'n'well she'll hope to come back with more than the latest in housewares and dress goods."

Mama mumbled something into her pillow.

"She'll try to get you-know-what, that's what I'm talkin' about. Pa won't pay for two rooms at the hotel and Love knows it. She's prob'ly been tryin' ever since their weddin' day to get him into her bed. This is her chance!"

"Loma, hush up!" cried Mama.

"I mean just what I'm sayin'. And, Sister, if That Woman has a baby, you know good'n'well she'll get her hooks on a whole lot more of Pa's money than she bargained with him for. Sister, you got to go to New York!"

"Well, I'm not. I don't even want to go now. I don't even feel like goin'."

Still and all, if Aunt Loma had kept her mouth shut, Mama might of had her trip. She didn't have a gnat's chance after Loma stormed into the store and gave her daddy down the country, blessing him out right in front of Papa, Uncle Camp, me, and two customers.

Grandpa let her rave till she shouted, "Pa, Love Simpson has earned the disrespect of everybody in town. And now she's go'n get everything she can out of you, startin' with New York City! But you, Pa, you're too blind to see!"

Grandpa held up his hand like a policeman—to stop her or slap her, I couldn't tell which—and shouted, "Good gosh a'mighty, Loma, ain't none a-this any a-yore dang bizness! Now go on home and be-have!"

Then he turned to my daddy and said in a harsh voice, "Hoyt, I wisht I'd a-knowed last night thet Mary Willis done changed her mind. But now it's jest too late."

I didn't see why it was too late.

I bet Papa felt like crying, or like knocking Grandpa to Kingdom Come and back, and Loma with him. But all he said was, "It's all right, Mr. Blakeslee. I'm sure Mary Willis understands."

Furious, I went back to the storage room to finish ripping open a crate of canned Alaska salmon. A few minutes later Grandpa yelled, "Will Tweedy? You come here, boy!"

As I soon found out, anger at me had been festering in him ever since yesterday, and Aunt Loma's fit brought it to a head. Standing behind the counter, he spoke sternly as I came towards him. "Will Tweedy, ain't I always treated you special?"

"Yessir?"

"Then how come, if'n you aim to be a dang farmer stead a-comin' in the store with me, how come you told it to a dang fool like Lias Foster? You ain't said pea-turkey to me bout it—you or yore daddy, either one. How you think it felt yesterd'y when I went to braggin' bout you takin' over the store some day and thet fool contradicted me? This here store's made a livin' for me and yore daddy, too, boy, and lots a-other folks. You think you go'n make a better livin' farmin'?"

"No, sir, that ain't it."

"Well, then maybe you think it's something noble to walk behind a dang plow and starve to death on five-cent cotton. Is thet it?"

I looked over at Papa, who was working on the ledger. His face was red as a beet, but he didn't put in a word for me. He was too upset about Mama losing her trip, I reckon, and anyhow he believed in a boy fighting his own battles. Without a word he went outside where the sacks of chicken grits were stacked against the show window and commenced talking to some old men sitting on the bench in the sun. I wished Papa had at least told me what Mr. Lias said I said. Later I found out he hadn't heard what Mr. Lias said I said.

The more Grandpa talked, the madder he got. "Why you want to be a no-count farmer?" he thundered.

"I ain't go'n be no-count, sir. I'm goin' to the Ag College over at the University and study new methods. I'm go'n make farmin' pay."

"I reckon you think I'll give you cheap credit." He said it sarcastic.

"Yessir, I do." I looked him straight in the eye. "Ain't you always talked like I was the same as your own son?"

A proud grin came on his face and his tone softened. "At least you smart enough to know how to get around me. But doggit, Will Tweedy, I thought you liked store work."

"I like bein' here with you, Grandpa. You and Papa." I

couldn't hardly stand it, seeing him let down. "But I'd rather work outdoors, sir. I like makin' things grow. Raisin' animals, gettin' up plants."

I didn't tell him that the reason I first started liking farm work was because I could make fifty cents a day hoeing cotton and fifty cents a hundred pounds picking it, whereas at the store I never even got a thank-you. What I did there was just expected. "Store work ain't excitin', Grandpa. But farmin' is just one great big old dice game. Else why would so many men stay in it, times like these?"

"What else can a farmer do cept farm? And heck fire, boy, you think they ain't no gamble to runnin' a store?"

"Yessir, some. But not much."

"You think it don't matter if'n I order something thet don't sell? Hit ain't gamblin' if'n I order ten ladies' dresses from New York and find out I could a-sold twenty-five? Answer me thet."

"Well, sir, but farmin's for bigger stakes, Grandpa. A ready-made dress or a can of salmon ain't near as big as a bale of cotton or a cow."

That made him laugh. Slapping his knee, he picked up the wholesale order form and I started back to the storage room. Then, with his pencil poised over the form, Grandpa looked up over his reading glasses and asked, "Son, why ain't you said nothin' bout this up to now?"

"I'm always talkin' bout farmin', Grandpa," I said boldly. "Maybe you just ain't been listenin'."

"Well, but you ain't talked bout not comin' in the store."

All of a sudden I didn't feel bold at all. "I reckon I was scared to," I mumbled. "Scared I wouldn't be your boy anymore, Grandpa."

He flushed, and in a gruff voice said, "You ain't old enough to know what in ding-dong you go'n want to do two-three year from now, Will Tweedy. Here I'm willin' to give you a chance in life and you say you don't want it. Gosh a'mighty, how I used to wish somebody'd give me a hand up. I had to make it all on my own, and it's a hard road, son. Well, time you git th'ew high school, you go'n be glad you got a job waitin' for you here at the store. In the meanwhile, don't be talkin' our bizness to Lias Foster."

Grandpa hadn't heard a word I said. He'd put the whole thing down to my being young and foolish and talking big. Like I hadn't said a word, he was still offering me the store, just like Aunt Loma offered me her blank book. Neither one of them cared what I wanted to be. Well, when the time came and somebody had to give in—him, her, or me—it sure dern wasn't going to be me.

Later I wondered if Miss Love had guessed how the fuss about the New York trip would turn out. Because despite she acted so willing to step aside after I told her the situation that morning, and despite it seemed like she took it for granted Mama and Papa would be the ones to go, when I went up there later that day to clean the stable, she had some gray and white striped taffeta cloth spread out on Granny's dining table and was pinning pattern pieces on it.

The pattern envelope said in big letters: TRAVELING DRESS.

She couldn't of known then that her trip was still on, since Grandpa had been too busy to come home to dinner that day and just ate sardines and crackers at the store. So who would of told her she was still going?

It really made me mad.

Still and all, when Miss Love looked at me and said how sweet I was to come clean out the stable for her, I felt almost as glad she was going as I was sorry that Mama wasn't. Cold Sassy really had been awful about her kissing Mr. McAllister.

No telling what they'd say about her going off to New York unchaperoned with a man she claimed she wasn't really married to. But at least she'd be away from the gossip for a while.

Grandpa had sense enough to know what folks were saying.

It was like he'd married Miss Love in the first place as a practical joke and couldn't understand why nobody bragged on him for thinking it up; and now he was furious because Cold Sassy was saying Miss Love stole Mama's trip to New York.

By next morning Grandpa had found a way to thumb his nose at the whole dang town, so pious and hypocritical: he started giving out invites to Sunday morning preachin' at his house.

When Mr. Predmore came in for pipe tobacco, for instance, Grandpa smiled big and friendly and said, "We havin' preachin' and communion agin at my house come Sunday. Miss Love and me, I mean. We'd be mighty proud to have you and yore fam'ly join us." Knowing he was being taunted, Mr. Predmore didn't answer. "Won't cost you a red cent," Grandpa called after him as he stalked out. "We don't pass no dang collection plate."

Uncle Lige whispered to Papa, "Thet in iteself would be a miracle—hearin' a sermon 'thout havin' to pay for it." Cudn Hope laughed, but Papa looked like he'd just heard heresy incarnate.

Showing off for customers, Uncle Lige kept making jokes about miracles, and Grandpa joked back. "Who knows, Lige, might be we'll even turn water into wine, haw! If'n we do, I'll save you some." Then, waving his arm to include several customers in the store, Grandpa called out like a dern circus barker, "Come one, come all y'all! Be glad to have you. We ain't havin' Sunday school, jest singin' and prayin' and preachin'. Miss Love's go'n make ten pound cakes to take care a-the communion crowd." Whacking a slab of cheese off the round for Thurman Osgood, the dwarf, Grandpa wrapped it and said as he handed down the package, "Join us Sunday mornin', son. We go'n have us a good time."

The church people of Cold Sassy, Georgia, didn't look at Sunday morning as the time to have a good time. As Grandpa expected and intended, they took it like he was making fun of

religion, or like he was asking folks to come to a house of ill re-
pute and call it church. People said it looked like Mr. Blakeslee
just wanted to make everybody mad. Which he did.

Mr. Flournoy said he and his wife would come, but most
folks either acted like they didn't hear the invite or else huffed
out of the store without buying a thing.

Finally Papa dared to say "Mr. Blakeslee, folks are mad about
you makin' fun of the Lord's Day. What if they quit buyin'
from us?"

Grandpa just laughed. "Ain't go'n happen. You think anybody's go'n hitch up and ride a buggy all the way to Commerce just for twenty pounds a-sugar or a dime's worth a-nails
at Hardman Hardware or Williford, Burns, and Rice? Naw,
Hoyt. Hit's easy to git mad, but it takes time to go over to
Commerce."

What my daddy didn't see was that Grandpa was madder
than anybody else in Cold Sassy. Grandpa had thought marrying Miss Love was a cheap way to get a white housekeeper
and not be a burden on his daughters, but now the town had
changed her from a nice pleasant milliner into a Mad Hatter
who cried all the time.

33

GRANDPA didn't preach the sermon at his second home church service. He asked Queenie's husband, Loomis, to do it.

Despite all the invites, the congregation didn't swell much that day. Only Mr. and Mrs. Cratic Flournoy came—probably because they liked Miss Love, but also because they liked to sing and couldn't bear the thought of trying to drag through another hymn with Miss Effie Belle feeling her way over the piano. But they claimed later they went to remind Cold Sassy in general and the Methodists in particular that God loves sinners and forgives them, "and we ought to, too."

Cold Sassy thought Grandpa had really stepped out of bounds, asking a Negro preacher to give the sermon. Old Loomis had preached many a one in the white kitchens of Cold Sassy. If he was bringing in stovewood and noticed a silver spoon that was tarnished, he'd say, "You know, white folks, 'ligion be jes lak dis here silver. You got to keep it polish reg'lar or it don' shine, naw suh."

Every June during the time of our school exhibition, the graduating class gave orations and dialogues on Friday night. Then on Saturday night the colored would make money for their church by putting on a show for us white folks. First they'd have a Negro minstrel, then a Negro sermon by Loomis, all dressed up in his dingy white vest, black pants, jimswing black tailcoat, and beaver hat. Later, after the spirituals, Loomis and old Uncle Lem would put on a debate, all in fun. Old Lem always took the "nigitive" and Loomis the "infirmity." I remember one time the evening ended with Loomis saying, "You know, white folks, when a man cast his bread pon de waters, it gwine come back buttered toast, praise Jesus." Passing his hat, he joked, "Tonight, I repersents de waters. So cast yo bread on me an' de good Lawd gwine bless yo gingerosity." Everybody laughed—and Loomis made some extra money.

But everybody knows there's a difference between a colored preacher preaching in a white kitchen or at the Negro entertainments and the same man preaching in a white parlor. Nobody blamed Loomis. He worked at the store, so he had to do what he was told. But Cold Sassy felt like Grandpa was slapping the town in the face, all over again, and nobody doubted Miss Love had put him up to it.

The Flournoys told it all over town, what Loomis said at the end of his parlor sermon. "Mr. Rucker, sir? Miss Love? Y'all scuse me fer sayin' so, but y'all white peoples knows better'n to ack lak dis. De Lawd God wonts peace mongst His peoples. He say git on back to yo own church an' quit dis here foolishment."

I, for one, had a lot rather been hearing Loomis up at Grandpa's house than listening to the Presbyterian preacher saying what's go'n happen to you if you dance, play cards, or spend your money on "adorn-ments," like fur coats. There wasn't a fur coat in Cold Sassy, but any time he talked about sin he brought up fur coats.

Mama and I weren't really listening that morning, though. We were worrying about my daddy. He had stayed home, and he wasn't sick.

Papa had been trying his best to cheer Mama up ever since

the Tuesday before, when, as Aunt Loma put it, "Miss Love grabbed Sister's ticket to New York." Wednesday at breakfast he even offered to take Mama to Atlanta for the day, but she said, "Hoyt Tweedy, I'm not bout to be disrespectful of the dead for just a li'l old seventy-mile trip."

The next night he actually stayed home with her instead of going to the Presbytery meeting. That worried Mama. She said, "Hoyt, you haven't missed a meetin' since you had the flu ten years ago. What will people think?"

He touched her cheek, real tender, and said, "I'm tired, Mary Willis. I thought maybe you and me could go to bed early to-night."

"Aw, shah, Hoyt," she said impatiently. But then she put her arms around his neck and her head on his shoulder and cried.

Friday morning Papa had taken the train to Atlanta. "Business," he explained, but wouldn't say any more. When he got home late that evening, he was all smiles. After breakfast Saturday morning, when Mama wiped her mouth for him to kiss her good-bye, he kissed her twice and then came back and kissed her twice again.

I wasn't the only one wondering what he was up to. Queenie said, "Lawd Jesus, Mr. Will, yo pa he ack lak he got a dimon ring in his pocket!"

Queenie fried a chicken and cooked up a mess of vegetables for dinner that day, but I don't think Papa knew what he was eating. He talked a mile a minute the whole meal. He was so chock full of news, Mama nor I could get in a word. "Oh, by the way, Will," he said, forking a drumstick onto his plate. "A mill girl came in the store today to buy some black goods for a dress. Said her daddy died. She ast if I knew you."

My heart thumped hard. "Did she say her name?"

"No. But she was a pretty little thing, and clean."

"Tow-headed?"

"Ain't they all tow-headed?" Papa swished buttermilk in his

mouth. I could tell he was watching me. Town people thought you couldn't be too careful when it was a question of your children hobnobbing with mill folks.

"It may have been the girl that hepped me off the trestle. You know, after the train ran over me," I said casually. "She's in my grade at school. Mama, can I have the chicken head?"

"Don't you always?" She suspicioned me, too.

"Well," said my daddy, "the girl ast me to tell you that her and her aunt are go'n take her daddy back home to the mountains for buryin'."

"On the train?"

He shrugged. "I reckon."

Queenie was clearing the table. Papa put out a hand to stop her as she reached for the chicken platter. "Mary Willis," he said to Mama, "just look at that platter!"

Was it dirty or something? Mama looked. Queenie looked. I looked. Near as I could tell, it was just a wing, a back, and a gizzard, laying lonely on the platter. "That's all we have left over," Papa complained. "Queenie, from now on if you fry a pullet this small, fry two."

"Yassuh, Mr. Hoyt!" To Queenie, that just meant more for her to take home. But Papa saw it as his providing a bounteous table.

I did admire his style that day. Some might think what difference did it make, who would know? Well, Queenie knew. And she would tell Loomis and her cousin Sissyretta and all her friends who did yard work or cooked in white kitchens or took in washing or nursed white children. Naturally they would all tell their white folks, and two days from now, everybody in town would know Mr. Hoyt Tweedy could afford more food than he needed.

Papa had always been looked up to in Cold Sassy as a good man with a flair for good living. You wouldn't say he put on airs or pretended to be what he wasn't, but unlike Grandpa

Blakeslee, he liked seeming well-off and "modrun." Unlike Mama, he didn't worry about folks thinking bad of him, but he always made sure they thought well of him.

When Papa went back to the store after dinner, he was whistling.

It wasn't till Sunday morning that Mama got really worried about him. After working till Saturday midnight at the store, he always bathed before he went to bed so he could sleep later on Sunday, and normally he was barely up in time to eat breakfast and get to Sunday school. But this Sabbath morning he was already dressed when I went out to milk the cow. I could hear him singing and whistling clear to the barn.

At breakfast, Mama said, "My, you feel good this mornin', don't you, Hoyt?" And she smiled at him across the breakfast table. She looked real pretty in a new black and white striped wrapper, and instead of having her hair pulled back in a plain knot, she had done it up for church in a pompadour.

You can imagine the shock when we got downstairs in our Sunday clothes, ready for Sunday school, and Papa said he wasn't go'n go.

It didn't make any sense. He was wearing his suit and had his Bible in his hand, but there he stood, saying he had to stay home. I noticed his hand shook a little, and his eyes sparkled.

We couldn't of been more dumfounded. Papa was a deacon. Papa was clerk of the session. Papa was church treasurer. Papa couldn't just not go, for gosh sake. While Mama stared at him with her mouth open, I offered to stay home with him.

"You will not," he said sternly. "Y'all go on now. Make haste, or you'll be late." He walked nervously to the door, looked up and down the street, then practically pushed us out onto the porch. When I looked back, he had sat down in the swing and opened his Bible.

Mama was all to pieces as we went down the walk. "Will, do you think he's gone crazy?" she whispered, her face pale.

After Sunday school, folks naturally asked where was Mr. Tweedy. Looking confused and flustered, which she was, Mama said weakly, "He seems to be ailin'." I opened my mouth to say he looked all right to me, but she poked me in the ribs.

When we got to our pew, Mama let me know what her real fear was. "I bet your daddy's up there with Pa and them," she whispered from behind the palm-frond fan she was fluttering like a house afire. I shrugged, which was supposed to mean that couldn't be it.

Tell the truth, that possibility was uppermost in my own mind, even though I couldn't believe it. Papa was anxious to please Grandpa, but not anxious enough to desecrate the Sabbath by singing songs like "Bird in a Gilded Cage" or "Waltz Me Around Again, Willie." Certainly not "Ta-Ra-Ra-Boom-de-Ay."

As the Presbyterian preacher commenced his sermon, I was puzzled by the behavior of Mr. French Gordy, who sat with Miss Sarah in front of us, smelling of soap as usual. He kept turning around during the sermon to grin at us, yet when church finally let out, he rushed past and didn't even wait for his wife, much less stop to ask Mama what my daddy was sick with.

Everybody else did, however. Mama looked embarrassed and upset as she said over and over, "I don't know. I just don't know what's wrong with Mr. Tweedy."

In a minute here Mr. French came back, his ruddy face beaming, and took my mother's arm. "Mary Willis, how I wish your ma was alive to see this miracle! You and Will come outside and look!" When she hesitated, kind of dazed, he pushed her toward the church's big open door. I ran ahead to go see.

If Santy Claus had been out there with his sleigh and his reindeer that hot Sunday morning, it wouldn't of been any more surprising than the sight of Papa grinning like a chessy cat from the driver's seat of a big shiny red Cadillac car! He was wearing a cap and goggles, and his Sunday suit just barely showed under a long linen coat.

The automobile had a black canvas roof, slotted rubber tires, and a brass horn, and was shimmying and shaking and backfiring to beat the band.

"Papa!" I yelled, forgetting I wasn't supposed to holler in the churchyard. Everybody else had forgot, too. I was the first to reach the motorcar, but the congregation quickly crowded around. "Mama!" I called, looking towards the church steps. "Come on!"

Mama stood there on Mr. French's arm like she was looking at a man with a tail. She was pure transfixed, mouth gaping, eyes shining. There must of been thirty or forty people crowded around, and they got quiet just from the sight of her. "Well, I declare. I declare, Hoyt, don't you beat all!" she said finally, and then, "Well, I swan. Won't Mary Toy have a fit!"

There wasn't a Presbyterian in Cold Sassy who wasn't proud for Mama at that moment. Something good had finally happened to Miss Mary Willis.

I opened a back door, jumped in, bounced on the seat, and started asking Papa questions. With all the engine racket, he couldn't hear a word I said. He was busy shaking hands with all the men, anyhow, and getting slapped on the back and being asked for a ride.

Boy howdy, that was some morning.

I'm not sure Mama ever would of made it to the Cadillac if Papa hadn't climbed out and gone to get her. The crowd parted like the Red Sea as he led her to his shaking red chariot. Picking up a new linen coat off the front seat, he held it out grandly for her to put on, then draped a big dust veil over her hat and face, and handed her in. When she turned toward the congregation and waved, everybody smiled and clapped.

About then the motor conked out. Papa was so excited he

like to never got it started again. He cranked, then showed me how, and I cranked, but nothing happened. "Let me check the directions," he said, reaching in his pocket to take out a little booklet.

It said he had forgot to use the gas feed.

Away we went at last. But we went away lots slower than if we'd had the horse and buggy. Papa hadn't practiced his driving but for a few minutes before church let out, so he wasn't all that sure he could remember where the foot brake was or how much gas to feed. Also, every time he saw a buggy or wagon coming, he had to stop the car and shut off the motor so the horses wouldn't bolt. It was a slow progress till we were out in the country.

As we got to going faster, a grand cloud of dust rose behind us and folks ran out of their houses to watch us go by. Every time we hit a bump or just missed a squawking chicken we'd laugh like children. Boy howdy, what a day! Mama yelled over the racket, "Hoyt, I just cain't believe it! When did you buy it? Can we afford it? Where did you have it hid? Does Pa know about it?"

I kept begging him to let me drive. "Naw!" he yelled. "I better learn how first myself, Will!"

Coming back into town, we passed Grandpa's house just as he and Miss Love came out on the front veranda with the Flournoys. Big Loomis, who naturally took his communion cake in the kitchen, was just coming around the house from the back door as Papa honked the brass horn and we all waved.

They were too dumfounded to wave back, I reckon, or maybe didn't recognize anybody but me, on account of the linen coats and Mama's veil and Papa's goggles. Papa didn't stop or so much as slow up. It was grand, the way we raced by!

"Oh, won't she be jealous!" Mama crowed when we got home. There was no doubt who was meant by *she*.

I felt real satisfied. I knew Miss Love would love to have

a motorcar, probably more than my mother wanted to go to New York City. So now they were just about even.

Which was what my daddy had in mind.

If you'd paid him to do it, Papa couldn't of stood up to Grandpa and argued to get Mama the trip. But he had the nerve to ride by Grandpa's house and not stop.

34

MAMA put dinner on the table that day while Papa rode Queenie around the block. After we ate, I started clearing out the barn shed for a garage, but couldn't make much headway for folks dropping by to see the automobile. They admired the shiny red paint, blew the horn, tried out the seats, and of course asked to ride. Some were jealous, I could tell. There is a price to pay for having the first something in town. But Lee Roy, Smiley, Pink, and Dunse McCall were as excited as if it was their folks' car. They asked me all kinds of questions: What's the choke for, and lemme see the toolbox, and how do you start it, and how do you stop it, and how fast will it go.

It helped feelings a lot when, by the next Sunday, Papa and I had practiced enough to take passengers out. Aunt Loma bid first, her and Uncle Camp. Papa took Aunt Carrie home after dinner, then let me drive Pink and them around the block by myself. Later we went and got Miss Effie Belle. Poor old Mr. Bubba, he wanted to go so bad, but Miss Effie Belle thought the excitement would be too much for anybody 102. I think that meant she was scared he might wet his pants.

Papa offered to ride Grandpa around, but Grandpa wouldn't even get in. "A car is a fool dangerous contraption. Worse'n a bicycle," he said. "I speck Miss Love would like to go, though."

Instead of asking her, Papa said, "I just remembered, Mr. Blakeslee, I told Mary Willis I'd be back by now." And we drove off. It was so pointed that I felt embarrassed for Miss Love's sake—but pleased for Mama's.

The next morning I hitched up Big Jack to the buggy and took Grandpa and Miss Love and a mountain of grips to the depot. They would go to Savannah by train and get a boat there for New York City. Standing in the shade of the Cold Sassy tree, I watched their train pull out, then drove Jack home, turned him into the pasture with Miss Love's horse, filled their feed boxes and the watering trough, fed the chickens, and got the Toy family Bible off the desk in the hall like Mama told me to. She had asked Grandpa for it and he'd said shore you can have it, come git it. But Mama thought it best to wait till they left for New York.

I hoped it would be years before she looked in that Bible and saw how Miss Love had written herself into the family.

I may have said already that on Wednesdays all the stores in Cold Sassy closed for the day at noon. On Wednesday that week, we left in the Cadillac right after dinner to drive out to Cudn Temp's and bring Mary Toy home. The trip was up one hill and down another on humpback roads, two feet deep in dust all the way. Papa worried about dark thunderheads in the distance. Lord knows we needed rain. But if the road got wet, we'd soon be two feet deep in red mud instead of dust. The clouds passed off, though, and we had only one puncture, and everybody at Cudn Temp's like to had a fit about the motorcar. Mary Toy just couldn't believe it was really ours.

The purple had faded out of her hair, but it was still a right peculiar shade of red.

We got home too late for prayer meeting, so after supper the four of us just sat out on the veranda together in the cool dark.

Mary Toy was curled up in Papa's lap in the swing, and Mama
sat content beside them. Sprawled on the top step, I leaned
against a turned post and listened to the swing's slow creaking. It felt like we were a real family again. "I'm glad you home,
Mary Toy," I said, and meant it.

"Will's tired of gatherin' eggs," Mama teased.

"But maybe Mary Toy's forgot how," said Papa, tickling her
ribs.

"I ain't, either. Cudn Temp's got a heap of layin' hens. Guess
what was in one of the nests, Mama? A great big black snake!"

"Lord hep us!" Mama shrieked.

"He was sound asleep," Mary Toy said. "Just nice as he could
be. Me and Sara Christine, we —"

"Sara Christine and I," Mama corrected, but I could tell her
mind was on the snake, not the grammar.

"We petted him."

"No!"

"Yes'm, and I put him in my apron and went and showed
him to Cudn Temp."

"Lord hep us!"

For a while all you could hear was crickets cricketing and the
swing creaking . . . back and forth, back and forth. Mary Toy
said sleepily, "Mama, what am I s'pose to call Miss Love? Do I
call her Granny?"

"Say Miss Love, just like you been doin'." Mama's voice was
hard. "She's not your grandmother by any stretch of the imagination. She's only your grandpa's wife, and there's a big difference."

On Sunday, which was the first Sunday in August, we drove
the Cadillac to the Presbyterian church out at Hebron for the
annual reunion and dinner on the grounds. Grandpa Tweedy
and Mrs. Jones were there, of course, and we took them to
ride.

The next Wednesday, Papa took the whole day off and we

went to Comer and back, which he thought had never been done before in one day.

If the Cadillac had been a circus elephant, it couldn't of done a better job of taking Mama's and Cold Sassy's mind off of Grandpa Blakeslee and Miss Love.

35

THE car was all Cold Sassy talked about, and all we talked about in the family. You'd think Grandpa and Miss Love had just disappeared, instead of being off in New York enjoying Mama's trip. Then Miss Love's picture postcards of Coney Island and Ellis Island started coming.

Most folks who take a trip send postcards. Usually they write, "Having wonderful time wish you were here," or "How are you fine I hope," or maybe just their name. What Miss Love did, she wrote every lady and schoolgirl in Cold Sassy about something special she'd found for her at the wholesale house.

Miss Vada Goosby was so pleased, she came down to show Mama her postcard. It said, "I've picked out the nicest pattern for you and some lovely crêpe de Chine that is just your best color! I can't wait for you to see it!"

Mrs. Boozer—Miss Alice Ann, not Miss Catherine—came in the store for some flour and sugar one day and told Papa she'd never got mail from as far away as New York City before. She was showing the card to everybody. Miss Love had written her about "a stylish cloak that is inexpensive but will look elegant on you."

Mrs. Flournoy reported that Miss Love had ordered a whole outfit with her in mind.

Loma's card said, "Your father wants to pay for a lovely dress I picked out for you! I can't wait to see if I guessed right on the size! You'll be the grandest lady in town next summer!"

Aunt Loma hooted. "Pa wants to pay for me a dress? That'll be the day. And why next summer? Why not now? Well, I'll believe it when I see it."

She half-believed she had a free dress, though, when here came a card to Mama saying Grandpa was buying her a black grosgrain coat. "It will look really ritzy when you ride to church in the new Cadillac this fall!" wrote Miss Love. "I've found all the materials to make a hat to go with it, too!"

Mary Toy heard only that Grandpa had "a surprise" for her, but Miss Love wrote other girls about a dress or pattern or a bolt of poky-dot material or some such. She knew this would make them start pestering their mamas as to when Miss Love would be back and when would the wholesale house ship the orders.

Mama and Aunt Loma grudgingly admired the postcard salesmanship. Papa was beside himself about it. I heard him tell Cudn Hope that the postcards were "a stroke of genius." With just a one-cent stamp apiece, Miss Love had let every lady and girl in Cold Sassy know she had been thought about way up in New York City. Papa said, "When word gets out that the shipment is in, it's go'n look like we're havin' the women's missionary meetin' down here."

I got a postcard. It said, "Your grandfather and I thank you from the bottom of our hearts for all you are doing at our house. I hope Mr. Beautiful is behaving. Yours, Miss Love."

I kissed Yours and then I kissed Miss Love—the words, I mean. But I felt let down. Everybody else in the family could look forward to presents from New York, but it seemed like I was doing all the work for just a thank-you.

Tell the truth, I wasn't doing near what I'd meant to, because when I wasn't busy at the store or hurrying through chores at home, I was out driving with Papa, either practicing or going somewhere, or else washing and polishing the Cadillac. It got a layer of dust every time we drove around the block.

Smiley and Pink and them worked on it about as much as I did. Lots of times Mama came out there to the barn shed and sat on the milking stool just to watch us. It was like she couldn't believe we really had a motorcar unless she could go to ride or sit and look at it, one.

Tell the truth, we none of us could quite believe it.

One morning I was just fixing to run up to Grandpa's and lead Miss Love's horse around some when here came fat Lee Roy Sleep, saying the Gypsy caravans were going through town.

The Gypsies always came in August—telling fortunes, selling lace, tarring barn roofs, trading horses and mules. It was a sight to see—the bright-painted wagons with little curtained windows, and the horses decorated with tassels and silver beads. Cold Sassy always turned out to watch. By time Lee Roy and I got downtown, the caravans had reached the public well near my granddaddy's store. Several Gypsy men were on horseback, riding ahead of or behind their wagons or leading strings of mules and horses. I still remember a pretty, olive-skinned girl I saw that day, riding on a big gray stallion behind a heavy-set man who was dusky black. At the well he reined in and the girl slid off to drink from the flowing pipe. Getting up my nerve, I walked over to her and asked politely, "Where are y'all from?"

She looked scared and mumbled in a foreign accent, "I do not know." Before she could say anything else or even get her a drink, the man spoke short to her in another language and jerked her back up on the horse, and they rode off to rejoin the caravans. When I told Papa about it, he said he wouldn't trust anybody who didn't know where they came from.

I still think about the Gypsy girl sometimes. Then as now, you hardly ever saw any olive-skinned people in Cold Sassy. And boy howdy, she was pretty.

I also still think about another girl I saw that day. Lightfoot

McLendon. Not more than an hour after the Gypsies passed through town, I saw Lightfoot walking the railroad tracks towards Mill Town.

I was driving the Cadillac, taking some corn and squash and tomatoes to old Mr. Slocum, who was laid up with a bad back. The car made a swell racket, and if I went slow, folks who heard me coming had plenty time to run out on the porch and watch me drive by. They'd wave, and I'd honk the horn.

I recognized Lightfoot even when she was way up ahead. But gosh, she was changed. I'd always thought of her as bounding along like a young mountain goat, but now she looked like any other mill hand. Shoulders slumped, head down, hair pulled back tight and plain. She turned as the auto came up behind her, and I saw that her face was thin and pale against the black of her mourning dress

Braking quick, I stopped beside the tracks and blew the horn at her. "Lightfoot!" I called. "Come 'ere a minute!"

She shaded her eyes against the sun. "Will? Thet you?"

"Come look-a-here at my automobile!"

She came running across the railroad ditch to the road and, like a wilted pot plant that just got watered, smiled up at me with the purest pleasure on her face. "Law, is this here yore'n?"

"Well, it's—ours. My daddy bought it."

"I ain't never been this close to a motorcar afore." She ran her hand over the red paint of the hood. "Don't it feel shiny! Kin I set in the seat fer jest a minute, Will?"

"Better'n that. I'll ride you down the road a piece. Hop in." As she stepped up on the running board, I nodded toward the basket of corn and tomatoes in the back seat. "I'm takin' those to a old man who lives over on the other side of the cemetery."

I wished I could give her the vegetables. It would kind of make up for that bucket of blackberries she lost. But her pride was in my way. It would be the same as saying I knew that nothing grew good in the hard-packed clay behind the mill houses, and that mill hands didn't have plows to cultivate the soil deep or money for guano.

Well, it was something, at least, to give Lightfoot her first ride in a car.

I tried to make conversation, but had to yell over the car racket, and she had such a thin voice I couldn't hear a word she said. Just before turning left at the corner house where Miss Alice Ann Boozer and Mr. Homer lived, I stopped to let her out—then had an idea. "I'm go'n turn up this street," I said, "but if you ain't in a hurry, we could drive into the cemetery and sit and talk a while."

Without waiting for an answer, I turned the corner and drove through the cemetery gates and down the narrow wagon road that wound around old graves and old trees. I didn't once think to wonder if Miss Alice Ann or Mr. Homer or anybody had seen me turn into the graveyard with a mill girl in the front seat.

From habit, I headed for the Toy burial plot. After I cut off the motor it was really quiet in there, and cool under the trees. Lightfoot said, "Jest listen to them birds sangin'. Hit shore is a pretty place, Will. And so peaceful."

"Well, it seems peaceful when I look at old graves like those." I pointed towards the moldy headstones of people I never knew, some of them born a hundred and fifty years ago or more in Scotland or Ireland or New Hope, Pennsylvania. "But, Lightfoot, I feel like I'm go'n suffocate when I think about Granny Blakeslee or my friend Bluford Jackson, layin' down there in the dark."

An uneasy look came on her face and she sighed a long sigh. "My daddy passed, Will."

"Yeah, Papa told me. Said you came in the store."

The silence hung heavy over us as I tried to think of something to say. Lightfoot kept rubbing the brass horn with her right thumb. Finally she looked at me kind of shy-like and asked if I'd been in any fights lately. "I seen you fightin' lots a-times at school. You're a good skull-knocker, Will."

I blushed under the compliment. "Well, I ain't had time for it lately," I said. "Anyhow, I mostly fight to keep from gettin' called a sissy. And it's a way to get my share of whippin's at school. If you don't get whippin's, they call you teacher's pet."

She laughed. "Ain't nobody go'n call you a sissy or teacher's pet, either one, Will."

"Well, I reckon. But I mostly fight for fun, like my grandfather does. If I feel like sayin' to somebody I bet I can lick you, I say it and we square off and all the boys crowd around, rootin' for one or the other of us, and everybody has a good time." I paused and added, "But it's a real fight when I'm tryin' to beat up Hosie Roach."

She rubbed the brass horn some more, and then said, without looking at me, "Why come you hate Hosie, Will?"

"I don't know. He's—well, snobby and smart-aleck. Always got a chip on his shoulder. And he's dirty."

She said real low, "He ain't got no bathtub like you."

I hated feeling ashamed for having a bathtub. "You seen Hosie this summer, Lightfoot?"

She blushed. "Ever day. He works same shift in the mill as me. Will, you'd like Hosie if'n you knowed him better. He's real smart—like you. Everbody at the mill thinks he's go'n amount to something some day. I mean, you know, get a job thet ain't at the mill."

"Yeah. Maybe."

Feeling around for something better than Hosie to talk about, I showed her how the gears worked, and the choke, and then thought to ask if she saw the covered wagons that came through Cold Sassy last week.

"Yeah. I went out on the highway to watch them pass. I 'as thinkin' it might be folks I knew from White County. But turned out they 'as from way up in the mountains. My folks is from the hills, not the mountains."

Silence. A breeze rustled the leaves overhead and cooled us some. Then Lightfoot said she came through Cold Sassy one time when she was little bitty. "They 'as ten or twelve fam'lies in our wagon train, takin' thangs south to sell in Washin'ton, Georgie. Quilts and arsh potatoes, you know, and them blue mountain cabbages, and apples and chinquapins and home-twist t'bacca. All like thet."

I grinned. "And moonshine?"

She grinned back. "Yeah, I reckon. I remember we stopped in Cold Sassy on the way back home. Went in a store and bought a cast-arn stove, and some piece goods and sugar and coffee. Might be it 'as yore grandpa's store. I always remembered Cold Sassy cause it 'as sech a funny name."

"It ain't funny if you know how it came about. You ever noticed that great big sassafras tree, Lightfoot? The one over by the depot?"

She nodded.

"Everybody calls it the Cold Sassy tree. Back a hundred years ago it was a big sassafras grove there, and the wagoners goin' through said that was the coldest spot between the mountains and Augusta. They all knew what was meant if somebody said let's camp at them cold sassy trees. By time settlers got to comin' in, Cold Sassy was its natural name."

"Hit still sounds funny, Will. Leastways to me it does," said Lightfoot.

"Lots of other folks think that. There's talk about changin' it to something prosperous-soundin', the way Harmony Grove was changed to Commerce a few years ago. Don't you think Commerce is a awful improvement over a pretty name like Harmony Grove?"

More silence, except for birds twittering and a dog barking somewhere. I felt uncomfortable. Aunt Loma's right, I thought. Southerners can't just sit and not say anything. I said, "My granny's great-granddaddy led a wagon train here from North Ca'lina. They were the first settlers."

"Had he heired the land?"

"Maybe, I don't know. I think he had a land grant for fightin' in the Revolution."

"Where I come from, most folks jest tuck it up. Their land, I mean. Maybe thet's what yore folks done."

Time lagged again till Lightfoot asked would anybody mind if she looked around some.

"Naw, course not." Jumping down, I ran around and helped her out, like she was Cinderella stepping out of a coach. I showed her Granny's unmarked grave. "The tombstone ain't come yet," I explained, embarrassed. "Grandpa ordered one from Sears, Roebuck, but it ain't come yet." Then I took her over to the Sheffield plot. Being as Mr. Sheffield owned the cotton mill, I thought she might like to see where some of his money went. "I'm go'n show you two big fancy headstones for men who weren't dead when they were buried," I said gaily.

"They warn't dead?" She was horrified, the way I'd felt when Granny told me about it. Stopping before a huge marble tombstone carved like a scroll, I said, "See? 'Daniel Bohannan Sheffield.' He was the Sheffields' only son."

"He got buried alive?"

"Naw, course not. Ain't nobody under there. Granny said Mr. Dan married a rich Jew lady in New York and was go'n bring her home to meet the fam'ly, but Miz Sheffield wrote him not to come. Said anybody who'd marry a Yankee or a Jew was the same as dead—specially if it was a Yankee Jew. Turned out the bride's family shut the door on her, too, but I don't know if they buried her. Anyhow, Mr. and Miz Sheffield put up this tombstone. See, it don't give a date. Just says 'Died in a foreign land.'"

"He still livin'?" Lightfoot looked around like she thought Mr. Dan might be standing behind her.

"Who knows? They don't talk about him. Now let me show you the other one. See that big carved marble angel over yonder?" As we walked toward it, I told her about Mrs. Sheffield's youngest brother. "Granny said he was around my age when the Yankee army came through. Just fourteen or fifteen. The Laceys lived on a big plantation, and they sent this boy down the Savannah River one dark night in a rowboat with a trunk full of money and silver and jewels—all like that. If he made it to Savannah, he was s'posed to buy passage on a ship to England and wait out the War over there. Which he did. But when it was over, he didn't come home. Granny said after Mr. Sheffield started the mill and they could afford it, Miz Sheffield hired her a lawyer over in England, and he found out her brother had squandered everything. He was workin' as a chim'ly sweep. Wanted to come home."

"Well, I reckon Miz Sheffield bought him passage."

"Naw. She buried him. See? 'Royal Garnet Lacey, Gone But Not Forgotten.'"

I plucked a leaf from the oak tree we were standing under and tore it in little bits while Lightfoot studied the gravestone. "Maybe he did die over in England," she said finally. "If Miz Sheffield said he 'as dead, he must a-been."

"Naw, he wasn't. Granny said he kept writin' letters for years." I laughed, but Lightfoot didn't. She stood for the longest kind of time, staring from one to the other of the expensive tombstones for live men. Then running her hand over the carved angel, she said, "I shore wisht I could get one a-them angels for Pa." She looked up at me, and I noticed for the first time the lavender-blue circles under her eyes.

I felt embarrassed, her wishing for such. Finally I mumbled, "Did you . . . uh, where's he buried at, Lightfoot?"

"Back home. Me and my aunt tuck him back to the hills on the train. I knowed he warn't go'n rest easy in no grave down here." With that, Lightfoot sank down on the empty grave of Mr. Royal Garnet Lacey, put her head against the angel's stomach, and cried and cried.

I didn't know what to do. I patted her shoulder and said I was sorry her pa died, but that just made her cry worse. She sobbed out that he 'as lucky to be dead; now he didn't have to work all day after coughin' all night, and didn't have to worry bout gittin' enough vittles.

"Was he . . . uh, did he have the TB, Lightfoot? Like your mama?"

She didn't answer. Just sat there and cried some more. Finally she wiped her eyes on the skirt of her black dress, trying hard to get aholt of herself. When she could talk, she said softly, "I think maybe Pa did have the TB. Pneumony's what kilt him, though. Hit come on him sudden like. He 'as deader'n Hell a day later." I hadn't ever before heard a girl say Hell, but she didn't even notice she'd said it. "I wanted to git a doctor, but my aunt, she said he 'as too fur gone. Said we didn' have no money to waste on no doctor when it couldn't do no good. . . . Oh, Will, I wisht I'd a-stayed with my sister after the funeral. Buster axed me to. Thet's her husband. I said thankee, but I ain't a-go'n be beholden to nobody. Buster said I'd earn my keep if'n I holped him in the fields."

"Why'n't you stay, then?"

"I didn't like the way Buster looked at me when he said I could holp him in the fields."

She picked up a stick and talked on, almost like I wasn't there. "Anyways, I wanted to come back here and go to school. Amount to something. We 'as halfway back to Cold Sassy on the train when my aunt she said, 'Now, Lightfoot, with yore pa dead 'n' all, I cain't keep you no more less'n you go in the mill full time an' pay yore part. Fast as you larn thangs, you'll be a-workin' both sides of the aisle in no time.' Will, I begged her and begged her, Please'm, let me git one more year a-school-in'.' But she said her chi'ren got two year apiece in school, and it ain't holped them a bit in the mill. Said if they'd a-been borned with books for brains, they'd be makin' bottom wages jest the same."

Over near Granny's grave a jaybird screeched. I stood drawing lines in the dirt with my big toe, saying nothing. Then all of a sudden Lightfoot hit Mr. Royal Garnet Lacey's marble angel hard as she could with her stick! Her eyes narrowed. "Here's somebody ain't even dead yet," she said, poking out her bottom lip, "and I bet his headstone cost more money than I or my people will ever see in our whole lives. Hit ain't fair!"

"No, it ain't, Lightfoot." I wanted to tell her about Blu Jackson dying so unfair young, but she started crying again. "Please, Lightfoot. Cryin' ain't go'n help. Hush up now."

"I don' want to hesh up. I'm a-go'n cry the r-r-rest a-my l-life. . . ."

"Look, I'll carry you home. In the car. Come on, Lightfoot. Quit cryin' and I'll ride you home." I caught her wrist and pulled her up.

And then I kissed her.

I swear I hadn't once thought of doing such a thing, and I'm sure she hadn't, either. But before you could say doodly-squat, my arms had circled her and she had flung her arms around my neck, and I could feel her wet cheek against mine. For what seemed like ages I just held her, thinking nothing but the purest thoughts, my heart aching for her, so poor and miserable and lonesome. And then I don't know what happened, I was kissing Lightfoot! Just like Mr. McAllister kissed Miss Love. On her mouth, her cheeks, her closed eyes, her neck. . . . She kept saying, "No, Will, no, no, no, no. . . ." But she didn't push me away.

My breath came in trembling gasps, and hers did, too. I felt dizzy. I was on fire. I pressed her against Mr. Royal Garnet Lacey's angel and wrapped my arms tight around her waist.

Just then God spoke out loud in the voice of Miss Alice Ann. "Will Tweedy, you ought to be ashamed!" said God. I looked up and there He stood in a pink and white poky-dot dress, pointing His plump forefinger at us.

Lightfoot put her arm across her face just like Eve in the garden when God saw her nakedness.

"You, girl, I don't know who you are," shouted God, "but

I can tell you're from Mill Town. Now you just git on home. Will's a good boy from a nice fam'ly. You ain't got no right to come to town like this and corrupt him." God was indignant as all get-out. "Soon as I seen y'all ride in here, I thought to myself they ain't up to no good. Will, I just hate to think what your daddy's go'n say."

"It ain't like you see it, Miss Alice Ann! We didn't mean to—"

"I got eyes, ain't I?" God retorted. "Your trouble, Will, you ain't got no shame! Imagine, actin' like that right in sight of your poor granny's grave!"

36

WHILE I was staring at Miss Alice Ann, my mouth open like a dummy, Lightfoot disappeared. Evaporated. Just like she had at the depot that day she helped me off the train trestle. She must of run across the cemetery and gone out through the woods at the back.

Then while I had my back turned, trying to crank up the Cadillac, Miss Alice Ann disappeared, too—I reckon to go spread the word.

I felt sick.

I took the vegetables to Mr. Slocum, and when I got back home, parked the car under the barn shed and sneaked up to the loft. I wanted to think about kissing Lightfoot McLendon before I had to think about a whipping. I wanted to remember my arms tight around her. I wanted to feel her lips on mine, her hands on my back, her breath coming in trembly gasps at my ear. Closing my eyes, I groaned and sank down in the hay.

Now I knew why Miss Love couldn't stop Mr. McAllister when he was kissing her, despite how bad she hated him. She had lost her senses. Well, I'd lost mine, too, and I wanted to stay that way. I wanted to keep aholt of all the feelings that kept passing over me in waves.

But I was also scareder and more ashamed than I had ever been in my life.

There was no point in worrying about Lightfoot. Nobody would go tell her aunt on her. Even if Miss Alice Ann knew where she lived, she wouldn't think a mill girl was worth the trouble. It was my sins that were as scarlet, not Lightfoot's.

I hated it that folks would talk about me. I knew now how Miss Love must feel. Lord, what would Mama say? I wished I was dead. I also wished Grandpa was home from New York. I could explain it to him, how I didn't mean to do wrong. But how could I explain to Papa or Mama? For that matter, how could I explain a thing like that to Pink and Smiley and them? They wouldn't believe it just happened, that I didn't plan it when I turned in those cemetery gates. They wouldn't understand or care that Lightfoot was crying and I only meant to comfort her. They'd just haw and guffaw and ask how it felt and did she kiss with her mouth open. She didn't, but they'd never believe it. They'd make the whole thing dirty.

All of a sudden I couldn't stand the suspense any longer—the waiting for Miss Alice Ann to get to Mama. I decided to go tell her myself, the way Miss Love told Grandpa before he could hear it from Miss Effie Belle Tate—or me.

There's no use going into all that followed. Telling on myself saved my pride somehow, but it didn't ease the punishment. I got my whipping from Papa, and my shaming from Mama to the point I tried to duck out of sight whenever I heard her coming. But what hurt, Papa decided I couldn't drive the Cadillac for two months.

He was really mad.

After the way I'd done bad and brought shame on the family, I deserved the whipping. But two months out from under the steering wheel was six weeks too much. Compared to being punished for kissing a mill girl, being in mourning for Granny had been like a picnic up at Tallulah Falls.

It occurred to me that mine and Mary Toy's punishments never had been equal. Whenever I misbehaved, Mama told Papa and he wore me out with the razor strop. But when occasionally Mama said to whip Mary Toy, why that was something else entirely. Taking a rolled-up newspaper, he would jerk her up to her room, and from downstairs we'd hear him speak harsh. "Now, young lady, bend over that bed!" Mama would cringe, hearing the blows fall. What she didn't know was that Papa would whisper to Mary Toy to start hollering, and then commence swatting the mattress instead of her. Mary Toy told me about it one time.

If I thought about Mama, that seemed like a good joke, but if I thought about me, it made me mad. I realized Papa was strict and hard on me because a boy had to amount to something, whereas Mary Toy didn't, being a girl. But just the same it made me mad.

I didn't go anywhere the next day except up to Grandpa's to feed and water the horse and mule and Granny's chickens. But the following day there was no way out of it; I had to help at the store.

It seems like everybody I saw took up for me, even Miss Effie Belle. She lectured me good, right there in the store, but it was about mill people. "Stay away from them folks, son. They all sorry and no-count and good for nothin'. You ain't a bad boy, Will. You was just led astray."

After she went out, Uncle Lige put his arm around my shoulders and said, "Natcherly you go'n sow some wild oats, boy. We all done it. But right now you jest a mite young. Wait till you old enough to be careful and not git caught."

Later Aunt Loma came in, carrying Campbell Junior, and patted my shoulder like she was forgiving me for doing evil. "Now, Will," she whispered, "be sure and write down about you and that mill girl."

Gosh, I wouldn't of written that down then for anything!

I left for dinner early. I didn't want to walk home with Papa. But as I hurried to cross the street just before reaching the depot, the old men playing checkers on a barrelhead under the Cold Sassy tree winked and grinned at me.

It's to my credit that when Smiley and them talked dirty about it and old men sniggered and spoke of wild oats, I felt even more ashamed than when I'd told Mama and then had to listen while she repeated it to Papa.

It's not to my credit that ever since Mr. McAllister came to town, I'd had a deep-down itch to kiss somebody the way he did it and see how it felt and all. I think I had Miss Love in mind, but I knew that would never happen. If I hadn't watched Mr. McAllister, I wouldn't even know about kissing like that. I might of put my arm around Lightfoot till she stopped crying, but probably I wouldn't of kissed her at all.

She was not a bad girl, or common, either, and I hated it that she would think I didn't respect her. She'd know I wouldn't kiss any girl from a nice town family the way I kissed her.

When Grandpa and Miss Love left for New York City, nobody knew how long they would be gone. "Hit jest depends," Grandpa had said when Papa asked. "But I gol-gar'ntee you I ain't a-go'n stay a day more'n I have to. I can stand them Yankees jest so long fore my arm goes to hurtin'."

They had been away for nearly two weeks ("Doin' no tellin' what," as Aunt Loma put it) when on August 13th Papa got a telegram that said: ARRIVING 11:40 A.M. AUG 16 E.R. BLAKESLEE. I tell you, on the morning of August 16th, we were all mighty excited.

I naturally got up early to go groom Miss Love's horse and see if everything was all right up there.

I don't know whether it was Mama's idea or Papa's, but it was decided to invite the travelers to dinner. Maybe what did it was Miss Love's postcard promises, but bygones almost seemed to be bygones as Mama and Queenie bustled about, fixing a Sunday dinner despite it was only Thursday.

Papa ordered ice from Athens for the lemonade. Mama put out the goblets and good china and good silver, and invited Aunt Loma and Uncle Camp and also Aunt Carrie, who was back from visiting her cousin in Athens. Aunt Carrie, remember, was the one who read poetry, studied Latin and Greek, talked cultured, believed in human excrement, and put mourning dye on Mary Toy's hair for Granny's funeral.

It really pleased me, seeing places set for Grandpa and Miss Love. She hadn't eaten at our house since before Granny took sick, and Grandpa hadn't been there for a meal since they got married. If Mama was letting Miss Love in the house, maybe she'd let her in the family, too.

Papa came home to get the Cadillac and drive it to the depot. "I know Mr. Blakeslee won't ride in it," he said as he left the house, "but I can bring Miss Love and their grips."

Right after he left, Mama looked up from peeling peaches and said, "Will, I just thought. Maybe you better go take the Toy Bible out of the parlor. Uh, let me think. Well, put it on my dresser upstairs."

I did as I was told. Laying it on the dresser, I felt a wave of grief for Granny, wishing she could be here today, with us eating on the good china and all. On an impulse I turned to where her life was recorded.

Gosh, no wonder Mama wanted me to hide that Bible! She had nearly wore out the page erasing *Enoch Rucker Blakeslee married Love Honour Simpson on July 5, 1906.*

Hearing the brass horn just a-honking, we all rushed out. There was Grandpa in the front seat by Papa; he was the one honking the horn! Miss Love was in the back, squeezed in between two mountains of grips, boxes, and hatboxes and boy howdy dressed fit to kill in a new fall outfit. She was probably hotter'n heck, but by dern she sure was fashionable.

Grandpa was so taken with the automobile he hardly noticed anybody except me. Stepping off the running board, he slapped me on the shoulder and said, "Gosh a'mighty Peter Rabbit, Will Tweedy, these here artermobiles is something else and then some!"

"Sir? I thought you liked mules better."

"Even a dummy can change his mind, son. I've rode ever dang artermobile in New York City. Stanley Steamers, Fords, Holsmans, Pierces, Buicks, Caddy-lacs, all of'm. Course Miss Love had to push me into the first car. Hit was a Franklin, and I'd jest soon been caught in the compress down yonder at the cotton gin. Scared me half to death. But you can git used to anythang." Catching Miss Love's eye, he grinned at her.

"Mr. Blakeslee held on like he thought that Franklin might fly," she said, teasing. "But next day he couldn't wait to try it again!" While everybody laughed, Mary Toy peeped out from behind Mama's skirt. "Why, Mary Toy!" said Miss Love. "You've come home!"

"Go kiss your grandpa, sugar," said Mama.

Grandpa bent down for the kiss, gave Mary Toy a penny and said how much she'd growed, then straightened up and slapped the hood of the Cadillac the way a horse-trader slaps the flank of a fine stallion. He said, "I done joined the dang twentieth century, folks! Gosh a'mighty, a motorcar is a marvel. A dang marvel! Hoyt, I shore am proud you got one!"

Queenie and Mama had dinner nearly ready to be served up, but Miss Love had brought some of the boxes in with her, and nothing would do Grandpa but to open them and pass out his presents. He had done so little gift-giving in his lifetime, he was like a child who's learned a new trick.

As Miss Love had promised, there was a black grosgrain coat for Mama, and for Loma a thin, expensive-looking white dress with big pastel flowers embroidered on it. Aunt Loma like to had a fit over that dress. While she danced around holding it up to her, Grandpa said proudly, "I got thet'n real cheap. Besides wholesale, it was marked down for end of season, which don't matter, cause what's end of season up North is jest right for August down South."

Mama and Papa both looked like they'd swallowed a straight pin. Mama said firmly, "Pa, have you forgot we're in mournin'? Loma cain't wear a white dress."

Miss Love defended herself. "Your pa was dead set on that dress. I figured—"

"A good-looker like Loma ought'n to wear black all the time," Grandpa interrupted. Aunt Loma's face prettied with pleasure at the compliment. "When you was little bitty, honey, yore ma was always makin' you flowerdy dresses."

"I figured it would keep till next summer," Miss Love put in real quick.

Aunt Loma's face fell a mile. "You did it on purpose, Love Simpson," she said, and burst out crying.

"Hesh up, Loma," Grandpa ordered.

Miss Love's face flushed. Closing her eyes for a second, she sighed, and then spoke like to a child. "Tell you what, Loma, I'll make you a big fashionable black hat with black ostrich plumes to wear this fall. Would you like that?" And Aunt Loma nodded through her tears.

There were presents all around. Derby hats for Papa and Uncle Camp, a little fur muff for Mary Toy that had a bunch of silk violets pinned on it, a book for Aunt Carrie, a beaded purse for Queenie—and for me a linen duster and driving cap with goggles, just like Papa's!

"Well, thet's it, folks," said Grandpa, real proud of himself. "Santy Claus is over. Now let's go eat some good Southern cookin'. Mary Willis, you ought to see what them folks in New York call fried chicken."

Nobody asked Miss Love to, but she explained about Yankee fried chicken. "They use only a little grease, and after the chicken pieces brown, they put water in the pan and let it steam."

"Another thang bout them Yankees," said Grandpa, heading for the dining room, "they never heard a-sweetmilk. When I ast for it, the waitress lady brought me some with *sugar* in it."

Papa said Lord make us thankful for these and all our blessin's for Christ sake a-men and started slicing the ham. Everybody was talking at once—except Mama. She was suspicioning, with funny-paper balloons hovering over her head. The first one said, *How come all those nice presents?* The next said, *Love's tryin' to buy a ticket into the fam'ly. But how'd she get him to spend so much?* The third balloon explained it: *He's sweet on her. They were together in that hotel in New York and now they feel guilty. They're hidin' guilt behind all that Santy Claus.*

But then Mama's mind came back to the fact she had dinner guests. She called Queenie to bring the hot rolls.

Papa kept trying to keep the talk away from New York, I guess thinking it would hurt Mama to have to listen to it. The whole time we ate, he was telling Grandpa about our motor trips. Described every puncture, every hill, every rut and gully.

"What I want to know," Grandpa said finally, turning to me, "did you do any a-the drivin', son?"

"Yessir. Drove all the way home from Comer."

He looked proud. "Hit shore is a wonder how young folks ketch on. Miss Love, now, she thinks she could drive a car." He grinned. "But I don't know as I'd ride with her or any other lady." That got Miss Love's goat, I could tell.

When it was time for dessert, Miss Love got up to help Mama and them clear the table. But Mama said keep your seat. By not letting her help, she made it clear that Miss Love was comp'ny, not fam'ly.

Grandpa, noticing, got back at Mama right quick. "Why don't you tell what all we done in New York, Miss Love? I mean besides ride artermobiles."

Miss Love said sweetly (too sweetly), "Mary Willis, your

daddy will try to say he didn't have a good time. But he had a real good time."

"I got to admit it, folks, it was a dang sight more fun with Miss Love than them times I went by myself."

"What all did you do?" asked Aunt Carrie. The flowers in her hair today were daisies.

Grandpa said, "You tell'm, Miss Love."

"Of course we were at the wholesale house most of the time. But we went to Coney Island one evening and walked on the beach. Another day we rode the ferry to Ellis Island, where they take in immigrants. And we visited a lot of churches and museums."

"I ain't talkin' bout them dang churches and museums when I say I had a good time, Miss Carrie," Grandpa said gaily. "What I liked was ridin' in them artermobiles and seein' them musical reviews and all like thet."

Miss Love shook her head at Grandpa like a mother trying to shush a child in public, but he chose not to notice. He didn't see the shocked looks that Mama and Papa exchanged, either.

Aunt Carrie said, "Did you hear that, Mary Willis? They went to a musical! How nice! Tell me, Rucker, did you see any theatricals? Any Shakespeare plays?"

"Naw, Miss Carrie, we didn't see no Shakespeare. But we seen a stage play. The main actress shore was a looker."

Aunt Loma came to life. "What was her name, Pa?"

"What was her name, Miss Love? Aw, it don't matter who she was. Well, and we went to a dance place. Miss Love, tell about us at thet dance place."

Miss Love, real flustered, said, "Why don't you tell about the big new department store we went in, Mr. Blakeslee?"

But Aunt Carrie was excited about the dance place. "Did you dance, Rucker?"

"You know I cain't dance, Miss Carrie." He laughed and slapped his knee. "I jest watched. Miss Love done the dancin'."

Aunt Loma looked interested. Mama's and Papa's faces turned fiery red. And Miss Love just about died as Aunt Carrie said, "Rucker, is it the style in New York these days for a lady to dance by herself?"

"Naw. At the dance hall they got extry men to dance with unescorted ladies. Miss Love kept astin' me to let's dance, so I give one a-them men a quarter to be her partner. She's a crackerjack dancer," Grandpa bragged. "I want her to learn me how."

Aunt Carrie didn't feel the chill in the air, and neither did Grandpa. "Did I ever tell you, Rucker," she asked him, "about the time another young lady and myself got caught dancing? It was when I was a student in Athens. We were just having fun, singing popular tunes, but the songs were not of the type approved by Madame Joubert. And then we started dancing. Of course somebody told on us and here came Madame. Oh, my, it was an awful scene. Papa gave Madame my mother's piano for her school and she let me stay, but I was restricted for the longest kind of time. The other young lady went home in disgrace and was turned out of her church. Oh, my, I don't like to remember all that. You were the smart one, Love. Always do your dancing out of town. . . . Thank you, Queenie," she said as the cook put dessert in front of her—coconut cake and fresh peaches.

Nobody said a word. Finally Aunt Carrie spoke again. "One should be allowed to dance if one wishes to. And read Greek poetry, and make use of human excrement for the beautification of God's earth." She spoke with a stiff dignity. It was the first time she'd ever let on that she knew Cold Sassy laughed at her behind her back, and that it bothered her.

I knew Mama and them were shocked at Aunt Carrie, but she made sense to me. Long as you didn't hurt anybody, why shouldn't you dance if you liked dancing, and marry again if you needed looking after, and go fishing or wear a flowerdy dress if it might lift your grief a little?

Yes, and hold and kiss a lonely mill girl.

37

AN UNEASY silence followed Aunt Carrie's little speech. Then Grandpa yelled toward the kitchen, "Queenie? Queenie!"

She came to the dining room with a clean vegetable bowl in one hand and a drying cloth in the other. "Yassuh, Mr. Rucker?"

"This here's the best coconut cake you ever made." He took another bite. "I want you to give Miss Love the receipt."

"I ain't made dat cake, Mr. Rucker. Miss Mary Willis made dat cake."

"Well, it shore is good, Mary Willis. I want Miss Love to make me one."

Mama picked up her dessert spoon. Her voice iced over as she said, "It's Ma's receipt, Pa."

"Well, copy it down, hear?" Grandpa pulled a cigar out of his shirt pocket, bit it, and spat the tip on the floor.

Taking a sip of lemonade, Mama looked right at Miss Love. "It's in that old brown shoebox in the pantry with all Ma's other receipts. Unless you threw the box out."

I could tell that Miss Love didn't remember any brown shoebox. There was a silence while Grandpa struck a match on the sole of his shoe, put it to the cigar, and changed the subject. "Y'all ain't even noticed my see-gar. In New York, Miss Love

kept tellin' me to try one. Said it's more modrun than plug tobacco and I'd like it better. I ain't smoked enough yet to know,
but a see-gar shore is tasty to chew. One thang bout smokin',
you don't have to spit so dang much." He looked over at Miss
Love and winked. I mean, he actually winked!

Plain as day, there was something new between the two of
them. Winking is not something an old man does at a lady who
only keeps house for him. They were excited, almost like two
children with a secret. I couldn't figure it out. I stole a glance at
Mama and I could tell she noticed, too. I didn't know if she was
wondering just how good a time they'd had in New York City
or worrying what folks would say if Grandpa told it at the store
about Miss Love dancing.

As usual, Papa finished his dessert first and tilted his chair
back on its hind legs. When everybody else was through, he let
the chair down and said, "Well, Camp, I reckon you and me
better get on back to the store."

"Yessir."

Mama folded her napkin carefully. "Don't you think you'd
better chauffeur our comp'ny home first, Hoyt?" I reckon she
was too nervous to want them there all day.

Papa laughed. "Law, I forgot. Y'all ready, Mr. Blakeslee?"

"Let Will Tweedy drive us," said Grandpa. "I want to see is
he any good at it."

Papa hesitated. He looked at Mama. I looked down at the
peach juice in my empty compote.

"What's the matter?" asked Grandpa. "He ain't hit a horse
or run th'ew somebody's parlor, is he?"

"Uh, no, sir, nothin' like that," said my daddy. Then he took
a deep breath and told me to drive Grandpa home but then
come straight back. "You hear? Straight back!"

"Yessir."

"He cain't come right straight back," said Grandpa. "I want
him to hep us git our thangs in."

"Well, soon as you can, Will," Papa said sternly.

"Yessir."

Mary Toy wanted to go, too, but Mama said no. "With all the baggage, honey, there's not room. Now kiss Grandpa bye and thank him for your present."

She didn't tell her to thank Miss Love, I noticed, and I didn't much blame her. Grandpa had rubbed in their good time a little too much.

Papa turned the crank for me. Just before the engine caught up, Miss Love leaned forward and whispered, "Will, your grandfather has saved the best surprise just for you!"

Grandpa opened his mouth to say something, but the motor drowned him out, so he shook Papa's hand and yelled above the racket, "I'll be down terreckly, Hoyt!"

"Mighty glad y'all are back, sir!" yelled Papa. "The store ain't the same with you gone!"

"Proud to hear it, Hoyt!" Grandpa yelled back. "Giddy-up now, son, let's see does it know gee from haw with you a-holdin' the reins. Hit run fine for yore daddy."

Soon as I shut off the motor in front of their house, Miss Love spoke up in an excited whisper. "Tell Will what you've done, Mr. B.!"

Like he was about to bust from holding back the news, Grandpa whispered, "I done bought me a dang artermobile, Will Tweedy! A Pierce!" Blue eyes dancing, he reached in his vest pocket and pulled out an advertising leaflet, covered with drawings of cars, and pointed to a black open sedan.

With him waving the paper about, I couldn't get a good look. But I saw good enough to be flabbergasted. "Boy howdy, Grandpa!"

"Sh-h-h, don't holler." Smoothing his thin mustache with thumb and forefinger, Grandpa grinned big. "Hit's a secret. Ain't tellin' nobody but you till it comes in on the train." Stepping to the ground, he opened the car door for Miss Love and reached for his grip, which was beside her on the back seat.

"Boy howdy, Grandpa!" I whispered, coming around the car.

He put the grip down and handed me the advertising leaflet. "See it? Thet'n right there. Thet's the one I bought. They sendin' it in a few weeks. When it's on the way, they go'n telegraph me which train to meet."

Grandpa and Miss Love stood there watching me read what it said under the picture: "PIERCE, 8 h.p., Geo. N. Pierce Co., Buffalo, N.Y. Price $900, without top; seats 4 persons, doors in back only; single, water-cooled cylinder; jump spark ignition, planetary transmission, 3 speeds; wt. 1,250 pounds."

Gosh, Grandpa had spent $900?

"We seen a Ford thet was jest half as much," he whispered. "Thet's the one I wanted. But it was a two-seater, and Miss Love said we got to have room to take folks to ride or we ain't go'n sell any. I saved by not buyin' one a-them canvas tops—hit costs extry—and they give me a dealer's discount, besides."

Seeing my puzzlement, Miss Love whispered, "Your grandfather's got his name on two dealerships: Pierce and Cadillac! What do you think of that?"

"You mean we go'n sell cars?"

Miss Love shushed me.

"Thet's jest what she means," whispered Grandpa. "We go'n sell artermobiles. Come on, y'all, let's go in the house. Talkin' like this is a-gittin' me hoarse."

"We go'n get rich or go broke, Grandpa?" I whispered.

"Get rich!" Miss Love said as we marched up the walk, her carrying hatboxes and us loaded with grips.

"No tellin'," Grandpa admitted. "One or th'other, for shore. . . . Howdy, Miss Effie Belle!" he called to what looked like a shadow just inside the Tates' front door.

"Howdy, Rucker," she called back, but didn't speak to Miss Love and didn't ask if they'd had a good time.

Soon as we were inside the house I said it'd be a miracle if we could sell more than one or two cars in Cold Sassy.

Grandpa laughed. "Thet's jest exackly what I told Miss Love, son. I said, 'How many folks is a-go'n shell out for a artermobile when they got a horse and buggy in the barn?' But Miss Love thinks she's figgered out the receipt for success in the motorcar business. And by dang, maybe she has!"

"Tell him what all you plan, Mr. B." We were still standing there in the front hall, so excited we hadn't even set down the boxes and grips. Miss Love was looking up at Grandpa like he was just the smartest man in the world.

"Well, I'm go'n keep my Pierce parked in front a-the store, and I want yore daddy to bring the Caddy-lac down there. Hit might not sell no cars, but it'll git folks here from Ila and Lula, and Pocatellago and Comer and Homer and Pendergrass. And after they git th'ew lookin' at them cars, they go'n come on in the store and buy fertilizer spreaders and chewin' tobacco and thangs."

"But it's the cars they'll go home talking about," said Miss Love. "Then first one and then another will buy one!"

They were chock full of ideas. Miss Love was planning a window display of linen dusters, dust veils, and driving caps with goggles. She'd already ordered some of those. Soon as they sold some cars, she was going to order sirens, hill holders, auto robes—"wind, water, dust, and oil proof"—and chain pulls for getting out of mud or sand.

"We'll let people sit out front in the cars all they want to," said Miss Love. Then she looked at me. "Uh, you haven't said much, Will. What do you think?"

I didn't think Papa would be all that glad to have folks pulling out the choke and flooding his engine, or turning the switch key on and off and using up his battery, or blowing his horn from morning to night. Not to mention how dusty the Cadillac would get, sitting out there on North Main.

But I didn't say all that. Because what could Papa do about it if Grandpa said to?

I had the feeling that displaying the automobiles was Miss Love's idea, not Grandpa's. No woman would understand how easy a machine can get out of fix. Well, for that matter, neither would my grandfather. He never did have any sense about machinery. Hitching up Big Jack to the buggy was about his limit. He hadn't the faintest idea how a motor worked. Didn't even understand a bicycle.

"What we standin' here holdin' all these grips for?" Grandpa said all of a sudden, laughing. "Let's unload first and talk second."

I followed Miss Love into the company room, set down her baggage, and went out to bring in the rest of it. As I came in again, she called to me from Grandpa's room. "We're back here, Will."

"Yeah, come on back, son," he echoed. "We ain't half th'ew talkin'."

"I need to get on home," I called, but after I put the grips down I went back there like he said to.

Miss Love was sitting on the blanket chest that Granny's angels had come out of. Grandpa had taken the cane-back rocking chair by Granny's side of the bed. "What we expect to do," said Miss Love, taking off her hat and fanning herself with it, "is make people want what they don't know they want. You call that salesmanship, Will."

"I call it hocus-pocus," said Grandpa, laughing at her.

"You'll see, sir." Getting up, she rumpled his hair so familiar it made me uncomfortable. "One way we'll make everybody want a car, Will, we're going places. And we'll take anybody out riding who wants to go. I'm sure Cold Sassy is already jealous as can be about your family taking all those nice trips. When Mr. Blakeslee's car arrives, they just won't be able to stand not having one."

Grandpa leaned forward in the rocking chair. "Thet's where you come in, Will Tweedy."

Granny's clock on the mantelpiece struck the hour. "Can I talk about it later, Grandpa? I got to get home like Papa said."

He didn't even hear me. "Son, when my black se-dan comes in at the depot, you go'n be the one to drive it to the store!"

"Me?"

"Besides that," said Miss Love, "you're going to teach us how to drive!"

"Me? Y'all?"

"That's right. If Mr. Blakeslee and I learn to drive, between us and you and your daddy there'll always be somebody around to demonstrate." She looked over at Grandpa. "Mr. Blakeslee, I just thought of something else! Let's offer free driving lessons! Once a man gets his hands on a steering wheel, he'd sell his wife and children, if need be, to get up the money to buy one!"

Just barely listening, I could feel my punishment for kissing Lightfoot closing in on me. I didn't think Papa would let me out of it, not even to please Grandpa. And I knew he wouldn't want any and everybody monkeying with his car or learning how to drive on it. "Giving lessons sounds good, Miss Love," I said finally. "But it ain't go'n work."

"Why not? The man in New York said it takes only a few minutes. You just show a person this and that and let him drive a few miles and then teach him how to patch an inner tube. That's all there is to it."

"Yes'm, but if you offer free lessons, every boy in town is go'n be sittin' around the store waitin' his turn, not to mention every man. And school's go'n start up again in a few weeks, Miss Love. I won't be at the store like I am now."

She thought for a minute. "Well, we could just have a drawing once a week. Yes, we'll have one every Saturday! Whoever gets drawn, we'll teach him to drive. Man or boy."

"Not ladies?" I grinned.

She looked surprised. "Yes, of course. Men, boys, ladies, girls."

I didn't say so, but I had my doubts about any lady being able to crank an engine or change a tire. If Miss Love managed to learn, I didn't think any gentleman customer would ride with her for a demonstration. I mean, for one thing she was a woman, and for another she was a woman who had married a widower when his wife wasn't hardly cold in the grave, got caught kissing another man, made a scene in public—and then dog if she hadn't gone off to New York City unchaperoned with a husband whose name she wouldn't use and whose bed she claimed not to be sleeping in. No man in Cold Sassy would dare ride in a car with Miss Love Simpson.

But nothing like that was worrying the two of them right then, and Grandpa had just about as many plans in his head as she did. Lowering his voice, he said, "Now, Will Tweedy, you ain't to tell a soul bout all this."

"Not even Papa?"

"Naw, not even him. I'm go'n tell him and everbody thet they's something big comin' in on the train in two-three weeks. And I'm go'n ast the town band and the Negro band both to come to the depot thet mornin', ready to play for a parade. But I ain't a-go'n say why. And don't you, either."

"Sir, what if somebody asts me?"

"Say you shore wisht you knew."

"What if nobody comes to the depot, Grandpa?"

"Soon as they telegraph me from New York, we go'n drape a big banner acrost the front of the store, tellin' what train to meet. And I gar'ntee you, Will Tweedy, everbody in Cold Sassy's go'n come, outer pure curiosity. And they go'n foller thet Pierce artermobile down to the store so they can see it up close. They mightn't sign up to buy one thet day, but like Miss Love says, they'll start to wantin' one. Now what you think a-all thet, son?"

What I thought was Papa would snatch me bald-headed if he saw me driving without his permission. And how could I get permission if I couldn't tell him about Grandpa's surprise?

Also, I worried whether it was possible to hop into a new automobile and drive it. What if it choked down or went dead, the whole town watching? "What if I cain't get the dern thing started?" I asked Grandpa. "Your Pierce ain't go'n start or run just like Papa's Cadillac, you know."

That didn't even give Grandpa pause. "I got a instruction book here in my grip, and you got plenty time to study it. You won't have no trouble, son. You'll drive jest dandy."

"Of course you will, Will," echoed Miss Love. She stood up. "Goodness, I'm hot. I need to get out of these clothes."

Racing my shadow home, I was almost too excited to think. I didn't know how I'd have time to go to school, give driving lessons, demonstrate cars, groom the Cadillac for Papa and the Pierce for Grandpa and the horse for Miss Love, and be Mama's colored boy and Grandpa's stockboy at the store. But I knew one thing: in a few weeks I would be at the wheel of a shiny black Pierce automobile, chauffeuring Miss Love and Grandpa and leading two bands and a parade of people down to the store.

If Papa didn't accept that Grandpa made me do it, why, I'd just take my whipping like a man.

38

"THET woman shore has got her a head for bizness,"
Grandpa said a few days later. He nodded in the direction of the kitchen, where Miss Love was washing up pans while waiting for her pound cake to get done. He picked a snag of chicken from his front teeth, sucked between tongue and teeth to clear out the rest of it, and then started telling me who all he aimed to sell a artermobile to.

I figured Miss Love was the one who suggested names to him. I bet she'd already figured out who would buy which car and what color, just like she knew who would buy which dress she picked out at the wholesale house in New York City. What I couldn't figure was how she got away with it. Grandpa always was one to admire business sense, but he'd never been one to let somebody else tell him what to do.

The cake wasn't out of the oven good before I got a glimpse of how Miss Love could lead him by the halter.

She came to the dining room door drying her hands and said sweetly, "Mr. B., I know now isn't the time or place to be talking about this, but don't you think it would be nice if the privy was nearer the house? Loomis could dig a pit and move it for us. What do you think?"

"I think it would stink."

"I read about some new chemicals to use."

"Doggit, woman, you got us eatin' in the dang dinin' room weekdays as well as Sundays; now you talkin' bout movin' the privy. Fore I know it, you'll be astin' for a bathroom!" He yelled that last. "Ain't I got enough to worry bout, buyin' thet dang artermobile, 'thout you talkin' bout no dang bathroom?"

Her dander went up like a flag. "Mr. Blakeslee, did I even mention a bathroom? I did not. I said let's move the privy closer to the house."

He grumped and sputtered, and then grinned at her. "Doggit, woman, I never seen the likes a-you." But he said it nice, and then swatted her on the behind as she walked past him to go get a plate for the cake.

It wasn't crude or anything, the way Grandpa flipped her, but the teasing look on his face somehow reminded me they'd been to New York together without a chaperone. And Miss Love took the flip as special, I could tell. She did a little dance all the way back to the kitchen.

I thought to myself that anybody who could get Grandpa to buy a car would have a bathroom in no time, and maybe even electric lights and a telephone. And if already, right now, she was in the family way and it was a boy, she was likely to get more out of Grandpa than Mama could stand—and heir more, too.

Gosh, having a baby uncle would be even worse than having Loma for an aunt. And where would it leave me? If Grandpa could make a pet out of Loma when she was little bitty and then just about throw her away after I was born, he sure-dog could lose track of me if he finally got him a boy of his own. Grandpa never could dote on two people at once.

Miss Love brought in the hot pound cake on Granny's best china plate, holding it high over her head, and set it down in front of Grandpa with a grand flourish. She was smiling big. "I hope it's just the very best you ever ate, Mr. B.," she said, as if she'd forgot me and wanted him to have the whole dang cake. "It's an old receipt, sir, but I added a little of this and that. I do hope you like it. The man who owns Cold Sassy's first Pierce deserves to eat Cold Sassy's best cake. Don't you think so, Will?"

Grandpa told her to quit the foolishness and cut the cake. But he grinned as he said it, and looked at her like the very air she breathed was made out of sugar and spice.

I could tell he'd already forgot about her wanting the privy moved and maybe hoping for a bathroom. But I knew she hadn't forgot. Like a cat smelling a rat, I sensed she was going to drop a hint here and an idea there and a big head-swelling compliment yonder—one this week, another next—till before Grandpa knew what happened, he would decide one day that it shore would be nice not to have to go out to Egypt on a rainy night or a cold winter morning. I didn't know how she would actually pry the money out of him, but she'd figure a way, and somehow make him like it.

Mama was in for a lot of headaches.

In the meanwhile, I had found out that a spate of kissing lasts only just so long. Like religion and silverware, it needs polishing up regular or it don't shine.

By that I mean this. For a few days after Lightfoot McLendon and I got caught in the cemetery, I could just think about kissing her and it was like we were still doing it. I could hear her little gasps and feel her arms around my neck, her body so thin and helpless against me, and as if it was happening right now, my eyes would go out of focus and I'd be breathing like I just made a home run. But the effect was wearing off fast.

And I knew Lightfoot would never kiss me again.

Still and all, when school started next week I could at least look at her and talk to her. I'd find some way to let her know she wasn't a cheap something in my eyes.

The day school started, I was so nervous I could hardly eat my breakfast. What if Lightfoot cut me down with a cold stare? What if she slapped me? But maybe—I dared to hope it—maybe her eyes would light up and she'd smile as if just seeing me was like mountain sunshine breaking through the gray mists of morning. I didn't believe for a minute that her aunt wouldn't let her come back to school. By the time I got there, all I could think about was finding a way to touch her hand or her arm without anybody seeing.

Lightfoot didn't come.

Hosie Roach hurried in just before the second bell. As usual, he was dirty and uncombed. Trying to sound casual, I managed to ask him at recess if Lightfoot McLendon had gone back to the mountains. He said, "Naw, she's a-workin' at the mill."

"She gettin' on all right?" I asked like you'd ask about somebody's grandmother, just being polite. But I made the mistake of blushing.

"What's it to you how she's a-gittin' on?"

"Gosh, Hosie, what's it to you? I just ast. I heard her daddy died and all and I'm just—astin'."

"Yeah, her daddy died. But that don't make it no town boy's bizness how she's gittin' on."

"Says who, linthead?" I snarled, and we went at it.

When Miss Bertha broke up the fight, for once she didn't send us to the principal for a whipping. Instead, she sent us next door to chop stovewood for old Mr. Billy Whisnant. Me first, then Hosie. Miss Bertha roomed upstairs at the Whisnants' house, so I figured Mr. Billy had put her up to it. Him being bent with rheumatism, he couldn't do work like that anymore himself.

Well, I fixed Mr. Billy. And when it was Hosie's turn with the ax I told him what I'd done and he laughed and did likewise. For three days straight, every time I or another boy misbehaved, we had to go over there and chop wood.

Then Mr. Billy chanced to take in an armload of it.

He came storming over to the schoolhouse, face red and fists clenched. Busting into Miss Bertha's Latin lesson, he yelled,

"Doggit to heck, I ain't go'n let no more a-you dang boys cut no more a-my dang stovewood!"

What we'd done, haw, and like I say it was my idea, we had cut every stick exactly four inches too long for the Whisnants' kitchen stove.

Worrying about driving Grandpa's automobile soon put Mr. Billy out of my mind. It even put Lightfoot out of my mind.

When Grandpa found out why I wasn't driving the Cadillac anymore, he just brushed it off. "I ain't heard yore daddy say you cain't drive my Pierce."

"No, sir, but he don't know about that."

"And long as he don't, he cain't say don't drive it."

Miss Love didn't fold her hands while waiting for word from the Pierce Company. She put up tomatoes and corn out of Granny's garden, made cucumber pickles, sewed new dining room curtains, made big black hats with black plumes for Mama and Aunt Loma, and got her horse broke to the bridle and bit.

It was Monday a week after school took in before the telegram came. I don't know how Miss Love managed it, but she got the telegraph operator to swear not to tell anybody what it said, namely, that the Pierce would arrive the following Saturday.

That would be a dandy day for it. Everybody came to town on Saturdays.

Miss Love made a banner out of white sheeting and painted big capital letters on it that said:

BLAKESLEE'S BIG SURPRISE
IS ON THE WAY
MEET THE 1:40 SATURDAY!
BANDS, PARADE, FREE GIFTS!

Grandpa had balked at free gifts, but Miss Love said the wholesale house in New York gave her a big boxful of sample thread, which would do for the ladies, and he could order stick candy and chewing gum to hand out to the men and children. Free gifts would get people into the store, she said.

Grandpa looked at her like she was just the smartest businessman in the world.

That night she and I went to the store and hung the banner out of a second-story window. Next morning everybody in Cold Sassy was talking about it—nobody more than Papa, Uncle Camp, Cudn Hope, and Uncle Lige, who were right put out with Grandpa for not letting them in on the secret. When Uncle Lige said so, Grandpa just grinned and said, "Hit's go'n be a grand fancy day. Y'all be sure and git to the depot on time."

Naturally, folks asked me what it was all about. A lie being an ever-present help in time of trouble, I just said, "Gosh, I wish I knew!"

Tuesday after school, walking through Grandpa's house on my way out back to clean the horse's stall, I saw Miss Love's New York traveling suit draped over the rocking chair in her room, airing out, and her linen duster and veil hung on a wall nail. She herself was in the dining room, pinning pattern pieces on a length of dark blue serge. She looked up at me and smiled. "I'm making Mr. Blakeslee a suit." Opening her scissors into a big V, she started cutting. "I want him to look modern and successful for the parade. It's good for business."

"Yes'm, I reckon."

I went down there again right after supper on Friday evening, before the big day. I was about to bust with excitement, and at home all I could say was "Wonder what Grandpa's plannin' tomorrow, Papa?" or, "I cain't wait to see what's comin' in on the train."

I had already eaten, but I sat down with them and had some blackberry jam and buttered biscuits while getting around to telling my idea. "You finished the suit, Miss Love?" I asked.

"All except hemming the pants."

"Grandpa?" I said then. "Why don't you get Papa to bring

his Cadillac to the depot? You don't have to tell him about your Pierce. Just say be there."

Miss Love took it right up. "And Mary Willis and Loma and Camp could ride with him! We can squeeze in Mary Toy between you and me, Mr. Blakeslee, and it will be a nice family affair!"

"Gosh a'mighty, why didn't we think a-this before, Miss Love? Two artermobiles is twice't as many as one!"

Tell the truth, the reason I wanted Papa to be in on it, I wouldn't have to worry so much. He might be mad about Grandpa making me break punishment, but if the dern thing wouldn't start, or broke down halfway to the store, he and I together might could figure out the trouble.

39

IF THE governor of Georgia was coming in, he wouldn't of drawn a bigger crowd around the Cold Sassy tree at the depot than Grandpa's surprise. I saw lots of country people in mule-drawn wagons. The town was full of cotton-buyers and they came. And so did just about everybody who lived in Cold Sassy, white and colored.

Looking for Miss Love and Grandpa, I saw some mill people and wondered if Lightfoot was there. But if she was, I couldn't find her in the crowd, which well before train time had swelled bigger than for our Southern Independence Day Parade on the Glorious Fourth.

Papa soon drove up in the Cadillac, Mary Toy in Mama's lap, Loma and Camp in the back seat, all of them dressed to the nines and Aunt Loma waving to the crowd like she was the queen of England. Mary Toy was wearing her funeral outfit. Everybody knew that underneath Mama's linen duster she had on mourning clothes, but she looked smart and stylish all the same.

But where were Grandpa and Miss Love?

I was really getting worried when here he came without her. He had on his old black trousers and an old white shirt and string tie, and he was mad as heck. Motioning Papa to park the Cadillac, he stalked onto the loading platform where I was waiting. "Where's Miss Love at, sir?" I asked, anxious. "And why ain't you got on your new suit?"

"Cause I don't feel like puttin' on no airs," he said, ignoring my first question. "Miss Love, she can carry off sech, but I feel like a dang fool in them fancy clothes when I ain't goin' nowhere but downtown. . . . Howdy, Mr. Horace. Howdy, Miz Boswell, how y'all gittin' on?"

I tugged at his sleeve. "Sir, where's Miss Love? She's go'n be late for the train!"

"She ain't a-comin'."

"Ain't comin'?" I couldn't believe it.

"She said she couldn't sleep last night for thinkin' what folks are go'n say. Said they'd say she talked me into buyin' thet big artermobile."

"Gosh, Grandpa. Gosh."

I wanted to ask him more, but he was busy greeting folks. "Howdy, Jedge. Howdy, Miz Landrum. Y'all doin' all right? Well, if it ain't Cudn George! I heerd you got li'l Sara Ann married off." His mouth stretched like he was smiling, but he wasn't. Waving and nodding to folks in the crowd, not looking at me, he said, "I told her to good-gosh-a'mighty let'm talk. I said she had to come. She said it wouldn't hep sell artermobiles if she did. I said I didn't care. She said she did."

A farm boy called up to him, "Mr. Blakeslee?"

"Yeah, son, how's it goin' with yore ma?"

"She's gittin' better. What's yore surprise, sir? Air it a thang or a person?"

Grandpa grinned. "You'll see, son. You'll see." Then he muttered to me, "Dang woman wouldn't budge. Said she'd walk to the store with the crowd. I said I ain't a-go'n let you humble yoreself like thet, but she said she was sick and tarred a-bein' called names."

Poor Grandpa. All the fun had gone out of it for him. But Miss Love was right. If folks saw her perched high and mighty beside him in the back seat of a shiny motorcar, they'd call her snooty, or grave-snatcher. They'd recollect that all Miss Mattie Lou ever had to ride in was a buggy pulled by a mule—unless you counted Mr. Birdsong's glass-sided hearse pulled by fine black horses that she'd rode to the cemetery in.

"Thet woman is stubborn, great goodness!" Grandpa sputtered. I knew the real reason he didn't wear the new suit was he was mad at her. Also, I could smell he'd had a snort.

Just then Grandpa sighted the train. "Here she comes, folks!" he shouted, excited despite himself, and the crowd cheered. As Mr. Tuttle motioned everybody back from the tracks, the town band struck up "Waltz Me Around Again, Willie," and Grandpa called, "Hoyt, y'all git up here on the platform! Here she comes!"

As "Waltz Me Around Again" faded out, the Negro band took over, root-a-toot-tootin' and rat-a-tat-tattin' from their mule-drawn wagon. Every man played a different beat and a different tune, but the music meshed together into one big happy sound.

Loomis wasn't on the bandwagon. He was up on the loading platform with some other colored men, all of them grinning big and waving to friends, white and colored. It being their job to get the surprise out of the boxcar, they would be the first to see what it was.

"Where's Miss Love at, Mr. Blakeslee?" my daddy asked. It was like he just mouthed the words. You couldn't hear them. His question was lost in noise as the train engine screeched to a stop, brass bell ringing and steam belching over the rails. That's when Grandpa yelled into Papa's ear about the Pierce.

"You want me to drive it, sir?" Papa yelled, so excited he hopped from foot to foot.

"Naw, Will Tweedy's go'n drive."

"What'd you say, sir?"

"I said WILL TWEEDY! He's go'n DRIVE!"

I couldn't tell if Papa heard that or not. Like everybody else, he was watching Mr. Tuttle signal the engineer. Grandpa's box-car stopped right where it was supposed to at the platform, and Mr. Tuttle helped Loomis open the big door. The crowd hushed as the big Negro took a quick peep inside. He shouted, "Lawdy, Lawdy, Mr. Rucker! Ain't you de one! Bless Jesus, you done got yo'se'f a chariot!"

As the colored men rolled the automobile out and down the ramp to the ground, I pulled the Pierce instruction book out of the pocket of my new Sunday suit and handed it to my daddy. While he studied it, I put on my linen duster and the driving cap with goggles, and big Loomis flipped a towel over the black sedan like he was shining a millionaire's boots. He bowed as the crowd whistled and whooped.

Grandpa didn't waste any time. After helping Mary Toy into the back seat, he climbed in beside her and stood waving as the crowd cheered. Papa had opened up the hood. We looked good to see if it was much different from the Cadillac, then I jumped behind the steering wheel and Papa leaned in to help me locate the ignition switch, gas feed, choke, brakes, and all like that.

With men crowding around to congratulate him, Grandpa got up on the back seat, raised his hand for silence, and shouted for everybody to follow us down to the store. After the word *store*, Mr. Goosby took it on himself to hit the big drum—and kept hitting it every time Grandpa finished a sentence. "I want y'all to git a good look at this here artermobile, folks!"—BAM—"See how she works!"—BAM—"I ain't aimin' to have the only Pierce in town for long! I'm a-go'n sell all y'all one!" BAM!

Seeing the question mark on Papa's face, Grandpa reached down and shook my daddy's hand. "Thet's right, Hoyt! I got the Pierce dealership, and we go'n sell Caddy-lacs, too. Folks, a new day's a-dawnin' for Cold Sassy!"—BAM—"We go'n put ever man in town behind a dang artermobile wheel!" BAM!

The crowd clapped and whistled like they thought Grandpa

was giving motorcars away. He raised his hand again. "Now, let's git on to the store! I got free thread for the ladies and lick-rish and peppermint sticks for all you chi'ren! Will Tweedy, son, start my dang artermobile!"—*Drum roll*—"Hoyt, start yore'n! Mary Willis? Loma? Y'all set? I'm ready to lead the dang parade!" BAM, BAM, BAM and another drum roll, and the bands struck up "Dixie."

I was scared to death the Pierce might not start. Turning the switch key, I pulled out the choke as Papa motioned big Loo-mis to turn the crank. The engine sputtered. He cranked again. The motor flipped over, sputtered, caught! The car shimmied and shook. Grandpa leaned forward and blew the horn, loud and long.

"Sit down, Grandpa! Here we go!" I yelled, and we were off. With drums beating, horn tooting, Mary Toy squealing, and Papa and them in the Cadillac right behind us, the crowd pushed forward toward Cold Sassy's new day dawnin'.

Except for me and Grandpa, I don't think a soul cared that Love Simpson wasn't in the party. But I expect a lot of folks no-ticed.

"You see her?" Grandpa asked, standing up to look as we chugged to a stop in front of the store. His eyes scanned the crowd. "I thought Miss Love would aw-ready be here, waitin'."

"I don't see her, sir," I said.

Mary Toy caught aholt of his knotted sleeve and tugged at it. "I saw her, sir, after you made your speech. She was goin' towards home. Why didn't Miss Love want to ride with us, Grandpa?"

He didn't answer.

In the store a few minutes later, Aunt Loma said to me, real smug, "I reckon Pa wouldn't let Love horn in on his big day."

"It wasn't like that," I said. "Miss Love, she—she's sick this mornin'."

"Well, good for her!" said Aunt Loma, pleased. "That's poetic justice, considerin'."

I thought Miss Love would come in after while, but she didn't. And nobody seemed to mind she wasn't there, especially not Mama and Aunt Loma, who got busy giving out thread samples and candy and had a swell time.

The store did a big trade in everything but cars that day. Lots of folks said they'd sure like to own one, but it was after five o'clock before anybody actually talked business. The man who did was Mr. Sheffield, president of the mill. He rode up on his white Thoroughbred.

Those crowded around the two cars parted for Mr. Sheffield as he kicked his horse up to the Pierce. Folks white and colored watched, silent and curious, as the rich man dismounted, leaned in, examined the seats and the steering wheel, ran his hand over the horn, then tied up his horse and went in the store. I saw him motion to Grandpa.

Five minutes later he came out with my daddy for a ride in the Cadillac. Then I took him out in the Pierce, with Grandpa in the back seat, shouting over the engine's putter that artermobiles is a dang marvel.

As Mr. Sheffield got back on his horse, he said he thought he'd rather have a Hanson touring car.

We all felt let down.

Just before dark, Grandpa told me to drive his car home and park it in the barn. Coming out to watch me crank up, he slapped his hand on the shimmying hood. "Be up home fore sunup, Will Tweedy!" he yelled. "You go'n learn me and her how to drive this here thang!"

"Tomorrow, sir? Tomorrow's Sunday!"

"Thet's right. Better tell Loomis to milk for you, son, cause we got to git a early start or we go'n run up on all them buggies and wagons comin' in for preachin'."

• • •

The sky was barely getting light and the birds just beginning to wake up and sing when I tiptoed downstairs in my Sunday suit and my new linen duster. Queenie hadn't even gotten there yet. After washing down a cold biscuit with some sweetmilk, I put on my driving cap and goggles and had just sneaked out the back door when Papa leaned out of his bedroom window upstairs. "Will?" he called softly.

Seen through my driving goggles, he looked dim in the half-light. "Sir?"

"Watch the time and don't be late gettin' back for Sunday school. You hear?"

"Yessir."

I ran all the way up to Grandpa's house.

Thirty minutes later we were on the Jefferson road, and it could of been Christmas, we were so excited.

There was no sign of leftover bad feelings between Grandpa and Miss Love. He had his new clothes on under his duster. Miss Love's gray fall suit barely showed under hers, and she wore the dust veil over her red hat. She said we looked like a fashion advertisement in the newspaper. But as the sun rose and the mist burned off, we really warmed up in our fashionable get-ups.

Grandpa was sitting up front with me to watch what I did. "Maybe we don't need the dang dusters!" he yelled, looking back at Miss Love.

Her answer was lost in the wind.

"What you say?" he yelled.

"I said somebody might see us!" she shouted, leaning forward. "The man said part of selling cars is looking the part! Wearing the uniform! Remember?"

When we got to a long stretch of newly graded road, I shut off the engine, and the sudden silence sounded like noise. "Sit forward so you can see, Miss Love," I said, feeling important. "I'm go'n show y'all where the foot brake is, and the hand brake and gas feed and switch key." When I thought they understood it all, I got out to walk around the car and Grandpa moved over to the right side behind the wheel. Stepping onto the running board and seating myself, I said, "Now, sir you got to get all these dohickies set right or else she ain't go'n start up."

I knew he didn't have the faintest notion why he was doing any of it, but he said, real impatient, "You ain't got to tell me but once't, Will Tweedy. What's next?"

"Next you got to give the crank a few hard turns."

"You go do thet for me."

"Sir, you need the practice. Crankin' up is part of drivin'."

Miss Love had been watching closely, her arms on the back of the driver's seat. As Grandpa stepped out, she said, "You forgot something, Mr. Blakeslee."

"I ain't forgot nothin'." He walked toward the front of the automobile.

"Yessir, you did, Grandpa," said I. "You didn't turn on the ignition."

"Gosh a'mighty, son, what's the ignition? You ain't mentioned thet'n."

"Yes, he did, sir," said Miss Love. "The ignition is what you turn on with the switch key."

"Well, doggit, whyn't you say so? Miss Love, reach over and turn the dang key."

She did. But as Grandpa bent to crank up the engine, she reached forward again and, with a chessy-cat grin at me, turned the switch back off! Naturally nothing happened when Grandpa cranked. Disgusted, he straightened up and bit off a plug of tobacco. "Hit must be outa gas-lene, Will Tweedy."

"Cain't be," said I, winking at Miss Love. "Come see if you set everything right, Grandpa." As he started toward us, head down in disgust, Miss Love quick reached forward and turned the key on. Grandpa leaned in, studied the board a minute, then said, "Will Tweedy? Everthang you told me to do, I done done. You see anythang I missed?"

"No, sir. I reckon you just ain't crankin' hard enough, Grandpa."

Soon as he turned his back, Miss Love shut off the switch again. We like to died, holding in laughter. Grandpa repeated his quick jerks of the crank, all for nothing. After he'd wore himself out up there, he kicked one of the front tires and said, "Giddy-up, you dang fool!"

Miss Love was laughing out loud now.

"Don't make fun a-me, woman!" yelled Grandpa. "Let's see you come have a try at it. You crank and I'll laugh."

As Miss Love sashayed to the front of the sedan, she looked back and winked at me, and I grinned and turned on the ignition. With one quick turn she had the engine putt-putting loud and pretty as you please. "It just needed a woman's touch!" she yelled sweetly. Grandpa swatted her behind as she went back to get in.

"I'm go'n shut it off now, Grandpa," I yelled. "You need to practice settin' all the dohickies, and I ain't sure you know how to crank it up yet. You get a knack for that by doin' it."

Glaring at me, Grandpa stalked back to the car, reached in, turned on the switch, pulled out the choke, spat, and went back to the front of the engine. Miss Love waited till he bent down to crank and then turned the key off again.

Crank, crank, *silence*. Crank, crank, *cuss*.

"Gosh a'mighty dang!" He raised up. "I never did like to do anythang I ain't done before!" Jerking off his linen duster and his cap and goggles, he threw them on the hood of the car and said he was a-go'n crank thet dang Pierce if'n it took all day. "Wisht I hadn't never heard the word artermobile."

The harder he cranked, the harder we laughed. Miss Love didn't see him coming towards us till he was nearly to the driver's seat. He caught her reaching for the switch key.

"I seen you! I seen what you done!" Grandpa shook his fist in her face and said, "Woman, if I ketch you doin' sech as thet again, you go'n walk home!"

I swear I don't know how she had the nerve, but she laughed in his face.

He walked backwards to the front of the auto, watching her, and then made her get out. This time when he cranked, the motor roared. "Now thet's more like!" yelled Grandpa. With a satisfied grin, he flung his duster and goggles into the back seat, put on his cap at a jaunty angle, climbed in, and yelled over the racket, "Now then, I'm a'go'n drive this son-of-a-gun. How fast will she go, Will Tweedy? How do I start off? What do I do after we git to goin'?"

"Release the hand brake first, Grandpa!" I yelled over the engine noise. "Now, sir, feed a little gas, . . . Not much. Just a little bit till you get the hang of it. Go slow now! . . . Grandpa, don't wiggle the steerin' wheel so much!"

"Thet's what you done, son!"

"Only enough to keep it goin' straight."

"Thet don't make no sense a-tall."

We crawled along for a mile or two, Grandpa having the time of his life. Then we reached the crest of a hill—and the road plunged down on the other side like a roller coaster! I saw Grandpa swallow his tobacco chew as we picked up speed. "What do I do, son?" he yelled. "Whoa, doggit, whoa!" He tried to hold the steering wheel with his arm stub while turning off the switch key and moving every lever his hand could find. "Will Tweedy, stop the dang thang!"

"The brake! Use the brake, Grandpa!"

Faster and faster we went, Miss Love screaming and me yelling for the brake. At the foot of the hill, the road curved. With a wild turn of the steering wheel, Grandpa landed us in a shallow ditch.

Nobody was hurt, but it sure knocked the pride out of us,

and it knocked the air out of the right front tire. It took me and Grandpa both to push the car onto the road, after which we just stood there looking at it. A crow called from a cornfield nearby. A fly buzzed around my ear. "We ought to brought Loomis along," I said, taking off the hot duster and my cap. "He could of just picked the car up and set it back on the road."

"If I'd a-had two good hands," said Grandpa, fuming, "I could a-kept it from happenin'."

I couldn't bring myself to remind Grandpa that he had two good feet, one of which should of found the brake.

While I patched the inner tube, Miss Love leaned against the hood of the car, looking like she might faint. Grandpa paced up and down scratching his head. Neither one watched what I was doing or tried to help me. Well, I'd teach them about inner tubes another day.

When I had the tire back on, I wiped my hands on a rag from the toolbox and said, "Now, Grandpa, you can crank her up again."

"Thet was my first and last time," he said, fishing in his pants pocket for his plug tobacco. "A artermobile ain't nothin' but a dang roller coaster. A mule's at least got sense of its own."

"Aw, Grandpa, come on." I tried to pull him toward the car. "It ain't hard, sir. You can learn."

"I'm shore I can, but I ain't a-goin' to. Anyhow, it's Miss Love's turn."

I motioned her towards the driver's seat, but she opened the back door and climbed in. "I think," she said in a weak voice, "that I'll wait my turn till later."

"Yes'm," I said, relieved. "It seems like maybe a good idea."

It looked like Miss Love was going to be a good driver. She wanted to practice without Grandpa in the car. The first time I took her out in the country, she just about sat on the brake and didn't go but two miles an hour, but she looked real stylish with her dust veil draped over Grandpa's driving cap and goggles, and she reeked of perfume. She said she always wore lots of perfume when she was nervous.

Two days later she speeded up considerable, and got brave enough to drive all the way home. We were in front of her house in no time, but instead of turning in, she kept right on going. "I want to drive to the store!" she yelled over the putt-putt. She was real excited. "I've been telling Mr. Blakeslee how easy driving is! I want him to see!"

It's just a pity that a bee got under Miss Love's dust veil about time she crept the car around the Confederate monument. I reckon it was the perfume did it. Probably the bee thought he'd found a flower. Then while Miss Love was slapping at him under her veil, the bee fell down the front of her dress! Got to crawling around on her bosom, I reckon, because she commenced screaming and hitting her chest, and the car went clean out of control! I grabbed for the wheel as Miss Love took her hands and feet off of everything and covered her eyes.

People screamed and ran, horses and mules screeched and rared. The Pierce bounced onto the curb of the monument, grazing the marble where it says OUR NOBLE DEAD, then ambled across the street and bumped to a stop against the sycamore tree near the cast-iron watering trough in front of Grandpa's store. Miss Love didn't even notice when I cut off the ignition. She was still fighting the bee. As Grandpa and my daddy rushed out, followed by a bunch of customers, Miss Love screamed. "He bit me! He bit me! Somebody help! Get him out of here!"

"Will Tweedy, be-have yoreself!" yelled Grandpa as Miss Love leaped out of the car and ran in the store.

"I ain't done nothin', sir! She's got a bee down her dress!"

We rushed into the store. Uncle Lige motioned towards the storage room. "She run in thar!" Grandpa found her behind a stack of ninety-five-pound sacks of cow feed. Her veil and linen duster were on the floor beside the bee, which she had stomped to death, and Miss Love was buttoning her shirtwaist. Turning her back to us, she sobbed. "I g-got stung, Mr. Blakeslee."

He looked helpless, like he didn't know what to do, then commenced patting her shoulder. "Hit's all right, Miss Love," he whispered. "Hit's all right."

I couldn't help thinking that though Miss Love could sass Mr. McAllister back to Texas and glare down a town full of folks sitting in judgment on her, with a bee in her bosom she was helpless as any lady I knew.

Finally she turned and faced Grandpa. Her cheeks were wet and she clutched her swelling breast with one hand, but she had control of her voice. "Mr. Blakeslee," she announced, "I'll not drive that or any car again. Ever."

"Now, Miss Love—"

"Sir, I mean it."

I couldn't hardly stand to see her give up. "You'll learn, Miss Love. It ain't like you go'n get a bee down you every time you drive."

She ignored that. "I guess we're alike, Mr. Blakeslee. I don't trust machinery. I don't understand how it works. I can talk to a horse and calm him down, but I can't talk to *that!*" She pointed in the general direction of the sycamore tree. "Oh, Mr. Blakeslee, I wanted a car so bad!" She started crying again. "How can we ever g-go m-motoring now!"

Grandpa, real agitated, looked over at me, where I stood leaning against a big wooden box. "Son," he said, "it 'pears to me like if thet dang Pierce ever sees the road agin, it's a-go'n have to be you at the wheel."

40

ANY mule head could see that the automobiles wouldn't last long parked in front of the store—children jumping on the seats, men and big boys monkeying with the wires and knobs trying to see which did what. Papa was real upset about it. I finally told Grandpa we ought to make room for the cars in the buggy-and-wagon shed behind the store, but he dismissed the idea with a backward flip of his hand. "I ain't a-go'n do thet. Two elephants tied out yonder wouldn't draw customers to the store as good as them artermobiles."

That was the Lord's truth. Cold Sassy never had been a whirlpool of excitement. If the preacher's wife's petticoat showed, the ladies could make that last a week as something to talk about. We had our share of cotton-gin fires, epidemics, storms, and lawsuits, of course, but the only diversion we could count on was protracted meetings, recitals, ice cream socials, fish fries, and lectures—a doctor talking up his cure for cancer, an old man telling how he tracked a mammoth moose for nineteen days back in 1856, a young fellow talking about "Across Asia on a Bicycle." It's easy to see why not even the scarlet of the Cold Sassy tree in autumn could equal our big shiny automobiles as something to rave about, especially with the open invite to come sit in them and take a ride.

By the end of the week, though, even Grandpa was worried. "I reckon maybe you better move'm on to the back, Will Tweedy," he said. He was let down about it, I could tell, but he made sure nobody forgot the cars were back there. Any time he had an audience of customers, Grandpa would say what a dang marvel a artermobile is, and then light in talking about car-owners taking all-day trips together, sending delegations to the Georgia legislature to talk up better roads, and having auto races "uphill, downhill, cross-country, and hind-part-before."

While Grandpa did the talking, Papa and I did the driving people around. It was my job to give a driving lesson every Saturday after our drawing.

Miss Love did what the man in New York called "pushing the merchandise." For one thing, she wanted to order a lady mannequin for the store window and dress it up in a linen duster and dust veil like one she saw at the Cadillac agency in New York City. Grandpa said, "Thet's jest fol-de-rol and foolish-ment. Them big dolls cost too much to think about, much less buy." But that wasn't the end of it.

Soon as the weather got cooler, Miss Love turned herself into a big doll. Sat in the store window nearly all day, wearing a veil, a duster, and a frozen smile. She'd be a statue till she had to scratch or something, then come outside for a few minutes and talk to folks about the latest in motorcar fashions.

Grandpa was really pleased, for Miss Love in the store window was a sight to behold. White folks and colored, too, stood in clumps staring at her. If she chanced to bat her eyes or yawn or shift a little in the chair, they'd poke one another in the ribs and haw and guffaw. Boys clowned and made faces trying to make her laugh, but she looked straight ahead and never even cracked a smile.

When Aunt Loma happened along, carrying the baby, she stared at Miss Love a minute, then flounced into the store and came over where I stood putting bars of Octagon soap on a shelf. "Love looks foolish," she grumped.

Loma was jealous. The store window being like a little stage and her having taken elocution, she considered herself the only person in Cold Sassy qualified to act like a dummy.

The county sheriff from over at Homer watched Miss Love a while and then went in and put down on a Pierce.

A country woman watched Miss Love and spent her egg money on a dust veil. Her husband was furious when he saw her draping the veil over her sunbonnet. Said you go git Mr. Blakeslee to give yore money back. But she wouldn't. Straightening up proud on her cut-off chair in the wagon, she said, "The same dust as gits on them fancy ladies in artermobiles gits on me when they go racin' by. I got jest as much right to look nice in a cloud a-dust as they do."

Late in September I drove Miss Love and Grandpa to the county fair over in Jefferson. Grandpa sold a car while Miss Love and I were on the Ferris wheel. Then he won the big prize at the rifle booth for three bull's eyes in a row. That really impressed Miss Love, and also the man who ran the booth. He wouldn't let Grandpa shoot again.

We had a swell time, just the three of us. I wrote down in my journal that night how pretty Miss Love looked. Her freckledy face was lit up with excitement all day, and seemed like Grandpa couldn't keep his eyes off of her.

I also wrote down that although he sat up front with me all the way to Jefferson—telling me when to slow down, when to speed up and, son, watch out for thet there bump in the road—coming home he sat with Miss Love, his right arm resting on the back of her seat.

Considering what happened soon after, it's interesting that I sensed it was worth noting in the journal how he sat with her on the trip home.

Early in October we had our first cold snap, and the next Monday, soon after I got to the store from school, Miss Love came in saying let's plan an overnight motoring trip for the weekend. "Weather permitting, of course. Wouldn't you like to take your family, Mr. Hoyt?"

Before Papa could answer, Grandpa said he'd rather take a day trip, get back to his own bed.

"That's a sign you're growing old, Mr. Blakeslee," she teased.

I could tell it made him mad. "Hit jest don't suit me to go off now. Anyhow, what's the hurry?"

"The hurry is because we can't count on many more nice weekends." Miss Love's fingers went to drumming on the counter. "Once winter sets in, that's the end of any real motoring till spring. We can't travel when it's freezing cold."

"Thet's one way a artermobile ain't no different from a horse and buggy, Miss Love. So you ain't tellin' us nothin' we don't know."

"But I so wanted—" She looked up at Grandpa like a little girl who's been told she can't play with her new doll.

Papa butted in. "It's out of the question for us both to be gone on Sarady right now, Miss Love. Farmers are comin' in to pay up credit accounts and seed and fertilizer loans, and I'm run ragged with the automobile bizness. And—"

"And me and Lige are knee-deep in cotton, buyin' and warehousin' it," Grandpa argued. "So it'll have to be jest a Sunday ride or not a-tall, Miss Love."

"Well, of course. I understand, Mr. Blakeslee. I guess . . . I guess it just seemed so—" Her mouth trembled like she might cry, but Grandpa didn't notice. He had got busy with a customer.

I tried to cheer her up. "If it's as cold next weekend as today, Miss Love, we cain't go anywhere anyhow."

On Friday it was still cold, with a strong wind. But Saturday turned off so warm you had to look at the reds and yellows and browns of the trees to remember how we'd shivered all week.

Papa thought it would be just as nice on Sunday, maybe better. "I'll get Mary Willis to fix enough food for all of us," he told Grandpa, "and we'll leave right after preachin'. Go out in the country and have a nice picnic together."

But Miss Love had a different idea. On my way home to milk, I met up with her and Mr. Beautiful, out for a late-evening canter. When she reined in, the horse prancing sideways and jerking the bit, she asked if I thought Papa and Mama would be willing to leave at daybreak. "That way we could go a long way."

"Yes'm, we could if Papa would miss Sunday school and preachin'. But he won't."

"Well, why don't we go then? Just you and Mr. Blakeslee and I."

Remembering the good time we'd had at the fair, I thought that was a swell idea. But I shook my head. "Papa ain't go'n let me miss, either, Miss Love."

The horse snorted, impatient. She patted his neck, spoke soft to him. "Whoa, baby. Whoa. . . . You could ask him, Will."

"Ain't no use."

And that's what I thought. But when my daddy and I got back to the store — Saturday nights being one of our busiest times — Grandpa said, "Hoyt, I know how you and Mary Willis feel bout missin' preachin', but I'd like to leave early t'morrer mornin'."

Papa wanted to, I could tell, and not only just to please Grandpa. But he pushed Satan behind him "Not this time, Mr. Blakeslee. Me bein' treasurer of the session, I got to be there t'morrer." He didn't mention Sin on Sunday, but I could feel the words hanging in the air.

About then old Mr. Billy Whisnant shuffled in and asked for a jar of lini-ment. "Hit shore heps my rheumatiz," he whined as Papa went to get it off the shelf. Mr. Billy looked around and saw me but didn't speak. He hadn't said pea-turkey to me, as a matter of fact, since I cut his wood too long.

But I wasn't studying him while Papa wrapped up the liniment and made change. I was thinking how lucky Miss Love and Grandpa were, going to church at home. The Flournoys having long since returned to the Methodists, it was just the two of them. They could run into the parlor, sing fast, pray quick, and be on the road before the rest of Cold Sassy got out its Sunday clothes.

I should explain that, though Grandpa never mentioned their preachin' service anymore or invited anybody to come, Cold Sassy knew the blasphemy was still going on. Miss Effie Belle could hear them singing when she got home from playing for the Methodists, and what she heard wasn't "Holy Spirit, Truth Divine."

After Mr. Billy shuffled out, Papa commenced toting up some figures, which meant the subject of an all-day motor trip was closed. But Grandpa didn't let it drop. "I respect yore position in the Presbytery, Hoyt, but I'd be much obliged if Will Tweedy could leave early to drive us." He laughed. "Miss Love is threatenin' to drive us if'n the boy cain't go." Not waiting for Papa to object, Grandpa turned to me. "Son, if you ain't up home by time we ready to eat, we'll save you some breakfast. I don't want yore ma gittin' up early to feed you."

Next morning when I got to Grandpa's, Miss Love had already fried a chicken for our picnic and was serving up fried ham, grits, scrambled eggs, and hot biscuits. After breakfast she packed a basket: chicken, peach pickles, fresh tomatoes, butterbeans in a jar, the leftover biscuits, and half a pecan pie.

I hurried out to the barn to crank up. The birds were singing as if life depended on making noise, and I didn't care at all that the Pierce would drown out their songs. It was going to be just the three of us! A really swell day!

As we rode off, bundled in coats and lap robes, Miss Effie Belle Tate came out on her porch. She couldn't help seeing that Grandpa was in the back seat with Miss Love, but in case she didn't notice, he reached over my shoulder and blew the horn at her and waved.

Miss Effie Belle didn't wave back.

I wondered if he'd want to go by our house for his snort, but he didn't mention it.

The single-track dirt road had deep wagon ruts, and it like to jolted us to pieces. There were chuckholes, too, and whenever I hit one, the rebound just about tossed Grandpa and Miss Love out of the car. I could brace myself with the steering wheel, but they didn't grab anything except each other. Being scared they might pitch out, I started swerving around the holes. I'd yell, "Hold on!" and Grandpa would whoop and hold Miss Love tighter, and she'd shriek and giggle like a schoolgirl.

Looking back on that day, I'm reminded of a story Loomis told me about his uncle in Macon who chauffeured a bride and groom around the state on their wedding trip. Everywhere they went, he'd say to folks as a joke, "We's on our honeymoon!" Well, we were on our honeymoon that day. Me and Grandpa and Miss Love. I don't think we knew it then. At least, I didn't. But even before we got out of Cold Sassy good, I felt left out. We were going to be two and one on this trip. Not three.

One time when I stopped to let the motor cool off and said something funny, they not only didn't laugh, they didn't even hear me. At some point Grandpa asked did I think we ought to let the air out of the tires and put in some fresh. He was just showing off for Miss Love, trying to be funny. And I don't think he said anything else to me all morning.

If they laughed, they never thought to tell me what the joke was. When I glanced back as we rode along, usually they were looking at each other, not at the fall leaves or the distant blue mountains. If Grandpa weren't so old, I'd swear he was sweet on Miss Love, and vice versa. Just like at the fair, he couldn't keep his eyes off of her.

Good thing Papa's Cadillac wasn't back there in our dust.

If Mama could of seen what I saw, it sure would of given her a headache.

We had the usual problems with punctures and the motor overheating, and though I tried to be careful, we scared our share of mules and horses. But it was another automobile that caused the accident.

We had eaten our picnic standing at a plank table in a country churchyard. They weren't having preachin' that Sunday, so we had the place all to ourselves. When we were stuffed full, we spread the lap robes on the ground and dozed in the warm sunshine a while—till Grandpa said he wanted to make it home by first dark so we better think about starting back. We had just got on the road again when a little two-seater black Ford pulled into the highway just ahead of us.

The driver blew his horn and the lady with him waved at us. I blew our horn and we waved back. "The automobile book calls this the cameraderie of the road!" Miss Love shouted. She was having a grand time.

"Yes'm!" I shouted back.

We soon found out that cameraderie of the road really means eating somebody's dust. After we'd gone two or three miles behind the Ford, Miss Love tapped me on the shoulder and yelled, "Will, honey, stop a few minutes and let them get on ahead of us! I can't stand it."

So we stopped, waving good-bye as the Ford went on. A good while later we rounded a curve and there it was again, just ahead, laying on its side like a dead horse. Grandpa shouted, "Watch out, Will Tweedy! Stop, son!" Miss Love screamed. I braked. But not in time. To miss the Ford I had to cut the steering wheel sharp left and plunge the car into a creek—really just a little shallow branch. It had a good gravel bottom, so I drove through the water till I got around the wreck, then went up the slanted red-clay bank and got back to the road.

Grandpa had grabbed Miss Love hard when I swerved into the creek; he still had aholt of her when I looked back to see if they were all right. Her face was white as cotton and her voice shaky as she said, "We'd better see if those people are hurt."

The man and lady were already walking towards us. "We was hopin' y'all would come along soon," said the man. "I don't think our car is damaged, but I cain't right it by myself. I done tried."

"I'm Rucker Blakeslee, Caddy-lac and Pierce dealer from over at Cold Sassy," said Grandpa. "This here's my wife and my grandboy."

Introducing himself, the man shook hands with Grandpa and me. He was from Athens.

"What happened, mister?" I asked.

"See yonder?" he pointed to a deep narrow cut that ran across the road. "Creek must of swole up after the last rain. Thet washout th'owed my car clean out a-control."

Grandpa stared at the washout and then at the dead Ford. "Come on, Will Tweedy. Let's set up the artermobile." Us and the man made short work of it. Watching them drive off, I felt puffed up and proud to of helped somebody in trouble.

It's just too bad we didn't know about the leaking radiator before they left. I didn't see it till after Grandpa and Miss Love climbed in the back seat and I went around to crank up. The radiator must of hit a rock in the creek. "Lord hep us," I said.

"What's the matter?" asked Miss Love.

"Ma'am, we got a hole in the radiator."

"Well, plug it up," said Grandpa.

"It ain't that simple, sir."

"Will she crank?" he asked, getting out to come look.

"I reckon," said I. "But she'll get too hot if we run her without any water in the radiator. We might could find a mechanic in Athens, but I don't know if the car will make it to Athens."

Miss Love smiled at Grandpa. "Well, you said it, Mr. B. All we have to do is think up some way to plug the hole."

"We could cool the engine some by keepin' on pourin' water in the radiator," I said. "But I ain't even got a bucket."

An old colored woman was walking across a pasture towards us. Likely she was curious to know what happened, or maybe she just wanted to look at a motorcar up close. "Auntie?" I called.

"Yassuh?" She had on a blue striped head rag and a dirty faded old feed-sack dress that blew in the wind against her knobby legs. She walked awful slow.

"Make haste, we need some hep!" I yelled. I don't know what I thought she could do. Give us a bucket, maybe.

"Yassuh, I's comin'! But I cain't make no haste."

While we waited, Miss Love had an idea. "The water in the radiator gets very hot, doesn't it, Will?"

"Yes'm. It boils."

"Why don't we ask the colored lady for some grits? I think—"

Grandpa hooted. "You thet hungry, Miss Love? Ain't we still got some fried chicken?"

"Oh, I'm not hungry. Certainly not for grits." I noticed that a day in the sun and wind had reddened her face and multiplied her freckles. "I'm thinking we could plug the leak with grits, if the lady has some." She nodded toward the colored woman, who was nearly to the ditch that separated the unfenced pasture from the road. "If Will puts water in the radiator and starts the engine, and when it gets hot he dumps in some grits, wouldn't it make a big stiff lump and stop up the hole? What do you think, Mr. Blakeslee?"

Grandpa thought it was a really swell idea.

If she'd asked what I thought, I'd of said, "Well, maybe." But she didn't ask me.

When the Negro woman got to the ditch, I told her what we wanted.

"Chicken grits or reg'lar eatin' grits?" she asked.

"I think regular eating grits," Miss Love answered.

"Yas'm, but mought be dey's weev'ly."

"That don't matter," I said. "Can you spare us some?"

"Yassuh, sho can." I know she thought we were crazy

Grandpa dug into his pocket and held out a dime. "Here you are, auntie."

Showing her bare mouth in a grin, the old woman spat snuff juice and put the dime in her pocket. "Son, I's gwine ax you to come up to de house wid me. My old feets, dey cain' make it back down heah agin today."

When I left the Negro shack, I was swinging a big old leaky enamel bucket with a cupful of grits in the bottom of it. I had paid the woman a nickel for the bucket.

Hurrying across the pasture, I saw Miss Love and Grandpa standing beside the car, just a-talking. When I was nearly to the big oak in the middle of the pasture, she turned away from him to climb back in the car. I was just fixing to holler that I got the grits when Grandpa put his hand on her arm and pulled her to him.

I didn't holler. I stood stock still and watched as Grandpa touched her cheek, then put his arms around her and kissed her long and hard—on the mouth! And Miss Love was kissing him back, no doubt about it. Same as if he'd been Mr. McAllister.

Not knowing what to do or say, I ducked behind the oak tree, feeling for the first time like Granny had been betrayed.

Miss Love had a house, a horse, and a piano—all the things she used to pray for—and now an automobile. Wasn't that enough? Hadn't God let her know once already that she couldn't have a husband?

Like Mama always said, I guess some folks just can't be satisfied. The more they get, the more they want.

41

BEING behind the tree, I didn't see it if Miss Love slapped Grandpa or pushed him away. By time I finally peeped around, they were back in the car. Miss Love was pinning her red hat on straight again, so I couldn't see her expression, but I could see Grandpa's, and he didn't look contrite or guilty, either one. He looked like a boy playing tops who has just won everybody's tobacco tags.

Before he could kiss her again and me have to wait it out behind the tree, I yelled, "I got the grits!" and hurried towards them.

After pouring the grits into a napkin out of the picnic basket so I could use the bucket, I filled the radiator from the creek and cranked up. I was just fixing to pour in the grits when I thought to wonder how in heck you could get cooked grits out of a radiator.

"I don't think we better try it, Miss Love," I said. I folded the napkin and held it out to her. "You want the grits, ma'am?"

"I reckon you got a better idea," Grandpa said, sarcastic. He was disappointed. Fixing a leak with grits would be something to tell and laugh about all week, like that time we ran out of inner-tube patching and rode home on a tire stuffed with a piece of old quilt.

"Well, it might plug the leak, Grandpa. I don't know. But I think it'd ruin the radiator. We can risk it, sir, if you willin' to buy a new radiator. But—"

"Let's try something else, Will Tweedy."

"Grandpa, the colored woman said we'd come to a town called Cushie Springs in about two miles. We just foller the creek at the next fork instead of stayin' on the Athens road. That way, we can keep gettin' water to pour in the radiator. And if we make it to the town, maybe we can find a mechanic with solderin' tools."

We made the two miles, but it was an awful drive on a narrow, rutted wagon road. On one side was the creek, on the other a ditch so deep that if you got in it you'd never get out without a mule team. In low spots we hit sand. I had to stay in low gear to get through that. In the meanwhile I was feeding oil to the cylinders and water to the radiator. Kept that bucket going the whole way. When we got there I was wore out, and the heat and burning oil had made a dirty brown mess out of the Pierce's neat new engine.

Cushie Springs was not what I'd call a town. It was just a handful of houses. Scant hope of finding a mechanic here. But probably we could hire a mule team to pull us into Athens.

Grandpa said let's ring up Mr. Shackleford and get him to send a mechanic. Mr. Shackleford had a garage over in Athens. I said, "You see any telephone poles in Cushie Springs, Grandpa?"

He looked around. "Naw, but what's thet got to do with anythang?"

"How can we telephone, sir, if Cushie Springs ain't got no telephones?"

"Don't be smart-aleck. Will. We'll think of something."

We stopped at the first house we saw. The young man who came to the door could hardly say howdy for trying to look around us at the automobile and at fashionable Miss Love, who was leaning out of the car to shake the dust from her veil.

Grandpa introduced himself and stated the situation. "You know anybody who could git a message over to Athens for us?"

The young man said he'd do it. Be glad to. "I work in Athens and I'm just fixin' to leave. Been down here seein' my folks. This is my mama," he said as an old lady came up behind him and said howdy.

"Howdy, ma'am," said Grandpa.

"And this here's my daddy," he said, smiling at a little old man who came around the house leading a big roan horse that was saddled up.

"Pleased to meet you, sir," said Grandpa, shaking hands. "Are you acquainted with Mr. Shackleford, son? We got a leakin' radiator."

The young man said he boarded right up the street from Mr. Shack's shop. Mounting the horse, he promised to go see him soon as he got back. "But I gar'ntee you, he ain't go'n send nobody over here to work on a Sunday."

"In thet case," said Grandpa, "I got another favor to ast." Writing his name and Papa's on a scrap of paper, he said to please ring up Hoyt Tweedy in Cold Sassy and say we'd be home some time t'morrer. He offered a quarter to pay for the call, but the young feller wouldn't take it. As he galloped off, his mother reached up to tidy her white hair, like we were real company, and said in a slow, drawly voice, "Looks to me like y'all got to spend the night some place, folks. We'd be mighty proud to put you up, wouldn't we, Mr. Nolly?"

It being the custom not to take anybody up on the first invite, Grandpa insisted we'd jest find us a ho-tel.

She laughed. "Ain't no ho-tel in Cushie Springs. Not even a boardin' house." Glancing at Grandpa's spiffy new suit and then at the car and Miss Love's motoring costume, she said, kind of embarrassed, "We ain't got no bathroom or lectric lights like all y'all in Cold Sassy. But if'n yore daughter don't mind, you welcome as can be."

"Hit's my wife, ma'am. And she won't mind." Grandpa motioned Miss Love to come up to the porch, which she did. After introductions all around, the old lady apologized again for the kerosene lamps and the privy. Of course Miss Love said that was all right. But she didn't once in the whole time we were there admit she had a privy, too, or mention her well water and lamplight.

The old lady's name was Miss Gussie. Mr. Nolly's real name, she said, was Knowledge Henry Jamison. I never heard a name like that before. When I got home, I put it down in my journal. What I heard later that night, I wouldn't of dared put down in my journal. But I didn't need to. I knew I'd never forget any of it.

The Jamisons wanted to look at the Pierce. What with all the mud and dust and oil stains, it wasn't much to show off, but they were real impressed, especially after Grandpa said we'd give them a ride when we got the radiator fixed.

Miss Love seemed upset and awful nervous. I reckon Miss Gussie noticed, because she told her to go set down on the porch. "Make yoreself to home, honey, and rest a spell. We just havin' sausage and cornmeal battercakes and soggum syrup. I don't need no hep."

But Miss Love went on to the kitchen anyway, I guess to get away from Grandpa. Considering her new prospects for the future, you'd think she'd be all smiles instead of upset.

As I learned later, she was upset because she thought she didn't want the kind of future that Grandpa had in mind.

Us men sat down on the back porch steps and watched the sun set behind the barn. After talking hard times a while, Mr. Nolly asked questions about the Pierce, and then politely inquired as to Grandpa's business.

"You got you a store? My brother Big Dawg had a store one time. Big Dawg's name is Early. We jest call him Big Dawg." Pointing way off across the fields to a little log house at the edge of the woods, he laughed and said, "Thet's Big Dawg's drinkin' place. His wife won't let him in the house when he's drunk, so he goes over yonder and she sends a colored boy name Fish to see after him."

Normally Grandpa would of come up with a joke or a story then, but he kept looking towards the kitchen. His mind was on Miss Love. Mr. Nolly was thinking about her, too, because he soon said, "Scuse me for astin', but ain't Miz Blakeslee a Yankee? She kind of talks like one."

After Grandpa explained she was from Baltimore, Mr. Nolly said, "We got a real Yankee here in the county. He's bow-leggid, great goodness! Thet damn son-of-a-gun come in here two-three year ago and bought up a farm at sheriff's sale. Painted the house red, white, and blue and then rode the train back up North and got marrit. All I got to say, thet woman must a-been hard up for a husband, comin' down here where ain't nobody go'n speak to her, to live in a red, white, and blue house with a bow-leggid man. She's bow-leggid herself, though, and horse-faced, so they ain't a bad match. Miss Gussie says she cain't wait to see the fruits a-thet harvest! Say, did you know W. T. Stoddard?" Mr. Nolly asked. "He moved over here from Cold Sassy. W. T. ain't much, if you ast me."

"Naw, nor his daddy, neither," said Grandpa. "His daddy's dead now. Last time I seen him, he'd jest set fire to a dog."

I didn't remember old Mr. Stoddard, but I'd heard about the dog on fire. "He was the one did that?" I asked.

"He was the one," said Grandpa, and then told Mr. Nolly how in summertime there's always a bunch of old men playing checkers on a barrelhead out under this great old big sassafras tree at the depot. "One day a starvin', mangy ole dog come along, scroungin' for a biscuit, and thet fool Stoddard decided to put him out'n his miz'ry with kerosene and a match. Whilst the pore thang howled and rolled and whirled in the flames, them old men set there jest a-laughin'. I happened by bout then. Pulled out my pistol, kilt the dog, and shot thet checker game to Kingdom Come." He shook his head. "I'm jest as glad young W. T. chose to locate over here."

At supper that night my napkin slid off my knee. Bending down to pick it up, I saw Grandpa squeeze Miss Love's hand that was in her lap.

When Miss Gussie said she'd show us our rooms, Grandpa looked so excited you'd think all he lived for was to go to bed at night. While we took turns at the privy, she got out a soft white nightgown for Miss Love. "It's the one I save for nice. I embroidered them roses on it myself," she said proudly, handing it over. Then she got some towels and washrags out of a cupboard in the hall and, carrying a lighted kerosene lamp, led us up the steep stairs.

"Now this here is yore'n and Mr. Blakeslee's room," she told Miss Love, holding her lamp high as she opened a door into a neat plain room with old-timy furniture and a 1903 Arm and Hammer baking soda calendar on the wall. "I see Mr. Nolly filled up yore water pitcher like I told him to."

Miss Love's face had flushed at the words "yore'n and Mr. Blakeslee's room." To hide her embarrassment, she moved to the bed and ran her hand over the heavy purple and black coverlet. "Who wove it, Miss Gussie?"

"Mama did, when she warn't but sixteen year old. Spun the wool and dyed it, weaved them panels, and stitched'm t'gether. Ain't it a beauty?" Miss Gussie put her lamp down on the washstand, struck a match, and lit the lamp on the bed table. "They's some quilts in the chest. Y'all might need'm. Mr. Nolly thinks it's go'n turn off cold t'night."

Just as I started to wonder where I was supposed to sleep, Miss Gussie opened a door over by the head of the bed. "This here used to be my sewin' room," she said. "But I fixed it up for my grand-boys, Horace and Ulysses. They's eight and ten year old now. They spend ever summer here with us, heppin' Mr.

Nolly around the place. Both them cots sleep good, son, so take yore pick." She lit a small lamp in there, then said good night and went back downstairs.

Miss Love looked at Grandpa. "Where do you want to sleep, sir?"

Like there wasn't any question, he nodded toward the big post bed and said, like teasing, "This here's where Miss Gussie said sleep. I reckon we better mind her."

Figuring they'd have to argue a while, I got a book off the bureau and took it to the little room. Though they lowered their voices, I distinctly heard Grandpa say, "One thang for shore, Miss Love. With two cots and a double bed, I ain't a-go'n sleep on the floor like I done in New York City."

(Well, so Mama and Aunt Loma had worried for nothing about New York City.)

Miss Love just laughed at him. "If you'd been willing to spend the money, sir, we could have had separate rooms. Weren't you lucky there were two berths on the boat!"

Peeping around the door, I saw him slap her behind, playful, and she laughed again. It was the first time all evening she'd seemed like her regular self. But then he got serious. "Cain't we jest sleep in here, Miss Love? Please?"

"Shh-h, don't talk so loud, Mr. Blakeslee."

I was about to pass out, I was so tired. "Where y'all want me to sleep?" I called from the little room.

"On one of the cots," Miss Love said quickly. "Mr. Blakeslee will sleep in there, too. I'll sleep in here."

"Thet's go'n look like Will Tweedy spent half the night on one cot and the rest of it on the other," said Grandpa. "Miss Gussie'll think he warn't comfortable."

The upshot was that Miss Love decided to sleep in the cot room and let me and Grandpa take the big bed. I couldn't help thinking how funny all this would sound to somebody who didn't know she was just his housekeeper.

There being only one washstand, Grandpa and I had to stay

in the little room with the door shut while Miss Love bathed. I laid down on one of the cots while we waited. Grandpa paced the floor. The whole time she was washing up, he stopped walking only long enough to hitch up his trousers and scratch his head—like if he scratched hard enough and fast enough he might think how to get his way.

We finally heard Miss Love pour her dirty water out of the washbowl into the waste pot on the floor. But it was some time before she knocked and said she was through. Grandpa rushed to open the door, and it was like he'd opened onto a flower garden, Miss Love had on so much perfume. She stood there in the doorway, holding the red hat in her hand and her clothes draped over one arm. The white gown peeped out above and below her coat, which she was using like a robe.

In the soft lamplight she looked real pretty. Her freckled face was flushed, her eyes bright in the frame of dark lashes, her hair plaited into a thick shiny braid that hung down the left side of her neck.

"I'm sorry it took me so long," she said, her voice steady.

Grandpa surprised me by leaning over and kissing her on the cheek. "G'night," he said. For a long moment they stood there staring at one another, like his eyes were steel and hers a dern magnet. Her lips trembled.

There being no way to get past them, I just sat there on the cot, half-asleep, watching them block the doorway. Finally Grandpa took a deep breath, which shook a little as he let it out. "I know you plumb wore out, Miss Love."

"No, not really. I feel fine. I—uh—feel fine. Are you very tired?"

"Gosh a'mighty, no. If I was a bull I could bust through a fence right now and never feel it." He touched her arm. She didn't move away. He laughed softly. "But I reckon I won't be a-doin' thet tonight. Well, Miss Love, sleep good, hear. Call me if'n you need anythang." They were still staring at one another. "Be sure and call me if they's anythang I can—"

"Thank you, I won't need anything, Mr. Blakeslee. Good night, sir."

She moved past him into the little room. I reckon she'd forgot all about me, because it startled her when I got up from the cot. "Uh, good night, Will."

"G'night, ma'am." She patted my arm as I went out. Then she shut the door.

Grandpa walked over to the washstand and poured some water into the big flowerdy bowl, but I just pulled off down to my union suit and turned back the covers. I was too tired to care about road dust. "Which side you want to sleep on, Grandpa? Left or right?"

"Hit don't matter, son. Like I used to tell yore granny, everwhich side I'm on is the right side. She always said hers was the one next to the cradle or closest to the kitchen."

I was standing on the side by the door to Miss Love's room, so I just got in there.

The wall between my head and hers was only one thin board, and I soon realized it might as well not be there. I heard her pull up the quilt, I heard her turn over, I heard her sigh.

I must of dropped right off to sleep. I didn't know when Grandpa came to bed. But I knew when he got up. The coil springs squeaked and waked me. I thought he just needed to use the pot, which he did, but then he moved around the bed. Every time a board creaked underfoot, he stopped and looked over at me.

It wasn't like Grandpa to notice or care if he was disturbing somebody. Plain as day, he didn't want me to wake up, so I didn't—not for him to know it. But I watched as he tiptoed over to the window where he'd laid his clothes on a chair and, standing in a long slanting rectangle of moonlight, put on his pants over his union suit and pulled up the suspenders.

Instead of knocking on Miss Love's door, he opened it, quiet as a burglar. I heard her gasp. He whispered, "Sh-h, it's me. I'm a-comin' in."

There wasn't any question mark in his voice, but she whispered, "Well, I . . . well, all right," and I heard her get up. Grandpa closed the door, but it didn't any more shut me out than if I was a ghost. I doubt they were standing more than two feet from my head when he grabbed her. "Oh, Lord, Miss Love! You don't know how long I been a-waitin' to hold you like this." His voice was muffled, as if his face was buried in her neck. "Seems like all my life."

She laughed kind of nervous, and whispered in a teasing way, "Now, Mr. Blakeslee, that's no way to talk to a housekeeper."

"I ain't a-talkin' to no dang housekeeper, Miss Love. I'm a-talkin' to my wife."

Still teasing, and I guess holding him off, she whispered, "I won't be the wife of anybody who calls me Miss and I have to call him Mister. So Mister Blakeslee, go back to bed."

He whispered right back. "If'n Miss and Mister is all thet's comin' betwixt us, I shore wisht you'd a-said so in New York City! Yore name's Love? Ain't no problem. My name's Rucker, pleased to meet you." And then before she could say pea-turkey, he grabbed her again. This time, if my ears heard right, she grabbed him, too.

After while she whispered, "Oh, dear God, what are we going to do?" I reckon Grandpa found her mouth before God could answer, because for the longest time the only sounds I heard were little moans and gasps and Grandpa's hard breathing. He sounded like it was all uphill in there.

Miss Love must of pulled away, to judge by her voice as she whispered, "Please, Mr. Blakeslee. If you knew—" And then she went to crying.

"Hesh now . . . sh-h . . . sh-h-h . . . ain't nothin' to cry about, Miss Love, less'n you don't love me, which if you said it I wouldn't believe you. Love. Love. Oh, Love. Hit ain't hard a-tall to call you Love. Or to say you're beautiful or how sweet you smell. You're like Miss Mattie Lou's rose garden, Miss—uh, I mean Love." They kissed again. "You're shiverin'," he said. "I could warm you up."

"I'm not cold. . . . Don't, Mr. Blakeslee! You'll tear Miss Gussie's gown!"

His whispered voice was hoarse. "Good God in Heaven . . ."

I thought he was about to say hit's time to pray. But for what seemed like an hour or two, all I heard was them breathing and kissing.

I won't try to say what I was feeling all that time.

"What are you doing? Don't . . ." she said all of a sudden, alarmed.

"I'm jest a-loosenin' yore braid. I ain't never seen yore hair down, Miss—uh, I mean Love. I want to feel it. I want to feel it on my face."

"Please go back to bed, sir. The boy might hear us."

He groaned. "I ain't studyin' him. He's dead asleep, anyhow. Listen to him."

Like I was in cahoots with Grandpa, I snored softly. I couldn't stand the embarrassment if they knew I was awake. They were silent a minute, then she whispered, "There's so much you don't know. . . ."

Smack. "Then say it, Love, but make haste. I been a-waitin' for you a million years. I cain't wait no longer!"

I was shocked, and she must of felt the same. "But . . . but you . . . but I only agreed to be your housekeeper!" Her whisper rose in pitch, an angry sound. "I will not be taken advantage of, Mr. Blakeslee! How dare you try to . . . to use me like I'm a. . . . Why, I trusted you!"

"I love you, Miss Love! Cain't you see thet? And today I . . . hit seemed like you loved me, too."

"What are you saying, Mr. Blakeslee?"

"You deaf? I'm sayin' I love you, dang it! I'm sayin' I want you to be my wife! I'm sayin' I been a-waitin' to hold you in my arms ever since the day we got married. . . . No, way longer than thet, Lord hep me. Miss Love—Love, I been a-waitin' for this minute ever since the day I laid eyes on you!"

It made me sick, hearing that.

"Please, Mr. Blakeslee, you don't know what you're saying." Her words were more softly spoken than whispered, and I could tell she had moved away from him, nearer the door. "I don't believe. . . . You never made one gesture, sir. Never said one word!"

"No, but ever time I looked at you, I thought it. God hep me, I been lovin' you and hatin' myself ever time I—"

"You never did anything wrong!" she protested, like she wanted to take up for him. Then she lowered her voice again. "I never once suspected. That's why I was so shocked when you asked me to marry you. I didn't think you'd even noticed me, Mr. Blakeslee."

"I was scairt to notice you. Scairt somebody would notice me noticin'. Scairt Miss Mattie Lou might, and I wouldn't a-hurt her—" I heard him sink heavily onto the cot, and he must of bent his head down, to judge by his voice. "Miss Mattie Lou knowed something was eatin' up my soul, Miss Love. She kept a-sayin', 'Mr. Blakeslee, tell me what's a-worryin' you so.' And when she took sick—"

"Sh-h, you're talking too loud, sir. Please don't wake up Will. Go on back to bed now and we'll talk when—"

"I got to talk now," he said, but minding her and dropping his voice to a whisper. "By time we git home I might a-lost my nerve. I used to beg God to take away my cravin' for you. When I'd git up off my knees, I'd feel better. But then the very next day I'd watch you workin' at yore table and . . . I couldn't hardly stand it, you was so beautiful. Then Miss Mattie Lou took sick, and I got scairt the Lord might take her to punish me for my sin. I ain't never believed God was thet mean. But what if'n He was? I commenced beggin' for forgiveness. When she was so sick, I got the notion if I didn't go down to the store where I'd see you, I could git you out a-my system. Miss Mattie Lou was. . . . She married me when I warn't nothin', Miss Love. She give me all she had when her daddy died. And she ruint her health havin' babies thet didn't live, tryin' to git me a son to carry on the name. She knowed how much—" His voice broke. "She would a-tried agin, but Doc said another baby'd kill her. So I made shore thet didn't happen. I loved Miss Mattie Lou very much. You unner-stand thet?"

I could hear tears in her voice as she whispered, "Yes. Yes, of course I do."

"She was part a-me. I could tell her anythang—cept bout you, a-course. It was jest like with Will Tweedy, and now you. I can cut the fool with anybody, but they ain't many folks I can really talk to. . . . Well, after what Doc said, I stayed off from her—"

"Mr. Blakeslee, it's not right to tell me all this."

"I got to tell somebody. You rather I tell Will Tweedy? Or Mary Willis or Loma? I'm sayin' I stayed off from her, and after while the fire went out. Seemed like she was jest my sister, my friend. Not my wife. It was like all the feelin's I ever felt—a man for a woman, I mean—they was jest dead. Then I went to the depot to git you when you come in on thet train from Baltimore, Miss Love. I took one look at you, so young and feisty, and hankered after you like a schoolboy."

"Hush, sir. Hush."

"You don't know what I been th'ew these two years, Miss Love. Lord, I wisht we didn't have to whisper. I'm a-gittin' hoarse."

"Go back to bed, Mr. Blakeslee. We'll talk later." It was like she was speaking to a child.

He paid no attention. "After you left off livin' at our house and went to the Crabtrees', Miss Love, I couldn't wait to git to the store ever mornin'. If'n I was sick, I went on anyways. I thought I'd die when a whole day went by and I didn't git to see you. Often as I dared to, I'd tell Miss Mattie Lou, 'Set a place for the milliner at Sunday dinner, hear. She's kind a-homesick.' Or, 'She don't git good cookin' at Miz Crabtree's. Not like yore'n.' You and me and her, we'd have sech a good time round thet pi-ana after dinner. Hit kind a-eased my guilty feelin's, seein' how fond a-you she was. But then, by George, you commenced keepin' comp'ny with thet fool Son Black! I couldn't hardly stand it."

"He didn't mean a thing to me. He was just—"

"How was I to know? And then . . . then Miss Mattie Lou was a-dyin'. I set there by her in thet rockin' chair day after day, lovin' her and grievin', but in the back side a-my mind I was wonderin' if'n you might up and marry thet son-of-a-gun jest when it looked like—"

"Sh-h, don't say it, Mr. Blakeslee. Please, let's stop talking. The boy—"

I coughed, and coughed again, like in my sleep, and then snorted and turned over.

"Hit'd take a earthquake to wake him up t'night." There was a pause. "Yore skin . . . hit's so soft, Love. See? Hit ain't hard a-tall to call you Love. Yore cheek, Love, it's like"—he laughed—"like a mule's nose. . . . Like velvet." She laughed, too. He kissed her gently. I know it was gently, because it didn't smack. "Love, when I set there with Miss Mattie Lou, I warn't jest beggin' God's forgiveness. I was prayin' she'd git well. But I was—"

"There's nothing wrong with that, Mr. Blakeslee. God wants us to ask for His healing hand on—"

"Let me finish. God don't want nobody to ast like I done. Gosh a'mighty, Miss Love, all the time I was prayin' Him to spare Miss Mattie Lou, like He was a dang Santy Claus, I was thinkin' thet if'n she died I could marry you!"

I swear I saw the ghost of Granny flit distraught around the room. I wanted to sic her on him, shout, "He ain't in here, Granny! He's in yonder with her! Go haint him!"

Soon as I thought it, I hoped she wouldn't. Back when she was alive and him lusting in his heart after another woman, it's a wonder God hadn't strung Grandpa up by his heels and split him down the middle. But I couldn't hate him now. And I hoped Granny up in Heaven didn't hate him, and I hoped Miss Love wouldn't. If a man's been horsewhipping himself for two years, it seemed to me like not even God would want to punish him anymore.

I couldn't hear everything they said that night, especially when they moved away from the door. I missed words and even sentences when occasionally I breathed deep or snored a little so they wouldn't guess I was awake. But I heard most of it.

After Grandpa's confession, Miss Love had tears in her voice. "You poor, dear man. I'm so sorry, so very sorry." She whispered it over and over, and then begged him to go back to bed.

But Grandpa said he warn't done talking.

"Miss Mattie Lou's last few days. . . . Well, the good Lord fine'ly set me free a'you, Miss Love. My mind and heart was all on her. I knowed she was go'n die, and all I wanted was for her to live. I kept thinkin' back over the years and knowed they was good years. I kept thinkin' how we used to talk in bed at night, how I was go'n miss thet . . . how I aw-ready missed it." He took a long breath. "But Miss Love, all sech didn't last past the funeral! After I wrote down her dyin' in the Bible, I turned around and seen you standin' there watchin' me, and from then on—"

"Oh, Mr. Blakeslee! As God is my witness, I never guessed it. Never encouraged—"

"I know thet. I jest wish you had a-encouraged me. Then I could a-risked waitin' a proper time to start courtin' you. As it was, I was twixt the rock and the hard place, afeared somebody else would git you in the meantime. Thet fool Son Black, for instance."

"I would never have married him."

"Well, I didn't know if you would or you wouldn't. On the

other hand, if'n I proposed right off, you'd think I was a dirty old man or thet Miss Mattie Lou hadn't meant nothin' to me. You wouldn't have no respect for me." He sighed, like he was lost in thought. Finally he said, "I commenced goin' by the cemetery ever night after I left the store, Miss Love."

"I know. I heard."

He laughed, soft and kind of rueful. "Hit warn't with me like with pore Miss Ernestine Tiplady. You never knowed her. Miss Ernestine would go to the cemetery ever evenin' to see old Mutt. Thet's what she called her husband. She'd tell him how she was feelin' and all, and any news she'd heard, and when she left she'd blow him a kiss and say, 'G'night, Mutt.' Folks seen her do it. Then after while Miss Ernestine got to sayin' g'night to everbody else in the graveyard, callin'm all by name. Pore thang fine'ly commenced passin' the time a-day with'm. Couldn't git home to fix supper for talkin' to dead folks."

He paused. "What I'm sayin', I didn't go to the cemetery to talk to Miss Mattie Lou. But seemed like bein' there calmed me down some." He coughed. "Gosh a'mighty, Miss Love, it's gittin' cold. And my throat's wore out from this here whisperin'. Will Tweedy's asleep. And if'n he ain't. . . . Well, I ain't studyin' Will Tweedy right now."

At the cemetery, he said, he did wonder sometimes what Miss Mattie Lou would tell him to do if she could talk. "Late one night I was so tired, Miss Love, I jest laid down on the cool fresh dirt. Right on her grave. Hit felt like when we used to lay in bed together talkin'. Uh, I reckon you think I was off in the head."

"No. No, I understand."

"Well, anyhow, it come to me something Miss Mattie Lou said long time ago, back when Mary Willis was on the way. She said, 'Mr. Blakeslee, if God takes me in childbed—' I remember tryin' to hesh her up, but she had it on her mind. She said, 'If'n I pass, I hope I done made livin' with a woman so sweet

thet. . . . Well, find you another wife and I'll take it as a compliment.'"

Miss Love started to speak, but he went on, talking low.
"Thet shore made it easier to think on marryin' you, Miss Love.
It was like she'd give me her blessin'. And whilst I was still a-
layin' over her in the dark night, I remembered something else
she said one time: 'If'n the Lord calls me first, Mr. Blakeslee,
don't be too stingy to hire you a colored woman. I cain't rest
easy Up There if you down here wearin' dirty clothes and nobody to see after you.' Thet's what give me the idea to ast you
to be my housekeeper."

He didn't say anything for a minute, or her, either. I reckon
they were kissing. Then he went on. "I figgered if'n I could jest
git you sewed up, I could do the courtin' later. But I knowed I'd
have to make it worth yore while, me bein' old and all the talk
and scandal of it. Took me bout two minutes to decide you'd go
against age and custom both for something big as a house."

She giggled, a little self-conscious. "I think I'd have done it
for the piano."

"The pi-ana cinched it. Then two days later here come Mr.
Texas. It like to kilt me, seein' you was still in love with him."

I heard Grandpa get up from the cot and start pacing the
floor. When he stopped, he breathed a long sigh that trembled
in the night air. "Stealin' Mary Willis's trip to New York City
was a selfish thang I done."

Miss Love plain admitted that it was her fault. "I thought
Mary Willis had definitely decided not to go. I—"

"Lord hep me, when I seen you wanted to go so bad, all I
could think was up there in New York I'd have you to myself,
with nobody around to cast looks, and maybe—"

"I'm beginning to hate myself, Mr. Blakeslee."

"For marryin' me?"

"For not guessing how you felt about me. I never even suspected it till we got to New York."

"I didn't know you caught on then, Miss Love."

"I didn't want you to know it."

"You might near as good a actress as Loma. I thought I'd jest lost the hang a-courtin'."

She didn't answer that. "Mr. Blakeslee, if you'd said you loved me when you proposed, I wouldn't have married you. I had decided never to marry . . . for reasons I can't speak of. For reasons no man would want to marry me. But you said—"

"They cain't be no reason any man wouldn't be proud to marry you, Miss Love."

"But you said you just wanted a housekeeper, Mr. Blakeslee. You don't know how I had longed for—prayed for—what you offered. A home, and to belong to a good, decent family. It was as if God had finally figured out a way to give it to me."

"Hit warn't God figgered it out, Love. Hit was me. And now I'm astin' you to be my wife." When she didn't answer, he said, "You cain't say you don't care for me."

"Of course I care for you, sir. But not like—that. I'm sorry."

"Thet ain't what yore arms said or yore lips said when I was a-kissin' you."

"I . . . I got carried away."

"Ain't gittin' carried away part a-what lovin' is?"

"You don't understand." She spoke stiff and formal. "Loving—being a wife—that door is closed to me. After Mr. McAllister, I promised God."

There was an awful silence. Then Grandpa exploded. "Promised God or promised yoreself? Gosh a'mighty, woman, God don't ast for no sech a promise!"

"It was the only way I could find peace. And now I don't want to talk about it anymore. I'm tired. . . . Mr. Blakeslee, please go to bed."

"What you and somebody else done, Love, thet's over with now. Same as my life with Miss Mattie Lou is over with—and thet hand I ain't got no more. Everwhat you done cain't be no worse than me lovin' you whilst I sat by her deathbed. But ain't no point in me givin' you up, now thet she cain't git hurt. And ain't no point in you messin' up what you and me could have jest cause you and thet dang Mr. Texas—"

"It wasn't him." Her whisper was so weak I barely heard. "But don't ask me to talk about it. Clayt couldn't take the knowledge. You couldn't, either."

"You told him what you won't tell me?"

"Yes. I thought"—she sounded about to cry—"I thought I shouldn't have any secrets from the man I was about to marry. I thought if Clayt really loved me. . . . How stupid I was!" I wondered if she meant stupid to tell him or stupid to think he wouldn't mind. "He'd thought I was so pure. Not like the oth-ers. You understand *pure*, Mr. Blakeslee? Undefiled?"

Silence.

"Defiled cain't be the right word for you, Love. Or don't them Methodist preachers talk none bout a forgivin' God? Ain't you heard how Jesus said go and sin no more? He didn't say go waller in yore sin!"

"I hadn't sinned."

Silence.

"Miss Love, you don't make no sense a-tall. Not to me. If'n you ain't sinned, how come all this here talk bout you ain't pure no more?"

"Sh-h-h, you're talking loud, Mr. Blakeslee." And she low-ered her own voice. "I can only say that Clayt . . . right after I told Mr. McAllister, he talked just like you. Said it didn't mat-ter. But—well, as you know, he finally broke the engagement. And you'd want to get out of being married to me, too, Mr. Blakeslee, if I told you."

"Then, gosh a-mighty, woman, don't tell me! I don't give a good doggone and I don't want to hear bout it. I jest want you to be my wife."

"No, no, please. Please, Mr. Blakeslee, don't touch me. Go back to bed. Please. . . ."

I snored softly as I heard Grandpa's hand on the doorknob.

I heard her whisper, "But I . . . I can't bear for you to think—I mean, what happened wasn't—I mean, I couldn't help what happened."

His hand left the doorknob. "Then it must a-been somebody you loved."

"Y-yes." She was crying.

"Well, dang it, why didn't you marry him? Good gosh a'mighty, Miss Love, are you sayin' you got mixed up with a married man?"

"It still wasn't my fault! But I thought you didn't care!"

"I don't! Livin' a lie like I done, I ain't got no call to th'ow no stones. And I ain't astin' are you pure. But I know I cain't stand it if'n you go'n hold a married man up in front a-me like a pitcher for the rest a-my life, sayin' I got to look at you and him. I ain't your Mr. Texas, but I cain't take it if'n you go'n dish out little bitty hints bout it ever time yore conscience starts to hurt. Thet'd keep me wonderin' and maybe jealous. God A'mighty, Miss Love, forgit all thet and jest let me love you and make you happy!" His whispered voice was angry. "Why'd you have to raise this up from the dead, anyhow? You go'n put the past on and wear it like sackcloth and ashes the rest a-yore days?"

Miss Love was crying. "Please, Mr. B-Blakeslee! Be fair. This wouldn't have c-come up if you had let me stay what I agreed to be. Just your h-housekeeper."

Grandpa left the room before Miss Love finished the word *housekeeper*. Came out and shut the door. I knew by the harsh breathing that he was furious. On the other side of the door, Miss Love laid down on the cot and muffled her crying in the pillow. I didn't see how in the world Grandpa could walk out on her like that.

He started to pace the floor, but the boards creaked and I reckon he was scared he'd wake me up. Shivering, he jerked his spiffy new suit coat off the back of the chair, put it around him, and stood at the window in the moonlight, trying to get aholt of himself. Every minute or so he'd scratch his head like he had cooties worse than Hosie Roach.

I must of dozed off, but I waked with a start when he turned the doorknob by my head and went back in there. I reckon Miss Love was too tired to get up. She whispered, "Go on to bed, Mr. Blakeslee. There's nothing more to say. I'll deed back the house and leave Cold Sassy soon as I can arrange it. Then you can get an annulment and marry that other lady."

"What you talkin' bout?" he whispered back. "What dang other lady?"

"You said there was one other woman in Cold Sassy you thought you could stand if I—"

"Oh, thet. I jest made her up—like a good salesman makes up thet somebody else is waitin' with the money if'n you don't take what he's sellin'. Miss Love, after all I done told you tonight, don't you know they ain't nobody in the world I want to live with cept you? Doggit, woman, I love you!"

And then he went down on the cot with her and they were kissing again.

At some point amid the sighs and moans and murmurs, Miss Love pulled away and whispered, "It was my. . . ." Her voice was shaking so I couldn't hear the word she said.

Grandpa didn't either. "What'd you say?"

"It was m-my f-f-father. My father. I said it was my f-father, Mr. Blakeslee!"

"You mean—?" He got up off the bed, and she did, too. "God A'mighty! Miss Love, you ain't got no call to tell me a thang like thet!" She couldn't talk for crying. "Sh-h-h-h," Grandpa whispered. "Sh-h-h-h. Hit don't matter now. Sh-h-h. . . ."

"Don't shush me. It does m-matter. And I'm . . . I'm g-going to stop cr-crying and tell you everything. Sir, please, don't s-say hush."

And she got aholt of herself and she talked. And she talked

and talked. Talked low and fast. "No matter what you say, Mr. Blakeslee, you won't want me for a wife. It's too—awful. But I'm going to tell you. When I finish, maybe you'll pity me or maybe you'll be sick of me, but at least you'll know I couldn't help it. Maybe you won't . . . be angry" Her voice shook so at first that she was hard to understand, but she got out that it happened when she was twelve years old.

"You don't have to tell me, Miss Love," Grandpa protested.

"I do have to. So don't interrupt."

I doubted she remembered that I was just two feet away, and I forgot about trying to sound asleep. But they wouldn't of noticed if I'd started banging on the wall.

"We lived in three rooms upstairs in somebody's house. I had a little cot like this one, in a small room next to what we used as a sitting room. Their bed was in the sitting room. Mama had heart trouble, Mr. Blakeslee. Everybody knew she was dying, and the lady and man downstairs helped her all they could. They had gone somewhere that night—I'm sure it wouldn't have happened if they'd been home. Well, I woke up when Father came in drunk, as usual, and I heard Mama coughing and crying. She asked him for some water, but, Mr. Blakeslee, Father just laughed. Laughed!"

"Don't Miss Love—"

She didn't hear him. Her voice had got mechanical, like she was reciting a story she'd read in the newspaper—one that didn't have anything to do with her. "After Mama's coughing subsided, she said, 'Timothy, when I'm gone, you will take care of Love, won't you?' I'd heard her say that sort of thing many times, and it always made him mad. I just thought he never wanted her to talk about dying, as if it wouldn't happen if she didn't say the words. But that night he suddenly screamed a man's name at her. 'He's her daddy, tell him to take care of her!'

"There was an awful silence, and then Mama said, 'Hush! Love might hear you. And you know it's not so, Timothy. He married somebody else, remember? Years before I even met you!' Father said that didn't prove a thing. He was so drunk, Mr. Blakeslee. He cursed and said, 'We were married exactly one week, Cleo, when you called me his name! I won't ever forget that.' Mama said it didn't mean she'd been seeing him, but Father wasn't listening. He said, 'You were carrying his baby. Admit it. Why else would you have married a man like me?' She was crying, but she got out something like 'God help me, I didn't know what you were like! But as God is my witness, I was not pregnant!' Father just laughed. 'Why was she born in eight months? Answer me that.' He shouted at her like she was deaf. 'She is his child. Ain't she?'"

"Hesh up, Miss Love," Grandpa pleaded. "You don't have to—"

"I have to. Mama was crying and went into the most awful fit of coughing, but he just cursed her. It was awful, listening to them. Then I heard Father stagger towards my room, yelling, 'By God, I'll show you what I think the truth is!' As he came in where I was, he was still yelling at Mama. I'll never forget his words. 'Would a man kill his own flesh and blood, Cleo?' I heard her scream, and I screamed. I tried to get under the cot, but he caught my arm. Then he said, 'Aw, she's too pretty just to kill! Cleo? Listen to me. Would I take my own daughter? No, by God. But, by God, I can take another man's daughter!'"

Miss Love's voice sunk to an awful whisper. "And then he—he raped me! Raped me, Mr. Blakeslee! I tried to fight him off, but he—"

Grandpa must of started shaking her. "I hear you, Miss Love! Don't say thet word agin!"

"The whole time, he was screaming, 'You know what I'm doing in here, Cleo?' But she didn't answer. Finally he left. Stumbled down the stairs and went away. When I got to Mama, she was on the floor in the hall, unconscious. I held her for what seemed like hours. When the people who lived below came home, they got the doctor."

She sighed a long sigh. "Mama had been trying to get to me, but she passed out. We talked about it later, she and I. She said I had two choices. I could dwell on this the rest of my life—let it make me scared of everybody and bitter against Father—or I could forgive him and put my hand in God's and live my life. Something she said. . . . Well, I realized Mama didn't know he had. . . . I realized she hadn't heard anything after he screamed would a man kill his own flesh and blood. So I never told her what really happened. She had suffered enough. But all the years after, I never forgot what she said about forgiving him. And I thought I had. I even got over feeling defiled—till I told Clayt and he did what he did. So, Mr. Blakeslee, now you know. You don't have to wonder. Just accept that I was defiled and hate it and I can never be anybody's wife. I don't even want to . . . be a wife. I'll leave Cold Sassy as soon as I can."

Grandpa's voice was hoarse. "Hit don't make no difference, Miss Love."

"I believed Mr. McAllister when he said that. Never again. . . . Leave me alone, Mr. Blakeslee! Go to bed and leave me alone!"

"Damnit, woman! Damnit, I. . . . Where's yore daddy now?"

"I don't know. Died drunk, probably. We never saw him again. He didn't come to Mama's funeral."

There was absolute silence in that room then, except they were both breathing hard. I thought sure Grandpa would try to comfort her. Make her see how much he loved her, how nothing mattered now except to forget all that and let him take care of her. Maybe he would have, but she said to him in a voice cold as metal, "*I said leave me alone!*" And he did.

Grandpa stalked out, shut the door, and stood there by the bed, shaking. I never saw him madder. I watched as he tiptoed over to the chest, raised the lid, pulled out a quilt, wrapped it around him. He stood by the window for the longest kind of a time, then knelt down by the windowsill and covered his face with his hand. Grandpa was crying, but he didn't make a sound except a hoarse gasp when he had to breathe. At some point I knew he had gone to praying.

It must of been an hour or more before he came to bed. I don't think he slept at all. I know I didn't.

Soon as I heard Miss Gussie in the kitchen, I bounced out of bed. "Better get up, Grandpa! Man from Athens might be here early. Boy howdy, I slept like a log! Hope I didn't root you, sir."

"I wouldn't know, son." He looked like he'd been beat up, but he said he slept like the dead.

"Reckon we better get Miss Love up?" I asked. Without waiting for his answer, I called through the door. "Miss Love? Hate to wake you up, but that mechanic could be here any time now. We slept like the dead in here. We rarin' to go!"

It was a nice breakfast with Miss Gussie and Mr. Nolly. Nobody would have guessed how mad Grandpa and Miss Love were at each other.

The mechanic came at seven o'clock. Soon as he fixed the radiator and cleaned the oil and grime off the engine, we took the Jamisons for a quick ride and then left Cushie Springs.

If Grandpa had ridden home in the back seat with his arm around Miss Love, I'd of thought everything I heard was just a bad dream.

But he rode up front with me.

42

MISS Love did a lot of horseback riding the next few weeks, and if she ever stopped to talk to anybody, I didn't hear about it. Whenever I went up there to clean the stable, I walked around the house, not through it. I didn't know what to say to her.

Grandpa? Hearing him joke and tease and tell tales down at the store, you wouldn't of known he had a care in the world, unless you studied his eyes. Since That Night, they were never merry. And he started to look bushy again, and older, and you could see his mean streak better.

For instance, there was the matter of Mr. Clem Crummy having a drawing to get a new name for the Cold Sassy Hotel, recently bought from old Mr. Boop. After sprucing it up a little, Mr. Clem advertised a drawing in the paper "for a name more befitting this fine, refurbished, modern establishment." The Crummys put a big shoebox on the hotel desk, and Cold Sassy filled it up with names like the Waldorf and the Savoy. Mama's entry was the Hotel Prince Edward. Mine was the Hotel Bedbug. Grandpa entered a name, but wouldn't say what it was.

At four o'clock on Sunday, less than two weeks before Thanksgiving, Mr. Clem held his drawing on the hotel piazza.

Nobody but him took it serious, but it was somewhere to go, so Cold Sassy went. Well, Miss Love didn't go. I remember that.

When Mr. Clem pulled his fat hand out of the shoebox and looked at the piece of paper, seemed like he couldn't believe what he saw. I was just sure he'd drawn the Hotel Bedbug! But he hadn't. "For pity sake, Rucker," he exploded, "if I'd a-wanted a name like that, I'd a-used my own!" Then he commenced to laugh. "Folks, Rucker here done named my place after his-self. The Rucker Blakeslee Ho-tel. Ain't he a card, though! I swanny, Rucker, you shore do know how to make a joke. Well, Miss Pauline, bring back the shoebox. I'll try agin."

While everybody laughed, Grandpa walked up so close to Mr. Clem they just about touched stomachs. "You done got you a name, Mr. Crummy. The Rucker Blakeslee Ho-tel."

The crowd got silent and uneasy. Mr. Clem looked like he didn't know what to say. "But . . . ain't it just a joke?"

"Hit was when I put it in the box," said Grandpa. "Hit was jest go'n be something to tell and laugh about, same as if'n you'd named it the Crummy Hotel. I never thought to git drawed." Though a smile was playing around under his mustache, his eyes were hard. "But now thet it's the one, I kind a-like the sound of it. You wanted a fine fancy name for yore establish-ment? A symbol of success and ca-racter? Well, sir, seems to me like you got one." Looking back at me, Grandpa grinned.

"You cain't make me do that!" Mr. Clem was sputtering. "It's my ho-tel!"

"But it's my name!" Grandpa put his forefinger on Mr. Crummy's big chest. "Yore ad said you'd use whatever name got drawed. If'n you don't carry out the drawin', I'll sue for breach a-promise. You can put 'Clem Crummy, Proprietor' on yore sign if you got a mind to, but what it's go'n be called is the Rucker Blakeslee Ho-tel."

Everybody thought Grandpa would take back the name after he'd had his fun. I knew he wouldn't. Like I said, he was not one to let go of a grudge, and several years back Mr. Clem had cheated him in a land deal. Well, now he'd got even — got even and then some. But that didn't mean he wasn't still mad about it.

The next evening, Grandpa came down sick. In a day or two he was coughing and said he thought it was a relapse of lung disease from war deprivation. He said his symptoms were just like what went through the 6th Georgia one winter, and sent word to the family that nobody was to come up there.

"Rucker says it's ketchin' as sin," Doc said. "I told Miss Love she better be careful. Boil his plate and fork and all. I don't want no epidemic gittin' started in this town."

Mama was real worried. Not being sure Miss Love knew how to tend the sick, she took some chicken soup up there for him. Grandpa liked the soup but wouldn't let her in the house. She might ketch what he had. Miss Love said he coughed and groaned a lot, but was eating well. "I just don't understand it," she told Mama.

Something seemed fishy to me, but I couldn't put my finger on it. Maybe he was really sick. On the other hand, if Miss Love had started packing to leave, he might just be playing sick to keep her there. If she'd decided to stay but still refused to be his wife, maybe he was pouting. Or maybe he was heartsick, hating her for what her daddy did to her but still not willing to give her up.

What I thought was that he loved her as much as ever and had decided to stay home till she gave in. I recalled him telling me one time, "When you don't know which way to turn, son, try something. Don't jest do nothin'."

The one time I saw Miss Love during his confinement, she said, "He groans all the time, but he eats enough for a regiment. I don't know whether to laugh or cry, ignore him or worry."

She must of decided to ignore him, because after about ten

days she got the idea of training Mr. Beautiful to old Jack's buggy. She'd hitch up and go off for hours. Grandpa soon let everybody know that the contagious period was over and insisted on going to ride with her. Said he was still weak, but the cold fresh air would be good for his lungs. After that, they were behind the horse every day, bundled up together under the automobile lap robes, her holding the reins and the whip, him sitting stiff and straight beside her. They would speak a greeting if they passed you, but as Miss Effie Belle said, it was like they didn't know each other or anybody else, either.

Before long, though, they were laughing and talking on their rides, and Grandpa was howdying and joking with everybody he saw.

He had become the grand duke of Cold Sassy again.

Like everybody else, Aunt Loma was relieved that her daddy was better. But, tell the truth, she'd been too busy directing the school's Christmas play to worry much about him.

Mama went over there one morning and found Loma sitting at the kitchen table writing in a tablet. She didn't seem to care that there were dust devils under the beds or that it was time for Uncle Camp to come to dinner. She said she had to work on the play. I expect it was the first time she'd been happy since she got married. Just before school let out every day, she'd bring Campbell Junior down to our house, hand him over to Queenie, and prance off to direct rehearsals like she'd got a call to do it from God Almighty Himself.

Aunt Loma didn't make me be in the play. But anything she needed she called on me and got so bossy I couldn't stand it hardly. Two weeks before play night, she told me to catch her a live mouse for Claude Wiggins to drop out of a shoebox in the third act.

The mouse was supposed to create pandemonium at a Christmas party on stage.

I think now that if Aunt Loma hadn't wanted the live mouse,

it never would of dawned on me to mess up the play. The way it happened, my cousin Doodle and Uncle Skinny came in from their farm in Banks County about three o'clock one Sunday evening to spend the night with us and pick up a wagonload of feed corn next morning at the store. Doodle and I had just gone out to the barn to pitch down hay for his mules when in strolled Pink Predmore, Lee Roy Sleep, and Smiley Snodgrass.

After a hard cold spell in late November, there's nothing like a nice warm day to make you restless. You just want to do something, for gosh sake!

Lying in the warm sunshine in the hayloft, we tried to think up something, but didn't have any luck. We were all kind of irritable. Doodle, who had his head resting on a horse collar, raised up to spit a stream of tobacco juice over Smiley's head, and Smiley got mad as heck. "You better be glad none a-that landed on me," he said, growling.

Doodle leaned over in the other direction and spat through the hay hole. Looking down below, he aimed next at the big barrel down there. "Damn," he muttered. "I missed it. Hey, Will, ain't thet the barrel with them drownded rats yore daddy said to bury?"

"Gosh, yeah." I had forgotten about it. Climbing down from the loft, we all went and looked at the three big stinking rats, floating in the barrel amongst the ears of corn that had been the bait.

Everybody knows that when a barn rat looks down into a barrel that seems half full of shucked corn, he never suspicions that it's really half full of water. By time he finds out, he's trapped. He can't climb up the rounded sides.

"Gosh, look how white they are," said Pink, poking one with a corn cob. "How come brown rats bleach out in the water?"

Lee Roy had a thought that made him shudder. "You reckon colored folks turn white like that if they drown?"

"Where you s'pose the color goes?" asked Smiley.

"I reckon it just dissolves," said I, gathering up the rats on a pitchfork. "Doodle, get that shovel over yonder, hear, and hep me dig a hole."

Pink was suddenly inspired. "Whoa!" he yelled, catching my arm. "Let's save the rats for Miss Loma! For the school play!"

"Haw, yeah!" echoed fat Lee Roy, clapping Pink on the back. "Cain't you just see them rats droppin' out of Claude's shoe-box?"

"Be mighty rank by then," said I. "School play's not till two weeks, you know." But they knew by my wide grin that in my mind I was seeing stinking dead rats on Aunt Loma's stage.

We hawed and guffawed, and then—I think because I'd taken off my shoes and it felt so warm and good and free with my bare toes twiddling in the dirt—it came to me that we should get Aunt Loma some live rats to keep her live mouse company. "We'll put shucked corn down in the barrel without any water," I explained as we went out to bury the dead. "We ought to be able to catch us a few by the night of the play."

What we got was nineteen, collecting sometimes two or three a night. One looked big as a cat. Smiley found a large metal cage in his attic and brought it over. We padded it with hay and put it in an empty stall in our barn, hidden under some dirty old croker sacks.

On the day of the play, Lee Roy and Smiley backed out. Put their tails down and slunk right out from under the best practical joke ever thought up by man or boy in Cold Sassy, Georgia. It really made me mad.

Pink said maybe backing out was a good idea.

"Well, you can back out, but I ain't." I was furious. If Pink didn't help me, there was no way I could get that heavy cage into the auditorium.

"I'll stick with you, Will," he said, miserable.

That night about first dark, he and I lifted the cage onto a wheelbarrow, covered it good with the croker sacks, and wheeled it around the house through the pecan grove. Mary Toy was playing hopscotch in the yard and like to had a fit to know what we had. "Something Aunt Loma wants for the play," I said. "But we cain't tell anybody. It would spoil the surprise."

As we humped the wheelbarrow over the railroad tracks, I looked back. Mary Toy was in the porch swing, watching us.

At the schoolhouse we had a time toting the cage up the outside steps that led backstage. Dern. Lee Roy and Smiley could of at least stayed with it this far.

There wasn't any real shortage of time, since Aunt Loma and everybody in the cast had gone home for early supper. We pushed the cage into a dark corner and tried to make it look like a natural part of the junk stored back there. Set an old globe on top of the croker sacks, and some cracked slates they kept for mill children to use, and two or three old window-shade maps of Europe that wouldn't let up and down anymore. In front of it all, we put two scuttles of dusty coal and a faded half-furled Confederate flag, saved last year when Cold Sassy's old wooden schoolhouse burned down.

We had a brand-new brick school now, and a brand-new Confederate flag out there on the stage. Aunt Loma's Christmas play was sure to have a packed crowd, because it would be the first entertainment held there at night, and everybody was anxious to see the electric lighting. Carbon bulbs were so dim that nobody thought you could light a stage that way.

Aunt Loma had told Chap Cheney she'd kill him if he didn't get the stage wired in time for the play. With her telling him exactly how she wanted it, he had wired for dozens of bulbs to be screwed into the floor at what she called stage front, and other bulbs dangled from the ceiling. Aunt Loma had put up a lot of mirrors on the walls of the set, which gave her twice as much light for the same number of bulbs.

That night when the heavy curtains parted to show the lit stage, the crowd yelled and clapped till Chap Cheney stood up, grinning, and took a bow.

The stage lights reflected on faces in the auditorium all the way to the back row, where I could see Papa and Mama and

Mary Toy sitting with Uncle Camp, him holding the baby. I
had a front row aisle seat, Pink right behind me.

Smiley and Lee Roy sat primly with their folks, acting like
they didn't even know us.

Among the latecomers hurrying in were Grandpa and Miss
Love. She was dolled up like a Christmas tree in a red velvet
skirt, a red and white striped waist, and a red velvet hat trimmed
in real holly. She seemed a little subdued, but Grandpa was
greeting everybody. This was their first time at a public func-
tion since he took sick. He still hadn't gone back to work, but I
thought he never looked haler or heartier, or neater or spiffier.
I sure was glad he got his health back in time for my rat joke.

Just after the curtains opened, Aunt Loma marched in from
backstage, dressed fit to kill in black silk and importance, and
sat down in the aisle seat that the Tuttles had saved for her.

I sat calm enough through the first act. But when Act II
started, my mind floated up to the stage and, like a ghost, went
through the painted set into the dark corner where we'd hidden the rats. I sure hoped they hadn't got to fighting or squealing back there.

Just like I planned it, when the auditorium went dark for
Act III, Pink and I slipped through a door by the stage and
tiptoed back where the rats were. During the Christmas party
scene, with all the actors singing carols at the top of their lungs,
we dragged the cage to the wings and waited till Claude Wiggins created pandemonium by dropping the live mouse out of
the shoebox. Soon as the mouse hit the floor we opened the
cage and shoved it onto the stage. Those big rats poured out of
there like a house afire!

Talk about pandemonium, we had it on stage and behind
stage and all over that school auditorium!

You never heard such screaming and hollering. When the
rats started leaping off into the audience, men were hitting out
with their hats and walking canes, women were jumping this
way and that or standing on their seats, some of which were

breaking, and good gosh everybody was trying to get out of there!

I saw the rat that looked big as a cat dive off the stage right into Aunt Loma's lap. She knocked him off, but then just sat there, too shocked to move.

I looked at Miss Love. Perched up on the back of her seat, she was shrieking with laughter, her red skirt bunched up nearly to her garters. Grandpa was laughing so hard he hurt—rocking back and forth in his seat, grabbing his stomach, slapping his leg, flopping his arms, and shouting like somebody getting religion at a camp meeting. When his left arm went up, it looked like the knotted empty sleeve was dancing. A rat must of jumped over Grandpa's foot, because he kicked out suddenly, but I expect he was laughing too hard to make contact.

To say we broke up the play was putting it mildly.

The lights came on just as I peeped farther around the curtain and saw Aunt Loma trying to push through the crowd to get to our folks. She stumbled along, crying, her hands over her face like somebody had beat her.

When I glanced toward the back of the auditorium, that brought me down some. I knew Mama and Papa hadn't a doubt who'd done it. They sat there just stunned—till all of a sudden Mama grabbed Mary Toy and they jumped up on their seats. By then, the audience was crowding all the exits, shoving to get out. A lady screamed, and Pink and I bolted for the backstage door. The live mouse and a rat or two scrambled out into the cold night with us as Pink flew off in his direction and me in mine.

I beat the folks home easy. Felt my way upstairs, groped for the light cord hanging near the foot of my bed, jerked the light on, put on my old long pants under my new ones, jerked the light off, and waited.

I couldn't help it; in a few minutes I was rolling on the floor with laughter. Every little bit, I'd stop to listen for the front door to open and Papa to roar out, "Will, you come 'ere!"

Then I'd think about Aunt Loma with that lapful of rat or my mother jumping up on the seat, and it was like I was a gun fired off. Laughter exploded out of me and couldn't any more be stopped than a bullet.

But laughing dies off pretty quick when you're by yourself, especially if it's way past your whipping and your folks still aren't home yet.

I was kind of sorry I'd messed up Aunt Loma's Christmas play. Oh, well, heck, if it weren't for my rats, Cold Sassy wouldn't remember that dern play past New Year's. As it was, everybody in town would be talking about it for years to come.

And heck, Aunt Loma could put it on again. It was still ten days before school would let out for the holidays. I could help her—

"Will Tweedy? Boy, you come 'ere! Right now!" Papa was shouting at me before he got in the house and had his belt off before my feet could drag me down the stairs.

I got whipped good. And next day he made me go over to Aunt Loma's to say I was sorry.

Except for telling her I was sorry about the bosom stories I made up, which didn't count since Aunt Loma wasn't mad, I had never apologized to anybody in my life. But for once I was soaked through with honest remorse. Not for what I'd done, but for what it did to Aunt Loma.

I found her in her bedroom upstairs, sitting in a rocking chair nursing Campbell Junior. Her eyelids were red and swollen.

Trying not to rouse the baby, I whispered, "Aunt Loma, uh, you ain't go'n believe it, but, uh, uh, I wish now I hadn't of done that about the rats. It was a real good play and I'm . . . I mean, I'll hep you if you want to put it on again next week. I, uh, I wish—" Something about her face plus having to whisper made me wind down.

I don't know what I expected. Maybe just a shrug of her

shoulders, acknowledging she heard what I said. I sure didn't expect her to smile at me. I guess I wanted her to say something noble, like "I deserved it, Will. I've always treated you awful. The one that should be apologizin' is myself."

Maybe I hoped she would handle it like God. I mean the Bible says if you tell God you're sincerely sorry, He puts His arms around you and forgives you.

Well, Aunt Loma was not God that day by a long shot. What she said, keeping her voice down to a whispered scream because of the baby, was "Don't you talk to me about doin' it again next week, Will Tweedy! Just get out of my sight!" She was shaking all over, tears of fury streaming down her flushed face. Naturally Campbell Junior stopped sucking and went to bawling. "Get out of my house!" she yelled above his frightened wails. "I'll hate you till my dyin' day! Get out! *Get out!*"

With that she leaped up, holding the baby tight, and slapped my face so hard I reeled backwards.

I slammed the door to her room as I went out, and kicked the cats that were asleep in a pile by the back door.

My first thought was I'll never say I'm sorry again as long as I live.

My second thought was if anybody ever says I'm sorry to me, I sure ain't go'n slap him or push him away.

My third thought surprised me: I realized it felt good to be back on familiar ground with Aunt Loma. Ever since that day we'd had such a good time laughing about the bosom stories, I hadn't quite known how to act around her. Last night I could hardly enjoy thinking about those rats flying off the stage for worrying about her crying. Well, if she was determined never to forgive me, I might as well enjoy hating her again.

By time I got home, I was whistling.

After that, Aunt Loma stayed in a bad humor with everybody, especially Uncle Camp. Just for instance, the next Sunday while she was helping Mama and Queenie take up dinner, Campbell Junior fell all the way down our stairs. "I swanny to

God, Campbell Williams!" she yelled. "Looks like you could at least see after your own son when I'm in the kitchen!"

"I'm sorry, Loma, I'm sorry," he said as he picked up the screaming baby.

"You sure are! You're just sorry!" screeched Aunt Loma, snatching Campbell Junior out of his arms. "That's the smartest thing you've said since the last time you said it."

When she wasn't fussing about him seeming glad to bring home the bent cans and weevily rice and flour we couldn't sell at the store, she was complaining about his not having any get-up-and-go. "You could at least *ast* Pa for a raise." After Grandpa went back to work just before Christmas, Aunt Loma had the gall to go ask him herself to raise Camp's pay.

Grandpa really blessed her out. "I don't even need Camp," he told her. "I shore cain't afford to pay him no more'n I awready do."

I don't know if Uncle Camp heard that, but I know he heard what was said a few hours later when Hosie Roach, the mill boy, came in to ask for a job. Hosie had washed himself and combed his hair and put on clean overalls, and I could tell Grandpa liked him. He even took Hosie back to the buggy shed to show him the cars. Hosie didn't get a job, but later Grandpa told Papa he shore wisht he could a-hired thet boy. "He'd be equal to three a-Camp."

At first I thought Grandpa didn't know Uncle Camp was standing right behind him. But maybe he did know and said it anyhow, hoping it would make Camp work harder.

The very next Saturday, Camp got some get-up-and-go and went. And the way he did it made my rat thing seem about like putting a frog in somebody's bed.

Aunt Loma never forgave him, either.

43

U NCLE Camp got away from Aunt Loma while she was
gone to Athens.

She had caught the train that Saturday morning, wearing
a black wool dress and the big hat with ostrich plumes that
Miss Love had made. She was to spend the day with her La-
Grange College roommate, Sue Lee Gresham, who was now
Mrs. Humphry Wright of Athens.

Uncle Camp had gone to work early that day, and since
Papa thought any lady taking a train should have somebody
see her off, he told me to drive Aunt Loma to the depot. To
my mind she didn't need a ride any more than if she was going
downtown, which she did every day, and besides, she was leaving Campbell Junior with Mama and Queenie. And naturally
I wasn't too crazy about being by myself with her. She might
take the occasion to raise Cain about the Christmas play. But
Papa said to, so I went and got her.

She was far from friendly, but her mind was on Athens, not
me or rats.

Aunt Loma really didn't want to go, or so she said as we
waited at the depot. "Sue Lee's just usin' me as an excuse to
have a luncheon. She hopes I'll be jealous of her. She's always
writin' about her big house and her big dinner parties, and her

husband bein' president of the bank. I don't call inheritin' a bank from your daddy any proof that you're smarter than the next fellow." Aunt Loma stepped back from the tracks as the train came in sight. "I just wish I hadn't told her I'd come."

I always thought ladies liked to be honor guests at a luncheon, and said so. "Besides, ain't nobody makin' you go."

"Camp made me," she said, real irritable.

"Well, I be-dog." Chalk up one for ole Camp.

"He promised to fix the faucet in the bathtub if I'd just get out of his way. Said he couldn't tackle the job with me standin' there watchin' him fail."

Poor ole Camp.

Papa said afterwards that Camp actually applied himself that morning at the store. Instead of waiting around to be told what to do, he put in a real good morning's work. And whereas he usually had about as much life in his eyes as a turtle, he seemed almost happy.

He and my daddy left together at dinnertime. On the way out the door, Camp asked Papa would he mind stopping by the house before going back to the store after dinner. Kind of apologetic, like he hated to take up Papa's time, he explained. "I'm fixin' to fix a leaky faucet, Mr. Hoyt, and I ain't never done one. I'd shore feel better if you'd come see did I do it right. I . . . well, you know how Loma is."

Papa did stop by, though grudging. I was with him. The door was open, despite it was a cold day, and we went on in. "Camp?" Papa called.

"I'm in the kitchen, Mr. Hoyt. Come on back, hear."

The shot rang out about time Papa set foot in the dining room. Neighbors said they heard somebody scream. It must of been me or Papa, one, though later I couldn't recall anything except the smell of gunpowder and, on the floor, a big long blob of blue and white checked oilcloth from the store. I didn't have to be told that Uncle Camp was under the oilcloth.

He had laid down on a length of it, pulled one end up over him like a sheet and the other end down over his head and chest, and after calling Papa to come on back, had put the pistol in his mouth and pulled the trigger.

I reckon he figured if all the blood and bits of bone and brains got trapped in the oilcloth, Loma Baby wouldn't be mad at him.

Papa lifted the part that was over Camp's head, put it down quick, and turned away, his face like ashes. I had seen, too. I stood there, shaking. Finally I said, "Papa, want me to run get Doc Slaughter?"

He could hardly speak. "Run get Mr. Birdsong, son."

Mr. Birdsong offered me a ride up beside him in the driver's seat of the old horse-drawn hearse, the one he called an ambulance if the person wasn't dead. Since neighbors were already gathering, he drove the horses around to the back door, where my daddy was waiting. Papa had closed the kitchen door and hadn't let anybody go in there.

Mr. Birdsong tied Uncle Camp up in that oilcloth like he was a dern side of beef. Me and Papa helped carry him out, and rode with him to the big old white-columned funeral parlor.

Mr. and Mrs. Birdsong and their nine children lived upstairs. Helping take Uncle Camp in there, I wondered how they could stand to live like that with dead bodies, especially when it was one that had committed suicide.

Papa hurried home to tell Mama and sent me to the store to tell Grandpa and them, but they had already heard. As I ran in, Grandpa met me at the door, grim of face. He asked me a few questions, then stalked off to the funeral parlor.

Soon as I could get away from the customers who pressed around, asking more questions, I ran back to Aunt Loma's. I wanted to make sure there wasn't any blood or anything on the floor.

If there was, Mrs. Brown next door had cleaned it up. But I

could still see Uncle Camp, same as if he was laying right there with his brains blowed out, and it made me sick. I felt about to faint. Leaving the kitchen, I rushed past the people whispering in the hall and went to the bathroom.

I nearly stumbled over the plumbing tools. Uncle Camp had left them on the floor by the tub.

Just what you'd expect, Camp not putting up his tools.

Then I saw a piece of paper stuck under the big wrench. I knew it was for Aunt Loma, but horses couldn't of kept me from reading it.

You can get the creeps, I tell you, reading what a dead man has just written. This is what it said:

> Loma baby i tryed to plan so as not to mess up yr kitchen. i loved you since the day i layed eyes on you you jus as pretty now as then. so it aint you Loma baby its i aint good for nuthin. which you know. its got so jus getin out of bed ever mornin is to much. i pact up my close and all in a box so you woodn have to fool with it. my leavin this werl dont have nuthin to do with you bein mad at me for not fixin the fawsit I bin aimin to do it a long time fore the fawsit went to leekin.
>
> plese save my gold pockit watch for Campbell Junior i leeve it to him i aired it from my grandedy you know. i love you an always will but now you can have some pese. tell mr. Blakesly i preshate him givin me the job like he done now he can fine him somebody who can do him a good dase work
>
> i hope god will forgive me so i can meet you in heven.
>
> plese dont be mad i have plan it so you wont be the one to fine me.
>
> yr lovin husban Campbell Williams.
>
> p.s. i fixt the fawsit
>
> p.s. i wont to be berit in cold sassy so you can vist me some time.
>
> yr lovin husban Campbell Williams.

The page blurred. I wished so bad I could of known Uncle Camp for the past three years like I knew him now that he was dead. But even as I stood there holding his sweet and lonely words, I heard water going *drip, drip, drip* into the bathtub.

I picked up the wrench and changed the washer. Nobody was go'n say Campbell Williams was so sorry that he couldn't even fix a faucet. It was a small thing to do for somebody brave enough to put a pistol in his mouth and shoot.

44

ALONG with half the town, my family met the late train from Athens.

Grandpa said later that folks just came to see how Loma would take the news, but I don't know. It seemed to me that going to the depot was the only way they could think of to show her they were sorry poor Camp had gone to Hell so young. Camp having committed suicide, and not living long enough afterwards to ask God to forgive him, there was no way he could ever be reunited with Loma or Campbell Junior in Paradise.

Naturally we all thought there would just be a quick private burying. Cold Sassy certainly never expected Camp would be brought home to lie in state.

But he was.

By first dark, Aunt Loma's little house was filling up with folks who had brought food and were waiting to speak to the new widow before settling in to eat. Loma was still upstairs in her room when here came Uncle Camp in a fine golden oak coffin with metal handles, riding in style in Mr. Birdsong's fine new glass-sided, gilt-trim black hearse drawn by two black horses with black plumes on their heads.

As soon as the horses stopped, Mr. Birdsong got down from

the driver's seat, went in the house, and asked everybody to leave the parlor. Then he and his three sons carried in the coffin, escorted by my grandfather. His grimness forbade any comment as he stalked across the yard behind the coffin. Those watching looked shocked, like it was as awful for Camp to be brought home like a regular corpse as for him to of shot himself in the first place.

Though the undertaker clearly disapproved, they toted Uncle Camp into Aunt Loma's little parlor as if he had a right to be there. I followed close behind Grandpa, who told me to come in and close the sliding double doors.

Mr. Birdsong unfolded his new collapsible casket stand and set it up right in front of the white mantelpiece that Uncle Camp had painted. I don't know why, but I walked over to see if the button, the pencil, and the cockroach were still there. They were, of course, just same as Granny's death was still in the Toy Bible.

Loma had hung the Saint-Cecilia-at-the-organ mirror above the mantel. I watched in it as the boys lifted the casket onto the stand and Mr. Birdsong laid a big wreath of wax flowers on top, about where Uncle Camp's hands that held the pistol would now be pressed together in prayer.

Mr. Birdsong always arranged dead hands like in prayer.

Hitching his trousers with his arm stub, Grandpa looked around and said, "Git thet marble-top table over yonder, Will Tweedy, and set it by the head of a-thet coffin. Then see can you find a kerosene lamp to put on it." He must of thought the carbon bulb hanging from the ceiling was too raw-looking for a settin'-up.

"Grandpa, you ain't go'n open the coffin, are you, sir?"

"No, course not. Camp ain't in no condition for viewin'." He spoke calm, but went to scratching his head like he had the itch. "Where's Loma at, and yore daddy and mother?"

"They all upstairs in the bedroom," I said. "Aunt Loma's still like she was at the depot. She don't even know what's goin' on.

Grandpa, I thought you didn't like embalmin' and funerals and all."

"I don't. But I don't like hypocrites, neither. I cain't stop folks from jedgin' Camp, but I ain't a-go'n let'm say how he's got to be buried. Where's Miss Love at?"

"In the kitchen."

"Go git her for me."

"Yessir."

"And bring a lamp."

"Yessir."

Wading through the crowd of silent people in the front hall, I found Miss Love busy getting out dishes. She knew Grandpa had brought Uncle Camp home. When she saw me at the kitchen door, she said, "Loma should be in there when people start paying their respects."

"You think anybody'll go in, Miss Love?"

"Yes. Because your grandfather will get his revolver if they don't." Turning to look at me as she reached for some dishes on a high shelf, Miss Love almost smiled. "But he won't have to, of course. Even grown people mind Mr. Blakeslee, Will—as if they had no choice."

I couldn't help wondering had she minded him. Let him have his way with her, as the saying goes.

I took a stack of plates out of her hands and set them on the kitchen table by a pile of papers that I recognized as copies of Loma's Christmas play. I reached for the lamp at the back of the table, where Loma had left it last time the lights went out. I felt awful. "Ma'am, do you think Uncle Camp might still be alive if Loma and Grandpa hadn't blessed him out so much? You think Grandpa is tryin' to make it up to him now?" I struck a match and put it to the lamp wick.

"Sh-h-h, Will. We'll never know. Not even your grandfather will know, because he won't let himself think that way."

"And couldn't admit it if he did?"

"And couldn't admit it if he did."

"Aunt Loma was the main one, I reckon, but she won't ever see how she treated him." In a low miserable voice I said, "Miss Love, I, uh, I didn't treat him so good myself."

"We'll talk about it later, Will. Not now." Miss Love took off her apron, I picked up the lamp, and we hurried out.

Mr. Birdsong and his boys were just leaving. I watched them walk across the gold cat-paw prints on the dining room floor and go out through the kitchen. Then we went on in the parlor, and Miss Love asked Grandpa if she should go get Loma and Mr. Hoyt and Mary Willis.

"I want you here by me, where you belong to be," said Grandpa. "Let Will Tweedy go. Tell your daddy to bring Loma on down, son. But first, open them doors. Hit won't do to keep folks a-waitin'. They might leave." As he took aholt of Miss Love's elbow, I pushed open the double doors and he stood glaring at the silent, uneasy crowd. "Y'all can come on in now," he said, as if it never occurred to him they might not want to.

All those Cold Sassy eyes moved past Grandpa and Miss Love and focused on the coffin. But nobody moved.

"Cratic?" Grandpa spoke in a soft voice. "You and Miz Flournoy come first. Camp always thought a lot a-y'all." Mr. Flournoy came forward like a puppet on a string.

Miss Love held out her hand to him. As Mr. Flournoy took it, he turned and looked back at his wife. "Mama?" he whispered. She looked nervous and uncertain, as if being in the same room with a suicide corpse might taint her. But she came on in and Mr. Flournoy ushered her forward.

I watched the Flournoys stare at the coffin. I knew they were wondering if Mr. Birdsong had been able to make Uncle Camp look nat'ral, considering the circumstances. But then Mrs. Flournoy commenced crying. "Daddy," she sobbed, "we c-could of been nicer to that p-poor boy. . . ."

One by one, then in groups, Cold Sassy came in to view the hidden remains. Watching them file by, I felt like their tears weren't just from gruesome imaginings of the blasted head under the golden oak coffin lid. They cried from real sorrow. Like me and Mrs. Flournoy, they knew they could of been nicer.

Hurrying out to go upstairs, I was surprised to see Grandpa following behind. "Hit's all right in the parlor now, son. I best see after Loma myself." As we pushed our way through the hall toward the stairs, I heard somebody ask where was the poor fatherless child. Somebody else said the baby was over at the Tweedys'. "The cook's keepin' him."

Papa was kneeling by the window, praying. Mama sat on the foot of the bed, holding a wet washrag to her forehead. Aunt Loma? Still in the dressy black wool outfit she'd worn to Sue Lee's, she walked the floor in front of the bureau, back and forth, forth and back. She didn't cry or carry on. She looked like a sleepwalker. Back and forth, and I don't believe she knew where she was or even that she paced.

"Loma?" Grandpa stood in the door. "I brung Camp's body home." My parents looked up, surprised, but Loma just kept pacing. He spoke louder. "Loma, I brung Camp's body home and folks are down there payin' their respects. They'll want to say their condolences to you." She kept walking. Back and forth, forth and back.

Mama got up from the bed and put her hand on Loma's arm. "Sugar, here's Pa," she said softly.

"Y'all go on down to the parlor," Grandpa told us. As we filed out, he was saying, "Loma? Come here to yore daddy, pet." I glanced back just as he caught her arm and pulled her to him. She looked slowly up, to see who had her. Then her eyes focused and tears ran down her cheeks. Clutching her arms around her daddy's waist, she hid her face against his chest. "Oh, Pa!" she cried. "Oh, Pa, I been so mean to him. . . . I fussed so about the faucet. . . ." She sounded like somebody lost. "Pa, I want to come home. Can I? Me and the baby? Please. . . ."

I didn't hear if he said yes or no, because I had to shut the door. But as I followed Mama and Papa down the stairs, I wondered would he let her. And would Miss Love let her? If she and Grandpa were romancing, it sure would put a crimp in things to have Jealousy Incarnate underfoot.

I couldn't help thinking that if all Grandpa needed was a housekeeper, Aunt Loma could keep house for him now. But even if he hadn't wanted Miss Love, it was just as well he didn't wait for Loma. If she had been born colored, not a soul would of hired her to clean up or cook, either one.

Anyhow, Grandpa hadn't hardly passed the time of day with Loma since they quarreled about her being an actress, and things got even worse between them after she disobeyed him and married Uncle Camp. When Campbell Junior was born, he did go see the baby and made a big to-do over it being a boy, which really pleased Aunt Loma. But that was the end of that. It didn't really change anything. Whenever the two of them were in the same room, it was like they didn't know enough English to carry on a conversation. They both could hold a grudge like it was a life work.

Well, it was awful to think what it had taken to make Grandpa treat Loma and Uncle Camp nice.

There hadn't been a suicide in Cold Sassy since the Crabtrees' son, Arthur, got drunk on a cold winter night, laid down across his sweetheart's grave, and took an overdose of laudanum. Next morning when he was found, the bottle was laying by his body.

Arthur never even got back home. The Crabtrees were so mad and hurt and ashamed, they took a pine casket out to the cemetery and put him right under, and to this day there isn't a marker on his grave. The burial service was just one sentence. The preacher said, "God won't forgive this awful thing he did." Dr. Slaughter thought it wasn't the laudanum that killed Arthur; it was laying out there all night in twenty-degree weather. But he was considered a suicide person just the same, since suicide was his clear intent. Two months before, when Arthur's sixteen-year-old sweetheart died of galloping consumption, the *Cold Sassy Weekly* had called her passing "the saddest and yet most beautiful death in memory, lamented in verse by her brother James, well-known invalid poet of Maysville, Georgia." The paper printed Brother James's whole long dern memorial poem about her. But poor Arthur got just two lines: "Young Arthur Crabtree of this city became deceased last Thursday."

Camp would of gone the same way as Arthur if it had been left up to his folks. The Williamses, I mean. Grandpa sent word to them right after it happened, but they sent word back saying they wouldn't come. That was the whole message. Despite Camp wrote in his letter that he wanted to be buried in Cold Sassy, Mama had hoped the Williamses would say bring our boy home. That was the usual thing to do when a young person died. "It would of saved a lot of embarrassment for Loma, considerin'," said Mama. "Not to mention the rest of the fam'ly."

But if Mama or Cold Sassy thought Campbell Williams would end up with a quick private burying like Arthur Crabtree's, it had another think coming. Sunday at three o'clock, Camp had him a nice, long regular-type funeral in the Baptist church. Brother Belie Jones didn't give any eulogy, but he asked God to comfort the young widow and raise the baby in the Bosom of the Lamb, and then he read Scriptures for an hour.

As the preacher finished the Twenty-third Psalm, he looked at Grandpa with a question mark on his face. Grandpa, who sat between Aunt Loma and Miss Love, glared hard at Brother Jones, and the preacher said, "Let us bow our heads a-gain in prayer." After reminding God that in the note to his wife, the deceased had asked His forgiveness, Brother Jones prayed, "Lord, Thou knowest this congregation is shocked and saddened by what has happened in our community. We know the Bible says it is a sin to take life, our own as much as anybody else's. But Lord, hep us to see that this boy was a poor lost soul and deservin' of our compassion."

Grandpa nodded grimly, and the funeral was over.

Nobody was sure that Camp's asking God's forgiveness before he pulled the trigger counted as much as if he had lived long enough to repent after doing the deed. But it was a comforting hope.

No suicide person in living memory had ever been treated nice as Uncle Camp. Papa even wondered if maybe Grandpa gave some money to the Baptist church to get it done right, but Mama said that idea was far-fetched—"stingy as Pa is." Anyhow, it was a grand send-off. And as if the church funeral and the fine coffin weren't enough, Grandpa not only insisted Camp be laid to rest in the Toy plot but had Loomis dig the grave right at Miss Mattie Lou's feet.

There were those who thought it was going far too far to put somebody who was already halfway to Hell at the feet of a lady who'd been a saint on earth if ever there was one. But Grandpa didn't ask anybody's permission.

Later that evening, when we were all at Aunt Loma's to eat supper, I asked him if he thought Uncle Camp could of got to Hell already. Grandpa told me to shut up. "They's plenty men thet are mean and hateful, son, or they cheat folks, or beat their wives and their colored, but when they die, them preachers cain't say enough nice thangs. Well, Camp he warn't evil or hateful, either one. He jest couldn't do nothin'. So doggit, Will Tweedy, ain't you or nobody else go'n say he's gone to Hell. He jest couldn't stand it no more. Would a lovin' God kick a boy unhappy enough to do what pore Camp did?"

Mama came up while Grandpa was talking. Right in front of her, he said he didn't want no funeral when he died. "I want a party, like them Irishmen have."

It made me proud, how Grandpa was that day.

But if I'd known from the beginning that Aunt Loma and

Campbell Junior would come live with us instead of with him and Miss Love, and me have to give up my room and sleep winter and summer on a sawed-off old bed out on our back porch, I'd of been too mad at Uncle Camp to fix the faucet for him.

45

I T WOULD of made a lot more sense for Loma to go live with her daddy and Miss Love. She and Campbell Junior could of had the upstairs room that was hers growing up.

Doing her duty, Miss Love gave her an invite the day after the funeral. But Grandpa spoke up before Loma could open her mouth. "Naw, you better go live with Sister and Hoyt," he said. "I'm too old to hep raise a youngun."

Despite Loma had begged to come home, I don't doubt she was relieved not to be going. Besides how she felt about Miss Love, there was how she felt about kerosene lamps, well water, and privies.

Still and all, I didn't see why she couldn't just stay on where she was, and said so.

"For pity sake, Will," said Mama, "I never thought to raise a boy so hardhearted. What fam'lies are for is to hep one another in time of trouble."

"Well'm, but it ain't like Aunt Loma's homeless."

"She cain't stay where she is. Not unless some older woman could go live with her, and I don't know who that would be. A widow pretty as Loma and not but twenty-one years old, what would people say? And how would she live? Lord knows, there's nothing under her mattress to fall back on."

What she would fall back on was Grandpa, of course. And since he owned her house as well as ours, it hadn't taken him two minutes to see that by putting the two families together and leasing out Loma's place, the rent money would just about equal her upkeep.

I know Aunt Loma didn't mind coming to our house a bit. She cried when Papa said she could bring only one cat, but losing the cats was nothing compared to gaining Queenie, who would help with the baby and do their washing and cook their food. Aunt Loma was a lot of things, but not dumb.

The first week or two at our house, she stayed in her room (my room), crying about treating poor Camp so mean. But it wasn't long till she was mourning instead for the way he had treated her.

During the Christmas holidays I went up to her room (my room) to see could I find my tobacco tags. I thought I had them in a Prince Albert can under a loose board near the fireplace in there. The door was open, so I went in, and there stood Aunt Loma in front of the mirror, staring at herself in the thin flowerdy dress Miss Love brought her from New York—the one she couldn't wear last summer because of being in mourning for Granny and couldn't wear next summer on account of being a widow.

Seeing me in the glass coming up behind her, she jerked around and started yelling about Uncle Camp killing himself. "The nerve of him, leavin' me like this! Beholden to my daddy and my brother-in-law for the very clothes on my back and the food in my mouth!"

"Aw, Aunt Loma, you don't have to feel beholden," I said, honestly trying to be a comfort. "Mama says that's what families are for."

Whereat she collapsed on the bed and went to crying. "Oh, Will, what's to become of m-me!"

As Aunt Loma got used to Camp being gone, though, she seemed to take on new life. And despite it was crowded at our house, we all settled down. She and I had a run-in every now and again, but even Aunt Loma could see it was to her advantage to be nice. Except for nursing the baby, she was more or less free to hold him or put him down, same as if she was his grandmother or a maiden aunt. She never had to look after him unless she was in a mood to, because if he wasn't toddling around after me, he was with Mary Toy, unless he was with Mama or Queenie. Life was just easier now for Aunt Loma.

Well, it wasn't easier for me. As always when things got behind in the family or at the store, I was the one who took up the slack. I never saw Pink and Lee Roy and Smiley except at school or church. I kept thinking I'd drive the Cadillac out toward Mill Town and see could I find Lightfoot McLendon and take her to ride, but I never got to.

I finally asked Mama why couldn't Aunt Loma make herself more useful. "That way I might could play baseball every year or two with Pink and them, or go fishing sometime."

Mama was at the sink, washing sweet potatoes to bake for supper. She said, not unkindly, "Don't talk bitter, Will. Loma's goin' through a bad time."

"Yes'm, but it sure would hep if she could milk the cow and bring in stovewood."

Mama bristled. "Yankee women do work like that, and colored women, and tenant farmers' wives and daughters. We don't. Loma heps in the house and that's enough."

Loma mostly stayed up in her room (my room) and did what she'd always wanted to, namely, write poems and plays. But pretending to be a writer wasn't much fun without an audience, so pretty soon she brought her pencil and paper down to the breakfast table. Once when the Muse was on her, she sat staring into space so long I got worried. "Reckon Aunt Loma's had a stroke?" I whispered to Queenie.

"Naw, suh, Mr. Will," she whispered back. "Miss Loma jes' be's sightin' on a poem. She do's lak dat lots a-time."

But it was easy to see the widow was restless, and before long she waylaid Grandpa, when he stopped by for his snort, to ask if she could come work at the store.

He said he'd think on it.

Lord knows he needed somebody, what with Miss Love gone to housekeeping, Uncle Camp gone to Hell, and spring just around the corner. Farmers would soon be coming in to arrange credit terms and buy seed and guano. Ladies were already picking through patterns and piece goods, planning their Easter dresses. And it looked like everybody and his brother was itching for an automobile. On a warm Saturday we could hardly wait on customers for taking folks to ride.

On the other hand, we couldn't afford to put them off, because the cars were beginning to sell. Grandpa read in the paper that in 1906 there were at least a thousand automobiles in Georgia, mostly owned by farmers, doctors, and residents of small towns. That really fired him up to try to sell a lot in 1907.

In the meantime, I was still the stable boy for Miss Love and Grandpa. I never had time to talk much when I went up there, but I couldn't help noticing she seemed happier lately, and that was a relief. Ever since That Night at Miss Gussie's house, I'd been scared we'd hear any day that she was leaving for Baltimore.

Or Texas.

I do remember complaining to her about the committee that had been set up to find a more modern name for Cold Sassy. "Papa's in favor," I grumped. "I don't see why he ain't noticed that the reason it's called Cold Sassy is because that's its name."

"Don't worry so, Will," said Miss Love, smiling her big-mouth smile. "You know your grandfather will never let it happen."

Miss Love was washing a kitchen window that looked clean to me already. It seemed like every time I went down there, she was washing floors or windows, one, despite she'd cleaned the whole house good last summer. "Miss Love, I reckon you ain't heard about fall and spring cleanin'," I said one day. She had come out on the back porch to empty her wash water just as I headed for the barn. I said, "In between spring and fall, and fall and spring, ma'am, you just s'posed to sweep and mop and use the feather duster and like that."

"I like the Yankee way better," she said, bristling. I reckon she thought Mama had criticized how she did. "Up North, ladies do extra cleaning every week in one room. Brush down the walls and wash the floor one week, maybe wash windows and curtains the next, and so on. When they get that room done, they start on another. The house stays nice year round, and it's not exhausting like doing all the heavy cleaning at once."

When I told Mama, she said, "I'd rather get worn out twice a year than stay worn out all the time."

The Rucker Blakeslee Hotel sign was finally up, and they said Mr. Clem Crummy just about got apoplexy every time a stranger asked was the ho-tel owned by the same feller had the brick store up the street. I knew Miss Love thought it was awful of Grandpa to hold Mr. Clem to the drawing, but he just laughed when she said so.

Then one day she came down to the store with a sign she had made. Grandpa read it and laughed. "Go on, put it in the winder," he said.

This is what was on it:

ATTENTION!
Drummers, Cotton Buyers, Railroad Men,
And Other Travelers!
Try the Elegant Refurbished
BLAKESLEE HOTEL
Fine Cuisine!
Clean, Bug-Free Beds!
Fiddle Music and Parlor Games Every Night!

The Crummys never even said thank you, but the sign got them some business that usually went to the boarding houses.

Miss Love's birthday was on Valentine's. (That's how come she was named Love.) The day before, Grandpa told me she had decided to give herself a present. She was going to use some of her savings to put in a bathroom, and of course a sink and faucet in the kitchen. "Hit's fol-de-rol and foolish-ment," he said, but he grinned proud.

That told me one thing. Whether Miss Love was now Grandpa's wife or still just his housekeeper, she wouldn't put her own money into plumbing if she was still thinking about leaving Cold Sassy. On the other hand, she had another think coming if she expected Grandpa to say "Don't spend yore money, let me give you the bathroom for your birthday." He had already bought her a present, a Home Graphophone. It cost five dollars from the Talking Machine Department at Sears, Roebuck and Co., and he'd ordered a dozen "best and loudest music records" to play on it.

A machine that could talk and play music was, as Grandpa kept saying, a dang marvel.

You can imagine that when Cold Sassy heard about the Graphophone, everybody remembered he never gave Miss Mattie Lou a birthday present. Granny had always insisted she didn't want one. "Birthdays is for chi'ren," she'd say. "I don't have to mark gittin' older. I can just look in the glass and tell." He did order Granny a coconut and a crate of oranges every Christmas to make him some ambrosia with, but his Christmas gift to Miss Love had been a new buggy top with side and back curtains, and now not two months later he'd bought her that Graphophone.

From Valentine's Day on, Grandpa never went back to the store after dinner on Wednesdays. Like I said, the stores in Cold Sassy closed every Wednesday around noon, but always before, he went back to work anyway. Said it was a good chance to ketch up on what needed doin'. But now it looked like he was ketchin' up on Miss Love.

Sometimes they'd go buggy-riding, closed up snug with the side and back curtains snapped shut. One freezing cold Wednesday I went through the house on my way to the barn and found them sitting in the warm kitchen, him in a rocking chair with his glasses on, reading to Miss Love while she sewed. One Sunday after dinner I went up there, just to visit a while, and Grandpa was laying on the daybed in the hall with Miss Love sitting right on the bed beside him, rubbing his forehead. When they saw me, she jumped like somebody caught stealing and hurried to the kitchen, and he sat up muttering something about a backache.

Plain as day, Grandpa was courting Miss Love. Why else would he be home with her so much? Why else would he have spent so much on the Graphophone and the records for it?

Despite I couldn't know if they still called each other Miss and Mister when it was just the two of them, I sensed a difference lately. They were always laughing and teasing, and whenever one came in a room where the other one was, you could read a book by the light on their faces.

To me they were like a book—a book with the last chapter missing. And I couldn't wait to know how it ended.

At school when we commenced studying *Romeo and Juliet*, the drama that might or might not be going on up at Grandpa's house laid itself down on every line Shakespeare wrote about love or marriage.

"Does she call him husband?" I read, and thought of Miss Love, not Juliet.

"Stony limits cannot hold love out!" That was Grandpa shouting at his Love. "O! I have bought the mansion of a love, but not possess'd it" was his lament.

But hark! Mayhap Miss Love doth use Juliet's words to tease: "If thou think'st I am too quickly won, I'll frown and be perverse and say thee nay, so thou wilt woo. . . ."

Well, Grandpa was wooing, no doubt about it. And seemed like Miss Love was enjoying being wooed. But was she yet saying him nay?

Whenever I was up at their house I'd go to wondering if she still slept in the spare room by herself, or did he come in there sometimes at night, or had she taken over Granny's side of his bed. It wasn't decent, the way I kept picturing in my mind what might or might not be going on and none of it any of my business. I just wished I knew one way or the other. Then maybe I could quit wondering and, as Papa would say, be-have myself.

One night I had to go take Grandpa a message from my daddy. As I ran up the front steps, I noticed the parlor draperies were pulled to. And despite the house was shut up tight, I could hear the music machine just a-going. Hurrying in, I saw they'd pushed all the parlor furniture back against the walls, Miss Love had put on a new dance record, and by golly she was teaching Grandpa the turkey trot!

He was bad to stumble, and kept stepping on her feet, but they were laughing and cutting up, just having the best time. I stood there grinning and they waved at me.

"I'm gittin' the hang of it, Will Tweedy!" bragged Grandpa, swinging her around. "Next time we go to New York City, I ain't go'n have to pay no partner for her! Here, Love, learn Will Tweedy how," he said, handing her over to me. "I got to rest a spell."

I was as stumbly as Grandpa, and kept stepping on her feet, too. But boy howdy, I had my arms around her and she was looking up at me, smiling, while Grandpa watched us and beat time to the music. When the machine started winding down, making funny groans and whines, we all three laughed like children.

Later I couldn't help but try and imagine what it would be like dancing with Lightfoot McLendon. In my mind I saw her in a silk ball gown, smiling up at me as I held her, and us circling and whirling.

I still thought about Lightfoot a lot, and still wondered sometimes if she hated me for kissing her. But I was too busy to moon over it much. Things had got real bad at the store.

Aunt Loma kept pestering Grandpa for a job. He didn't pay her any mind, but he did start saying he had to hire somebody. One morning before school I was stacking big sacks of cow feed and guano outside against the brick wall of the store when Grandpa ambled out, spat brown tobacco juice through a crack in the board sidewalk, and said, "Will Tweedy, you know the mill boy thet come in here a while back wantin' a job? What's his name, son?"

I knew right off who and what he had in mind, and it made me mad as heck. But all I said was, "Hosie Roach?"

"Thet's the one. Is he in school this term?"

"Yessir."

"How old you reckon Hosie is? He ain't a real big boy, as I recollect. But he's some older'n you, ain't he?"

"Yessir. He's prob'ly twenty. Maybe twenty-one." I couldn't help adding, "And still ain't finished school."

"Well, he seemed right smart to me." Grandpa had sense enough to know the reason Hosie hadn't graduated was that he worked a lot at the cotton mill and couldn't get to school regular. "I liked thet boy. Tell him to come see me this evenin', son. I got to git me some more hep."

I told Hosie what Grandpa said. He didn't jump up and down about it like I thought he would. Didn't even let on he was excited. But he couldn't hide the deep flush that came on his face.

"Tell Mr. Blakeslee I cain't come today," he said, putting his scaly hands in the pockets of his dirty, ragged overalls. "Tell him I'll be by t'morrer."

"He ain't go'n like it, you not comin' when he said to." I spoke hateful. "He's used to folks sayin' yessir when he tells'm something."

Hosie flushed again. I swear he looked like my dog T.R. when he's ashamed and trying to wag his tail and drag his belly at the same time. "Will," said Hosie, "be shore and say I'll see him t'morrer, hear. Tell him I'll be by fore school takes in."

I fell in step with Grandpa next morning as he left our house after his snort. "I'm goin' by the store and get me a pencil," I said.

Crossing North Main, with T.R. trotting ahead, I decided to speak up about Hosie Roach. "There ain't but four things wrong with him, Grandpa."

"What, son? Besides he's a mill boy."

"Some folks in Cold Sassy will think when it comes to workin' at your store, him bein' a linthead is enough and too much." I was being real smart-aleck. "Main thing, sir, he's got cooties and the itch and he stinks."

"He was clean as you thet day he come in astin' for a job."

"Well, he ain't clean when he comes to school. He don't grow much beard, but his hair's so long and tangled and dirty it looks like a dern cootie stable, haw!"

Hosie was waiting in front of the store when we got there. I didn't hardly recognize him.

Naturally he was barefooted, and his feet were cracked and bleeding from the cold. But he had on new overalls and a clean long-sleeved denim shirt. His face was shaved smooth and scrubbed raw, the tow hair clean and wet-combed.

I knew now why Hosie wouldn't stop by yesterday. He was too proud to show up dirty. He must of scrubbed himself from suppertime to midnight.

"I come to see about the job, sir," he said as Grandpa unlocked the big door. "Sir, I hope you ain't a'ready hired somebody."

"Come on in, son." I knew Grandpa was surprised at Hosie being so clean, after what I said, but I could see it pleased him.

While he went behind the counter to unlock the cash register, I walked over to the rack where the tablets and pencils were. But of course all I really had on my mind was Hosie Roach.

If he got hired, it wouldn't be Uncle Camp he'd be replacing. It would be me. He'd get the floors swept and the stock put out every morning in no time. Within a week he would find a hundred ways to make himself useful. Without being asked, he'd get the chickens crated up to ship to Atlanta, and the cars washed, and I don't know what all. Lord, smart as Hosie was, it wouldn't be any time before he'd know how to drive and start taking people out for demonstration rides. And unless folks didn't want his hands on their foodstuff, he'd soon be weighing up sugar and flour and drawing molasses out of the barrel.

Hosie wasn't any better worker than me. But whereas I always had to go home in time to milk and bring in stovewood, he could stay all night if Grandpa wanted him to. And whereas my daddy always asked how much Latin or geometry I had to do that night, and lots of times made me go home early to get at it, Hosie would of course quit school if he got the job.

Bad as he wanted to leave the mill and amount to something, Hosie would be equal to ten of Uncle Camp plus maybe two of me, and Grandpa would respect him. Jealousy rose in me like a pain as I heard them talking terms.

Grandpa had sense enough to know how cheap a linthead would work. However little he paid, it would be more than Hosie made at the mill. He would cost more than me, since I didn't get paid anything, being in the family, but he would be cheaper than Uncle Camp, who had to be paid enough for him and Aunt Loma to live on.

The whole idea of it made me mad.

I was fixing to call the dog and go on to school when I heard Grandpa ask Hosie if he had cooties.

Hosie would of hit any town boy at school who even mentioned such. I stood there hoping he'd hit Grandpa. Because if he did, that would be the end of that.

"I ain't wantin' to shame you, boy," Grandpa said, propping his left elbow on the oak counter top and leaning forward. "I jest got to make shore. If'n we bring cooties in here, or the seven-year itch, I ain't go'n have no customers."

"Yessir. I unner-stand, sir." And Hosie turned to leave.

"Wait a minute now. I ain't said I cain't hire you, son. But most folks gits the itch now and agin, so lemme tell you what to do—if'n you got it or if'n you git it. Will Tweedy?" Hosie jerked around. He must not of known I was still there. "Go in the storeroom, Will, and open up thet case a-Siticide. Bring me a bottle for Hosie."

Why did he have to say that? Oh, well, let him make Hosie mad. Nothing I'd welcome more than to take on Hosie Roach at recess today.

"You heard about Siticide?" asked Grandpa.

"Naw, sir."

"Well, it's itch medicine. Use it at night, not when you comin' to work, cause it's the stinkin'est stuff you ever come acrost in yore life. Got sulfur in it. Makes the skin yaller and you'll smell like a rotten aigg. But by dang it'll cure the itch. Dr. Lem Sharp over in Harmony Grove invented it—Commerce, you know. Dr. Lem ships the stuff all over the United States of America, so it's got to be good."

"Yessir." Hope was rising in Hosie's face.

"Now bout cooties. I ain't a-sayin' you got'm, but we cain't be too careful. What you want to do is git yore ma to cut yore hair short—short as mine. Wash yore head with lye soap ever night for a while, and use you one a-them fine-tooth combs to git the nits out. Y'all got one them combs, boy?"

"Naw, sir."

Grandpa reached up on the shelf back of him, but the comb box was empty. "I'll order some from the wholesale house, son. We do a real good bizness in fine-tooth combs. Lots a-town folks got trouble with them critters." He didn't say that town people with cooties were usually teachers or children who'd caught them at school from lintheads.

Hosie bent over to pet T.R., I guess so his red face wouldn't show. Finally he said, "Mr. Blakeslee, I can start work today. I'm ready and willin', sir."

"Naw, not today," said Grandpa. "Naw, you go git squared away at school, son, and git yore hair cut and all. T'morrer will be jest fine."

Like I said, Grandpa could get away with anything.

And he had finally done what the school superintendent never could. He'd made Hosie Roach willing to quit school.

Mama had a fit when Papa told her about Hosie being hired. She said Grandpa was crazy to think town folks would accept a mill boy in the store. "Well, maybe y'all can keep him in the back," she decided. "You really got to have some hep."

Papa and Cudn Hopewell Stump opened up next morning, but Hosie was there ahead of them. He had found a broom out back and was sweeping the board sidewalk in front of the store when they walked up. "Lord, Mary Willis, we didn't know who he was!" Papa said at dinner. "That boy was bald as a newborn babe!"

Hosie hadn't just got his hair cut. He'd shaved his head. I really resented him wanting to please all that bad. Especially after

Papa asked could I spare an old cap so Hosie wouldn't look so funny.

Papa was real impressed with Hosie.

The next week Miss Love told Grandpa the store ought to have a milliner, and offered to teach Loma. She thought Loma might have a real knack for hats. Grandpa didn't exactly promise the job, but he said it shore would be nice if she could earn her keep, which may of been what Miss Love had in mind. Anyhow, it wasn't long before the two of them came down to the store and set up the millinery table again, and Miss Love put a sign in the window saying Mrs. Loma Williams was under her tutelage and was ready to accommodate customers for new Easter hats at a special low price.

Loma was in hog heaven, being out in public again. I never knew she could act so nice to people. The ladies of Cold Sassy were only too glad to help her get started, knowing Miss Love would lay a hand on every hat, and all the men asked Grandpa how come he waited so long to bring his pretty daughter into the store.

"Jest never thought to," said Grandpa, grinning proud and draping his arm around Loma's shoulders. "If'n she'd a-been a boy, I'd a-had her down here from the day she was born."

Loma looked pleased. I hadn't really hated her for a good while, but I hated her right then. I knew if she worked hard she could worm her way into Grandpa's good graces. And the same with Hosie. Between the two of them, Grandpa might not even notice when I went off to the University.

And would the store ever be quite the same, now that two of the people I couldn't stand were there every day?

46

I SHAVED for the first time on my fifteenth birthday. Went to school with little pieces of paper stuck on my face to stop the bleeding.

That was the thirtieth day of April. Peonies and flag lilies and poppies were blooming in people's yards, and roses and sweet William, mountain laurel and bleeding heart. And boy howdy, I was fifteen years old!

Smiley and them gave me fifteen licks at recess, one for each year. Then after school they rubbed smut on my face. When I went to the boys' washroom to get it off, I looked in the mirror and, gosh, it was like I'd grown a black beard.

What it was, they were jealous of me being the first to shave.

I like to of never got the smut off. My face was still streaked when I headed for the store. I was already late, and as I hurried by the Presbyterian church, a girl's voice called from behind a big beauty bush in full bloom. "Will?"

It was Lightfoot!

"Will, kin you talk a minute?" She peeped around the beauty bush. "You got time? Jest for a minute?"

Glancing quickly up and down the street, I ducked around where she was. Gosh, she looked pretty! Her face wasn't pinched from thinness and sorrow like the last time I saw her.

The ivory skin glowed against the deep blue of her dress. Like in my dreams, her hair hung loose and shone like platinum.

"Lightfoot?" I'd thought so many times what I'd say when I finally saw her again, but now I was tongue-tied and embarrassed. "Uh, you all right?"

"Yeah, I'm fine. I knowed you ne'ly always come by here goin' to the store from school, but I 'as jest fixin' to give you up. You must a-had to stay in."

"Naw, I just had to wash my face." I rubbed my chin. "Boys put smut on me. It's my birthday today. I'm fifteen."

"Well, thet's nice. I 'as fifteen two months ago."

Gosh, I hadn't thought about her being older than me. "Uh, you gettin' on all right, Lightfoot?" I asked again.

"Pretty good. How you doin', Will?"

"Fine. Uh, my grandpa bought a Pierce car and I drive it for him."

"Yeah, I heerd."

"You did?"

"Hosie told me."

"Oh. Well, uh, with the weather gettin' nice I reckon we go'n be takin' trips again soon. Uh, Lightfoot, I been hopin' to see you again. I wanted, uh, I mean I owe you a apology for—you know, in the cemetery that day. I didn't mean to do it. I—"

"Thet's over and done with, Will." She put her hand on my arm. "And it's one reason I come. You so nice, I knowed you'd feel bad bout thet day. I shore was sorry the lady had sech a fit at you, but I ain't sorry you wanted to comfort me. Maybe I oughtn't to say it, but I ain't never go'n forgit thet time with you."

I dared to put my hand on her hand that was on my arm, and where it had seemed like a million years since I kissed her, all of a sudden it was no more than a day. "Lightfoot, if you ain't mad, why'd you wait so long to say so? Why you sayin' it now?"

"Will, uh—" She flushed and pulled away. "I jest wanted

you to know before—" She faltered. "Uh, how's Miss Neppie? She 'as real nice to me."

"She's fine. But she ain't my teacher now. You go'n get to come back to school next year?"

"No. But I been studyin' Hosie's books, Will. I ain't go'n quit larnin', no matter what."

"School ain't been the same with you not there."

Smiling, she put her hand in her pocket and held out a big buckeye. "Would you take it, Will? For luck, and to remember me by? I brung it with me from White County when we come down here. I, uh, I ain't a-go'n need it no more now."

Something about her tone made me suspicion what this was all about. "Lightfoot, are you sayin' good-bye to me?"

She said, "Will, I . . . I mostly come to make thangs right betwixt us, whilst I'm still free to. I wanted you to know I never thought hard a-you for—you know. And yeah, I reckon thet's it. I come to say good-bye."

"Where you goin'? Back to White County?" I thought I couldn't stand it, not ever to see her again.

"Will, I'm a-go'n git marrit."

The sky wobbled. "Get married?"

"I didn't want you to hear it from nobody else. I'm a-go'n marry Hosie."

Oh, good gosh a'mighty!

"We couldn't even think on it fore yore granddeddy give him thet job. Hosie's got a chance in life now, Will. We'll always feel beholden to Mr. Blakeslee. He shore is a fine man. I better go now, but I ain't never go'n forgit you and please don't forgit me, Will. Thet's why I give you the buckeye. Look at it ever now and agin and remember—"

She kissed me quick, on the cheek. Her eyes were brimming with tears. Next thing I knew, she had disappeared.

As if a chance in life wasn't enough, the next day Grandpa let Hosie off work early to go over to Jefferson for the license, and even lent him his mule for the trip. Also raised his wages fifty cents a week.

It like to killed me.

I felt by myself in a way I never had in my life. Miss Love just had eyes for Grandpa, and Grandpa was taken up with her, and now Lightfoot was about to marry Hosie Roach.

Maybe something would stop it. Maybe something would happen to Hosie. Maybe—

School was out for the summer on Friday that week, and they got married on Sunday, at the little Baptist church in Mill Town. "We jest went up after preachin'," Hosie told Grandpa, "and got the knot tied."

The one that something happened to was Grandpa.

47

G RANDPA worked late the following Friday night. Hosie Roach worked late, too, naturally, but went home
to Lightfoot about nine o'clock, a good hour before Grandpa
locked up to go home to Miss Love.

Just as he turned the door key, a man stuck a Harrington and
Richardson revolver to the back of his head, and a rough voice
said, "Unlock thet door, Mr. Blakeslee. Hit ain't quite time to
close up yet."

There were two of them, one big and burly, the other a
younger fellow with a slight build. Despite they had dirty white
handkerchiefs over their faces, Grandpa recognized them right
off as the strangers who'd come in the store that morning
claiming to be cotton buyers.

They made him unlock the cash register, despite he said
it was empty, and it *was* empty. Then they sat him down in
a straight chair by the potbellied stove, out of sight from the
street, and tied him to the chair with a length of medium rope
cut from the store's big coil. All that time, Grandpa kept saying how pore he was. "I ain't got no more cash money'n a one-
horse farmer," he insisted. "The store don't bring in enough
these days for nobody to bother stealin' it."

"Tell thet to somebody ain't got no sense," said the big burly one. "A man ain't pore thet owns two artermobiles and a store and a ho-tel." He nodded towards Miss Love's fine-cuisine sign in the window. "Luther, tie thet last knot tighter. Now, sir, whar's yore safe?"

"They ain't a dime in thet safe," roared Grandpa, struggling against the rope. He was really mad.

As the burly one slapped him across the face, Luther spied the safe. "Now call out the combination," ordered the big fellow. "And if I was you, sir, I wouldn't give no wrong numbers."

"Have it yore way, but it's a waste a-time," Grandpa insisted. "I used to keep cash money in there. But not since I read bout somebody breakin' in a store in Atlanta and cartin' off the safe to blow up later. I don't—"

"Say the combination for Luther here," the big fellow ordered again. "Say it slow. He ain't too bright."

So Grandpa said the numbers. But Luther being a little bit drunk and his hands shaking like the palsy from nervousness, he couldn't work it. They decided to untie Grandpa and make him do it.

Just like he said, the safe was empty—except for his will and a letter and some stock certificates, land deeds, and other legal papers. The robbers were mad, boy howdy! "Now, sir! You tell us where thet money is or git ready to die, one!" the big fellow yelled, waving his revolver in Grandpa's face.

"I shore didn't waste no time mindin' them boogers," Grandpa said the next morning when he was telling us all about the robbery. "Gosh a'mighty, I couldn't hardly wait to upturn my dang nail keg!"

He was lying on his left side in Granny's big bed. Miss Love sat in the rocking chair facing him. The rest of us stood behind her—I and Mama and Papa, Aunt Loma, Mary Toy, and Aunt Carrie, who had come over offering to help.

"Well, sir, I dumped the nail keg and—ow!" Grandpa, try-ing to turn onto his back, quickly eased back to his left side, which was where the broke ribs were. Doc had bound his chest tight with strips of old sheets to keep the broke ribs from moving every time he breathed. "Hit don't hurt so bad as long as I stay like this," he said, his face twisted with pain. "Ain't I a pretty sight, Will Tweedy?" He tried to grin.

I could hardly bear to look at him. Besides a big ugly knot on his forehead, he had two black eyes, his nose was swelled up huge—broke for the fourth time in his life—and Doc had bandaged a bad gash above his left eye. Besides all that, his right knee was bad twisted, and he was sore and bruised all over.

My daddy got him back to talking about the highwaymen. "Did they get all the money, sir?"

"I reckon, Hoyt. Like I say, I dumped the keg, nails and all, and besides the day's earnin's, out fell all them silver dollars and gold pieces I had in there. Must a-been a hundred and fifty dollars' worth, and them coins rollin' ever whichaway!" Grandpa spread his right arm wide to indicate the whole store, but I noticed he was mindful of his broke ribs. "Gosh a'mighty, they was greedy! Went down on hands and knees and crawled around jest a-grabbin'! They'd been drinkin', you know, and they warn't any too bright, and was new at the game, too, I reckon, cause they plumb forgot I wasn't still tied up. All I had to do was watch my chance and whack each one acrost the back of the neck with the side of my hand—*thonk*, *thonk*. By time they come to, I was a-settin' on the counter with their dang Harrington and Richardson pointed right at'm."

Grandpa usually kept his own revolver under the counter, a Smith and Wesson, but had taken it home for cleaning.

First he made his prisoners take off their handkerchief masks. "Why, I thought y'all was men!" he exclaimed, making like he was surprised. "But dang if you ain't monkeys!" Grandpa was having the time of his life. He said, "Well, jest in case y'all got in mind to start some monkey bizness, I'll do a little target

practice. See thet there cardboard advertise-ment?" He nodded toward a cutout of a pretty lady holding a box of Pearline
Washing Compound. It hung by a string from the ceiling just
above where the robbers were sitting on the floor but, being
dazed and dumfounded, they looked all around and didn't see
what he was talking about.

"Hit's a-hangin' right over y'all's heads," jeered Grandpa.
The men looked up just as he shot the string half in two, dropping the cardboard lady to the floor at their feet. "Now then, I
reckon y'all go'n be-have whilst I ring up Pearl Potter, our po-
lice. Thet's *Mister* Pearl Potter, for yore information."

But with just the one hand, Grandpa would have had to lay
down the revolver to talk on the phone. Not being that big of
a fool, he told Luther to do the calling. "Say to Mr. Pearl, 'Me
and my buddy been tryin' to rob Blakeslee's store, so come git
us and put us in the calaboose!' Make haste, now, Luther. I got
to git on home. Gosh a'mighty, I bet Mr. Pearl ain't never got
a call like this'n before," he said, laughing.

Luther stood up real slow, eyeing the telephone.

"You ain't never seen a telephone?" Grandpa was trying to
goad him. "All you do, you turn thet crank, then you pick up
thet dohickey and put it up to yore ear and wait till Central answers. What you talk th'ew is thet thang stickin' out of the box.
Tell her Rucker Blakeslee is a-holdin' you and yore partner and
you want to speak to Mr. Pearl Potter."

The robber was naturally mad as heck, being made fun of
like that, but he did like he was told to — then just stood there
and stood there.

"Why ain't you talkin'?" asked Grandpa.

"Cause she don't answer," said Luther.

"Dang!" said Grandpa, "Miss Lucille must a-gone to the
bathroom. Crank it agin, sonny boy."

All of a sudden he noticed that the other fellow, the burly
one, had stood up and moved a step forward. "You want a bul-

let th'ew that mole on yore chin, buster?" he yelled, waving the revolver. "Move one more step and I'll put it there. Or maybe you rather watch me shoot another string half in two."

He saw the men exchange quick glances when he said that, but as he himself admitted later, he was havin' sech a good time he never thought nothin' of it.

Instead of stepping back, the big hunky fellow sneered and said, "Thet with the string was jest a lucky shot. You cain't do it agin."

"Less'n yore revolver don't aim true, I can do it any number a-times." Still sitting on the counter, not taking his eyes off the big fellow, Grandpa said, "Keep on crankin' thet phone, Luther."

"A gun cain't shoot no better than the feller aimin' it," said the big hunky one, and eased forward a little.

Grandpa saw that. "Go to dancin', buster!" he yelled, firing off a bullet that grazed the toe of the man's boot. Even before he pulled the trigger again and got a click instead of a bang, young Luther had dropped the receiver, leaving it dangling by the cord. Crouching low, like a bobcat ready to spring, he grabbed Grandpa's right knee, turned quick, and jerked him off the counter just as his partner raised a chair high and crashed it over Grandpa's head.

48

W E ALL wondered if the robbers meant to kill
Grandpa. "He shore looked dead when I come in the
store," said Mr. Pearl. "Out cold and bleedin' like a hog."

Dr. Slaughter said it was just a good thing Miss Lucille got
back to her switchboard in time to plug into the fight, and then
had the good sense to ring up him and Mr. Pearl.

If Miss Love had had a telephone, she would of been called
next instead of us. As it was, she'd just started wondering why
Grandpa hadn't come on home when she heard Mr. Birdsong's
old horse-drawn hearse rattle into her drive — the one he took
Uncle Camp to the morgue in but called an ambulance if the
person wasn't dead yet. Miss Love didn't have any way to know
for sure which it was when Doc climbed out and said he'd
brought Rucker home.

Papa and I got there in the Cadillac a minute or two later. I
won't ever forget the look on Miss Love's face as she watched
us bring Grandpa in on the stretcher. You'd think he'd been
under a rock all his life, he was so pale. The knot on his forehead was big as a double-yolk egg. The gash over his left eye
was still bleeding, and his face was a twist of pain. But as we
carried him towards the bedroom — Miss Love holding a lamp

high to light our way down the hall—Grandpa looked up at her with a weak grin and said, "Don't worry, hear. I'll be up in the mornin' fore the water boils. I got outsmarted, is all."

Then he coughed, and yelped with pain from the broke ribs.

Before I got inside his house good on Saturday night after it happened on Friday night, Grandpa called from the sickroom, "Thet you, Will Tweedy? Anythang new happen down at the store? They ketch them robbers? Come in here, son!"

His room smelled of turpentine, which Doc had prescribed as a liniment for the pulled ligament. Grandpa was sitting on the side of the bed in his nightshirt, holding a pack of steaming hot towels to his knee. By then he was tired of hurting and madder'n heck at the robbers. "If'n I ever meet up with them two agin," he yelled, shaking his fist, "I'll kill'm!"

"Better wait till you feel better, Grandpa," I said, joking.

That just made him madder. But he had to get aholt of himself, because the ranting and raving made his ribs hurt. Groaning, he eased back down on the bed, turning onto his left side. "Hit ain't so bad . . . long as I lay still and breathe shaller."

"Dr. Slaughter says you must breathe deep," Miss Love reminded him, coming in with a supper tray.

"Gosh a'mighty, woman, I'd like to see him breathe deep in my condition! All this wouldn't a-happened, Will Tweedy, if'n I'd jest knowed what them dang robbers knowed—thet warn't but two bullets in their dang revolver."

Miss Love set the tray on a towel on the bed so Grandpa could eat laying on his side. "You couldn't have known about the bullets," she said, patting his shoulder.

"Don't pat me when I'm mad, woman! I would a-knowed bout them bullets if I'd a-looked." He groaned, reaching down to rub his knee. "And I would a-looked," he added, "if'n I hadn't a-been talkin' so big and showin' off."

"Dear, try to stay calm. Dr. Slaughter said—"

"Let Doc stay calm. I'm mad and hurtin' and I need to git on to the store." Grandpa took a bite of cornbread and kept right on fussing. "If'n they'd a-fought fair, with fists, I could a-licked them boogers! Either one or both of 'm!"

He wasn't just mad. He was embarrassed. What hurt most —worse than the broke ribs, broke nose, banged head, and twisted knee all put together—was his pride. The only fight he'd ever lost before was the War Between the States.

Miss Love bent over him and touched his cheek. "You're alive," she whispered. "That's all I care about."

"Well, it ain't all I care about. Doggit—no, damnit, by gosh—I never thought to git done in by a dang settin' chair. If I'd a-seen it comin', I could a-ducked." He groaned.

My mother was coming down the hall as I left Grandpa's room to hurry back to the Saturday night customers at the store. "I thought maybe I could hep some way," she told Miss Love. "Maybe wash your supper dishes. And I'll take the soiled sheets home for Queenie to wash and iron." Almost timidly, she peered in at Grandpa lying in the bed. "Pa?" she said sweetly. "Would you like me to come sit with you a few minutes?"

He was still mad at the robbers. "I reckon, Mary Willis," he grumped, "if'n you'll set over in the corner and not say nothin' and not cry. I cain't stand it when you mother-hen me."

I just knew she'd burst into tears. Instead, she snapped back at him like she'd been taking lessons from Aunt Loma. "Just cause you didn't get your way with the robbers is no reason to talk to me like that, Pa. And I don't have to stay and listen to it." She turned to stalk out.

"Aw, Mary Willis honey, come on in here and set down." Motioning toward the rocking chair, he grinned up at her. "Did you bring me a snort, by any chance? Miss Love ain't no diff'rent from yore ma when it comes to whiskey in the closet."

Mama actually burst out laughing. I did, too, and so did Miss Love. Grandpa almost laughed but had to keep it to a smirk. Laughing hurt his ribs.

I knew Mama had come mostly to be with her daddy. Miss Love was not one she had in mind when she said what fam'lies are for is to hep in time of trouble. But Miss Love seemed real glad to have her there.

I didn't get back again till after dinner Sunday. By then the whole house smelled like turpentine.

Thinking Grandpa might be asleep, I tiptoed down the hall instead of calling out. Just as I was about to peep into his room, I heard him and Miss Love talking soft and easy in there, the way people do when they're resting and in no hurry.

I knew I ought to announce my presence. But instead, drawing back behind the open door, I looked at them through the slit between it and the door frame. I could see them easy. Miss Love, in a pretty yellow dress, was lying a-top the sheet on Granny's side of the bed, her head cradled in the crook of Grandpa's left elbow. He lay on his left side, a thin nightshirt over the tight binding around his chest, the sheet pulled up to his waist. And gosh, he had his right arm laid across Miss Love's stomach! His eyes were closed.

To save me, I couldn't move or speak.

"Are you about to go to sleep, Rucker?" she asked softly.

He said, "Naw, I'm jest lookin' at the inside a-my eyelids."

"What?"

"I got my eyes shet and I'm a-lookin'. Which ain't the same as jest havin' yore eyes closed. Did you know you can shet yore eyes and see in the dark? At night it's like lookin' at a moldy old prune—jest all kinds a-gray dots and lines and curlicues amidst the blackness." Turning his face towards the window, which was a block of bright sunshine, he exclaimed, "But gosh a'mighty, Love honey, it's so much more to look at now! Hit's like watchin' a dang sunset. Mostly red and orange, but they's streaks a-brown, too, and a big purple blob thet moves, and here come some little green dots!"

"What on earth are you talking about?" Miss Love thought

Grandpa was joking. I did, too. I near bout laughed out loud.

His eyes still closed, he grinned. "Shet yore eyes and look. You'll see."

Miss Love did what she was told, turning her head towards the window as her black lashes brushed her freckled cheeks.

I shut my eyes, too. In order to see the sunshine, I held my face up close to the crack in the door.

"I see what you mean!" she exclaimed. "Why, it's beautiful, Rucker! I never noticed before! Goodness, it would make a lovely design for dress goods. But . . . what's the point?"

"Ain't no point. Jest something to do when you cain't sleep. Leastways thet's how I got onto it last night. When I went to lookin', and marvelin' how much I could see in the dark, I quit thinkin' words and then I started to git sleepy. The surprise was when God come into the pitcher. I don't mean I saw God. I . . . well, I felt him, like He was inside a-me, or at least closer than my nose, stead a-bein' way off up in the clouds somewhere thet I cain't reach to." His voice softened. "Hit feels like thet now, Love. Hit must be what the Bible means by 'Peace, be still,' or 'Be still and know thet I am God.'"

For a while neither one said anything. Then Miss Love asked, "Are you praying now, Rucker?"

"No'm. Like I say, I'm jest a-starin' at my eyelids. If'n I went to prayin', I'd be sayin' words, thinkin' bout myself and what I want and what I'm scairt of. This way I ain't thinkin' nothin'. I'm jest feelin' God's presence. Hit makes me feel safe—like I can do anythang I got to, includin' stand all this dang pain. I reckon it sounds like foolish-ment. You prob'ly think I'm off in the head, Love, like them folks that has visions."

"No," she said softly, "because I feel it, too."

"Don't it seem like yore brain ain't cluttered up? Like if'n the Lord wanted to tell you something, you'd know what it was?"

"Yes, it feels like that," she murmured.

A covey of goosebumps thrilled up the backs of my arms, be-cause it felt like that to me, too.

"Well, let's say a-men now. I'm th'ew lookin' at my eyelids. I rather look at you a while."

Opening my own eyes, I saw Miss Love smile, and him smile back, so tender. They lay there a few minutes, neither one speaking. Then, rubbing his whiskers, he said, "Is this Sunday?"

She nodded.

"Then I ain't shaved in ne'ly three days. Hit's got so I cain't stand whiskers, Love." He grinned at her. "See what you done? I used to didn't care." Another silence, and he said, "You miss goin' to the Methodist church, don't you?"

She hesitated. "Sometimes. Well, every Sunday. It's the way I was brought up."

"You miss thet collection plate goin' around, and Miss Effie Belle plowin' up and down the pi-ana? And all them dull an-nounce-ments, not to mention them dull sermons?"

"I wouldn't swap one of your sermons to have all that." She laughed, then got serious. "But I like being part of a congrega-tion. I miss the people, Rucker."

"All them dang hypocrites?"

"My mother always said never expect church members to be perfect. Christians are still people."

"Well, she spoke the truth there."

"Most of us Christians need to go to church, Rucker. By ourselves, we feel uneasy about God, and we're too bashful to pray except when we're sick or scared. We read our Bibles, but we never think things out the way you do. But you—it's a won-der God didn't call you to preach, Rucker."

"Ain't I been preachin' to you?"

"I mean in a church. I mean really preach." She smiled at him so sweet.

I was getting restless. I wanted to leave. But a board creaked the first step I took, so I decided to wait a little. It being Sunday, they'd probably go on to sleep. Long as I could remember, Mama and Papa had gone to their room every Sunday after dinner and shut the door, and we knew better than to wake them up.

"I got called to preach one time," said Grandpa. "Up in the mountains when I was a-peddlin'." He laughed. "But it warn't the Lord thet called me. I done the callin'. Called myself Brother Blakeslee, itinerant Baptist preacher and peddler of fine merchandise."

"Oh, you didn't!" Grinning, she raised up on her elbow to look at him. "Why in the—"

"I'd jest come out of the War. I'd had my fill a-sleepin' in the woods and cookin' over a dang campfire. I reasoned thet them mountain folks would feed a preacher and put him up, and then buy his blankets and needles to hep with the Lord's work. Well'm, it shore did backfire! I got me a invite to preach, but I warn't into my sermon hardly when a mean-eyed man on the front row stood up and cussed me out. Said I must be the Devil Incarnate, or at least his agent, cause I shore warn't no True Believer. A-mens rose up all over thet little room."

"Goodness! What did you do?"

"Thought fast, I tell you. 'Wait a minute, folks!' I shouted. 'All what I jest said, thet was s'posed to be the Devil a-talkin'. Now if y'all will shet up, I'll tell you what God said back to thet old fork-tail varmint.' I warn't go'n let a bunch a-dang hill people run me off. I went at it, makin' up stories bout sinners thet God had punished, and spoutin' hellfire and damnation and all the other preacher stuff I could think of." He grinned. "Didn't make a dang bit a-sense, but they liked it. Wanted me back next Sunday. But I'd learnt my lesson, Love. I vowed it was the last time I'd try to tell bout my Jesus and my God to folks with rock minds."

He blew at a curl near her ear. She shivered, giggled. "Quit. That tickles."

"You rather me preach? I wisht I felt up to havin' our Sunday time in the parlor. I got a good sermon worked out for you."

"Well, I could go play some hymns."

Oh my gosh, where could I hide right quick?

"Not now, Love," said Grandpa. "I rather have you layin' here by me. You hep me forgit the pain, and I don't feel so sick."

Another silence. "What's it about?" She sounded lazy, sleepy. "The sermon, I mean."

"Something Will Tweedy's been questionin'. He don't unnerstand why Jesus said, 'Ast, and it shall be given.' He says why would Jesus say sech a thang when it ain't always so?"

"That's easy to explain, Rucker. Tell Will that sometimes God has to say no for our own good, or to teach us something, or show His power. Sometimes it's just not His will to give us a certain thing. Or He wants to test our faith and see if we trust Him no matter what."

Grandpa laughed. "Love, you sound like ever preacher I ever heard. But Jesus didn't say God might say no when we say gimme. He said God's go'n say yes. Anythang we ast for, we go'n git it. Well, hungry folks pray for food, but they shore don't all git fed. And sick folks beg Him for healin', but lots of'm die, or maybe live on in bed. Jesus had to mean something diff'rent from what folks think He meant, else to my mind He was a dang fool to go round promisin' what God wouldn't do. But Jesus warn't no fool, Love. So what did He mean?"

Distressed, she sat up and said to Grandpa, "Please, Rucker. Don't talk sacrilege."

"Hit ain't sacrilege. Miss Effie Belle says when she cain't think what to have for dinner, she asts God and right off He gives her a idea. To my thinkin', thet's sacrilege."

Miss Love really laughed. "There's not a woman in the world who hasn't prayed what to cook for dinner, Rucker!"

"Well, God give y'all cookbooks for thet. Anyhow, when I got to ponderin' on it last night, the word *ast* commenced to jump at me like sheep comin' over a fence. *Ast. Ast. Ast.* But ast for what? For meat and bread? For healin' miracles? Are we s'posed to ast 'Lord, give me the answers on the arithmetic test,' 'Lord git me hired over the next feller,' 'Lord, give me a son'? Gosh a'mighty, how I used to ast thet'n, Love!" He looked long and tender at her, and kissed her cheek.

"And didn't God send you Will Tweedy?"

Gosh, I hadn't thought of that!

"Maybe He did," said Grandpa. "Then agin maybe He sent me you so I could have another crack at it." I could see Miss Love blush, and, out in the hall, I blushed. Grandpa didn't. "But I don't think He planned Will Tweedy for me. I don't even think He sent me you. You and Will jest happened in the way of thangs. God ain't said you won't git nothin' good less'n you pray for it. But I'm shore thankful for you, Love." He touched a finger to her chin and her mouth, then rested his hand on her cheek.

His voice softened as he went on. "Another thang to think on: some folks ain't said pea-turkey to God in years. They don't ast Him for nothin', don't specially try to be good, and don't love nobody the way Jesus said to—cept their own self. But they go'n git jest bout as much or as little in the way a-earthly goods as the rest of us. They go'n have sorrows and joys, failures and good times. And when they come down sick they go'n git well or die, one, jest same as the prayin' folks. So don't thet tell you something bout prayin'? Ain't the best prayin' jest bein' with God and talkin' a while, like He's a good friend, stead a-like he runs a store and you've come in a-hopin' to git a bargain?"

Miss Love frowned. "Rucker, you can't write Holy Scripture. It's already been written."

"Well, I shore can question what it means." With a heavy

groan, trying to shift a little to get comfortable, he put his arm across her stomach again. "And hit fine'ly come to me in the night, what Jesus must a-meant by *ast*. You want to be like them folks with rock brains, or you want to hear it?"

She smiled. "I want to hear it."

I put in my journal all the above. Also the answer that had come to Grandpa.

"When Jesus said ast and ye shall receive, I don't think He meant us to pray 'Lord, spare my child,' or 'Make it rain for the crops,' or 'Don't let my bizness fail.' I don't even think Jesus meant us to ast for—"

"—for a house or a piano?" She put her hand on his open palm. He laughed, and lifted her hand and kissed it.

"Naw, and not even for a husband or any other sech favor. The Lord's Prayer does say, 'Give us this day our daily bread,' but thet's the only dang thang Jesus ast for in the whole prayer thet you can *tetch*. They ain't nothin' in the Lord's Prayer says 'Make me well.' I'm tempted to pray thet right now, hurtin' like I am. But I don't think Jesus meant us to think we can git healed jest by beggin' for it." Grandpa laughed kind of rueful. "God made us so we want to stay alive. He put healin' power in our bodies. We don't have to beg Him to save us. All we got to do is accept bein' sick, do what Doc says, and trust thet God wants us to git well if'n we can."

Miss Love broke in. "In the Bible, Jesus only healed the people who asked Him to—and believed He could. If Jesus could heal, can't God? If we pray and have faith?"

"Well'm, faith ain't no magic wand or money-back gar'ntee, either one. Hit's jest a way a-livin'. Hit means you don't worry th'ew the days. Hit means you go'n be holdin' on to God in good or bad times, and you accept whatever happens. Hit means you respect life like it is—like God made it—even when it ain't what you'd order from the wholesale house. Faith don't mean the Lord is go'n make lions lay down with lambs jest cause you ast him to, or make fire not burn. Some folks, when they pray to git well and don't even git better, they say God let'm down. But I say thet warn't even what Jesus was a-talkin' bout. When Jesus said ast and you'll git it, He was givin' a gar'ntee a-spiritual healin', not body healin'. He was sayin' thet if'n you git beat down—scairt to death you cain't do what you got to, or scairt you go'n die, or scairt folks won't like you—why, all you got to do is put yore hand in God's and He'll lift you up. I know it for a fact, Love. I can pray, 'Lord, hep me not be scairt,' and I don't know how, but it's like a eraser wipes the fears away. And I found out long time ago, when I look on what I got to stand as a dang hardship or a burden, it seems too heavy to carry. But when I look on the same dang thang as a challenge, why, standin' it or acceptin' it is like you done entered a contest. Hit even gits excitin', waitin' to see how everthang's go'n turn out."

Grandpa stopped to move a little and his face twisted with pain. But he went on. "Jesus meant us to ast God to hep us stand the pain, not beg Him to take the pain away. We can ast for comfort and hope and patience and courage, and to be gracious when thangs ain't goin' our way, and we'll git what we ast for. They ain't no gar'ntee thet we ain't go'n have no troubles and ain't go'n die. But shore as frogs croak and cows bellow, God'll forgive us if'n we ast Him to."

"He will also help us be forgiving," said Miss Love, smiling. "Rucker, why don't you try to forgive Clem Crummy? You really ought to take your name off his hotel. You got even with him. Isn't that enough?"

Grandpa laughed. "Not quite. I want to rub his face in the dirt a while fore I let him up, Love. Somebody's got to learn him better than to cheat folks, else he's liable to land in jail. Besides, me and God ain't got time for Clem right now. We too busy tryin' to make a challenge out a-them broke ribs and this here twisted knee. And I'm busy tryin' to accept the loss a-my dignity."

Out there in the cool hall, afraid even to wiggle my foot lest they hear me, I wondered if I could ever accept Lightfoot McLendon marrying Hosie Roach.

"Well, Miz Blakeslee," Grandpa said, running his hand down the side of her waist and hip and thigh, "do you think thet's what Jesus might a-meant? Don't it make sense?"

She thought a minute. "If you talked like this at a Wednesday night prayer meeting, Rucker, most people would walk out. They'd say you're not a Christian and shouldn't be allowed to speak in God's house. But to me it makes beautiful sense. Thank you for it."

"Remind me to tell Will Tweedy, hear."

I slid down to the floor. Just by peeping around the door frame, I could still see them if I wanted to. But what I wanted to do was ponder what all Grandpa had just said.

Then Miss Love changed the subject and I had to listen instead of think. "Rucker, do you know they've made up a committee to find a new name for Cold Sassy?"

"I heard. But they'll change Cold Sassy over my dead body."

"What if they named it Blakeslee? Wouldn't you like that? Our name being on the map might help us sell cars."

He laughed. "Blakeslee is too much like Blakely. Thet's a town in south Georgia. Anyhow, the Blakeslees warn't nothin' special to the town."

"You're special to the town."

"Yeah, but not like Miss Mattie Lou. Now she was descended from two pioneer fam'lies, the Toys and the Willises both. But Toy would be a silly name for a town, and Willis ain't much better." Grandpa paused. "Will Tweedy's name ain't William, you know. Hit's Willis."

Trying again to get comfortable, Grandpa moved his arm up from Miss Love's stomach and by gosh let his hand rest right between her bosoms! And like she didn't even notice where his hand was, she moved her head over on his shoulder. Her breath quickened as his fingers traced the curve of her neck and wandered careless toward the soft flesh below.

"God hep me, Love," he said softly, "I ain't so bad hurt I don't feel nothin'!"

She didn't say a word. The smile left her face and her lips parted.

If you thought about it, me spying on them through the slit of space between the open door and the door frame was right humorous. But what was funny as heck was Grandpa with that bruised, swelled-up nose, the big knot like a horn on his forehead, the black eyes like a dern raccoon's mask, the scab over one eye like a sword slash on a pirate, the itchy three-day sprouting of gray whiskers—and Miss Love gazing at him like he was Prince Charming come to the costume ball dressed up as a toady frog.

"What do you think about Enterprise?" she asked sleepily. "Or Progressive City? What about Sheffield? Those were suggested in last week's paper."

"Any one a-them names on a postmark would bore me to death, jest like Commerce does. They say a Englishman come th'ew Harmony Grove in nineteen aught-one, sellin' silverware. The next year he come th'ew agin and like to had a fit when he seen 'Welcome to Commerce' where it used to say 'Welcome to Harmony Grove.' He'd sent in Harmony Grove to name a new park over in England and it won him a five-hundret-dollar prize, but over on this side a-the ocean, folks thought it sounded tacky and countrified."

"Cold Sassy wouldn't win a prize anywhere," Miss Love said. "Admit that."

"Naw, it wouldn't. But it suits the town."

"You suit me, Rucker." Her eyes all shiny, she looked at him and murmured, "The last few months with you . . ." Her lips trembled. "Dear Rucker, I think you know, but I want to say it. This has been the only really happy time of my whole life."

Grandpa smiled and touched her hair. "I cain't say it's the onliest happy time for me, ma'am. But they shore ain't never been any to equal it!"

She giggled. "Now quit sayin' *ma'am* to me. That's what people call old ladies, or their betters."

"You're my better."

"No, I ain't, I'm just your—" A look of surprise crossed her face and she burst out laughing. "Good Lord, Rucker, I just said *ain't!* Before you know it I'll be saying *hit ain't!*"

He tried not to laugh, to save his ribs. "Well, come 'ere, honey. Learn me how to talk right." Wincing, Grandpa pulled her close and kissed her, hard. Then, keeping his mouth on hers, he loosed the pins from her hair. Just as it fell around her neck in a wavy brown mass, he jerked away. "Yore dang nose!" he yelped. "Hit hit my nose!" Quick tears filled his eyes. Then he whispered, "Didn't hurt a-tall," and kissed her again—but a lot more careful.

Long minutes later, I heard her whisper, "If I held you tight as I want to, Rucker, your nose and your ribs and your knee couldn't stand the pain."

"Then don't do it," he whispered back, kissing each freckled cheek. "I can tell you, pain don't do nothin' for ro-mance!"

"Remember that when you rub stiff whiskers on my face and I say *ouch* instead of *oh darling.*"

He rubbed his chin against her cheek. "Well'm, they ain't stiff now."

"Don't say *well'm.*"

"All right'm." He laughed, and kissed her again.

"Oh, dear, dear man. I love you. I love you."

They quit talking then, and drifted off to sleep, and I tiptoed out.

I was ashamed of myself, and embarrassed. But by golly, I

had my missing last chapter. If Grandpa and Miss Love weren't already living happy ever after, they would be soon as he got well.

But the last chapter wasn't finished.

By middle of the week, Grandpa was coughing and running a little fever. By Friday it hurt him to breathe and it like to killed him when he coughed. Mama went down and stayed all day. Doc came by every chance he could.

Saturday morning, just as we sat down to breakfast, here came little Timmy Hopkins, saying Miz Blakeslee wanted Mr. Hoyt to ring up Dr. Slaughter. Said tell him Mr. Blakeslee was having a bad chill and he'd coughed up some dark, rusty sputum.

49

I WENT in the Cadillac to fetch Doc, who began fussing at Grandpa before he got in the room hardly. "I don't care if it does hurt to breathe, Rucker, you got to git some air down there." He put his hand on Grandpa's forehead. "Hot as a firecracker!"

Despite all the blankets on him, Grandpa was shaking like a dog pulled out of a frozen pond. As Dr. Slaughter bent over him with the stethoscope, he asked, "Wh-wh-what you th-think I g-got, D-Doc?"

"Shet up, Rucker. I cain't hear with you a-talkin'."

Doc listened all over his chest and his back, too. "Where does it hurt when you cough?"

"B-b-between my sh-shoulder blades. You r-reckon it's a t-tetch a-pleurisy?"

Doc straightened up. "Naw, it's a tetch of pneumonia, Rucker. More'n a tetch, tell you the truth. I can hear the rales. But you're strong as a ox, you know. You go'n pull th'ew all right."

Out in the hall, though, Dr. Slaughter told us he was worried. "Rucker's tough, but losin' all thet blood ain't go'n hep, and he shore could do without them broke ribs. He could do without the pneumonia, for thet matter." He sighed.

"I don't understand," said Miss Love, dazed. "I thought I was doing all I should for him. But he got worse so fast."

"Hit ain't your fault, honey. Thet's the way pneumonia is. Hit comes on with a bang, then it has to run its course, and we won't know which way it'll go till the crisis comes." Doc put on his hat. "Now listen to me, Miss Love," he said. "Rucker's fever is aw-ready a hundret and five. Hit could go lots higher. For shore, he's go'n git lots worse fore he gits better. So you let Mary Willis and Loma come up here and hep with the nursin'. You hear me?"

"I couldn't ask them to do that."

"You ain't got to ast'm. You jest got to let'm. Soon as he gits over the chill, y'all go'n be spongin' him off night and day. We got to keep his fever down, else it might cook his brains. You understand, Miss Love? And keep the windows open. He needs fresh air. Don't let the whole dang fam'ly set in there around the bed, usin' up the oxygen."

My mother and Aunt Loma arrived right after he left, just as Doc knew they would. After school I went to the store as usual, but Papa told me to go on to Grandpa's and stay there. "Get the chores done," he said, "and be there in case they need to send for hep. Too bad Miss Love ain't got a telephone."

It was awful, listening to Grandpa cough and hack and moan. I was glad to go get busy outside. In my mind I can still picture Granny's rose garden that day, the bushes decorated with buds and blossoms. But at the time I just glanced at the garden and went on to the barn to see after the animals.

While I was pitching hay, Miss Love came out and stood by the pasture gate. I climbed down from the loft to see if she needed anything, but she just shook her head, watching as Mr. Beautiful galloped up and put his head over the railing to be petted. She rubbed his ears and stroked his neck, but her mind wasn't on him.

"If your grandfather dies," she said bitterly, "I won't stay in

Cold Sassy any longer than it takes to sell the house. I hate this town. It's like life. It gives, and then it takes away."

I couldn't bear the thought of Cold Sassy without Grandpa or her, either one. As we started back to the house, I begged her, "Ma'am, don't give up on him. Like Doc said, he's strong. He's go'n get well. Hear?"

That night we were all there for supper, even Mary Toy and Campbell Junior. Miss Love sponged Grandpa off while the rest of us ate.

Mama was just leaving the table to take her turn with him when we heard Grandpa say, real loud, "Miss Love, you better git on back to the store now. . . ." He paused for breath. "We're much obliged, but Miss Mattie Lou don't need no more hep."

Forks clattered onto plates as Papa and Aunt Loma and I jumped up and dashed to the sickroom, leaving Mary Toy and poor little Campbell Junior sitting there, confused and scared. We got to the bedroom door in time to hear Grandpa say, "Best go on now, Miss Love. They short-handed at the store."

"But I live here, Rucker! Remember? I'm your—"

"Miss Mattie Lou?" Looking toward the door, not seeing us at all, he said brightly, "You want to serve Miss Love some cake? She's got to get back to the store terreckly."

Grandpa had a bad spell of coughing then. Soon as he could speak, he said, "Did you ever git Miss Pauline's hat finished, Miss Love? She come in yesterd'y, astin' bout it."

"Call me Love, Rucker," she begged, kneeling down by the bed so she could look right in his face. "Please, call me Love!"

Trying hard not to cough again—it hurt so bad—and looking right at her, he asked Miss Mattie Lou for some water.

At that, Miss Love rose to her feet, tears streaming down her cheeks. My mother reached out like to a hurt child, and Miss Love stumbled into her arms.

I couldn't stand it. I fled to the back porch, knelt down by the tall slab table, and begged God to let Grandpa get well.

· · ·

Mama and I stayed all night, her taking turns with Miss Love at the sickbed. The fever raged despite all the sponging, and Grandpa couldn't sleep for coughing and talking. Sometimes he just mumbled gibberish. Other times it was real sentences, but they didn't make sense. Then again he'd speak clear as anything, telling jokes or carrying on a conversation with some person we couldn't see.

For a while Grandpa was back in the War with his daddy. There would be a handful of words; then he'd get quiet and Miss Love would say he's gone to sleep, thank God, But soon he'd take up where he left off. I remember him mumbling something about a battlefield. "Hit was awful, Pa. . . . All them dead Yankees layin' there. I tried to find you . . . some boots, but they jest warn't none left. . . . Our boys had done hepped theirselves."

He talked about seeing a Yankee balloon. "Pa, you reckon they spotted our battle-ments? If'n they did, Lord hep us!" And Grandpa sat bolt upright in the bed. I helped Miss Love ease him back down on his side. "Who're you, ma'am?" he asked as his eyes focused.

Remembering that Grandpa had been a boy like me in the War, she said, "I'm your nurse, son. They—uh, they brought you to the hospital."

"Where's my daddy at?"

"Uh, on the next cot. But let's don't wake him up. He's worn out."

"We ain't go'n march t'morrer?" He pulled nervous at his whiskers.

"No. Don't talk anymore now. Try to rest."

I brought in another pan of water. Miss Love wrung out the towel again and slowly, so weary, she wiped his back and his neck, his face and arms and then his legs. After while he seemed to sleep, but in no time was coughing again and talking.

He wasn't in the War now. He was with Miss Mattie Lou —coughing and mumbling disconnected sentences picked out of the air from this or that time in their life. He was a Graphophone record kept on a shelf for thirty years and getting played again now. His eyes were unnatural bright, his breathing short and fast and difficult, and what he coughed up was tinged with bright red blood.

About ten o'clock, Mama talked Miss Love into lying down a while, "even if you cain't sleep."

As Mama bent over the wash basin on the floor to wring out a towel, Grandpa fixed his eyes on her. But it was Granny that he saw. "Miss Mattie Lou . . . they's something I got to confess, hon. . . . You deserve . . . to know what kind a-man . . . you done pledged yoreself to marry."

Oh, law, was Mama fixing to hear how he'd loved Miss Love from the minute he laid eyes on her?

"I been shamed to tell you . . . but I ne'ly . . . got run out a-them hills . . . last month." Then he told her bout callin' hisself to preach. With her and him fixin' to git married, it was go'n be his last peddlin' walk th'ew the mountains and he was jest sick and tarred a-sleepin' on the ground. Figgered the church folks would put a preacher up and feed him, too. "I acted a lie, Miss Mattie Lou . . . and it shore did . . . backfire. Fore I was hardly . . . into my sermon. . . ."

His voice trailed off.

"Hush now, Pa," said my mother, wiping his chest as best she could around the binding, which wasn't easy, with him lying on his left side to favor the broke ribs.

I sure wished Granny was here. She could always think of something to do for a sick person. But that night Mama was like Granny. "Pa, try to take some water," she'd say, lifting his head and holding a glass to his cracked, parched lips. Then she'd rub his mouth with Mentholatum, or maybe lay a wet washrag over his eyes.

"Sit down and rest, Mama," I finally told her. "I'll wash him."

Staring right at me, pulling at his whiskers kind of frantic, Grandpa said, "Miss Mattie Lou?"

"I'm Will, sir. I'm your boy. . . ."

Granny's clock had just chimed midnight when Miss Love came back in, her eyes dark-circled, her green print dress wrinkled. "I'm afraid I dozed off, Mary Willis," she whispered. "Is he better? Has he slept any?"

My mother shook her head. "No, he cain't rest for talkin'. I cain't understand why Dr. Slaughter don't come. He said he'd come."

"He said he'd come if he could. Miss Herma is having her baby. I guess he couldn't leave her. I'll take over now, Mary Willis. You try to get some sleep. Use the bed in the front room." Miss Love had become businesslike and mechanical. "Will, you go lie down on the daybed in the hall."

"I ain't tired, Miss Love. I'll stay."

Grandpa drifted into a fitful sleep, then waked with a start about two-thirty and between gasps for breath went to raging at something or somebody, all the time pulling at his whiskers.

"We've got to get him quiet," said Miss Love. "Will, can you manage by yourself?" I nodded and reached for the wet towel. She tiptoed out, and in a minute there came to my ears—and to Grandpa's, I could tell—the sound of piano music. Miss Love played hymn after hymn. "Faith of Our Fathers," "A Mighty Fortress Is Our God," "Rock of Ages," "Abide With Me." All his favorites, chording slower and slower, quieter and quieter. And Grandpa calmed down.

At daybreak the fever was still high. He was back with Granny when Dr. Slaughter arrived.

Mama had gone on home. Aunt Loma arrived to fix our breakfast and then took over the sponging so we could eat, but we all carried our plates to the sickroom. Miss Love let her eggs turn cold while she hovered over Grandpa.

Finally he spoke to her. Spoke her name. "Miss Love?" he whispered. Oh, she was so excited. "Miss Love, make . . . Miss Mattie Lou . . . rest some, hear. . . . She's been up . . . all night, seein' . . . after me."

Miss Love looked like she'd been slapped. "I feel sick, Loma," she said, and left the room crying.

When she didn't come back and didn't come back, I said, "Aunt Loma, you think I ought to go see about her?"

"Maybe you better."

I figured she was out at the barn, and she was. The black gelding had trotted up to her, but she paid him no mind. She heard me coming and turned quick toward me. "Will! He's not—"

"No'm."

"Dr. Slaughter thinks he won't make it. He said so this morning. Will, he just can't die! Oh . . . I've got to tell him something. Something I can't say with Miss Mattie Lou always in there!"

She burst out crying, then all of a sudden threw her head back and went to laughing! Laughed like a crazy woman. Like she couldn't stop. Finally I got mad and shook her. "Stop, Miss Love! Ain't nothin' funny!"

"Oh, you just don't know!" Out there in the May morning she could hardly talk for laughing. "I'll tell you, Will, so you can laugh, too. You see this second wife?" She pointed to herself. "She thought she was going to have a baby, but she wasn't sure. After she was sure, she decided to wait till her husband's birthday to tell him. But"—Miss Love stopped laughing, her voice went flat—"but now he's dying, and I can't tell him because . . . dear God in heaven, Will, how can I tell your grandpa right in front of your granny that he has fathered my child! He'd hate me! He wouldn't believe it was possible. Will, he has forgotten all about me and him!"

Gosh, a baby! It was going to end up just like Mama and Aunt Loma said it would.

"I can't bear it if . . . if he dies without knowing. And knowing might even make him fight to live!"

"He's already fightin' to live, Miss Love. He'll fight to his last breath."

"But if he knew this, it might make all the difference!" And she burst into tears.

I didn't know what to do. Finally I said, "Miss Love, hush up. Hear?" I sounded just like Grandpa. "Ma'am, he always says when you don't know which way to turn, do something. Don't do nothin'. Listen, ain't it the fever causin' him to be funny-turned? I mean the delirium; ain't that from the high fever?"

She nodded, holding both hands to her cheeks. "We m-manage to cool him down some, but it's n-never enough."

"What if we could cool him down quicker? If he came to himself even for a minute, you could talk to him! Why don't we put him in the bathtub? It'd soak him cool a lot quicker than all that spongin'. Wouldn't it?"

"I never heard of doing that!" She was excited, then worried. "But it might chill him too much. We'd have to ask Dr. Slaughter first."

"But don't it make sense?"

"Let me think, Will." Out there by the pasture gate, she quickly took the pins out of her tousled hair, pulled it back, twisted it into a knot at the back of her head, and pinned it tight. Even with her hair so plain and her eyelids swollen from crying, Miss Love looked beautiful to me, for she had come alive!

"I could run get Loomis," I went on, excited. "Loomis could pick Grandpa up like a rag doll, Miss Love. Not jostle his ribs or anything. Just bend over easy and lay him in the water."

Hope upon us, we ran back to the house. It scared me to death when Aunt Loma rushed to meet us at the back door. "He's had a big sweat!" she shouted. "Drenched the bed! The fever's down, Love! At least for now, and he's gone to sleep! He knew me, Love!"

"Oh, thank God!" Miss Love's eyes filled with tears. "But—oh, Will, what if I've missed my chance!"

Loma said she'd go on home and tell Sister and Brother Hoyt the good news. "You stay here, Will, just in case. Love, try to get some rest."

I thought Miss Love would want to sit there alone with him, but she asked me to stay. Grandpa was laying on his left side, as usual. She sat beside the bed, facing him, in the same rocking chair he had sat in to watch Granny.

Sometimes she would lay her head on the mattress and stretch out her hand just to touch him. I know she prayed; I could see her lips move. Every few minutes she'd feel of his forehead or his arm. At some point she murmured, "I'm dying to wake him up, but I don't dare. This sleep could make all the difference. . . . Will, honey, won't he be thrilled if it's a boy? I just know it will be a boy."

I didn't tell her, but Mama used to say Granny was always sure it would be a boy.

She got up to pace the room. "Will, what if the fever goes way up again before he wakes?"

At that moment Grandpa went to coughing. His eyes opened wide as he gasped for breath. Miss Love looked at the sputum he spat into a rag. "It's so bloody, Will," she whispered.

When the coughing subsided, Grandpa started to drift away again, but she called him back. "Rucker, look at me!"

He opened his eyes. "You . . . so beautiful," he mumbled.

"How do you feel, dear?" She spoke softly.

"Well, I'm . . . takin' it leisurely. . . ." He pulled at his whiskers.

She leaned over the bed to get her face close to his. "I've got something wonderful to tell you, Rucker. Can you hear me, dear?"

Gazing at her, his face softened. He put his hand on her hair, and something like a weak grin passed over his face. "I'm

Rucker. . . . Pleased to . . . meet you, Love. . . . Oh, Love, I'm so sick. I jest cain't . . . git . . . enough . . . air. . . ."

"You're going to get well, Rucker. I'll make you get well! Don't go back to sleep yet. Please. I've got to tell you what I have for your birthday. The most wonderful thing has happened, Rucker. . . ."

It's to my credit that I left the room. I didn't stand out there in the hall and listen, either. I went to the kitchen and drank some milk, then mixed some meal and water for Granny's chickens and went out to dump it in their pan. They ran up to me, clucking and shoving, and then here came old T.R. Sensing my joy, he jumped up on me and licked my face, and I hugged him good, pulling his ears and scratching his belly.

Church bells were beginning to ring all over town. I wondered would Papa attend preachin', now that Loma would of told them that Grandpa was better.

I thought I ought to go back in and see if he was still awake. I couldn't wait to hear what he'd say about the baby. I went in the house, tiptoed up the hall.

It looked like he was sleeping again, and Miss Love, too. She had stretched out on the bed beside him, her hand on his. The house was quiet and peaceful at last, and I was wore out.

I thought I'd just go lay down on the daybed a few minutes. . . .

I don't know how long I slept. Miss Love's scream woke me up. Grandpa was dead.

50

I RAN in there. Miss Love, still on the bed, was raised up on one arm, staring at him. I waited for her to say something, but she just kept staring.

I heard somebody come in the front hall. "Miss Love? Mary Willis?" It was Miss Effie Belle.

"Oh, God help me!" whispered Miss Love. "Keep her talking out there, Will. I've got to . . . oh, God, just a minute more."

Miss Effie Belle had heard the scream as she was coming in from church. Her pink lip wart quivering, she said, "Rucker's passed on, ain't he, Will?"

"Yes'm."

"Well, God knows best." Her eyes misting, she touched my face with her wizened hand. "You go'n take it hardest, Will. You was his favorite in all the world."

I thought I ought to say that Miss Love was his favorite now, but what was the use?

"One time when your granddaddy was a baby, I helt him in my lap. Who'd a-thought I'd outlive him!" she said, trying hard to keep aholt of herself. "And we been next-door neighbors for I don't know how long. Lord, why couldn't it of been Bubba? I'm so tired, and Bubba just cain't seem to die." She sighed and patted my shoulder. "I'd like to go in and see him, Will."

At that moment we heard the bedroom door close, and Miss Love came up the hall. She looked like stone. Her eyes were dark-circled and her skin pale. There was no expression at all on her face as she said, "Will, you'd better hurry home and tell your family. They'll have to call Dr. Slaughter."

"Yes'm. I was just fixin' to go. Here's Miss Effie Belle to see you."

The wizened hand reached out to pat Miss Love's arm. "I'll be more'n glad to stay with you till Mary Willis and them git here."

"You're very kind. But I . . . I'd like to be alone right now. I hope you understand?"

Granny's clock chimed half-past noon as I followed Miss Effie Belle out of Grandpa's house and ran home.

Papa had attended morning preachin', but he was already back home when I rushed in.

Dead must of been written all over my face, because I didn't have to say a word except how and when.

"Run clean up and put on your suit, Will," said Papa. "Folks go'n be comin' in all day. Out of respect for your granddaddy you ought to look presentable. But make haste."

As the family hurried out to the car, Papa said we had to go by the store.

"Are you crazy, Hoyt?" asked Mama. She had cried all the time she was getting dressed, and looked it.

"There's a sealed letter in the safe," he said, taking the driver's seat. "Your daddy told me about it a month or more ago. Said if anything happened to him, I was to get the letter out and read it to the fam'ly." He motioned me to turn the crank. The engine sputtered but didn't catch.

"Cain't it wait, Brother Hoyt?" Loma screeched. "I want to see Pa!"

"No, it cain't wait. If you want to know exactly how your daddy put it, he said, 'Git thet letter fore my body's cold, and don't let nobody move me till it's read.'"

Miss Love came out of the room where Grandpa was and walked slowly up the hall to greet us. She hadn't fixed herself up or anything while I was gone. Smelling a little of turpentine, she was still in the soiled green print dress she'd worn all yesterday and all last night and all this morning. She hugged everybody, the way folks do when they don't know what to say, but she did it as if there was nothing to be said.

Mama whispered, "Can we see him?"

"Certainly. Of course," said Miss Love. Leading the way, she said Dr. Slaughter had already come and gone. "He said to convey his condolences, and tell you he was sorry not to stay. Miss Herma is having a bad labor."

I couldn't believe the change in Grandpa! He was turned on his back, his head on a single pillow, his right arm outside the fresh clean sheet that had been spread over him and the bed. His face was shaved, the mustache trimmed to a neat pencil line again, the hair combed and slicked down. Miss Love must of used some of her freckle-cover cream to fade the bruises and lighten the blackness around his eyes.

"Don't he look nat'ral," Mama whispered.

My throat swelled till I could hardly get my breath. To me he looked spiffy, and I just wanted so bad to tell him.

I saw that Papa, holding Campbell Junior, was having just as hard a time as I was. Whereas I was grieving for my grandpa who had died, Papa was mourning for the man who had given him his chance in life. I don't know why, but right then it finally dawned on me that Papa had wanted to please Grandpa out of respect and gratitude, not from kowtowing. I watched as he tried not to cry. All of a sudden, still carrying the baby, he left the room.

Aunt Loma, Mary Toy, and Mama stood around the bed, crying. Miss Love stood there dry-eyed, looking down on the father of her unborn child.

I found Papa in the parlor. He had lifted Campbell Junior up to the window so he could watch a hen leading her baby chicks towards the front yard. "See the biddies?" asked Papa, and little Camp jumped with delight.

"What do we do now, sir?" I asked. "Call Mr. Birdsong?"

"Not yet, son." He sighed deep. "I have to read that letter first. I reckon we better go back in there and start."

For the reading, Miss Love sat down in the rocking chair, pulled as close to Grandpa as she could get it. Papa had handed over the baby to Aunt Loma. She stood jiggling him in her arms to keep him quiet. Mama was holding Mary Toy's hand, but my little sister begged, "Will, stay by me," and I put my arm around her, held her close. Papa walked around to Granny's side of the bed and tore open the envelope.

"Mr. Blakeslee didn't tell me what's in this," he began. "He just said if anything happened to him I was to get the letter out of the safe and read it to y'all right away." He looked over at the widow. "Are you all right, Miss Love? You rather go in the parlor?"

"No, Mr. Hoyt. Please read it." She placed her hand on Grandpa's shoulder.

The letter was in his big sprawling hand on a long ruled sheet torn out of the store's ledger book. I copied it later, word for word like Grandpa had it.

"To my dearly beloved wife Love Simpson Blakeslee, to my beloved daughters Mary Willis Blakeslee Tweedy and Loma Blakeslee Williams, to my beloved son-in-law Hoyt Tweedy, who is like a son to me"—Papa had to wait a minute before he could go on—"to my grandsons Hoyt Willis Tweedy and Campbell Williams Junior, and to my granddaughter Mary Toy Tweedy:

"This is about the disposal of my earthly remains.

"Please recollect the funeral I gave Miss Mattie Lou. I tried to make it a nice thank-you to her for living. Likewise I gave Camp a nice funeral. I believe God means us to stand up to suffering, not end it with a bullet. A man killing himself aint nothing I can understand. But I can forgive it. Anyhow, I wanted Camp's funeral to say 'Judge not that ye be not judged.'"

I could hear Aunt Loma snuffling.

"Now I want my burying to remind folks that death aint always awful. God invented death. Its in God's plan for it to happen. So when my time comes I dont want no trip to Birdsong's Emporium or any other. Dressing somebody up to look alive don't make it so."

My daddy paused. I could tell he was reading ahead to himself, because his face flushed all of a sudden and he had to take a deep breath before he could go on.

"I dont want no casket. Its a waste of money. What I would really like is to be wrapped in two or three feed sacks and laid right in the ground. But that would bother you all, so use the pine box upstairs at the store that Miss Mattie Lou's coffin come in. I been saving it. And tho I just as soon be planted in the vegetable patch as anywhere, I dont think anybody would ever eat what growed there, after. Anyhow, take me right from home to the cemetery.

"Aint no use paying Birdsong for that hearse. Get Loomis to use his wagon. Specially if it is hot weather, my advisement is dont waste no time."

Mama, scandalized, had both hands up to her mouth. Mary Toy had turned white as a sheet. I held her tight. Aunt Loma seemed excited, like when watching a spooky stage play. I felt excited myself. I wondered was this Grandpa's idea of a practical joke or was it a sermon. Maybe after he made his point, he'd put a postscript saying that when he was dead it really wouldn't matter to him what kind of funeral he had. But I doubted it.

Miss Love? She kept her eyes on Grandpa, lying there so unnatural quiet, so unnatural still.

Papa read on. "I want Loomis and them to dig my grave right next to Miss Mattie Lou. I dont want no other preacher there but him, but don't let him give a sermon. It would go on for hours. Just let him pray for God to comfort my family.

"I would like Will Tweedy to read some Bible verses, and I want you all to sing 'Blessed Be the Tie That Binds.' Also I want Hoyt to read some verses I am going to copy on another sheet and put in with this letter. The title is 'Be Still, My Soul.' I want Miss Love to know that the line in the poem about 'Love's purest joys restored' means I want her to try to find a way to be happy after I am gone. I expect her to outlive me by some years, and I dont want her to live drab. I want folks to say there goes Rucker Blakeslees happy, good-looking, piana-playing widder. I dont want them to say she sure has gone downhill since he passed."

All eyes turned on Miss Love, but she sat like stone.

Papa read on. "I dont want nobody at the burial except you all and them at the store that want to come. Dont put *Not Dead But Sleeping* on my stone. Write it *Dead, Not Sleeping*. Being dead under six foot of dirt wont bother me a-tall, but I hate for it to sound like I been buried alive.

"Now then, the funeral party. In case you all aint noticed, the first three letters of the word funeral spells FUN. So a week or two after I die, you all have dinner on the grounds at one of the churches, or if they aint in favor, have it at the ball park. I dont care which. I think a Wednesday at one o'clock would be fine since the stores close anyhow. I hope everybody in Cold Sassy will come, white and colored. Have a happy get-together with kinfolks and old friends. Tell funny stories about me and such.

"I would like for you all to ask the town band and the Negro band to come play parade music and also tunes like 'Ta-Ra-Ra-

Boom-de-Ay' and lively hymns like 'When They Ring Them Golden Bells.' Get everybody to sing out on *Don't you hear the bells now ringing, Don't you hear the angels singing? Tis the glory hallelujah Jubilee-ee-ee.* And so on.

"Let it be known ahead that we going to have favors. That will bring out the crowd. But dont buy nothing that cost much. Unless its in the cold wintertime, lets set up apple bobbing and dunking booths for the children. Maybe have a shooting gallery for the men. And lets have a hog-calling contest and a crowing contest, funny things that will make folks laugh. See can you get some little colored boys to do buck-and-wing dancing. Maybe we can have a backwards automobile race, and race bicycles backwards too. Oh, it's going to be a fine fancy day!

"Now you all can cry and wear black at my burying if you want to, but I dont want nobody at the funeral party to wear black or cry either one. Dont go if you cant be pleasant. If you do go, dress up and act happy. You can cry later.

"Anybody who dont foller my wishes as written here is out of my will. I do not wish my will to be read till after the funeral party.

"Well, thats all I can think of. I hope it will be a long time between this writing and when Hoyt has to read it. I want all of you to always remember what my family meant to me and how blessed I was to have two such fine wives. I think they was both dang marvels. Enoch Rucker Blakeslee."

The paper was signed, dated, sealed, and witnessed.

There was no choice but to hurry with the burying, despite folks were already bringing in food and sad faces. Loomis got his two oldest sons to go dig the grave. Then, while Cold Sassy gathered on the front veranda and in the parlor, we gathered in there around the deathbed with the door closed, watching as Loomis, weeping, lifted Grandpa and gently laid him in the coffin box. Miss Love had fixed a sort of padding out of clean feed sacks printed in bright red and white checks. It liked to killed Mama, those feed sacks, but Miss Love acted like they were the usual thing for a coffin liner.

After my daddy said a prayer, she draped two more of the checked feed sacks over his body and then, hesitating only a moment, covered his face. Loomis nailed the box shut, and he and Papa and I toted Grandpa out the back door to the wagon.

It sure would of tickled him to see all the neighbors on his front porch staring with their mouths open as Loomis drove the mule team towards the street.

Miss Love rode in the wagon with Grandpa. Besides lots of perfume, she had on the black dress she wore to church that time Cold Sassy criticized her for acting like she was in mourning for Granny. As expressionless as the time she was a store mannequin, she sat in the wagon on a sawed-off chair, bracing herself with one hand on the driver's plank and the other on the coffin box.

Behind the wagon came the two cars, me driving the Pierce, Papa the Cadillac, and all of us looking straight ahead. It's no credit to me or Aunt Loma that we were enjoying our roles in this melodrama. Mama and Papa sure didn't feel that way. They were ashamed. But if Miss Love was feeling anything like shame, she didn't show it.

What Grandpa would of really enjoyed, haw, was the sight of Mr. Birdsong reining in the black horses pulling his ambulance-hearse just as our procession turned into the street!

Cudn Hope, Uncle Lige, and Hosie were waiting for us at the cemetery gates. I could tell that Hosie had been crying.

It was awful, the burying. Such a pitiful little band of mourners, so bumbling without Mr. Birdsong or anybody else to tell us what to do.

There hadn't been time to think or feel much of anything except disbelief while we were making all the arrangements. Now that we were actually here in the cemetery, we felt shocked and helpless.

Grandpa had only considered what he wanted when he

wrote all those instructions; he didn't give a thought to what it would be like for us to gather around a gaping hole before we'd hardly realized he was dead, before we'd hardly even got started on the grieving.

And what were we supposed to do? How was the service supposed to start?

I could tell the spirit was on Loomis to help us out, but he knew white folks' funerals aren't like colored funerals. He was scared we might not like him taking over.

As Papa put one arm around Mama and the other around Mary Toy, Miss Love's composure crumbled and she went to crying. I got the wagon chair for her to sit in, and stood by her while she sobbed and wailed. What to do? Black Loomis knew what to do. He lifted his face to the sky and sang, "Swing low, sweet chariot, comin' for to carry me home. . . ."

By time the last hum of the word *home* drifted in and out among the tombstones, all of us felt calmer, and Miss Love hushed as Loomis prayed "for Missus an' all us in de fam'ly. We asts You to hol' us in Yo Bosom, Lawd. Hol' us 'n' comfort us, till we's able to git up 'n' carry on in de lan' ob de livin', bless Jesus a-men."

Then Papa pulled the letter out of his pocket. "I will now read this poem of Mr. Blakeslee's choosing. He wrote that he found it in a old book." He cleared his throat.

> *"Be still my soul: the Lord is on thy side;*
> > *Bear patiently the cross of grief or pain;*
> *Leave to thy God to order and provide;*
> > *In every change He faithful will remain.*
> *Be still, my soul; thy best, thy heav'nly Friend*
> > *Thro' thorny ways leads to a joyful end.*

> *Be still, my soul: thy God doth undertake*
> > *To guide the future as He has the past.*
> *Thy hope, thy confidence let nothing shake;*

All now mysterious shall be bright at last.
Be still my soul: the waves and winds still know
His voice who ruled them while He dwelt below."

Papa said, "Here Mr. Blakeslee wrote that he was tired of copying, but he thought the third verse was the best one of all for a funeral.

"Be still, my soul: the hour is hast'ning on
When we shall be forever with the Lord,
When disappointment, grief, and fear are gone,
Sorrow forgot, love's purest joys restored.
Be still my soul: when change and tears are past,
All safe and blessed we shall meet at last."

I hadn't really decided which Bible verses to recite. One thing boys and girls growing up in Cold Sassy know a lot of is Bible verses. Maybe I'd do the Twenty-third Psalm. They always say that at funerals. . . . But then like a light turned on, it came to me what Grandpa might like.

"'Ask, and it shall be given you,'" I began. "'Seek and ye shall find; knock, and it shall be opened unto you; For every one that asketh receiveth; and he that seeketh findeth; and to him that knocketh it shall be opened.' We have the same message in the Book of Saint John," I said, sounding for all the world like a preacher. "'If ye abide in me, and my words abide in you, ye shall ask what ye will, and it shall be done unto you. . . . Verily, verily, I say unto you, Whatsoever ye shall ask the Father in my name, He will give it you. Hitherto have ye asked nothing in my name: ask, and ye shall receive, that your joy may be full.'"

Well, but how could I just stop there? Those words were worse than nothing if I didn't tell what they meant to Grandpa. Looking at the long rough box, I spoke timid, in a mumbled voice. Not preachified at all. "Grandpa didn't think Jesus meant, by that, that we should ast God for things, or for special favors. He said we could trust that in the nature of things, without astin', we'll get lots of blessin's and happy surprises and maybe a miracle or two. When Jesus said ast and you'll get it, He meant things of the spirit, not the flesh. Right now, for instance, I could ast, 'Lord, please raise Grandpa from the dead,' but it wouldn't happen. But I can say, 'Please, God, comfort me,' and I'll get heart's ease. Grandpa said Jesus meant us to ast for hope, forgiveness, and all like that. Ast, 'Hep us not be scared, hep us not be greedy, give us courage to try.'" I was really carried away. "Ast any such and God will give it to you. But don't ast Him not to let fire burn, or say spare me from death. At least, uh, that's what Grandpa said."

Right then it dawned on me. By some of what I was saying, I had just revealed to Miss Love that I had spied on them last Sunday. She would know I heard not only Grandpa's sermon, but probably everything else that he said and she said. I couldn't look at her.

Later, when I did, she smiled a little smile at me, like saying it didn't matter now.

I couldn't go to sleep that night for wondering would it put Mama in the bed when she heard about Miss Love's baby. I knew she'd be upset, but I doubted she would talk about it to anybody except Papa, because whereas Miss Love had just been her daddy's wife, now she would be the mother of Mama's half sister or brother. That would put her in the family. And in our family, we don't talk against each other to outsiders.

Tossing and turning, I kept remembering the look on Mr. Birdsong's face as he watched our procession move off. But I also remembered our embarrassment and shame at the cemetery, and wondered how much Grandpa had really cared about all he made us do. I bet he just wanted to stir up Cold Sassy one last time. Give folks something to gossip about.

I didn't wonder why nobody in my family even questioned burying him the way he said to. If Grandpa wanted to keep his whiskey in your closet, marry three weeks after Granny died, and be buried in feed sacks in a coffin box, if you couldn't say yessir you didn't say no sir. Him saying what he did about cutting anybody out of his will who tried to interfere was entirely unnecessary.

Oh, law, we forgot to sing "Blessed Be the Tie That Binds."

The store stayed closed on Monday. Miss Love made a big black satin wreath for the door and I went down there and hung it. I meant to go on to school, but for once in my life I didn't want to see Smiley or Pink or Lee Roy or Dunse or anybody. I didn't want to have to answer dumb questions about the burial.

I wished so much for Bluford Jackson. If he were here, he would just sit with me, and not talk or ask anything. Well, that's what he was doing in his grave: not talking or asking anything. Likewise Granny and Uncle Camp and now Grandpa.

I sure didn't want to go sit around at Grandpa's house and listen to Cold Sassy pay its respects. I'd done enough and too much of that the past year.

What I ended up doing that morning, I went over to old Mr. Billy Whisnant's, next to the schoolyard, and knocked on the door. The winter hadn't been kind to his rheumatism. He was more bent than ever. "What you want, boy?" he asked, looking real suspicious when he saw who it was.

I said, "Sir, if you'll trust me to do it right, I want to cut you some stovewood. I don't mean for pay. I . . . well, I just want to."

The next Sunday morning, Miss Love went back to the Methodist church. She wore a navy blue dress and lots of perfume. There were those who said she ought to have on black no matter what Mr. Blakeslee wanted, and they didn't think it was fittin' for her to be out in public so soon after buryin' her husband. But as everybody knew by then, Rucker Blakeslee had seen to it that nothin' about his passin' was fittin'. So what did it really matter what his widder did?

The following Wednesday she wore a red dress and lots of perfume and her brightest big-mouth smile to the ball park for Grandpa's funeral party. She and Aunt Loma were the prettiest ladies there by far. Loma was all dolled up in the flowerdy dress from New York.

Mama didn't wear black, but she didn't wear red or anything flowerdy. She wore gray.

I never saw so much food or so many smiling people. Nobody approved of the party, but knowing what the family was up against, they weren't about to make it worse for us by not coming.

Tell the truth, they wouldn't of missed it.

With the band music and all, it was like a festival. Miss Love got Mary Toy and me and Pink Predmore and the other boys to give out balloons and stick candy. She first thought of chewing gum, but Mama said nobody but common people would chew it.

I overheard Miss Alice Ann Boozer say it served Rucker right, after the way he done Miss Mattie Lou. "Married that Yankee and didn't live a year."

You ought to've heard Miss Effie Belle take up for him: "I never thought to say it, Alice Ann, but I'm glad now he married her. Miss Love kept his house nice and seems like she made him happy."

In between the crowing contest, the backwards bicycle race, and all that, you'd see folks gathered together, talking and laughing. One group I went up to, for instance, somebody was telling that Grandpa was the best knuckle-knocker in school when he was a boy. Somebody else told about him gettin' up in church and prayin', "Lord, forgive me for fittin' thet man, even though if'n I had it to do over agin I'd hit him harder." Somebody else said, "Ever hear bout the time he beat Wildcat Lindsay in a fist fight? Funniest fight you ever seen."

Mr. Pearl was telling another group about the time Rucker turned over the privy at the depot with a Yankee railroad president in there, "and the Yankee offered a fifty-dollar re-ward to anybody who'd tell him who did it. But nobody would," said Mr. Pearl. "Rucker said he needed the money and was go'n go claim the re-ward hisself. But Miss Mattie Lou wouldn't let him." Everybody died laughing about that, and then they joked about Grandpa naming Mr. Clem's hotel after hisself.

But nobody joked about him saying, when he married Miss Love three weeks after Granny died, that Miss Mattie Lou was as dead as she'd ever be. At least not in my hearing.

Mama had been scared folks would criticize and say the family didn't show proper respect, not having Grandpa embalmed and not having a church funeral, and then getting up a party. To make sure that everybody understood the circumstances, she had showed certain people his letter ordering the cheap burial, and then she let the *Cold Sassy Weekly* print Grandpa's plans for the funeral party, including, of course, that the whole town was invited.

So not only was it written up ahead of time, but it got a big write-up afterwards.

"Just as the deceased had requested," said the paper, "a good time was had by all. It's just too bad that the one who would have enjoyed it most couldn't be there."

The family gathered at Grandpa's house that night after supper for the reading of the will. The lawyer was Mr. Predmore, Pink's daddy.

My daddy was named executor.

First the document reminded us that the old Toy house and furnishings had been deeded over "to my beloved wife, Love Simpson Blakeslee" at the time of their marriage. "I also leave her one thousand dollars, as promised at the time of said marriage." He left Mama the house we were living in and a thousand dollars. Loma would get a thousand, too, "and the house on Julius Street, now rented, which I believe to be of equal value to the others." After payment of all debts and certain bequests, and after the rest of the estate was sold, including houses, farmland, and stock—but not the store—the money was to be divided, share and share alike, between Miss Love, Mama, and Aunt Loma.

Well, that would be less for Miss Love than Mama and them had feared, but a lot more than Miss Love had bargained for back when she said I do. Still and all, to me it seemed fitting, her having moved up from housekeeper to *bona fide* widow.

But wait. "In the event that I should have another child or children born or unborn at the time of my death, the estate will be divided, share and share alike, between my wife, my two grown daughters, and this other child or children, if living. Should any of these heirs precede me in death, the deceased's share will go to her (or his) offspring. If there be no offspring, born or unborn, said share will revert to the estate."

Mama and Papa and Aunt Loma didn't bat an eyelash at that. But then they didn't know what I knew. Gosh, what if Miss Love had twins!

I waited for her to speak up about the baby, but she didn't.

Now Mr. Predmore was reading about the store. Grandpa wanted it to be owned jointly by his widow and children, share and share alike. Papa was to serve as manager for as long as he wanted the job.

The first of the individual bequests was for four hundred dollars "to my grandson Hoyt Willis Tweedy for his education, provided he agrees to come into the store as an associate for a period of at least ten years after leaving college." Grandpa didn't leave Campbell Junior or Mary Toy a dime. I guess he just forgot about them.

To the First Baptist Chuch of Cold Sassy he left "the sum of one dollar in appreciation of its kindness in the matter of my son-in-law Campbell Williams's funeral." Mr. Predmore read that with a straight face. Boy howdy, what I'd give to be at the deacons' meeting after they heard about the dollar!

But there was a sop for the deacons: two hundred dollars "in memory of my late beloved wife, Mattie Lou Toy Blakeslee." Grandpa left the same amount to the Methodist Episcopal Church, South, of Cold Sassy "in honor of my beloved wife, Love Simpson Blakeslee."

The last bequest was for Loomis Toy, "the sum of fifty dollars in appreciation of his loyal service to the store and my family."

Not much was said after the reading. It's to my family's credit that when we got home, nobody spoke out loud what I'm sure we were thinking about, namely, Miss Love's share of the estate. Naturally I didn't say that most likely she was going to get half of it instead of a third. I wondered when she would tell them about the baby. It would have to be soon.

Gosh, what if sure enough the baby *was* a boy? I couldn't help thinking how in that case, if Granny Blakeslee was alive she would call it worth mentioning that Grandpa finally got what he wanted most in life after he died.

I wondered when Miss Love would leave Cold Sassy. Probably not till the baby was born and the estate settled. I wondered if she'd try to sell hers and the baby's interest in the store to my daddy. I wondered if he could afford to buy it.

I wanted to talk to Papa and them about my four hundred dollars, but it hardly seemed like the time. It really made me mad, Grandpa thinking he could buy me like I was Uncle Camp's funeral. It was all right with me if he wanted to pave the way with money for Miss Love to get welcomed back to the Methodist fold, but if I wouldn't spend my life in the store despite caring so much about him, I sure wasn't go'n do it for a bribe. Dead or alive, he meant to have his way. Well, in the matter of my future, I meant to have mine.

· · ·

Miss Love came down to our house to tell the family about Grandpa's baby, and I drove her home. We sat there in the car talking, and that's when she told me she had decided not to leave Cold Sassy.

"For one thing," she said, matter of fact, "where would I go? And why should I leave the only family my son will ever have? No matter how your folks feel about me, Will, they'll do right by their baby brother. That's the kind of people they are. They'll make room for him in the family and bring him into the life of the town. He'll know people who enjoyed and re-spected his father. And he'll know you, Will. You can show him how to fish, play ball, work hard, drive a car—all the things a boy needs to know that I can't teach him. Oh, Will"—her voice trembled—"you're so like Rucker! Knowing you, my son will know his father."

The child and I were keeping Grandpa alive for Miss Love. Who would keep him alive for me?

Grandpa had said Cold Sassy's name would be changed "over my dead body," and that is exactly what happened. A month af-ter we buried him in the coffin box, the U.S. Post Office ap-proved a new name, and Cold Sassy became Progressive City.

The next spring the town council voted to widen the road on each side of the railroad tracks, which meant the Cold Sassy tree had to go. It was taken down and the roots chopped up, and I think everybody in town took some home to boil for sas-safras tea.

I still have a piece of that root, put away in a box with my journal, my can of tobacco tags, the newspaper write-up when I got run over by the train, a photograph of me and Miss Love and Grandpa in the Pierce, my Ag College diploma from the University—and the buckeye that Lightfoot gave me.

Leaving Cold Sassy

THE UNFINISHED SEQUEL TO
Cold Sassy Tree

WITH A REMINISCENCE BY
KATRINA KENISON

A Note from the Publisher

At the time of her death in 1990, Olive Ann Burns had been working for five years on a sequel to her best-selling novel, *Cold Sassy Tree*. Since its publication in 1984, *Cold Sassy Tree* has become a phenomenon, taking its place alongside such American classics as *The Adventures of Tom Sawyer* and *To Kill a Mockingbird*. It is the story of life in a small Georgia town at the turn of the century, as seen through the eyes of fourteen-year-old Will Tweedy. In the course of three momentous weeks, Will mourns his grandmother's death and then watches as his grandfather scandalizes all of Cold Sassy by up and marrying a fresh-faced young milliner thirty years his junior.

In *Time, Dirt, and Money* (the working title for her novel), Olive Ann picks up Will's story in 1917, just as he is falling in love with his own wife-to-be and grappling with the changes time has wrought in his beloved hometown. Fifteen chapters of the novel are complete, and Olive Ann had mapped out the rest of the story in her mind. Despite a long battle with cancer and congestive heart failure, she continued to write with tremendous energy and pleasure.

To the end of her life Olive Ann Burns was passionately interested in Will Tweedy's future—as were her thousands of fans, who have waited eagerly for a second book. In large part, we are publishing her unfinished novel for those readers. Anyone who came under the spell of *Cold Sassy Tree* will welcome this glimpse of Will Tweedy, now on the brink of adulthood; of the feisty young school-teacher who captures his heart; and of Cold Sassy itself, a town that has claimed a permanent place in our imaginations.

We would not undertake such a publication were we not certain that Olive Ann herself wished it. For years, Olive Ann promised her readers a sequel; she dictated the first draft when she became too ill to write. She endured nearly three years of complete bedrest without complaint, for she spent long afternoons in Cold Sassy, Georgia, chronicling the adventures of our old friends. But during her last hospitalization, she realized that she might not live to complete the novel. Late on the night of June 22, 1990, while lying awake in the Georgia Baptist Hospital, she dictated a letter to her next-door neighbor, Norma Duncan. It said, in part, "I've figured out a way that if I don't get to finish the novel it might still be marketed as a small book." With this publication, we fulfill Olive Ann's wish to let people know what happened to Will Tweedy, and we trust that her many fans will welcome her final pages.

Time, Dirt, and Money

I

I THOUGHT I was roaring into Sanna Klein's life, but if I'd been on tiptoe instead of a motorcycle, it wouldn't have made any difference. She didn't even hear me coming. Everybody in Cold Sassy was at the watermelon cutting that Sunday afternoon except the bedsick, and to her, meeting them was more of an ordeal than a party.

The school board always put on a watermelon social the day before school started in September to introduce the new teachers to the townspeople. I'd never missed one, but this year I wasn't going. I didn't much feel like facing that many homefolks. It was 1917, the United States had got itself into a world war, and I was twenty-five years old and not even in uniform. While some of the fellows I grew up with were already dying in France, I was working for the University of Georgia over in Athens, twenty-three miles from Cold Sassy. I told myself I'd outgrown a small-town watermelon cutting. But the truth is, I didn't have the nerve to go. Then on Thursday I ran into my old friend Smiley Snodgrass at the Athens Hardware Store. "Well, if it ain't Will Tweedy!" he yelled, slapping me on the back. "Hey, Will, you go'n get over to P.C. for the watermelon cuttin' Sunday?"

I need to explain "P.C." Back in 1907 our town council decided Cold Sassy sounded too countrified for an up-and-coming business community, and they changed the name to Progressive City. My Grandpa Blakeslee wouldn't have allowed it, but he was dead. In the nearly ten years since, the town had progressed, but the new name still hadn't caught on. Progressive City sounded silly and took too long to say. Those of us who didn't keep calling it Cold Sassy just called it P.C. Old Doc Slaughter still had COLD SASSY, GEORGIA, on his office letterhead. "Anybody you hear callin' our town Progressive City," he said, "you know he's just passin' th'ew."

Anyhow, here was Smiley, come to Athens to buy some plumbing pipes. Smiley was bursting with news. "I done got you a teacher picked out, Will. Her name's Miss Klein and she's from over in Mitchellville. We ain't got but three new teachers this year," he added.

"Yeah, Papa told me." Papa was head of the school board.

"I reckon I'll see you there."

"Cain't make it this year, Smiley. I'll meet her later."

"Well, I'll gar'ntee you, Will Tweedy, if your later ain't soon, somebody's go'n beat you to her. She's a pure-T beauty, Will. Real foreign-lookin'. I-talian maybe. Or Spanish. Might could even be a Gypsy. Anyhow, she's got heavy black hair, and black eyes, and her eyelids—law, they's so smoky-dark it's like she reached in the f'arplace and got herself some sut and smeared it on."

When I didn't say anything, he added, "I reckon you know that her and them other two teachers are rentin' the upstairs rooms at Miss Love's house."

"Yeah, I know."

"I built a bathroom up there so Miss Love could rent to'm."

"I've seen it. How'd you think up puttin' it on the roof?"

"Miss Love thunk it up, to save space indoors."

The bathroom was set into an L-shaped corner of the roof. From the street it looked like a playhouse. Had a roof, a porch, a corner column, banisters, a door, and two little windows. Smiley had cut a door to the bathroom porch from the upstairs hall. This bathroom was an improvement over the backyard privy Miss Love had to use when she married Grandpa Blakeslee, but nobody would look forward to going out there on a freezing-cold, rainy night.

The clerk came over to Smiley. "I've got up your order, sir, and toted the sum. You want to come see is it right?"

Smiley started to follow, then turned back to me.

"Well, anyhow, but . . . well, you know . . ." Smiley kept the conjunctions coming whenever he was trying to think what he wanted to say. "Well, ain't it about time you quit bein' hurt about Trulu Philpot or whatever her name was?"

"You tend to your business and I'll tend to mine."

He shrugged. "Well, so anyhow, yesterd'y I took Miss Klein's trunk and thangs upstairs to her room, and I'm sayin' you better latch on to her."

I picked up a tenpenny nail, tossed it, caught it, and put it back in the barrel. "I know I'm God's gift to women, Smiley, but you met her first. How come you're so willin' to give her to me?"

"Shoot dog, Will, Miss Klein is—well, refined as heck. She wouldn't give somebody like me a second look. Now I don't go so far as to say you're refined, but, uh . . . at least you're educated."

Smiley wasn't the only one who already had me matched up with Sanna Klein. The next day I got a note from Miss Love, my grandpa's widow. The word *widow* sounds like "old woman," but Miss Love was still high-style and beautiful, and looked young despite the fact her hair turned solid white in the month after Grandpa died. Every widower and bachelor in town would be courting her if she'd give them half a chance.

As usual, she began the letter "Dear Will Tweedy." Grandpa Blakeslee used to call me both names, and Miss Love had kept it up—in his memory, so to speak. Maybe it was in his memory that we both still called our town Cold Sassy instead of Progressive City or P.C.

> Dear Will Tweedy,
> You must come meet "my girls"—all twenty-two years old. The first to arrive was Miss Isa Belle Hazelhurst, from Ty Ty. She has dimples and a sweet face, but is a little empty and silly, I'm afraid. You'll be interested in her south Georgia accent. She pronounces the "i" in "nice" and "ice" like the sound of "i" in "bicycle." Those sixthgraders will be mocking her from the first day, poor thing. "Isa Belle" is pronounced like "Isa-belle" but she says just call her Issie.
>
> She is sharing the large upstairs bedroom with Miss Lucy Mercer Clack from Clarkesville, a nice plain sensible young lady.
>
> Miss Sanna Klein has the small bedroom by herself. I think you may be really interested in her, Will. She's a beautiful little brunette.
>
> Judging by the quality of her clothes and her manners, she obviously has what your mother would call "background." She's from Mitchellville and is to teach fourth grade. Just a lovely girl.
>
> See you at the watermelon cutting if not before.
> > Hastily,
> > Love Simpson Blakeslee
> P.S. I guess you've heard that your Aunt Loma came in on the train Tuesday.

Two years before, Aunt Loma had gone off to New York City to seek fame and fortune on the stage, leaving her son, Campbell Junior, for my parents to raise. She claimed to feel guilty about it and had just gone back to New York after being home for a month "to be with my boy." But from what I heard, she didn't spend any time with Campbell Junior except to tuck him in bed at night like he was still little bitty instead of twelve years old.

I wondered briefly why Aunt Loma was back again so soon. But I was more interested in Miss Sanna Klein. Sanna . . . Sanna . . . What an odd name. Vaguely familiar, though I was sure I'd never known a Sanna before.

Sanna Klein was exotic and beautiful. She was refined. Miss Love approved of her. Suddenly nothing this side of dropping dead could have kept me away from the watermelon cutting.

Usually when I went home, I took the train from Athens and used Papa's car after I got to Cold Sassy. But that Sunday I rode my motorcycle, with the sidecar attached so I could take two pillowcases full of dirty clothes for Mama's washerwoman to do up. There's nothing like a Harley-Davidson for getting around mud holes, rocks, and wagon ruts on dirt roads—or for making an impression on girls. I stopped by home, left the clothes on the back porch, and went directly to Sheffield Park.

Saddle horses and buggy horses were tied under trees on the far side of the baseball field. Cars sat in a straggly row near the wagon road into the park, so as not to scare the horses or make dust. I stopped the Harley-Davidson between Miss Love's old black Pierce automobile and Wildcat Lindsey's new Model-T Ford, and lit up a cigar. Most of the university students smoked cigarettes, but I favored Tampa Nuggets.

Then I headed over toward the town band, already playing in the big eight-sided pavilion for the crowd gathered in the shade of some huge oak trees. The dusty, dried-up grass was thick with low-hovering yellow jackets, but I barely noticed them. My mind was on Sanna Klein.

2

I T COULD have been a scene in a moving picture show
—except I was walking into the picture. And instead of everything being black and white or gray, I was seeing blue sky, green trees, and ladies in bright-striped or flowerdy dresses, dazzling in the sunlight.

It was a hot day. The very old sat on benches in the shade, some holding babies, all tapping their feet to the band music, and all smiling except for poor old Dr. Hedge Rufesel, the dentist, who used to travel from town to town, filling teeth and making dental plates right in people's homes. A year after finally settling in Cold Sassy, he'd had a stroke. Today Dr. Rufesel's wheelchair was parked beside the bench where Miss Effie Belle Tate had sat at the watermelon cutting in 1914, not long before she died. A Negro man was pushing bits of watermelon into his mouth.

Long planks had been laid across sawhorses to make tables, and people stood around in clusters, talking. Every few minutes they parted like the waters to let one of the Negro men get through with a huge watermelon that had been cooling in the creek. With much laughter and howdy-doing, the colored men would tote melons to the tables and slash them open with a flourish of their big sharp knives. The slices fell like red dinner plates on each table, as neat as place settings.

Loomis Toy saw me before I saw him. "Hey, Mist' Will! How you doin', son?" I loved Loomis, a very tall, very black man who had worked for my family for as long as I could remember. He taught me how to garden long before the university's School of Agriculture taught me to farm.

"I heard your little girl took sick last week, Loomis." I'd never noticed the sprinkle of gray in his hair before.

"Yassuh, Mist' Will, but she doin' mo better now, yassuh. And she sho 'preciate that doll Miss Mary Toy sont her. Lawdy, I 'member Miss Mary Toy playin' wid dat doll her ownself. Don't seem lak that long ago, does it?"

Mrs. Avery came up from the creek with some wet towels. "For when folks are ready to wipe their hands," she said, smiling at me. "Will, go put'm on that sycamore stump over yonder."

Near the stump I saw the Widow Abernathy and her eight children lined up at a table in front of eight watermelon slices, like dairy cows at their feeding troughs. The mother opened her purse, took eight spoons out of a napkin, and handed one to each child.

I wondered where Sampson was. Several young boys were dodging out from behind trees to spit watermelon seeds at each other, but he wasn't with them. Nor was he among the clusters of parents and children who stood with favorite teachers from years past. My own favorite, Miss Neppie, had died of appendicitis in the spring.

I headed for the biggest oak tree, where the rest of Cold Sassy would already be waiting in line to meet the new teachers. Snatches of conversation drifted in the air:

A young woman jiggling a fretful baby was talking to Mrs. Means. "I don't know if he's teethin' or just tired."

"Most babies are teethin' or tired, one. Unless they're hungry or wet. What I call a good baby is one that's asleep. I never have . . ."

"In the paper it says we 'sposed to join the Women's Army Against Waste. What in the world's the Women's Army?"

"It's just a way a-talkin', honey. What the gov'ment really wants, they want us women to serve less meat. They say raise more hogs and chickens, quit fryin' the pullets, let'm grow up to hens. Can more vegetables. They say quit cookin' light bread and biscuits. Save the wheat for our soldier boys, and . . ."

". . . seen that new teacher?"

"Miss Klein? The dark-complected one? She's a pretty little thang, ain't she?"

Mrs. Snodgrass, Smiley's mama, was talking to two women I didn't know. One had a voice like a crab. "You wouldn't think mill hands would come to a town social," she rasped.

"They got chi'ren in the school same as us," said the third lady.

"But they ain't comf'table here," said Mrs. Snodgrass. "Look at 'em, standin' off to theirselves, starin' at all us. Not to change the subject, but have y'all seen that great big diamond Loma Blakeslee Williams is flashin'? I hear her fee-ance is a rich Yankee banker!"

"It's all right to marry rich, Wi-nona, but anybody marries a Yankee is a lost cause. Loma's daddy fought in the War, for heaven's sake!"

"Sometimes I wonder bout Loma," said Mrs. Snodgrass. "It's like her corn bread didn't git done in the middle."

This was my Aunt Loma they were talking about. I paused to relight my cigar, took some slow puffs, tried to act like I was looking for somebody.

". . . Well, Loma left here two year ago to make her fortune in New York City," the crab-voiced lady commented, "and if'n that diamond is any measure, Wi-nona, I reckon she has did it."

"She's also took up smokin'," said old Mrs. Calvert, joining the group.

"No!" exclaimed Miss Winona. "Who told you that?"

"Miss Hazel's cook smelt it on her."

Mrs. Tabor, walking by, heard that and said, "But y'all, she whistled for the Presbyterians at preachin' this mornin'. It was real pretty."

Miss Winona was incensed. "Now, Miz Tabor. What could a vaudeville whistler possibly whistle in church?"

"Why, Wi-nona, you should a-been there! She done 'Whisperin' Hope.' She whistled it in two-part harmony—like doin' a duet with herself!"

"What I heard was she looked mighty peculiar doin' it," said Mrs. Crab-Voice. "Kept pokin' on her mouth and cheeks with her hands and fingers the whole time."

"Well, she did look funny. But it was bout the prettiest sound I nearly ever heard. Sent chills up the back of my neck. Why, there's Will Tweedy! Where you been keepin' yourself, sugar?"

Greetings and handshakes came thick as I made my way through gaps in the crowd. "Hey, Will Tweedy, you old son of a gun! Come 'ere, boy!" "Goodness, Will, ain't seen you in too long!"

A group of excited boys and young men were carrying on about the war. Old Mr. Henry Botts put his arm around one in uniform and said, "We go'n have the Kaiser on the run in no time, ain't we, son?"

The Army boy was Harkness Predmore. Last time I saw Harkness he looked barely old enough to shave. "Hey, Will!" he called to me. "I enlisted!"

"Congratulations, Harkness. Take care of yourself," I called back, and walked on—faster. . .

Nobody had asked why I wasn't in the Army. They may have wondered, but nobody asked.

Fat little Mr. Homer Boozer was already eating watermelon at a table shaded by the big oak tree. Fat little Miss Alice Ann saw me, poked Mr. Homer, pointed in my direction, and called out, "Will Tweedy, come say howdy!" I went over and said howdy, then excused myself to join those waiting under the tree to meet the new teachers.

I couldn't see Papa for the people, but I knew he was there. When I did catch sight of him, I felt the usual twinge of shame, but I also marveled how he could keep on in his role as community and church leader despite what he'd done—as if it hadn't even happened. There he was, prosperous and dignified, standing with four other school board members. By craning my neck I could see two of the young ladies. But not the dark-complected one.

Instead, I saw Lightfoot and Hosie Roach with their four children, all holding hands as they headed for a plank table already set with watermelon slices. I wanted to go speak, but let the moment pass.

In high school when I was so crazy about her, Lightfoot was skinny, tow-headed, fresh from the mountains, eager to learn. But she had to leave school and work in the mill, and at fifteen she married Hosie Roach, a twenty-two-year-old mill hand who had gone to work for Grandpa Blakeslee at the store. Lightfoot was kind of fat now and her hair had darkened, but from where I stood she looked proud and happy.

I used to hate Hosie. He always was smart, no denying, and a few years ago, he and Lightfoot had started a store of their own in a little shack at the edge of Mill Town. Townspeople called them uppity, which meant they were making a go of it. Their oldest child was about nine now, a pretty little white-haired girl named Precious.

Precious Roach. Good Lord!

Watching the family stroll away, I wondered if Precious would be in Miss Klein's fourth grade.

I heard someone call out, "Will!" and turned to see my Aunt Loma, hurrying to catch up with me. The way Loma was dressed you'd think she'd got Cold Sassy confused with New

York City. Her curly red hair, cut short in the new style, was almost hidden under a gold-colored cloche hat. She had on a pale green silk dress, a short dress, way short enough to get talked about. Talk, talk, talk. Loma reveled in it. In Cold Sassy the ladies were just daring to show their ankles.

And that engagement ring! The diamond was big as a fat black-eyed pea! As if to keep her balance, she walked with her left hand held forward, wiggling her fingers, flashing the diamond in the sunshine.

"Hi, Will!" she said, a little out of breath.

"Hey, Aunt Loma."

"Hay is what horses eat, Southern boy," she said.

"And hi means you think Northerners are way up above us down here." I was teasing, but all that put-on Yankee accent irked me. Taking her hand, I bent down close to the diamond. "That's a nice piece of glass you got there, Aunt Loma."

"Glass, my foot. Don't show off your ignorance, Will." She laughed and took her hand back. I gave her a little hug and we walked on. She wiggled her ring finger at me again. "Are you impressed?"

"Well, yes, I admit I am."

"It's three and a half carats."

"Tell me about him," I said, "and tell me how come you're back in Cold Sassy so soon."

Before she could answer, I saw Miss Klein!

It's not too much to say that to me, at that moment, Sanna Klein looked like a bride, dressed head to foot in summer white except for the blue ribbons and blue silk roses on her white straw hat and a wide blue satin sash at her waist. She wore a thin cotton dress you could see through over an embroidered petticoat. The dress had long embroidered sleeves and a high collar. Her lips were the color of ripe raspberries and her hair was jet black, done up in a thick braid. She was the darkest white person I ever saw.

After Smiley's description, I had sort of pictured her as a refined Gypsy dancing-girl type, but there was no sparkle in these dark eyes. She looked anxious, like a little girl traveling alone and scared of losing her train ticket. She smiled nice and all, and stooped down to hug the little children. But it was easy to see that she wasn't having anywhere near as much fun as the folks who had come out to meet her.

Aunt Loma got to Miss Klein before I did. At thirty-one, Loma was still pretty, with eyes blue as Grandpa's and those short saucy curls of red hair peeping out from under her hat. But as always she talked catty, and talking catty with a Northern accent just made it worse. I'm sure she said what she did to Miss Klein just to call attention to herself. She talked real gushy. "I hear you have cousins in Germany, Miss Klein! I know you must be worried about them."

Papa's face turned red. Loma was questioning Miss Klein's patriotism, right out in public, which was the same as saying he shouldn't have hired her.

He spoke quickly. "Miss Klein, meet my sister-in-law, Mrs. Williams. She lives in New York City," he said, as if that explained everything.

"I'm very pleased to meet you, Mrs. Williams," Miss Klein said politely. Then, just as politely—but loud enough for those around her to hear—she said she guessed there were cousins somewhere in Germany, "but I really don't know them. My people came to this country in seventeen-twenty, back in the days when immigrants had to pledge loyalty to the Crown of England. When did your ancestors come, Mrs. Williams?" Loma looked confused and didn't try to answer. Then Miss Klein turned to Mrs. Means and little Ronald, waiting to be introduced.

At that exact moment an overripe slice of watermelon dropped out of the tree and landed on Miss Klein's shoulder, splattering her white dress with pink juice and dotting it with black seeds. Everybody jumped back as if she had exploded; then all eyes turned upwards.

"Sampson, he done it!" yelled little Ada Foster, hopping around like a chicken with its head cut off. "Hit's Sampson Blakeslee, Miss Klein! See him? Up in the tree?" She pointed as two bare feet disappeared above a wide limb high overhead.

"Sampson, you come down from there!" Papa yelled.

The handsome, sun-browned face of nine-year-old Sampson appeared among the oak leaves. This was Miss Love's boy. The son Grandpa Blakeslee always wanted but didn't live to see get born. Half-brother to my mother and Aunt Loma.

My half-uncle.

Straddling the wide limb, Sampson grabbed a branch with one hand and leaned towards us so his innocence could be seen.

The band had stopped playing, a politician started giving a speech, and everybody under the tree was staring up at Sampson. "Gosh, Miss Klein, did it hit you?" he called down. Miss Klein was too angry to speak. Jerking off her hat, she picked furiously at bits of red watermelon nestled among the blue silk flowers.

"I am a-SHAMED of you, boy!" yelled Papa. Still looking up, he put his hand under the sticky wetness of Miss Klein's elbow to steady her.

"I didn't mean to, sir. That old watermelon, it just slid right . . ."

Little Ada was dancing again. "Sampson, here comes yore mama! I bet she's go'n git you good!"

"Naw, she ain't," mumbled Mr. Homer Boozer, speaking to everybody and nobody. With a hunk of watermelon heart in one hand and a salt shaker in the other, he had pushed through to see what the commotion was about. "Half the boy's trouble is Miss Love don't never git him good. Just gives him a talkin' to." Gesturing with his watermelon towards Sampson's perch in the tree, he said, "Ain't thet right, Will Tweedy? The Widder Blakeslee spares the rod and spiles the chil'.."

What the child had spoilt was the vision of Miss Klein's loveliness. But he didn't need any hard words from me on top of what he was about to get, for here came Miss Love, yelling up the tree before she even got to it. "Simpson Rucker Blakeslee! What have you done now!" Then she saw Miss Klein, who had drooped with embarrassment, like a wet cat. "Good Lord, Sampson, what. . . ?"

"I didn't mean to, Mother." His voice sounded small and lonely in the sudden quiet under the tree.

Miss Love's hands were on her hips. "Why in the world did you have that watermelon up there in the first place?"

"I—I wanted to eat it in the tree. I hauled it up here! See?" He spoke proudly, holding out a zinc bucket with a long rope tied to the handle.

"You let that bucket down right now!" Miss Love shouted. "Before it falls on somebody!"

"Yes, ma'am."

In seconds the bucket was dangling in Miss Klein's face. Miss Love grabbed it out of the air. "Now you get down from there yourself!" I looked up just in time to see Sampson swing to a lower limb, squat, and poise himself to jump to the ground.

Miss Klein gasped. "Oh, mercy, he'll break his neck!"

"Naw, he won't," said Mr. Boozer, taking a bite of his watermelon. "Thet boy's middle name is Circus. Wait'll you see him standin' on his mama's horse and hit a-gallopin'!"

WHUMP! Sampson landed on his feet, almost colliding with Aunt Loma.

"Smart aleck!" Loma snapped, her face flushing.

"Wasn't that a grand leap?" he asked her with a wide smile, as if expecting applause.

Miss Love was trying to dry off the teacher's arm with a lace handkerchief. "I'm just so sorry," she kept murmuring. Then she turned to Sampson. "Now I want to hear you apologize to Miss Klein," she ordered.

"I already did. Didn't I, Miss Klein?" With a bare foot he kicked aside the broken watermelon slice where yellow jackets were already crawling, and looked boldly at the wet dress. "Gosh, ma'am, I really am sorry."

Maybe he meant it, but there was the glimmer of a smirk on his face when he glanced around to see if everybody was looking at him. To old Mr. Boozer he said, "Did you watch me jump, sir?"

Just then Sampson saw and leaped on me, wrapping his arms around my neck and his legs around my waist. "Uncle Will!" he said happily. "Did you see me jump?"

"Yes, I saw." Untwining him, I lowered him by his arms, and spoke sternly. "Now you get up that busted watermelon and put it in the barrel over yonder."

"Yes, sir, Uncle Will."

"And then go get Miss Klein one of those wet towels off of the sycamore stump."

While the boy picked up the mess with a great show of being busy, Papa made introductions. "Miss Klein, Miss Clack, Miss Hazelhurst, this is my son, Will Tweedy." He said my name proudly, as if I'd just made the honor roll. "Will, these fine young ladies are our new teachers." Then he noticed that Miss Klein was busy waving off yellow jackets. "Son," said Papa, "you better carry her on home."

"You can use my car," Miss Love offered.

"I'm too sticky," protested Miss Klein.

"I've got my motorsickle," I said. "Bein' sticky won't . . ."

"Oh, no, I couldn't!" The prospect seemed to horrify her. "I mean I haven't finished meeting people. I mean thank you but . . . o-o-oh!" She shrank from a yellow jacket hovering near her cheek.

"I've got the sidecar hitched on, Miss Klein."

Sampson had come back from the trash barrel. Waving the towel, he started hopping. "Can I ride, too, Uncle Will? Please, Uncle Will? Please?"

"Hush up beggin', Sampson. Here's the towel, Miss Klein. It might help." I wiped her face and hands and dabbed at the stickiness of the long sleeves, then handed the towel to Miss Love.

Miss Hazelhurst and Miss Clack and Papa turned back to the job at hand—greeting and meeting townspeople—and I took Miss Klein's arm. But she turned back to the boy. "I've got a thing or two to say first. Simpson Blakeslee?"

"Ma'am? You mean me?"

Miss Klein was already acquainted with Sampson, of course, being as she was living at Miss Love's house. They were bound to have talked, since he talked to everybody. Talked friendly, I'm sure. But right now the teacher was fearsome to behold.

Using her hat to fan off yellow jackets, she grabbed Sampson by the hand and marched him away from the tree and the crowd. Miss Love looked at me. I nodded. Miss Klein didn't notice us following at a distance. When the teacher stopped, Sampson stood contrite and apprehensive before her. She plopped the hat back on her head. "You look here at me," she demanded, almost whispering, but that didn't hide her anger. "I said look at me. Not at the ground. That's better. Now, my rollbook says your name is Simpson Rucker Blakeslee, so in my classroom, you will be called Simpson."

"Yes, ma'am."

"Now, Simpson, I want to know if you think you're smart."

He looked surprised. After glancing back at his mother and me, he said respectfully, "Yes, ma'am. Everybody in town says I'm smart—like my daddy was."

"Can you name me the nations of the world?"

Hesitating, the boy glanced around again. "Uh, we haven't studied the nations yet, Miss Klein."

"Do you know nine times seven, Simpson?" She slapped at a yellow jacket on her arm. Killed him dead.

"Uh, no, ma'am. We haven't learned the nines." Poor Uncle Simpson. He dug his bare toes in the grass. "I'm s'posed to learn the nines this year, in fourth grade." Boldly: "You s'posed to teach them to me, ma'am."

Her voice softened. "You've had the sevens, Simpson. If seven times nine is sixty-three, what is nine times seven?"

He looked up, puzzled, then beamed. "Nine times seven is sixty-three?"

"That's good, Simpson, Now I want you to understand something else. I hope we'll be friends at home, but there are fifty-five names in my rollbook. That's a lot of children, and I'm supposed to teach all of you, and y'all are all going to learn. My classroom will not be yours or anybody else's playground."

"Yes, ma'am. I mean, no, ma'am. I mean, yes'm, I understand."

Loma had strolled over. She patted him on the cheek and said, "Simpson, sugar, I think you've just met your match."

He glared at her.

Stepping up behind him, I hung my arms around his shoulders and asked, "Miss Klein, ma'am, may we still call him Sampson after school?"

She couldn't help laughing, and Miss Love laughed, and Loma, and then Sampson did. He tugged at my arm. "I need to tell you somethin', Uncle Will."

"Well, OK, but make haste, son."

"I got to whisper it."

His mother shook her head. "Simpson, it's not polite to tell secrets in front of other people. You know that."

I winked at her. "Just this once, Step-Grandma?"

"Oh, Will, you . . . you . . ." Miss Love was blustering. "You're always undermining my discipline."

"Yes'm." I smiled at her, shrugging my shoulders, and she stalked off, back to the party. Squatting down, I cupped my right ear forward with my hand. "All right, Uncle Sampson, the cave's open. Send in your secret." Miss Klein and Loma were watching, and I was showing off.

Sampson whispered in my ear. I tried to look disapproving. He whispered again. I grinned, nodded, and gave him a playful jab in the stomach. "OK, son, now go play."

When I stood up, Aunt Loma was right in front of me, her arms crossed. "You spoil him worse than Love does."

I tapped her diamond with a fingernail. "Looks to me like that Yankee spoils you."

"It's time somebody did," she snapped back.

A yellow jacket was buzzing around Miss Klein in circles. "Please, Mr. Tweedy, I think I'd better . . ."

"Will," said Aunt Loma, "I hope you don't really expect her to ride in that silly sidecar. She won't have a dab of dignity left."

"Are you willin', Miss Klein? If you'd rather not, I'll . . ."

"Anything, Mr. Tweedy. Oh, Lord, here's two more! No matter which way I turn, they're hanging in the air!"

"We'll walk around the crowd, through these woods, to get where I'm parked." With my hand on her elbow, I looked back and said, "Bye, Aunt Loma. See you later."

3

THE harrrumph, harrrumph seemed deafening as we headed down the wagon road towards the park entrance. Despite I didn't go fast, Miss Klein was scared to death —braced herself in the sidecar and shut her eyes tight.

At Miss Love's house we *varoomed* around to the backyard, where I stopped under the big elm. In the quiet after I shut off the engine, a cow lowed somewhere far off and a rooster crowed. When Miss Klein opened her eyes, she looked up to the roof of leaves above us and murmured, "What a beautiful tree!"

I told her it was my Grandpa Blakeslee's favorite. "He always said *el-lum* tree, like it had two syllables, so naturally I said *el-lum*, too. Then a botany professor over at the university set me straight."

A mockingbird lit on a high branch and commenced his song. She watched him for a minute, then lowered her gaze and smiled at me. "It wasn't a bad ride," she said, taking off her hat. "Bumpy, but not scary. Well, Mr. Tweedy, thank you." But she made no move to go. Her black hair glinted blue in a dapple of sunlight. A breeze stirred a loose wisp of hair across a seed that had dried on her cheek. She smelled like warm watermelon.

"You know somethin'?" I said. "Watermelon is very be-comin'—to you, I mean. I don't think it would improve me any."

She smiled again. "Maybe you don't need improving."

"The U.S. Army says I do."

"What do you mean?"

"They won't let me join up unless I get fat. I'm six-foot-one and weigh about fifty pounds, which . . ."

She laughed. "Nobody's that skinny."

"Well, I guess a hundred pounds."

"That can't be. I weigh a hundred and twelve myself and I'm just five-three, and . . . oh, you're teasing!"

"Actually, a hundred and twenty-five according to the scales they use at Papa's store to weigh out cow feed and guano. Still, that doesn't suit the Army. Like I told the recruitin' officer, if I was a hog, it'd make sense to fatten me up for slaughter. But as a soldier boy, the thinner I get, the harder I'll be to hit." I meant to sound light-hearted, but I couldn't laugh. My hands tight-ened on the handlebars. "Last week in Atlanta I saw a frater-nity brother. He was in Army uniform with a corporal's stripes. I hadn't laid eyes on him in a year and we were good friends at the university, but I crossed the street hopin' he wouldn't see me."

I hadn't meant to say all that. Miss Klein looked embar-rassed for me. After an awkward silence, she said, "I really must go in, Mr. Tweedy."

I pretended not to hear her. Leaning back from the handle-bars, I let my hands drop to my knees. "Over in Athens they say my work is important to the war."

"Then you must have a very responsible position."

"I'm what they call a county agent."

"A what?"

"The School of Agriculture thought it up two years ago, just before I graduated. They made me county agent for Clarke County." Miss Klein leaned forward, her hand on the handle of the sidecar's little door, but I kept talking. "I tell farmers how to farm."

She turned towards me again. "You're a farmer?"

"No, this is a salaried job. But it's the biggest joke I ever got into. Farmers aren't exactly thrilled over havin' a fool college boy claimin' to know better than they do. When the professor hired me, I said, 'Sir, even the hired hands will see I don't know what I'm doin'.' He said, 'If somebody has a problem you can't solve, don't admit it. Stall till you can find out what to do.'" I paused. "But you aren't interested in all this, Miss Klein. I better let you . . ."

"Oh, but I really am interested, Mr. Tweedy. I was born on a farm. My daddy was a farmer. My brother is, and . . ."

Surprised, I said, "I bet you miss it, don't you? The farm, I mean. And the quiet, and the smell of fresh-cut hay and fresh-turned soil, and watchin' newborn lambs and calves frolic, and . . ."

"I don't miss any of that." Miss Klein shook her head. "I don't miss drawing well water, either. I will never ever live out in the country again. A man trying to make a decent living on the land? That's a lot bigger joke than what you do, Mr. Tweedy. Farming is nothing but hard work and high hopes, debt and disappointment."

"But I'll know all the new methods. Farmin' is a gamble, all right. Still, that's what keeps it excitin'."

"I hate excitement. That's just another word for worry."

"Farmin' lets a man work outdoors. I couldn't stand bein' cooped up in a store or office the rest of my life. Right now, though, I just want to enlist. Bein' a county agent won't mean pea-turkey to the fightin' men, the ones over here, or over there either." I itched to pluck that watermelon seed off her cheek. "Want me to give you a for-instance, Miss Klein? Yesterday I was out in the county advisin' an old fool named Duck Lassiter how to get one row of cotton picked. How's that go'n hep beat the Kaiser?"

She looked puzzled. "One row?"

"Old Duck plowed his field in a spiral, like a snail shell, and bragged that it was go'n be the world's longest gol-durn cotton row. His field hands hoed it, and they slopped the stalks with arsenic and molasses to kill the boll weevils, but they don't want to pick the cotton." I laughed. "Cotton pickers like to take a row apiece and move down a field together. If they have to space themselves out, that's lonesome pickin'. And it'll be heavy totin' and a lot of wasted time if they have to cut across the spiral to get to the cotton wagon. I told Duck he'd have to make a road across the spiral, but he said that'd mess up his row."

Miss Klein was really laughing. She didn't notice a yellow jacket closing in on her scent.

"Now tomorrow evenin', I'll be talkin' to a dozen or so farmers about crop rotation, which just might hep feed my frat brother. If the war lasts long enough." I couldn't resist any longer. I plucked the seed off her cheek and held it out to her. "A souvenir," I said.

Her smile was rueful. "I don't think I want it."

"Then I do," said I, and put it in my shirt pocket.

At that moment, Miss Klein stood up, frantic, waving off the yellow jackets with her hat. Right quick I helped her out of the sidecar and followed her up the back steps. After Miss Klein dodged inside the screen door, I asked if I could take her to church the next Sunday night. "By then," I said through the screen, "I can tell you if I figured out how to get the world's longest row of cotton picked without messin' it up."

She hesitated. "I'm sorry, Mr. Tweedy. I'm going over to Jefferson Saturday. It'll be late when I get back Sunday. I'll . . . uh, I will be visiting my sweetheart's family."

She hesitated again, then blurted out, "I'll be meeting them for the first time, Mr. Tweedy, and I'm scared to death!"

Her perfume of watermelon drifted through the screen, and two yellow jackets crawled across it, looking for a way to get to her—like me. Trying to sound casual, I said, "You go'n marry this feller?"

"I'm . . . not sure." My spirits rose. She kind of smiled. "He did ask me one time if I could cook. That seemed encouraging."

"Can you? Cook?"

"I told him I could make real good mayonnaise and divinity candy. I don't think he was impressed."

"I am. Nothin' in the world better than divinity candy dipped in mayonnaise."

She half-laughed, traced her right index finger down the screen. "I just wish I knew where I stand with him. He writes me love letters and recites love sonnets, and he wants me to meet his family, and last time he was in Mitchellville, just before he left he said, 'If I asked you to marry me, would you?' He said it like teasing. There's only one answer to a sideways question like that. I said, 'Well, I might.' That made him mad, Mr. Tweedy! Heavens, did he expect me to say 'Oh, goody!' or beg him 'Please, ask me'? Now his mother has invited me to a family dinner party, and I don't know what that's supposed to mean. Am I being auditioned for a place in the family, or am I just invited because Hugh wants me there? I don't know how I'm supposed to act."

"You could practice on my folks," I offered. "I'll take you over home for supper tonight."

She laughed. A nervous little laugh. "I guess I just never have liked meeting people I don't know."

"You sound like my Grandpa Blakeslee. He used to say he didn't like to go anywhere he hadn't been. You really want to marry this feller, don't you?" A stupid question, but she answered it.

"I think I do. I feel so proud when I'm with him, Mr. Tweedy. Before him, I never even met anybody who went to Harvard. He remembers every name and date in history. He can quote whole acts of Shakespeare. And he . . . he actually enjoys me! When I said that to my Sister Maggie—that he seems to enjoy me—she said, 'Why wouldn't he? He does all the talking.'"

"He sounds like a friend of mine," I said. "Pink Predmore. Old Pink went to Harvard. Went there a nice feller, came out a snob with a silly accent."

Her reply was defensive. "Hugh isn't like that. He's . . ." She cut off the subject. "I don't know why I'm telling you this. And it's inconsiderate of me to keep you standing there talking through a screen door."

"I like talkin' through screen doors. But I expect you need to wash off, Miss Klein, and I got to go by home and see my sister. She's leavin' tomorrow for college." I had turned and was headed down the steps when I remembered something. "You want to hear Sampson's secret?"

"Why, Mr. Tweedy! You wouldn't tell a child's secret!"

"He said to. Said tell you he was aimin' at Loma with that watermelon. You met Loma, Miz Williams. She's his half-sister and my aunt, and neither one of us is crazy about her. He felt bad bout hittin' you, but I think he felt worse bout missin' her. You sure did shut Aunt Loma up, Miss Klein."

"What?"

"About those German ancestors, how they came over in the seventeen-hundreds."

"Would she be impressed if I told her one of them got a land grant from the King of England?"

"Yeah, that would impress Loma."

She laughed. "But then I'd have to un-impress her by admitting he couldn't write, and that he lost his land in a wrestling match."

"I think even Loma would rather have a German wrastler in the family than somebody like our Cudn Hortense, the wife of a Blakeslee cousin. She's traced her ancestry back to British royalty. Claims her parlor furniture came from Lord Baltimore, and she's got ribbons tied across the chair arms so nobody can sit in them. Cudn Hortense looks down on anybody whose name isn't English or French."

Miss Klein sighed. "There are a mighty lot of folks like her, Mr. Tweedy. With a four-year-college degree I thought it would be easy to get a teaching job, but three towns turned me down. One school superintendent claimed the places were all filled, but a friend of mine who teaches there said they still had two openings. She thought the problem was my German name." Miss Klein was staring down at her hands. "Mama used to be so proud of our being German, because Germans are said to be smart. Since the war started, she never mentions it."

I wanted to see her laugh again. "They tell it on my Cudn T.D. how last year he refused to go to his daughter's weddin'. Said, 'I cain't bear to see Ethel git marrit to a man from Texas named Ertzberger.' His wife, Cudn Huldah, said, 'T. D., how could you forgit that you marrit a Holtzkaemper!' He said things were way different back then.

"Well, Miss Klein, I better get on over home. Like I said, my little sister's leavin' for college in the mornin'. I'll be seein' you soon, I hope?"

4

M Y SISTER, Mary Toy, was nineteen and a senior at Cox College in College Park, Georgia, near Atlanta. When I got home I found her in her room, packing for school. She'd come home early from the watermelon cutting.

Mama hadn't gone at all, despite Papa being president of the school board. She was in the kitchen, reaching into the warming oven above the big iron cookstove, taking out bowls of fried chicken, black-eyed peas, string beans, and a sweet potato soufflé. Mama never cooked at night on Sundays except maybe to slice tomatoes, since Queenie always cooked enough dinner to have it for supper. Still, there was always a rush to get it on the table early on account of Sunday night preaching.

"I cain't go to church with y'all tonight, Mama," I said. Lifting the thin linen cloth that kept flies off the bread, I picked up a cornstick. "I'll have to get on back to Athens. After dark it's slow goin' on a motorsickle."

"But you'll stay to supper, won't you, Will?" Mama didn't say it like an invite. More like an urgent plea. I realized she'd been crying.

"What's the matter, Mama?"

"I've got one of my sick headaches," she said, and burst into new tears. "Son, Loma's go'n go back to New York Wednesday mornin', and she's takin' . . . Will, she's takin' poor li'l . . ." When she got hold of herself, she looked towards the breakfast room door to be sure nobody was coming, and said in a low voice, "Will, the Yankee that Loma's engaged to, he's got a name so foreign I cain't pronounce it. And he's old! Will, what she came home for, she's go'n take Campbell Junior back up North with her!"

Campbell Junior had been staying with Mama and Papa for two years, ever since Aunt Loma set out on what she called her career. "Well," I reminded Mama, "you been sayin' the boy ought to be with his mother."

"But he's not go'n be with her! Will, that man she's engaged to? He's go'n pay for Campbell Junior at one of those military schools for rich boys. A boardin' school that's a hundred miles or more from New York City!"

"Good Lord! Loma don't know upside down from sideways! Campbell Junior cain't even hold his own with the boys here in Cold Sassy. Him in military school? He's never had a gun in his hands. Cain't stand thinkin' bout a bird or rabbit gettin' shot. Him in military school?"

Mama took it up. "They'll make fun of him for bein' fat and they'll mock his Southern accent, and . . . and I don't know what all." She looked around again at the door. Lowering her voice still more, she said, "If you ast me, he'll die on the vine up there, or cry his eyes out, one. He's bright as a penny and makes good marks but . . ."

"But he don't know beans bout bein' a boy."

"He's such a little gentleman. They'll make fun of his manners."

Campbell Junior wasn't a little gentleman. He was a little lady. That was the trouble. He'd grown up around too many women. Papa treated him like his own, but Papa was always at the store or at a church meeting.

"Will, stay to supper and talk Loma out of it," Mama begged. "Campbell Junior is petrified."

I knew that anything I said would just make Aunt Loma more determined. "I'll try to come back Tuesday, Mama, and talk to him." I pulled out my pocket watch. "I really cain't stay long now, but since supper's ready I'll eat with y'all."

Mama splashed some water on her face, blew her nose, told me to bring the sweet potato soufflé, and picked up the platter of fried chicken. "What with the shame of his daddy shootin' himself dead and all," she muttered, "that poor boy's had more'n his share already."

The family gathered, and we hadn't sat down at the table good before Aunt Loma said in her put-on Northern accent, "You must have felt like a white knight this afternoon, Will, rescuing that poor maiden from those great big old mean yellow jackets."

Loma always did know how to get my goat. When she was twelve and I was six, she decided to make me call her Aunt Loma. Mama, Papa, Granny, and even Grandpa had backed her up. They said she was a young lady now and I must show her proper respect.

Ever since I got grown, and especially after she got to be thirty, she'd been trying to make me go back to calling her just Loma. I could feel sorry for any woman worrying about getting old, even Aunt Loma. So I knew how to get back at her. Whenever I felt hateful, I'd stick my face in hers and say, "Ain't you my Aint Loma?"

That night around the supper table I said, "What I want to know, Aint Loma, is about this rich old Yankee you go'n marry. What's his name, and just how old is he? And how rich?"

"That's how rich!" Reaching across the table, Aunt Loma made a fist of her left hand and wagged that big old diamond ring at me.

Campbell Junior interrupted. "Cudn Will, I don't want to go up North," he whined, and bit glumly into a drumstick. I was his last hope. "Tell Mama I ain't go'n go to no military school."

"You'll like it once you get there," his mother said, not un-kindly. "But you might as well quit saying 'ain't' right now. And start cutting up your chicken. New York people don't say 'ain't' and they don't eat chicken with their fingers."

"Not even fried chicken?"

"They don't have fried chicken. They flour it and brown it and then steam it awhile. That's what they call fried chicken."

Campbell Junior stared at her, unbelieving, and slowly low-ered the drumstick to his plate.

"Never mind," Loma said. "Honey, you're going to have a daddy."

"I don't want a daddy. Uncle Hoyt is my daddy."

Smiling very sweetly at him, Loma said in exaggerated Southern, "Honey chile, you just go'n love Mr. Vitch."

"Mr. Vitch?" Papa repeated.

"The man I'm going to marry." She rattled off a twenty-syl-lable last name that I couldn't understand then and never could remember later. "Our friends call him Vitch. But when it's just us, I call him Mr. Rich Vitch. He likes that."

"Is he a Bolshevik?" asked Papa.

"Don't be silly, Brother Hoyt. Rich men aren't Bolsheviks."

"With a name like that he could be anything," said Papa.

Campbell Junior just sat there pushing his black-eyed peas into a mound with his fork and a cornstick.

"How," I asked, "did this man Itch make his money?"

Loma's face flushed. "I said Vitch. *Vitch.* I think he made it in the steel business. Or maybe coal. I'm not sure. But he told me he's doubled his money in the stock market."

I felt ornery enough to want to rake her a little. "You haven't said how old he is."

Loma hedged. "Wasn't Pa fifty-nine when he married Miss Love? I'd say Mr. Vitch is a little older than that. Maybe two or three years older."

I started to ask if it was more like five years or ten or maybe twenty, but I chanced to look over at Mama. She couldn't stand it when conversation got tense at the table—or anywhere else, for that matter.

Mary Toy spoke up. "Aunt Loma whistled at church this morning, Will. It was just beautiful!"

Loma blushed with pleasure. As if suddenly realizing Mary Toy was somebody she cared about, she asked, "What are you majoring in, honey?"

"Latin."

"Latin? I majored in elocution and it's gotten me all the way to the New York stage. But, Lord, what in the world can you do with Latin?"

Papa, about to bite into the pulley bone, waved it in protest. "Mary Toy's go'n teach Latin, Loma. That's what."

For a few minutes everybody just ate. I found myself staring at my blue-eyed, auburn-haired sister. She was flowering at college. Her face was plain, like Mama's, but radiant in a special way. She and I liked each other.

I glanced then from Mama at one end of the table to Papa at the other, noticing with surprise, as if I hadn't been around lately, that Mama looked several years older than Miss Love, though they were the same age, and that Papa, at forty-eight, had gone from stocky to portly. Most prosperous middle-aged men got portly, as if it took a protruding stomach to show off a gold watch fob.

The store had survived the depression of 1914. When farmers made money, the store did too and the war had sent cotton prices soaring, easing Papa's worries. He'd started talking about buying the farm in Banks County from his father and giving it to me.

Papa still didn't have a sense of humor. People said if Mr. Hoyt heard something funny in the morning, it was night before he laughed. I knew he was a good man though, except for that one never-mentioned event that hung in the air at home. I wished he'd talk about it to me so I could tell him I didn't really hold it against him. Well, maybe he knew I didn't. We had got a lot closer since Grandpa Blakeslee died. When I was a boy I never noticed how Papa doted on me. I was too busy doting on Grandpa, despite Papa was always saying I made him proud.

What hung in the air right now was the family's unspoken objection to Mr. Vitch. Campbell Junior's fork screeched across his plate, Mama set her tea glass in its coaster, Mary Toy fiddled with her napkin ring. The loudness of these small sounds was finally interrupted by Loma's voice.

She didn't start off talking loud, just tight and bitter. "Y'all don't want Campbell Junior to get the education he deserves, do you? Here he's got a chance to go to a fine boarding school and you want to keep him stuck in P.C.—a backward town if I ever saw one."

Papa was indignant. Speaking as president of the school board, he said, "For Pete's sake, Loma, Campbell Junior cain't get a better education anywhere than right here. Mary Toy, pass the sugar. Chi'ren are lucky who grow up in a small town."

Loma snapped back at him, "You're the epitome of small town, Brother Hoyt. You think the city limits of P.C. are the boundary of the world. Even Atlanta"—she sputtered—"to you Atlanta is just the Southeastern Fair every fall. And you think New York is on the other side of the moon."

"I've been to New York City, you know. How you think we'd stock the store if I didn't go up there? But I tell you one thing, young lady. Anybody who'd deliberately go live in New York City is . . ."

"See what I mean? What this is all about tonight is y'all never did want me to go to New York, and now you don't want me to marry a Yankee." She glared around the table. "Y'all are so smug—you more than anybody, Will." Really gearing up, she had lapsed into Southern. "Why do y'all hate me? Why cain't . . . why cain't I live my life like I want to? Y'all are all like Pa. I had my big chance years ago, when that tourin' Shakespeare company asked me to join the troupe. But, oh no, Pa said, 'Loma, you ain't go'n be no actress, so hesh up. I ain't ago'n let you do it.' I'll never forget the way he said it, like he was puttin' his foot down on me, and squashin' me. Then everybody in town had to have their say. 'Lord hep Loma if'n she ends up a actress.' I said someday I'll be doin' command performances for King Edward the Seventh, and they said even if I did, I'd never live down the taint. Why does everybody hate me?"

"Now, Loma," I said. "Now, Loma, don't . . ."

"Don't you don't me, Will Tweedy! It's all y'all's fault I married Campbell Williams. Pa said, 'You ain't marryin' thet fool, Loma. I ain't a-go'n let you.' Well, I showed Pa. But I'd have thought twice if he'd left me alone."

Campbell Junior's head hung down like a rosebud that had withered before it could open. Nobody said a word. As I'd just been reminded, if you talked back to Aunt Loma, it only fed the fire.

"Everybody said I couldn't make a livin' in New York City, but I did."

"Now, Loma," said Mama. "We just think you ought to marry your own kind."

"Mr. Vitch is my own kind. He cares about the finer things of life. And I'm go'n marry him. And I'm go'n keep on with my career, no matter what he or anybody else says. I found out there's not much future for an actress with a Southern accent who can only play Shakespeare and Abraham Lincoln's wife. But I'm not just any two-bit bo-hem'en. You'd know that if any of you had ever bothered to come see me perform. Y'all say you're too busy to come. Main thing, y'all are ashamed of my bein' an actress. You may like to know I've been offered a part in a real play! Mr. Vitch thinks I ought to quit the theater when we marry, but I've told him and told him . . ."

She stopped. Her face was steamy red. In a frenzy, she raked her fingers through the short red curls, then clutched her forehead and threw her head back like in a New York melodrama. "I asked why y'all hate me. But I know why. Y'all are jealous.

You'd like to be out of this hick town too, wouldn't you? Well, Campbell Junior's go'n be out of it, and have a chance to be somebody. He's not . . ."

"Loma Williams, shut up!" yelled Papa, banging his fist on the table.

I thought she'd start crying or light into Papa, one. But she didn't do either. Just pursed her lips and raised her chin—and shut us all out.

It was Mama who looked ready to break apart.

We all fell to eating again, or trying to. For once I couldn't think of a thing to say. But Mary Toy did.

With a forkful of string beans suspended halfway to her mouth, she grinned around the table as if Loma had just been chattering about somebody's mah-jongg party or the price of French perfume. "Let me tell the funniest thing!" said Mary Toy, then took time to chew her beans before she told it. "You know I went over to Athens last week? I went for a lecture by a famous woman Latin scholar. She read from a prepared speech. But all of a sudden she stopped, just stood there staring at her paper. Finally, shaking her head she said, 'This is certainly strange. Here's a word I never heard of. I can't imagine what it means, but it's in my handwriting! It's spelled H-E-R-E.'"

The faces around our supper table went blank. Campbell Junior was the first to laugh. He never had been dull-witted.

"H-E-R-E," Mama murmured. "H-E-R-E." Then it dawned on her—and the rest of us. "That spells *here!* Just plain old HERE!"

"Hear, hear!" I said, and even Aunt Loma got off her high horse and laughed. All of us did.

Then Mary Toy changed the subject again. "On the train ride home," she said, looking at me, "I saw that redheaded Sorrows boy. You remember the Sorrowses, Will."

"Yeah, they moved to Commerce a few years ago. Julian Sorrows was in my class. We called him Julie."

"That's right. Julie. He's the one I saw. He told me he had enlisted in the Army. He seemed so proud."

I knew what Mary Toy was saying: why hadn't I enlisted yet. And I knew Mama and Papa were sitting there hoping I never would. Her question and their dread hung in the air. Even to my own family I was embarrassed to admit I got turned down just for being skinny. Mary Toy and Loma wouldn't believe it, and Mama and Papa would want to starve me to death.

I marveled how easy it had been to tell Sanna Klein.

Of course I was registered for the draft—one of 120,000 white boys registered in Georgia. "Did you know that more'n a hundred thousand Georgia Negroes are registered?" I asked casually. "If they keep callin' up our colored boys, Southern farmers sure will be hurtin' for wages hands. Already are hurtin' from so many colored families movin' up North, and now they're worried about the Army's draftin' jarheads."

"Jarheads?" asked Campbell Junior.

"I'm talkin' about mules, son. Last week the paper said the United States has already shipped a hundred thousand mules to France, and three hundred thousand horses. They pull artillery and ammunition wagons."

Papa was always uneasy with war talk, whereas Mary Toy was obsessed with it. She had a sweetheart, an engineering student at Georgia Tech in Atlanta. Now she said he'd written that aviators were being trained on the Tech campus, and that he wanted to apply to be one.

"That's what I'd like to do," I said. "Fly an air machine. I expect they want lightweight aviators." I glanced at Papa. When he didn't say anything, I added, "I expect aerial fightin' will get more and more important as the war goes on."

Mary Toy put in eagerly, "Remember what Grandpa Blakeslee said his granddaddy said? How someday people would ride through the air? Grandpa said folks thought the old man had lost his mind."

"I wish it was still just a prediction," said Mama. "Imagine, flyin' through the sky! The very idea scares me half to death."

Campbell Junior nodded. "Me too. I'd just bout soon fly, though, as go to a old military school full of Yankees."

Sitting beside him, I patted his knee, then pushed back my chair. "Son, I got to head on back to Athens. But Tuesday I'm go'n come to Cold Sassy, and I'm go'n take you to the drugstore and we'll get some ice cream. I'll buy you the big dish. Mama, I hate to eat and run, but I don't want to let the road get dark on me. Aint Loma, I'll see you Tuesday too. I'll kiss you good-bye then."

She always knew when I was teasing. "You don't exactly have to kiss me Tuesday, either," she said, smiling as I stood up. "But I hope you will." She wagged her left hand in my face again, and the diamond sparkled.

5

I HAD already set up Tuesday to go see Mr. Ambrose Hall, whose one-horse farm was just south of Cold Sassy on the road to Commerce. To get there I took the early afternoon freight train from Athens, riding high in the cab with the engineer, Mr. Talkington. We'd been friends ever since I saved him from killing me on Blind Tillie Trestle when I was fourteen. I was fooling around up there on the trestle when his train came thundering onto the tracks, headed right towards me. I quick stretched myself out thin between the rails and the train ran over me, but I lived to tell it. All of which happened the same day Grandpa Blakeslee eloped with Miss Love. Now I rode with Mr. Talkington anytime I couldn't wait for the passenger train to Cold Sassy.

I said good-bye to Mr. Talkington in Cold Sassy, borrowed Papa's Buick, drove out to see Mr. Ambrose, then back to Cold Sassy, where Campbell Junior was waiting for me on Papa's front steps.

When we got to the drugstore, Dr. Clarke, the pharmacist, was behind the counter. He piled an extra scoop on Campbell Junior's big-dish ice cream. "That ought to hold you from here to New York City," he said, sliding it across the counter. "You want a big dish, Will?"

"Yessir. I got to fatten up."

"You been eatin' like a horse ever since you got legs, Will, but you still look like a crane. You'll use up this much ice cream just twitchin' your shoulders."

"I reckon I picked up that habit from my granddaddy. He was a champion shoulder-twitcher."

"For a fact he was," said the druggist. "But, Will, if you want to gain weight, my advice is get married. I never knew a young man didn't gain after the weddin'. I was up twenty pounds in three months. Campbell Junior, how bout a Co-Cola?"

The boy looked at me. I nodded and said we'd both have a Coke.

Dr. Clarke put each Coca-Cola glass under the syrup spout, then under the carbonated water spout, stirred with a long spoon, chipped some ice off the big block, spooned it in, and handed over the drinks.

"No charge, Will. I mean for the boy's extra scoop and his Co-Cola. Campbell Junior, do yourself proud in that Yankee school, hear? And when you get back home, come tell me if they make Co-Colas up yonder as good as I do."

"Yessir. Thank you, sir. But maybe they don't drink Co-Colas up North, Dr. Clarke. Mama says they don't eat fried chicken."

"Everybody drinks Co-Colas, son. Even Yankees."

As we sat down at one of the little round tables, white-topped on black iron legs, I nodded towards the ceiling fan. "Eat fast, Campbell Junior. The breeze feels mighty good, but it sure can melt ice cream."

While we ate, I told him about going to New York City with Papa on a buying trip for the store. I didn't tell him how scared I was, being only seven and having heard all my life how mean damnyankees were.

Campbell Junior got a little excited while I was raving on about the wonders of New York. But then he started talking about leaving home and all. "Miss Willa had a good-bye party for me today," he said sadly. "She made a cake for the whole class. She gave me the biggest piece, Cudn Will, and she ain't been my teacher but two days! I begged Mama to let me go to school in the mornin', just till time for the train, but she says I cain't."

When we got back to the house, I stood on the veranda with him, trying to think how to cheer him up. Then I remembered my buckeye. I pulled it out of my pants pocket and handed it to him. "For luck, son."

"Thank you, Cudn Will. Gosh, that makes forty-two!"

"Forty-two?"

"Wait a minute, can you?" He disappeared into the house and came back holding up a cloth tobacco sack. It bulged with buckeyes. "Everybody in my class brought me one today," he said proudly. "For luck in my new school."

"Well, that ought to do it, Campbell Junior. If you run short of money, you can sell some to those Yankee boys."

"I bet they never heard of a buckeye," he said.

We shook hands, man to man. But then I hugged him. Hard.

"You'll do fine, big boy. Just remember where you're from and who your folks are. Act proud."

He went inside, trying to be brave.

Aunt Loma was in the backyard out near Mama's flower pit, digging up a magnolia seedling. It was only a foot high, but it had five or six big waxy green leaves.

Lighting a cigar, I watched a minute, then asked, "What you doin', Aunt Loma?"

"I'm gettin' me a magnolia tree." She didn't sound Yankee at all. Her short red hair, damp with sweat, had shrunk into tight curls.

"You go'n carry it on the train?"

"In my lap all the way, if I have to."

I took the trowel out of her hands. "Let me do that. You need a bigger pot."

"I cain't hold too big a pot," she protested.

"But if it's too little a pot you won't have enough dirt to nourish the tree. I'll get one out of the flower pit. And we need some good black dirt instead of this red clay."

She stood there watching, rubbing her hands together to get off the dirt, while I dug up the seedling and potted it with black dirt from out by the cowshed. "Don't let it dry out," I said, watering it from the rain barrel, "and give it plenty of light. Do you have a window facin' south?"

"How do you tell south?"

I explained as simply as I knew how. "If sun comes in a window in the mornin', that's the east side of the buildin'. If it's sunny in the afternoon, that's the west side. If it doesn't come in at all, that's north. The best exposure is southern. Come winter, sunlight will flood into a south window." I didn't say how dumb it was for anybody to be thirty-one years old and not know such, though I was tempted. "I hope you don't expect to show off this li'l old thing. It won't impress anybody."

Brushing dirt off the pot with my hands, I looked at Aunt Loma. She was wiping her eyes. "I'm not takin' it to impress anybody," she said, her lip quivering. "I'm takin' it for myself. It. . . . I need somethin' to remind me of home."

I handed her the seedling. "Mama has a scrap left over from that new oilcloth on the kitchen table. Tie some around the pot, why don't you? So it won't get your dress dirty. Well, good-bye, Aunt Loma." I put my arms around both of them—her and the baby magnolia. "Look after this good, hear, and look after your boy. And you look after yourself."

"You too, Will. Do you still see Trulu?"

"No," I said firmly.

"Just asking. You're too good for her anyway. Well, good-bye, Will."

"You haven't said when you're gettin' married."

"Some time next month. In New York, of course. Not here."

"Mama will have a conniption fit."

"It can't be helped." Her tone was formal, defensive.

"I don't know as I can get off work long enough to make the trip."

"It won't be a family kind of wedding," she said quickly, "Just the two of us, and a justice of the peace. And Campbell Junior, of course, and two of our friends for witnesses."

I was about to say nobody in our family had ever got hitched in a courthouse when she added, "Pa and Miss Love did it that way, remember." Raising her chin, she said again, "Good-bye, Will," and started up the back steps with her magnolia tree.

Campbell Junior wasn't the only one trying to act brave.

"Aunt Loma?" I called after her. "Uh, take the oilcloth off when you get there, hear? The roots'll rot if it cain't drain."

She nodded.

I called again. "Don't worry if the leaves fall off. That won't mean it's dead."

Though it wasn't anywhere near train time, I didn't want to hang around. I'd had about all the sad good-byes I could take. I decided to amble on up to Miss Love's. Check over the animals. See who was home.

On the way I met Sampson. "What you got there, son?" I asked.

"A present for Campbell Junior." He proudly held up a big contraption of nailed-together wood scraps. "See, sir, he can mash this and that and that, and then turn this magic wand down towards Georgia and wish himself right back home. If he does everything right, the wish will come true. I invented it!"

After inspecting and admiring and not saying it had about as much chance of going to New York as Campbell Junior had of staying here, I asked Sampson if he thought Miss Klein was a good teacher.

He said she sure was strict.

I asked if Miss Klein and Miss Clack and Miss Hazelhurst had got home yet.

"No, sir. All the teachers stayed in after school. They had to go to the principal's office," he said, spinning a loosely nailed stick on his invention. "I don't think they've been bad. They just had to go meet."

"Yeah, well, son, I'm on my way to your house. It's time to inspect the livestock." Every so often I'd stop by to check over Papa's cow, Grandpa's old mule, Miss Love's gelding, known as Mr. Beautiful, and Sampson's pony, Miss H, named by him when he was four and learning the alphabet. "You still puttin' that salve on H's leg?" I asked.

The boy hedged. "Uh, most of the time Loomis does it, Uncle Will. Mother pays him to feed and water, so I just asked him to doctor H's leg, too, while he's at it."

"It's not your place to tell Loomis what to do."

"He said he'd be glad to. Just glad to."

"Well, you're old enough now to do all the stable work. You're not even feedin' and curryin' the pony?"

"Why should I, Uncle Will? I don't ride her anymore. She's got so little, and all she wants to do is walk or trot. Hey, just let me run give this to Campbell Junior. I'll be right back. I want to show you my new circus trick on Mr. Beautiful!"

"You're gettin' too big for your britches, but you're not big enough for that tall horse. Stay off of him, Sampson."

His face reddened. "Mother lets me. I don't have to mind you."

"And I don't have to fool with a smart aleck named Simpson." I turned to walk away. He grabbed my arm.

"Please don't call me Simpson, Uncle Will. Cause of Miss Klein, everybody at school calls me Simpleton now. Please, Uncle Will? I was just mad at you. I didn't mean it, sir."

I looked at him hard. "Try being a friend to Campbell Junior this afternoon, Sampson. He's in bad need of one right now."

6

WHEN I got back to Miss Love's house after checking the animals, I was naturally hoping Sanna Klein would be there. She wasn't, and it occurred to me that even if she came in before I had to leave, she probably wouldn't be by herself. So I sat down at the kitchen table and wrote her a note, using my office stationery with the letterhead *Cooperative Extension Service, Georgia State College of Agriculture, Athens, Georgia.*

> Dear Miss Klein,
> I would still like to see you Sunday night provided you get in from Jefferson early enough. I plan on being in Cold Sassy anyway, so you don't need to let me know ahead. I'll come down to Miss Love's right after supper to see if you're back yet, and we can go to church. I often spend Sunday night with my folks and ride the early freight train back to Athens next morning.
>
> Please excuse the eccentric appearance of this paper. It's been folded up in my pants pocket.
>
> Hoyt Willis Tweedy

Miss Love kept envelopes on top of her desk. I wrote "To Miss Klein" on one and dropped the letter in the teachers' mail basket on the hall table by the stairs. I couldn't help noticing Miss Klein had a letter there from Mrs. Henry K. Jolley in Mitchellville, and two more in long business envelopes with the embossed return address *Blankenship, Crowe, and Blankenship, Attorneys-at-Law, Jefferson, Georgia.* In a bold scrawl above the print was written "Hugh A. Blankenship, Jr."

I knew about the legal firm of Blankenship and Crowe. I used to go over to Jefferson sometimes for court week with Pink Predmore and his lawyer-daddy, and if it was a trial that amounted to anything, you could count on Mr. Blankenship or Mr. Crowe representing one side or the other. I was discouraged for a second or two but tossed my note in the basket anyway.

I blame everything that's happened between Sanna and me on the sight of that name scrawled so bold and confident, as if he and his daddy's firm had legal rights to her. Before that moment I'd only been smitten by Sanna Klein's beauty. Suddenly I was determined to marry her.

That's what I was thinking as I headed for the front door, but I stopped in my tracks when I realized that the veranda was occupied. I recognized the voice of Miss Alice Ann Boozer. "Did you know Loma Blakeslee Williams come in on the train last week from New York City?"

"Everybody this side the cemetery knows it," said a voice I couldn't quite place. "Why you think I wouldn't know a thing like that?"

"Cause you been gone, Miz Jones," said Miss Alice Ann.

Of course. The other lady was the wife of the Reverend Brother Belie Jones.

I knew I ought to go speak to them, but not being in much of a mood for woman talk, I tiptoed over to Miss Love's wing chair by the window and sat down with a magazine. But I couldn't read with those voices floating right in. I heard Miss Alice Ann ask Mrs. Jones how was her sister.

"Sister's really on the down-go," said the preacher's wife.

"But I couldn't just stay on there till Kingdom Come. Like I told her, Brother Jones needs lookin' after too. So yesterd'y I hired her a colored girl and took the train home."

"Where is it she lives? I never can remember."

"A little coal-minin' town — Brilliant, in Alabama."

"Funny name."

I could hear rocking chairs just going to town out there. Then one stopped and Miss Alice Ann spoke again. "When's Miss Love go'n git here?"

"Any minute now. I 'phoned down at the store, and she said meet her here, she'd be on terreckly. I've got my good fall hat in this hatbox. She's go'n make it over. I'm sure glad you happened along to keep me comp'ny."

With the chairs going *rockity-rockity-rockity*, I didn't have to be out there to see Mrs. Jones, a tall stout lady in her sixties with swimmy eyes and a red face, probably fanning herself with a piece of cardboard, or Miss Alice Ann, so fat she didn't have a lap and so short her little feet barely touched the floor.

Years ago Miss Alice Ann had caught me kissing Lightfoot McLendon in the cemetery and told it all over town. I hated her back then, but now she was just an old lady. Suddenly she said, "I bet you ain't heard about Loma Williams splashin' her bare chest with cold well water, Miz Jones. I mean BARE chest! Done it out on the Tweedys' back porch!"

"My land!"

"And she was wearin' her shirtwaist tucked into some long baggy purple pants! I seen a movin' pitcher show one time with some ha-reem women dancin' in thin baggy pants. That's all right for heathen women, I reckon, but it don't speak well of a Christian lady to wear such."

"No, it don't."

"Anyhow, Queenie said Loma splashed water on herself awhile and then buttoned up that shirtwaist and commenced to stretch. This-a-way and that-a-way, up, down, and sideways.

Queenie told Miz Predmore she got skeered Miss Loma'd had a stroke, she went to breathin' so hard! Time she got done she was downright raspin'—like a peach seed had got stuck in her th'oat!" Sitting inside by the open window, I nearly laughed out loud. Mama hadn't told me all this.

"Loma told Queenie how in New York City she stands in front of a open window to splash herself—even when hit's a-snowin'. Said you sho do feel good when you git th'ew."

"It don't take a genius to know why you'd feel good to git th'ew," said Mrs. Jones, "but it'd take a fool to think it up in the first place. All I got to say, folks sure do turn strange when they go live in New York City."

"I reckon you know Loma's done got herself engaged to one a-them Yankees. Shoo, now. Git away!" she yelled all of a sudden. "I think God invented yellow jackets just to drive folks off of their porches. Specially in hot muggy weather like we been havin'. Shoo, shoo! Git! Shoo! What Loma ought to do, she ought to come on back to P.C. where she belongs."

"I don't know as she belongs down here anymore," Mrs. Jones put in. "A woman who'd smoke and wear pants? And make her livin' on a vaudeville stage?"

Almost in hugging distance of the conversation, I wanted in the worst way to go join in. But I knew if I went out there, they'd just go to talking about the weather.

"Of course she don't admit she works in vaudeville," Miss Alice Ann was saying. "Loma calls it a the-ater. But lately she's been doin' mannequin work, too!"

"No!"

"Yes'm! She told somebody that's how she met this man that she's a-go'n marry. Her and some other ladies was modelin' Gossard corsets one mornin', s'posed to be just lady buyers in the auditorium, but halfway th'ew, somebody spied a man hidin' under a seat off to the side, and hit was him! Loma told it herself. She thinks it's funny."

I sure thought it was funny. But not one hee-hee or ha-ha came from the preacher's wife. "I bet he got hustled out in a hurry," she said with disgust.

"I speck he did. But Loma said he come backstage later and ast her to go eat with him, and Lord if she didn't have any better sense'n to do it! He took her to one a-them fancy rest'rants. I reckon with him bein' so old, and hit daylight and a nice place, Loma figured he couldn't do her no harm."

So that's how Aunt Loma got her diamond.

"Too bad she didn't stay here and marry Herbert Sloan back when he ast her to. Li'l Herbert, I mean. Not his daddy. But they say Loma said Li'l Herbert was pussy-footy—and besides, she couldn't stand the name Herbert, and anyhow she wouldn't marry anybody short as him if his name was Valentino."

Mrs. Jones snorted. "I bet if Loma had of known Li'l Herbert would inherit that pile of money, he'd of looked two feet taller. All I got to say is anybody mean enough to say a thing like that about such a sweet little man deserves to marry a Yankee. I never could understand how she's had so many men chasin' after her. I got to admit it, though, she's helt on to her looks."

"Maybe so. But not her brains," said Miss Alice Ann.

"You know what she's come home for? To git Campbell Junior and—"

The big clock in the hall struck. Mrs. Jones said, "I wonder what's helt Miss Love up. I got to git on home."

Miss Alice Ann said she needed to get on, too. I heard the chairs rock free, knew the ladies had stood up, and decided to go out there and say howdy.

Just as I was about to open the screen door, I heard the preacher's wife say, "I didn't get to the watermelon cuttin'. Did you? Did you meet the new teachers?" She lowered her voice to a whisper. "They say one of'm is real foreign-lookin'."

"That's Miss Klein," Miss Alice Ann whispered back.

"C-L-I-N-E?" Miss Jones whispered. "That's an Irish name. We don't need any Irish Catholics in Progressive City."

"Hit ain't spelt C-L-I-N-E. Hit's spelt K-L-E-I-N."

I heard them sink back down into the rockers.

"Must be she's a Jew girl."

"Sh-h-h, Miz Jones. Might be she's to home."

"Only Jew we ever had here was Mr. Izzie Lieberman, who had the furniture store," Mrs. Jones whispered. "They say he drank hot tea out of a tall glass. But everybody liked him."

"Miss Klein ain't no Jewess. She went to the Methodist church with Miss Love Sunday."

"Well, she must be some kind of hyphenated American," said the preacher's wife.

"What you mean, hyph'nated?"

"Oh, there's Irish-Americans and German-Americans, and British-Americans, and I-talian-Americans and—well, hyphenated is what the politicians call all those."

The chairs commenced rocking.

"Wonder why we don't say Indian-Americans instead of American Indians," Miss Alice Ann mused. "Maybe because they got here first. What are we, Miz Jones? American-Americans?"

"Think, Miss Alice Ann. The hyphenateds aren't us. They're the immigrants. Like those Irish Catholics. They came over to this country starvin'. A potato famine drove'm here, and they ought to be thankin' the hands that fed them. But no, they're sidin' with the Kaiser in the war."

"Why come?"

"Cause Ireland hates England. Always has. I read how up North a Irish-American will get yellow paint slapped on their house if they don't buy Liberty Bonds. German-Americans too, of course. I can see why German-Americans are pro-tes-tin' us gettin' in the war—after all, we're fightin' their brothers and cousins. Still, if Miss Klein's got kinfolks in the German Army, it don't make sense to pay her forty dollars a month to teach school in Progressive City. Not with our boys over there in France gettin' gassed by the Kaiser and dyin' and all."

For a minute or two neither lady spoke. Then Miss Alice Ann said, "I'm thinkin' on Mr. Izzie. Wonderin' why he went back to Germany."

"They say he went back to get marrit."

"Wonder is he fightin' in the Kaiser's army?"

"I doubt it. The Kaiser don't like Jews."

"You know, Miz Jones, ever since Mr. Izzie left to go back to Germany, they ain't been any dark-skinned white folks in this town—not less'n you count that Armenian in the graveyard. Remember him? Come here sellin' perfume soap and died on us, and weren't nothin' to do but bury him?"

"Law, I'd clean forgot about him!" exclaimed Mrs. Jones. "Remember the big fuss about whether he ought to be buried in the cemetery? Somebody had heard that Armenians are Christians, but nobody knew for certain."

Miss Alice Ann sighed. "LeGrand Tribble donated his extra lot, remember? Said weren't nobody left in his fam'ly to put there, or to get mad at him for invitin' a stranger in, either one. And Brother Jones sure give that man a nice graveside ceremony, Miz Jones."

"He thought it was the right thing. I mean in case he was a Christian."

"Mr. Boozer said the reason all us ladies insisted on it, we liked his soap and he had them foreign good looks." A moment of silence for the dead, and she added, "I don't see as he'll ever git a marker, though. Who'd pay for it?"

They stood up again, and I was halfway to the door when Mrs. Jones said, "Oh, I meant to ast you. What about Will Tweedy?" I drew back as they moved towards the steps. "Did he join the Army while I was gone?"

"Not as I know of."

"I just don't see how he's managed to stay out. Nothin's wrong with him."

Miss Alice Ann said the trouble was my daddy. "Mr. Hoyt just goes to pieces when anybody asts has Will joined up. Claims Will is a heap more use to the war on the home front than if he was a-totin' a gun."

Mrs. Jones had just one question. "What could be more use to the war than him doin' his patriotic duty?"

I wanted to stalk out there and take up for myself and Papa too, but what could I say? "I've always been crazy about that boy," added the preacher's wife, "but even before I left to go see about Sister, folks were sayin' looks like Will's a slacker. I don't think Mr. Hoyt ought to carry on so. He ain't the only daddy that cain't bear to think of his boy in foreign trenches."

I retreated. Sneaked down the hall, out the back door and down the steps, and wandered into what used to be Granny Blakeslee's rose garden.

For the first time in my life I hated Cold Sassy and all it stood for. Call it Progressive City or Branch Water, I didn't care. "I don't belong here anymore," I muttered to the rose bushes among the tangled expanse of jimson weed, honeysuckle, trumpet vine, and Johnson grass. I took a cigar and a match out of my shirt pocket, scratched the match across a rock, lit up, and stood there puffing smoke and staring—at nothing. I was suddenly overwhelmed by a great homesickness for Granny Blakeslee and Grandpa.

Granny had died when I was fourteen. Grandpa and I were out here cutting roses at daybreak on the morning of her funeral. I remembered how he had straightened up, indicating the dewy splendor of color around us with the stub of his left arm, and said, "Miss Mattie Lou shore was a fool about roses. Did you know, boy, she's got over sixty different kinds?" Later, as he was lining the open grave pit with roses, tears had spilled down on his cheeks.

That was June the fourteenth, 1906. Three weeks later, Grandpa Blakeslee told my mother and Aunt Loma he aimed to marry Miss Love Simpson, the young milliner at his store. He said Miss Mattie Lou was dead as she'd ever be and he needed him a housekeeper, and a wife would just be cheaper than hiring a colored woman. That afternoon he took Miss Love over to Jefferson in his mule-drawn buggy. They got married at the courthouse.

When Grandpa died the next May, I overheard Miss Alice Ann Boozer say, "It serves him right, after the way he done Miss Mattie Lou. Married that Yankee woman and didn't live a year." Cold Sassy eventually accepted the fact of the marriage. But even now, ten years later, nobody ever let anybody forget it.

Her first summer as a widow, Miss Love told me she intended to keep up Miss Mattie Lou's rose garden. But her talent was making hats and money, not growing roses. After Sampson was born, in February 1908, the sixty varieties were on their own—or, as we say in the South, "own their own."

I could have waited for Miss Sanna Klein another fifteen minutes and still made the train, but could I really compete with a Harvard lawyer named Blankenship who could quote Shakespeare? I didn't even like Shakespeare. I might have if the teachers hadn't made us read all those footnotes. I could do a pretty good job quoting "To a Daffodil" or "To a Mouse"—*Wee, sleekit, cow'rin, tim'rous beastie, o what a panic's in thy breastie*—but that's hardly a love sonnet.

If this Hugh Junior was so smart, why wasn't he in the Army? I bet his daddy was busy pulling strings to get him a cushy lawyer job in Washington.

I left Granny's garden and cut through a gap in the hedge to the backyard of the house next door, where Miss Effie Belle Tate and Mr. Bubba used to live. Their niece, Miss Hyta Mae Brown, had a few boarders and ran a public dining room. Miss Love's three teachers took all their meals over there.

The smell of vegetable soup drifted from the kitchen window as I walked by. One of the cooks, Evaline, came out to the side of the back porch and poured her soapy dish water on the fig bush. "Evenin', Mist' Will!" she called. "Dish water sho' do make figs grow. You wont som'a my good ole soup and cawn-bread, son? Come on in de kitchen, I dish you up some. Hit'll put meat on dem bones you got for laigs."

"That's hard to pass up, Evaline, but I got to catch a train." I walked as far as Miss Hyta Mae's pigeon cote before I turned towards South Main, far enough to avoid being seen from Miss Love's veranda.

If I passed anybody on the sidewalk, if any children were playing in their yards, if any lady waved at me from her porch, I didn't notice. Walking fast, puffing furiously on the cigar, I kept repeating the name Progressive City, over and over. At the depot, I stared at the sign as if it had been put up only that morning. For ten years it had declared this was PROGRESSIVE CITY to train passengers, and for ten years I'd kept reading it COLD SASSY.

Well, no more. All of a sudden the name Cold Sassy was as dead as Grandpa and Granny, and my old dog T.R., and Miss Effie Belle and Mr. Bubba. Growing up, I'd been made to feel like I was the town's great hope for the future. Everybody proud of me, ready to make allowances. Now this was Progressive City, and I was just somebody who used to live here. My home town had gone on without me in the six years I'd been in Athens. And I had gone on without it, except for family.

The truth was, I had outgrown Progressive City. I wondered why I never understood that before.

The next day I saw the house in Mitchellville where Sanna Klein's sister lived, and where Sanna had grown up.

7

THERE'S no direct railroad line to Mitchellville. You got there by train; then somebody has to meet you five miles away at the depot in 1888, Georgia, a town named for the year it got incorporated. When my train pulled in, old Mr. Charlie Cadenhead was already there, waiting in a battered Model-T Ford.

Mr. Charlie ran a dairy farm just south of Mitchellville and had done considerable cross-breeding of cattle. And Professor Harris, who ran the county agent program, wanted the dairyman's figures regarding increase or decrease in milk production.

Mr. Charlie was a short, white-haired, peculiar-shaped man. Had a big square head, thick neck, massive chest, bulging stomach, small hips, short arms, and short thin legs. He had on a blue denim shirt, a big straw hat, and overalls, and he smelled of chewing tobacco and hay.

Soon as he found out my home town was Progressive City, he said, "Y'all got a new teacher this year, Miss Sanna Klein. She's the prettiest little thang I ever seen. You met her yet?"

"Yessir."

He didn't give me time to say more. Spitting out the window as we bounced on a rough dirt road with nothing but woods and farmland to either side, he shouted above the motor's racket, "I tell you what, Mr. Tweedy. Iffen I was fifteen year younger and not marrit, little Sanna wouldn't never have even got to P.C. I said so to her, on the steps of the post office, day before she left here. She just smiled and patted my arm." Mr. Charlie honked at two boys walking on the road, and waved as we passed, leaving them in a wake of dust. "I told her, 'I reckon you heard how teachers don't last more'n a year in that town.' Just teasin', you know, but Miss Sanna thought I meant they git fired. I told her, 'No'm, they git marrit.' She cain't blush, Mr. Tweedy, on account of she's got that dark complexion. But she looked mighty flustered, sayin' marriage was the fartherest thang from her mind. I said, 'Yes'm, but everybody knows a town's got to keep gittin' in good new bloodlines if it's go'n keep a-growin'—just like me with my dairy herd.'"

We were on the little wagon road that led up to his farmhouse, and Mr. Charlie turned to give me a wide grin and a wink. "Are you a single man, Mr. Tweedy?"

"Look out, sir!" I shouted. A big white hen, frantic and squawking, was back-and-forthing across the road not knowing which way to go. But when she decided the only way to go was up, she nearly hit the windshield in a panic of squawks and flailing wings.

Mr. Charlie stuck his head out the window and shouted back at her, "You dang dummy!" Then he turned to me and grumped, "That one's ready for the pot. Too old to lay aiggs, but she's Miss Emma's pet."

I saw the herd, copied Mr. Charlie's figures, helped him and Miss Emma eat a big dinner, and asked her if she'd give me the recipe for her whipped cream and chocolate pie for my mama—"that is, if you don't keep it secret."

Driving back through Mitchellville, Mr. Charlie went down a side street and slowed almost to a stop in front of a large white frame house. "That's where little Miss Sanna Klein growed up," he explained. "Come here when she was a little girl to live with the Henry Jolleys. Miss Maggie is her older sister. Mr. Henry's mayor of Mitchellville and has got his hands in just about every business around here. Owns the bank and sawmill and a little factory makin' shuttles out of dogwood for textile mills, and a furniture factory. That one's turnin' out rifle butts now for the U.S. Army. The mayor owns considerable land, too. Buys it cheap on the courthouse square whenever his bank forecloses on somebody. They's some that faults him, with good reason, but he shore done right by little Sanna, sendin' her th'ew four year at college like she was his blood kin. Well, you got a train to ketch."

Going on through town, Mr. Charlie waved towards a building and said that was Mayor Jolley's bank.

"The mayor is sump'm to see. Must weigh four hundret pounds. Everthin' bout him is big, cept he ain't tall. His whole face and head is fat—fat ears, fat lips, and his eyelids so swole up with fat you cain't hardly see his eyes. His face is always red, mainly cause he's bad to drank. That's his main fault. He thinks bootleggers are man's best friend. They say he told the sheriff to let them stills alone long as the boys don't hurt nobody. They pay him back in free moonshine.

"Now, Mitchellville ain't a place to think well of folks drankin' licker, but he's so friendly-like and heps so many folks, they just keep a-votin' for him. Course it heps a politician if he's got plenty of money and spreads it around. Like on Sarady mornin' . . . well, ever Friday night he and his drinkin' cronies play cards in Miss Maggie's parlor, which she don't like, but on Sarady mornin' he goes uptown, after a little nip to cure his hangover, full of jokes and generosity. He's really funny when he's had a little to drank. The deadbeats lay in wait for him. Always got hard-luck stories, and he's always ready for 'em with a pocketful of bills. I mean, he's ready for them and they ready for him.

"He's always had a soft heart for young folks. But it ain't just Miss Sanna he's hepped go to school. Many a boy with folks

havin' hard times—well, who ain't these days—he heps 'em
finish high school. I heard about a family on hard times, their
boy got the promise of a job in the freight yards in Atlanta, but
they couldn't scrape up enough train fare to get him there. He
ast the mayor to lend him ten dollars for his ticket and to see
him through the first week. He said Mr. Jolley give him twelve
and said, 'You don't owe it back. Just go make sump'm of yourself.'

"You never saw anybody want chi'ren bad as the Jolleys.
They always used to be takin' in somebody—orphans and
nieces and nephews and all like that. Then Miss Maggie, she
adopted her a little baby boy they call Lonzo. His mama died
when he was born and nobody thought the baby could live
and the daddy said she could take him if she wanted him. Well,
that baby warn't no bigger'n a fryin'-size chicken. Miss Maggie brought him home on the train on a pillow, and wadn't
nothin' but her wantin' that baby so bad kept him alive. Bout a
year later they finally had a little girl of their own. Annie Laurie started at Shorter College last week, and Lonzo is a junior
at Mercer. And Miss Sanna, well now, she's gone, too."

I looked at that big white house and tried to imagine Sanna
Klein as a little girl, maybe sleeping upstairs while the mayor
of Mitchellville got drunk and played cards in the parlor below.
I had no idea, then, that I'd soon be spending a night in that
house myself.

8

AT THE time I met Sanna, I'd been a county agent for two years.

Part of the job was treating sick livestock. Since farmers didn't trust college boys or book learning either one, they never sent for me till an animal was about dead.

Tell the truth, I didn't know all that much about veterinary medicine. The way I got by, I'd examine a sick cow and say to the farmer, "You called me too late. But I'll try to save her." That way, if she died it was his fault. If she lived, I was the greatest doctor in the world. The Ag School furnished me just one medicine, and no matter what the disease, I drenched with it. Drenching means you put the liquid medicine in a bottle, pull the animal's head way up, and pour the stuff down its throat. My first week as a county agent I found out you can't drench a hog. A hog will choke if you try to make him swallow with his head up. They never taught me that at the university.

Eventually I was doing everything from breeding and midwifing cows to castrating bulls, horses, and hogs. Most of them lived.

Manufacturers would send fertilizer or cow feed to the Ag School so we could give out samples to farmers. A lot of politics was involved. The college wanted the commissioners to support its new county agent program, so in actual fact it was the custom for free shipments of fertilizer or other products to go right to the commissioners for their own fields. We'd invite other farmers in the area to come see it poured on, and later to see the results.

Of course part of my job was talking. What Clarke County farmers didn't know from experience, they were supposed to learn from me, based on work being done at the agricultural experiment stations. I'd hold night meetings at schoolhouses for these strong men with rough hands and leathered faces, who came in the same overalls, denim shirts, and mud-caked brogans they'd worn in the fields all day. I'd tell them how to feed out their hogs and cattle to get more meat in a shorter time, when and what variety of corn to plant for the best yield, why they ought to quit pulling fodder for cattle when the corn is still green. "As all y'all know, the kernels are bigger if you let the ears mature," I explained. "And in the long run you'll produce more animal feed. We've proved it."

Naturally I talked about ways to head off the boll weevil. "Plant your cotton early, fertilize it good, and cultivate once a week so your crop will grow faster. Destroy the old cotton stalks this winter, and get rid of weeds and rubbish."

Because of the boll weevil, the 1917 cotton crop in south Georgia was off by more than three-fourths. In northeast Georgia half the cotton was damaged. That was reason enough to urge farmers to start diversifying. Go to hogs, beef cattle, more grain crops, field peas, white potatoes, watermelons, turnips, sugar cane. Some cotton farmers didn't even raise enough hay or corn for their own livestock feed, much less to have any to sell. With no cash crops, they had to let their cotton go on the market as soon as it got ginned and baled, regardless of price.

Farm labor was becoming a serious problem. In the past year and a half, sixty to seventy thousand Negroes had left Georgia and moved to cities like Cincinnati and Philadelphia. Once I made the mistake of trying to sympathize. "With so many col-ored folks leavin' and so many enlistin' in the Army or gettin' drafted, y'all are kind of up against it."

Angry voices rumbled in the room. "That shore is the truth!" yelled one man, his face flushing red. "How them colored think we can run a farm without no hep?"

"It makes me madder'n hell," said another, "the way they sneak off in the night. Anybody sneaks off, they know they doin' wrong. If we find out a nigger's plottin' to leave, Mr. Tweedy, we git us up a posse and go to the depot with guns."

"Yeah," said another. "Yeah, them colored boys git the mes-sage real quick. Real quick. They see us a-comin', they know they go'n miss that train."

A giant-size farmer, laughing, added, "And them that do git away, what's go'n happen to'm up North? They ain't go'n know nobody. Ain't go'n have no pickled pig feet or hambone or fat-back, ain't go'n have no collards, no turnip salat. And come winter, they go'n freeze to death."

A short stocky man stood up. "Well, now, how I look at it, are we Christians or ain't we? They got a right to go if'n . . ."

"Set down, Worth Haley! We talkin' bout crops rottin' in the fields. We talkin' bout plowin' for spring plantin'. A whole fam'ly of cotton pickers left out from my place the night I paid'm off, and never a thank-you to nobody for all that's been done for 'em."

"The State Department of Agriculture," I said, talking loud, "is lookin' into ways of addressin' this problem. They're en-couragin' white mill hands to try sharecroppin', or hire out for field work. Most used to live in the mountains, and—"

"Mr. Tweedy, I'd a long sight rather have colored hands and tenants than sour-lookin' whites," retorted the red-faced man. "Last year a sorry no-count white sharecropper on my farm shot his wife in the chicken yard and then kilt hisself in the hog pen. That goes to show what kind of trash they was. I'd of lost half a-their crop if I hadn't set my own farmhands to pickin' the dead man's cotton."

There aren't any better people in the world than farmers. But these men felt betrayed. The colored could leave, but they couldn't. I didn't bring up that subject again anywhere.

I spoke often to meetings of farm wives, telling them how to store corn for the family by brining, urging them to dry more fruits and vegetables. "And y'all put Leghorns in your hen houses. They're the best layers."

One night a gray-headed lady in a dress made out of feed sacks got up and told how to get rid of flies. She said, "Spray lavender water. Put it in one a-them glass atomizers, you know like per-fume comes in? I spray it all over my kitchen and dinin' room. They say flies jest cain't stand it, the smell, I mean. My husband says he cain't stand it either, and I ain't sure it heps, but the *Progressive Farmer* magazine said so. What you think, Mr. Tweedy?"

"Since your husband don't like lavender water, try using blue tablecloths. Flies really hate the color blue." They knew I was joking. "Or try to get you some screens for the windows."

"I know a lady got screens," said the woman, "and she is forever chasin' after flies with a swatter. You git screens, them flies cain't git out."

That just about covers my experience with county agenting. On October 2, 1917, I got fired.

In actual fact I was asked to take up a state job with the Agricultural Extension Service.

In the new job I traveled over the whole state, helping farmers and students learn how to build barns and silos and chicken houses, put in drainage ditches, and so forth.

One of my first assignments was at Young Harris College in Towns County. Boys studying agriculture had put up framing for a cow barn, and their professor wanted me to come cut the pattern for a gambrel roof—which I didn't know how to do. I found blueprints for a dairy barn but not for any gambrel roof. So I went out to Banks County to see old Mr. Luthie Fletcher, a carpenter. He used to take me fishing on the Hudson River when I was a boy. I said to him, "Mr. Luthie, let's go up to the mountains next Monday. I got to mark off timbers for a barn roof, but if you hep me, we can get in some fishin'."

I didn't tell him I'd never designed a gambrel roof. I put the emphasis on time to fish.

We got to Young Harris real early Monday morning and I handed him a pencil and said, "Now, Mr. Luthie, I'll look over my blueprints while you mark off timbers for a pattern. Do it light, and then I'll mark over them again while the students watch." Mr. Luthie grinned at me. He knew what I was up to. But he marked the timbers light, and when the boys arrived, I'd ask one to bring me a plank and I'd go over the marks, and pretty soon me and Mr. Luthie were off fishing.

When we got back to Young Harris, those students had cut and mounted the timbers and were ready to nail on the tin. Prettiest thing you ever saw. The president of the college wrote me a letter saying it all fit just perfect.

People wanted blueprints for everything, houses and privies, barns and chicken houses. The president of the Central of Georgia Railroad had a farm at Orchard Hill and he wanted a concrete silo. I'd never even seen one. Silos had always been made out of wood. I didn't know what I'd do, but I just happened to see an ad in the paper for a company in Atlanta that had started selling steel forms for concrete silos. I got to Atlanta early the next morning and presented myself as a representative of the University of Georgia's Agricultural School.

"We're doin' a demonstration project at Orchard Hill for the president of the Central of Georgia Railroad," I said, "and I think it would be the best advertisement in the world for y'all if you'd build it with your new form."

The day they started on it we had a crowd of farmers over

there. The steel form was like a doughnut with a big hole. They'd pour in the concrete, let it set up, then raise the form and pour in some more. They did that over and over, clear to the top.

If that silo is still standing, it's got my name on it. I scratched it in the concrete. I thought about adding Sanna's name to mine, but I didn't do it, even though I had already asked her to marry me. But all that came later.

9

I SPENT the week after the watermelon cutting hoping that Miss Sanna Klein would get cold feet and not go to Jefferson, in which case she'd have to attend Sunday school and preaching in P.C., as is expected of teachers. In that case, I meant to be waiting when she and Miss Love and Sampson came in from the Methodist service. I took the train to P.C. Sunday morning and walked up to Miss Love's house. Sunday school hadn't let out yet, much less church, so I sat down on the porch swing, lit a cigar, and opened the *Atlanta Journal* wide.

I had sense enough to know Miss Klein had probably spent last night with the Blankenships. But even if she had, at least I had an excuse to spend the morning enjoying the newspaper instead of wiggling and shoulder twitching through a long Presbyterian sermon with my folks.

Fools in love get fool hopes. My idea was if Miss Klein hadn't gone to Jefferson, I could save her from an afternoon of misery in her room alone. A few hours with me would surely seem better than nothing. I'd thought of taking her to ride, maybe out to my Grandpa Tweedy's farm in Banks County. I knew I could use Papa's car, since kinfolks were coming for Sunday dinner and would sit visiting all afternoon.

Concentrating on the newspaper wasn't easy, nervous as I

was and distracted by hope and cooking smells from Miss Hyta Mae's boarding house next door and a squirrel in the fig tree who kept barking at a cat. Finally my eyes lit on an item that interested me:

> The Rev. Mr. Jared Elder, age 70, has dug his own grave in Silver Shoal Community and lined the sides with Portland Cement. He is in good health, so expects to wait a few years before occupying the home he has prepared for his body. But he brags that when the final hour comes, his neighbors will not have to be summoned to dig a hole. Mr. Elder did a good job, but it does not look inviting.

I tore that out, and also a little boxed-off story about base pay for soldiers in different countries. I already knew American privates were drawing thirty-three dollars a month, but I never imagined that French privates got only a dollar-fifty, a soldier of the same grade in Russia thirty-two cents, and in Germany sixty-five cents. It said the British Army was paying seven dollars and sixty cents a month plus extra for service in France. Japanese privates earned eight dollars a year.

Then I noticed a little item I'd almost missed:

> Miss Trulu Philpot, formerly of Athens, will be honored as Miss Liberty Bond at a gala in the nation's capital on Saturday night, October 3, to raise money for the War Effort. This is "The Event" of Washington's social season.
>
> According to Miss Philpot's mother, Mrs. Cason R. Philpot, her daughter's "court" will include her escort, Captain Horace Luck, a U.S. Army aviator who leaves soon for France, and some of his fellow aviators.
>
> Miss Philpot is staying with her maternal aunt and is one of this year's most sought-after debutantes in Washington.

Lord, I was tired of Trulu intruding on everything I did. Trulu Philpot was a modern girl with hypnotic blue eyes and golden hair. Before Sanna, I never looked twice at a dark-haired girl. If you only dated blondes, I figured, you were sure to marry a blonde. I'd loved blondes ever since Lightfoot's hair shone like an angel's in the sunlight as she bent over me on Blind Tillie Trestle the day the train ran over me. Tru was a vamp and flirted with everybody, but I was the only one she fell in love with, and we got engaged. It had been announced and everything.

Tru's grandfather was a major general in the War Between the States and he was the man who built the white-columned mansion in Athens where Trulu and her family lived. That impressed Papa and Mama, and they were even more impressed when I said the whole Philpot family made the grand tour of Europe and Russia in 1910.

They were less impressed when they met her. She'd just got her blond hair cut short—that was sometime before Loma cut hers—and though Tru didn't smoke that day, Mama smelled it on her clothes. "I'm sure she's just sweet as she can be," said Mama later, "but I don't know, Will. I'm just not used to these modrun ladies. She don't seem like somebody who'd be happy on a farm."

"Oh, we've talked a lot about that," I said. "I don't reckon she'll be sweepin' the yard or feedin' the chickens, but she'll keep friends comin' out for weekends in the country. I doubt she'll be bored." I guess Mama and Papa had the same unspoken thoughts I did. When I got ready to quit my job in Athens and move to Banks County, Tru's daddy would put money into my farm. After all, she was his only child.

A flea had more common sense than I did around Tru. All my life I'd dreamed of taking over Grandpa Tweedy's farm, but Trulu Philpot got me to promise I'd keep my job in Athens. "We can use the farm for house parties," she said. "Everybody loves to go to the country."

I didn't tell Mama and Papa she was a great dancer. I'd never even told them what a great dancer I was. They thought dancing was a sin, like playing cards. Everything was a sin if you did it on Sunday—except church, Bible reading, big Sunday dinners, and swapping gossip. What Sunday afternoons were for was visiting kinfolks and neighbors. I couldn't tell them I didn't believe in sin anymore, or that Trulu had hold of me, body and soul, or that I was "wild" about her. Trulu was wild in the most literal sense of the word *wild*. She got expelled from the normal school in Athens. She didn't plan to be a teacher anyhow.

I closed the newspaper in disgust, checked my pocket watch, and settled down to wait for a girl who was everything Trulu was not.

I didn't have to wait long. Minutes later a big fancy touring car slowed to a stop in front of the house. I watched as the driver, a middle-aged man, escorted Sanna up the steps, set her grip down, and said gruffly, "I'm sorry it turned out this way, Miss Klein. Maybe next time things will . . ." His voice trailed off.

Neither one smiled. She thanked him for bringing her home, said good-bye, and watched till he drove off. Then she started for the door.

The face she turned towards me was a portrait of fatigue and misery. Circles dark as bruises made a mask around dull black eyes. "Why, Mr. Tweedy, I . . . I didn't expect . . ."

I asked did she have a good time.

"Yes, thank you," she murmured. "I had a v-very nice t-t-time." Her lower lip quivered on the last words and her eyes brimmed with tears.

"What happened? Is he sick or something?"

She didn't answer. Just opened the screen door and hurried in. I followed her, bringing the grip. "You forgot this," I called as she rushed for the stairs. "What's happened, Miss Klein?" I asked again, like it was any of my business.

"I . . . he . . . I . . . I t-took a b-b-bath!" she wailed, and sank down on the bottom step, sobbing. The long navy blue skirt of her travel suit hid high-buttoned shoes. Her hands hid her face. Whenever Mama or Loma used to tune up like that around Grandpa Blakeslee, he'd say, "Iffen they's one thang I cain't stand, it's a woman cryin'. So hesh up!" Even when I was real young, I could see that such talk didn't turn off any faucets. Soon as Miss Klein's sobbing let up enough for her to hear me, I asked by way of changing the subject if the Blankenships lived in a big old Victorian house set way back on the street on the outskirts. "Tan-colored? Gold trim, brown shutters?"

With new tears running down her cheeks, she nodded. I had passed that house many a time. Papa thought it was built soon after the War Between the States by a rich man from Philadelphia. It had three stories, a tall turret on one side, gingerbread doodads on porches and balconies, and stained glass panels in the front door. I was torn between curiosity about Miss Klein's awful bath and the hope that I could get her calmed down enough to tell me about it.

"Did the family pass?" I asked suddenly.

"Wh-what?" She looked up at me from her seat on the bottom step, kind of dazed.

"I mean, do you approve of this feller's folks? Are they good enough for you?"

"Oh, they're very"—she searched for the right word—"very n-n-nice." Miss Klein wiped her eyes with a handkerchief and drew a deep, steadying breath. I could see then that she needed to talk worse than she needed to cry, so I asked her about the bath. And sure enough, it was pretty awful.

As Sanna told it, Mrs. Blankenship had come hurrying up from the back hall before she got in the house good, arms outstretched in greeting and with a big smile. "So this is Miss Klein! May I call you Sanna? I'm so glad you could come, dear." Then Hugh introduced their "maid," Missouri, who showed Sanna upstairs to the company room where she would sleep.

Not saying a word, Missouri opened what looked like a small closet door, but inside was a lavatory. The bathtub was in one corner of the bedroom behind a Chinese screen. "It was the shortest, fattest little tub you ever saw," Miss Klein told me.

"Missouri's silence was getting on my nerves, so I said, 'What a funny little tub!' Without even looking at me, she answered back, 'De drain, it ain't been workin' right here lately. Miz Blankenship, she keep aimin' to call Mr. Amos, but she ain't did it yet.'

"Mr. Tweedy, Missouri had on a white uniform and Hugh had introduced her as 'our maid.' But she treated me as if she knew I'd never known anybody whose help wore a white uniform and was called a maid. And I haven't."

"Me neither," I lied. At Trulu's home in Athens they had three Negro servants who wore white uniforms and got called maid. And, according to Mama, Aunt Loma claimed Mr. Vitch had a whole bunch of maids—white maids who wore black uniforms.

"She treated me as if she knew I wasn't used to formal dinner parties." A tiny flash of anger stifled her tears for a minute.

"Who is?" I asked, trying to make light of it. "Most folks I know never even heard of a dinner party." That was true. Everybody in Cold Sassy used the good tablecloths and the good china, silver, and goblets on Sunday, and usually invited kinfolks or the preacher's family or neighbors. Mama was always saying she "owed" somebody a meal, and if Mama's watermelon pickle or sweet tomato sauce or fried eggplant was their favorite, you could count on that being on the table along with eight or ten more dishes, hot yeast rolls, and everything good you ever thought of eating. But it was just called Sunday dinner, not dinner party. If you had a party at night, it was a barbecue or fish fry.

The truth was, I almost got used to fancy dinner parties when I was engaged to Trulu, and now I confessed to one of them.

"You want to hear about it, Miss Klein? Well, I'll tell you

about mine if you'll tell me about yours," I said, leaning back against the wall. "This rich family in Athens, see, they needed an extra man to balance out the table. The hostess . . . uh, I was told it would be a black tie affair. I didn't have one, and didn't know it meant wear a tux either, till I got there. The hostess said never mind, so I didn't. No point letting a little thing like that spoil your dinner. They had Negro men waiters who didn't just wear uniforms, they wore white gloves to serve the food. And I don't mean they just brought everything to the table for us to pass around. They served it from behind you. Here would come this meat on a silver tray or a bowl of vegetables, and a waiter would stick it between you and the next person and you had to take what they forked over. Well . . ."

Miss Klein was staring up at me, almost forgetting her own troubles for a moment. "Well," I continued, "I don't remember what all we ate, but when we got through with the main meal and the homemade ice cream, the waiter they called the butler reached between two folks and picked up the ice swan and started serving it. I don't know why he started with me, but I took a bunch of grapes. Then he offered it to the lady next to me and she ran her fingers over the swan's back and then wiped them real dainty on her napkin. It was quiet around the table like everybody thought I ought to put the grapes back. I'd heard of finger bowls, but I'd never seen anybody use one, much less an ice swan."

I could tell by Miss Klein's face that she thought I'd never get asked back again to that house. "How awful! You must have felt like crawling under the table."

"No, I just said to the butler, 'Hey, uh, how bout bringin' that back? I don't want to miss anything!' And everybody just laughed. That was the first time everybody at the table had laughed. Before, they all were just talking quiet to who they were sittin' next to."

Miss Klein actually smiled. Almost laughed. "I'd have been mortified to death, Mr. Tweedy. I wish I could be like that."

I propped an elbow on the newel post and smiled down at her. "You want to tell me what your dinner party was like? Who all came?" I was trying to prime the pump, keep her talking.

"Oh, his parents, of course. Mr. Blankenship, he's not handsome like Hugh, but he's lean and strong-looking. His sister and her doctor-husband were there. Neither one of them said much. I guess I didn't say much either." Miss Klein spoke carefully, as if assuming I really wanted to know. "And his grandmother. She was dressed like a genteel old lady, but she talked country. I liked her. Mr. Crowe was there, the law partner, a tight-looking little man with a pencil mustache. Mrs. Crowe was nice, but talked through her nose. And Judge Fuss of the circuit court was there. He was big and fat, from sitting so much, I guess. Oh, and Hugh's Aunt Trudy from Virginia."

Everybody had gathered in the parlor, a room full of Victorian furniture, ornately carved tables with marble tops, big electric lamps with globe shades, fringed velvet pillows on the sofa, and dark draperies. Framed photographs and watercolor country scenes covered the walls. Figurines and vases of peacock feathers or silk roses and books were crowded on the mantel, the tables, and the top of the big, heavily carved upright grand piano.

As I listened I realized that taking a bath had the worst consequences for Miss Klein but it wasn't her only mistake. The first one was when Missouri came around with a tray full of little glasses of sherry wine and offered it to Miss Klein. Instead of just murmuring no thank you, she said, too loud, "I don't drink." Hugh shot her a disapproving glance.

The elegant deaf grandmother, who hadn't heard the I-don't-drink remark, said in a loud country voice, "Ain't it been a hot day?"

"Ain't it been hot all week?" echoed Judge Fuss. "If y'all think it's hot settin' on the screen porch, you ought a-been in my courtroom this week. Packed with everybody and his cousin and hotter'n hell. Excuse me, ladies, but it was. But maybe the court ain't any hotter'n your classroom, Miss Klein, less'n you ain't got but ten pupils."

She said, "I have fifty-five pupils," and gratefully took a bite of her little cucumber sandwich.

Judge Fuss, who was sitting next to her, leaned close and said, "I taught school. After two weeks of it I vowed if I could just get through that year I'd never set foot in a classroom again. That's when I decided to go to law school. Law school was easy after that year."

After some more conversation, Hugh and his daddy got up and recited "Jabberwocky" together. It was an amazing feat. They took turns with each verse, till close to the end they joined together and got faster and faster and faster.

Then Mrs. Blankenship, who had studied music in New York, played a long, heavy piece on the big piano.

The concert finally crescendoed to a stop, and before the smacks of applause died down, Missouri pushed the twin sliding doors apart and called out, "Y'all come on to supper . . . uh, I, whut I mean to say, DINNER IS SERVE!"

Considering it was already first dark, and the dining room lit only with candles and a circle of tiny electric bulbs in the huge crystal chandelier, it's no wonder Miss Klein was nervous at dinner. In the soft flickering light, she wasn't sure till she tasted it whether Missouri had served her rice or creamed corn.

"None of it was as splendid as the dinner party you went to must have been, Mr. Tweedy, but it was at least as grand as Sister Maggie's Thanksgiving dinner and Christmas dinner and Easter dinner put together. Everything just so glittery and beautiful. Vases of flowers everywhere. And cut-glass goblets and heavy scrolled silverware reflecting the light."

The centerpiece was red roses in a large silver bowl, and the china was gold-and-white Spode.

Suddenly Miss Love's big hall clock bonged the noon hour, echoing in the stairwell. We listened to the twelve strikes. Then, as the last one died away, Miss Klein blew her nose and stood up. Reaching for her leather grip, she mounted a few stairs. Paused. Leaned wearily against the wall. "I'm so t-tired, Mr. Tweedy. I didn't sleep last night after . . . I was . . . oh, it was all just awful! I c-can't . . ."

I interrupted before she could move on upstairs or go to crying again. "You mean . . . your bath?"

"It . . . wasn't the bath." She took a deep breath, let it out in a long shaky sigh. "It was what h-happened afterwards. Mr. Tweedy, at dinner I was actually having a good time. They are nice people, and the table conversation . . . well, it wasn't highbrow the way I expected—I mean, with Hugh being so intellectual and all." There had been a lot of talk about the war news, until Mrs. Blankenship said she'd rather hear the men talk politics than war, and Miss Klein was asked questions like where was she born and where did she go to college. Then the lawyers swapped stories about colored folks and country hicks they'd dealt with in their practice.

Maybe the people didn't act highbrow, but the food sounded mighty la-di-dah to me. No field peas or turnip salad and cornbread on that table. Green tomato pickles, a bowl of sliced fresh tomatoes with raw onion, and a congealed fruit salad on lettuce were on the table, but, as at Trulu's family dinner parties, the food was served to each guest from behind by Missouri and the cook, who had taken off her kitchen apron and put on a clean white maid's uniform.

Miss Klein told me the menu like a fourth-grader reciting the names of United States Presidents: first, a shallow bowl of creamed onion soup, followed by smothered chicken, smoked ham slices, rice, baked dressing that was chock-full of Apalachicola oysters, chicken gravy, fried eggplant, a sweet potato soufflé, and a big silver vase-shaped pot of hot yeast rolls.

By the time the eating and talking were in full swing, Miss Klein was thinking she could get used to all this. Then she was startled by the sight of a drop of water that splatted down onto a red rose in the centerpiece. A few petals danced, then danced again, then again. For a minute Miss Klein just stared, puzzled, and finally looked up. The ceiling plaster was wet!

She nudged Hugh, and he glanced at the ceiling, but just said *sh-h-h-h*. He wanted to hear Judge Fuss tell about his first legal client, a chicken thief called Two Fingers.

But the judge never got to say what happened at Two Finger's trial. He stopped in midsentence, staring up as those first drops became a stream. The dim electric lights flickered, went out! Before anybody could duck or dodge, the crystal chandelier crashed down with a mess of wet plaster. Women screamed and men cursed, and the colored women in their white uniforms flew in. Missouri looked up and shouted, "Lawd a mercy, de bed gwine come down nex'!"

Miss Klein, sobbing anew, said, "It was j-just the biggest m-m-mess you ever saw, Mr. Tweedy!" The candles on the sideboard and buffet gave enough light to show plaster and food all over the lace tablecloth, roses scattered, cut-glass goblets and china plates broken. Everything was crushed, and the chandelier sprawled over the table like a big dead octopus.

Judge Fuss's shoulders were drenched with water and crumbled plaster. A piece of oyster clung to Mr. Crowe's vest. One arm of the chandelier dripped gravy. A green tomato pickle was impaled on the jagged glass of a broken electric light bulb. Miss Klein discovered she had wet congealed salad in her lap.

Mr. Blankenship jumped up and shouted at his wife, "That fool tub! How come you didn't call Mr. Amos like I told you to!"

Hugh grabbed Miss Klein's shoulder and said, "Sanna! Did you take a bath?" Then he dashed upstairs behind his daddy.

Miss Klein was too shocked to speak.

Missouri shook her fist at the ceiling. "I'se been a-tellin' you, Miz 'Ships, dem faucets and dem drainpipes, dey ain' nothin' but RUST. An' all dat fine china busted!" She waved her arms towards the table. "Lawd hep us. Whut we go'n do, Miz 'Ships?"

As if rising from a stupor, Mrs. Blankenship got up and said, "We're going to clean it up."

Sanna was weeping by then. "It's all m-my f-fault! I took a bath!"

"No, it's mine. I just kept putting off calling Mr. Amos. Sanna, see if you can help Aunt Trudy wipe the soufflé off her neck."

I could tell that Sanna Klein was reliving all this now, after reliving it all the time she should have been sleeping the night before. "And you do see, Mr. Tweedy," she wailed, "why no matter how much Mrs. Blankenship tried to comfort me, it was all—all—m-my f-f-fault! I just f-felt so hot and d-dusty after the ride over! I hated to p-put on my nice dress f-for the p-party when I was so sweaty—I mean, perspiring so much. I . . ."

She had completely run out of steam.

My way of comforting probably wasn't like Mrs. Blankenship's. I said, "It strikes me as how this would make a fine scene in a movie film, Miss Klein. Comedy or tragedy, either one."

She didn't say anything. Just kept crying.

"Gosh, Miss Klein," I said finally, "from now on you'd better watch out."

"Wh-what?" she spoke from the middle of a sob.

"I mean, you may be in real danger. One day you're under a tree and a watermelon drops out of it and hits you, and a week later a chandelier crashes down onto a dinner table and splashes you with congealed salad!"

A moment of stunned silence on her part, then as I started laughing, Miss Klein's mouth turned up at the corners. But not for long. "I wish I could see something funny about the rest of last night." She looked at me and went to laughing again. As the big clock bonged for twelve-thirty, I heard a clatter of voices and high heels on the front porch.

"Must be Miss Love and them, Miss Klein, comin' in from church."

"Oh, my," she whispered, distressed. "I don't . . . can you just tell Miss Love I'm back, Mr. Tweedy? And . . ." she reached out and touched my hand, "and thank you." With that, she grabbed her bag and disappeared up the stairs.

During Sanna Klein's miserable recital of broken glass and gravy stains I had begun to feel as if this were something we were in together. But walking home for dinner with my folks, I kept puzzling. None of what Miss Klein told me explained why she'd come back so early in the day, or why it was the daddy who brought her home. Why not the sweetheart?

She couldn't have flunked out of the fancy family. If so, Mr. Blankenship wouldn't have sounded so kind and sad, saying he wished things had turned out different.

What did it all mean? It was months before I found out.

Cudn Milford and his wife, Cudn Zena, had arrived by buggy, in time to go to church with Mama and Papa. When I got home they were on the front porch with Papa. They lived in Pocatelago Community, better known as Poky, which was eight miles from P.C. All Poky amounted to was a large general store at the crossroads and farms all around. One of those farms was where Grandpa Blakeslee grew up.

Cudn Zena's face was lop-sided from a stroke. Her right eye and cheek drooped and the right side of her mouth, which made her *f*'s come out like *h*'s. But that didn't stop her from talking.

"My, don't you look hine, Will!" she said as I came up the steps. "Spittin' image of Cudn Rucker, ain't he, Mr. Milhord. But, son, you need some weight on you. Skinniest, long-leggedest thang I ever seen. Come 'ere and hug this old lady!"

"How you been doin', Cudn Zena," I asked, reaching down to her in a bear hug.

"Well, my hace ain't too good, but the rest of me is as good as common, thank you, thank you." Cudn Zena always was a talker, once she got started, and right then she got started telling Papa and me her latest hope for a cure. "Y'all know Porter Springs, don't you, up in the mountains near Dahlonega? Other day I got to rememberin' my Uncle Alva, how he was so afflicted with the rheumatism, he dragged his heet around like an alligator. And he got well at Porter Springs. Told me he stayed three days in a boardin' house up thar and drank two gallons a day of that mineral water, and when he come home, he could walk just hine and go about his worldly bizness."

Cudn Milford butted in. "She wants me to take her up yonder, but I cain't afford it. Miss Zena, I'm willin' if you're willin' to sleep in a tent."

"I got my aigg money," she replied from the good side of her mouth.

"Maybe he likes you the way you are," I said cheerfully.

"Well, I don't. Lookin' like a clown don't matter much, but my eye hurts. Hit cain't blink. I have to keep my hand over it like this and tie a rag across it at night. Uncle Alva told me bout lots of sick holks he met up there, stayin' in them little cottages or the boardin' house or the ho-tel and drankin' the water. Just miracles. One man had piles in the worst way, and he spent hive days on the spring water and his piles was healed. A lady who'd had laig sores for seven years got cured in a two-week period. Now, listen to this, Hoyt—a man from White County had the dropsy? You know, somethin' wrong with his heart and him swole up all over? Uncle Alva said the man at the ho-tel said the man come up there swole up all over like he'd bust if you stuck a pin in him. Weighed three hun-dret pound if he weighed a ounce. And drankin' that water made him start shrinkin'. In just three weeks he was down to a hundret and thirty. The ho-tel man swore on a Bible that time he was ready to leave, this man could run, wrestle, li't thangs like anybody else! I don't know i' Porter Springs is the hancy summer resort it used to be back then, but there's still places to stay, I know that."

A tear rolled down her cheek from the drooped eye. But she

wiped it off, and though the right side of her face drooped in despair, a smile of hope brightened the good side. About then Mama called us in to dinner. Once we'd passed all the food and got to eating good, Cudn Zena started talking about my Grandpa Blakeslee.

"Remember that old log cabin your daddy was born in?" she asked Mama. "You know, up on that woody clay hill between Poky and Erastus? Well, we went over there to see it—I reckon it was a year ago January, wadn't it, Mr. Milford?"

He nodded and said the cabin had plumb rotted down.

"Vines growin' betwist and between the logs," said Cudn Zena. "Them vines had just pulled it apart."

Everybody was sad to hear that, but then we had a good time swapping stories about Grandpa Blakeslee. The Poky folks told some I'd never heard before. Like for instance when Grandpa was about twelve years old and stayed out possum hunting on Saturday night and went to sleep on the bench next morning at church. "The preacher noticed," said Cudn Zena, "and right in the middle of his sermon he said real loud, 'Rucker Blakeslee, I'm askin' you to pray.' Remember Aunt Lula Pritchett? Well, Aunt Lula, she punched Rucker and said, 'Git up and pray, son.'" Grandpa, stumbling to his feet, said *Lordmakeusthankfulfortheseandallourmanyblessin's.Amen.* Then he sat down and went back to sleep.

I told about the Halloween night Grandpa pushed over the privy at the Cold Sassy depot, knowing the Yankee president of the railroad was in there, and how the man offered a fifty-dollar reward to anybody who'd tell who did it. Nobody would. Mama and Queenie were clearing off the table by then, ready to bring in Cudn Zena's pecan pie.

I sat there wishing Mary Toy and Aunt Loma and Campbell Junior were still here. The table seemed suddenly lonesome without them.

And without Granny and Grandpa . . .

I didn't look forward to an afternoon hearing about who

all in the family was sick, so when Mr. Talmadge from Athens stopped by in his automobile to see Papa and offered me a ride back, I took him up on it.

That night I spent an hour writing a five-sentence letter to Sanna Klein:

> Dear Miss Klein,
> I'm sitting here in my rented room eating sardines and crackers whereas I had hoped to be with you. If it's in order, I would like to take you to church next Sunday night. Please let me know if that is OK. I hope you don't have a "previous." You already seem like an old acquaintance.
> Hoyt Willis Tweedy

10

MORE than seventeen years passed between the September night I wrote that letter and the Monday night last November when I read it again, in a dingy one-room cabin at the Rest-Easy Motor Court near Shellman, Georgia.

In desperation I had taken a cotton-buying job as one of four field men in a new farmers' cooperative. When I started traveling in south Georgia for forty-five dollars a month, all I had in the world was a wife, four children, a milk cow, a bird dog, a worn-out Model-A Ford, and an expense account for gas plus two dollars and fifty cents a day for food and lodging.

If I happened to be talking to a farmer anywhere near noon, I could count on his wife inviting me to dinner. If I slept in the car two nights, I could save enough expense money to buy gas and get home to Progressive City for a weekend. If it wasn't a hot night, sleeping in the car was real pleasant. Plenty of fresh air, no roaches, and not many more mosquitoes than in a cheap hotel room.

In the car I had to sleep folded up, but that wasn't much worse than sleeping at the Rest-Easy Motor Court, where the mattress was thin and the springs as rusty and sagging as my spirits.

I was lonely, tired to the bone, too restless to sleep. My

shoulders kept twitching, and my eyes were red and sore from driving all day on dusty roads.

I wished I hadn't gone home for the weekend—home now being an upstairs apartment in P.C., rented from a silent old man and a sharp-tongued old lady who didn't like children fussing and banging doors. I wasn't used to that anymore myself. The children made me nervous as heck, Sanna was a witch, and the dog was whining and limping from a thorn in his foot that had begun to fester.

I got the thorn out and soaked Pup's foot in Epsom salts water, but there was no balm for the anger that was festering in Sanna.

I didn't blame her. Responsibility for the children was a heavy weight to bear alone. They had always gone to school and church in P.C., so they already had friends there. But my losing the farm and our new house had broken Sanna's heart and my pride. Change of any kind was hard on Sanna, but she always said she was never happier than out there in the country having babies—four born in less than five years—with me coming in for meals, helping any way I could. It was hard on her when I had to quit farming and start traveling. It was a lot worse when she was looking after four rowdy children by herself—trying to sound brave but worrying by herself, sleeping by herself, trying to make my little salary last till the end of the month and feeling disliked by my mama.

But good Lord, it wasn't easy on me either. I was really by myself. The first time I had to leave her for south Georgia, neither Sanna nor I slept the night before, and at four A.M. I said, "There's no point waitin' for the clock to ring. I'm gettin' up." Sanna had packed my bags the night before. She fixed me a good breakfast, and by first light I was raring to be off.

"Do you want to look in on the children?" Sanna asked.

"I'll never leave if I do," I said. We went hand in hand down the stairs, tiptoeing so as not to wake anybody.

I kissed Sanna good-bye, but we kept clinging to each other.

Leaving her and the children was like having my arms and legs torn off. My heart ached. I held her head to my chest and stroked her hair. Then with a deep sigh, trying to make my voice cheerful, I said, "I'll be back this weekend, hon. Or at least by the next weekend. It won't seem so long."

"It will to me," she said. "Will, I hate living in P.C. when we owe everybody in town. What if something happens to one of the children? What if . . ."

"Mama and Papa are just three blocks away, and Miss Love says she'll help you. All you got to do is ask."

Taking her hands in mine, I kissed them. I got past the screen door then, but couldn't walk away. Her on one side of the screen, me on the other, and we were both crying. We both knew things would never be the same again.

They haven't been.

But by the time the Model-A hit the city limits of Progressive City, my spirits rose like a balloon. Ahead lay new places, new people, new challenges. I had a job, by gosh, and it had a future. "God help me, I'm go'n make a livin' for my fam'ly! Dear God, I got to get my self-respect back."

With my foot heavy on the gas pedal, the car picked up speed and I let out a yell. "Boy howdy, God!" I hadn't said boy howdy in years. I hadn't *felt* like saying boy howdy in years.

I had quit farming in 1928, when the banks foreclosed. Before we knew what hit us, we'd lost the farm and were renting rooms in town. When I first went to work for a former county agent who organized a Georgia cotton cooperative, I had to travel, but I could make it home most nights. That venture failed, but Mr. Downes formed a new cooperative, and I agreed to take south Georgia as my territory. Sanna said I should have insisted on the northeast territory. I told her I'd never get ahead if I made demands, but I guess I was wrong. The northeast went to a man whose wife refused ever to move. Sanna always resented that.

Long before the end of the cotton season in south Georgia, I'd stopped trying to get home every single weekend. I was working eighteen hours a day and sometimes couldn't get off before two o'clock Saturday afternoon. Heading for home, I'd be so excited about seeing Sanna I wouldn't stop for supper, just maybe get a Co-Cola and a moon pie when I stopped for gas. If I didn't have a blow-out and the roads weren't slick, I'd get in around ten at night, worn out and hungry for supper. I did try for every other weekend, but the longer we lived apart, the more my life in south Georgia seemed to be the real thing, and my family in Progressive City a little remote. When I'd let myself worry about home, I couldn't do my job. When I did go home, after a night with Sanna and seeing that she and the children were all right, and how the money was holding out, then it seemed like I might as well just go on back. I'd leave right after Sunday dinner, which we always had at Mama and Papa's house. That made Sanna anxious, because she knew they didn't approve of the way she was raising the children. On Monday I'd start the week already worn out.

Part of my job was to buy cotton, but the most important part was to try to sell the farmers on the advantages of belonging to a cooperative, instead of selling to middlemen who tried to buy cheap and could hold the bales in warehouses till the price went up and then sell high to the mills. It cost an individual farmer a lot to warehouse his cotton crop. "You go with the co-ops," I told them, "and whatever profit gets made will come back to you, according to how much cotton you sell through us. And when spring comes we'll sell you seed and fertilizer, and whatever else you need, at a discount, and at the end of the year whatever we've made above expenses goes back to you." To show how we kept down operating expenses, I always managed to get in how much the wives of us field men fussed about how low our salaries were. And that was the truth. Sanna couldn't see that we'd lose the farmers' trust if we drove big cars or stayed in high-priced hotels. I kept reminding her I'd have more time at home when the fall cotton session wound down.

I found the letters just before I left on Sunday, when I was looking through drawers for a screwdriver to tighten a doorknob for Sanna, but I didn't try to read any till I got to Shellman the next night. The only light in the little room was a bulb hanging from the ceiling on a long cord. I turned the pillows to the foot of the bed and untied the faded blue ribbon. I think what I was hoping for was some understanding of the difference between what Sanna and I had in the beginning and this mixed-up mess we were in now. Part of it, of course, was being separated, but that wasn't all.

Sanna had them sorted according to postmark date. Her letters and mine. I reckon she kept every letter I ever wrote her, which is not exactly surprising. She can't throw away an old grocery list, much less the dentist bill from 1929 that we still haven't paid and may never be able to.

Before Sanna, the only letters I ever tried to keep were from Trulu Philpot. A week after our engagement was announced in the newspaper, I called it off. That great love affair ended at a house party in the mountains. We all went out to pick blackberries and were scattered along the roadside when a thunderstorm came up. I ran under a bridge to get out of the rain, and there was Trulu, kissing one of my fraternity brothers. Right then and there I demanded my ring back. It like to killed me.

There's nobody quite as mad as an old flame when she gives you back your letters and your picture and demands hers, and you have to admit you never saved them. When Trulu asked me for her letters, I got some satisfaction out of telling her I'd been using them to get fires going in my fireplace. It wasn't so, but I said it. Then for spite I passed them around the Sigma Chi house for the boys to read and laugh at. It was a mean thing to do, but I did it.

That happened a year before I met Sanna. I'd be excited, opening a letter from Trulu, but I don't remember ever reading one twice. From the beginning I knew it was different, how I felt about Sanna, because I'd keep reading her words over and over till the next letter came.

They haven't lost any of their magic, but not many are here in the collection. I know I tried to keep all Sanna's letters, but I'm sure many got left behind in hotel rooms—lost from pure carelessness.

Now, holding Sanna's packet of letters, I grieve for all those she wrote that aren't here.

My second letter to Sanna was written after our first "date"—the evening service at church.

Wednesday, September 19, 1917

Dear Sanna,

I hope you don't mind if I call you Sanna. I've known you a long time now—two whole weeks and three days.

This is circus day in Athens. Everybody from everywhere is in the big tent, including the people I'm supposed to work with, so I'm sitting at my desk with nothing to do but write up reports. It was like a light came on in here when I decided to write to you instead.

I certainly did enjoy that long-drawn-out sermon Sunday night, and our chat after we carried the others home. I hope you don't mind the way I filled up Papa's car with friends. The more people, see, the closer I can sit to you. Too bad our number keeps diminishing. If this war keeps up and everybody but me gets to go, I'll be looking after all you girls by myself. Call it a slacker's paradise. I'm equal to it and I'd take pleasure in doing my duty. But I wouldn't take pride in it.

This is some busy week. I've already been everywhere except Mitchellville and would have gone there if you could have gone with me.

Had a telegram yesterday from my Aunt Loma in New

York (you met her at the watermelon cutting) saying she had tied the knot. Her new husband is rich and old and a Yankee, and most likely a Republican. Mama is real upset about it. Miss Alice Ann Boozer (have you met her?) says, "Anythang that's outlandish, Loma has did it." I think marrying a Yankee takes the cake when it comes to outlandish.

I like the way "Dear Sanna" looks on paper. I've been practicing the way it sounds. I never heard the name Sanna before. Were you named for a grandmother or somebody?

May I impose on you for a date Saturday night?

Please write that it's OK.

Sincerely,
Will T.

Sanna's answer is the next letter in the stack. Reading my name on the envelope, I feel again the same rush of excitement I always did when an envelope came addressed in her handwriting. Now as then, I can picture her sitting down to write at the oak table in her upstairs room at Miss Love's house. Her long black hair is braided for the night. The drapey silk shade on the lamp casts a soft glow on her dark skin, and her small lovely hand is graceful as she dips the pen into the ink bottle.

Dear Will T.,

Your letter was in the mail basket when I got in from school today. I'm pleased to say I have no plans for Saturday night.

No, I didn't mind "the crowd." They were all so nice to me. I'm a rather shy person, but they were easy to be with, and you saw to it that I and everybody else had a good time.

This was a hard day. I had to paddle two boys. With fifty-five fourth-graders I don't have an easy job, but I am not discouraged. The main problem is the animosity between town children and mill children. We didn't have that in Mitchellville, though poor farm children are looked down on there—people say they're "from over the river."

Your Uncle Sampson is trying very hard to be good, but he still talks instead of listening, and he distracts the class. He's always plotting mischief. But he is bright and charming and at home we are good friends. Little Precious Roach is a delight. I hope she doesn't come to hate her name the way I used to hate mine.

You asked how I happen to be called Sanna.

My mother, named Flora, gave flower names to all six children ahead of me. The first three were grown and married before I was born—Blossom, Lily Maude, and Magnolia. Magnolia, called Maggie, raised me from the time I was ten years old. After them came Zinnia, Violet, and Joe Pye. (I'm sure you know the big dusky-pink Joe Pye weed that grows by the roadside. When Joe Pye was a boy, everybody called him "Weed" and he never minded. I'd have hated it.)

There was another boy, born before me. He died of pneumonia at six months so I never knew him. His name was Welcome Peter George Klein. Mrs. Herndon, our neighbor across the road, says that when he was born she asked Mama, "Miss Flora, how come you named him Welcome Peter George? You ain't near run out of flowers yet. Not even boy flowers." She says Mama told her, "One name sounds good as another when you get to be forty years old. I reckon I'm just tired of gardenin'. From here on out I'll just reach up and pick me one out of the air."

Mama was forty-three when I was born. She picked my name out of the air. It made me feel different in the family, and at school, too.

Little Sophronia came four years later, and Mama named her for a childhood friend at Brick Store Community in Newton County where she grew up. Poor Sophie was what the country people speak of as "illy formed." Her head was too big, and she never sat up by herself or talked. I have only one memory of her, lying on a blue blanket near the hearth like a limp doll, watching the logs flicker. Sophie lived only eighteen months.

When Mama was forty-seven, she had Carrie, called Tattie, and made a pet out of her. Mrs. Herndon says Tattie was the first child Mama had time to spoil.

Ever since my papa died, when I was thirteen and I went to live with Sister Maggie and Brother Hen in Mitchellville, their house has seemed more like home than the farm does.

I have papers to grade so I will close by saying I look forward to Saturday night. You forgot to tell me what time.

Sincerely,
Sanna K.

11

AT THE time, all I really knew about Sister Maggie and her husband, Mr. Henry Jolley, was the gossip I'd heard from Mr. Charlie in Mitchellville. But Sanna had told me how much they had done for her. Mayor Jolley had sent her through Shorter, a Baptist college for girls in Rome, Georgia, from which she graduated in 1915 with a degree in mathematics. Then she'd lived with them and taught fourth grade for two years in Mitchellville before coming to P.C.

"But I got so restless," she'd told me as we sat on Miss Love's porch swing after church Sunday night. "Most of my friends were married and gone, and I wanted to make a new life for myself. One Sunday a missionary who was home from Africa talked at our church, hoping to recruit young people to the mission field, and I wanted to go. A college friend of mine had married a missionary and they went to China. Every time I had a letter from her, I'd say I'm going to be a missionary someday. Imagine, teaching heathen people about the love of Jesus Christ, and teaching them to read! All the time the man was talking about Africa, I felt God was calling me, telling me to go there. Even showing me the way. How to apply, where to get training."

"But you didn't do it," I said.

Sanna gave a helpless little shrug. "Sister Maggie wouldn't hear of it. She kept saying, 'You'll just end up an old maid in the jungle. With you being so particular, I can't imagine you living in a dirty hut in a village full of savages. They don't have any dentists or doctors in Africa. You'll get leprosy and jungle fever and I don't know what all.' Sister Maggie told me about a young missionary lady who got all her teeth pulled on a visit home so she wouldn't have to worry about toothaches in Africa. Will, I'm ashamed to admit it, but after Sister Maggie said that, God's call got weaker."

I told Sanna I was glad she didn't end up in the jungle, since I wouldn't be there.

"I felt so guilty. Jesus said, 'Go ye into all the world,' but Sister Maggie kept saying, 'Don't go, don't rot your life away after all the advantages we've given you.' I couldn't bring myself to go, with her so opposed. It seemed unappreciative. But I've always regretted it."

I knew what it was like to have somebody pushing and pulling at you. "Grandpa Blakeslee always expected me to come into his store business," I told her. "He had a fit when I said I wanted to be a farmer."

"I can see why," she said, wrinkling her nose as if she'd had a whiff of pigpen.

"Grandpa died when I was fifteen, so it never came to a head. The choice, I mean. But if Grandpa had lived and kept aggravatin' me about the store, I'd have just got more hard-headed. I'm that much like him."

She smiled. "Well, I'd hate to see you get old behind a mule, Will. This way you aren't exactly wasting your degree, and you get paid every month."

"I aim to farm someday." I said it real firm. "Soon as the war's over, Papa's go'n buy the land and the home place from his daddy out in Banks County and give it to me. I'll take you out there one day, Sanna, to see Grandpa Tweedy. He's the world's laziest man. He married a widow woman named Miz

Jones, and that's what he still calls her. Too lazy to change it. He used to sit on the porch all day swattin' flies, and he had a pet hen to peck up the dead ones. Now the hen's dead, so he just sits there."

"I think you like him," she said with a laugh.

"I hated him when I was a boy. But I don't have to mind him now."

Sanna hadn't mentioned Hugh again. You don't help somebody forget anybody if you keep bringing up the subject, so I didn't, and pretty soon I forgot about him myself. But I did ask Miss Love one day if Sanna was getting much mail from Jefferson.

"No," she said. "Sanna told me she wouldn't be seeing the young man anymore. I never thought that would be the end of it, but I guess it was."

Miss Love took the opportunity to tell me how nice Sanna was, how she kept her room neat as a pin and her clothes immaculate. "She reminds me of Mrs. Villy, a woman I knew in Baltimore. After every rain Mrs. Villy got out a stepladder and wiped off the outside of all her windows. I really like Sanna," Miss Love continued. "She never complains about anything, which is more than I can say about the others, especially Issie. Issie says her mattress is too hard, it's hot up there, she wishes she didn't have to go next door for meals, and she fusses about Sanna hogging the bathroom. Sanna can spend an hour in the tub, it's true, and she's forever washing her hands. I didn't expect girls to be spilling over into my bathroom when I rented those rooms, but I've told them they can if they have to."

That was the closest Miss Love ever came to criticizing Sanna. Mostly she kept trying to sell her to me, as if she was selling a hat or a car at the store. Any time she wasn't bragging about how neat Sanna kept her room, she was saying what beautiful taste she had in clothes. "Her Sister Maggie makes most of them, you know. Sanna says when she was learning to sew, if a seam was the least bit crooked, her sister made her take it out and stitch it again. Now she makes herself do that. I think it's admirable, don't you, Will?"

"It sounds tedious to me."

"I mean, to try that hard, and be conscientious enough to take the time."

One afternoon Miss Love said that when she got home from the store, Sanna was in the parlor playing the piano. "Sanna played very competently, but when she saw me, she quit."

Later, when I asked Sanna to play me a piece, she wouldn't. Her lovely eyes were cast down and she was picking at her thumb with a fingernail. "Will, I've never told—well, my piano teacher at Shorter asked me once if I'd heard much music as a child. I said no, and she said she thought not. She thought I played mechanically, said I worried so much about getting the right notes, I couldn't play with feeling. I've never had much confidence since then—about my music. If anybody's listening, I just can't play."

We were sitting together on Miss Love's loveseat in the parlor.

"Me neither," I said. "Not if somebody's listenin', or if they aren't. I count it as one of my blessings, Sanna. I'm crazy about dance music, especially the way Miss Love plays it, but the most miserable six weeks of my life was that time Papa traded twenty pounds of cornmeal for a clarinet. Folks were always bringin' in things like that to the store. One time a troupe of midget clowns got financially strapped here and talked him into swappin' some tobacco and canned goods for a clown costume. He brought it home for Mary Toy to play dress-up in."

"But what about the clarinet?"

I shifted a little on the loveseat. In her direction. "A man came to town sellin' band instruments and givin' lessons, and we had the clarinet, so Mama made me take them. Practicin' was about as prickly and borin' as pickin' up sweetgum balls. I told my teacher I hated practicin'. He said, 'Just play a little while and then walk around the house and then practice some more.' The piece I learned on was 'Abide With Me.' It got so I couldn't abide 'Abide With Me,' much less the clarinet. One day I traded it to Pink Predmore for a pair of skates. Mama fussed, but I think it was a relief to her and everybody."

By now we were somehow sitting right close on the loveseat, and she was looking up at me, saying how much more fun life would be if she were more like me, taking things as they come and not being scared to fail.

"Oh, I don't take kindly to failin', as they say in the country." I eased my arm across the back of the loveseat behind her, getting set to casually touch her shoulder. "But if one thing won't work, I try another. It's a challenge," I said softly. Our eyes met. The raspberry lips parted slightly. I could feel her warm breath. My arm was around her. "Like for instance," I whispered, "I've tried a dozen times to kiss you, and you . . ."

She pushed me away firmly and stood up. "It's late, Will. I think you'd better go."

I got up, stood looking down at her, moved a step closer. Slowly, slowly, I bent forward.

She moved a step back. "I thought you were different from other men, Will. Why do you keep . . ."

"I love you, Sanna. I love you."

"Nobody can really be in love this fast."

"I can. I am."

"Then quit trying to force yourself on me. Please, Will." She was very upset.

"I don't want to force anything. I just . . ."

"Good night, Will." She gave me a quivery little smile.

I followed her to the parlor door and watched as she ran quickly up the stairs.

12

*E*DITOR'S *note: During the fall of* 1917, *with Will constantly on the road, he and Sanna fell in love through their letters. In the first draft of the manuscript, Olive Ann Burns told much of the story through these letters, but in her revision she intended to replace some of them with scenes in which Sanna and Will learned about each other face to face.*

In the following letters Will declares his love for Sanna and makes plans to accompany her to Thanksgiving dinner in Mitchellville.

October 31, 1917

My dear Sanna,

I bet you haven't written me one line, but I'm going to Macon tomorrow just to find out.

I left Athens Monday, got to Camilla at ten on Tuesday, built a barn, and came on to Vidalia. We had a food-conservation meeting tonight at which Yours Truly presided and told all he knew in two minutes. We'll hold another tomorrow morning at the schoolhouse to try to get the kids to save waste paper and eat a little less of the foods needed by the Army and Navy for my boyhood pals and fraternity brothers in uniform.

I'll leave here tomorrow afternoon for Macon to get my precious letter from you, be there thirty minutes, go on to Tifton, hold meetings, go on from there to Barnesville, hold meetings, then back to Athens and then P.C. Saturday evening, when I hope to find you without a date. That's my program for the week and I'll complete it or bust.

Vidalia is a quaint little south Georgia town, with the same old moon that rides above your room at Miss Love's house. It's a beautiful night, almost perfect, but not perfect because you're not with me. I didn't really know how much I could miss you until I came way off down here.

Sanna, I know you think I'm the biggest fool in the world, but I can't help saying I love you. I knew it almost from the moment I saw Sampson's watermelon explode on your shoulder. I've tried to hold back, Lord knows. I can tell it makes you uneasy. But it's hard to have self-control when I love you so much. You'll pardon me saying all this, won't you, Sanna? Please at least consider me a true friend who's always ready and willing to help you any way I can. Ask me to do anything that will be of help to you or give you pleasure. I will do it. You are the sweetest, truest, best person I have ever known.

It's after one o'clock, so be good and don't forget—

Will T.

Sunday, November 18, 1917

Dear Sanna,
Little ole girl, I like to talk to you, I love to think of you and be with you. I don't ask for all your time or thoughts. I just want a little of your love, though I'm not worthy of even your friendship.

I'm trying to live a better life from knowing you, and because I love you so and want to be worthy of you. Girl, you don't know how much difference you have made in me. There are things I would have done did I not know you. When thoughts come that shouldn't be in my mind, I picture your own dear self—your happy smile, your beautiful sparkling black eyes—and your image drives temptation away.

This is one dark gloomy day. Even the clouds sigh for you. When autumn leaves were in color I loved hearing you exclaim, "Oh, look at the beautiful trees!" You have brought so much sunshine into my life that this morning I noticed for the first time how dead with winter everything looks. By spring, when the maple tree outside my office window dangles its transparent yellow-green winged fruit, lit by sunlight, I hope love for me will have begun to light up your heart . . .

Sanna, please thank your sister for the kind invitation to stay over for Thanksgiving dinner. I'll try to make Mama and Papa see how important this is to me. If it's freezing cold or raining and you have to go on the train, I'll come to Mitchellville to get you on Sunday, weather permitting. Otherwise, I'll meet your train in Athens and ride with you to Progressive City.

Back when I was in high school, Sanna, I had a girl in any direction—Jefferson, Franklin Springs, Wilson's Chapel, Royston. I'd hitch up old Jack, Grandpa Blakeslee's mule, and leave in the morning to reach Royston by five in the afternoon. At eight or nine o'clock I'd start back. It took all night to get back, but of course the mule knew the way home. I could just turn old Jack's reins loose, go to sleep, and wake up at Grandpa's stable. Us boys and our dogs had a lot of night life in those days. We were always slipping out to go possum or coon hunting.

Right now I'd better get to work.

As ever,
Will

In reply to my letter she wrote:

Dear Will,

I am indeed grateful for your offer to carry me to Mitch-ellville the day before Thanksgiving. Of course I realize you can't drive through the country if it's freezing cold or the roads are muddy and slick. I know it will disappoint your parents for you not to be at home, so I will certainly understand if you can't.

Will, I see why every girl in P.C. has been in love with you at one time or another (or so I am told) and probably half the girls in Athens. You're so anxious to please, you make people laugh and have a good time, you put your-self out for everybody, young or old. You are wonderful to Simpson. You are something of a flirt, of course, but ev-erybody knows it's partly just your way of being friendly. I wish I could be the way you are with strangers. In two minutes it's as if they're old acquaintances.

As I've told you, I really enjoy the food at the boarding house, but now I'm not sure I can keep eating there — not since I found out the monkey can get in the kitchen.

Yesterday I finally had a real visit with Miss Hyta. She had asked me to come by for coffee after school, and we sat talking at one end of that long dining table. I've won-dered about her Greek name. She said her father was a Greek scholar and it was his idea to call her Hyta. I said I'd heard she was a direct descendant of George Washington. "Who told you that?" she snapped. I said Will Tweedy, and she said, "You tell Will to get his facts straight. Ev-erybody knows George Washington had no children, so a statement like that impugns his character." She said Pres-ident Washington was her great-great-great-uncle. His sister Betty married Fielding Lewis and they had eight children, and one of those was her grandfather's father.

So, Will, you are now set straight.

I am impressed that she is also kin to the King of England and Chief Justice John Marshall, but I liked her better after she said her mama always told her a family tree should be like a potato vine, with the best part underground. "Of course I'm proud to be descended from the Washington family, but nobody else cares about that except the D.A.R. I'm more interested in the United Daughters of the Confederacy than the D.A.R."

I begged Miss Hyta to come talk to my class about George Washington, but she says everybody already knows about her and him. She offered to come talk about the women's suffrage movement or the Women's Christian Temperance Union, but warned me that certain men in Progressive City would want me fired if she did either one.

I was about to ask her about living in the Panama Canal Zone when one of the cooks rushed in and said, "Lawdy, Miss Hyta, come quick! Yo monkey loose in de kitchen! He done made a gran' mess wid my custard!"

You'd told me about the monkey, but I thought he stayed in a cage in the barn. It gives me the creeps just thinking about him. I can't even stand a dog in the house.

With best regards,
Sanna

I was crazy about Hyta Mae Brown. I think I halfway fell in love with her when she came to Cold Sassy in 1910. I was eighteen then, and I guess she was about ten years older. Not pretty or anything, but there was something quick and special about her, almost electric, and she had sad eyes.

I'd never known a lady before who said exactly what she thought about anything and everything, as if she had nothing to lose anymore. Her mouth was usually going ninety-to-nothing, but you never learned much about her except the George Washington stuff and her life in the Canal Zone. Her mother was dead, and she had gone to Panama to keep house for her daddy. That was in 1904. The French had given up on digging the canal because of yellow fever and malaria, and her daddy, a civil engineer, went there to help clear out the swamps where mosquitoes bred. There were no schools. Miss Hyta tutored a bunch of American children in the French cottage where they lived. She liked telling how termites ate up the floors every two or three years and government carpenters replaced them free.

Other than such as that you never heard Miss Hyta talk about herself. Nothing personal, I mean. Frolic Flournoy, the postmaster in P.C., said she mailed a letter every Monday to a man in the Canal Zone named Mr. G. Leeds Wildman, and letters came from him to her, sometimes two or three at a time, but nobody dared ask her who he was, and she never mentioned him.

As I explained to Sanna, Miss Hyta was still an outsider in Progressive City, her and the squirrel monkey both, despite they'd been here seven years. Miss Hyta's daddy had died of malaria and she came to P.C. to live with Miss Effie Belle Tate and Mr. Bubba, her mother's sister and brother. Mr. Bubba died the next year at age 105, and that's when Miss Effie Belle started renting out rooms.

One paying guest I remember was an old lady named Mrs. Merkle. If she was going somewhere, even for just an hour, she'd take a spool of black thread and run it from the knob of her hall door to the bedposts and through drawer pulls on the dresser, all around the room to her closet door. The thread was never broken. One time four old maids were rooming there, Miss Rachel, Miss Jessie, Miss Grace, and Miss Bessie. Miss Grace had stock in the Coca-Cola Company and lived on her dividends. When she got too old to go down for meals, Miss Hyta or Miss Effie Belle took her a tray upstairs three times a day with no extra pay for it. Miss Grace kept saying she'd leave Miss Effie Belle her Coca-Cola stock, but when she died her will said it was to go to the American Red Cross.

After she died and Miss Bessie went to live with her sister, Miss Hyta and Miss Effie Belle decided to fix up two apartments, meaning a tiny stove and sink were installed. Mrs. Eubanks lived in one of them. She put coffee grounds and water in a pan and hard-boiled an egg in it while the coffee brewed. We always hoped she washed the egg good first. She also sprinkled psilum seeds on her oatmeal. Psilum, which she called persilum, was for her colon. She's the only woman I ever heard talk about her colon. "The seeds swell up in the digestive track," she said. "They keep me reg'lar."

I once had to go get a dead rat out of the closet for Mrs. Eubanks.

A retired Baptist preacher and his wife lived in the other apartment, upstairs. The lady was crazy. One day she got tired of washing dishes and just threw the dish-pan out the window, soapy water and dishes included. The dishes were English Wedgwood brought from the Canal Zone.

After that, Miss Effie Belle changed the apartments back to rooms and decided to start a boarding house. On account of Miss Hyta's monkey, it wasn't easy to hire help or get customers. But good food soon outweighed the zoo, and people from all over town got to coming there for dinner. When Miss Effie Belle died in 1914, Miss Hyta inherited the house and business.

Which is why she and Sanna were talking in the dining room that day after school.

13

THE Wednesday before Thanksgiving turned out rainy and cold, which meant driving to Mitchellville was out of the question. However, by then it had been decided that, rain or shine, I would be eating my turkey with the Jolleys. Sanna was to leave P.C. Wednesday afternoon and I would join her at the station in Athens, where she had to change trains.

The Athens depot was an anthill of goings and comings. University students, old folks, and families were all trying to get somewhere for Thanksgiving. I watched one tattered poorwhite family running single file across the tracks, scared they'd missed their train. The daddy was first, followed by the mama and a string of stairstep younguns. The littlest one, struggling to keep up, kept yelling, "Wait for baby, dod-dammit! Wait for baby!"

Sanna and I managed to get seats together in the passenger car. "Just think," I said, "I've got you all to myself!"

She laughed. "Look around, Will. We aren't exactly alone."

The seats were all full. The conductor was taking up tickets. "Don't see a soul," I said, and touched her cheek.

Moments later, a stout farm woman wearing a big toothless smile and a man's old wool overcoat lumbered down the aisle, aimed right at us. Above the *whoosh* of steam and grinding of wheels as the train pulled out of the station, she shouted, "Lawd, if it ain't li'l Sanna Maria Klein!"

"Why, it's Mrs. Herndon!" Sanna exclaimed. She rose quickly, held out her arms. They hugged like long-lost relatives. "Oh, I'm so glad to see you! It's been years!"

I stood up too, of course.

"Lemme look at you, Sanna Maria!" Holding on to a seat, Mrs. Herndon stepped back a little. "Lawd, if you ain't done growed up and got ladyfied! But I'd know you for one a-them Klein girls anywheres. All y'all got yore mama's looks—black-headed, and that brunette skin and them black eyes. Who's your mister?"

"Oh, I'm sorry." Sanna put her hand on my arm and introduced me. "Mrs. Herndon, this is Mr. Tweedy."

"Hidy-do, sir."

"Mrs. Herndon lives down the road a piece from Mama," Sanna explained. To Mrs. Herndon she said, "We're, uh, on our way to . . . to Mitchellville. For Thanksgiving."

"You ought to be a-goin' home for Thanksgivin', Sanna Maria."

"How's Mama?"

"Good as common, I reckon. But she complains she don't see you much since yore daddy died."

"Well, it's hard to get there and—I mean, I stay so busy . . ."

"Hit grieves her, Sanna Maria. She thinks you done got shamed of the fam'ly."

I could tell that Sanna was flustered. She said, "You know that's not so."

"I know it and you know it. But she don't."

It was an awkward moment. I said, "Take my seat, Miz Herndon, so y'all can visit."

"Thank you, sir, but I got a seat of my own, and it looks like I better go on back to it." The passenger car started rocking. She turned and staggered up the aisle.

Sanna called after her, "Tell Mama you saw me, hear? And give my best to Li'l George and them when you get home."

Without looking back she shouted, "Yes'm, I'll do that."

As we settled into our seats again, I wondered about Sanna and her mama. Had Sanna thought about going to the farm for Thanksgiving? "You're twitching your shoulders, Will. What's bothering you?"

"Nothin'. Just thinkin' about Miz Herndon." I smiled at her. "You know, right now you remind me of a chicken that just got its head pecked by a brood hen."

She didn't like that. There was a long silence between us, underlaid by train sounds and sprinkled with coughs and chatter from other passengers. Somebody going to the next car opened the end door, letting in a blast of cold damp air and loud clickety-clacks.

"Hey, Sanna Maria Klein." I leaned my head close to hers. "You never did tell me how your mama picked that name out of the air."

She didn't answer. Just sat watching trees move backwards past the train window. Then, rifling through her handbag, she pulled out a little mirror, surveyed her face, tucked a loose strand of black hair under her red hat. I tried again. "I don't know why, but Sanna Maria sounds kind of familiar."

She had gone back to staring out the window. Still not looking at me, she said, "Do you remember the names of Columbus's ships?"

"What's that got to do with it?"

"Just tell me the names of Columbus's ships."

"Okay, they were the *Nina*, the *Pinta*, and the *Sanna Maria*." I pronounced the last one without the *t*, the way I'd always said and heard it. Light dawned as the train car rocked in a sudden buffet of rain and wind. "You mean. . . ?"

With a little sigh, she said, "I'm afraid so. I was born on Columbus Day, and Mama was still trying to decide on a name when Lily Maude came home from school, singsonging, 'The-Nina-the-Pinta-and-the-Sanna-Maria.' She went on like that all afternoon—'the-Nina-the-Pinta-the-Sanna-Maria'—and Mama started thinking that Nina or Sanna Maria, either one, would make a pretty name for the baby. Me."

Sanna still wasn't looking at me. She was staring through the rain that now sheeted the train windows. "I've hated my name ever since Columbus Day in the first grade."

"I don't see . . ."

"The teacher wrote the names of the ships on the blackboard and made us recite them out loud over and over, just the way Lily Maude had done. 'The-Nina-the-Pinta-and-the-Sanna-Maria.' I remember Miss Dot slapping out the beat with a yardstick."

Trees kept sailing backwards, followed by more trees and cotton fields and an occasional lonely unpainted farmhouse, but Sanna didn't see them. She was looking inside herself. "You may not believe it, Will, but I was a very shy child. It took a lot of nerve, but that day I halfway raised my hand, and Miss Dot nodded. I stood up and proudly announced, 'Today is my birthday. I'm six years old. I was named for Columbus's ship!' I thought Miss Dot would say how nice. What she said was, 'In that case, your name's not spelled right.' She turned to the blackboard and underlined the *Santa* part of *Santa Maria* and told me to copy it thirty times. All the children laughed. This was a one-room school, Will—first through seventh grades—and everybody laughed. Even my brother, Joe Pye. Even Lily Maude."

The train slowed as we passed a small community of wood frame houses, then screeched and hissed to a stop across the road from a little store and a small church named Hard Creek Baptist. When the door opened to let an old man get off, cold air swept through the car and set us shivering. We were moving again before Sanna said, "From that day, I never opened my mouth in class unless I got called on. If I didn't speak, I couldn't say anything stupid and get laughed at. Will, there's a little girl in my class now, shyest child you ever saw. She makes perfect grades on her papers, but if I call on her, she can't say a word. I've quit calling on her."

She looked up at me with a little smile that turned off as quickly as it had turned on. "I copied *Santa Maria* thirty times, but that night I got out the family Bible and found the names. Of course the only one I could read was mine: Sanna Maria Klein. That's how Mama had written it, so that was my name—no matter what Miss Dot said."

I ached for the shy little girl she'd been. I longed to take her in my arms, soothe her with tender kisses, stroke her hair. But we were on a train, and she wouldn't have let me touch her anyhow. So I just asked what did her mother say about it.

"I didn't tell Mama," said Sanna. "None of us ever went to Mama about anything. We went to Papa. That night he wrote a note for me to take Miss Dot, saying he wanted the spelling to stay the way it was. That didn't stop the children, though. For weeks they taunted me. I hated them and I hated my name. When I went to live with Sister Maggie, I asked her to please just call me Sanna, and that's been my name ever since. I guess I'll always be Sanna Maria to Mama and Mrs. Herndon and everybody else in Mount Sinai Community—the same way Progressive City is still Cold Sassy to Miss Love and Doc Slaughter—and you."

"Not to me. Not anymore. Anyway, at least you've got one thing to be thankful for, Sanna."

She looked up at me, puzzled.

"What if you'd been born on Christmas Day? You might have been named Santa Claus and called Sannie Claus."

"Don't make fun of me, Will."

"I love you, Sanna. If your name was Issie or Pocahontas or King George, I'd still love you." I put my hand on hers and she let it stay—for about two seconds.

"You want to hear my mother's name, Will? Mama had a

great-uncle, Wilhelm Barnhart, and when she was born he declared her a special child. 'Like one born with a caul over her face,' he said, and claimed the right to name her. What he came up with was Flora Plantena Lemma Sadai Zetta Susannah Greta Margarethe Utilly Meety Keesy Barnhart. It's all there in the Barnhart family Bible. When Mama was little she'd have to recite all her names for preachers and visiting relatives, and she enjoyed the attention. She was just called Flora. Being Flora was why she got so interested in flower names . . ." She sighed again.

"You think your mother will come for Thanksgiving dinner?" As soon as I asked, I knew I should have kept my mouth shut.

"She never comes to Mitchellville," Sanna said bitterly. Then, brightening, she added, "Will, you don't know what it means to me that you'll finally get to meet my people—I mean the ones who've made all the difference in my life. I wouldn't be anything if it weren't for Sister Maggie and Brother Henry.

"From my first day in school I wanted to be a teacher. Mount Sinai only had seven grades and wasn't much of a school, but Mitchellville had a high school. So Sister Maggie asked Papa if he'd let me spend the school year with them and go home for holidays and summer vacations, and he said yes.

"I'd been promoted to sixth grade, but I had to take tests in Mitchellville, and as soon as I saw the math test I knew I couldn't pass it and asked to stay back. I had a wonderful girl-hood in Mitchellville. Sister Maggie taught me to sew and paid for piano lessons and had parties for me and saw that I had nice friends.

"And then Brother Henry sent me to college. Paid all my expenses, and me just his sister-in-law. I wasn't even theirs, the way Annie Laurie and Lonzo are."

At that moment the engineer blew the whistle, and with much screeching and grinding of wheels, the train stopped and the woman who had been sitting across the aisle from us hurried to the door.

It took Mrs. Herndon less than a minute to seize the opportunity. She landed in the vacated seat with a lapful of boxes, sacks, and bundles. Leaning across the aisle, she tapped Sanna on the shoulder. "How's Maggie? She feelin' all right?"

Sanna's answer was brief. "Yes'm, except she's been sneezing ever since August."

"Her and yore mama both. Once they git a-goin', they can sneeze their heads off. I seen Miss Flora just fore I left to go visit Helen'n'em in Commerce. Hit were on a Tuesday. No, Wednesday. No, hit was a Tuesday, cause that was the day Mr. Paul Pur-due tuck a wagonload of corn to the gristmill. You remember Mr. Pur-due. When I went in, Miss Flora was sneezin' like hit was pepper up her nose. Eyes a-runnin', nose a-runnin', her face broke out red all over and hit a-itchin'. Said she'd been sweepin'. Sweepin' always gits her goin'." The train slowed to plod up a steep grade. "I shore do hope hit don't stall," said Mrs. Herndon. "When I rid this thang to Commerce, hit hit a artermobile at a crossin'. Didn't nobody git hurt, but we waited the longest kind a-time. Well, I cain't git over you bein' so fancy, Sanna Maria. You still little-bitty, though. Ain't tall like Maggie and Blossom."

"No, ma'am, I'm not."

The train picked up speed again. A baby started crying. A child's voice wailed, "Papa, I'm cold." There was loud laughter from a group of soldiers at the front of the car. Sanna took a book out of her handbag, but Mrs. Herndon wasn't about to be cut off. Placing her feet in the aisle, she leaned forward the better to see me, and said, "Mr. Tweedy, ain't Sanna Maria just the prettiest thang you ever seen? You ought've seed her when she was a baby. Law, I remember one day, I reckon she warn't no more'n eight month old, and her sisters brought in a big dishpan full of blackberries, fresh-picked and shiny, with lots of red'ns to make the jelly firm up right." The book was still open but I knew Sanna was listening. "Honey, you got so excited. Kicked yore li'l ole legs and bounced in Miss Flora's lap a-pointin' to them red berries and just a-crowin'! You was tryin' to say, 'See? See?' What come out was 'Tee? Tee?' Hit 'as the first time you'd tried to talk. Miss Flora, she was real proud."

Sanna, delighted, said she'd never heard that story before.

Mrs. Herndon knew how to keep an audience once she got hold of it. "I recollect another time," she said. "It was a Sunday afternoon, and Miss Flora was still dressed up cause the preacher was there, him and his wife both. Miss Flora was a beautiful lady then, Sanna Maria, not all wore out like now. She had on the prettiest dressin' sack, lots of lace on it. I can see her now, a-holdin' on to yore li'l dress to hep you balance. You was just larnin' to walk."

Sanna had planted her feet in the aisle too, almost touching Mrs. Herndon's, but their conversation was interrupted by a shiny-faced young soldier standing in the aisle. "Excuse me, ladies, I got to get by." The doughboy looked pressed and proud in his new uniform. You'd have thought he was a general, they made way for him so quick. In my Sunday suit, I felt like a fool.

After he passed, I leaned around Sanna and asked Mrs. Herndon if she was going home for Thanksgiving.

"I reckon. Though I ain't shore where home's at no more."

Sanna looked surprised. "Didn't you stay on at the farm after, uh . . ."

"You mean after Big George walked out on me? Yes'm. But I couldn't keep thangs goin' by myself. So when Bertie Ruth and her husband offered to move in and take over, I said, 'Hep yoreself, and welcome.' Sanna Maria, you remember Bertie Ruth. She married a man old as her daddy. Dance O'Neill, that's his name. I knowed Mr. O'Neill was in the loggin' business, but hit shore did surprise me when he went to loggin' my woods stead of farmin' my land. Pretty soon their oldest boy, he moved in with his bride. Said he 'as go'n grow him some cotton. Said hit'd be all the same to me whether he farmed hit or I let the fields lie fallow, and I couldn't argue with that. And then Katie, she come with her husband—he works for the railroad—and pretty soon t'warn't my house.

"They wouldn't let me do nothin' cept rock babies. I couldn't wring a chicken or pick a chicken, neither one. Hit makes me proud, the way they treated me so nice, but like I told Bertie Ruth, I can rest in the grave. Hit 'as like I was just comp'ny. So three or more weeks ago I went to see Helen over in Commerce. Sanna Maria, you remember Helen."

"Oh, yes, we used to study together. She was really smart, Mrs. Herndon."

"She still is. Works her head off. Her and her husband, Richard, they both do twelve-hour shifts in the mill, and they was mighty proud to see me, I tell you. They let me do all the cookin' and the washin' and the cleanin', and by me bein' thar, the oldest chi'ren could go to school reg'lar cause I could hep to see after the li'l uns. Helen's got eight chi'ren already, Sanna Maria, and another'n on the way that looks like twins. Well, that li'l ole sorry mill house felt a lot more like home than my farm, but I did get right tarred a-not restin'. So when Bertie Ruth wrote and begged me to come spend Thanksgivin', I was right ready to."

"So you go'n stay on at Mount Sinai?" I asked.

"I don't know. I been a-livin' in that house nigh on fifty year, but, well, we'll see."

The train jerked and a box on Mrs. Herndon's lap toppled into the aisle. Reaching for it, she said, "I got some shuttles in here. Broke ones. They tho'm out at the mill, and so Helen, she brings'm home for the babies to play with. I'm takin' these here to Bertie Ruth's crowd, and I'll give some to the colored chi'ren."

"How many does Bertie Ruth have?" Sanna asked.

"Fifteen. Ain't none of her girls had to get marrit, but they's a few boys I call speckled. I mean they ain't bad but they ain't

good either. Out of that many, they cain't all turn out good."
She laughed. "Want to hear sump'm awful, Sanna Maria? Bertie Ruth, she wrote me last week a colored hand on old Baldwin's place up and ran off in the night. His wife, she said he'd
deserted her and the chi'ren, but one a-her boys, the uppity
one—he's go'n git hisself shot if he don' be careful—he said
his daddy had gone to Cincinnati. Said his daddy could make
a decent livin' up North and was a-go'n send for the whole
fam'ly later. Mr. Baldwin got so mad he might-near turned'm
all out right then and thar, but he thought twice. Knowed he'd
be in a pickle if they left fore hog killin'. The way them colored
ack here lately, I'm bout ready to move up North myself, just
to git away from'm."

Sanna bristled. "You can't blame them. Jesus said—"

"Jesus didn't say nothin' bout farm hands leavin' their white
folks in the lurch. Jesus said do unto others as you would have
them do unto you." Staring straight ahead, Mrs. Herndon was
quiet for a while. Then she said again, "I still think you ought
to be goin' home for Thanksgivin', Sanna Maria. You go see
Maggie'n'em all the time."

Sanna didn't answer. She just opened her book again. Ten
minutes later the train steamed into the depot at Greensboro.
It looked like the whole town had come to meet somebody.
Families waved and hollered when they spotted the passenger
they were waiting for, especially if it was a college student or
a man in uniform. It wasn't hard to locate Mr. Henry Jolley.
A huge man, much taller than I was, and built like a hog. Big
head, fat face and lips, and small eyes squinting through folds
of fat. No neck you could see, ham-sized arms, big fat hands,
massive chest, and a stomach that led the rest of him.

"Sanna! Here, girl!" he called, waving a big cigar.

Her face brightened, and, forgetting me, she ran towards
him, arms outstretched.

Even as he hugged her to him, I could tell he was drunk.

14

BESIDE Mayor Jolley's bigness, Sanna's smallness struck me. Her head barely came to his chest as he folded her into a tight hug. That's when her glowing smile faded to dismay and embarrassment, then anger. He smelled of whiskey, and he staggered against her as she tried to guide him away from the depot's crush of people. When she introduced us, his fat lips stretched into a silly grin. He was holding his cigar in the hand he extended, and that just made him giggle. He leaned on Sanna as we hurried on towards his new seven-passenger touring car in the cold mist of late afternoon.

It was easy to picture us freezing to death in a ditch or stuck in the mud or worse, so I said I'd sure like to get the feel of the steering wheel if he didn't mind my driving. "By all means, Mr. Tweedy," he said, and was asleep in the back seat before we reached the road to Mitchellville. Supper was a mix of good hot food and imitation gaiety, a lame attempt by everybody to cover up the fact that the big man at the head of the table was besotted. He belched loudly, flirted with Sarah, his daughter Annie Laurie's friend from Shorter College, fussed at Lonzo about his grades in front of the two boys he had brought home from Mercer, and asked Mrs. Jolley where in hell did she get that sausage. "You know I like hot sausage," he said, "and this lye hominy, I don't see one piece of red pepper in it."

"Well, the girls are here," said Mrs. Jolley, a tall, plump, matronly woman with dark eyes like Sanna's. Her brown hair was plaited and wound around her head. "You know, Mr. Jolley, they don't like hot sausage, and—"

"You could have cooked some of both." He glared at her. Nobody spoke while the lye hominy was being passed, and the stewed tomatoes and butter beans.

Sanna asked Annie Laurie and Sarah if teachers she'd had were still at Shorter. And she told about the time it was announced that senior girls could have the privilege of not going to supper on Sunday night. "A friend and I thought you should take advantage of any special privilege, so we didn't go to supper and then about nine o'clock we were starving. We went around to every room hoping that somebody had something to eat and finally a girl gave us a five-cent package of crackers. We didn't ever skip Sunday night supper again."

Mr. Jolley couldn't reach his food if he sat straight in front of the table. He had to sit sideways to keep that big stomach out in front and his right hand close to the nearest plate. Everybody was pointedly ignoring him, so I said, "When I was at the University of Georgia, we had pressing clubs. You had to join and it cost a dollar a month. I joined one month and my friend Frank would join the next and somebody else the next. We'd all send our clothes in on one membership."

Mr. Jolley got on Lonzo about his grades again, and I looked at the mayor and said, "When I was leavin' for college, old Loomis Toy, who worked for us, brought my trunk up there to the depot in a wheelbarrow and my daddy came to see me off. That day Papa told me he didn't know anything bout college and never heard of one until he was grown, but he said, 'I understand there is a lot more to college than what you get out of books and I want you to get it all.' Maybe Lonzo's just tryin' to get it all, sir."

Tall like her mother, Annie Laurie was a plump girl with mischievous eyes. Sanna asked her if she'd been invited yet to the president's house as she had. "Dr. Van Hoose was a sweet man," she said. "He and his wife had a pretty house down the hill from the college and they'd invite a few girls to their home for Sunday dinner sometimes."

I noticed that every time Mr. Jolley tried to say something, Mrs. Jolley said something else. She seemed furious at him for getting drunk. When supper was over and the girls had cleared the table, Mrs. Jolley brought in a coconut pie. Mr. Jolley stared at Annie Laurie and said, "Sugar, you've put on weight."

Sanna said, "All girls do that their freshman year, Brother Hen."

"Maybe you'd better let me eat your piece of pie, honey," he said.

"If you want to talk about weight, Papa, I think you've put on some too. How bout letting me eat *your* pie?"

His face turned red, and suddenly he got up and left the room. There was an embarrassed silence. Finally Mrs. Jolley said, "I hope y'all will excuse him. He hasn't been himself lately."

At that moment he came back in. Flailing a hacksaw in the air, Mayor Jolley pushed his chair aside with his foot and said, "I'm sick and tired of sittin' sideways to eat." With everybody watching, eyes wide and mouths open, he proceeded to cut out a half-moon at his place at the mahogany table. When he was almost through, his wife covered her face with her hands and started to cry. He ignored her.

"All right, now," he said as the cut-out piece clattered to the floor. "A table had ought to fit the man that provisions it." He sat down, pulled his chair up, and his stomach fitted the hole perfectly. He pulled his pie and a cup of coffee to the right of his stomach, ate the pie, sucked up the coffee, and lit a cigar, wearing a triumphant smile.

After supper, while Miss Maggie and the girls were washing,

drying, and putting away dishes and setting out plate scrapings for the dog, Mr. Henry and the boys and I smoked in the parlor.

Mr. Henry was in charge, and seemed to have sobered up a little, but he was still belligerent. "I understand you studied agriculture at the university," he said to me, puffing to get his cigar started again.

"Yessir."

"Would you like to manage one of my farms over in Twiggs County? Or maybe you are about to get drafted. You trying to get in the Army or trying to stay out?"

"Tryin' to get in, sir." I almost told him I was too skinny, but in the presence of his bulk, I lacked the nerve.

"Well, if you get rejected, my offer stands. It's mighty hard to get good overseers."

I thanked him, but told him about the Tweedy farm in Banks County that I wanted to farm when the war was over.

Later, after Brother Hen and Sister Maggie had said good night, Sanna came into the parlor. We could hear loud talk from their bedroom—mean talk.

As we stood together in front of the fire, Sanna suddenly began to cry. I put my arms around her, and she rested her head on my chest as sobs racked her body. I kissed her forehead but had the good sense not to try for more. She never raised her face to mine, just sobbed. Finally I put my arm around her and guided her to the couch that was drawn up near the fire.

"How could he do this to Sister Maggie?" she said, with the tears still running down her cheeks. "As long as I can remember he got drunk on weekends, but never like this. He's never done anything like this. She's so humiliated, so ashamed. And she's heartbroken at the mess he's made of her dining table. She's always been so proud of the dining room suite.

"Right now I just hate him. He—I guess there haven't been many Friday nights he didn't get drunk, but not on weekdays and not when our friends were here. I just can't understand how he could be the mayor, sworn to uphold Georgia law, and we've got this Prohibition Act and he thinks nothing of violating it.

"To him the bootleggers are man's best friend. He's told the sheriff to let them alone as long as they don't hurt anybody, so the moonshiners come in the night and leave jars of moonshine behind the sacks of cow feed in the milk shed. 'As long as it doesn't hurt anybody.' It just about kills Sister Maggie, and Annie Laurie and Lonzo and I have lived with it all our lives here. He's such a good, kind, wonderful man when he's sober, but a drink of whiskey makes him mean as he can be. Sister Maggie's never complained, she's never even admitted to us that he drinks, as if we wouldn't know it if she didn't say so."

Sanna told me about Mr. Jolley's Friday night card games with his drinking cronies. She said her sister was helpless to put an end to them.

One night Sister Maggie got so mad she screamed at him, "No more card games here! I'm putting my foot down!" The next morning, she was groaning in pain as she limped to the breakfast table. "She told Annie Laurie and me that she dropped a heavy picture frame on her foot the night before, but we knew better. That's what she told everybody in town. When Sister Maggie realized that Brother Hen was either pretending not to know that he'd stepped on her foot and broken it, or that he really didn't remember, she told him the same story she'd told everybody else.

"But Annie Laurie had heard the whole thing the night before.

"I don't know what Sister Maggie will tell everybody at Thanksgiving dinner about what he did tonight. Of course, when he realizes how much he's upset her, he'll be sorry and he'll offer to buy her a new table. He can't buy what this one means to her, though. It was our grandmother's table." Sanna was quiet for a moment, staring into the flames.

Then she said, "Annie Laurie and I have always vowed we would never marry a man who would even take a drink. Sister Maggie says if a man has habits you can't live with, and he doesn't love you enough to change before the wedding, don't expect him to change later. She had to learn that the hard way. I've learned it the hard way too. Will, I didn't really tell you what happened that night with Hugh in Jefferson, did I? You remember what I told you about the tub running over and the mess the dinner party became, and I told you that I wished the rest of what had happened was as funny? Hugh got mad with me that night, Will, and I was mad with him, and he got drunk. He stayed up drinking after everybody went to bed, and I didn't sleep a wink either. In the middle of the night I smelled smoke and ran out to the hall, and his mother and father were already rushing towards the parlor with blankets and buckets of water. Hugh had gone to sleep smoking a cigarette and the upholstery had caught fire. He and his father had an awful row when it was all over and I wasn't supposed to know any of it. Hugh didn't come down to breakfast the next morning and everybody was upset—the way it's going to be here in the morning—and when Mr. Blankenship offered to bring me on back home—he said Hugh was sick—well, you were there when I arrived.

"I vowed never to marry a man who drinks, and I'm not going to."

I was driven to confess. "Sanna, there's a lot of drinkin' goes on at frat houses. One night I took a drink and I guess I took another and another, but I started feelin' sick and went to my room. Sometime in the night I woke up in a pool of vomit. I couldn't believe it. I'd thrown up all that stinkin' stuff and was too drunk even to wake up."

She went pale and her face tensed. Before she could say anything, I said, "I tried to drink a few times since then, Sanna. I've found out that one drink makes me sick. Every time. I can't even finish a drink, in fact. So now I have a good excuse not to.

I just tell people it makes me sick, and then I don't feel so awkward, or like, because I'm not drinkin', I'm passin' judgment on what other people are doin'. So you see, that's not anything you have to worry about with me, now or ever. I can't drink and I know it, and all my friends know it."

Mr. Henry had very little to say at breakfast and looked awful, fitted into his semicircle at the table. He was gone most of the morning to get his two cousins from his farm near Mitchellville. The boys went over to see a friend of Lonzo's, and the girls helped in the kitchen.

I met Maybelle, the cook, a sweet, dignified brown-colored woman with scant hair and no teeth. I could tell she had been crying. Later, when I was reading in the parlor, I could hear Sanna and Maybelle through the open doors of the dining room. They were at the buffet, taking out silver and linens for the table. Maybelle said, "Miss Sanna, ever'body in town go'n be laughin' at us. Dey go'n ax me do it be so, did Mr. Henry cut up Miss Maggie's table, but I ain' go'n tell nobody nuthin'. I des go'n make lak I don' hear, or I go'n say, 'What Mist' Henry do or doan do ain' none my bizness.' But I go'n be shamed, Miss Sanna, and po' Miss Maggie, she go'n be mighty shamed."

The rain had stopped, and the day was cold and darkly overcast. But the dinner Miss Maggie served that afternoon was splendid. The turkey was a huge torn, and the dressing was the best I think I ever ate, baked and browned, crisp, but what I was most thankful for at that dinner was the good cheer. It was as if a quick rain had cleared out the strain and anger at Mr. Henry that had spoiled the air ever since I arrived. I'm sure it began as just courtesy, with everyone trying not to bring hard feelings to the festivities, but the festivities took over as soon as Mr. Henry got back with the two old cousins. I remember how happy the young people were, and how the strained looks on Sanna's and Miss Maggie's faces lifted, and how even Mr. Henry joined in. His morning-after misery seemed to have eased, and he was the jovial, twinkled-eyed fat man I had expected him to be. He sat in the curve of that whacked-out semicircle as casually as if the table had been designed and built that way.

I'm sure we talked about the war—everybody did in those days—and I remember the old ladies talked about their ailments. Everybody talked about past Thanksgivings, and I did my best to liven things up anywhere I could. Mr. Henry's two old cousins, Cudn Em and Cudn Abby, both had heavy mustaches, and Cudn Em had a humped back. Sanna said later they never went anywhere except to see close relatives because they were so embarrassed about their mustaches. I asked her why they didn't just shave, but she said they thought that's the way the Lord meant for them to look and to change it would be a sin.

Cudn Em was especially taken with sin. She had a Bible covered in faded red calico that she kept in her lap. The hump on her back reminded me of a man who came through Cold Sassy once selling blankets. He carried them on his back the way Cudn Em carried her hump. Sanna said Cudn Em felt the Lord was punishing her with the bent back for some sin. She never could figure out what the sin was, but she'd got the notion that if she kept opening the Bible, closed her eyes, then looked where her finger landed on a page, it might give her a clue about her sin. I liked her. Her head was bent so far forward she couldn't hold it up, but every now and then she'd look at me sideways with a shy little smile.

Another guest, Mrs. Faunt, was a neighbor whose husband had died on the Fourth of July. The Jolleys invited her for dinner when they heard she would be alone for Thanksgiving. She had an ear trumpet, which she aimed in the direction of whoever was speaking. She was a beautiful old lady in a navy blue wool dress, with a heavy shawl around her shoulders. Her face was powdered, her thick gray hair piled fashionably atop her head. She was the one who started the liveliest conversation of the day, about storms. The lightning we'd had the day before was unusual, and Mrs. Faunt said she was scared to death.

"That lightnin' yesterday brings to mind the time we was all settin' on the porch after dinner," she said. "That was in the summertime, and all-a sudden it come up a storm, a real bad one, with lightnin' flashin' and thunder thunderin' somethin' awful. We all went inside, and the dogs and cats tried to get in the house too, but Mama said, 'Don't let them animals come in! They'll draw the lightnin'!' We had a big old rooster named Uncle Lenox and that rooster flew up on the porch to get out of the rain, but Mama went out and shooed him off. Then he flew up on the iron gate and Mama told Lem to go make him get down. 'He'll draw lightnin',' but Lem said, 'Roosters ain't animals, they birds. And birds don't draw no lightnin'.' He said he could prove it, and he yelled out the door, 'All right, rooster, draw. Draw! I say draw that lightnin', Uncle Lenox!' And bless patty, down come a single bolt and down fell Uncle Lenox! We had him for supper that night."

Maybelle was passing her big yeast rolls. "I heerd that a white man got hit by lightnin'," she said, "and he turnt black. But I doan know as he stayed black."

Cudn Abby, hiding her mustache with her hand, said, "I had a teacher got hit one time and from then on her neck was twisted to one side. Good thing lightnin' never strikes twice in the same place." She laughed. "If Miss Mable had got hit in the neck again, she'd a-been lookin' backwards the rest of her life."

"Well, it can strike twice," said Mr. Henry. "Miss Maggie will back me up on it. The Quillians over on Fourth Street, their chimney got struck by lightnin' fifteen years ago and it happened again just a short while back, sometime last year."

"That's right," said Miss Maggie. "They say brick and ashes fell down all over Mrs. Quillian's living room furniture."

I got in on that. "One night we had an electrical storm so bad," I said, with the last of my turkey poised on my fork, "that next morning our neighbor came to the back door with a long coil of pine bark in his hand. 'I think this belongs to y'all,' he told Mama. Lightnin' had struck the big tree that straddles the fence between our house and his. I kind of collect stories about weather, so I remember."

Sanna went with us that evening when Mr. Henry drove me to the depot in Greensboro. It was black dark when I got home, and there was a Western union telegram under my door.

Received at 7:50 P.M. — Air F430

New York, New York
11/28/17

Mr. H. W. Tweedy
c/o Mayfield Boarding House
Athens, Georgia

ARRIVING MORNING TRAIN SATURDAY WITH
CAMPBELL JUNIOR STOP
BEG YOU BREAK NEWS TO FAMILY STOP
LOMA

15

THERE was no way to break news like that gently to Mama and Papa. With the office closed, I had planned on spending Friday and Saturday with them in P.C., so I just took the telegram with me and said, "Mama, looks like you don't have to worry about Campbell Junior up there with the Yankees anymore."

"Will, do you think this means Loma's gettin' a divorce? What . . ."

"Maybe it's the old man that's gettin' a divorce. But if you notice, she didn't say anything about divorce. Maybe she'll just do like lots of people and come home for a while and then they'll make up and off she'll go again, specially if he waves some money in her direction. You know what they say. A dollar is the fastest flyin' machine yet known."

Mama always was one to worry about what everybody would think, but I believe it was Aunt Loma she was worrying about while we waited at the depot for the train to come in on Saturday.

They arrived, just like the telegram said they would. Campbell Junior looked like he had grown an inch since September and lost some of that fat. You never saw a boy so happy to be home.

Aunt Loma had dark circles under her eyes, and her clothes looked like she'd slept in them all night, which she had. The only thing looked good about her was the fur coat she was wearing, and that diamond flashing in the sunlight. Within a day or so I learned that what was troubling Loma was something clean clothes and a good night's sleep couldn't put right. Loma was depressed. Whenever Mama saw her coming, she'd go lie down on the black leather daybed. "I can just take Loma better if I'm layin' down," she told me.

To Mama and Papa and the rest of the town she had nothing much to say. But Loma needed to talk; and by her second day home she'd realized I was probably the closest friend she had. "Will, I guess you think I was crazy in the first place, but I didn't marry him just for his money. I mean, I married him a lot for his money, but I was really very fond of him." Loma got herself a glass of tap water and sat down at the kitchen table with a dramatic sigh.

"He claimed he was a Russian count. He had a wife and four children, and when he was still young they all died in a typhoid epidemic. He came to America in eighteen eighty-nine with twelve dollars in gold coins in his pocket and got a job in a New York factory.

"If you remember," she said bitterly, "Pa never knew I existed from the time you were born. You had two daddies, your grandpa and your pa. I never had any. Vitch didn't treat me like a daughter. It was more like I was a princess. He even called me Princess, and I found myself acting like one. When he'd have a party and I was his hostess, I'd pretend I was really a princess, kind of like stage acting, and it gave me a feeling of pride in myself. I liked that."

Mama was taking a nap upstairs and Daddy was out visiting with Campbell Junior, showing off all the changes in town. It occurred to me that if I just kept quiet, Loma would tell me everything. I set some of Mama's leftover Thanksgiving pie out on the table, got out two forks and plates, and settled down to listen.

"He never came to see me without bringing a gift, perfume or earrings," Loma said dreamily. "Once he brought me a little lap dog. I made him take that back. I just couldn't look after a little dog like that in an apartment when I was gone so much.

"He came to every performance I was in. I guess you heard about him being at my performance when I was modeling corsets. That's when we met." She laughed. "He was so gallant and his foreign accent made him seem glamorous. He had all this money he'd made in America. And he talked all the time about the castle he grew up in, and the toys he'd had, and the servants, and the literary parties his parents put on. I just was too . . . he . . . it was just a world I used to read about and couldn't believe existed. I'm not sure it ever did, even for Vitch.

"He'd kiss my hand when we met and he acted so proud of me. When he talked about us marrying, he said he'd build a mansion for me away from the noise and grime of New York City."

I tried to picture Loma living in a mansion, bossing servants around.

"I respected him and I felt he respected me. It wasn't like with Camp. I knew I couldn't step all over Vitch the way I did Camp. Oh, Will, I was so disgusted by Camp, and then after he died I was so ashamed of the way I'd treated him." Loma blushed, and I knew she was wondering if she should go on. But she was in too deep to stop now. I nodded to her, and then pretended to study my pie.

"But, Will, from the first night after I married Vitch, I knew . . . I couldn't stand . . . I mean, he was like a coal miner or somebody. Good Lord, Will, you've got a degree in agriculture. You must know all about animal husbandry. I don't know why it's so hard for me to tell you. Well, let's say that my rich, gallant Mr. Vitch's idea of husbandry was very animal."

Loma said after the second night she was so repulsed and so mad, she told Vitch never to set foot in her room again. He got mean. "He said he'd take my name out of his will. He finally admitted that the main reason he wanted to marry me instead of just courting the rest of his life was because he wanted heirs. The next night I locked my bedroom door and he got a key and unlocked it. I didn't have to fight him off then. He was so cold and calm. He said, 'You will not leave this room until you grant me my rights.' And he took my key and left and locked the door behind him."

For a week he sent the maid in with Loma's meals. Even though the maid was afraid she'd lose her job if she didn't lock the door behind her, at last she felt so sorry for Loma, she did leave the door open. Loma packed a bag and was sneaking down the steps when Vitch saw her and forced her back to her room. The next day there were gardeners working outside near her window. She called to them that she was being kept prisoner and asked them to bring her a ladder. She threw a diamond pin down to them, then put the rest of her jewelry in a drawstring bag that she tied around her waist, stuffed a few clothes in a small satchel, climbed down the ladder, and got away in a taxi.

She sent a telegram to the headmaster at Campbell Junior's school, saying she had to take him out early for the holidays because of illness in the family. She met his train in New York after hocking her gold pins in a pawnshop so she could buy their train tickets to Cold Sassy.

I never doubted Loma would find a way to get back at Mr. Vitch. She was so vindictive that Grandpa once said if he wanted to make a raid on Hell, he would make Loma his first lieutenant.

Editor's note: *Although Olive Ann worked on several scenes that were to appear later in the novel, the chronological narrative ends here. We know from her notes for the rest of this chapter that the fol-*

lowing Sunday was going to be a beautiful day and that Will was going to borrow his papa's car to pick up Sanna in Mitchellville and drive her back to Cold Sassy.

From Olive Ann Burns's Chapter Notes:

On the way home Sanna is going to tell Will more about the situation in Mitchellville—in fact, this may be when she tells him some of the stuff that I have her telling him the night before. May somehow get around to her telling him about the day Papa got hooked by the bull. Want as fast as possible for him to learn more about her and her family, but there are things she won't tell him until she knows they are going to marry and she knows she has got to tell him about her family.

Feed in some of the information about Loma and her husband in letters home—the braggy things she can write home about so that her returning home is totally unexpected. That way she won't have so much to tell Will, and it will keep Loma alive in the minds of the reader if there are little dribbles of it from the time she comes home to get Campbell Junior to go back North with her. Now Loma is left high and dry in New York, as far as the reader is concerned, except for the letter saying that she has just gotten married.

Note: Actually I think what I'm going to do is have Loma say nothing about why she's home. Just say she's homesick and wanted to come home and Campbell Junior wanted to come back there to school and she's obviously very upset, though she tells everybody else in town. . . . Want her to have time after arriving to get the word out around town that she's just homesick, and then the Sunday paper (maybe of Thanksgiving weekend or the following), the headlines in the Atlanta newspaper, pick up a story in great detail from New York telling all the gory details about this rich man, and his wife having to escape from him by climbing down a ladder and being helped by two gardeners and how she claims she was locked in her room. Saw this story in a paper about 1895—have notes on this with more details—look up and concentrate on getting details—in 1917 same kind of yellow journalism, though in a local weekly they would not—they would protect the people—let this be a shock to Cold Sassy, not only the details but her name given and her home town, where according to the paper her husband suspects she may have gone.

Note: When Loma left to go to New York City, she knew she would have to finance herself because she couldn't be sure of getting enough work in the entertainment field. Loma has her house rented. Will asks if she's going to live there. "You could pretend you're a widow. I heard about a widow who painted her house black the week after her husband died." She sold her interest in the store to Hoyt. Miss Love and Sampson own half the store and Hoyt owns the other half and runs the store, which he would love to do anyway, so when she's back she has these jewels but she's not going to be there long, so she rents rooms at Miss Hyta Mae's boarding house for herself and Camp—maybe at this point Camp's room and the room she had used before she went to New York—maybe Mama has rented it to a teacher or someone. In those days people were always renting rooms, so it may not be available for her to come back to and she doesn't want to either, because she doesn't think she'll be there long—and this will get Miss Hyta Mae back into the reader's mind. I want her to be a running character through the book, because she's interesting. I don't know what wonderful or awful things will be happening to her, but I think when Will is through with the Army and comes back to farm, it will be the Depression, and I think Miss Hyta Mae and Miss Love and Will's mother will all be calling on him to do the kinds of things that need doing around the house that a woman can't do or thinks she can't do, and that's going to be a bone of contention with Sanna because maybe he needs to fix fences on the farm and instead he goes over to do little things for all these women who depend on him.

Notes

S ANNA—a perfectionist and a worrier. Obsessed with idea of finding happiness, and for her, happiness means being first with somebody, having her own home, being loved by a perfect man and perfect, loving children. She will never have to have second place there, will be secure, life will be happily ever after, no more misery or problems. She never feels secure with new people or in new situations—doesn't want change—and revels in the way Will is easy with people and never fazed by the unexpected. In fact, the harder things are, the more he is excited and challenged. She thought all troubles would be over if she found the right man. Marries Will—hard time of war months—pregnant, etc.

The theme of Sanna is disillusionment—her life is the pursuit of happiness and perfection, but she finds happiness and perfection impossible to obtain—her idea of happiness is constant joy, no changes.

Will's idea of life is to be challenged. Loves trying anything new, loves change, is impatient with Sanna. Living is a matter of making things work if you can, seeing if you can make things work.

At end of book he is leaving home, happy and excited to have a job, to be able to hope to support his family. Hates leaving Sanna and children, but he's not just off to Dawson, he's off on a new adventure.

Soon after arriving in Cold Sassy and causing trouble with Sanna, Loma has a car accident and breaks her back. [Editor's note: *Although there are no written notes on this, Olive Ann said that she wanted Loma to undergo a personality change through her suffering, to be able to walk again and pay all her medical bills, and then to settle down in Cold Sassy and teach elocution.*]

Perhaps Miss Love's father, sick and dying, age 70 to 75, comes to P.C. for her to look after, and she does it. He has to be waited on, bedridden. Sanna helps her.

Sampson falls in love with Precious, child of Lightfoot and Hosie Roach. Used to getting his way, marries her at end of book despite family feelings.

Loma tells Sanna, "It's just common, like po' white trash, the way you get pregnant every year. Just *common*. I can't imagine anybody smart as you think you are not knowing how to keep from getting that way. You've embarrassed the whole family."

SANNA: Well, I've got three things to say to *you*. Number one, you're crude and mean and your side of my family has just as much to do with it as I do. *Will*, I mean. Number two, it's *our* business, not any of yours. I never wanted a baby every year—I'm *tired*. But it's none of your business. And if you want to talk about embarrassing the family, look in the mirror. You think everybody is proud of your smoking and drinking cocktails and getting a *divorce?*

LOMA: I'll smoke and drink and get a divorce any time I want to.

SANNA: And Will and I will have babies if we want to. One thing I know, I'll never have to get a divorce.

LOMA: Don't you know the talk in town? How often Will goes by to see Carrie Summers?

The book will be the story of Sanna and Will, and Sanna and Loma, and Sanna and Miss Love and the boy Sampson, Sanna and the Depression, Sanna and her perfectionism and anxiety and obsessiveness and possessiveness.

It will show Loma doggedly determined not only to walk again, but to repay all medical bills.

It will show Sanna caught in yet another situation where she feels second—except with the children. She centers her life on them. So does Will, so this is their togetherness. Their separateness comes from his being pulled between his family and Sanna, and conflicts over money.

Miss Love is a sort of catalyst. She says things like "I put a dimmer light at my mirror. I don't like wrinkles."

She tells Sanna: "Be kind to Will."

Sanna tells her: "I read some psychology books in college. Everything that's supposed to warp a child happened to me."

Miss Love: "Everything that could warp a child happened to me, too. But understanding that doesn't help. It's interesting, but it doesn't help. I figure that what you do with your life now is all that counts. I try not to look back."

About Papa's affair:

Mama and Papa had been praying for another baby for years, and hadn't had any, but when I was twenty and Mary Toy fourteen and Mama was forty-two . . . She was so happy. After it came out about Papa and that young woman, it was like she hated her own baby. She didn't make any clothes for it, and even before she started showing, she quit going anywhere, not even to church or missionary circle, and she never smiled or hardly ate. She didn't talk about Papa, of course. But she was too shamed to face anybody, and angry to the core.

Miss Mabry went back home and married an old man who'd been after her, and nobody would have known the scandal if Miss Mabry hadn't got so upset she told his best friend. After Mama heard the baby was a healthy boy, she cleaned a big closet. Lifting and reaching up to high shelves. She thought the reaching did it. That night the pains started and the baby was born dead, the cord around his neck. She never forgave herself.

If she'd wanted to punish Papa, she did it. Punished all of us. I'd have loved having a little brother.

There are the family scandals that hurt so — Papa's baby; Papa dies, had life insurance for the other woman.

Then Brother Henry writes letter so Will marries Sanna even though he realizes it as a mistake, and he tries to be a good husband. (Papa got a special delivery letter from Brother Henry saying if I put off the wedding again, he would send the sheriff after me to put me in jail and sue me for breach of promise.) He will never hurt her, he vows to her and himself. At first he transfers his love from Trulu to Sanna. Only after he is engaged does he realize she doesn't provoke the wild passion Trulu did. He's sorry he acted in haste, but knows he couldn't have trusted Trulu.

Talking to Sanna after Jefferson, he doesn't tell her that the grand party was celebrating his engagement to Trulu. He sat to Mrs. Philpot's right — there was an orchestra (give its name).

Loma divorces finally, comes home after Will and Sanna's marriage, miserable — accuses Sanna of being snobbish, above everybody else. Sanna judging Loma for divorce and smoking and drinking.

Loma says awful things to Sanna. When Loma breaks her back, Sanna has to ride in ambulance with her.

Will thinks he won Sanna. Really it's that she broke up with Hugh — drinking, near-rape. Will learns this after engaged. Hugh becomes politician, runs for government. Sanna doesn't know about Brother Henry's letter, believes Army duties caused two postponements of wedding.

Will is proud of Sanna, feels great tenderness and appreciation of Sanna, enjoys being with her. Kind of girl he'd always hoped to marry. He is also challenged by her being hard to get — first kiss is dynamic. After he proposes, he meets Sanna's family — prejudiced — loses that feeling on next date. Always remembers Trulu, how she made him feel, how he still yearns for her. He sees her in Athens and is bitter: knew he couldn't trust her, knew she was no good, but wishes . . . All through the years he longs for her.

She marries an aviator; he is killed in air crash in WWI. Will goes to see her when she invites him. This is after he quits farming, maybe 1929—her father has lost his money.

In Dawson, Will rents room and takes meals with couple who have no children. She fascinates him. Husband mean. "I never did anythin', but I'm sure the attraction was mutual. Of course I didn't dare let her husband know." But Sanna came down with him for a week and *she* knew. Didn't say anything, but Will knew she knew.

Trulu, who has married again (first husband killed in war) and lives in Milledgeville, no money, comes back into his life (like Norma). Will hides behind Sanna's skirts—can't divorce and hurt her.

Sanna finds out, breaks it up, decides divorce better than living like that, but if the affair ends she will be happier in an imperfect marriage than most divorcees.

Old man decided he was going to die, no use bothering to eat. Turned on his side, facing wall. Two days later, when he hadn't died, he decided to eat again. Got well.

Old lady had such tender feet, hospital attendants investigated—doctor had told her twenty-five years before to stay in bed. She never asked if she could get up, he never told her to, and now she really couldn't.

It's not hard to forgive a person after he's no longer a threat.—Sanna

Story of two people who marry, love, respect, appreciate, but are not *in love*.

Toward end of book (maybe *at* the end) Will goes home for weekend. Sanna has settled his "affair," which he insists to her and to readers was just bad judgment, not really an affair. She says: "I'm sorry you married me. You would be much happier with a modern woman. It disappoints you that I don't drive, I don't wear tailored clothes, and I don't wear jewelry or make-up. I don't get permanent waves, my skin breaks out, and I itch and scratch. I don't dance. I watch you dancing with other women at parties and see how much you enjoy dancing. A lot of what I don't do is because we can't afford it. I don't have dinner parties because it costs money, but mostly, I guess, because I go to pieces worrying about whether the food will taste good and will it be enough and we don't have fine china and lace tablecloths, and because by the time I do all the housework and look after the children, I'm worn out. But I know some women could do all I do and have time and energy to entertain. I don't really care about all that, but I'd like to because you enjoy people so. I wish I didn't worry about time or dirt or money. I wish I weren't anxious all the time, afraid of what tomorrow will bring.

"I'm mostly sorry I can't approve of everything you say or do. I can't say I'm glad you paid thirty-five dollars for a pedigreed bird dog when we owe so much money. I can't say it was all right for you to plan for us to move in with your mother without consulting her or me. I can't say I'm willing to move into a boarding house with old men because it's cheaper.

"I can say I love your zest for life. I love and appreciate how hard you work to make a living for us. I envy your talent with people. I love to go places with you. I marvel that you never meet a stranger. I love your having so many friends.

"I've thought about divorce. It would set you free to marry the kind of person who would suit you better. But I know you care deeply about your family. You would be embarrassed to be divorced even though you wouldn't be lonely long. The women would swarm, and you'd revel in the attention, and you'd marry quickly.

"But you love your family and your children, and most second wives don't like to give time and energy and divide money with a man's children. Her resentment would make you miserable. I've noticed most men who remarry get weaned away from their own children, even other kinfolks, because they spend more time with the second wife's relatives than their own and the second wife's children and grandchildren.

"As for myself, I see that women who divorce are no happier than I am. I was so miserable when the jeweler said my diamond had cracked. Now I know that an imperfect marriage is better than divorce. I got to the point I couldn't live with you and the other woman, but with that over, I can settle for imperfection. If you can."

Papa and the Bull
(*Sanna in a conversation with Will*)

I WAS eight years old and quiet, shy. I had drawn a bucket of cold well water and was standing at the shelf on the back porch, drinking from the tin dipper and watching Papa. He was working just inside the nearby pasture, hammering a loose board on the milk shed.

"Papa was small and stringy. He wasn't old, but his hair was white and silky, and so was his long beard, which he had tied in a loose knot that afternoon to keep out of his way. I adored him.

"When he looked up and saw I was home from school, he waved, and I waved the dipper, sloshing water everywhere. I decided to take Papa a drink, and poured some water into a fruit jar.

"I saw that our big Jersey bull was plodding towards him, but I wasn't alarmed. Shoot, that was just old Sultan. I laughed when the bull nudged Papa from behind. Papa turned around, smiled, and scratched Sultan between his horns, where he liked it. Then he wiped his forehead on his shirt sleeve, took off his big straw hat, and commenced fanning himself with it.

"Everyone agreed later, it must have been the movement of the hat that aroused the bull.

"Sultan backed off, lowered his head, and snorted. I could

tell that my papa hadn't noticed. He had gone back to his work and was bent over picking up nails when Sultan hooked him in the stomach and tossed him like a sack of potatoes onto the tin roof of the milk shed. Papa rolled down like a log. He tried to grab something, but there was nothing to grab and he dropped right back onto those horns, as if they were loving arms waiting to receive him.

"I still don't know if I was crying or screaming, or what, but I saw the bull toss him up again, higher, almost over the roof peak.

"Afterwards I told Sister Maggie it was like Sultan thought he'd made up a game. Like he thought Papa was a play-pretty. When Papa hit the ground, Sultan turned away and ambled off towards his cows standing in the creek to get cool.

"I was halfway to Papa when I tripped over a root and fell, but as I was getting up I thought to run back and ring the big farm bell. We had a bell that called the field hands to dinner and called quitting time at sundown. It would never be rung at four in the evening unless for something awful. I grabbed the bell rope, jerked it hard, and with each clang screamed, 'Papa! Papa!'

"Mama came running from the side yard, carrying Tattie, who was four then, and she saw immediately what had happened. She set Tattie down among the chickens and the cats and raced towards the milk shed. Violet and Daisy came out on the back porch and Zinnie ran from the privy. Scrawny, bowlegged Possum rushed out of the kitchen and down the steps. Her husband, called Christmas for being so slow, hobbled up from the back of the barn.

"Everybody's eyes were on me, ringing the bell. They didn't see Papa bleeding on the pasture grass or Mama running towards him out of the milk shed, holding a pitchfork to slay whatever had got him down.

"'It's Papa! Sultan hurt him!' I pointed, and all eyes followed my finger. The girls ran for the shed. Old Christmas followed them, but Possum stayed with me, and we rang in everybody from the cotton fields—the colored wages hands and share-croppers, their wives, their children, some with cotton sacks still slung over their shoulders.

"I was still ringing the bell, and crying for my papa not to die, when Violet came back from the pasture and twisted the bell rope out of my hands. 'Stop it! Stop rangin' that bell! They all comin' now, honey. Gimme the rope. Turn it loose.' She picked me up and ran towards the pasture.

"Little Tattie was left alone, bawling, wandering about the yard. Mama heard her and yelled, 'Daisy? Sanna Maria? One a-y'all go git the baby!' But not one of us went, cause Papa had started groaning. I leaned over the fence and saw that the front of his overalls was soaked with blood. There was a red spot on the white beard where it was knotted.

"He suddenly rolled onto his side, facing us, and pulled his knees up. Vi whispered to me, 'He's bent double with pain.'

"Papa was mumbling. 'Don't . . . let nobody . . . hurt . . . my bull. We . . . need him . . .' Then he went limp.

"I buried my face against Vi's stomach and screamed again. Mama glared at me. 'Shut up, young'un.'

"'Papa's dead!' I wailed.

"Mama said, 'No, he ain't.'

"I begged her not to let him die and she said, 'He ain't a-go'n to.' Then Mama turned to the field hands. 'How come all y'all standin' there like fence posts? I got to git him in the house.'

"Mama hadn't seen old Christmas standing behind her, his hat off. 'I'm here, Miss Flo,' said Christmas. Christmas lifted Papa like he would a hurt dog. With Mama leading the way, he carried him out through the shed and past the silent watchers.

"I ran and grabbed Mama's skirt. She slapped my hand. 'Turn me loose, Sanna Maria!' she said, and rushed to pick up Tattie, who was squalling. 'Po' li'l lamb,' she crooned. 'Ain't anybody got sense enough to see to you? Here, Lily, take her. Possum?

Don't just stand there wringin' your hands. Go be gittin' out
some clean rags and some turp'mtime, and th'ow a clean sheet
over my bed.'

"I pulled at Mama's arm and said, 'Don't let him die, hear,
Mama?'

"Mama said, 'Git out of the way, girl. Yore pa ain't go'n die.'"

"And he didn't. He lived five more years. But he was never
the same after that day.

"And nothing was ever the same again for me either, Will.
That was the day I realized that I was yesterday's child.

"I had got slapped. Tattie had got comforted.

"Joe Pye, sixteen, had to come home from Gordon Military School to run the farm. Papa supervised. He scheduled the
plowing and plantings and kept the books. But he never again
nailed a board or plowed a field. He just got weaker and weaker.
No doctor guessed why. I heard him say to Mama, 'Miss Flora,
we could make it if we'd had nine boys and one girl instead of
nine girls and one boy.' If a man owned his land, his daughters
couldn't work in the fields or go to market or do carpentry or
fix fences. I helped him put on his shirt and socks and shoes,
but he finally got so he couldn't walk alone.

"My mama, harder worked than ever, turned me over to my
big sister Zinnie. Zinnie did all the sewing for the family—the
sheets, the dresses, Papa's shirts, everything. She was nineteen
years old, beautiful, the way all my sisters were beautiful, with
dark eyes and black hair, and a bright mind and agile fingers.
But Sister Zinnie had no beaus and no hope. Never would have
a beau out there in the country, and no way to meet anybody.
Sometimes I think my mama wanted to keep her there. She
had finished the seven grades of school at thirteen and had
been minding children and sewing ever since. As soon as Zinnie was big enough to hold a bolt of cloth, Mama put her to
making sheets, then Papa's shirts, and then dresses. I think she
felt trapped by the sewing machine.

"If I ran down the hall, Zinnie might make me sit beside her at the sewing machine all day long—just for running down the hall, for heaven's sake. I started to hate her and I wouldn't mind her unless Mama was around. One day Joe Pye chanced to come in when Zinnie was going after me with the buggy whip. He grabbed the whip and raised it at Zinnie. 'You touch that baby, dammit, and I'll beat you to hell,' he shouted, and Zinnie never raised a hand to me again. From that day on, Joe Pye was my hero.

"The other one I loved was Sister Maggie. She and Brother Hen had been married for nine or ten years, with no children. So they finally adopted a premature baby boy whose mother died in childbirth. Sister Maggie had a heart big enough for all the orphans of the world."

"When I was ten an awful thing happened in the family. Violet was having a baby and wasn't married. Sister Maggie's husband came down and *made* the boy marry her. The next morning Sister Maggie found me crying in the privy and asked me if I'd like to come live with them in Mitchellville. 'The school is so much better,' she said. 'You want to be a teacher, it matters to go to a good school.'

"I wiped my eyes and asked, 'At the new school, will you say my name is Sanna? Not Sanna Maria?'

"'Yes, if you want to be just Sanna.'

"'Will you ask Mama can I go? She's got Tattie. She loves Tattie better'n me.'

"'I already did. Come on, precious, let's go get up your things.'

"'But I don't want to leave Papa. I help him put on his shirt and shoes and socks.'

"'You'll come home for Christmas and summer vacation.'

"'I hate the farm. It'd be so nice to be in town and have a bathroom and go to parties. It's awful here. One thing I know, I ain't go'n marry no farmer. I wouldn't have to mind Zinnie anymore?'

"'Only when you're home.'

"Even now that I'm grown, I've thought bitterly and often that Mama certainly never had spoiled me. The Christmas before I left home to go live at Sister Maggie's house, Mama gave Tattie a little gold ring with a tiny diamond in it, a real 'sho-nuff' diamond. Her present to me was a dollar bill, not even wrapped up. She just took it out of her apron pocket and said, 'Here.'

"Mama didn't come to my graduation from Mitchellville High School. She didn't come to my college graduation, either, though I went out home and begged her to. 'Sister Maggie said tell you she'll make you a new dress to wear, Mama, and buy you a hat and shoes to go with it.'

"Mama's expression didn't change. 'Y'all don't need me,' she said, then leaned forward in her rocking chair and spat into the fireplace."

"I hated that Mama dipped snuff."

Olive Ann Burns

A REMINISCENCE

OLIVE Ann Burns lived sixty-five years and completed only one book. Since its publication in 1984, *Cold Sassy Tree* has become an American classic, selling over a million copies worldwide and still going strong. It has inspired accolades and fan letters from readers young and old, from all walks of life. Schoolchildren and cancer patients, Broadway producers and country farmers have written to say that their lives were touched, even changed, by this remarkable novel. Barbara Bush named *Cold Sassy Tree* one of her favorite books; Oprah Winfrey, Craig Claiborne, and B.F. Skinner wrote grateful letters to its author.

Now, nearly ten years after its publication, *Cold Sassy Tree* is widely regarded as one of the best-loved novels of our time. It is required reading in English classes across the country; it still appears on best-seller lists, from Washington state to the East Coast, and fan letters continue to arrive, from people who have fallen in love with fourteen-year-old Will Tweedy and the story he tells of life in a small Georgia town at the turn of the century. Over the years, there have been literally hundreds of such letters, and rare is the one that doesn't ask for a sequel to *Cold Sassy Tree*. People who read Olive Ann's book can't help feeling they know her—that she must be just like them, except that she happened to write this wonderful novel. That is how Olive Ann herself felt. "If I can write a book," she often said, "anybody can."

I met Olive Ann Burns for the first time in Atlanta, on the day *Cold Sassy Tree* was published. But by the time we finally met in person we were already fast friends. During the preceding year we had talked on the phone every few days, and we had embarked on a correspondence that was to transcend a typical author-editor relationship, if there is such a thing. The first thing she said to me, when we were face to face at last, was, "I thought you would be plump!" "And I thought you would be old," I blurted out. Well, I wasn't plump, and Olive Ann certainly didn't seem old. In fact, she was beautiful—tall and slender, with enormous brown eyes and curly dark hair. She wore red lipstick and a silvery blue dress, long dangly earrings and a sparkly necklace—and, underneath it all, flat sensible shoes.

Surely our friendship was an unlikely one. I was a novice, a twenty-five-year-old editor from New Hampshire, making my way in New York City. She was a born storyteller from the Deep South who was about to publish her first novel at the age of sixty. I knew just a bit more than she did about how books get published, and she knew far more than I did about the things that really matter—life and death, for example. While I helped her cut some two hundred pages out of her manuscript, she taught me lessons that have helped determine the course of my life. We discussed punctuation, publicity, and print runs, of course, but we spent more time talking about husbands and children, the books we loved and the ones we didn't, the secret of a tasty casserole and the key to happiness on this earth. At times I provided her a link to the publishing process that she found so fascinating and so much fun; at other times, she offered me motherly advice, shared stories about her next-door neighbors or distant ancestors, and brought me up to date on the goings-on in her family. Always, she was an inspiration to me in her ability to see the humor, and even the joy, in any situation.

Olive Ann battled cancer on and off for ten years and spent the last three years of her life confined to bed with congestive heart failure. And yet, in the midst of her illness, she was able to look back on the previous year, a year during which she had left the house exactly twice — once to vote, and once to see the fall leaves — and say, "This has been a happy year." She joked about someone who had referred to her bedridden condition as her "lifestyle," as if it were something she had chosen. But she took issue with another friend, who had tried to sympathize with her "horrendous ordeal." "I'm not trying to be brave or put a happy face on it," she wrote, "but it has not been horrendous. Working on *Time, Dirt, and Money* gives structure to my days, and so many friends keep me integrated with the outside world." Knowing that she would probably spend the rest of her life in bed, hooked up to an IV tube, Olive Ann never felt sorry for herself, and her enthusiasm for writing never waned.

She worked on the novel for almost five years, years during which she also had to cope with the demands of fame, with a recurrence of cancer and debilitating rounds of chemotherapy, and finally with the death of her beloved husband, Andrew Sparks, following his own long battle with cancer. Given the obstacles she confronted, it is a wonder she was able to work at all.

As readers of *Cold Sassy Tree* may know, the irrepressible character of Will Tweedy is based on Olive Ann's father, William Arnold Burns, who was fourteen years old in 1906, when the events in the novel take place. In *Time, Dirt, and Money*, Olive Ann introduces us to Will ten years later, and to the young woman he is about to marry, Sanna Maria Klein, who is based on Olive Ann's mother. The novel was to be the story of her parents — of how they met, fell in love, and raised a family during the Depression. Above all, it was to be a portrait of their marriage, a marriage that was nearly destroyed by poverty, disillusion, and disappointment, but that survived and flourished again, years after both husband and wife had all but given up on finding happiness together.

Time, Dirt, and Money was due to be delivered to Ticknor & Fields on January 1, 1991. Olive Ann knew she wasn't going to make the deadline, but she always believed that she would finish the book. During the last years of her life, she so perfected the art of being both sick and productive that it was hard to imagine she wouldn't always be there, in her bed at 161 Bolling Road, a lacy afghan over her legs, a basket of letters to answer at her side, a Dictaphone or a pen in her hand. Andy once said that Olive Ann could be sicker than anyone else ever was, and he was right. But she had been desperately ill, and had pulled through, so many times that the news of her death, on July 4, 1990, came as a shock. She had just been talking about *Time, Dirt, and Money,* and I'm sure that her dying surprised her as much as it did everyone else—just as becoming a published author had surprised her. "I always thought selling a book was rather like dying," she once said, "something that happened to other people, but never to me."

Even now, as I read through the chapters published here, it's hard to accept that there are no more to come. Illness may have slowed Olive Ann down, but it never stopped her imagination or dulled her passion for storytelling. Months might go by, but then there would be another letter, full of funny anecdotes and wisdom. And there would be another batch of chapters to read after any long silence, miraculously produced through her painstaking process of jotting notes by hand, dictating, editing, and rewriting. (She never sent anything that was less than perfect—and she could never resist the urge to pick up her pen and start improving an impeccably typed page.)

Only during her final hospitalization did it occur to Olive Ann that she might not live to finish her book. Sometime after midnight, on June 22, 1990, she dictated a letter to her close friend and neighbor Norma Duncan, who had transcribed all the tapes for *Time, Dirt, and Money*. If she couldn't finish the book, she said, she hoped that the chapters she had already written would be published. Olive Ann was thinking of all those readers who wanted to know about Miss Love's baby and how Will Tweedy turned out. She had promised them a sequel, and she didn't want to let them down. This book, then, is Olive Ann's gift to her readers, and it is one way of saying good-bye, both to her and to the unforgettable characters she created.

Olive Ann started *Time, Dirt, and Money* the summer after *Cold Sassy Tree* was published. By the time she died, she had completed these chapters, had notes on several others, and had the rest of the novel in her mind. It was a story she knew well—in fact, she had already written the story of the real Will and Sanna. Long before she thought seriously of writing a novel, Olive Ann undertook to record the stories of her parents' lives as a keepsake for herself and her family. She began early in 1972, shortly after she learned that her mother was dying. That year, Olive Ann spent countless hours with her, asking her to recall her childhood and the early years of her marriage. Olive Ann took notes as her mother spoke, and the long afternoons drew them close, diverting their attention from pain and illness. They also indulged Olive Ann's lifelong love of storytelling.

Ruby Celestia Hight Burns died that September, but by then Olive Ann had become engrossed in her project. "What hooked me on family history was not names and dates," she said, "it was the handed-down stories that bring the dead back to life." She interviewed aging aunts and uncles, siblings and cousins. She found and copied love letters her parents had written during World War I and grocery bills dating from the Great Depression, which had somehow survived in the family possessions. Report cards, telegrams, early photographs, letters, and anecdotes contributed by other relatives—even a floor plan of the family home—all went into the book, evoking an era that

Olive Ann knew would soon be lost forever, save for these memories and mementoes.

With her mother gone, Olive Ann turned to her father, a man who "could always make a good story better in the telling." Mourning the loss of his wife and in failing health himself, Arnold Burns still found enormous pleasure in practical jokes and funny stories. "I'm sure he could have made a million dollars as a stand-up comic on television," Olive Ann said. Now, he embellished the tales she had heard all her life, some of which had assumed the proportion of myth, and he recalled events he had forgotten but that came forth with her gentle urging and well-placed questions. Arnold's voice later became Olive Ann's inspiration for Will Tweedy, and many of Will's boyhood adventures can be found, in their original versions, among Arnold Burns's most delightful recollections. He painted a vivid picture of Commerce, Georgia, at the turn of the century, a picture that later served as a model for Cold Sassy. And one of his favorite stories was about his Grandpa Power, a store owner in Commerce, who got married again three weeks after his wife died. According to Arnold, Grandpa Power said he "had loved Miss Annie, but she was as dead as she'd ever be and he had to git him another wife or hire a housekeeper, and it would just be cheaper to git married." Olive Ann recalled that, even as she heard her father tell the story, she thought it would make a fine first chapter in a novel. "But I never thought I would write it," she said.

Arnold Burns died less than a year after his wife, and finishing the family history became a way for Olive Ann to cope with the loss of her parents and to preserve their voices for her own two children. She had taken down their stories in their own words, exactly as they told them, adding her recollections and contributions from other family members as she went. The result is two typewritten volumes crammed with letters, photos, and countless other small treasures, and brought to life by a chorus of voices from the past, preserved in all their raw beauty, humor, and eccentricity. "Details matter," Olive Ann often said, and she paid attention to them. In searching for her ancestors, she wrote, "I was after the facts of their lives, of course, but also for anything anybody remembered about someone's habits, sayings, or physical appearance." She called the book *Yellow Paint on the Cows' Tails . . . and other Stories,* in reference to one of Arnold's boyhood pranks, and she dedicated it "to the memory of my parents and all those who come after them."

When she began to write *Cold Sassy Tree,* Olive Ann found the family history an invaluable source for the authentic expressions and anecdotes that give the novel its flavor. Much as she loved to write, Olive Ann's real passion was collecting such bits and pieces. Whenever she heard a phrase that captured her fancy, she jotted it down and saved it; she kept lists of colorful country names and local expressions, and slap-dash files of amusing stories, dialect, superstitions, and lore. Like a quilter with a bulging bag of scraps, she loved to find ways to work these colorful fragments into her large design. As her daughter, Becky, observed, "Mother wrote backward. She had all these little bits and pieces, and she was always trying to find places to use them."

A year after Olive Ann's death, I spent several days in Atlanta going through her papers. It was hard to know where to begin. With the boxes of fan mail stacked up in her neighbor's spare bedroom? With the piles of revised manuscript pages that represented so many years of work on *Cold Sassy Tree* and *Time, Dirt, and Money*? With all those scraps of paper and backs of envelopes on which Olive Ann had written bits of dialogue, ideas for scenes, and lists of funny names? With the files of correspondence to and from her family and friends? That first morning, I poked around just enough to become overwhelmed by the sheer amount of material and by sadness. I remembered the hours Olive Ann and I had spent one afternoon, side by side on the sofa, with the family history open in her lap. As we paged through it, she pointed to a photograph here, a letter there, and told the story behind it. Now, faced with the task of telling some of Olive Ann's story, I realized that the family history was the place to start, for it holds not only the seeds of both *Cold Sassy Tree* and *Time, Dirt, and Money*, but also an account of Olive Ann's own beginnings, on a hardscrabble farm in Banks County, Georgia.

Olive Ann Burns was born in 1924 on land originally farmed by her great-great-grandfather. According to her mother's recollections in the family history, "The pains started in the night and we called Dr. Rogers about six. He came about nine, said, 'Oh, it'll be several days before she's born.' He gave me a shot, I went back to sleep, and about two your daddy called the doctor to come back. It was forty-five minutes before he arrived, and you had been here five minutes. Your daddy pulled the film off your face and sat down to read the paper to show me he wasn't upset. I said to him, 'Honey, you're reading the paper upside down, that's how calm you are.' He later told it that the paper wasn't upside down, that I was looking at an ad for the circus with a clown standing on his head. Anyway, we could hear the doctor's car across the covered bridge at the river, so daddy went to the front door to meet him and left me with the baby. Your daddy laid you on some newspapers with the cord still uncut. You were born easy, you were always easygoing and good-humored, just the way you came into the world. That was on July 17, 1924, at two-forty. I only had three hard pains."

Ruby Burns gave birth to four children in four years, creating a strain on her new marriage and on the family finances. She had never planned to have so many babies so fast. She and Arnold were married on September 8, 1918; Margaret was born one year later. Ruby confessed that she had screamed all after-

noon. "It's a good thing I was out in the country," she told Olive Ann. "There was nobody to hear me." In April 1921, Emma
Jean appeared, and then Billy in 1922. Olive Ann was the baby
of the family. "I realized there were ways to keep from having
babies," Ruby said, "but we didn't know anything but old wives'
tales, like keeping a pan of water under the bed, which I knew
couldn't help. Anything that's a mystery always has untruths
told about it, so I didn't pay any attention to all the things people told me about that. But I read everything I could find, about
not having babies and about having them and what to do with
them."

Ruby said she never could have survived those early years
without Arnold's help. When it was time to bathe the children,
they set up an assembly line, with Arnold washing and Ruby
drying and dressing. Olive Ann recalled that her father cooked
breakfast every day, was around for any emergency, and had a
wonderful way with children. "He was always an imaginative
and flamboyant father," she wrote. "Even after the Depression
hit, he didn't act poor. He bought a pony named Beauty and
brought her out to the farm in the back of the car, with the seat
out."

But money was a constant problem, and the farm on which
Arnold—like Will Tweedy—had pinned all his dreams was a
losing proposition. Recalling her earliest childhood, Olive Ann
wrote, "In my mind I still see what meant country then—red
dirt roads, dilapidated unpainted houses and barns, porch
flowers growing in old coffee cans, mules in the pastures, shy,
scrawny children with white rags tied around impetigo sores
playing in swept dirt yards, and on hot Sunday afternoons,
tenant families sitting on the porch watching cars go by and
yearning for the fast lane."

In 1931, the family could no longer afford to stay on the
farm and were forced to rent it out while they moved in with
Arnold's mother in Commerce, where Olive Ann attended

school through fourth grade. Two years later, Arnold took a job in Dawson, and Ruby and the children moved into a tiny rented apartment in the home of some Commerce neighbors. The year of separation took a harsh toll on her parents, and Olive Ann intended to draw on her own memories of that time to show the initial strains between Will and Sanna. "They were both so lonesome," Olive Ann wrote in the family history, "and so worried about money — they owed everybody in Commerce — and for Mother it was hard, having all the responsibility of the children." When Arnold did make it home, he was often impatient and distracted, with little tolerance for his boisterous children. Once he stung Ruby by telling her that she was raising the worst children he had ever seen. But he loved her as much as ever, and pined for her when he was away. In one letter, written after a brief stop at home and preserved in the family history, he said, "You don't know how much I did enjoy being with you last night and how I hated to leave this morning . . . I just miss you so I can't hardly stand it."

Olive Ann missed the farm — the cows, the sheep, the woods, the sound of the river. One Christmas, the renters gave the family a surprise: they were going away for two weeks and would let the Burnses move back in for the holidays. "It felt strange, seeing somebody else's furniture where ours had been," Olive Ann wrote later. "Maybe that was part of the magic, but part of it was being seven and full of Christmas hope."

When she was nine years old, Olive Ann began to keep a diary. But all it amounted to, she said, was, "Got up, ate breakfast, went to school, came home, studied, ate supper, read my book, went to bed, and prayed for everything." It wasn't until she got to high school that she began to take writing seriously. The family was reunited in Macon, Georgia, where Arnold was working for a cotton cooperative, and it was here, Olive Ann wrote, "that we all grew up." For her, that meant thinking about a career as a writer. Her first encouragement came from her ninth-grade teacher, who was teaching the class to write similes.

"*Violin* was one of the words she put on the board, and the one I picked out," Olive Ann recalled. "I wrote, 'A violin sounds like a refined sawmill.' The teacher thought that was wonderful and made me feel I was a poet or something. She told the woman who ran the high school newspaper to put me to work. So, really, those seven words changed my life." The award-winning school newspaper was a good training ground. From the beginning, a by-line meant something to Olive Ann—no sloppy work. For a while, she also dreamed of being a doctor, but said, "I knew I wasn't efficient enough to be a mother and a wife and a doctor, and I wasn't willing to study that hard. . . . Besides, I was more interested in catching a husband."

By 1942, neighbors were calling the Burns house "little USO." There was a brother in the Army and three pretty sisters at home, so it was not surprising that a steady stream of soldiers and air cadets came to call from nearby Camp Wheeler and Cochran Field. Olive Ann recorded her memories of that time in the family history: "Some weeks we went to as many as five dances a week, in the summer especially. To the three of us, names like Art, Jim, Clay, Jacobson, and Ralph have special meaning. At dances, all the dark-complexioned men lined up to dance with Margaret. [She was the sister on whose looks Olive Ann modeled Sanna Klein's.] Whatever they were—Jewish, Italian, French, Spanish, etc.—they were sure that's what she was. There weren't many dark people in the South then, except Negroes, of course. We were all in and out of love many times," she wrote, "and it was a time when you grew up fast. We had been so insulated in the South. . . . When all these Yankees came to town it was a tremendous integration of former enemies. . . . Oh, the hours we argued the Civil War with those boys, and the hours we argued Protestant versus Catholic with those of the Roman faith."

That fall, Olive Ann entered Mercer University, a small Baptist school in Macon, where she edited the campus literary magazine. After her sophomore year she transferred to the University of North Carolina, at Chapel Hill, to major in journalism. Having read that it was not enough to get training for just one job, and having watched her father struggle to stay in work during the Depression, Olive Ann got a teacher's certificate in addition to her journalism degree. "I was so practical," she said, "just awfully practical. My family had a long background in teaching—my mother taught, and my sister—and I had loved teachers all the way through school." As a result of her practicality—which required that she split her course work between education and journalism—Olive Ann never took a literature course in college, something she always regretted.

By the time she graduated, in 1946, her parents were living in Atlanta, and Olive Ann joined them there, in their modest brick house at 161 Bolling Road. In addition to her degree, she brought home from college some newly formed opinions about politics and about racial matters in particular. "Racial slurs and anti-Semitic remarks made me livid," she recalled years later. A Methodist, she had fallen in love with a Jewish boy at Chapel Hill, but had ended the romance when she realized that she lacked the nerve to tell her parents about it. "I was very much in love," she said, "but I wasn't strong enough to face the difficulties with his family or with mine." Instead, she proudly proclaimed herself a liberal and was adamant about her opinions, which she aired at every opportunity. Her father told her she was going down a one-way street and had lost sight of the fact that some people have to go the other way. The criticism hit home. "He wasn't a philosophical man, but he made me realize I was prejudiced against people who were prejudiced, and that my prejudice was as bad as theirs. And this freed me to live among all kinds of people and accept them as they are."

Within a year, Olive Ann had landed a job as a staff writer at the *Atlanta Journal Sunday Magazine*, under its founding editor, Angus Perkerson. A remarkable editor with a sure instinct for what people would read, Perkerson was already legendary, known for his magnificent tantrums and respected as a great teacher. Although dour and shy by nature, he was fully capable of letting rip a stream of profanity that would leave even seasoned newspapermen trembling. Olive Ann always remembered him with great affection, but she also admitted, "Mr. Perk fired me three times in the first six months and scared me to death for five years." Angus Perkerson had given a young Margaret Mitchell her first job, in 1922, and he remained in charge of the magazine for most of Olive Ann's ten years there. She gave him full credit for turning her into a writer.

"Everything I know about writing began with Mr. Perkerson," she said. "He never rewrote a writer. You had to do it yourself. You learned not to be sensitive about the *x's* he put in the margins. He'd go through the copy with you like this: 'Don't you think a *the* would be better than an *a* here?' 'Dammit, that whole page is boring.' 'This word is too long. We ain't putting out the magazine for Ph.D.s.' 'You used the same word five times in two sentences.' (Once when I said I repeated a word on purpose, for emphasis, he said, 'Hell, it's bad enough to be careless without being stupid.') If he said, 'That's funny,' he meant suggestive; being young and unworldly, I was often 'funny.' He never gave praise. You knew he liked your story if he put it up front in the magazine. He was obsessive about two things: being interesting and being accurate. Once he asked me when George Washington's birthday was. I said, 'February twenty-second.' 'Well, call the reference department and make sure.'"

Much as she loved her job, Olive Ann had no confidence in herself; it often took her two or three weeks to write a story—a pace that wouldn't cut the mustard at a weekly magazine. Whenever Angus Perkerson couldn't stand her pained efforts any longer, he'd come over to her desk and yell, "Hell, Olive, if you don't finish that story by three o'clock, I'm goin' throw it in the trash can." In 1952, she accompanied her family on a trip to Europe, despite Perkerson's opposition. This time she was sure he meant it when he told her she was through. But when she returned two and a half months later, she found that he had kept up her payments to Social Security and that the job was still hers. Once she realized that Perkerson had confidence in her, Olive Ann was able to laugh when he scolded, "Olive, you gnaw on a story like an old dog gnawing on a bone," or "You rewrite so much, your copy looks as if you wrote it by hand and corrected it on the typewriter." She came to love him very much. She also credited her newspaper work with giving her the tools she needed to write a novel. "I was used to listening to what people said and how they said it, quoting dialogue exactly the way it was said and paraphrasing only when a speech was boring or too long. Also, newspaper work made me think and look for what was interesting. If it's not interesting, readers put that newspaper down! And they may plod on through a book for three pages if it starts out boring, but then they put it back on the shelf."

The memory of Margaret Mitchell still cast a spell over Atlanta in the 1950s. Although it was nearly twenty years since *Gone with the Wind* had been published, readers had continued to hope right up until her death in 1949 that Peggy Mitchell might write a sequel, and her many friends continued to talk about her as if she had been with them just yesterday. Certainly, for any young writer in Atlanta in those days, Mitchell's legendary success was vivid. She had come out of obscurity with a novel that had taken the entire country, if not the world, by storm, and that had gone on to sell more copies than any piece of fiction before or since. Little wonder, then, that Atlanta was a fine town in which to be an aspiring novelist, or that a group of young hopefuls banded together to read and criticize one another's work.

The Plot Club convened on the shady front porch of the home of Wylly Folk St. John, who later became a successful children's book author, as well as one of Olive Ann's most treasured friends and supporters. Other members were Margaret Long, Celestine Sibley, Robert Burch, Genevieve Holden Pou, and Mary Cobb Bugg—published writers all. Olive Ann was pleased to be included—indeed, she was a member of the group for thirty-five years. But she never thought she would write a novel, and, according to one veteran of the club, neither did anyone else. She had never read Faulkner or Hemingway or any "important" writer; she was too restrained, too innocent, "the wide-eyed one." Olive Ann herself claimed that she never took her writing seriously. "I was too busy dating to write more than two or three pages for those evenings, and I never finished anything I started," she said. "I figured I'd never get married if I spent every night at the typewriter."

Getting married was very much on Olive Ann's mind, for she was over thirty, and, although she had plenty of dates, there was no serious beau in sight. She had, however, become friends with Andy Sparks, a fellow staff writer at the magazine, who was the first person she met when she came to the *Atlanta Journal and Constitution* to apply for a job. Angus Perkerson was out, so she handed her portfolio of college stories to the handsome young man behind the desk. They worked side by side for the next nine years, and Andy thought she was so funny that he sometimes took notes on things she said at the office. He planned to use them, he teased, for the role of the ingenue in a play he was writing that would be called *Peachtree Island*. One line he thought worth saving was Olive Ann's confession that "at cocktail parties, I never know whether to order ginger ale, so people will think I'm drinking, or milk, so they'll know I'm not." On another occasion, she told her colleagues that she had been kissing a man she wasn't in love with. "I just wanted to teach him how," she said. "I think it's a pity, a thirty-year-old man, so uneducated. I'm just doing it for the sake of the girl he'll really fall for someday." (After Andy's death, Olive Ann found his transcription of this line among his things. On the scrap of paper he had saved, she wrote, "How silly can a young girl be?")

Olive Ann was always willing to provide a full account of her previous night's date, good or bad. One day Andy remarked, "If you and I ever fall in love, I don't want you to tell ANYBODY at the office what I said last night and what you said." "All right," she promised, taken aback.

On New Year's Day 1956, Olive Ann was interviewed on a local radio show, "a young-girl-reporter sort of thing," she recalled. Andy was listening as the host asked his guest what she wanted most in the year to come. "Well," Olive Ann replied, "I just want to get married." As soon as the show was off the air, Andy was on the phone. "Why didn't you ever tell me that's what you wanted?" he asked. He picked her up at the station, and at midnight they kissed for the first time. And then, said Olive Ann, "the magic started." She kept her word, and "didn't tell anybody anything." Their colleagues at the office didn't even know they were dating, much less in love, and when they went together to tell the Perkersons they were getting married, Medora Perkerson was shocked — she thought that Olive Ann was in love with someone else. Arnold Burns was glad to hear that his youngest daughter was finally leaving the nest. "Good," he said when she told him the news. "That will be someplace else to go."

The wedding took place on August 11,1956; Olive Ann was thirty-two and Andy thirty-seven. She continued to write for the magazine, using her maiden name because, as she explained it, "two hot names like Burns and Sparks would look silly together in a by-line." Several weeks after the wedding, Andy developed mononucleosis and was told to stay away from his new bride lest he infect her. Olive Ann was convinced that he had gotten the "kissing disease" by kissing every girl who had offered her cheek at the wedding, and she found their enforced separation hard to take. Finally, in desperation, she held a piece of plastic wrap over her mouth and said, "Kiss me, Andy. I can't stand it anymore." "It wasn't very effective," she said later, "but it made us laugh." For them, being in love meant always being able to laugh, no matter what, and one of the things they most appreciated in each other was a sense of humor. As one close friend observed, "They might come close to having words, but they could never do it — they would always end up giggling instead. They just adored each other."

On December 6, 1957, Olive Ann gave birth to a daughter. She had Becky under hypnosis. At a time when women were routinely drugged for labor and delivery, Olive Ann knew that she wanted to experience fully the birth of her baby. "Not even an aspirin," she wrote. Afterwards, she was alone for a few minutes in the delivery room, "after the OB, nurses, assistants, and gallery of OB observers (who didn't believe it would work) had all left. The big lights were off, and an old Negro man came in to mop the floor. I was crying with joy. I told him everything was fine, I was just happy. He said in the sweetest voice, 'You jes' go on and cry, ma'am. Yes, hep yo'sef.' "

On February 1, 1960, Olive Ann gave birth to a son, John. During those years, she didn't write much at all. "Although I'm not a great housekeeper (I use a dust cloth when I can see the dust without my glasses)," she admitted, "I care about the house being a home. I don't resent the fact that cooking, cleaning, and washing clothes has to be part of homemaking, but I do wish I were more effective at it."

When Medora Perkerson died, Olive Ann was offered her job as the newspaper's advice columnist, "Amy Larkin." She snapped up the chance to work at home, and for the next seven years, she said, she "lived like a queen. I had a full-time maid and cook. I took care of the children and wrote the column, even when I was sick. It's easier to write than vacuum when you're sick, and I was always getting sick with sinus or chest infections." At times she was too ill to care for the children, and John and Becky would go off to stay with their grandparents on Bolling Road, or at Olive Ann's sister Jean's. Even then, she realized that there was one great advantage to illness — it created space and time for writing. The mail to Amy Larkin made Olive Ann shock-proof and taught her much about human nature. But she knew that as long as she was answering letters, nothing more substantial would come from her typewriter. So she gave up the column and resumed writing three or four stories a year for the magazine.

In the fall of 1971, Olive Ann's mother underwent surgery for stomach cancer. On the morning of the operation, Olive Ann prayed all the way to the hospital, "Dear God, please don't let it be inoperable." But the cancer had already spread. Afterward Olive Ann reflected that, of course, her mother's cancer was inoperable regardless of her prayer; it was simply too late for God to change it. These thoughts marked a turning point for her, for it occurred to her that she had always prayed wrong, that almost everybody did. It was a mistake to ask God for material things, "like Cadillacs, and a pay raise, and for the body to get well." Still, it would be several more years before she carried this idea any further, or before she moved beyond what she called "appreciation prayers" — "Thank you, God, for this; thank you, God, for that."

Because Ruby Burns was susceptible to bouts of depression and anxiety, the doctor suggested that she not be told the outcome of the operation, and Arnold agreed. Olive Ann thought that the challenge of keeping the truth from his wife was part of what sustained her father over the following months. "Deception for a cause never bothered him at all," she said. The doctor predicted that Ruby would have one or two good months following the surgery, after which it would all be downhill. At the most, he thought, she had about six months to live. For Olive Ann, the hardest part was lying to her mother. "I seldom had in my life," she explained. She also felt Ruby was fully capable of handling the truth. "She had always been the kind to go to pieces over a Disposall not working or a water heater exploding," Olive Ann wrote, "but the big things she could stand. I knew she could stand anything if Daddy was holding her hand and loving her out loud. But I couldn't tell her if Daddy didn't want to, and what if he did know best?"

After Ruby's surgery, the family history became a family project and, as Olive Ann wrote later, "we had a wonderful winter and spring." A relative had already worked on early genealogies, which Olive Ann's sister Margaret began collating and typing.

When Ruby Burns died in September 1972, Olive Ann wrote, "I have to mention Mother's beauty—physical beauty. As she lost weight in the last weeks I thought I had never seen anybody so beautiful. Her bone structure, her face, was an artist's perfection. It was the beauty of youth; I could now imagine how absolutely perfect her beauty must have been when she and Daddy married. She was five foot three and only weighed 112 when she married, but in maturity she had always been overweight, and though glowing and lovely, her face was just not revealed. I shall never forget her on her birthday—so physically beautiful, her dark eyes alive and sparkling with hope and love."

By the time Olive Ann's father died, the next July, the family history was nearly complete. Olive Ann ended it with a eulogy for both of her parents, now "side by side in the twin beds of death." Her mother's death was the first she had ever experienced in her immediate family. "After all that's happened," she wrote to friends of her parents, "it almost seems now that Daddy died within weeks instead of ten months later, and that grief for one was all wrapped up with grief for the other, as if it were all one package."

Olive Ann and Andy bought Arnold and Ruby's house on Bolling Road and moved in the next spring. There, Olive Ann typed the final pages of the family history. "It's fall now," she wrote, "and we Sparkses have lived in Daddy's house for six months. Outside we've got turnip greens planted—he was always generous with turnip greens, which he planted in his flower beds. And there are two blossoms on his roses. Every morning he would pick a bouquet for Mother and hand them to her and kiss her. He could write about love, but he couldn't talk about it much, and she always felt the roses were a special thing between them. When the season was ending he might have only one or two for her, and he'd always say, 'These are the last ones, I guess,' but then he'd find another the next day. I think maybe what is out there now may be the last ones; I wish I knew how to keep them thriving and prolific, as he did."

By 1974, Olive Ann Burns had lost her mother and watched as her sister grew desperately ill from chemotherapy treatments. Now, cancer was about to strike even closer. At a routine physical that October, her doctor detected a blood abnormality that led him to predict that, within the next two months to two years, Olive Ann would develop either leukemia or lymphoma. Olive Ann listened carefully to his explanation, wondering just how she could sit at home *waiting* to get cancer. Clearly, she would need something to keep her mind off her white blood cells and her own mortality. And then it came to her—she would write a novel. The idea, she said afterward, surprised her even more than the diagnosis. Before she left the building, she found a phone and called Andy at his office. "I may get cancer," she told him, "but I am definitely going to write a novel." Back home, she spotted her neighbor in the backyard. She told Norma Duncan the same thing, adding, "And I don't want you to feel sorry for me." Norma could tell that Olive Ann was serious. "From that day on," she said, "we would talk about the book, but she never gave me the chance to pity her."

From her father, Olive Ann had gained a lively sense of what it was like to grow up in a small town in Georgia at the turn of the century. And she already had an idea for a first chapter—the story of Grandpa Power. She would call him Enoch Rucker Blakeslee and give him one arm, a physical detail inspired by Andy's mother's recollection of a one-armed relative who had tickled her with his stump when she was a little girl.

Olive Ann figured she should start the book the way she had learned to start a magazine article: by grabbing the reader in the first paragraph. If any passage seemed slow or boring, she rewrote it. But, she confessed to her fellow Plot Club member Wylly Folk St. John, "I don't know anything about plot." "Well," her friend advised, "don't worry about plot. You just get your characters into trouble, and then you get them out." So Olive Ann got Miss Love and Grandpa in trouble right in the first chapter and forged ahead, aware that she really didn't know the first thing about writing a novel. "I never knew that the bookstores had shelf after shelf of books about how to write novels," she later admitted. "I could have saved myself a lot of time."

She finished the first chapter while visiting her sister Margaret in Pennsylvania, and sent it home to Andy, who was by then the editor of the *Sunday Magazine*. He returned it with a note: "I think you had better try again." Back in Atlanta, she reworked the beginning, added more chapters, and showed them to Norma, whose judgment she also trusted. "You're just trying to tell all those funny stories your daddy told you," Norma observed. "You've got thirty-five pages of Will Tweedy and the boys putting rats out at the school play while I'm wondering what's happened to Grandpa and Miss Love." Norma had more useful criticism: "Every time you introduce a character," she said, "you write an article, instead of feeding the information into the action."

Another friend, who taught writing, read the early chapters and observed that there were flashbacks within flashbacks within flashbacks. Olive Ann knew she was floundering. She began to watch a soap opera and followed it for a year, learning how to weave plots and subplots together, and to keep the action moving. "And where at first I made all the characters into people I could like and respect," Olive Ann recalled, "I noticed that the soaps always had a main character that viewers can hate. Hating is still a problem for me. I made Aunt Loma an unsympathetic character and I hated how she was, but I kept trying to help the reader understand her."

When she was ready for more feedback, she read a few portions of the manuscript to the Plot Club. "I was surprised," one member admitted. "I had no idea she could write something . . . so *good.*" Then, in December 1976, her monthly blood test brought the dreaded news. She had lymphoma, and she would need to undergo chemotherapy.

By this time, Olive Ann was having a fine time in Cold Sassy, Georgia, but the prospect of chemotherapy and its possible side effects terrified her. She was already running a high fever, and she knew there was no turning back. The worst thing that could happen was not that she would die; she had already accepted that. The worst thing would be to go on living with terrible fear—to be afraid any time she wasn't busy; to wake up in the middle of the night, "cold and shivering in the pit of my soul." On the gray January day before she was to begin treatment, Olive Ann knelt down alone in her living room and began to pray as she had never prayed before. She knew now that she could not ask God to make her well. Instead, she prayed with all her heart for courage. "Lord God," she said over and over, "please help me not to be afraid." A half hour went by, and Olive Ann rose from her knees with the realization that her prayer had been answered. The fear was gone. It was a moment she would remember with awe and gratitude; in the years that followed, she said, she never had to repeat that prayer.

As it turned out, this first round of chemotherapy consisted of a monthly dose of twelve tiny pills—not much to fear after all. The treatment didn't make her sick, but it did cause her white blood cell count to drop, making her particularly vulnerable to infection. As a result, she was forced to stay at home and to stay rested—which meant that she could spend a good deal of her time working on the novel. Years before, a doctor treating her for arthritis had advised her not to vacuum anymore. Olive Ann was always grateful to him, for he had, in effect, granted her permission to spend less time on housework. Now, she tried to see her confinement in a positive light. "I realized that if I was going to be sick a long time, it would be hard on my family, so I'd better try to be as cheerful as possible," she wrote.

Soon after the day she had prayed to be released from her fear, Olive Ann had a sudden insight into how to cope with her loss of health. On a sheet of yellow lined paper, which I found in her files, she told herself that instead of thinking of her cancer as a *burden*, which seemed intolerable, she would think of it as a *challenge*. "Each time of life has its peculiar problems," she wrote. "A young girl doesn't think of finding the right husband as a burden—she sees it as a challenge." Rather than resent her cancer, she would figure out a way to get through it with grace. "A challenge is something to be faced and met. A burden is just heavy, and unbearable if it goes on too long. When seen as the biggest challenge I had ever faced, not only the illness itself, but my attitude about it—I felt that my spiritual resources were marshaled, not beaten down."

Olive Ann had to summon those resources again and again in the months and years to come. As the chemotherapy progressed, she lost all of her hair and was plagued by a constant fever. The fever she dealt with as best she could, refusing to let it keep her down. "I got great pride in keeping the clothes washed and the supper cooked," she said. "I would lie in bed and string beans, and when the fever went down I'd go fix a salad or put on a chicken, then go back to bed to write or read, then get up and empty the dishwasher." Going bald presented its own challenge. She dealt with it by maintaining her sense of humor. In an article for the *Sunday Magazine* called "Co-Ed in the Bald Club," Olive Ann wrote, "I hated being bald. I saw myself as a side-show, right up there with the tattooed lady and the two-headed calf. I'd like to say that I bore the affliction with grace. I certainly never felt that hair was more important than life." Exactly two weeks after her first chemo treatment, Olive Ann noticed that her brush was thick with hair and, she said, she literally went weak in the knees. That night, she wrote, she told fifteen-year-old John that she was molting.

> "Aw, MOM!" John groaned, then with a sick look on his face said, "Well, please don't talk about it."
> "Don't you care?"
> "Yes. But I know you. You won't just lose your hair, you'll tell everybody—even show them."
> "Tell, yes. Show, never." There was an awkward moment as he stood miserably munching his Pop-Tart, avoiding the sight of my thinning hair. "Think of it as a new style," I said brightly.
> "Don't make jokes, Mom. It's not funny."
> "Had you rather I cry? I could cry for hours any minute." I don't know why I expected my son to like the prospect of having a bald-headed mamma when I hated the prospect of being one.

Olive Ann's vanity never got in the way of a good story, and she wasn't shy about telling this one. "There are said to be 100,000 follicles on the average human head," she wrote. "Imagine the nuisance when they all start migrating from your scalp to your mouth or down your back, sticking like Velcro to clothing, upholstery, blankets, sheets, and pillowcases." When she was completely bald, Olive Ann realized that covering her pate was a matter of necessity as well as esthetics—it was winter, and it was cold. She first tried a lace-trimmed white Colonial cap she'd bought in Williamsburg—"fetching," she wrote, "but not as warm as the stretchy blue cut-off pajama leg I pulled out of the dustrag bag. This knit tube didn't shift around, gave me a madonna look, as in Bible pictures, and prevented sinus headaches in cold weather if I slept with it pulled down over my eyes to the end of my nose." Andy called it the Hooded Falcon Look.

Finally, she got herself a wig, although she never got over feeling "fakey" in it, as if she were pretending she wasn't bald. Because she couldn't go out to a store to try wigs on, friends and neighbors threw her a wig shower, hauling out their old bouffant hairpieces from the 1960s—over a dozen in all, from blazing orange to jet black to prim and proper iron gray. Olive Ann arranged them all in the bedroom until Andy complained that it looked like a headhunter's trophy room. Six months after she had molted, Olive Ann began to sprout baby-fine black hair that gradually covered her head. In another three months, she wrote, "I had go-anywhere hair." But there was nowhere to go. The doctor still wouldn't let her out of the house.

Throughout that winter, Olive Ann's goal had been to accept her illness, come what may. She took comfort in reminding herself that "any person in Atlanta, including me, could be dead on the highway next week." But as the weather warmed and green shoots began to push through the earth in Andy's garden, it occurred to her that perhaps she had been too accepting. "At first I was happily fatalistic," she wrote. "I was so sure that whatever happened was all right that I forgot we're here on earth to *live*. I accepted so totally, and was indeed content with my lot, that I forgot for a while how much life matters. Then all of a sudden, when spring came I was *consumed* with the joy of living. I accepted the illness, but I wanted to live, and every new day seemed like a treasure or like a passion that couldn't be satiated."

A few weeks before Christmas in 1977, Olive Ann's doctor told her that the chemotherapy appeared to be working. After more than ten months of fever, her temperature was back to normal, and, although her white blood cell count was still low, she felt well. In a letter to the Sunday school class that she and Andy attended throughout their marriage, she wrote, "You must be mighty tired of hearing how I am. It's been hard for me to keep a sustained interest in it. So I will report, once and for all, that as far as day-to-day living goes, I am now a well person. I can wash windows, cook casseroles, and run the dishwasher and typewriter with the best of you."

She said she loved to hear about art exhibits or shops that were so unsuccessful that nobody went—because then she could go. But the year at home had been a happy one, she said. "I'm convinced true fulfillment is living in God's world one day at a time, savoring it, leaving today's disappointments behind and borrowing no troubles from tomorrow. It's done not only by accepting life, fever, and things that go bump in the night, but also by cultivating love and new and old friendships, and especially by finding a new work or project that makes it exciting just to get up in the morning."

Working on the novel made it exciting for Olive Ann to get up in the morning. Day after day she sat at her kitchen table, surrounded by notes she had made on scraps of paper. She wrote on the old Royal typewriter on which she had composed her magazine features and her advice column. She edited and rewrote as painstakingly as ever, covering every typed page with dense scribbles in ink, always "cutting out the dull stuff." She had taken her early readers' advice to heart and by the middle of 1978 had several hundred typed pages that she felt good about. When Andy read them, he said, "Stop writing articles and finish the book." It was all the encouragement she needed. She sent the chapters to an editor in New York, who turned them down, gently. Olive Ann took the rejection in stride. "I have to hope that in its finished form the book will seem salable to some other editor," she responded. "Meanwhile I take encouragement from your appraisal that it is 'splendidly written,' for when I started I had no idea how to structure a novel. Even if it doesn't sell, I will have learned a lot, and I've never had more fun."

Olive Ann was hooked on her story and determined to go

on with it, but she was also realistic about her prospects as a first-time novelist. Rather than set her sights on publication, she thought of the novel as "just a hobby." "Who would want to publish a novel by someone who doesn't know how to write one?" she asked herself. "I thought if I finished it, I would just make some Xerox copies and give them to my family for Christmas presents. I really wasn't sure I'd ever finish it, though. If I lived to be ninety, I might not finish it at the rate I was going."

Oddly, it was a clean bill of health that slowed her down. After three years of on-and-off chemotherapy, a blood test showed that Olive Ann's lymphoma had gone into remission. It was time for her to turn her attention away from Cold Sassy and back to the world—and to all the things she had missed during her confinement. Now she had choices to make. "I wrote when I wasn't busy doing something else," she said. "If I wanted to go camping with the family for three weeks, I didn't say, 'Oh no, I have to stay with my novel.' I might go for weeks without writing; I might write every day for a while. Real writers tend to get up at four or five in the morning and write until they have to go to work, or they start at eight and that is their work, and they write steadily until about two or three o'clock."

When Olive Ann was well enough to fulfill her responsibilities as a wife, mother, and homemaker, there was often little time or energy left for writing. It was being well that now presented the challenge. "My surprise, after conquering cancer, is to find that renewed health is something to cope with," she wrote to the Sunday school class. "I've got postpartum blues! All the time I was sick I was happier than ever in my life. I *accepted*. I had everything to gain by fully and joyfully living one day at a time and worrying about nothing, not even the cancer. Viewed in the light of cancer, other problems never seemed worth a worry. Now that it has remissed, I'm realizing that I've gradually withdrawn from that sense of spiritual well-being. In other words, I've become a chronic worrier again, always impatient for progress. Cancer teaches that life is too short to be lived like that; you take your knocks when they come, not in advance.

"So my current project is to deprogram myself as a worrier. I find I can *notice* when I'm depressed or anxious and switch on another attitude—the way a man on an expense account can freely choose shrimp scampi over hamburger. Andy, who has always taken life in full stride, isn't much help in the project. After I put a card on the bathroom mirror that said WHY WORRY? in big letters, he wrote under it WHY NOT?"

Friends who watched Olive Ann cope with cancer and the side effects of chemotherapy would not have characterized her as a worrier. She could always see the positive side of her illness, even saying, "It's almost worth being sick awhile to come to such glorious joy and realization of how great it is to live." She could transform any problem into an anecdote; she found the humor in every situation. But the stories themselves were often a means of prevailing over her worries. She believed that she had inherited her tendency toward anxiety from her mother. "I worried about my children's problems," she admitted. "I had no patience to just let their lives evolve; I wanted to make things happen. And I worried about not getting the house dusted and things like that." Getting back to work on the novel provided a necessary distraction.

And so, instead of worrying about things she couldn't change, she stewed over tricky scenes and bits of dialogue, turning them over in her mind until she had them right, jotting them down, and then fiddling some more. She struggled to make the dialect authentic, convinced that if you get a person's words right, you don't have to go on and on describing his or her personality. She loved to find ways to use the pieces of real life that seemed stranger and more wonderful than fiction could ever be. Granny Blakeslee's hallucinations on her death bed, for example, were inspired by visions Andy's mother had seen shortly before her death in 1978. After visiting with her in the hospital one day, Andy came home and told Olive Ann that his mother had grabbed him and tried to pull him right down onto the bed. The room was full of angels, she told him. Couldn't he see them? Olive Ann comforted her husband. She also got him to elaborate on what had taken place, and later sat down and told the story of Granny Blakeslee's death through Will Tweedy's eyes.

At the end of the novel, when Grandpa is critically injured during a hold-up at the store, he is as feisty as Olive Ann's own father had been after a bad fall. Nearly eighty and unwell, Arnold had stumbled on the front walk on the way to the car. He called Olive Ann and told her that he had broken his nose, cut his forehead, and was bleeding like a hog, but was going fishing anyway. When his daughter suggested that he stay home and rest, Arnold replied, "Haven't you ever noticed? Folks die in bed." Olive Ann jotted that down—and she remembered it when Grandpa broke his nose and ribs, banged his head, and twisted his knee.

All her life, Olive Ann had written down bits of conversation that interested and amused her. One country aunt, a particularly colorful speaker, once got so put out with her niece that she warned, "If you don't stop takin' down notes, I'm goin' stop talkin'." Olive Ann later said, "Well, I didn't stop taking notes, and my aunt couldn't stop talking." Now, all those years of listening and paying attention to detail were bearing fruit. She had a feeling that the novel was finally coming together, and the reactions of others confirmed it.

In 1980 she spent time at a writers' colony on Ossabaw Island. One evening she read some chapters aloud. Her fellow writers, she said, "were mostly Yankees who couldn't understand my Southern accent. When I asked if they thought the dialect was overdone, a man said, 'We can't tell how much is the way you pronounce things and how much is the way it's written, but it sounds great.'" One member of the group was Menachem Perry, a publisher and professor of literary criticism at the University of Tel Aviv. "He insisted on reading the whole manuscript," Olive Ann said, "and shocked me by comparing it with Mark Twain's work. He said it was not a regional novel, but a universal love story. He said a lot else—enough to make me believe that I had somehow stumbled into learning how to structure a novel. After that, I took the writing seriously."

She bought herself a computer and set it up down in the basement, in the pine-paneled room her father had built. With the help of her son, she learned how to use the word processor, and realized that now she could rewrite and edit to her heart's content. What's more, she could steal away to this little room at all hours of the day, put on some classical music in the background, and lose herself in writing, without the sight of dishes piled in the sink or unmade beds to make her feel guilty.

Having made up her mind to finish the book, Olive Ann arranged to spend a month at the Hambidge Center, an artists' retreat in the north Georgia mountains. Away from the familiar routines of home and family, however, she found it difficult to work. Later, she wrote an article about her experience there: "Whenever I hit a snag in the writing, the need for human companionship became overwhelming, but nobody lived within hollering distance of the Hopper House. I found myself neglecting the novel to write extravagantly long letters. I talked out loud to myself, and whenever I wasn't working, I turned on the radio. Hungry for other voices, hungry for news, I listened eagerly to country music, school doings, even funeral news on 'The Obituary Column of the Air.' Only late at night was there good reception out of Atlanta or Chicago or New York—usually hard rock music that set me dancing like a teenager. Dancing gave me something to do and somebody to watch: surrounded by night, the kitchen windows became black mirrors in which my gyrating image was indistinct. Not quite me, a woman with grown children, but instead a lithe and lovely girl who, if I do say so myself, seemed rather winsome." Olive Ann admitted that there were times during that month that she almost gave up and went home, but she stuck it out. In the end, the affection she felt for her characters was more powerful than her loneliness and isolation.

During those years of writing, Olive Ann had never made publication her goal. All she really wanted, she insisted, was to perfect the dialect, to tell a good story, and to have fun doing it. "I wasn't trying to preach or write a sociological study," she said. "I wanted it to be funny. I'm tired of a world so dead serious, in which silliness passes for humor. I wanted to present fictional characters who are human but fundamentally decent. I wanted Grandpa to be true to himself and care about work and goodness, yet be free of the burden of perfectionism. I wanted him to live with courage and gusto, and know how to look death in the eye."

There is so much passion, so much life and humor, and so much wisdom in *Cold Sassy Tree* that it is hard to imagine that Olive Ann might have finished her novel only to circulate it among her family and friends. As it happened, a publisher was practically delivered to her doorstep.

In 1982, Anne Edwards was in Atlanta doing research for her biography of Margaret Mitchell. One day, Andy gave her a tour of the *Sunday Magazine* office and helped her locate copies of the feature stories that Peggy Mitchell had written under Angus Perkerson. Grateful for his help, Anne and her husband invited Andy and Olive Ann out for dinner. The two couples hit it off, and before they parted, Olive Ann suggested that Anne be their guest the next time she came to Atlanta. As Olive Ann admitted later, she didn't realize it might be an imposition to ask an author to read a manuscript in progress. When Anne returned and stayed with the Sparkses, Olive Ann said to her, "If you'd like to read a chapter or two of my novel, you'll know me better." Anne was complimentary, but, Olive Ann said, "I didn't dream she'd ever remember it."

Anne did remember, though. A year later, in May 1983, Ticknor & Fields launched Anne Edwards's *Road to Tara* with a publication party at the Atlanta Historical Society. Although it was her night to celebrate, Anne also wanted to do some matchmaking between Olive Ann and the president of Ticknor & Fields, Chester Kerr.

Chester Kerr had become the president of Ticknor & Fields after a distinguished career as the director of the Yale University Press. On his retirement from Yale, he had been invited by Houghton Mifflin Company of Boston to preside over a new trade book subsidiary that would resurrect a famous nineteenth-century firm that Henry Houghton had acquired in 1880. In its heyday, Ticknor & Fields had published such American writers as Emerson, Thoreau, Holmes, Longfellow, Whittier, and Harriet Beecher Stowe, and had imported from England the works of Tennyson and Dickens. Under Chester Kerr's leadership, the revived imprint published its first titles in the spring of 1980, out of a modest office in New Haven, Connecticut. (Three years later, the offices were moved to New York.) In January 1981, I came to work at Ticknor & Fields as an editorial assistant.

Anne Edwards's biography was an important addition to our 1983 list, and Chester and his small staff were determined to do everything right. Anne was pleased by Chester's attention to detail, and she suspected that Ticknor & Fields might be just the right place for Olive Ann's novel. On the plane trip to Atlanta she told Chester and his wife, Joan, about Olive Ann and her manuscript; she was eager for the Kerrs to meet her.

Olive Ann loved to recall her first impression of the man who was to become her publisher: "He was a tall, big man, with a shock of white hair and a shock of white mustache, and very dignified. . . . I thought he was the kind of person you should call 'Your Eminence' when you speak to him."

While Chester was busy making introductions for Anne Edwards, Anne's husband introduced Olive Ann to Joan Kerr, who put the aspiring author immediately at ease. "Oh, tell me about your book," Joan prompted. "Can you describe the characters and what it's about?"

"I did," Olive Ann wrote afterwards, "and she said, 'Will you send it to us?'"

When Olive Ann asked if she should finish it first, Joan told her not to bother. "Send it tomorrow," she said.

Olive Ann knew she couldn't send it tomorrow—"it was the biggest mess"—but she now had a great incentive to get the manuscript in shape. "I had already spent eight years on the novel, and it was really time to wind it up," she said. A month after their meeting, she wrote to Joan Kerr, "I plan to send my manuscript as soon as possible. In the rhythm of the South (actually my rhythm), that is not as fast as it sounds."

But by the middle of August, she was almost done. She typed a title page for the novel, then entitled *Call Me Love*, packed up the manuscript (minus the ending, which she had yet to write), and sent it to Joan Kerr in New Haven. "The book will be about 825 pages, finished," Olive Ann predicted, "but I am quite willing to cut it. I am also willing to tone down the colloquialisms and the Southern accents if they seem overdone. . . . I think (fear) that submitting a manuscript is a lot like entering a Reader's Digest Sweepstakes!" She enclosed a check to cover the cost of shipping the manuscript back to Atlanta.

Joan Kerr was not on her husband's staff, but she *had* encouraged this charming Southern woman to submit her unfinished novel and she was eager to see if her hunch was right. It didn't take eight hundred pages for Joan to know she had had the right instinct in urging Olive Ann Burns to send her book. The novel was too long, it sagged a bit in the middle—but there was certainly something special here and Joan felt certain that we should publish it. She asked me whether I would take the manuscript home over Labor Day weekend and read it.

I will always remember meeting Will Tweedy on that early fall weekend. Thanks to him, I had to abandon my holiday plans—yet any regret I may have felt melted away as I fell under the spell of this extraordinary novel. I remember feeling privileged to be among its first readers, privileged even to hold those pages in my hands. I had left the office on Friday afternoon with a pile of unexpected work, and I returned on Tuesday morning carrying one of the best books I had ever read.

Olive Ann told us that when she received Joan Kerr's letter the following week, she was so happy, she cried. "Boy howdy," it began, "that is a fine book you have sent us. Katrina Kenison, our editor, and I can hardly wait for the concluding chapters!" Olive Ann had never let herself set her sights on getting published; now she had a publisher eagerly awaiting the rest of her manuscript. "Hurry up with the conclusion," Joan wrote, "so Katrina and I can take the ms. to Chester for preparation of an offer. And congratulations on a superb job."

Olive Ann treasured this letter for the rest of her life. "Reading your warm, encouraging letter," she wrote to Joan, "is the most exciting thing that has happened to me since Andy and I got married and had babies." She estimated that it would take her till mid-November to finish the book, depending on how much rewriting she decided to do. "I have never seen a first-draft sentence that couldn't be improved," she wrote. "As you can imagine, your letter has put wings on my imagination." But while Chester and Joan waited in New Haven, Olive Ann found herself waylaid in Atlanta.

As would be the case all too often in the years ahead, her inspiration and good intentions were thwarted by illness. After a week of high fever, she ended up in the hospital with an infection. Then, just as she felt up to working again, an inner ear problem brought on a few days of dizziness. "That too is passing," Olive Ann wrote to Chester, "but so is time. If I were not a wife, mother, and housekeeper, and if I did less rewriting, I could go like a nine-day wonder and still finish before Thanksgiving. As it is, a more realistic deadline is mid-December."

It was worth the wait. "If you think it is unsatisfactory in any way," Olive Ann wrote, "I will try again." In fact, there was remarkably little to be done. All those years of polishing had paid off. Olive Ann may have created Grandpa "free of the burden of perfectionism," but she allowed herself no such freedom. She had been as meticulous with the details as Angus Perkerson himself might have been, carefully checking all the historical facts, confirming the authenticity of the dialect, and scouring the manuscript for typographical errors. She had also taken Anne Edwards's advice and engaged an agent in New York. Five days before Christmas 1983, Chester called her to say he was ready to make an offer.

That day, in a gesture so characteristic of her, Olive Ann took the time to share her good news with her old Plot Club friend, Wylly Folk St. John, now widowed and in a nursing home. "Today has been a red-telephone day," she wrote. "The first thing I could think of after calling Andy was to write you and thank you for saying all those years, 'If I could do it, you can too.' I never believed that made it so, because you knew instinctively what I had to write for eight years to learn—how to put together a novel. But your encouragement—back when writing a novel was not even a gleam in my eye—has meant everything to my keeping on trying. One thing I have to accept is that I can't tell Mother and Daddy or Ma Sparks or Tom [Wylly's husband] about it. But accept we must in the death part of life."

The encouragement of others meant a great deal to Olive Ann. Now that Chester had actually offered to buy her novel, Olive Ann wrote to Joan, "I think anybody who suffers from low self-esteem should get letters from you, Joan. I feel quite confident as an article writer but one reason I had to work on this book for eight and a half years is that I was, and felt like, a total amateur at fiction. So to have you tell me enthusiastically and warmly that things I tried have mostly worked is very gratifying."

Eight years after she had begun to write, with the threat of cancer hanging over her, Olive Ann Burns found herself in remission from lymphoma, a finished novel to her credit, and an enthusiastic offer from the very first publisher to have read it. *Cold Sassy Tree*, as we now agreed to call it, would be published in the fall of 1984.

After so many years of working alone, Olive Ann loved the collaboration of the editing process, which we began the day after New Year's, 1984. I knew from our first telephone conversation that this would be more than a business relationship. That day, I took a deep breath and picked up the phone to tell our new author that, much as I loved her book, I thought it could be made even better if we cut it by about a fourth; there were too many incidents that did nothing to advance the plot. "I'm game if you are," she said, adding, "I look at it as a challenge to cut and at the same time make the book better."

It was clear that all of this was simply great fun for her. Business would be done, of course, but above all, we would have a good time. For Olive Ann, that meant getting to know each other. I wanted to hear all about her and how her book had come to be—but Olive Ann said, in her gently insistent and irresistible Southern accent, "Tell me about *you*." Years later, as I sorted through her papers after her death, I found notes she had made during that very first phone call—about our publication plans for her book, yes, but also about where I was born, where I went to college, and how many people were in my family. Even then, in that first rush of excitement at becoming a published author, Olive Ann was as interested in the people she would be working with as she was in what would happen to her book. She was tremendously happy that *Cold Sassy Tree* was going to be published at last, but she was not at all impressed—and she knew there was a difference.

The next day, Olive Ann sat down and wrote a letter answering all my questions—and some I never would have presumed to ask. She described her childhood in Banks County and in Commerce. She wrote, "1906 is a whole generation before my time, of course, but it is interesting that even in 1934 they still could produce a few tottery old Confederate veterans in uniform to sit on the stage for our Southern Memorial Day exercises at school, and there was always a Confederate flag—though by 1934 they had a U.S. flag, too. The war was still bitterly discussed on front porches, and I never met a Yankee till I was in high school in Macon, Georgia. When I told my mother's mother I was in love with a Yankee (she was five years old when Sherman's soldiers ransacked her home), she said there must be a few good ones." I think this was her way of letting me know that, despite my own Yankee heritage, she would be willing to give me the benefit of the doubt, and would consider me a "good one" until she was proven wrong.

We had decided that I would suggest cuts and editorial changes on one copy of the manuscript while she made her own on another, and then we would put both versions together and decide what should go and what should stay. Despite her fear that the dialect might be overdone, I felt she had written it to perfection—that it was, in fact, one of the novel's greatest achievements. We worked to hone the story line while preserving as many as possible of what Olive Ann called "the nonessential stories and dialogue that make the characters alive and what they do believable, and that also help to color the time and place."

She was particularly fond of her "dying stories." Andy described *Cold Sassy Tree* as "a funny book about death"—a theme that had never occurred to Olive Ann. As she said, "There's just no way to avoid the fact of life called death in a book set in the year 1906. Folks died a lot back then." But it wasn't quite that simple. Like many Southerners, Olive Ann had a well-developed appreciation for good dying stories. "If Southerners get going on dying and funeral stories," she said once, "a party can last till 3:00 A.M." After Granny Blakeslee dies, at the beginning of the novel, Will Tweedy spends a morning alone in her house, missing her. He says, "One thing I got on to that morning, with the house full of Granny and empty of her at the same time, was the notion that she'd have hated dying so plain. Like doctors and undertakers, she really told good dying stories. There wasn't a grown person in Cold Sassy who couldn't pass away the time after Sunday dinner by recollecting who'd died of what when, but Granny was the only one I ever heard be interesting about it." Needless to say, Olive Ann could be pretty interesting on the subject herself. In the end, we arrived at a compromise—her favorite dying stories would remain intact, and the ones she could bear to sacrifice would go, in the interests of space and pacing. Typically, Olive Ann turned our deliberations into a good story; she loved to tell how her Yankee editor had never heard anyone tell dying stories and couldn't understand why there were so many of them in the book. That would always set people shaking their heads, asking "You mean, you had stories that she made you take out of the book? Well, what were they?" One way or another, Olive Ann got to tell her dying stories; after the book came out, she even wrote a *Sunday Magazine* article on the subject.

During the spring of 1984, we sent revisions back and forth and talked on the phone almost daily. Olive Ann loved every minute of it, but her happiness was tempered by the discovery that Andy now had lymphoma himself. She had suffered from side effects during chemotherapy, but she had never been terribly sick. Andy endured the treatments with his usual good grace and humor, but, in addition to losing every hair on his body, he was violently ill almost continuously for two or three days after every treatment. In February, he was hospitalized, and Olive Ann sat at his bedside, editing the manuscript. She sent the first batch back to me right on schedule. "I look back in amazement to all I've done besides be a compassionate wife in the five weeks since Andy went to the hospital," she wrote. "Sitting with him at the hospital, I went through the first 600 pages, coordinating your copy and mine. Counting the above, I have read through and revised it five times since the original I sent you, including the revisions I made as I ran it through the computer again twice. Much has been smoothed out that way, including the cut parts, and I had a grand time doing it, despite fatigue."

Before, Olive Ann had written for her own pleasure; now she had a book contract and deadlines to meet. The sense of urgency was new to her, and she rose to the challenge. Olive Ann met every deadline and she went through the entire manuscript yet again to respond to the copy editor's queries and suggestions. She also managed to take care of Andy, attend an aunt's funeral, and help her son pack his belongings for a move to Colorado. ("He left home this morning and I haven't even had time to cry yet," she wrote in one letter.) Little wonder that, nearly nine years after beginning to write, she took pride in the fact her job was done; *Cold Sassy Tree* was finally ready to go to the printer. "You have to understand that I am not a workhorse type," she wrote to me. "Besides writing and cooking and housework, I take naps and camping trips and go swimming and read. All such has taken a backseat lately to what in this household is called 'Mother's Book.' I have really enjoyed the push, though I still find it hard to believe I could do so much."

Olive Ann added a P.S. to this letter: "I am about to get so I don't shout when I talk to you all in New York. I could say I talk loud so you can hear me way up there. The truth is, I think, that I'm feeling more at home with you all and am getting over the shock and surprise of being publishable as a fiction writer." For her, one of the best things about having her book published was that it led to friendships with people she never would have known otherwise. She was delighted to find herself suddenly in the company of all these "Yankees," and she loved to hear the details of the Kerrs' lives in New Haven and mine in New York City—a name she always said with some awe, as if it were as far away and as foreign as the moon.

With the editing done and the manuscript out of her hands, Olive Ann had only to sit back and wait for the second installment of her advance. "I look forward to getting the second check," she wrote to her agent in New York. "I'm going to have the sofa re-covered and buy an electric skillet with mine. What are you going to do with yours?"

Now that her novel was about to be published, well-meaning friends warned her not to have high expectations. "Most first novels sell only about five thousand copies," several Atlanta authors told her, and she had no reason to expect that hers would be different. In a letter to Chester she wrote, "I find myself hoping that the book is a success for all of you even more than for myself. Fame and fortune have come to few writers that I know, so I have no illusions or delusions or frivolous expectations. Having had a marvelous time writing it, and never having thought it would get finished, much less published, I can't lose. But I want it to make enough money to justify the time and enthusiasm you all are bringing to the project."

Years ago, she and Andy had decided they would live off his salary, and that any money she made from writing would be for nice "extras." Now, she assured us that "making gobs of money or becoming famous myself isn't even in my daydreams. This sounds naïve or insincere, since obviously if T&F makes a lot of money, I will make some too. The point I'm trying to make is that, having no craving for fame and fortune, I expect whatever I do in the way of promotion will just be fun, not a time of anxiety or overblown expectations."

Just because Olive Ann didn't have any illusions about publicity didn't mean that we weren't thinking about it. We had already decided to pique interest in *Cold Sassy Tree* by producing a thousand bound samples of the first sixteen chapters. In an accompanying letter, Chester Kerr wrote, "When a cheese seller has faith in his cheese, chances are he'll offer you a taste before you buy. We have faith in *Cold Sassy Tree*—in fact we're ebullient about it—and that's why we want to give you a taste of it now. We're sure these pages will whet your appetite for more." He was right. As soon as these "teasers" were distrib-

uted at the American Booksellers convention that May, word
began to travel among booksellers that Olive Ann Burns was
a first novelist to watch. Early readers of the manuscript were
responding with glowing letters and phone calls. Olive Ann
claimed that she wasn't "looking any farther ahead than the
next project, which will be the galley proofs and getting the
house cleaned up," but it was becoming clear that we would
be able to drum up attention for our first-time novelist. Olive
Ann was more than willing to help, but she was also wondering what to expect. In a letter to the Ticknor & Fields publicist,
Gwen Reiss, she wrote, "Since I'm such a neophyte in this business and have no idea what to expect next fall, could you tell me
when the publicity will start? . . . I assume there will be a lot of
autographings in and around Atlanta, and around Georgia, but
do you think I'll have to go farther than that? And does that
usually slack off, say, in a month, or had I better get my Christmas presents bought before then?"

"Incidentally," she added, "I will be sixty in July, and if there's
any reason to use that fact, I certainly don't mind. I'd rather be
sixty than dead, and also I realize I couldn't have written *Cold
Sassy Tree* when I was thirty. I didn't know enough about life.
Anyhow, I've only just begun to realize I'm middle-aged . . . I
don't really think I'm old enough for my age to help promote
the book. If I were a hundred, that would be something you
could make hay out of."

As far as we knew then, even if *Cold Sassy Tree* did enjoy
modest success, Olive Ann wouldn't have to worry about finding time to do her Christmas shopping. Despite a generous
handful of prepublication comments, we figured that *Cold Sassy
Tree*, like any first novel, would need every push we could give
it. But with publication still several months away, there was not
much more to be done, so at the end of June, Olive Ann and
Andy set off for two weeks in England, for a reunion of Andy's
World War II military unit — a luxury paid for by her advance.

Andy had grown accustomed to his chemotherapy treatments, eventually scheduling them for late on Thursday afternoons so that he could be sick Friday and all weekend, and still be able to go to work on Monday morning. But the drugs had taken a toll. Andy Sparks was the embodiment of an old-time gentleman journalist, with his lively blue eyes beneath scraggly, bushy eyebrows. He wore snappy ties, hats that would have looked silly on anyone else, and a mustache that only emphasized the width of his smile. He had boundless energy and enthusiasm, and was one of those rare men who can work all their lives in one job and yet never assume the demeanor—the tired posture, the tension, the lines of worry or resignation—of a working man. He loved his life and he loved his work, and he radiated happiness. Whether he was on his way to the office downtown or to his beloved garden in the backyard, he walked with a bounce in his step and a look of anticipation on his face, like a kid stepping into Saturday morning.

Now, for the first time, he looked his age. And without those eyebrows or the mustache, not to mention the hair on his head, he didn't look like Andy. In a letter to John just before they left for England, Olive Ann wrote, "A strange thing has happened about Dad. About me, really. Until recently I have felt I had a new husband from the skin out—he looked so different. I'd find myself just sitting staring at him, trying to get used to it. Because he has gained weight, the lines in his face have filled out and he really does look good, but he doesn't look like Andy. Now I guess I've become used to the difference, because I'm really enjoying the new him all of a sudden. I can't remember how he looked before!"

Olive Ann had nursed Andy through the worst of it, telling him that she wished they could just trade places; she had learned to be such a good cancer patient, she felt, that it would be easier on her than it was for him. "No," he told her, "you had your turn; now it's mine." Olive Ann found that it was harder for her to deal with Andy's illness than her own. "I could face the possibility of dying myself," she said, "but I didn't want to live without him." Throughout the spring, Andy kept assuring her that the book was more important than his throwing up; that's what they would focus on. "It's something to remember," Olive Ann wrote to John. "If you ever have a prolonged problem, do something that gives you something else to think about—like have your wife publish a book, or the two of you go off to England for a second honeymoon."

By the time they returned, the prepublication excitement had prompted Chester to move the publication date up from November to October. Gwen Reiss was busy scheduling autographings and interviews, and the Book-of-the-Month Club had named *Cold Sassy Tree* a featured alternate for October. Gwen wrote to Olive Ann and asked how she felt about public speaking, for it was becoming apparent that *Cold Sassy Tree* was generating more attention than a typical first novel. "I found out long ago that talking to a thousand or two hundred or ten is all the same," Olive Ann replied. "I mean it doesn't scare me, and if it's a small group I enjoy the ones who are there instead of lamenting that it isn't a crowd."

She did want us to know, however, that she was not a "fancy speaker." "I don't declaim," she wrote, explaining that her talks were "really kind of like *Cold Sassy Tree*—funny, with stories and throwaway comments, but carrying significant and, I hope, inspiring messages. I don't mean I try to be inspiring, but when I say things that are heartfelt, things that other people are surely dealing with, too, they seem to respond. Also, I don't try to act brilliant or as if I take myself to be the world's greatest gift to audiences. If I did, I'd feel like a fool and fall on my face. As it is, they take me for one of them and it seems to be effective."

Characteristically, she wanted to make sure that Ticknor & Fields didn't incur any extra expense on her account. Olive Ann prided herself on never spending a penny she didn't have, and she certainly didn't expect her publisher to spend any more than necessary on accommodations. "My ego needs are small," she assured us. "Being Andy's wife and a fulfilled person are enough, and all this is just icing on the cake. I can be just as happy about talking to the little literary club in Cornelia, Georgia, as to more important groups. And I don't need any VIP treatment. Do whatever you need to for T&F's image, but limos and ultra hotels are unimportant to me. I'm game for anything that will make the promotion budget stretch. To me, ordinary taxis will be a luxury because driving tires me if I've never been there before and have to feel my way, and any place to sleep will be fine if it's not on a busy highway beside an uphill curve where trucks scream into lower gear all night long."

The only thing she insisted on was some time to lie down in the middle of a busy day, and a taxi instead of the services of "a little old-lady driver who drives scatter-brain or tailgates and with whom I must carry on a conversation. I like such conversation," she said, "but I would arrive out of breath at my destination."

She meant what she said: Olive Ann loved to talk and she could somehow ask questions and tell a funny story at the same time. She once told me that her talking had caused one of the few arguments she and Andy had, when, early in their marriage, he suggested on the way to a party that she try to keep her mouth shut that night. If she could do it, he told her, she might hear something interesting. Much as Olive Ann talked, I never once heard her say anything that wasn't worth listening to. It was impossible for her to be boring. And her letters were almost as wonderful as Olive Ann in person—long and leisurely, funny and intimate, and thoroughly entertaining. When she returned her author questionnaire with a ten-page single-spaced essay about her intentions while writing *Cold Sassy Tree*, everyone in the office gathered round to read it. "I think what I've written is more than you want to know about anybody," she apologized, "and certainly more than you need to know for publicity purposes. But I decided to send it on as is. At least you'll have some idea of what you're dealing with."

Her essay became a publishing story in itself. "I don't know if it will help sales to say *Cold Sassy Tree* isn't a dirty book," Olive Ann wrote, "but I don't think I'm the only person who is tired of sordid stories about unsavory people. I'm tired of books and movies full of paper-doll characters you don't care about, who have no self-respect and no respect for anybody or any institution. I hope this book is compelling and realistically sensual; I have great respect for human sexuality. But I'm tired of authors so lacking in sensitivity that they wallow in vulgarity and prostitute sex—making exhibitionists out of the characters and peeping Toms out of the readers. And I don't want to sound preachy or Victorian, but I'm tired of amorality in fiction and real life. Immorality is a fascinating human dilemma that creates suspense for the readers and tension for the characters, but where is the tension in an amoral situation? When people have no personal code, nothing is threatening and nothing is meaningful."

Olive Ann's words were far more captivating than any sales line we might produce. Here, Chester realized, was the perfect way to introduce Olive Ann Burns to everyone else in the company; to let them know, as she put it, "what they were dealing with." He sent copies of this letter to all of the Houghton Mifflin sales reps, and they, in turn, started showing it to booksellers they knew. Everyone was charmed and intrigued. B. Dalton Company, a large bookselling chain, reprinted six pages of the questionnaire in their merchandising newsletter. By early September, the *New York Times* and the *Washington Post* had both caught wind of the story and responded with features about Olive Ann and *Cold Sassy Tree*—several weeks before books were in the stores. "It remains to be seen whether the book has any merits," Jonathan Yardley wrote in the *Post*, "but there can be no doubt that its author does."

On September 27, the first copies of *Cold Sassy Tree* came off the press. Already there had been a cover story in the *Sunday Magazine* (now renamed the *Atlanta Weekly*) and a special boxed review in *Publishers Weekly*, proclaiming Will Tweedy "one of the most entertaining narrators since Huck Finn." The advance reviewers were unanimous in their praise, and early readers of *Cold Sassy Tree* concurred. Ferrol Sams, author *of Run with the Horseman*, said simply, "Olive Ann Burns has laid claim to all the literary territory between *Tobacco Road* and *Gone with the Wind*." The Georgia governor, Joe Frank Harris, announced that October 18, publication date, would be Cold Sassy Tree Day in Georgia. When Olive Ann received the first copies of her book, she set them all up on top of the hunt board and the mantelpiece in her living room so that Andy would see them as soon as he walked through the front door. She was delighted that the colors on the book jacket perfectly matched the autumn hues of her upholstery. "Sometimes I feel like Cinderella," Olive Ann wrote to a friend, "scared I'll forget to leave the ball before my coach turns back into a pumpkin. But I'm about to believe I will at least get to the ball."

The ball was a party at the Atlanta Historical Society, attended by over 150 people, including about twenty-five of Olive Ann and Andy's relatives; the former first lady Rosalynn Carter and the governor's wife, Elizabeth Harris; Joan and Chester Kerr and four of us staff members from Ticknor & Fields; and an assortment of local writers, booksellers, and friends. *Cold Sassy Tree* was already a hit—the first printing of twenty-two thousand copies was nearly gone and we had gone back to press for twenty thousand more the day before—and the party was really a celebration of Olive Ann and her success.

When Chester Kerr stood to introduce his "star" author, she admitted that she had been more than a little intimidated by him when they first met, at Anne Edwards's party. Chester took the ribbing in stride, delighted that in a year's time Olive Ann had gone from thinking of him as "Your Eminence" to being able to joke with him in front of a crowd.

Although he had retired from Ticknor & Fields five months earlier, Chester was clearly the host of Olive Ann's publication party in Atlanta—in the very room in which they had first been introduced. The Kerrs and Olive Ann remained good friends and correspondents, and Olive Ann never forgot that it was they who had given her the confidence she needed to finish her manuscript. "If the Kerrs hadn't encouraged me," she told one interviewer, "I might have gone on like Miss Santmyer did with . . . *And Ladies of the Club.*" Olive Ann always recalled the day that she opened that very first enthusiastic letter from Joan Kerr as one of the high points of her life. "My joy at receiving that letter would rate at least twelve on a scale of one to ten," she said.

Just the year before, Olive Ann Burns had stood in this room trying to describe her sprawling, unfinished manuscript to a stranger; now she was the guest of honor at Atlanta's literary event of the season. She had a wonderful time. For a few hours Olive Ann seemed to forget that writing a 600-page novel had actually been hard work; she was having so much fun entertaining her friends and family. "I think everyone should write a book," she said happily.

Later that evening, all of us from Ticknor & Fields sat around Olive Ann and Andy's living room, getting acquainted in person at last. Norma and Charlie Duncan came over from next door, and we had another party, reliving the first one. I don't remember all that we talked about, but I do remember that Olive Ann and Andy and Norma began to tell dying stories, just so we Yankees could see that Southerners really do entertain one another with accounts of dramatic deaths and good funerals. Later Olive Ann told me that she and Andy had lain awake most of the night. She was almost as happy and excited as she had been on her wedding night, she said, knowing that she was surrounded by people who loved her as she embarked on a new life, not as a bride this time, but as a published author.

She was about to discover just what that meant. The next morning, the first autographing party for *Cold Sassy Tree* was held at one of Rich's department stores. Olive Ann had asked

Norma to come, because she had been warned that sometimes no one shows up at book signings. When Olive Ann and I arrived a half hour early, people were already lined up, holding their books. Most of them had two copies, and one woman had a Rich's shopping bag full of books: she was going to give *Cold Sassy Tree* to everyone on her Christmas list. Olive Ann talked and signed, signed and talked, until we were out of books and time. It was only the beginning. Rich's had arranged for the first autographings to be held at their stores, and they had placed an initial order for twenty-five hundred books. According to the former bookstore manager, Faith Brunson, "It should have been five thousand."

Faith Brunson had been with Rich's, Atlanta's largest department store, since 1945 and had a reputation as one of the shrewdest buyers in the industry. As soon as she read a bound galley of *Cold Sassy Tree*, she knew we would have a best seller on our hands. She requested galleys for every bookstore clerk and made the book required reading. "After that," she recalled, "it was a snap." Over the years, Faith had built a formidable book department on her ability to get people excited, and she went all out talking up *Cold Sassy Tree* to her employees and customers. In the first few days after publication, Olive Ann autographed books at each Rich's store, and there was a crowd every time. People came because they knew Olive Ann—from church, from her days at the magazine, even from grade school or high school or college. They came because they loved the book and wanted to meet the woman who had written it, or because they had heard about *Cold Sassy Tree* and wanted to find out what all the fuss was about. All over Atlanta, bookstores sold out their initial orders, and many people showed up at autographings with books that they had stayed up all night reading. Most came with their own stories to tell—about growing up in small towns and how things really hadn't changed, or about parents or grandparents who were just like the folk in Cold Sassy, Georgia.

The stories Olive Ann enjoyed most were the ones about relatives who, like Grandpa Blakeslee, had married scandalously soon after a spouse's death. She wrote to us about meeting a young woman who said, "My parents were Grandpa and Miss Love. I'm the product of the union. They married six weeks after his first wife died." Another woman said that her father was a fifty-five-year-old bachelor when he married her twenty-four-year-old mother. Her family protested that she would spend her life taking care of a sick old man. "The mother died at forty-eight," Olive Ann reported. "He was healthy and died two years later at eighty-one." Olive Ann had something to say to everyone; she asked questions and cracked jokes and made sure that the people who had come out to meet her were all having as good a time as she was.

Within a week of publication, Olive Ann had talked herself hoarse. Exhausted and unaccustomed to such a relentless schedule, she landed in bed with a racking cough. But, true to form, she took a week off, marshaled her resources, and declared at the end of October, "I'm coming back to life."

In the months that followed, she attended parties and autographings almost every day. Norma remembers how wonderful it was to look out the window and see her neighbor all dressed up and heading off to another event in her honor, after so many years of sickness and confinement. Several weeks after publication, Olive Ann wrote, "I think I'm going to like being an author. I'm now looking at my schedule as a job instead of as an interruption of writing or as an intrusion on this do-my-own-thing life I've had." For her, the best part was not the pile of glowing reviews, which continued to grow, or her sudden fame and popularity; it was meeting new people every day. The most interesting ones found their way into her letters—more stories and characters for her collection. "Saturday in Fayetteville," she wrote, "I met a ninety-one-year-old lady who grew up in Commerce and worked for my great-grandfather when the store was Power and Williford. She was a milliner! Trained by Miss Love herself—by a milliner who came to the store from a hat company in Baltimore." She was excited about attending a homecoming reception in Commerce, which was suddenly famous itself as the model for Cold Sassy. "I am to give a talk, eat homemade cookies, and sign books—all from 7 to 9 P.M.," she wrote, "and *everybody* plans to come."

Cold Sassy Tree was a phenomenon in the South. The reviewer for the *Atlanta Journal and Constitution* admitted, "About a quarter of the way through Olive Ann Burns's *Cold Sassy Tree*, I stopped taking notes. But I continued reading, and now, several hours after finishing the book, I am still searching—sweating, if not blood, at least the last good drops of several pots of black coffee—for the words to do it justice. This is the best I can do: *Cold Sassy Tree* is simply great. And Atlanta's Olive Ann Burns, who suddenly has bloomed into a novelist at age sixty, is as good a writer about the South as you're going to read for a long, long time."

Still, Olive Ann and Andy were amazed to see the book in the number one spot on the *Atlanta Journal's* best-seller list week after week. By Christmas, it was popping up on best-seller lists across the country. "Not since Flannery O'Connor has the state of Georgia produced a storyteller to compare with Olive Ann Burns," wrote one reviewer. "Not since Eudora Welty and Alice Walker has the whole country spawned an author with so flawless an ear." The *Boston Globe* called *Cold Sassy Tree* "no less than brilliant," and the *Washington Post* described Will Tweedy as a "rare literary character who is so perfect that his existence can be credited only to magic." Readers agreed. At the end of the year Ticknor & Fields had fifty thousand copies of *Cold Sassy Tree* in print, and we were waiting for the fourth printing to arrive. Paperback rights were about to be auctioned off, and inquiries were coming in from foreign publishers and the film industry. Olive Ann had appearances booked throughout the spring and into the summer, and the mailman was delivering her fan mail in bags.

In January, in a letter to Chester and Joan, she wrote, "Somebody quoted Will Campbell, the folk hero of the civil rights movement, as saying you don't need to worry about success. 'Fame don't mean much,' he said, 'and it don't last long.' I'm so naive about books that I don't even know what success really means. Five thousand books would have been success to me. Fifty thousand is hard to believe." She still expected that the dust would settle before long, and that she would be able to resume some semblance of normal life. "I began the winter in bookstores," she said, "and I hope to end it working on the next book."

The next month, Andy retired from the editorship of the *Atlanta Weekly*, after thirty-nine years, and celebrated his final chemotherapy treatment. "Around here," Olive Ann wrote, "that is even bigger news than paperback rights." There was still evidence of lymphoma in his bone marrow, however. "We feel disappointed that he isn't well," she wrote, "but we're delighted that he'll have a chance to recuperate from the treatment awhile before diving back in." Andy embarked on retirement with as much zest as he had brought to his work on the magazine. In his first three weeks at home, he wrote three articles and conducted an interview in South Carolina, and Olive Ann joked that she was beginning to think he wouldn't get the kitchen painted after all. Andy always claimed he was thankful that he didn't want to write a book—he knew better than anyone how hard Olive Ann had worked on hers. But he was a first-rate writer himself and, in addition to the articles he continued to do for the magazine, he composed long, delightful letters to friends scattered all over the country. He carried on a passionate gardening correspondence with the writer Mary Hood, and he stayed in touch with members of his Eighth Air Force unit from World War II. He was enormously proud of Olive Ann and didn't mind it a bit when people referred to him as "the husband of Olive Ann Burns," or even as "Mr. Burns." In February he wrote to a friend, "Olive Ann told her publisher

that she was going to start her second book in January and so
far she hasn't written a word. She is running here and there to
autographings and speechmakings, and generally having fun."

"Running" was just the word for it, too. Between the middle
of March and the first of June, Olive Ann attended three library
receptions in her honor, over half a dozen autographings, and
one concert. She addressed four writers' clubs, students at five
schools, and the Sunday school class of over a hundred members at her church. She preached one Methodist sermon, in
Thomasville, Georgia, and she did a TV interview in Macon.
She was the featured speaker at one luncheon and two dinners, did two days of publicity in Tallahassee, Florida, taught
a three-day course in novel writing at the Hambidge Center,
signed books and performed at a three-day literary symposium
at the University of Georgia in Athens, and spent a week teaching writing on St. Simon Island. She and Andy also found time
to fly to Colorado to spend a week visiting John. In April she
flew to Virginia to give a dinner speech for a library fund raiser.
"Imagine anyone that far away thinking I can draw a crowd,"
she marveled. "But they say the book has caused a stir there.
Isn't that something?" There was one day on which she gave
both breakfast and dinner speeches, at two different locations.
"Some of those weeks are really overloaded," she conceded,
"but I think I will enjoy them." Still, she was beginning to realize that she could easily spend the rest of her life on the road
promoting *Cold Sassy Tree*. "Anybody else who calls," she said,
"I'm saying call me back next year, or in two or three years. At
my age it is important to get on with the next book if I intend
to write it."

One of Olive Ann's favorite opening lines in her talks was "I
now know the difference between a writer and an author. Writers write, and authors speak." She told everyone that she didn't
intend to be an author much longer. But even with her good
intentions, it was hard to say no and return to the lonely life
of a novelist. Writing *Cold Sassy Tree* had been tremendously

fulfilling; it had given her a new identity. "Writing the book was like getting born again as ME instead of remaining forever a wife and mother," she wrote. "I like wifery and motherhood, but it's like being young again to create something of one's own—young again, only better." She was having a grand time taking advantage of this second youth. In the course of autographing books all over the state of Georgia, she claimed, she had seen every boyfriend she'd ever had—"all those that hadn't died." Some of them came accompanied by wives, who didn't believe that their husbands had actually dated the author of *Cold Sassy Tree*. She even signed a book for a man who told her, "Well, I'm glad you didn't marry me. My last name is Olive." Olive Ann laughed and said she was too old for him anyway.

If Olive Ann had had to say what pleased her most about the success of *Cold Sassy Tree*, the fact that her book was read by schoolchildren would surely have been at the top of her list. Her favorite audiences were "the eager ones among high school and college students," because she could encourage them to pursue their own writing. She was living proof that anyone with the determination to stick with it could write a novel. Now that she had published a book herself, she was delighted to share what she had learned, lessons gleaned not from any writing workshops, but learned during forty years of journalism and nearly a decade at her own desk, as she figured out for herself how to write a novel.

"Use words that make pictures," she would tell every group of schoolchildren. "If you say the word *animal*, you can't see it. You don't know what it looks like. If you say *horse*, you can see it very well. If you say somebody is riding the horse, you don't know who. If you say the word *boy*, it makes a picture."

Even before *Cold Sassy Tree* was published, Andy's sister Jane, a high school English teacher in College Park, Georgia, had invited Olive Ann to visit her classroom. Not only did Olive Ann encourage Jane's students to write; she urged them to seek out stories from their families just as she had done in her family history. "Stories bring the dead back to life," she told them. "With only a name and dates, all you can see is a tombstone. Yet if all you find out is that Uncle Quillian was short and his wife tall, you can see them."

Inspired by Olive Ann's visits to their classroom, the students embarked on an oral history project, honoring their black heritage by interviewing relatives and members of their community, who described a vanishing way of life. The annual magazine that grew out of these efforts was a source of great pride to Olive Ann—she knew that, in a small way, she had made a difference in these students' lives. *Cold Sassy Tree* provided her with countless such opportunities to reach out to children, and she seized them all. She was just as happy talking with a group of sixth-graders as she was giving a dinner speech or being interviewed. She cherished the letters she received from schoolchildren and made a point of answering each one personally. When the American Library Association and the New York Public Library put *Cold Sassy Tree* on its list of books recommended for teenagers, Olive Ann was unabashedly thrilled. "The New York list had my name right there between Emily Brontë and Willa Cather," she exclaimed. "Think of that!"

Reading through the letters Olive Ann wrote during 1985, I'm struck by how happy she was. In the midst of all the publicity she once said, "It's as if everybody I know is dancing with me." She meant it when she said that fame was never important to her, and never once did she write to inquire about sales figures or advertising plans. Instead, she wrote to tell us about her adventures with *Cold Sassy Tree*. She was the first to admit that she loved being in front of an audience, and she found herself in steady demand. "I said no to invitations three times today," she announced in one letter, "but last week I said yes to PREACH at a morning service in a Methodist church. I've always wanted to write a book entitled *Flattery Will Get You Somewhere*. It got me to say yes to this." The same day, her aunt called to say that a professional speaker had come to her church to review the book. "Maybe I can cut out all my going and just let other people talk about it," she joked. But in the next sentence she said, "I never knew there were so many literary clubs. It's ego-stroking to attend one—all those excited women coming in with my book under an arm."

When a woman hurried up to her at a writers' conference and exclaimed, "You've changed my life!" Olive Ann admitted, "Oh, I felt so important. I thought one of Grandpa's sermons in the book did it." But no, that wasn't it. The woman continued, "I read that interview with you in the paper where you said you wear all your underwear inside out. I tried it, and sure enough, it is more comfortable to have the inside outside 'cause it's smoother." "That's what I said," Olive Ann conceded. "I didn't think about anybody remembering that, but she did."

Someone told Olive Ann that "the real pros" accept only one speaking engagement a month after their book promotion tours are over. "Unfortunately," she admitted, "I keep accepting invitations because they are so attractive—like going to Mercer for two days, and to the University of Georgia where I can see, hear, and touch Mr. Erskine Caldwell, not to mention James Dickey. . . . And I do indeed love to talk to the eager ones among high school and college students, and to old folks, as at Cornelia, Georgia, last week—lots of them were cousins I'd never met. I got a teacher's certificate in college as well as the degree in journalism, and this has been my first chance to indulge. Also, it is exhilarating to get out of my basement hole and back in the world again. I was such a hermit for so long that at first I felt resentful of the calendar ordering me to be here today and there tomorrow instead of at home doing whatever I pleased. But I do look forward now to almost every place I speak. I am a ham."

The book continued to sell steadily, and the invitations showed no sign of abating, but we all agreed that the best thing Olive Ann could do for her fans now was begin on novel number two. She decided that June would be her cut-off point for "speaking wholesale," as she called it. "It has been and still is a very happy experience," Olive Ann wrote to a friend, "and I have had a grand time speaking. (I really always wanted to be a stand-up comedienne or an actress, and I really can make an audience laugh. They connect with me. What fun!) But I've stopped it all for the time being, and I am emotionally and physically ready just to be me, housewife and writer. I have no itch for any more attention. I am satiated with it. I know that I'll be a one-shot writer if I don't say no to most invitations next year, and I'm already finding it hard; libraries and schools are gearing up for fall and winter and the invitations keep coming, and saying no to them is a little like a girl having to stop kissing a boy she's crazy about. Maybe my pleasure in talking (I don't really give speeches) is a little like Marjorie Kinnan Rawlings's and Betty Smith's thirst for drink, but I don't think for the same reasons. Also I know that I really enjoy writing more, so once I get the book going I'll be more tempted to be right here in front of a computer instead of in front of an audience."

Certainly Olive Ann hoped that would be true. "I plan to start the new novel the last week of June," she wrote to me, "when all my commitments will be done with. I have now run the gamut of life as a new author—everything except starting to write again." She got home from a week of teaching on June 22, and on June 23 she sat down in her basement room and began to write. The next morning, however, she couldn't go on. Instead, she sent me a letter. "I've learned that when I feel blocked," she said, "it's always because what I've done is not going to work, and my subconscious knows it." She spent a week rereading her family history, thinking, and planning; she read *Cold Sassy Tree* cover to cover (and admitted that she was surprised by how good it was); she turned over ideas for the first chapter, but she couldn't seem to go back to it. She had begun to write *Cold Sassy Tree* out of desperation, knowing that she was facing, as she put it, "nausea, pain, and death—the great uncertainty." But in the summer of 1985, she had no such crisis to back her against the wall. Indeed, life was offering all sorts of new pleasures and adventures. In addition to the invitations to speak and travel, she and Andy were embarking on a project together. They had decided to build a small vacation cabin in the mountains about two hours north of Atlanta.

"Mostly," Olive Ann wrote to a friend, "it will be a writing place. I'm not so famous that I need an unlisted number or that anybody bothers me here at home (fan mail is no bother!), but the house and all I need to do here besides write are always pulling me this way and that." The cabin would be a quiet retreat for work. Meanwhile, planning and building and furnishing it together would be more fun than sitting alone in the basement, facing a computer screen. For the first time in her life, Olive Ann felt that she could relax about money—which is not to say that sixty years of thriftiness could be abandoned overnight. She often said that, for her, being rich meant being able to throw away a soup that didn't work; usually, if a pot of soup didn't turn out well, she kept adding things, trying to make it better. John would always complain, "Mom, you're not making it better; you're just making it BIGGER." Being rich, she went on, "is buying fish and fruit without feeling guilty, buying books and nice gifts for friends without worrying about the cost, buying maid help." After *Cold Sassy Tree* was published, Olive Ann and Andy began to allow themselves all these things, but they still seemed like indulgences.

Once, writing had been Olive Ann's indulgence; now the success of *Cold Sassy Tree* had brought her unexpected fame and, at the same time, the pressure to produce another novel. She was no longer a cancer patient with a hobby; she was a best-selling author with an audience. In some ways, the latter role was more of a challenge.

Olive Ann knew the story she wanted to tell in *Time, Dirt, and Money*, but she kept changing her mind about how best to tell it. She had felt confident writing *Cold Sassy Tree* from Will's point of view as a fourteen-year-old; she had her father's stories, told in his own words, to inspire her. This time, though, she wanted to write in a different voice—that of Sanna Klein, Will's wife. "I have already figured out everything that will happen to each character in the new book," she assured me, "and I KNOW the characters—not only those left over from *Cold Sassy Tree*, like Miss Love and Will and his family, but also the new ones."

She hoped that a month at the Hambidge Center, free of all other temptations, would enable her to get "a big glump of writing done." In fact, the weeks she spent there were difficult ones, as she grappled not only with the first chapter of her novel, but with a return to the discipline and isolation of writing. She was surprised by her own lack of confidence. "I had a good writing day today," she reported to Andy and Becky two days after arriving. "Redid the first chapter and I now believe I can still write (more than yesterday). I remember now that I do my best writing off the top of my head and *then* developing it further later." But before she sent the letter, she added a P.S.: "It was a faulty remembrance. I tried it today and got bored to death." She tried writing in Sanna's voice, and stopped after five pages. She turned on the radio and danced to rock music; she ate meals with friends, attended a bluegrass concert, and wrote more letters home. After two weeks, she went home herself, sick with a fever and feeling that she had made little real progress. She now had four different first chapters and didn't like any of them.

Though she was not feeling well, Olive Ann made a trip to New York on September 9, 1985, to speak at the annual dinner of the Bookbinders Guild. She had accepted this invitation because it meant that she and Andy could have a holiday in the city, and they had been looking forward to it for months, planning trips to museums, meetings with Olive Ann's agent and her paperback publisher, and visits with old friends. When Gwen Reiss and I arrived at their hotel to take them out to

dinner on the first night, Olive Ann was running a temperature and hadn't been able to eat for several days. Nevertheless, she was determined to enjoy herself—and she did. I think
she was as surprised as the rest of us when she handily put
away two good-sized lamb chops at the Yale Club that night,
and her speech the next evening was a smashing success. She
stood before a crowd of well-fed businessmen, most of whom
had never read her book, and won their hearts. "The Yankees
laughed as hard as they do in the South," she wrote afterward.
But she spent most of the rest of her time in New York in bed.
Back home, she signed books and gave speeches. But every day
that she spent before an audience was a day that she was not
working on her novel. At the end of September she returned to
the Hambidge Center, hoping that this time inspiration would
strike.

All of the other residents had left by the time she arrived,
and the retreat was about to close for the winter. This time Olive Ann really was alone; she cooked her own meals in her tiny
cabin. "It is a beautiful time here," she wrote, "fall nip in the
air, leaves beginning to turn." She suspected that she had had
so much trouble those first two weeks because she was sick and
getting sicker without being aware of it. Now she felt strong,
but still not sure of her direction. "I could really get all my correspondence done now," she wrote to a friend. "It is so easy and
gratifying, and starting the book is so hard." Three days later,
she wrote to me, "I seriously sat myself down the first day back
here and asked myself, 'Do you really want to write a novel?
You've done that.' I asked myself if it wouldn't be fun just to
take a year off from have-to's and just cook good food and go to
Italy with Andy and read lots of books, and get my kicks with a
speech here and there."

She was still pondering that question when a letter arrived from Mary Hood, the Georgia writer who had become a
friend. Mary knew that Olive Ann was still rewriting Chapter
1, and she enclosed a copy of an essay by Robert Pope entitled

"Beginnings," about authors' efforts to write first lines. "Beginnings may be entrances to a time and place, a culture and a faith, a moment, an eternity," Pope wrote. "The struggle to find first words creates great anticipation, if not great anxiety, in the writer searching for the voice in which to speak, for each writer hopes to reach that voice inside himself which is immortal." It was the right thing at the right time. "How can I ever thank you?" Olive Ann wrote back. "I was actually about to give up and come home. I haven't liked anything I've tried. It wasn't alive. And of all the things you might have copied from writing philosophers, you chose the one that made me see what was wrong . . . I realized suddenly that I was using the wrong voice to tell the story."

Sanna Klein may be the main character, Olive Ann realized, but that didn't necessarily mean that Sanna should narrate the story. "Sanna is modeled after my mother," she wrote in her letter to Mary, "who was beautiful, and good, shy, often depressed, always trying so hard, always doing *the right thing*, a brilliant woman, under-used intellectually, a chronic worrier; I loved her very much and thought of her as my best friend—we had many interests in common, I valued her thinking, she was intellectually stimulating. But from the time I was a teenager it exhausted me to be with her, listening to her and trying to pull her up from depression, anxiety, endless rumination about all her problems from childhood to now. Because I was her therapist, her telling me so many details of her life [gave] me a sense, and understanding, of what she was like and why. She was an amazing person, and her family was unbelievable, and I couldn't have made up such a person without knowing her. Sanna will be different in ways, but I think I was afraid of dragging the reader down as I was often drug down."

Reading Pope's essay had forced Olive Ann to confront the fact that she simply didn't want to assume her mother's voice, as she had her father's. "To write as Sanna would be to BE her for two or three years," she wrote, "and I felt exhausted by the prospect. And I realized I wanted to keep on writing as Will Tweedy. My father had so little understanding of my mother, and she knew him inside out, but he had a zest for life and challenges and change that made him very appealing. Without Grandpa Blakeslee to grab the book and run away with it, Will and Sanna will have a chance to have their own troubles and triumphs—and there is no doubt that the way Sanna is is a challenge to him."

For the first time, Olive Ann knew in her heart not only that she wanted to write another book, but that she could do it in her own way and feel good about it. Having decided that she would be Will Tweedy again after all, she sat down at her typewriter and "wrote some first words, and words following words—so free and spontaneous and alive that I felt resurrected." At last she was having fun again. "I had almost forgotten that writing can feel wonderful," she wrote to Mary. "I don't think I'll worry any more about whether it gets published than I did about *Cold Sassy*. I've always been a perfectionist about writing—wanting to make it my best and all that—but I haven't really been ambitious. Ambition can be a spur, but if it uses up energy it can be a cruel taskmaster." It wasn't ambition that Olive Ann discovered at Hambidge; it was a renewed confidence. Even though she didn't come home with a tall stack of manuscript pages, she had done something just as important: she had decided that she would write another book because she *wanted* to, not because the world expected it of her.

It would be a mistake to assume that *Time, Dirt, and Money* would have been strictly a biographical novel, for while her parents' marriage was certainly to be at its heart, from the very beginning Olive Ann was taking liberties with their story in the name of fiction. Real life was her jumping-off point, it was even the basis for her plot, but it would not have been the whole story. She had learned how to weave fact and fiction together while writing *Cold Sassy Tree*. Although she began that book thinking Will would be her father, she quickly discovered that he needed a life of his own. "After three pages," she said, "I realized I couldn't keep trying to recreate my father because then I couldn't let Will become himself—a person, not a reminiscence." In the same way, Sanna Klein is both Olive Ann's mother and her own creation, and she is all the more compelling for that.

Olive Ann said that her parents' marriage was a great love story. She thought of *Time, Dirt, and Money* as a love story, too. The title came from a psychiatrist friend, who had once told her that the three things worriers worry about most are time, dirt, and money. "What about sex?" Olive Ann asked. No, her friend assured her, sex wasn't in the top three. The phrase captured Olive Ann's imagination, and she knew that she could create a character whose worries would threaten to deprive her of any real happiness. Will and Sanna would meet, be attracted to each other, and marry. But they would not be *in* love. True love would come to them years later, once they had learned to accept each other just as they were, for better or worse, and for all time. When we leave Will and Sanna at the end of Chapter 15 their life together is just beginning. However, the family history does shed some light on the challenges they were to face, and it provides a glimpse of their final reconciliation. It is also a fascinating document in its own right; it reveals how Olive Ann drew on real life to write her fiction. Here, for example, are Ruby Burns's memories of meeting her future husband, from which Olive Ann created Chapter 1 of *Time, Dirt, and Money:*

> I met Arnold at a watermelon cutting in the park. The school board gave the party for the teachers, and a lot of young men came because there were a lot of new teachers. Arnold was working in Athens and brought several friends with him from the college. There were quite a lot of attractive young men there that day. I was impressed

with Arnold Burns, but not overly. I didn't think he was exactly handsome, he was so skinny. He just weighed 135. But I knew I liked him. The next Sunday he asked me for a date and I had a date with him every Sunday from then till summer, when he went to the Army. He had a motorcycle when I first met him, but he always used his father's car for dates and I never remember having a date with him by myself. He always filled up the car. He wasn't too good at talking in those days—I mean saying sweet things or handing out a line. Arnold was good at DOING. I mean he showed me how he felt, by wanting to be with me.

That's Will Tweedy, all right, but only Olive Ann could bring him to life. Her notes for the novel make it clear that Ruby Burns's struggles were to provide some of the book's major themes—namely, Sanna's lifelong search for a sense of belonging, and her need for constant reassurance that she came first in her husband's heart.

Ruby Burns told Olive Ann that she didn't let Arnold kiss her until the day she told him she would marry him. "She always said she thought part of what kept Arnold after her was being hard to get," Olive Ann wrote in the family history. "He was so popular and attractive that girls had always fallen for him and he wasn't used to anybody as feisty and independent as she was."

If Ruby was feisty and independent, it was because she had been forced to be. Her life had been shaped by her father's early death and by her mother's rejection of her. "Ruby's father got sick when she was eight," Olive Ann wrote, "and after that nothing was ever right again . . . From then on she always expected the worst to happen, not the best." Sanna's childhood was based on Ruby's as Olive Ann had recorded it. "When Ruby was ten," she wrote in the family history, "Sister Ollie and Brother Ed invited her to stay with them in Greensboro so she could go to a better school. This made a good education possible for her, yet it was the beginning of an isolation complex from which she still suffered as an adult. To belong somewhere became an obsession. Her education cost her a mother, for she never again felt that Mama was interested even."

Olive Ann had grown up hearing about the unloved little girl who was given just a dollar for Christmas while her six-year-old sister received a diamond ring; whose mother hadn't attended her high school graduation or her wedding. "I went to see my mother when school was out," Ruby told Olive Ann, "and showed her my engagement ring and she didn't say anything. She just looked at it. Arnold and I were married on the eighth of September at Sister Ollie's house. Mama didn't come to the wedding." Olive Ann found it hard to believe that any mother could reject a daughter like this. Such experiences went a long way toward explaining Ruby's bouts of moodiness and anxiety, and the sometimes unreasonable demands she made on those around her. In creating Sanna, Olive Ann tried to see the world as her mother had seen it. Soon after she returned from the Hambidge Center, she sent me a photograph of her mother, taken when she was a dark-haired young beauty with large, sad eyes. "This is Sanna," Olive Ann wrote.

Olive Ann describes Sanna as "a perfectionist and a worrier." She is obsessed with the idea of finding happiness, and for her, as Olive Ann wrote in her notes for the novel, "happiness means being first with somebody, having her own home, being loved by a perfect man and perfect, loving children." Much of the dramatic tension was to come from the difference between Will and Sanna, each wanting such different things from their marriage. Rejected by her mother, Sanna spends the rest of her life seeking love and acceptance. "The theme of Sanna is disillusionment," Olive Ann wrote. "Her life is the pursuit of happiness and perfection, but she finds happiness and perfection impossible to obtain—her idea of happiness is constant joy, no changes."

By contrast, "Will's idea of life is to be challenged. [He] loves trying anything new, loves change—is impatient with Sanna—living is a matter of making things work if you can. . . . In fact, the harder things are, the more he is excited and challenged."

Ten days before their wedding, Arnold Burns sent Ruby Celestia Hight a diamond engagement ring. Olive Ann wrote in the family history, "All her life she treasured the fact that it was a perfect stone. Then perhaps five years before she died the jeweler who cleaned it said it had a crack—he said a diamond can survive all manner of licks and then get hit just the right way, maybe on a sink, and crack like that. It was a great blow to Ruby, who treasured perfection. But to me—I wear it now—it is a symbol that a marriage that was a victim of the Depression, and the fact that these two, so in love in the beginning and so in love in the end, with so many troubles in between and personalities so opposite—it's a symbol that an imperfect marriage can still survive and be good, and much good can come out of it. And if any grandchildren or great-grandchildren reading this has a cracked marriage and is thinking of divorce, remember Ruby and Arnold and try harder before you give up."

The Depression nearly crushed the fragile bond between Arnold and Ruby; he had to struggle just to keep food on the table, and Ruby yearned for romance and affection. Her dreams of perfect married life were replaced by a reality that included four rambunctious children, piles of unpaid bills, cramped rented rooms, and a husband who was away from home five nights a week. Olive Ann remembered those years all too well; she had sympathized with both her parents. Her notes for the novel show that Will, like her father, was stretched too thin, trying to help his parents, to earn a living, and to be a good husband and father. But Sanna wants all of him. Olive Ann intended to show "Sanna caught in another situation where she feels second, except with the children. She centers her life in them. So does Will, so this is their togetherness. Their separateness comes from his being pulled between his family and Sanna, and from conflicts over money."

At one point, trying to explain her unhappiness, Sanna was to say to Miss Love, "I read some psychology books in college. Everything that's supposed to warp a child happened to me." Miss Love, who had been raped as an adolescent, replies, "Everything that could warp a child happened to me, too. But understanding that doesn't help. It's interesting but it doesn't help. I figure that what you do with your life now is all that counts. I try not to look back."

This is Will's philosophy, too. Much as he loves Sanna, he can't understand her constant brooding, and he cannot bear the feeling that no matter what he does, he can never meet her expectations. Olive Ann knew how hard her own father had tried to make her mother happy, and she saw the disappointment on both sides. In the family history, she transcribed a 1943 letter that Arnold had written to Ruby from a hotel in Alabama, where he was working for a cotton cooperative. "Dearest Ruby," it began, "so tomorrow's your birthday and the night when you took me for better or worse 25 years ago. Well, I guess it's been worse for you, but if I had it all to go thru again my pick of all the women would be the same. You have been a wonderful mother and a very patient woman to put up with me. You could probably have done much better, as your life with me has been one continued hardship. About the only good thing I can think of, is you have never actually gone hungry, even tho for six months your only meat was rabbit. I am enclosing a little plain ring. [Olive Ann added: "Her original wedding band wore so thin it broke. For years she had only had the engagement ring and looked divorced."] It's not what I wanted for you," Arnold apologized; "it should be filled with diamonds and made of the finest platinum, but with so much to buy and the war on I'll have to put off just what I wanted to get you until later. You have four diamonds around you and after seeing other people's children I am satisfied they are the finest in the world. You deserve all the credit. I'll be thinking of you tomorrow and Wednesday, and of the vow I took 25 years ago, 'Until death do us part,' and I'll make the same vow again."

Ruby and Arnold did indeed stay together until death intervened, but they were sorely tested. Olive Ann had figured out how she would test Will and Sanna, too, from the influenza epidemic of 1918 to the grinding poverty of the Depression. She also knew that she would take Will and Sanna to the brink of divorce.

In her notes for the novel, Olive Ann refers to two women who were to enter Will's life at a time when his foundering marriage had made him particularly vulnerable. One of them is his college love, Trulu Philpot, who is living nearby, unhappily married, with no money. Although Will assures Sanna that their affair means nothing, that it was only bad judgment on his part, Sanna is devastated. "Sanna finds out," Olive Ann writes in her notes, "breaks it up, decides divorce is better than living like that." In time, though, Sanna informs Will that if he gives his word that the affair is over, she will stay with him, having concluded that she will probably be "happier in an imperfect marriage than most divorcees are."

Ruby Burns had come to the same conclusion. In the family history, Olive Ann recalls an extraordinary afternoon she spent with her mother shortly before her death. One of Ruby's grandchildren was there, with a young friend, and everyone was sitting around the dining room table. Ruby said that she wished young people wouldn't give up so easily. "There was a time when your granddaddy and I just couldn't get along," she admitted. "It was as much my fault as his, and it started with the Depression. Before that, nobody could have been happier than we were. Plenty of things happened that I resented, and I'm sure he didn't like everything I did, but we were so in love it didn't affect our relationship. But then we lost everything we had and his father went bankrupt—you see, in his family there had always been money, and the family pride was based on what they had as well as their prominence in the life of the town. . . . To lose everything humiliated Arnold. We owed everybody in Commerce when we left. MONEY became the cross of our lives. When he was upset over bills he fussed at me and I fussed back, until finally I lost my spirit."

Ruby believed that Arnold would be better off with a different kind of person. "I told him that we had to either change or separate," she said, "and that's when he made his decision. He didn't become an angel overnight and he's still not an easy person to live with, and I'm certainly not easy for him to live with. We are just as different as we ever were. I'm such an awful perfectionist, and he really doesn't care whether a job is perfect or not, just so it's done. He still is totally concentrated on whatever he's busy at, whether it's a drive to sell more debentures at the office or getting ready for a fishing trip, so that I still don't get the attention I need to really feel secure. But when I have needed him most, since I've been sick, it is me he has been concentrated on."

Olive Ann was moved by her mother's reflections, and she never forgot that afternoon; it prompted her to look at her parents' marriage in a new light, and to feel that the pain they had endured had not been for nothing. Not only had they survived it, but, toward the end of their lives, they rediscovered the best in each other and fell in love all over again.

According to Olive Ann, Ruby finished telling her story "with the most beautiful glow on her face." At last, she felt the love and security she had been seeking all her life. "So I've gone from thinking I couldn't possibly keep living with him to knowing, now, that he is the one thing I don't want to live without—can't live without. He is my whole reason for living. He always has been, of course. I've never stopped being in love with him. When he would be sweet and affectionate to me the whole world seemed mine. When he ignored me or was irritable I was shattered. That's why it mattered so much. I couldn't ignore him. So don't give up too quickly when you marry and things aren't right. I wish long ago I could have accepted your granddaddy as he is, not as I wanted him to be. I might have made him happier too. I was not the person he needed, I know that, but I thank God we have lived long enough to love each other again."

Arnold felt the same way. He had never stopped loving Ruby, and when he finally realized that she felt her life had become intolerable, he did everything in his power to win her back. He tried to find ways to show her, every day, that he was thinking of her, that her happiness was the most important thing in the world to him. When he was sixty-two, he wrote her, "I am looking forward now, not to 63 or 64 but to 65. Then I'll quit this job and fish and piddle and sit and watch you. You are just as sweet, pretty, and lovable as you were in 1918 . . . I don't know of one thing I would want changed in my life and the only thing in yours I would change would be from a pessimist sometimes to an optimist. Just think, if it's raining today, the sun will be shining tomorrow, and just remember that I'll be loving you every day until that day when there's no tomorrow for either of us."

Olive Ann adored her father and shared with him a sense of humor and a love of storytelling that led her to write the novel that changed her life. And she knew that there was nothing she couldn't share with her mother. With her talent for listening and for drawing people out, Olive Ann felt she had come to know and understand both of her parents even better than they knew each other. Their marriage shaped her, and in the end, it astonished her. Watching her father, sick himself, care for her mother during the last year of her life, Olive Ann felt a new respect for both of them, and for the amazing power of love. "And all the time there was Daddy," Olive Ann wrote. "Always there at the hospital, bringing her cantaloupe, which she could eat, and wine, and making jokes that made her laugh. There were times, of course, in their life together when he had failed her, as she had him, but no woman ever felt more loved and secure and supported than she did when it mattered most. She said one day, 'I couldn't have stood it if it hadn't been for all of you. I've felt as if the arms of God and everybody I love have been around me, holding me, and your daddy most of all.'"

This was the story Olive Ann wanted to tell in *Time, Dirt, and Money*, and she worked hard on it because she was determined to do it justice. "I want to write this book because it can say something," she wrote from the Hambidge Center. "I don't need any more fame or fortune than I have and have never craved it. But when I thought about NOT writing this book, I knew it would haunt me. I think I've been writing it all my life—Sanna and Will, I mean. I think it can say something to all these people who have problems or are mismatched and just give up and get divorces."

Back in Atlanta in October, Olive Ann was still saying no to speaking invitations at least once a day; now, though, it was easier, because she was genuinely eager to keep writing. But she also wanted to make time to enjoy life, the great gift that had been handed back to her. She would work steadily, she decided, but not let herself feel guilty about taking time off for naps, for friends and family, or for the occasional *Cold Sassy Tree* appearance. Bookstores were already gearing up for Christmas. Olive Ann agreed to do a round of holiday autographings and publicity, and *Cold Sassy Tree* jumped right back onto the Atlanta best-seller list. This time, most of the people who appeared at her signing parties were already loyal fans, out buying more copies of their favorite book. Olive Ann wrote about meeting a mother and her fifteen-year-old son, who were buying two books as gifts. "We already own six," the mother explained. "We lend them out."

Over a year after publication, *Cold Sassy Tree* had taken on a life of its own. It seemed that publicity, or even appearances by Olive Ann herself, had little to do with it. The word simply traveled. Nearly everyone who read *Cold Sassy Tree* passed it on to someone else; teachers used it in their classrooms; ministers preached it from the pulpit. After selling the hardcover for a year, Faith Brunson reported that *Cold Sassy Tree* had sold more copies at Rich's than any other fiction except *Gone with the Wind*, which had a forty-five-year head start. The actress Faye Dunaway bought the movie rights to the novel, in January 1986, and announced her plans to play Miss Love in a film version. After the *Atlanta Journal* quoted Olive Ann's agent as saying that the deal had been in the six figures, the author reported that everyone in Atlanta now thought she was rich. She also began getting telephone calls from stage mothers wanting her to arrange auditions for their children.

Any notion Olive Ann may have had in the fall about sticking to a regular writing schedule became moot that winter, when she found herself seduced by a whole new batch of invitations. "Yesterday I got a call to teach at a writers' conference for a week on a horse farm in Kentucky, which I turned down," she wrote to me in February, "and then an invitation to go to New York for lunch, which I accepted." She couldn't imagine why the Georgia Department of Industry and Trade was willing to send a bunch of Southern writers all the way to Manhattan for lunch at the Russian Tea Room, but she couldn't pass up the opportunity. "I don't personally see how we are famous enough outside of Georgia to interest a bunch of Yankees, even if they're hungry," she said, "unless they're just mad to hear Southern accents." The tourism board would put them up for two days. Olive Ann conceded, "Now conscientious fiction writers would let it go at that and come on home and get to work. Being me, and like my father, I can't imagine not extending the trip, hoping that this time I will be in action instead of in bed. . . . After being a hermit so many years, what with doctor's orders not to go anywhere and then really trying to finish the book, it's as if I'm starved to go places."

That year, there were lots of places to go. She and Andy contemplated another trip to Europe, and they made plans to attend the American Booksellers Association convention in New Orleans in May. The paperback edition of *Cold Sassy Tree* was due out that summer, and the publisher, Dell, was launching it at the ABA with a special luncheon for booksellers. Olive Ann hadn't been to New Orleans since 1952, on a trip with her parents; this time, Andy would be her escort and she would be a guest of honor. "I'm sure you understand why, for me, going is more delightful with him than without him," she wrote. "I am not a helpless female who can't carry my own bag or weight, but with him even a simple trip is sprinkled with starlight."

Happy as she was visiting all of us in New York and being wined and dined by booksellers and publishers in New Orleans, these two trips were also sobering for Olive Ann; they made her realize that she didn't have the strength to do everything she wanted. She already had had to cancel a couple of appearances and talks that spring because of the mumps, of all things. ("But just on one side," as Andy kept reminding her.) Mysterious fevers continued to come and go. And five days of bookstores, Broadway shows, galleries, and socializing in New York landed her in bed on the last day.

"I am finally facing the fact that I need an afternoon nap just as much in New York or New Orleans as at home," she wrote me when she got back to Atlanta. "New York made me sick." After a week of bed rest she felt better, but knew that a trip to Europe was out of the question. That summer, *Cold Sassy Tree* was once again climbing the best-seller lists—now as a paperback—and Olive Ann Burns was as much in demand as ever. A fifth-grade student wrote her a fan letter, after reading the book for school, and begged for a reply: "Please answer this letter. If you do, I'll get extra credit, and I need all the help I can get." ("I answered the letter," Olive Ann reported.) On Sunset Boulevard in Los Angeles, a huge *Cold Sassy Tree* billboard advised California drivers to "leave the fast lane for a country road." Olive Ann was pleased that *Cold Sassy Tree* was suddenly being read by thousands more people, and she would have loved to be out and about, meeting some of her new fans, but in December she confessed that she didn't feel well enough to write *or* do publicity. It was one of the few times I ever heard her sound discouraged about her health.

Ever since she was first diagnosed with cancer Olive Ann had thought about one day writing a book called *How to Be Sick*, for people with terminal or chronic illness. Now she joked that she had been unwillingly gathering material for *How to Be Sick* all fall. "But," she said, "it isn't meant to be for people with intestinal bugs, mumps, vertigo, bronchitis (my latest ailment), or too much New York or New Orleans." Reading her letters, one might be tempted to accuse Olive Ann of being a hypochondriac; there was always something wrong. In the fall of 1986, she had run a fever every day for a month. Standing up made her dizzy, and two days of watching work progress on the mountain house had landed her in bed with bronchitis. She didn't complain; instead, she wrote about how much fun it had been to sit outside in a director's chair and watch as the backhoes and front-end loaders felled trees and dug trenches for the drain field and septic tank. Norma said that no matter how bad she felt, Olive Ann could find something to enjoy in every day, and that was certainly true.

The day after she wrote to me that she had not been feeling well enough to work, I received another letter, titled "Chapter II—Dec. 7, 1986." It read, in part: "Now as for the sequel, I think circumstances are giving me a chance to make my fiction-writing career repeat itself. Five weeks ago I had a bone marrow biopsy that showed some evidence of lymphoma (the first time in eight years!), but it didn't seem worth mentioning since it might be months or years before chemo. But I've been running fever with the bronchitis that should have been long over. Trying to be sure of the situation, the doctor ordered a CAT scan that revealed a mass (probably of tumor-laden lymph nodes) at the back of the abdomen." She was scheduled for a biopsy and surgery the week before Christmas, after which she was to undergo more chemotherapy and radiation. The day she got the news, Olive Ann said, she had been so busy cheering up relatives that the fact that her cancer had recurred didn't even sink in. But later she realized that she was scared. "I admitted this to Andy," she wrote, "and I haven't felt scared since we talked about it. Hooray for an in-house therapist—one who can hold me." But, in parentheses, she added, "He said he was a little scared, too."

As one of their friends has observed, Olive Ann and Andy weren't cheerful just by nature; they were cheerful by policy. Certainly Olive Ann summoned all her resources in an effort to view this new development in a positive light. "I'm really not much dismayed or upset right now," she wrote, perhaps trying to convince herself, too. "I've had lots of practice living one day at a time and accepting the unacceptable. This is one more adventure in living—another challenge—and what a difference to know for sure that I can deal with it. It has *not* been easy to deal with feeling bad most of the time."

As usual, Olive Ann knew that what she needed from her friends was not sympathy but encouragement. And after all those years of living next door to Olive Ann, Norma Duncan knew that the best thing she could do for her now was urge her to get back to work on her book. After making Olive Ann promise not to die, Norma said to her, "Well, maybe we'll get another *Cold Sassy Tree* out of this." Olive Ann had already had the same thought. "That is exactly my intention," she wrote to me. "A few letters to do now, and Christmas presents to wrap and mail, and then I expect to get to work in earnest—before that biopsy next week. I really haven't felt like getting at anything lately, but I had *better*." Ferrol Sams liked to tease Olive Ann by saying, "Some writers need to get drunk in order to work. Olive Ann Burns needs to get cancer." She thought this was a wonderful joke; I suspect she also believed that there was a grain of truth in it.

Unfortunately, cancer was not much of a help this time around. Olive Ann was out of the hospital for Christmas but was back within days. "I felt what dying must feel like," she wrote. As it turned out, she was severely anemic and dehydrated. But worst of all, her abdomen had swollen up so much after the surgery that, as she joked in one letter, "it looked as if the surgeon did a caesarean and put the baby back in." She was in the hospital for almost two months, sicker than ever before, and it was then, I think, that I realized that she was not indomitable after all. Always before she had done such a good job of coping with illness that I had come to see it as just another part of her life, something she accepted with good humor, but not something to worry about. Even now, she was referring to the hospital as her "health spa," so extended was her stay turning out to be.

She didn't come home until March. "I had chemo on Tuesday," she wrote, "a bigger dose than before, but as Andy pointed out, only the cat threw up that night." She believed that she could beat lymphoma again as she had beat it before, so she set about choosing appliances, carpets, and cabinets for the mountain cabin. They were calling it the Write House in honor of all the writing that she and Andy intended to do there. Reading through Olive Ann's letters from the spring of 1987 is in itself a lesson in living in the moment, for they are an odd juxtaposition of alarming health bulletins and lovely plans for the future. At the end of March, Andy had an enlarged lymph gland removed from his neck; it proved to be malignant. Now he and Olive Ann were both receiving chemotherapy, alternating treatments so that one of them would be well enough to cook and keep house while the other was sick from chemo.

Olive Ann described one night when Andy began throwing up and didn't stop until four-thirty the next afternoon, at which point the Prednisone he was taking kicked in and produced such a high that he couldn't sit down. "He tackled every project in the house and garden, both here and at the mountain house, and without sleep," Olive Ann wrote. "By the time he finished the pills on Sunday he was getting a little tired but had had a good time. At one point I was afraid we'd give out of work to do and I'd have to hire him out." Olive Ann herself was in and out of the hospital for blood transfusions and was confined to the house after each round of chemo until her white blood cell count rose to an acceptable level. Hearing all of this, I began to fear that if I didn't make a trip to Atlanta soon, I might not get another chance to see either Olive Ann or Andy. Even though her letters were upbeat—she wrote about meeting a fan who had bought forty hardcover copies of *Cold Sassy Tree*, about Dell's seventh printing of the paperback, about her cozy writing loft in the Write House—I also sensed a precariousness, as if either one of them might be snatched away at any moment.

So my fiancé and I planned a visit for May, timing it so that we would arrive just before one of Olive Ann's chemotherapy treatments. "Just before treatment time," she advised us, "the white count is always 5000 or 6000, and I can do wild things in public." She didn't do anything wild, but she and Andy did take us to the Write House for lunch. What I remember most about that trip to Skylake was how much life and laughter and vitality could emanate from someone who appeared so frail. Olive Ann covered her bald head with a colorful turban rather than a wig, but she wore it with style, complemented by long, swingy earrings. Her eyes were enormous in her thin face, magnified even more by her large glasses. She didn't look healthy, but she certainly looked happy, so it was easy to forget how sick she was. We had a wonderful time. She joked and told stories and asked questions all the way to the mountains, and then she and Andy proudly showed us around their little house—including their bright red bathroom. There was no furniture yet, and the electricity hadn't been hooked up, and just as we arrived the day darkened and it began to rain. We set up a makeshift table on the screened porch, covered it with an old cotton tablecloth, and sat down to a meal of fried chicken, Vidalia onions, and iced tea that Olive Ann had brought from home. The spring rain fell all around us, thunder rumbled in the distance, and we all agreed that it was a beautiful afternoon. Olive Ann and Andy knew how to make a rainy-day picnic into a festive occasion, just as they knew how to turn cancer into an adventure in living. I remember that meal, and that day, with great pleasure and with more than a little awe. We had come to Atlanta with the notion of perhaps saying farewell to two sick friends; instead, they orchestrated a party in our honor and thoroughly enjoyed themselves in the process.

That summer Olive Ann did feel well enough to get back to work on the book. What's more, after nearly a year of poor health and little or no progress on the novel, she was excited again. Just after our visit, she wrote, "Sunday morning I woke up at 3 o'clock and just suddenly I, who could once honestly say I didn't understand what a theme meant, suddenly saw where I wanted to go with this book. I had everything before—setting, characters, incidents, scenes, conflicts—but I hadn't decided what I wanted the book to say, so I just saw endless writing days ahead. Now it's as clear as looking out a newly washed window."

A month later, Olive Ann and Andy's dream of a writing retreat finally came true. She got her computer set up at the Write House, and they spent a peaceful week there, returning to Atlanta for chemotherapy treatments and then heading right back to the mountains. "I wish you were here with us now," she wrote, "the house fully furnished and the tree frogs outside an antiphone chorus so loud we have to raise our voices to be heard clearly. . . . I got interrupted on the writing last week by a high fever (an infection) . . . but I'm still excited about what I've written and am writing, and I feel really good." She and Andy were planning to come to Maine that September for my wedding, and they were confident that they could not only make the trip, but do some sightseeing and visiting as well. Olive

Ann's doctor had told her that the lymphoma appeared to be in remission again; she would need only one more chemotherapy treatment, three weeks before the wedding. "That should leave me in good shape," she wrote. "Andy will have three more after the wedding, but the doctor will let him put one off for a week, for the occasion." She added, "I expect my eyebrows to be in for the wedding. I have missed them."

Olive Ann *had* beaten lymphoma, but a couple of days after she wrote this letter, it became clear that something else was terribly wrong. She was too weak to do anything but sit at the computer for a couple of hours, and when she went in for her weekly blood study, the doctor warned that her white blood cell count was low again. The next day she was weaker still and was having trouble getting her breath. The diagnosis was congestive heart failure. In a letter to a friend, Andy wrote, "I am not sure when she will be home, but soon I hope. It is awfully quiet around here at 4:30 A.M. which is about as late as the Prednisone will let me sleep, even with a sleeping pill." To me he wrote, "September 12 on Bailey Island has been a dream for us just as it has for you and Steve. We even got a New England guidebook from the library and dug out our old camping road atlas. But we've had an unexpected change of plans."

According to Olive Ann's doctor, Andy wrote, the only cure for a weakened heart was rest. That meant no walking, no sitting, not even talking. Olive Ann always got a laugh in speeches when she told about the arthritis doctor who had advised her never to vacuum again. "Now," she would say, "if I could only get one to say I shouldn't cook . . ." She remembered that joke now, hearing her doctor's orders for complete bed rest. "Be careful what you wish for," she said to Andy. Still, she hoped that the bed-rest sentence would result in progress on the book, and she inscribed a copy of *Cold Sassy Tree* "to the doctor who says I can do nothing but write." At the end of Andy's letter to me, she added her own handwritten note: "I have to not think about all we will be missing in Maine . . . I learned long ago to accept what has to be and not waste energy on what cannot be changed. There are good things to everything. Since I've been in the hospital I figured out how to put Loma on page one, and I'm giving her a pet monkey and snake, the better to make her even more inconsiderate, and suddenly the whole book has a life and focus and excitement I didn't feel when Will and Sanna were carrying it by themselves."

From the first time I saw Olive Ann and Andy together, they had been an inspiration to me. Here were two people who had been married for over thirty years and who still got starry-eyed looking at each other. They were each other's best audience, equally matched in their storytelling abilities and in their appreciation of a good joke. Even when Olive Ann was telling a story Andy had heard a hundred times before, he would listen with full, adoring attention, stopping whatever he was doing to gaze at his wife as she spoke. Sometimes Olive Ann would turn to him, and say, "Andy, tell the one about . . ." just because she wanted to hear his voice. The pleasure they took in each other's company was unmistakable and absolute, and I often told them that I aspired to a marriage like theirs. Having discovered true love at the office herself, Olive Ann presided over my romance and my engagement to a Houghton Mifflin colleague in fine Amy Larkin style, sharing our happiness and dispensing romantic advice at the same time. She and Andy had looked forward to being at our wedding just as much as we had looked forward to having them there. Now, trying to put the best face on her having to spend September 12 in the hospital instead of on an island in Maine, Olive Ann suggested that we freeze some fish chowder for her and Andy. "If you were our daughter we wouldn't love you more or be any happier for you and Steve," she wrote. She hoped that she would be going home the day after she and Andy sent this letter. Instead, she took a sudden turn for the worse, and two days before the wedding she slipped into a coma. Just as I was packing my wedding gown into the car to head for Maine, Andy called to say that

Olive Ann's doctor didn't expect her to live through the night. His voice breaking, he told me that he and Olive Ann would be there in spirit when we said our vows.

The next day, we heard nothing from Atlanta. And so, first thing on the morning of our wedding, I called the hospital, not knowing whether Olive Ann was alive or dead. Andy answered the phone in her room, and his voice held the answer. She had opened her eyes that morning and asked if she could have her hair washed. Hours later, as sun broke through the clouds on Bailey Island, the first glass of champagne was raised to Olive Ann Burns.

Olive Ann remained in the hospital until just before Thanksgiving, and there were many more days when the doctor summoned the family to her bedside, as her blood pressure dipped dangerously low. When she finally did come home, she was so weak that she could barely talk. She couldn't leave the hospital bed that they set up for her downstairs, and she couldn't have company. As Norma said, "For someone as gregarious as Olive Ann, that was hard." Of course, "company" didn't include Norma, who was almost part of the household, always there to do a load of laundry, drop off a casserole, or share in the daily reading of the fan mail and get-well cards. Olive Ann often said that God must have put Norma Duncan in the house next to hers, so grateful was she for Norma's presence in their lives. But Norma herself takes no such mystical view. "I was just their neighbor," she says simply.

Surely, if there was ever a time when Olive Ann needed Norma's love and encouragement, it was that fall, when even holding a pen was too much effort for her, and when day after day went by with no improvement. Though he was just finishing his own chemotherapy and not feeling well, Andy was determined to take care of Olive Ann himself, and he did. Olive Ann knew how hard it was for him. And feeling that she was a burden on Andy was more difficult for her to handle than being sick. Later, she recalled that shortly before she went to the hospital, Andy had said, "If I had to prepare three meals a day, I'd eat out." "Now," Olive Ann quipped, "he cooks three meals a day."

Olive Ann was never one to waste much time or energy worrying about her health, but that fall she did worry about money, and with good reason. Her hospital and medical bills had been astronomical, and she had run through her insurance. From now on, she and Andy would have to pay all her expenses themselves, a frightening prospect. Royalty checks came twice a year and were earmarked for medical bills, but it still wasn't enough. Even the day-to-day cost of home care was staggering, because Olive Ann couldn't leave her bed, and the doctors made house calls. She required a hospital bed, a wheelchair, and a variety of expensive medications; the daily cost of the oxygen alone was nearly a hundred dollars.

Olive Ann and Norma and Andy often talked about *Time, Dirt, and Money,* and about how she would get back to it when she was feeling better, but, recalls Norma, "it seemed to be taking an awfully long time." Late that fall, Norma went over to check on Olive Ann one afternoon and found her reading a pamphlet on congestive heart failure. "I guess I had just had enough," Norma says. "I asked her if she would be willing to try dictating the sequel, because I thought that would be a lot more fun than reading about heart failure."

At first, Olive Ann didn't think she could do it; she was accustomed to typing, to having the words come through her fingers, not out of her mouth. Norma suggested that Olive Ann just pretend she was talking to her; then Norma would transcribe the tape and give the typed page to Olive Ann to revise by hand. They arranged to try a dictating machine for a month, and, Norma says, "We started off, not with the novel, but by answering fan mail."

"I wish now that I had kept one of those early tapes," she says. "Olive Ann's voice was so weak and the sound of the oxygen so grim that I would have to type a little bit and then cry a little bit. But as she got stronger and started having fun with what she called 'the dictator,' I could type and laugh, not only at what she was writing in letters, but at the asides she would make to me, sometimes complete with punctuation."

When she began to dictate in January, Olive Ann had five months' worth of fan letters to answer, not to mention correspondence to resume with countless friends and relatives. She composed what Andy called "a generic letter" to her "Dear Loved Ones," explaining that, although she was once again in remission from cancer, she was also bedridden, and the end of that was not in sight. "I did have a period of despair about it," she admitted, "but I've accepted future limitations and am aware of an inner joy and peace that a low-salt diet and backaches can't alter."

That done, she tackled the fan mail, finally agreeing to write an all-purpose letter to her readers, too. Even so, she couldn't resist adding personal notes when Norma brought the letters back for her to sign. "Andy and I would tease her that we wouldn't give her the mail until she had dictated a chapter of the book," Norma recalls, "but that fan mail was as important to her as writing, and she answered every letter."

At the end of January, Olive Ann reported, "If I can dictate the book as easily as I can dictate letters, this is going to be no problem at all. Norma knows how much I rewrite and says that won't bother her a bit. I can just talk it out any way I want to and she will double-space it and I can correct and rewrite and she will do it again. . . . What a great, great blessing! It has already changed my life. All of a sudden I have something to do instead of lie here with my mind turned on to most anything or nothing, whiling away four hours a day on 'All Things Considered.'"

It may sound dramatic to suggest that *Time, Dirt, and Money* saved Olive Ann's life, but it certainly gave her the escape she needed, for the only way she could get away from her bed, her financial worries, and her physical discomfort was on the wings of her own imagination. Her hair was just beginning to grow back, but, by her own admission, she looked like "a ridiculous refugee, with rib cage and arms being just skin and bones, and this huge stomach." She had been unable to eat normally for months, but her weight had gone up as high as 151 pounds—all from fluid retained in her abdomen. The pressure was so great that it was all she could do to sit up for a half hour before backache forced her to lie down again. With the dictating machine as a means of communication, Olive Ann began to feel a certain pride in her ability not only to cope, but to enjoy life in spite of all the obstacles. She found a great sense of accomplishment in answering a hundred fan letters that month, and she was deeply moved by a book about a blind leader of the French Resistance movement in Paris, who had overcome his handicap with joy—even when he was imprisoned in a concentration camp. "The impact it had on me was partly because I realize that—wherever it came from—I have this kind of joy, too," she wrote to me. "My back can hurt, but I am still undismayed. A lot of it comes from acceptance, but I know that's not all of it, and I hadn't realized this before. The longest I can be depressed is about two hours and that's not often. I was depressed for about a month when I got home from the hospital with this problem—the congestive heart failure—because I realized I might never get to write the book and because I might be more or less bedridden for the rest of my life. At some point I did accept this and was back to my usual self." She promised that she would have some chapters ready for me to read "any minute now."

Working on the book turned out to be much harder than doing letters, but Norma was patient, transcribing every page twice, once as a rough draft, and then again after Olive Ann had edited it by hand and read it back into the machine. "For the first time I believe it will work!" Olive Ann wrote happily.

It did work, but in fits and starts. Just when she would get on a roll with the writing, the pain in her back and shoulder would flare up, and, as Olive Ann said, she would feel "waylaid as a person and as a writer." Her back hurt if she got up, and her shoulder hurt in bed, and a few days of this, combined with lack of sleep, would result in another setback. Progress—on the book and on getting well—was slow indeed. "I still look as if I'm carrying surrogate twin grandchildren," she said in one letter.

As spring rolled around, Andy began to make day trips to the Write House, and Olive Ann realized that any hope she might have of accompanying him would lead only to disappointment. Instead, she took pleasure in the way the world seemed to come to her. Craig Claiborne wrote her a fan letter, and they became pen pals, a new friendship that she enjoyed immensely. Faye Dunaway called to introduce herself and to say that she would love to come to Atlanta and talk with Olive Ann about turning her novel into a film. Meanwhile, *Cold Sassy Tree* was banned in a high school in Florida, which only resulted in more publicity as parents and teachers came forth to defend its virtues. (Much to Olive Ann's amusement, the principal of the school appeared on television to explain why the book was banned. "With hands shaking, she said, 'It's just an awful book. Full of rape, incest, and SOUTHERN DIALECT!'") One day Oprah Winfrey announced on her show that she was reading a great novel called *Cold Sassy Tree*; that night Olive Ann heard from every friend in Atlanta who had seen the program. "But I decided I had really arrived," she wrote in a letter to Chester and Joan Kerr, "when I heard that last summer a high school girl went into a bookstore and asked for the Cliff Notes on *Cold Sassy*, which was required summer reading in her school."

Being bedridden may have been the greatest challenge Olive Ann had faced so far, but every day brought its own reminder that she continued to touch people's lives. What's more, after three years in which she had made almost no real progress on her novel, she was now in a situation where the only thing she *could* do was write. She had a good laugh when a friend called to say she had heard that Olive Ann's publisher had sent a secretary down to Atlanta for her to dictate the sequel to. "Thanks but no thanks!" she wrote. "Norma suits me just fine, and I think she'd shoot anyone who tried to take her job. The ms. is now 40 pages." Norma never complained when Olive Ann scribbled all over her perfectly typed pages. More important, she knew just when to urge her to keep writing and when to insist that she rest. "I know if it weren't for Norma I would still be wishing I could write but not doing it," Olive Ann admitted in one letter. "Maybe planning scenes, but not writing them."

Olive Ann's goal that spring and summer was to perfect a hundred pages to send to Ticknor & Fields. As long as she had a telephone and a commode by the bed, she could be alone for a few hours, and she looked forward to that time for dictating and rewriting. When Olive Ann had two finished chapters, she gave the first to Andy one night to print out on her computer. "In the morning," she wrote me, "he waked me like Prince Charming with a kiss and the words 'I read the first chapter and I think it's delightful. I knew you could do it.' Isn't that a nice way to wake up?" In August, John came home for a visit from Colorado and read several versions of the first chapter. Olive Ann was still in a quandary over how the book should begin, but it helped her to have a fresh pair of eyes on the manuscript. She reread one of her old beginnings, written in the third person, and felt that it worked. "I can't wait to get this all together and see what you think," she wrote. "I'm more excited about *TDM* now than ever before. Not from anything John said but from my own confidence. At last."

On October 5, Olive Ann sent me 113 pages of *Time, Dirt, and Money* for my birthday. It was the best present an editor could have received. Olive Ann felt that she, too, had been given a great gift—the courage and the inspiration to keep writing. Finally, she had something to show for all those nights of lying awake, planning scenes in her mind; for all those hours spent dictating; for all those first chapters. "As I've told you before," she wrote, "anybody who ever worked for Angus Perkerson can't get hurt feelings from criticism, so you don't need to try to veil your words in kindness." A stack of manuscript pages wasn't the only thing Olive Ann had to celebrate. She felt stronger, and she was finally able to get up and walk from one room to another. "The fluid retention in my stomach has been reduced to about the size of a large baking hen," she reported. Olive Ann's doctor was impressed by her progress; he told her he had never been able to get a patient to stay in bed this long. As Olive Ann wryly observed, "It was no temptation to be up. Between the backache and the fact that I had a definite forward list when I walked, it was easy to stay in bed."

After a whole year of that, though, it felt wonderful not to have to be waited on for every little thing. "Now, other than the fact that Jack (the cat) and I have fleas — we've got a flea collar for him and we may well get one for me — everything here is going well," she wrote. When Steve and I went to visit that fall, Norma cooked the meal for our reunion dinner, but Olive Ann and Andy were definitely the hosts. They opened a bottle of homemade scuppernong wine in honor of the occasion, set out the fine china and lit candles in the dining room, and talked of the past year as if it had been one of the happiest of their lives. After dinner, Andy read a funny scene from T.R. Pearson's novel *A Short History of a Small Place*. He was a marvelous reader, with a rich, expressive voice, and he knew just how to play up the humor, but he couldn't keep a straight face himself. Once he started to laugh, he couldn't stop, The more he read, the harder he laughed, and that laughter was so infectious that all of us ended up gasping for breath, urging him on. Sitting around the table that night, it was hard even to imagine what Olive Ann and Andy had just been through; not a mention was made of pain or hardship.

In a November letter to her *Cold Sassy Tree* fans, Olive Ann said, "I'm up more now. I've been out once to ride, I've had on lipstick seven times and a dress five times, I've put on a chicken to roast, last night I fried some fish, and the doctors think the heart muscle is getting well, not just better. (They say the only way to be sure is with an autopsy, but I say never mind being so sure!)" The same day, however, she wrote to me that about ten pounds of the abdominal fluid had reinstated themselves. After just a month of the very mildest activity, she was being sent back to bed. It didn't seem to faze her. This time, she knew she could handle it and, besides, she had work to do. Ticknor & Fields had made an offer for the novel based on the first hundred pages of manuscript, and Olive Ann now had a contract in hand and a deadline toward which to work. "Just knowing about it has liberated me," she wrote. "Suddenly I don't want to read the newspaper in the morning before I even think about writing. The first two chapters are already improved, and I'm now on chapter five."

Although she had tried out several different narrative voices, the chapters Olive Ann had sent in October were written in the third person. Will's voice was nowhere to be heard. When I told Olive Ann that I missed Will, she admitted she missed him, too. It was hard to suggest that she start all over again, knowing how much effort and sheer force of will it had cost her to produce these chapters, but I also knew that she wanted a truthful reaction and that she could handle the criticism. She did handle it, magnificently. In fact, she hardly needed to hear it, for her instincts were telling her the same thing I was. Andy, who had watched the painstaking writing process day by day, was moved and deeply impressed by Olive Ann's willingness to go back to square one. In a letter to friends he wrote, 'Olive Ann sent 113 pages to her editor, who said she liked it, but would she mind starting over. . . . So Olive Ann started over, writing as Will as an older young man, and says the book is much more fun. She said she had written herself into a corner, having to explain everything from the girl's point of view, when Will can just dive in. She now has 85 pages that she is happy with, although she keeps rewriting. Norma and I say, 'Get on with Chapter 7.'"

That winter of 1988–1989, the continuing success of *Cold Sassy Tree* and Olive Ann's "fat contract" for *Time, Dirt, and Money* seemed to be the only bright spots. Shortly after our October visit, Andy began to feel pain in his lower back. Late in December tests revealed that his lymphoma had come back yet a third time, now in the form of a large tumor pressing against his lower vertebrae. In February he underwent four weeks of radiation, to be followed by nine months of chemotherapy. "We are now a two-wheelchair family," Olive Ann wrote.

She wanted to care for Andy as he had taken care of her over the past two years, but with both of them in wheelchairs, the day-to-day tasks that they had just managed before were now impossible. Friends and relatives all pitched in to help, and members of Olive Ann and Andy's Sunday school class took up the cause. This group of nearly a hundred friends organized themselves, drew up a schedule, and saw to it that hot food arrived at Olive Ann and Andy's doorstep several times a week. When they were too ill for company, the cook would drop off his or her wares and slip out quietly; when Olive Ann and Andy were up to it, they would visit and catch up on news of the outside world. "All those Sunday school class people who bought books by the dozen at Rich's are bringing soup and casseroles," Olive Ann wrote. "I am still amazed by what *Cold Sassy* has done and now I'm even more amazed by the kindness of people and by how many friends in various places we have who care and help. And Norma is our mainstay. She is typing this, of course, and I'm not saying it just so she'll hear it and clean out the dishwasher real quick."

On days that she felt well, Olive Ann undertook some of the cooking and housework herself, but she wasn't able to combine being up and about with any writing. Every exertion tired her, and besides, as she said, "How could I retire into Cold Sassy when Andy was hurting?" That spring, she sent out a letter to "special friends," bringing them up to date on her health and Andy's and on other events at 161 Bolling Road. "The doctors say my heart is working fine," she wrote, "and I've lost all of the abdominal fluid. I don't look like Tweedledum or a California raisin anymore." She hoped that her return to a normal shape meant that she would begin to feel stronger; nevertheless, she had grown almost accustomed to a universe that extended no farther than her living room. "In October Andy took me to see the fall leaves," she wrote, "and I sat outside on the front lawn three times, but otherwise I haven't been out of the house since November of 1987, when I got home from the hospital. But I don't feel lonely or cut off from the outside world, partly because of *Cold Sassy Tree* and the mail it brings, and partly because so many people come here. Somebody said yesterday, 'You and Andy have such a wonderful attitude!' We have a whole houseful of attitude, and most of the time it sustains."

Even with Andy sicker than he had ever been, Olive Ann could look around her and feel grateful. In a letter that March, she wrote about signing a contract for a Hebrew translation of *Cold Sassy Tree*, about the paperback edition coming out in Great Britain, about the Turner Network Television company's plans to start filming for the movie that spring, and about her son John's engagement to be married. The wedding was to be in the fall, in Olive Ann and Andy's backyard, so that they could both attend. Meanwhile, Olive Ann's sister Margaret had come from Pennsylvania and was "keeping the house going, making oatmeal cookies, whole wheat rolls, and anything else she can think of to fatten us up." That meant Olive Ann could conserve her energy and get back to her writing; she hoped to send a hundred revised pages to me within a week. "The suspense of waiting for so long for Andy's treatment, and the difficulty of accepting seeing him feel bad, is not conducive to writing," she admitted. "On the other hand, it's the other world I can go to without leaving the house. He and Norma keep me at it."

By the time Margaret returned north to her family, after three months in Atlanta, Olive Ann and Andy were able to manage on their own. For the first time in nearly two years, Olive Ann felt well enough to sleep at night in her own bed with Andy. They used her hospital bed and a twin bed in the guest room for resting during the day. "We may be the only couple in Atlanta who has his bed, my bed, and our bed," Olive Ann joked, adding, "It's wonderful to be together again." Once a week, Olive Ann's sister Jean and her husband came by to help around the house, buy groceries, and run other errands. With the help of Meals on Wheels, they could feel somewhat independent, knowing that a hot meal would be delivered once a day. Olive Ann loved that she could be on the phone with Craig Claiborne one minute, hearing about his most recent culinary explorations in China, and then tuck into her own plate of plain fare from Bradshaw's Feedmill the next. "If we had our choice we wouldn't eat at the Feedmill five days a week," she conceded, "but it's good average cooking."

Andy never did feel well that spring, but he was able to go out back and lose himself in his garden, just as Olive Ann could turn on her dictating machine and escape to Cold Sassy. John's October wedding gave Andy a goal, and he was determined that by fall the backyard would be more beautiful than ever before. His chemotherapy wasn't making him nauseated, as it had in the past, but he was terribly frail and often in pain. One day he came in from the garden, complaining of being weak. "I don't know what's wrong with me," he said. Olive Ann replied, "Well, I do. You've got lymphoma, you're taking chemotherapy, you're very anemic, and you've been hauling concrete blocks in the garden." Andy hadn't lost his sense of humor. "Oh, good," he said, "I thought it might be old age."

In May Olive Ann sent me the new version of the opening chapters, now written from Will's point of view. She had never once questioned the wisdom of starting over, and now, six months later, she felt good about what she had done and was eager to keep going. "Of course I look forward to hearing what you think," she wrote. "Please remember you don't have to tip-toe around my feelings. If this beginning is too slow or you want something more exotic to start with, I can put Will and Sanna at the Army camp where everybody's dying of the 1918 influenza epidemic—really strong stuff. I'd just as soon have that in the next hundred pages, but I can't be sure this (what I've done) grabs the reader the way I want it to. I like it, but is that enough? Please tell me if there's any section that seems slow. I'm not going to work on this (chapters 1–5) for a while. Norma and Andy both say I've got to get on with chapters six, seven, eight, nine, ten, eleven, twelve. Andy said one way to get ahead was to let Will pretend he lost one chapter and just skip from chapter five to chapter seven. But I've already done chapter six, so I'll save that idea for a real emergency."

It was a good thing that Olive Ann finished five chapters and got them sent off that May, for just a week later shooting began for the TV movie version of *Cold Sassy Tree*, and every day brought new visitors and distractions. The movie company set up camp in Concord, Georgia, a little town about seventy miles from Atlanta that Olive Ann said hadn't changed since the Civil War. Olive Ann and Andy had been invited to be on site for the filming, but they had to decline. As it happened, though, a close friend was hired to be the dialect coach, and he kept them supplied with regular briefings from the front lines.

"I wish you could see the beehive of activity in Concord," Charles Hadley wrote. "The production office, set up in a lovely old home, is awash in traffic of stars, crew, secretaries, producers, make-up artists, wardrobe people, etc. Out front a sign says 'Welcome to Cold Sassy Tree, population 586.'" For Olive Ann and Andy, Charles Hadley's "secret communications" were almost as good as being there in person, for he took time from his own busy schedule to describe the scene and all the goings on. "Strickland's old country store now reads

'Blakeslee,'" he wrote, "and tons of dirt have covered the paved street in front of it. Set designers have transformed the interior into something marvelously 1906! All is about ready for the turkey trot come Wednesday. Costumes from London are being fitted, hairdos and beards are appearing. Poor Lightfoot has undergone a chopping that left her near tears. Both she and Will T. begin the shoot with the cemetery kissing scene on Tuesday and are scared to death. They should be—I'm having trouble getting the Yankee out of their speech and there has been so little time to work. Effie Belle, Alice Ann, Mrs. Predmore, and Mr. Means, however, are a hoot! It is all ultra-exciting to see this huge operation in full swing. You would burst with pride if you could see how beloved and famous you are. Can there be a soul left who doesn't know your name? I do get so much mileage out of telling that I know you in person!"

Cast and crew members alike took advantage of breaks in the filming to come to Atlanta to meet Olive Ann. She welcomed them all, signed their well-thumbed copies of *Cold Sassy Tree*, and listened to their accounts of life on the set. When she first read the movie script, Olive Ann had been surprised and disappointed that all vestiges of Southern dialect had been removed. Even the rhythm of Southern speech—which she had worked so hard to capture precisely—had been lost. Olive Ann was sure *Cold Sassy Tree* was such a success in part because she had put every line to the supreme test by having Andy read the manuscript aloud. Whenever she was fussing over a tricky bit of dialect, she would listen carefully as Andy read, making changes as he went so that every sentence *sounded* right. Now the film producers seemed ready to disregard her efforts. "The script was written as if everybody in Cold Sassy was educated and had at least an A.B.," she said when she saw it. Grandpa Tweedy's "Good goshamighty, she's dead as she'll ever be, ain't she?" had become "Good gosh almighty. She is as dead as she is ever going to be." Not only was the poetry gone, but so was the authenticity. "Southerners are just too lazy to say that many extra words," Olive Ann pointed out. She quickly realized that she would be wise to take Chester Kerr's advice concerning the film—namely, Be happy that a movie was made at all, and don't waste a moment's time or energy fretting over the final product. That done, Olive Ann was able to enjoy both the film itself and the people who worked on it. For a brief time, she even became something of a Hollywood celebrity, a role which amused her thoroughly.

Certainly having actors and actresses in for tea was a good way to divert one's attention from red and white blood cell counts or the rough spots in Chapter 7, and it was good for the ego, too. Olive Ann was delighted when two visiting actresses greeted her with "You couldn't have been born in 1924; you don't have a wrinkle!" One afternoon Faye Dunaway herself came to call—an event staged mainly for the benefit of some national reporters and photographers. The story of the movie star making friends with the author of *Cold Sassy Tree* did result in some fine publicity, but Andy's version of that memorable day was by far the most entertaining. Later Olive Ann even sent a copy of Andy's account to Faye.

The photographer had come a few days in advance to scout the location and plan his shots; Faye was expected on Sunday at five. "By Sunday afternoon," Andy wrote, "we had white magnolias at one end of our antique white sofa and white hydrangeas at the other; tables were waxed and excess books and magazines banished out of sight. Things did look good, if I say so myself. Until the photographers came back. I told them they could move anything. They had enough equipment to cover half of the dining room floor. They moved furniture to install strobe lights on top of the cornices over the windows and the tall clock on the mantel. They strung extension cords from the garage to the back of the garden to have some blue hydrangeas in the background for a possible cover picture outdoors.

"Then they shot Olive Ann in bed, with her tiny dictating equipment and the red telephone and pages of manuscript.

They shot her in the living room, with those bookshelves in the distance, and in the dining room with a photograph of her real great-grandfather hanging on the wall beside the grandfather clock.

"Then we started waiting for Faye."

The writer from *Southpoint* magazine, which had orchestrated this momentous meeting, confided that Miss Dunaway's requirements included a hired limousine, a suite at the Ritz-Carlton for the night, and $800 worth of make-up. Once Faye arrived, the writer explained, her German make-up artist would require two hours to get the star ready to be photographed. Olive Ann joked that she had done her own make-up and that it had taken ten minutes. At quarter of seven, a long black Cadillac pulled into the driveway at 161 Bolling Road. As Andy told it, "Doug [the writer] went out to tell Faye the arrangements—I was to open the front door, introduce her to Olive Ann, and get out of the way. The black driver got out first. Then out stepped a man who must have seemed to Doug like the enemy climbing out of the Trojan horse; he was a writer from *TV Guide* who had had two hours to interview Faye in the limousine at Doug's expense. Then Faye got out, wearing a white T-shirt, rumpled gray slacks, and a wind-blown (air-conditioner blown?) blond wig. Doug must have thought, where did my $800 go?"

Faye said she would have to go inside and change her clothes before the meeting, so Olive Ann and Andy hid in the kitchen while Faye and her assistant disappeared into the back bedroom, carrying a boxful of clothes and a large make-up case. "When Faye reappeared," Andy wrote, "she wore neat gray slacks, a tailored plaid jacket, and Miss Love's blond wig, made of real human hair by the German artist and beautiful. With those cheekbones, Faye could look beautiful in anything, and now she really did."

The writer guided Faye back out the front door, Olive Ann and Andy emerged from the kitchen, Faye dashed back in and threw her arms around Olive Ann as the photographer flashed away. According to Andy, Olive Ann and Faye chatted for the next hour or so like old friends while the reporters took notes and the photographers took pictures. A young TNT vice president arrived dressed in a tuxedo, with a glamorous blond woman on his arm; Olive Ann's sister and brother-in-law set out a gallon of iced tea and sliced some cake; the writer from *TV Guide* slipped away; and, in the last light of day, everyone descended to the backyard, where they swatted at mosquitoes while the photographer tried to get a shot worthy of a magazine cover. Faye began to scratch, but Olive Ann and Andy weren't bothered a bit. "Fortunately those biting insects hate people who are taking chemotherapy," Andy wrote.

By the time the filming was over and the Hollywood folk had packed up and gone home, Olive Ann and Andy were ready to settle back into what he called their "un-star-studded normalcy." Still, that summer of 1989 was a happy one, and all of Olive Ann's letters brimmed with movie news and wedding plans. "We really did enjoy all the visits," Olive Ann wrote, "and that afternoon with Faye was like a three-ring circus." She mentioned Andy's anemia and his difficulties with chemotherapy, of course, but there was no way for distant friends to know just how weak he had become. His own letters, as the account of Faye Dunaway's visit attests, were full of vitality and humor. As one close friend of Andy's later wrote, "No one ever knew when he was in pain, because that's the way he wanted it." "If you smile," Andy always said, "no one will know." He did admit to Celestine Sibley, a long-time friend and fellow newspaper writer, that he was "too weak to dig holes in the backyard, as I would like to, and almost too weak to walk up our not-too-steep driveway from the backyard."

Those who knew Olive Ann and Andy had come to think of her as the invalid and of Andy as the ever-present, good-natured caretaker. That summer, almost imperceptibly, the tables turned. In July, Olive Ann's doctor gave her permission to spend a quiet weekend at their mountain house. The house had been finished and uninhabited for two years, ever since Olive Ann had left there and ended up in the hospital, in August of 1987. Now, a weekend at Skylake seemed cause for celebration—they were in their beloved retreat at last, and even though she was still in bed much of the time, Olive Ann could begin to imagine a more normal future. "It is not the Write House yet," Andy wrote, "but it will be!" They had furnished it with old pieces from 161 Bolling Road and, as Andy observed, "they look good with the natural white-pine walls, especially painted things like an old red-and-black chest from New England, a little blue blanket chest we use as a coffee table, and a black chair from Madison that Olive Ann sat in to write much of the book." Andy had always planned to collect wildflowers and native shrubs from their property at Skylake and bring them back to Atlanta, to grow in what he called his "final wheelchair garden." But, he joked, this was before he knew they'd *have* wheelchairs. Now, he wasn't strong enough to dig holes and transplant shrubs, but he did walk all over the lot, examining every tree and flower, and thinking about the gardening he would do once his chemotherapy was over.

Back in Atlanta, he read one gardening book after another, pored over seed catalogues, and made occasional visits to the nursery. We sent him gardening books from Houghton Mifflin, and he sent back enthusiastic reviews, happily correcting mistakes that had eluded our proofreaders. Olive Ann was working, too. In one letter Andy reported, "Yesterday O. A. had a fine time in bed going through her boxes of 'goodies,' words, ideas, anecdotes, and letters from the real Will Tweedy to Ruby Hight to see what she can use in upcoming chapters. This is one way she kept rewriting the first book, making it better. Believe me, she hasn't left those first 113 pages alone, Katrina, so it's a good thing you didn't do extensive editing. But she loves the process."

Late in August Olive Ann and Andy considered a friend's offer to drive them to Skylake again, but this time it was Olive Ann who looked at Andy and questioned whether he should make the trip. "I don't think Andy's up to it," she confided. "He really has gotten very weak, and the low white blood count from chemotherapy has kept him from going places and doing things where there are people who might have a germ or virus to give away." In the end, they did decide to make an overnight visit to the Write House. It was to be their last together.

About a week before Andy's final chemotherapy treatment, Steve and I spent an evening with Olive Ann and Andy and Becky. We arrived with a huge lasagna dinner, heated it up in batches in the microwave, and served it on their good china. Olive Ann looked almost like her old self, all dressed up and delighted to be presiding over a party in her own dining room. Andy conceded that the summer had been hard—but all that was behind him now, he assured us; the chemotherapy had worked its exacting magic once again, and now he expected to see some of his hair and some of his strength return. After dinner, Norma and Charlie appeared for dessert, and we all sat in the living room, telling stories and getting caught up on *Cold Sassy Tree* news. Olive Ann read a fan letter from B.F. Skinner, and admitted that it had pleased her as much as the one from a farm woman in Virginia, who had written to say that she'd named her prize hen Olive Ann. The mood was wonderfully festive. I was nearly seven months pregnant, so there were baby stories to tell, and Olive Ann and Andy were both in high spirits, looking forward to John's October wedding and to the Atlanta premiere of *Cold Sassy Tree*, which would occur the same weekend. The wedding guests would be served Brunswick stew and barbecue on Friday night on Norma's deck, and then attend the movie premiere the following day, where they would see Faye Dunaway herself arrive in a horse-drawn carriage. "It's Ted Turner's party, naturally," Olive Ann said, "but it's heaven-sent for entertaining wedding guests!" She and Andy planned to skip that celebration so that they could really enjoy the wedding.

At one point in the evening, as Olive Ann was telling a funny anecdote she planned to use in *Time, Dirt, and Money*, I happened to look across the room at Andy. He was seated on the edge of his chair, leaning forward, his hands clasped between his knees, listening with full attention to Olive Ann's every word. On his face there was a smile of pure delight. It was impossible to look at Andy and think of him as a sick man; he was a happy man—and that's what showed. Later, Olive Ann told me that much as she had enjoyed that evening, the high point for her was just after they had closed the door behind us. Then, Andy took her in his arms and said, "Wasn't that a wonderful party!"

A week later, on September 17, 1989, Andy died. Olive Ann believed that she could accept almost anything, but she never expected that she would have to accept the death of her husband. If there was a "dying story" to tell here, it was that after all those years of nursing Olive Ann, Andy was the first to go. All summer, Olive Ann had looked forward to attending John's wedding; it was to be her first real outing in over two years, and she had every reason to believe that Andy would be at her side. Now, she was going to his memorial service instead. She managed it, and afterward she invited family and friends back to the house. That afternoon, she admitted that she hadn't slept at all the night before. Lying in bed, she realized that she had to decide whether life was worth living without Andy; it would be so easy to just give up now and follow him. By morning, she knew that wasn't the answer. One by one, she told us, "I've decided that I want to live." The way she said those words, there was no doubt in anyone's mind that she meant them. Losing Andy took an enormous toll on Olive Ann, but his death did not diminish her zest for life. There were still too many things she wanted to do.

A few days after Andy's service, Olive Ann wrote a note to a little boy down the street who had come to offer his condolences. "Dear Clark," it said, "it's not easy to say good-bye to someone you love. It helps me to know that a boy like you cares that I am sad, and I want you to know that thinking about Mr. Sparks makes me smile. He enjoyed your visits. You brought sunshine into our house. Ask your mother to make this cake for your next birthday. It is big! It is so big you could ask 799 children to the party and still have a big piece left for your mom and dad and your brother and your sister. It makes 800 pieces of cake." She enclosed a recipe that Andy had saved from the mess galley of the battleship U.S.S. *North Carolina*.

In the weeks after Andy's death, friends and relatives gathered round to make sure that Olive Ann was well taken care of. Characteristically, she thanked everyone with a letter—a letter that was also intended to let us all know that she would be all right. "Andy assumed he'd get well this time," she wrote, "just like twice before. 'If I don't, it won't be for not trying.' In the spring, he laughed and said, 'I know the chemo is working. It has taken most of my hair, my white cells, my red cells, and my energy.' But he did beat the lymphoma, as it turned out, and despite having chemotherapy that last week he looked and felt better every day. What caused heart failure and death was an overwhelming infection that started with a chill late Saturday night. He died at 8:30 the next morning.

"But we had a good year," she continued. "There's something to be said for living dangerously! We didn't waste much time worrying, we cherished the fact that we were still together, we had some really good times with friends, got to the mountain house twice, enjoyed hearing about the goings-on in our Sunday school class and with the *Cold Sassy Tree* filming, and our hearts were constantly warmed by all that was being done to help us.

"Andy's garden was never lovelier. And there was great joy in looking forward to John and Judy's wedding. Sometime in July, on a bad day, he said, 'If I don't make it to the wedding, I want you to see that it goes on exactly as planned.' I promised, but he was obviously so much better in general that I never once thought he wouldn't make it. As planned, three weeks after he didn't make it, the wedding took place in College Park at the home of Andy's sister, Jane Willingham. The house was built by their grandfather in 1904, and their mother and father married there in 1912. It was a lovely day.

"There is now something wonderful about knowing for sure that I can cope with whatever happens. Andy taught me how. It hasn't been hard for me to accept that Andy has died, though I think I don't quite believe it. It's just that he has disappeared and I miss him. Acceptance doesn't mean I haven't cried—a lot. But I never have to remind myself that we had much to be thankful for, and I still do, most especially for our family, neighbors, friends, and doctors."

Olive Ann did go to John's wedding, but by the time it was over it was clear that the stress of the preceding month had affected her heart. Some of the fluid had returned, and her doctor ordered her back to bed. Now, in addition to having to adjust to a world without Andy, Olive Ann had to get used to someone else taking care of her. There were decisions to make, financial affairs to settle, and tasks to be done—from finding someone to make her breakfast in the morning to cleaning out Andy's closet. She hired a cook-housekeeper to come in five mornings a week, and she spent some time with her brother-in-law and an investment broker, organizing her finances and arranging for a regular monthly income from the *Cold Sassy Tree* profits. As Olive Ann wrote in a letter to John and Judy, "To have the money question sorted out for me and to have the housekeeper and cooking problems solved seems like huge progress and a lot off my mind."

One Sunday morning, two months after Andy's death, Olive Ann wrote that she had woken up at six o'clock and, for the first time, was able to think about him without crying. "It was a joy and a delight to think about him," she said. "I think one reason I've missed him so is having to try not to, in order not to cry all day. I guess I'm healing, at least emotionally."

By November she was catching up on her correspondence and getting ready to go back to work on the novel. She wrote a long letter to Faye Dunaway, complimenting her work on the movie and recalling the day they had spent together. "For myself," she wrote, "it was enough to be with you as a delightful human being, so interesting that we could both forget photographers. It really was a lovely day, which Andy enjoyed as much as I did. The whole time that you were in Concord, we were getting reports and photographs of what was going on and felt we were a part of it. It really added a great sense of fun to those last months. He has disappeared now, and I miss him, but I'll soon be back to the sequel, and writing has always been my best escape, my best therapy, and my most pleasure."

In the months that followed, Olive Ann did get back to work on her book. As always before, fiction transported her to a place where she could call all the shots. Having lost first her own health and now her husband of thirty-three years, she was glad to have at least one aspect of her life in her control. Although she was almost completely bedridden again, she spent the afternoons alone in the house, dictating and editing. "I do enjoy the afternoons by myself," Olive Ann wrote to me, "and that's usually when I get around to working on the book." Her deadline was just a year away, but, as she told us, "My first job is to stay alive, so there's no chance I'll be burning the midnight oil to make up for lost time during the last few months." Olive Ann's doctors gave her permission to sit up but said that she mustn't walk any more than was absolutely necessary. "For the most part my walks now are to the bathroom and to the front door once a day to let Jack out, Jack being the cat," she wrote.

To some, such a life might seem little more than a prison sentence, but Olive Ann didn't think of it that way. That winter, she indulged herself and wrote long, thoughtful letters, something that she truly loved to do. In answer to a letter from a young woman who had worked on the film of *Cold Sassy Tree*, Olive Ann wrote, "If balancing a career and family ever puts too much pressure on you, don't mind lightening up on the career for a few years. It's better than chronic exhaustion." My Christmas letter from Olive Ann was full of memories of the first camping trip she and Andy had made with John and Becky, and reflections on being a parent. "The wonderful thing, I think, about children is that you see the world all new through their eyes," she wrote, "whenever you try to show the world to them, whether it be a red maple leaf, a ladybug, dinosaur tracks, or the Metropolitan Museum. That's what it really is all about—that and love."

On December 18, 1989, my husband called Olive Ann from my hospital room to let her know that I had just given birth to a baby boy. Over the next few months I sent more photos than letters to Bolling Road, and Olive Ann devoted herself to her book. She was feeling well enough to write and was determined to make "real headway now." Rather than dictating the first draft, she was jotting down lines and paragraphs on scrap paper, fiddling with them till they were the way she wanted them, and then dictating them for Norma to type. "That way I have something on paper that I can see and work from," she explained, "and I think it will cut out the necessity for so much rewriting of the first draft." Arduous as the process might be, Olive Ann still refused to settle for anything that was less than perfect; she had worked out a method that enabled her to tinker more while Norma typed less. It seemed a good sign.

The eight-page, single-spaced letter Olive Ann sent me in March 1990 was, it turned out, the last. It seems a fitting farewell. As Olive Ann herself warned, "You may have to read this letter in sections between feedings. Unless my voice gives out, it will have all the things I've stored up that I've thought about and wanted to tell you since last fall." She began by reflecting on the friendship with Norma and what it had meant to her and Andy over the years. "I really love each person in my family, and we are all very close," she wrote, "but Norma being next door and being over here so much washing dishes and cooking when we needed her, and typing, and needing Andy's advice about gardening, I think she — like you and Steve — had much in common with Andy and enjoyed and really experienced him in the same way I did. It was always a merry threesome whenever she came over."

In fact, this letter is full of stories and recollections of happy times, from the days she and Andy had spent at the *Sunday Magazine* to the magical connections and friendships that had come about as a result of *Cold Sassy Tree*. Olive Ann described the afternoon she and Andy had spent with Jessica Tandy, who came to visit while she was in Atlanta filming *Driving Miss Daisy*. She gave a progress report on *Time, Dirt, and Money*, and brought me up to date on *Cold Sassy Tree* news, concluding, "*Cold Sassy Tree* does seem to have a life of its own, like a river with lots of little branches — or maybe I should say like a sassafras tree with many branches."

And, much as she missed Andy, Olive Ann also wanted me to know that she was growing accustomed to life without him. "At first I had the feeling that Andy's death was a dream and I would wake up," she said. "When I did wake up, my feeling was as if a meteorite had hit the earth in September and killed every witty, interesting, sweet, cheerful, courageous, loving, exciting, sometimes irritable, determined man of seventy who lived at 161 Bolling Road. It doesn't hit like that anymore, and I'm very grateful for the kind of marriage we had. We were married for thirty-three years but worked together every day for nine years before that." Still, she felt that her recovery was occurring in stages, and that the process was a continuing one.

"The first few weeks, every morning when I woke up I had to remind myself, with surprise and amazement and often out loud, that 'Andy is dead!'" she admitted. "Then for four months

I hardly ever thought about him. I couldn't let myself. Any time I ever thought about him I cried, and even with a good heart it's exhausting to cry all day. I looked forward to the nights because I would sleep and not have to try so hard not to think."

Once all of the legal and financial affairs were tended to, Olive Ann decided it was time to go through Andy's things, something she had dreaded. "It seemed like just another painful, overwhelming widow-type task," she wrote, "until it dawned on me this was something I could do for him! He did hate to go through stuff, as is clearly evident when one opens his closet door or his drawers or his desk. I started with the desk, and it's turning out to be a happy time. The desk is like a profile of Andy and his life and his interests, with constant interesting or funny surprises."

She found Andy's uncle's gold pocket watch; a box of coal ash containing the burned remains of a diamond ring that Andy's Aunt Mamie had wrapped in a piece of paper and accidentally thrown in the fire; a box of gold inlays ("Years ago I heard inlays are worth something, so whenever I had to have one replaced I'd make the dentist give me the old one. Even Andy, who was embarrassed by such, started asking for his"); and two stamped envelopes from Andy's mother's Aunt Em, mailed during the Civil War. "This desk work has been like being with Andy again," Olive Ann wrote. "Too interesting to cry about, and full of memories of happy times, including my love letters that I didn't know he'd kept, and notes from the children when they were little. It's amazing what a difference it's made—feeling I'm doing something for Andy, almost with him. I bring batches out of the pigeonholes to my bed to go through, and I'm having a good time. But, oh, law, he's got two file cabinets full in the basement!"

Written words were never discarded in Olive Ann and Andy's household, and Olive Ann's going through Andy's desk didn't necessarily mean that she was throwing anything away; in fact, she was annotating, as I discovered a year later when I sorted through many of these same papers. To a bundle of tender and funny notes that Olive Ann had written to Andy over the years, and that he had saved, she added this explanation: "Whenever Andy was away overnight, I would tuck a card or a note into his suitcase. I never knew he kept them."

"I really am being long-winded," Olive Ann exclaimed toward the end of this extraordinary letter, so full of looking back. "Most of all I want to express my joy in everything about yours and Steve's and Henry's new life. My feeling is a little like something said by Ray Moore, a local TV newscaster whom I dated for four years—seriously but not exclusively. I never dated anybody exclusively until I told Andy I'd marry him. But the night I told Ray I was in love with Andy, he thought a minute and said, 'I envy Andy, but I'm not jealous of him.' He and Andy and I stayed good friends, and the last time he called I reminded him of what he said, thinking it was such a genius way of delineating the difference between our friendship love, which had been romantic at times, and what I then felt for Andy. He didn't remember that, or that shortly before we married, he took Andy and me out to lunch and said, 'I can't come to the wedding because the three of us will be the only people in Atlanta who will know I wasn't jilted.' The point of all this is to say I envy you all right now, but I'm not jealous. Actually I don't think I envy—I'm just happy for you. I've had my turn."

In addition to her own eight pages, Olive Ann enclosed all the letters I had written her during my pregnancy and after Henry's birth, explaining, "You may have been too busy or too tired to have kept a journal in this period. *It is hard to part with them*, they make such pictures of you and Steve and little Henry, but they could go in your baby book." And at the end she added a final note: "The doctor made a house call after I finished this—heart much better, and he said by all means accept an offer from a retired doctor-friend and his wife to take me and all food to the mountain house for a few days!"

Olive Ann made that trip, but by the time she got home

she had caught a cold. Over the next weeks, she felt worse and worse, and by May she was in the hospital with bronchitis, which took a severe toll on her already weakened heart. Olive Ann believed that, with time and patience, she would rally, as she had so many times before. But in June she was in intensive care, and the doctors were considering a heart transplant. Mercifully, they concluded that she was too weak to undergo the surgery. It is impossible to know what Olive Ann thought about as she lay in her hospital bed while doctors deliberated her fate, but I don't doubt that she found some comfort in words she had written herself, for Grandpa Blakeslee to say to Will Tweedy after the boy narrowly escaped getting crushed by a train:

"Life bullies us, son, but God don't. He had good reasons for fixin' it where if'n you git too sick or too hurt to live, why, you can die, same as a sick chicken. I've knowed a few really sick chickens to git well, and lots a-folks git well thet nobody ever thought to see out a-bed agin cept in a coffin. Still and all, common sense tells you this much: everwhat makes a wheel run over a track will make it run over a boy if'n he's in the way. If'n you'd a got kilt, it'd mean you jest didn't move fast enough, like a rabbit that gits caught by a hound dog . . . When it comes to prayin', we got it all over the other animals, but we ain't no different when it comes to livin' and dyin'. If'n you give God the credit when somebody don't die, you go'n blame Him when they do die? Call it His will? Ever noticed we git well all the time and don't die but once't? Thet has to mean God always wants us to live if'n we can. Hit ain't never His *will for us to die*—cept in the big sense. In the sense He was smart enough not to make life eternal on this here earth, with people and bees and elephants and dogs piled up in squirmin' mounds like Loma's dang cats tryin' to keep warm in the wintertime."

In a letter she wrote just before she got sick in March, Olive Ann had said, "I guess what gracious living all comes down to is acceptance and forgiveness. Forgiveness has never been a problem for me and now acceptance isn't either." Everyone who visited Olive Ann in the hospital that June remembers that, sick as she was, she never seemed to despair. The last time that Andy's sister, Jane, saw Olive Ann, they spoke about the possibility of an afterlife. "I wish it were true," Olive Ann said. "That would be wonderful. But if it's not, that's all right too."

One day Olive Ann's brother Billy went to see her in the intensive care unit. She was having a terrible day, was very sick, breathing through an oxygen mask, and unable to talk much at all. After a short time Billy concluded that she might be better off just resting alone. But as he headed for the door, Olive Ann spoke. "Just a minute," she whispered.

"What is it?" he asked, turning back.

"I just wanted you to see me smile," she said. And she did. *That* was Olive Ann.

When Norma came to visit, on June 22, Olive Ann tried to talk with her about her hopes for *Time, Dirt, and Money* if she was unable to finish it. "There's no need to discuss that now," Norma assured her. "Of course you'll get back to work on it." But Olive Ann was not to be put off that easily. She would not give up hope, but she would be practical, too, and she knew she could rely on Norma to do whatever needed to be done. Late that night, she picked up her dictating machine and began to speak: "Norma, this is Olive Ann. Your visit and Charlie's was just like a great gift . . . I've figured out a way that if I don't get to finish the novel it might still be marketable as a small book." She expected that she would be able to revise the first six chapters, and when she got home, she said, she planned to work on a synopsis—"which won't hurt me to do—I may even write faster if I've got it, everything written down and decided." She referred Norma to several scenes that were among her notes, and said she hoped that some of these could be used and that she would have time to write an ending. That way, even if the novel itself was not finished, there would be enough to satisfy those people who were interested in what happened. "In the meantime," she concluded, "I'll just keep working on the book, and aren't you glad it's in a fairly good state of repair?" Finally, yawning, she said, "Now this is the middle of the night, Norma, Friday night, and I'm getting sleepy so I'll send this over to you . . . And so good night now."

Less than two weeks later, early on Independence Day 1990, Olive Ann Burns died. She had come home from the hospital four days before, accompanied by a portable IV tube that was to administer medicine continually for the rest of her life. She had declined the suggestion that she employ a home nurse, confident that Becky, a part-time housekeeper, and a few friends and relatives could manage the IV and oxygen. Olive Ann was delighted to be home, and she was eager to get back to work. On the morning of July 3, Billy's wife, Rosalind, had come to stay with her while the housekeeper went out to run errands. "Olive Ann was scribbling notes for her book when I arrived," Rosalind recalled. "She thought that she was missing a chapter, and I began to look around for it. We talked about the novel, and also about a book I had loaned her from my church library, called *Better Health with Fewer Pills.*" Olive Ann said she had read the book cover to cover, and she was so impressed that she'd asked a friend to buy two copies, one for Rosalind and one for herself.

In his introduction to *Better Health with Fewer Pills,* Louis Shattuck Baer quotes Socrates: "If the head and body are to be well, you must begin by curing the soul." Sick as she was, Olive Ann was inspired by the author's conviction that faith and a positive outlook are as important to health and happiness as any medicine. This was one of the best books she had ever read, Olive Ann told Rosalind, and she wanted to inscribe a copy of it for her sister-in-law. Rosalind handed her one of the new books, and Olive Ann wrote, "For Rosalind . . ." She stopped. "I feel dizzy," she said, and turned her head away, closing her eyes. Olive Ann would have thought it worth mentioning that she